嫌われ松子の一生（下）

山田宗樹

五一〇

鏡の孤城

目次

第三章 罪

1

昭和四十九年一月

わたしは助手席に、身体を投げ出した。力任せにドアを閉める。乾いた音が、脂臭い空気を震わせた。

「おつかれさん」

小野寺が、ラークの箱を差し出した。わたしは一本取り、口にくわえた。小野寺が、金張りのライターで火を点ける。顔が炎に照らされた。

「ライター、換えたの?」

「デュポン。ジッポは田舎臭くて駄目だ」

わたしは、煙を吐き出した。シートにもたれ、目を閉じる。

「ヒーター、消してくれない？」

「熱いか」

小野寺が、左手をキャビネットに伸ばし、ヒーターのスイッチを切った。送風音が消え、エンジンの振動だけが残った。ギアの入る音がして、車が動きだす。

「ここ、ちろりん村っていうんだってな」

「なに、それ」

「知らねえ。でもよ、なんか似合ってるって気がしねえか」

わたしは目を開けた。

メインストリートに並ぶ建物は、形も大きさも色合いもばらばら。城郭風あり、西洋の宮殿風あり、意味不明のものあり。

はじめてこの地を目にしたときを思い出す。小野寺のクーペに乗り、寄り道をしながら、三日かけての旅だった。京都から逢坂山を越え、浜大津を抜け、琵琶湖を右手に眺めながら国道一六一号線を北上しているとき、水田の広がる平野の彼方に、建物の群落が現れた。その建物はみな、見たこともないような奇妙な形をしていて、わたしは遊園地でもあるのだろうと思った。しかしそれこそ、小野寺が話していた、雄琴のトルコ団地だった。大正寺川と

琵琶湖西岸に面する一角が、トルコ風呂許可地域になっているとかで、当時すでに十軒のトルコ風呂が林立していた。いまも新しい店の建築が至るところで進んでいて、一年後にはトルコ風呂だけで四十軒を超すらしい。

この一帯にまともな民家はない。あるのはトルコ風呂と、その従業員とトルコ嬢が住むマンションやモーテル、ヒモがたむろする麻雀屋、そして彼らの胃袋を満たすレストランだけだった。

「ちろりん村……ね」

車が、雄琴のメインストリートから、国道一六一号に出た。ここを左折して大正寺川を越えたところに、四階建てのマンションがある。土地成金となった農家が、トルコ嬢目当てに建てたものだそうだ。そこの二〇二号室が、わたしと小野寺の住処だった。六畳と四畳半の居間に、四畳程度の板張りのダイニングキッチン。バス・トイレ付き。わたしは六畳の部屋を使い、小野寺が四畳半で寝起きしていた。

マンションに戻ってから、きょうの稼ぎ分を小野寺に渡した。小野寺がそれを数えてから、自分の四畳半の部屋に向かう。わたしは水道水を一杯飲んでから、六畳の部屋に入った。衣服を脱いで、ベッドにせに俯せになる。ほどなく小野寺も入ってきた。ベッドに乗り、わたしのマッサージを始めた。肩、背中、腰、腿、ふくらはぎ。疲れが揉み出され、ベッドに吸い取

られていく。

「どうする?」

小野寺の声。

「寝る」

「エアコンは?」

「つけたままにしておいて」

小野寺がベッドをおりた。わたしの身体に布団をかけて、電気を消した。部屋を出ていく気配。わたしは息を吐く。

また一日が過ぎてしまった、と思った。

正午近くに目が覚めた。じっとりと汗をかいていた。喉が痛い。エアコンを消し忘れたらしい。下着の上にセーターを被り、エアコンのスイッチを切ってから、部屋を出た。

キッチンの食卓に、書き置きを見つけた。冷蔵庫を開けて、ラップに包まれたサンドイッチを取り出した。ラップを剥がし、サンドイッチを頬ばる。卵焼きと刻んだキュウリに、マスタードをたっぷり効かせたマヨネーズ。小野寺は見かけによらず、料理上手だった。殊に魚を捌くときの包丁づかいは、なかなかのものだ。

冷蔵庫から牛乳パックを出し、喉に流しこんだ。牛乳が口の端から溢れた。口のまわりを掌で拭う。トイレを済ませてから、セーターと下着を脱ぎ、シャワーを浴びた。

胸にバスタオルを巻いて、浴室を出た。少し迷ってから、コップに水道水を満たした。冷蔵庫から、○・一グラム入りのパケと、耳かきと、注射器を取り出す。耳かきを使い、パケから米粒くらいの塊をすくいあげ、注射器の中に落とした。中筒の棒をコップの水に浸してから、注射器にセットし、塊を押し潰す。コップに針を浸けて水を吸い上げ、筒を指で擦る。左の上腕をタオルで縛り、血管を指で叩く。右手に注射器を持ち、怒張した血管に針を添える。

ああ、また打とうとしている。だめだな。

一瞬の呵責を消し去り、針を血管に突き通す。中筒の棒を引くと、血液が逆流して、注射器が赤く染まった。口でタオルを外してから、中筒をゆっくりと押しこむ。

目を閉じる。

足もとが冷たくなる。

鳥肌が立つ。

髪がざわりと波打つ。

身体が宙に浮かぶ。

目を開けた。

世界が鮮明になった。

「お、やってるな」

ドアに小野寺が立っていた。今朝いちばんで銀行に行き、きのうの稼ぎ分を預け入れてきたはずだ。小野寺が、自分の部屋に入った。金庫の扉を開閉する音が聞こえる。すぐに戻ってきた。

「ちょうどいいや。俺も」

小野寺が、慣れた手つきで準備をして、自分の腕に注射した。窪（くぼ）んだ目が、爛々（らんらん）と輝き始める。鼻息が荒くなる。

「わたしたち、打ちすぎじゃないかしら?」

「このくらいは平気さ。ほんもののポン中は、一日に二回も三回も打つものだ。それにシャブが身体によくないのは、食事をとらなくなるからだ。ちゃんと食べていれば、気にすることはない」

「きょうもまた麻雀?」

「ああ」

「よく飽きないわね」

「ほかにすることがないからな」

「そうかしら」

わたしは、胸のバスタオルを外して、床に落とした。

小野寺がにやりとして、わたしを抱きあげた。六畳の部屋に入り、ベッドに倒れこんだ。

店の手前の角で、小野寺のクーペを降りた。

通りを歩いていると、似たような二人が、似たような光景を演じている。車はみな国産高級車か外国車。男はイタリアかフランス製のスーツに、何万もしそうなシャツを着こんでいる。

わたしは、黒地に金文字で「帝王」と大書された看板をくぐった。「帝王」は雄琴に来て最初に面接に行った店だった。面接したマネージャーは五十代の女性。金髪に厚化粧で、豊満な肉体を紫色のラメ入りワンピースに包んでいた。わたしが中洲の南新地で働いていたと告げると、鼻からタバコの煙を噴いて、

「あそこは遅れてるからねえ」

と、不機嫌な声を漏らした。

これにはわたしもかちんときて、実際に自分の技術を見てくれと迫った。そこで、マネー

ジャー補佐である四十代半ばの男を相手に、実演することになった。マネージャー補佐は十分もしないうちに射精してしまい、わたしはめでたく採用となった。源氏名は、雪乃にしてもらった。

採用とはなったが、トルコ嬢間の競争は厳しく、ナンバーワンにはなれなかった。マネージャーの話では、雄琴にはススキノ、川崎、横浜、千葉など、全国のトルコ風呂先進地域からベテラントルコ嬢が集結していて、毎日のように新しい技が編み出されているという。中洲の「白夜」でナンバーワンになれたわたしも、ここではその他大勢の一人に過ぎなかった。

もっとも、ナンバーワンになれなくとも、収入は倍増した。客一人あたりの単価が高いうえ、一日にこなす数が半端ではなかったのだ。

この日の一人目の客は、地元の土地成金だった。腹の出たハゲで、笑うと金歯が光った。

一通り済んだとき、このハゲがにやにやしながら、

「どうや。手当を三十万あげるから、わしの愛人にならんけ」

と言いだした。

「うちの人に聞いてからね」

そっけなく答えると、とたんに面白くなさそうな顔をして、

「なんや、ヒモ付きかいな。ほな、別の探そ」

と、さっさと帰っていった。この御仁はトルコ嬢のあいだでは有名人だそうで、やたらと愛人を囲いたがるという。噂によると、奥さんは奥さんで、京都で若い男を買い漁っているとか。

二人目の客は、出張で大津に来ているサラリーマン。一見すると真面目そうなタイプだが、出張先では必ず地元のトルコ風呂を訪れるという好き者だった。わたしが博多の南新地から移ってきたと言うと、博多のトルコ嬢は情が濃くて最高だったと誉めてくれた。わたしも嬉しくなって、うんとサービスをした。

三人目は外回り中の営業マン。身体は細く、顔は青瓢箪のようで、若いのに愚痴をこぼしてばかりいた。そのくせベッドインとなると、あれこれと横柄に命令して、乱暴に扱おうとする。さすがに痛くなって、優しくしてくれと頼むと、こんどは逆上しそうになる。もう少しで店の男の子を呼ぼうかと思ったほどだった。

四人目は、一目でそれとわかるスジ者。どうせどこかのトルコ嬢のヒモで、暇にあかせて来ているのだろう。仕事柄というのも変だが、この手のタイプは女性に優しい。チップも弾んでくれる。わたしも肩の力を抜いてプレイできた。

五人目も似たようなタイプだったが、何度か指名してくれている常連だった。わたしが、やんわりと外で会おうと持ちかけてくる。どうやら、ヒモに取り入りたいらしい。わたしが、やんわりと

断ると、

「オレ、あんたのヒモ、知ってるぜ。あんたは知らんだろうが、山科のマンションに女を囲っている。しかも十九歳の素人娘、女子学生だ」

ときた。誰がそんな話を真に受けるか。

いつも五人目を終えるあたりから、疲労が溜まってあそこが痺れ、足腰が重くなってくる。

六人目は酔客だった。顔を赤くした四十がらみのサラリーマン。酒が入っているわりにはおとなしく帰っていった。

七人目も酔っぱらい。五十過ぎのデブ。祇園で同僚と飲んでいて、タクシーを飛ばしてこまで来たという。偉ぶっていて、いちばん嫌いなタイプだった。

八人目は素面で、ほっとした。若くて学生らしかった。場慣れしていないのか、終始どぎまぎしていた。

九人目はまた酔っぱらい。声も態度もでかい。きょうは厄日だ。

十人目。酔っぱらい。この時間になると、素面の客を期待するほうが無理か。酒臭い息が顔にかかるたびに、死ね、と心で叫んだ。精神的にも肉体的にも限界だったが、表面では笑顔をつくった。

十一人目。若い酔っぱらい。潰れる寸前で、脱衣所に入るなり眠ってしまった。こちらも

と、

　仕事だから起こそうとしたが、駄目だった。終わりの時間が来てしまい、そのことを告げる

と、

「きょうこそ童貞を捨てたかったのに」

と、泣きだした。

　わたしは口では慰めながら、やれやれ助かったと、こっそり舌を出した。

　最後の客を送ってから、入念にシャワーを浴びて、泡踊りで使ったローションを洗い流す。

これが肌に残っていると、たちまち荒れてしまう。

　仕事着からまともな衣服に着替えるころには、精も根も尽き果てていた。きょうの稼ぎ分

をマネージャーから手渡され、店を出たのが午前二時。店から三十メートルくらい離れた路

上に、小野寺のクーペが待っていた。近づくと、ドアが開いた。わたしは深く息を吐きなが

ら、助手席に身体を投げ出した。

「おつかれさん」

　小野寺が、ラークを差し出す。わたしは首を横に振った。小野寺が、ラークを引っこめた。

車が発進する。

「知ってるか、ここ、ちろりん村って呼ばれてんだってさ」

「なにそれ」

「知らない。でも、なんか似合ってるじゃねえか」

「ちろりん村ね」

わたしは、車窓の外に目をやった。

「その話、前にもしなかった?」

「そうかな。したかな」

「したわ。二回目よ」

いや、三回目だったかも知れない。

どうでもいいか……。

「明日の休みはどうする?　また琵琶湖を回るか?」

「もう飽きた」

「京都見物は?」

首を振る。

「疲れたか?」

「当たり前でしょ」

「稼ぎは?」

「十五万、チップも入れてね」

小野寺が口笛を吹く。

「口笛を吹かないで」

「わるい」

「今月いくら稼いだ?」

「二百五十万は超えた」

「新記録?」

「間違いない」

「疲れるわけね」

「シャブ、新しいの仕入れておいたぜ。こんどのはいいぞ。水に落とすと、しゅるしゅる音をたてて走りやがる」

小野寺が愉快そうに言った。

わたしはシャブよりも、一カ月くらいのんびりしたい、と思った。

正午を過ぎてもベッドを出なかった。食事もとらず、布団にくるまっていた。小野寺がしつこく求めてきたが、拒んだ。小野寺は機嫌を損ねて、出かけていった。また麻雀か、トルコ風呂にでも行ったのだろうか。せっかくの休みに相手をしてあげられなくて悪いと思った

が、身体が言うことを聞かなかった。

電話のベルが鳴った。居留守を決めこむことにした。小野寺からだったら、シャワーを浴

びていたと言い訳しよう。

ベルは鳴り続けている。耳に障ってくる。

ベッドをおりた。セーターを被り、キッチンに出て、受話器を取る。

「誰?」

『雪乃か?』

目を見開いた。聞き覚えのある声。懐かしい声。

まさか……。

「赤木さん?」

『憶えていてくれたか』

「赤木さん? ほんとうに赤木さんなの?」

『ああ、赤木だよ。起こしちまったようだな』

「だいじょうぶです。起きようと思ってたところですから」

『元気そうだな、雪乃。いや、いまはどんな名前で出てるか知らないが』

「いまも雪乃です。赤木さん、お元気でしたか? いまも北海道で?」

『ああ、おかげさんでな。北海道で、地味に暮らしてるよ。雪乃は？』

「なんとか……」

「よかった。ほっとしたぜ」

「よくここがわかりましたね」

『綾乃に聞いていたんだ』

「ああ、綾乃姐さん！　懐かしいなあ。どうしてるだろう。すっかりご無沙汰してるけど」

『あのなあ、雪乃……』

赤木の声が、低くなる。

わたしは、無意識のうちに、身を固くしていた。

『綾乃は……死んだよ』

息が止まった。

「うそ」

『雪乃にだけは、知らせておいたほうがいいと思ってな』

「うそでしょ……うそよ、赤木さんまた……冗談にしちゃ酷すぎるわよ、ほんとうにっ」

『冗談じゃないんだ』

黒い電話機を見おろした。ダイヤルの数字を目で追っていく。心臓の鼓動が徐々に激しく

　なる。

『……雪乃?』

『……どうして』

『男に刺されたそうだ』

　息を吸いこんだ。

『浅野輝彦を憶えてるか?』

『浅野?』

『「白夜」にいた若いやつだ』

　脳裏に、床磨きをしている若い男の横顔が浮かんだ。二十歳そこそこだったろうか。仕事ぶりは真面目だったが、無口で、仕事以外で言葉を交わした憶えはない。そういえば、綾乃が「白夜」を辞めたすぐあとに、浅野も店に来なくなった。

『あの浅野くんが、綾乃姐さんと……?』

『仙台のマンションで、いっしょに暮らしていたらしい。あのころから付き合っていたのか、店を辞めてから付き合いだしたのかはわからん。たぶん、店を辞めてからじゃないかな』

「でも、どうして浅野くんが……」

『浅野のやつ、シャブに手を出してやがった』

背すじに冷気が奔る。

『シャブで頭がいかれちまってな……マンションの外まで綾乃を追いかけて、道の真ん中で刺したそうだ。綾乃は胸を刺されて、ほとんど即死だったらしい』

「……綾乃姐さんも、シャブを?」

『いや、綾乃は、やっていなかったようだ』

綾乃自身がシャブを使っていなかったことは、せめてもの救いだった。

『雪乃?』

「いつですか、綾乃姐さんが亡くなったのは?」

『二週間前だそうだ。じつは最近になって、綾乃の夢を見てな、あんまりいい夢じゃなかったんで、ずっと気になってたところに、吉富から電話があった。浅野がシャブ中になって綾乃を刺したらしい。きょう警察が店に来て、綾乃と浅野のことを調べていった。そっちにも警察が行くかも知れないから、店には関係ないと言ってくれ、ってな。関係も何も、そっちにも『白夜』ではシャブ厳禁だった。浅野だって、あのころは使っていなかったはずだ。シャブをやっている奴は、目を見ればわかるからな』

「……浅野くん、いまは?」

『警察にいる』

『……』

『こんなこと、伝えたくはなかったんだが』

『いえ……ありがとうございました』

『雪乃、おまえも無理するなよ。雄琴は忙しいって聞いてるけど、シャブにだけは手を出す
な』

『……』

『おい、まさか、雪乃……』

『いえ、わたしは、だいじょうぶです。『白夜』で赤木さんに教えられたことを、ちゃんと
守っていますから』

『そうか。それならいい』

『すみません、ご心配かけて』

『水くさいこと言うな。いいか、雪乃。なにか困ったことがあったら、遠慮なく言うんだぞ。
いつでも飛んでいってやる。住所と電話番号を言っておくから、控えてくれ』

赤木に言われるまま、メモ書きした。

『……雪乃、おれはな』

『はい』

『おまえのことが、好きだったよ』

「うん」

『だから、おまえには、幸せになって欲しいんだ』

「……ありがとう、赤木さん」

　受話器の向こうから、鼻を啜る音が漏れてきた。続いて、無理につくったような笑い声。

『すまねえ。似合わねえこと口にしちまった』

「そんなこと、ないです」

『まあ、そういうわけだ。せいぜい達者でいてくれよ』

「赤木さんも、お元気で」

『ありがとよ。じゃあな』

「さようなら」

　静かに切れた。

　わたしは、自分の部屋に戻り、鏡台の抽出から手帳を出した。住所録を開けて、電話機に戻る。スミ子の実家の番号を確認しながら、ダイヤルを回した。

　呼び出し音が四回鳴って、相手が出た。

『はい』

中年女性の声。聞き覚えはない。

「斉藤さんのお宅でしょうか？」

『そうですけど』

「……わたしは、スミ子さんの中学の同級生で、川尻という者です。スミ子さん、ご在宅ですか？」

『何のご用？』

「あの……同窓会を開こうって話が出ているので、その案内を」

『スミ子は、死にました』

　目を閉じた。唇を嚙んだ。

「亡くなったのですか……」

『ええ、親の顔に泥を塗って、死んでいきましたっ』

　切れた。

　受話器を耳から離し、電話機に戻した。動けなくなった。

　手紙を書くと約束したのに、転居通知を出したきりだった。電話もしなかった。まだ半年も経っていないのに、綾乃の顔を思い出すことさえ、なくなっていた。

　わたしは、へたりこんだ。

泣いた。

涙が涸れてから、部屋の中を見渡した。乱れたベッド。脱ぎ散らかした下着。仄かに漂う、自分たちの体液の匂い。冷蔵庫には覚せい剤。明日になればまた店に出て、十人以上の見知らぬ男に身体を売る。疲れて部屋に戻り、目が覚めたらシャブを打って、小野寺と抱き合って、店に出て客を取る。ずっとその繰り返し。仕事をしている充実感など、かけらもない。

心と身体を、ひたすら摩耗していく毎日。

こんなところで、なにやってんだろ、わたし。

その夜、小野寺は帰ってこなかった。

わたしは一晩中、食卓の椅子に座ったまま、ぼんやりと過ごした。

窓の外が、明るくなってきた。

一条の朱色が、射しこんでくる。

静かに漂う埃が、光に浮かんだ。

朝日を浴びるのは、何年ぶりだろう。身体は干からび、神経が擦り切れていたが、食べようとも眠ろうとも、思わなかった。シャブを打てば、一発で気分爽快になる。それはわかっ

ていたが、綾乃を殺したシャブを、この身体に入れる気には、ならなかった。赤木に嘘をつ

いた、後ろめたさもあった。

午前十時過ぎになって、マンションのドアが開いた。小野寺が鼻歌まじりで現れた。

小野寺がわたしを見て、気まずそうに笑った。

「なんだ、起きてたのか。早いじゃねえか」

小野寺が、流しで口をすすいだ。痰を切り、排水口に吐き出す。備え付けのタオルで口を

拭った。

「どうした、元気ねえな。まだ打ってないのか、こんどのは抜群だぜ。水に落とすとしゅる

しゅる音が……」

「ねえ、小野寺」

「なんだ」

「話があるの。ちょっと座って」

「どうしたんだよ？」

小野寺が鼻を鳴らして、正面の椅子に座った。わたしの顔をちらと見て、目を伏せる。

「なんだよ、そんな硬い顔して」

「あのね、わたしもう、辞めようと思うんだけど」

「なにを?」

「仕事よ。トルコ嬢」

小野寺の眉が、すっと上がった。

「辞めてどうする?」

わたしは、両肘を食卓に突き、身を乗り出した。

「小野寺さ」

「おう?」

「調理師の免許を取る気ない?」

「調理師?」

「それで、二人で小料理屋を開くの。小野寺が料理をつくって、わたしが接客するわ。もちろん、わたしも調理師の免許を取って、料理するわよ。そうすれば、儲けは知れてるけど、二人で息の長い商売ができる。ね、いい考えでしょ」

小野寺が、横向きに座り直した。背もたれに肘を乗せる。

「店を出すには金がかかるぞ」

「そのくらいのお金は貯まっているでしょ。三千万円はあるはずよ。それだけあれば小さな店くらい……」

小野寺が目を逸らす。

わたしは自分の顔から、血の気が引いていくのがわかった。

「小野寺」

声が震えた。

「なんだよ」

「預金通帳、見せて」

「いまか？」

「そう。いますぐ」

「どうして？　金のことは俺に任せるって言ったじゃねえか」

「確かめておきたいの、いまいくらあるのか」

小野寺が、ため息を吐く。舌打ちをする。

「早く見せてっ」

小野寺が、渋りきった顔で、腰をあげた。自分の部屋に入り、ほどなく戻ってくる。手には預金通帳。わたしの前に放り投げた。

わたしは通帳を開いた。

並ぶ数字を見つめる。

目をあげる。

小野寺は、ふてくされたように横を向いていた。

「なに、これ?」

「通帳だよ、見りゃわかるだろ」

「そんなこと聞いてるんじゃないの、どうして預金残高が減ってるのよっ!」

わたしは立ちあがった。椅子が後ろにひっくり返り、大きな音をたてた。

小野寺が、横目で睨みあげた。

「しょうがねえだろっ、とにかく世の中は不景気で、何もかも値上がりしてる。この家賃だって払わなきゃならないし、シャブだって高いんだぞ」

「もっともらしい理屈並べたってだめよ。毎月二百何十万も収入があったのよっ」

小野寺が、不機嫌な唸りをあげる。

「そんな声を出したって誤魔化されないわよ。何に使ったの?」

小野寺が、歯を剝き出して、笑顔をつくった。

「悪いな、麻雀で負けて」

「ふざけないで!」

「ほんとだよ、ほんとうに麻雀で……」

「女ね」

小野寺の笑顔が、固まった。

「わたしのほかに、女がいるのね、その女に注ぎこんだのね、そうなのねっ」

「お、おい、なに言ってんだよ。そんな女、いるわけねえだろうが。毎日いっしょにいるのに」

「山科のマンションに、十九歳の女子学生を住まわせているんだって？」

小野寺の顔が、蒼白になった。

わたしは、小野寺の反応に、戸惑った。笑い飛ばされるとばかり思っていた。ばかばかしい、わけのわからんことを言うな。そんな言葉が返ってくるはずだった。

それなのに、この小野寺の青ざめた顔は……。

「……そうなの？　ほんとうに、そうなの？　わたしがほかの男に抱かれているあいだに、ほんとうに峠を越えて、そんな女に会いに行っていたの？」

「いや……それはだな、そうじゃなくて」

小野寺の目が忙しなく動く。どうしたらいいのか、わからないでいる。

わたしは床に泣き崩れた。

「ひどい……わたしの身体で稼いだお金を、そんな小娘に注ぎこんで……わたしを何だと思

ってるのっ！　馬鹿にしないでよっ！」

小野寺が、わたしの横にしゃがんだ。わたしの肩を抱いた。

「悪かったよ、すまなかった」

「さわらないでっ！」

「もう浮気はしない。あんな小便くさい女とはきれいさっぱり別れる。これからはおまえだ

けだよ。だから、あと一年だけ、やれよ。こんどこそ貯めておくから。そうしたら、いっし

ょに小料理屋を開こう、な」

「もういや。できない。わたし、疲れたのよ。肌だって荒れてきたし、体型だって崩れてき

てるし」

「雪乃はまだまだいける。あ、そうだ」

小野寺が立ちあがった。冷蔵庫から、注射器とシャブを出した。いつものように注射器に

入れ、中筒で潰し、水道水で溶かす。

「雪乃、いくら疲れてても、これさえ打てば元気が出る。な、いつもの雪乃に戻れよ」

小野寺が針を上に向けた。先から液体が飛んだ。

わたしは、首を振りながら、後ずさった。

「もういや、打たないで……シャブはもういい……」

小野寺が、信じられないという目で、わたしを見る。

「どうして？ こんどのは最高なんだから、いままでとは違うんだから」

「もういやなの……シャブはもういやなのよっ」

小野寺が、わたしの腕をつかんだ。

「とにかく一度試してみろって、絶対気に入るから」

「いやっ、放して」

「おとなしくしろっ」

「いやあっ！」

わたしは小野寺の顔を引っ掻いた。

小野寺が悲鳴をあげた。わたしは小野寺の手を逃れた。

「雪乃、このやろうっ」

わたしは食卓を回って、流しに飛びついた。足もとの扉を開け、木の柄をつかんで引き抜く。ずっしりとした手応えを目の前に掲げ、小野寺と対峙した。

小野寺が、口の端を曲げて、にたりとする。

「ほお、出刃包丁とおいでなすったか」

わたしは肩で息をしながら、小野寺を睨んだ。

「こりゃ面白れ。やってみろよ、刺せるもんならやってみろよ」

わたしは小野寺に向かって走った。目を瞑って包丁を突き出した。

「男をなめんじゃねえ」

手首をつかまれ、ねじられた。動けなくなった。目の前に、小野寺の顔。

「おら、どうした？　そんなへっぴり腰じゃ、人は刺せねえぞ、おら」

悔しくて涙が溢れた。小野寺の顔に唾を吐いた。粘液が小野寺の頬に垂れる。

小野寺が、哀れむような目で、わたしを見た。

「潮時だな、俺たちも。悪いけど俺は、その山科の女子大生、利香子っていうんだけどな、彼女のところに行かせてもらうよ。利香子も俺といっしょに住みたいって、前から言ってくれてたし、俺も利香子となら、長くやっていけそうな気がする」

小野寺の瞳に、悪意が光る。

「利香子はな、おまえと違って、素直なんだよ、健気なんだよ、清純なんだよ。わかるか？　だいたいおまえはさ、トルコ嬢のくせに生意気なんだよ。売女がいい女ぶって、カッコつけやがって。この際おまえも、新しい男を見つけてやり直したらどうだ？　じつを言うと、おまえを譲って欲しいって話があってな。そいつに話を通しておいてやってもいいぞ。それがお互いのためだ。な、そうだろ？」

「ちっくしょう……殺してやる、殺してやるぅ……」

「馬鹿が」

手首を締めあげられた。指から力が抜けていく。包丁が手から離れる。床に落ちる。

次の瞬間、小野寺が、大きく口を開けた。悲鳴が迸った。わたしを突き放した。

手から落ちた包丁の切っ先が、小野寺の足の甲に刺さっていた。小野寺がしゃがみこみ、

包丁を引き抜いた。血が滴った。

「いでぇ、くっそう、いでぇっ!」

小野寺が、足を押さえて、のたうち回った。床に、引き抜かれた包丁が、落ちていた。先

端が赤く染まっていた。わたしは、拾いあげた。両手で握った。思い切り振りかぶった。

「雪乃、雪乃、医者、医者を呼んでくれ、おい……!」

見あげる小野寺の顔が、凍りついた。わたしは、叫びながら、打ちおろした。首と右肩の

境目に、刃が食いこんだ。両手で柄を握ったまま、引き抜いた。小野寺の首

から、鮮血が噴きあがった。小野寺が、目を剥いた。口をぱくぱくと動かした。スローモー

ションのようにゆっくりと、横倒しになった。心臓の拍動に合わせて、血が溢れ出た。

「きゅ……救急車……」

弱々しい声が、漏れてきた。

小野寺の手足が、痙攣（けいれん）を始めた。

やがて、それも、止まった。

静かだった。

床や壁に、赤い飛沫（しぶき）が、散っていた。

足もとには、大きな血だまり。

わたしは、小野寺の傍らに、しゃがんだ。

「小野寺……小野寺？」

小野寺は、答えなかった。

わたしは、立ちあがった。包丁を床に投げた。ごとりと音がして、転がった。息を吐いた。

震えていた。

終わっちゃったな、わたしの人生。

血に染まった下着を、脱ぎ捨てた。浴室に入って、鏡を見る。青白い顔で、長い髪を振り乱し、目を吊りあげ、口を半開きにした女が、映っていた。頰には血が、こびりついている。

シャワーを浴びて、血を洗い流した。浴室から出ると、汚臭が漂っていた。血に染まった

小野寺は、まだ目を見開いて、倒れている。瞼だけでも閉じてあげようかと思ったが、やめた。

自分の部屋に戻り、ドライヤーで髪を乾かした。新品の下着をつけ、化粧をする。洋服ダンスを開け、服を選んだ。タンスの隅に、灰色のジャンパーが掛かっていた。引っぱり出す。

徹也のお古。博多で着ていたもの。まだ捨てていなかったのだ。

あのころは、よかったな。

お金はなかったけれど、徹也がいてくれた。ときどき乱暴されたけど、徹也はわたしを必要としてくれていたし、わたしにも徹也が必要だった。いまから思えば、互いの傷を舐め合うような日々。それがどうして、こんなにも甘美なのだろう。わたしの胸で、子供のように泣きじゃくった徹也。ほかの男と寝たり、覚せい剤を打つことで、刹那の快楽は得られたが、あのときほど満ち足りた気持ちになることは、とうとうなかった。

服を決めた。ボトムはジーパン、トップは白いブラウスに手編みのセーター、そして徹也のジャンパー。ちぐはぐな格好だが、いちばんわたしらしい。ねえ、徹也?

下着と、ありったけの現金と、預金通帳と、その他細々としたものを、スポーツバッグに詰めた。

電話でタクシーを呼んだ。電話の横に、きのう書き付けたメモがあった。赤木の住所と電

話番号。その紙切れを、見つめた。長いあいだ、見つめた。そして、ちりぢりに破り、トイレに流した。

クラクションが聞こえた。バッグを持って、ドアに走った。ドアノブに手をかけたところで、振り返る。小野寺は、マネキン人形のような目を、天井に向けている。

「じゃあね、小野寺。わたしもすぐに行くけど、あなたのところじゃないわ。さようなら」

そして、少し迷ってから、付け加えた。

「ごめんね。でも、小野寺も悪いんだよ」

ドアを開けると、日光が降り注いでいた。足早にマンションを出て、タクシーに乗りこむ。

「雄琴温泉駅まで」

運転手に告げた。

雄琴温泉駅で、ヂーゼル列車に乗った。琵琶湖西岸を南下し、大津で降りる。ここで国鉄に乗り換えるつもりだった。しかし死に場所をどこにするかは、決めていない。

駅舎内を、あてもなく歩く。人の流れから外れ、柱の陰に立った。ざわめきが途切れることなく、まとわりついてくる。「みどりの窓口」という表示が、目に入った。

わたしはまだ、新幹線に乗ったことがなかった。博多まで通るのはまだ先だし、雄琴に来

るときは小野寺のクーペに乗ってきたので、新幹線は使わなかった。テレビでしか見たことのない夢の超特急。それに乗れば、ほんの数時間で、東京に行ける。

東京。

まだ一度も行ったことのない大都会。そこに行けば、何かが変わるかも知れない。すべての過去から、逃げられるかも知れない。

わたしは、みどりの窓口で、東京行きの切符を買った。乗車券、指定席の特急券合わせて、四千円ちょっとだった。

大津から東海道本線に乗り、京都で降りた。ホームから階段をのぼり、跨線橋を渡って、東京方面と書かれた新幹線ホームにおりる。

午後一時十三分、「ひかり三十二号」東京行きが入線した。胸の鼓動を感じながら、ひかり号に足を踏み入れる。わたしの指定席は、通路左列の窓際。隣は空いていた。座席に腰を落とし、バッグを膝に抱える。ひかり号が静かに動きだす。

身体を背もたれに沈めた。頭の中が空白になり、眠りに落ちた。

目が覚めたとき、嫌な夢を見た、と思った。

男の人を包丁で殺すなんて、どうしてそんな夢を見たのだろう。小野寺という名前まで覚

えている。それにしても、わたしがトルコ嬢になっているなんて、すごい夢だった。徹也？

ああ、そんな男の子も出てきた。一つ年下の、とても可愛い子だった。赤木というおじさんもいた。顔は怖いけど、根は優しい人だったような気がする。もう一人出てきたけど、名前を思い出せない。どうでもいいか。そろそろ起きなきゃ。学校に遅刻してしまう。

違う。この振動と音。わたしは列車に乗っている。どうして？　ああ、そうだ。修学旅行の下見？　いや、これが修学旅行の本番？　もう終わったのではなかったか。

目を開ける。

車窓の向こうに、富士山が聳えていた。青々とした山肌に、真っ白な頂。眠気が吹き飛んだ。息を呑むような美しさに、目を奪われた。

どうして富士山が……。まだ夢の中なのだろうか。

自分の服装を見た。膝に抱えているスポーツバッグを見た。手を見た。爪の中に、赤黒い汚れが残っていた。それはすべて、現実だった。

絶望が、腹の底から、せりあがってくる。

ジャンパーの襟をつかみ、ぎゅっと閉じた。ジャンパーに染みついた匂いを、吸いこんだ。徹也といっしょにいるような気がした。目頭が熱くなる。

徹也。

わたしの心は、潰れようとしていた。救いようもなく、徹也を求めていた。

そしてわたしは、自分の死に場所を、見つけた。

午後四時過ぎに、東京に降り立った。駅員を捕まえ、三鷹への行き方を尋ねた。教えられたとおり、中央線に乗り換える。四十分ほどで、三鷹に着いた。すでに陽が沈みかけていた。

三鷹駅のホームから階段をおり、改札口を出たところに、周辺地図の看板が掲げてある。

駅前の商店名などが書かれていた。地図によると玉川上水は、駅のすぐ脇を流れている。

徹也が太宰治の生まれ変わりなら、わたしは山崎富栄なのだ。どうしてあのとき、徹也の後を追わなかったのだろう。いっしょに死んでいれば、こんな目にあわなくて済んだのに。

でも、もういい。ここが終着駅。そしてわたしは、徹也のところに行く。徹也はきっと、痺れを切らしている。

駅舎を出て、左に曲がった。歩道沿いに、桜と思しき立木が並んでいた。枝越しに見おろすと、緩く傾斜した土手肌が見えた。その底に、石材を組んで造られた、水路らしき溝が横たわっている。幅二、三メートル、深さは一メートルくらい。しかし肝腎の水は、流れていない。太宰が入水したのは、どのあたりだろう。自殺できるほどなのだから、かなりの水量が流れているはずだ。

夕闇（ゆうやみ）が濃くなる中、玉川上水沿いを歩いた。どこまで歩いても、太宰治と山崎富栄が入水した地点を示す、碑のようなものはなかった。水の流れる音も聞こえない。そしてどこまで行っても、水路に水は現れなかった。桜の枝の合間から見える水路の底には、泥のこびりついた樹木の根のようなものが、干からびて絡み合っているだけ。

間違えたのだろうか。これは玉川上水とは別の何かなのだろうか。

戸惑いながら、歩き続けた。水路は、駅前の商店街から、田畑の広がる一帯に出た。ゆるいカーブを描いてから、公園らしき森に入る。その森を抜けたころには、すっかり陽が落ちていた。

街灯がないため、足もとも見にくかった。

森を出てしばらく歩いたところに、石橋が架かっていた。欄干には、新橋と刻まれている。新橋のたもとではなかったか。互いの腰を、赤い紐で結んでいたという。

太宰治と山崎富栄の遺体が発見されたのが、新橋のたもとではなかったか。互いの腰を、赤い紐で結んでいたという。

橋の真ん中に立ち、眼下の闇を見おろした。三メートル下を走っているはずの水路からは、何も聞こえなかった。聞こえるのは、ときおり橋を渡る自動車の音だけ。

「あんた、なにやってるの？」

はっとして振り向くと、小太りの男が立っていた。年齢は四十歳くらいか。くすんだ色のジャンパーを着ている。背はわたしより少し低い。髪は短く刈り上げられ、顔の輪郭は角張

っているが、眼差しはどこか哀しげだった。薄い唇を真一文字に結び、前屈み気味にわたしを見ている。

「あなた、誰?」

「おれはこの先で店をやってるもんだけど、あんた、このあたりじゃ見かけない顔だし、そうやって辛気くさい顔で橋に佇んでいるのを見たら、気になっちまって……迷惑だったらごめんよ」

わたしは首を横に振った。

「ねえ、よかったら教えてほしいんだけど」

「なんだい」

「ここ、玉川上水でしょ」

「そうだよ」

「太宰治と山崎富栄が入水した」

「あんたも太宰のファンかい?」

男が、ふっと笑う。男の肩から力が抜けたのが、見てとれた。男の目が、川底に向く。

「そうか。水がないから、期待はずれだったわけか。ここも以前は、抹茶色の水が、ゆったりと流れていたもんだよ。川幅が狭く見えても、けっこう深くて、底になるほど流れが速い。

落ちたが最後、まず這い上がれないものだから、自殺の名所になって、人喰い川なんて呼ばれたこともある。地元の人に聞いた話じゃ、太宰が死んだころには、年に三十人くらいは土左衛門があがって、子供にとっては近づくのも怖かったそうだ。それが七、八年前だったかな、上流の取水場が閉じられて、それ以来、水が流れてこなくなって、このとおりだよ」

「じゃあ玉川上水って、もう水が流れていないの?」

「そういうこと」

わたしは呆然とした。ぷっと吹き出した。堪えきれず、しゃがみこんだ。バッグを抱え、笑い続けた。腹がよじれて痛くなる。息苦しくなる。それでも笑いの衝動は、収まらなかった。

どのくらい笑っていただろう。呼吸を整え、顔をあげた。男はまだ、立っていた。不安げな笑みを浮かべて、わたしを見ている。ときおり車のヘッドライトが、男の姿を照らした。

「ごめんなさい、あんまり可笑しかったものだから。こんなに笑ったの、何年ぶりかしら」

わたしは立ちあがった。髪を後ろに払った。

「あんた、九州の人かい?」

「わかるの?」

「言葉がね、なんとなく。おれも長崎生まれだから」

46

「わたしは福岡、といっても、佐賀に近いところなんだけど」

「どこ？」

「大川市ってわかる？」

「知ってるよ。家具で有名なところだな」

「そう。わたしの家は、大野島といって、筑後川と早津江川に挟まれた三角州にあった。有明海が近くてね。朝、目を覚ますと、遠くから漁船のエンジンの音が聞こえてきて……」

わたしは、息を深く吸った。

「わたしね、ここで、死ぬつもりだった」

男が、うなずく。

「あなた、それで声をかけてくれたの？」

「入水自殺は無理でも、ここから飛び降りれば大怪我をする。動けなくなったら、寒さで死んでしまうかも知れない」

「ありがとう。もうだいじょうぶ。死のうなんて気持ち、どこかに行っちゃったわ」

「泊まるところはあるのかい？」

「死ぬつもりだったのよ、わたし」

「よかったら、うちに来るか？」

「ご家族に悪いわ」

「一人暮らしだよ。狭い家だけど、寝る場所ぐらいはある」

わたしは、男の顔を見つめた。

男が、決まり悪そうに目を逸らす。

「誤解するなよ。別に下心があるわけじゃない。おれはただ、あんたが困っているんじゃないかと思って……」

「わかってる」

男がわたしを見た。

「ありがとう。お言葉に甘えるわ」

「おれは島津賢治。名前、聞いていいかい?」

「わたしは雪……」

「ゆき?」

「いえ、松子。川尻松子が、わたしの名前よ」

島津賢治の家は、理容店だった。表のトリコロールは、止まっていた。ガラス張りのドアには『定休日』の札。ドアの上に掲げてある看板には『理容しまづ』とあった。

島津賢治が、鍵を使ってドアを開けた。入ると、整髪料の匂いがした。蛍光灯が点った。

左手一面の鏡の前に、セット椅子が二つ並んでいる。

わたしは、鏡に映った自分を見た。長すぎる髪を、手でつまんだ。

男が、ストーブに火を入れた。薬缶に水を入れ、ストーブの上に載せる。水色の仕事着に、

腕を通した。

「座りなよ。注文を聞かせてくれ。あまり洒落た髪型は苦手だけどな」

「いいの？　定休日なんでしょ」

「特別サービス」

わたしは、ふっと笑って、椅子に座った。

「とにかく短くして。髪型はお任せする」

「それならお安いご用だ」

島津が後ろに立った。わたしの首にタオルを巻き、白いケープをかける。

「苦しくないかい？」

「だいじょうぶ」

島津は霧吹きで髪を湿らせた。髪をほぐしてから、髪の束を指のあいだに挟む。先をハサ

ミで切る。黒い塊がばさりと落ちる。島津の指が、魔法をかけられたように、動きだした。

わたしの頭から、黒いものが次々と、落ちていく。

目を瞑った。リズミカルなハサミの音と、島津の指の感触に、身を任せた。

時計の秒針の音が聞こえる。店の壁にでも掛かっているのだろう。

「わたしのこと、聞かないの?」

「なにを?」

「どうして死のうと思ったのか」

「言いたけりゃ自分から言うと思った」

「あなたのこと、聞いていい?」

「ああ、いいぜ」

「一人で住んでいるの?」

「一人だ」

「家族は?」

「女房と六歳の息子がいたが、二人とも三年前に死んだ。交通事故だ」

「ごめんなさい」

「かまわないよ」

「聞いてくれる?」

「ああ」

「わたし、好きな人がいた。その人は自分を、太宰治の生まれ変わりだって言っていた。その人、自殺したの。電車に飛びこんで」

島津の指は、わたしの髪の中で、黙々と動いていた。

「そのあと、いろいろあって……わたしも死ぬことにした。その人のところに行きたくて、玉川上水で死のうと思った。彼が太宰の生まれ変わりなら、太宰の死んだ玉川上水で死ねば、彼のところに行けるんじゃないかって。ところが来てみたら、玉川上水には水がなかったってわけ。とんだ山崎富栄だわ……ね、馬鹿みたいでしょ」

「洗髪するよ」

「うん」

「美容院と違って、前屈みになってもらうけど」

島津が鏡の下の取っ手を手前に倒すと、洗髪台が現れた。わたしは上半身をかがめた。シャワーのあと、シャンプー、リンスと続く。島津が黙って、自分の仕事をこなしていく。リンスを洗い流してから、タオルで水気を拭き、ドライヤーで乾かす。髪型を整えて、整髪料をスプレーする。

「さあ、できた」

わたしは目を開けた。思わず歓声をあげた。生まれて初めてのショートボブ。髪はサイドに流してあり、前髪が軽く額にかかっている。知的で、清楚で、別人に生まれ変わったようだった。鏡の中の自分が、微笑んでいた。

わたしは、右、左、と顔の向きを変えた。

「よく似合うと思うんだがな」

「ありがとう。素敵だわ」

「よかった」

「おいくら？」

「いらないよ」

「そういかないわ」

島津のお腹が、大きく鳴った。島津が気まずそうに、頭を掻いた。

「ほんと言うと、さっきは行きつけの小料理屋に、飯を食いに行くところだったんだ」

わたしのお腹も鳴った。

「そういえばわたしも、きのうから何も口にしていなかった。そうだ。何かつくってあげようか」

「あまり自炊しないから、ろくなもんがないよ。駅前まで歩けば、遅くまでやってる居酒屋

「三鷹駅（みたかえき）？」

「いや、井の頭線の、井の頭公園駅。歩いて五分くらい」

「行きましょ。わたしが奢（おご）るわ。髪を切ってもらったお礼に」

「いや、それには……」

「その前にちょっと待ってくれる？」

「どうしたんだい？」

「せっかくだから、お化粧したいわ。洗髪のときに落ちちゃったみたい」

居酒屋の軒先には、赤ちょうちんが揺れていた。カウンター席が四つと、幼稚園児が使うようなテーブルが二つあるだけの、こぢんまりとした店だった。客は三人。みな、仕事帰りらしき男だった。

わたしと島津は、テーブル席に着いた。注文は島津に任せた。ビールで乾杯し、やきとり、肉じゃが、つくね、マグロの刺身、焼きおにぎりと続く。島津はよほど腹が減っていたのか、がつがつと口に運んでいた。その喰いっぷりは豪快で、見とれるほどだった。わたしもつられるように、料理を口にした。美味しい、と思った。

島津は、わたしのことをあれこれ詮索しようとはせず、もっぱら理容師になりたてのころの話をしてくれた。

「最初は丁稚奉公みたいなものでさ、小遣いみたいな給料で、朝早くから夜遅くまで、一日十五時間くらい働いていた。眠る時間もわずかなもんだった。まさに職人の世界だったよ」

「辞めようとは思わなかったの？」

「うちは祖父さんの代から床屋だったから、ほかの職業に就くなんて考えもしなかったな」

「ご実家のお店は？」

「兄貴たちが継いでる。暖簾分けもして、地元ではけっこう大きくなっているらしい」

「そのお店を手伝ったりしないの？」

「いろいろあって、飛び出してきたんだよ。こっちにも意地があるから、いまさら帰れない」

島津が、子供のように口を尖らせた。

「ずいぶん帰ってないの？」

「十四、五年になるかな」

「帰りたいとは思わない？」

「……親がどうしてるか、それだけかな、気になるのは」

「わたしも、三年前に家を飛び出したの」

「それで東京に？」

「東京はきょう来たばかり。それまでは、あっちこっちにね」

腹を満たし、ほどよく酔って、店を出る。勘定はわたしが払った。島津が払おうとしたが、わたしが睨んだら、おとなしく引きさがった。

わたしと島津は、肩をすぼめ、震えながら、家に戻った。

島津が風呂を沸かしてくれた。わたしは島津の後に入浴した。自分の家では男が先に入るものだったと言ったら、島津も納得してくれた。

風呂からあがると、浴衣が用意してあった。

「よかったら、使ってくれ」

声が聞こえた。少し湿っぽかったが、使わせてもらうことにした。亡くなった奥さんのものだろうかと、ちらと思った。

島津が、テレビのある六畳の部屋に、案内してくれた。すでに布団が一組、敷いてあった。抽出の四つある箪笥の上には、薬箱や観光土産らしき人形が飾ってある。壁際には、ちゃぶ台が立ててあった。

「ここを使ってくれ。狭くて悪いけど。電気あんかを入れておいたから」

「あなたは?」

「向こうの座敷で寝てる」

「そう。いろいろと、ありがとう」

「おやすみ」

「おやすみなさい」

島津が、ガラス戸を閉めた。

わたしは、紐を引っぱって、電灯を消した。布団の上に正座し、耳をすませた。

考えてみれば、普通の民家に寝泊まりするのは、久しぶりだった。大野島の家を飛び出して以来、ずっとアパートやマンション暮らしだったのだ。家にはそれぞれ、住んできた人間の、生活の匂いが染みついている。家族の歴史が、刻まれている。それは決して、嫌なものではないな、と思った。

家のどこかにあるのだろう。柱時計が、午後十一時を告げた。

わたしは、立ちあがった。ガラス戸を開け、廊下に出た。冷たかった。襖の閉まった部屋の前で、腰を落とす。耳をすます。両手を襖に添え、静かに開けた。杏色の常夜灯が、点っていた。島津は布団の中で、目を閉じていた。胸がゆっくりと、上下している。

わたしは部屋に入り、襖を閉じた。部屋の奥には、仏壇があった。わたしはその前まで、

進んだ。女性と男の子の写真が、立ててある。わたしはその写真を、静かに伏せた。仏壇の扉を、閉めた。島津のほうへ向き直り、浴衣を脱いだ。下着を外し、畳に落とした。島津が目を開けた。わたしの裸体を見あげて、目を剝いた。

「あんた……」

わたしは腰を落とし、布団をめくった。

「待ってくれ、おれは、そんなつもりじゃ……」

わたしは島津の口に、人差し指を立てた。

「おねがい、恥をかかせないで」

囁<ruby>囁<rt>ささや</rt></ruby>いて、島津の身体に寄り添った。

翌日から、店の手伝いを始めた。掃除の仕方から、蒸しタオルの準備、レジの精算まで、一つ一つ教えてもらいながら、覚えていった。どれもが新鮮で、おもしろかった。島津からは、要領の呑みこみが早いと誉められた。

店は古いなりに、固定客がついているらしい。ほとんどが男性で、注文はたいてい、いつものようにしてくれ、だった。

そういう人たちにとって、わたしの存在は衝撃的だったらしい。島津も、わたしをどう説

明していいものか迷ったらしいが、遠い親戚の娘でしばらく預かることになった、と苦しい言い訳をしていた。客の中にはそれで納得しない人も多く、小松刈りの大工の棟梁からは、

「おい、賢ちゃん。いつのまに嫁さんをもらったんだ？」

と冷やかされ、島津が顔を赤くしていた。結局は、親戚の娘などではなく、同棲の相手ということがばれてしまったが、それで客の評判を落とすでもなく、逆に贔屓の客から、

「これで俺も一安心だ。賢ちゃんのこと、よろしく頼むぜ」

と言葉をかけてもらったりした。

島津との日々は、信じられないくらい平穏だった。朝はいっしょに起きて、島津は開店準備、わたしは朝御飯をつくる。朝八時から夜七時までの営業時間は、島津が調髪をし、わたしが洗髪やレジを担当する。仕事の後は掃除や片づけを済ませ、夕食をとる。日曜日の晩には、外でお酒を飲む。夜はいっしょに入浴し、床で愛し合う。心地よい疲労を感じながらぐっすりと眠り、日の出とともに目を覚ます。そんな二カ月が、幻のように過ぎていった。

わたしは、お代わりの御飯を茶碗に盛り、島津に渡した。島津が、サンキュ、と言って、受け取る。

島津はいつも、御飯を喉に押しこむように食べる。頬を目いっぱいに膨らませ、猛烈な早さで咀嚼して、呑みこむ。まるでフィルムの早回しだった。

島津が、頬を膨らませたまま、目をあげた。なに見てるんだ、と言ったらしかったが、御飯が口に詰まっていて、はひひへふは、と聞こえた。

わたしは、くすりと笑った。

「男らしい食べ方だなあと思って」

島津が、ふんと鼻を鳴らして、咀嚼を再開した。お茶で流しこんでから、「おれは六人兄弟の五番目で、早く食べないと飯がなかった。だから子供のときから早く食べる癖がついてしまった。この歳になったら直せないよ」

「直さなくてもいいけど、喉に詰まらせたりしないの?」

島津が、真面目くさった顔で言う。わたしは、うふふ、と笑った。

「年に二、三回かな」

「ねえ、お店で、賢治さんのことを何て呼んだらいいかしら?」

「賢治さんでいいんじゃないか?」

「でも仕事と私生活は、きちんとけじめをつけたほうがいいんじゃない?」

「堅苦しいことを言うんだな。どう呼びたいんだ?」

「わたし考えたんだけど、先生っていうのは?」

島津が、飲みかけたお茶を、ぶっと噴き出した。

「おれが先生?　勘弁してくれよ」

「そうかしら。わたしの行っていた美容室では、みんな先生って呼ばせていたわ」

「おれはそんな余所余所しい言い方より、賢治さんとか、あなたとか、親しみをこめて呼ばれるほうが好きだな。たとえ仕事場でも」

「あなた、っていうのは、ちょっと図々しいわ。奥さんでもないのに」

島津が箸を置いた。神妙な顔で、両手を膝の上に揃える。

「そのことなんだけど」

「え」

「けじめをつけるというのなら、この際ちゃんと、籍を入れたらどうかと思うんだ」

わたしは、島津の顔を見つめた。持っていた茶碗と箸を、下に置く。両手を前で重ねた。

「それ、結婚しようって、言ってるの?」

「そうだ。もちろん、君が嫌だと言うのなら、どうしようもないけど。見てのとおり、おれは若くはないし、一介の町の床屋に過ぎない。断られても、仕方がないと思っている」

島津が、自信なさげに、目を伏せる。

わたしは心臓が高鳴った。舞いあがりそうな心を叱りつけ、押しとどめる。懸命に笑みをつくった。

「賢治さん、まだわたしのこと、よく知らないくせに。わたしがどんな女なのか知ったら、きっと軽蔑するわ。わたし、あなたに相応しい女じゃないもの」

「君がどんな過去を背負っているのか、おれにはわからない。でも、昔のことを話したくないのなら、何も話さなくていい。過去のことはどうだっていい。おれはただ……君とずっといっしょに、暮らしたいだけなんだ」

わたしは、こみあげてくるものを、抑えられなかった。無理に笑おうとしても、頰が震えた。

「まいったなあ、そんなこと言われるなんて、考えもしなかった」

わたしは、目を瞑って、俯いた。

息を吸い、吐いた。

夢を見よう。いまだけは、夢を見よう。どんなに大きな悲哀が、後からやって来ようとも。

わたしは、覚悟を決めた。

目を開けて、島津を見た。

「きちんと言ってみて」

「なにを?」

「プロポーズの言葉」

島津が、背すじを伸ばす。

わたしの目を、まっすぐ見る。

「松子、おれと、結婚してくれ」

わたしは、胸を膨らませた。

「はい」

島津を見つめたまま、涙をぽろぽろと零した。

台所に入ると、外から鳥の囀りが聞こえてきた。朝日を浴びた窓は、黄金に輝いている。

そろそろ玉川上水沿いの桜も、花を綻ばせるだろうか。

わたしはエプロンを着け、米びつから米を取り、流しで研いだ。炊飯器のスイッチを入れてから、ナベに水を張って、火にかける。その間に大根をまな板にのせ、イチョウ切りにする。大根をたっぷり入れた味噌汁が、島津の好物だった。

昨夜の会話を思い出すと、頬が緩む。プロポーズを受けた後、わたしは島津と、将来のことを話し合った。島津は、いずれはわたしも、理容師か美容師の資格を取ったらどうかと言

った。そうすればわたしも、一緒に調髪ができるし、もし美容師の資格を取れれば、新たに女性客を呼びこむこともできる。お金が貯まったら、美容院を別につくってもいい。それは思ってもいないアイデアだった。そして、とても素敵なアイデアだった。わたしにとって、夢ができたのだ。

ナベの水が煮立ってきた。鰹節を加え、ふわりと吹き上がったところで、火を止めて鰹節を濾し上げた。真っ白い湯気とともに、濃厚な旨味が立ちのぼる。わたしは胸一杯に、吸いこんだ。ふたたび火を点け、ナベに大根を落としたときだった。

「なんだよ、あんたら！」

店から、島津の怒声が響いた。わたしは、身を固くした。まだ開店には間がある。それに島津が声を荒らげるなど、めったにない。

わたしはガスの火を止め、エプロンをしたまま、店に出た。

「あなた、どうしたの？」

店に、背広姿の男が二人と、婦人警官が一人、立っていた。三人の視線が、わたしを射た。

「中に入ってろ！」

島津が振り向いて、怒鳴った。顔面は、熱湯を被ったように赤かった。

「川尻松子だね」

男の一人が言った。

わたしは、うなずいた。　脚が震えていた。

男が警察手帳を出す。

「一月二十八日、滋賀県大津市のマンションで、小野寺保、三十一歳が刺し殺された事件で、逮捕状が出てる」

もう一人の刑事が、一枚の紙切れを示した。

「裏にも警官を置いてある。　観念しなよ」

わたしは、島津の顔を見た。　島津は口を開け、瞬きもせずに、わたしを見つめていた。わたしは刑事に向き直り、

「わかりました。　用意しますので、お待ちください」

婦人警官が前に出た。　背が低く色白だが、体つきは逞しく、ふくらはぎは聖護院かぶらを思わせる。

「わたくしもごいっしょします」

「わたしは逃げません」

「いえ、ごいっしょさせていただきます。　取り返しのつかないことが起こるといけませんの

で」

わたしは、婦人警官と睨み合った。わたしが先に、目を逸らした。

「おい、いったい、なんなんだ。松子が何をしたんだ！」

島津が、わたしと刑事たちを、交互に見た。

婦人警官が、島津の横を通り過ぎようとしたとき、

「おいっ！」

島津が遮ろうとしたが、二人の刑事に止められた。婦人警官が平然と、わたしの腕を取っ

た。

「早くしてね。人が集まってくるわよ」

婦人警官が、前を見たまま、言った。

「わたしが自殺すると思ってるんですか？」

答は返ってこない。

わたしは、奥に入った。背後から、島津の声が聞こえる。泣いていた。

「あなた、自分が全国に指名手配されてるって、気づかなかったの？」

婦人警官が静かに言った。

「せめて偽名を使おうとは、思わなかったの？」

わたしは答えず、身の回りのものを、スポーツバッグに入れた。鏡の前に座り、口紅を引いた。鏡の中の婦人警官は、わたしが口紅を呑みこむとでも疑っているのか、厳しい目を向けている。

「終わった？」

「もう少し」

今朝届いたばかりの新聞から、広告を引き抜いた。裏が空白で、厚手のものを選び出した。

そこに口紅で、置き手紙を書いた。

ありがとう。短い間だったけど、しあわせでした。わたしのことは、忘れてください。

松子

2

「いちばんいい女だったってなぁ……」

さすがオフィス街の真ん中にあるホテルらしく、ロビーにはビジネスマン風の外国人が多かった。俺は、高級ホテルに足を踏み入れること自体が初めてで、居心地が悪かった。つまみ出されるんじゃないかと冷や冷やしながら、臙脂色の絨毯を歩いているうちに、太い角柱の陰にソファを見つけたので、とりあえずそこに腰をおろした。

周りは、スーツや正装で決めた人たちばかり。耳に入ってくる言葉は、日本語よりも英語のほうが多いくらいだ。フロント係やボーイさんたちも、涼しい顔で英語を話している。

俺は沢村社長に電話をかけたあと、ひかり荘に戻ってヒゲ野郎の部屋に跳び蹴りを喰らわせてから、北千住駅に向かった。まだ時間があったので、駅前の「ロッテリア」に入った。

ひかり荘を初めて訪れる朝に、明日香と朝食をとった店だ。考えてみれば、あれから二日しか経っていないのだ。

ハンバーガーとフライドポテトとコーラで腹を満たしてから、日暮里に出て山手線で東京駅まで行った。丸の内中央口を出たところの交番で場所を確認し、排気ガスあふれる永代通

りを歩き、パレスホテルに到着したのだった。

時計を見ると、もうすぐ約束の四時になる。電話での口ぶりからして、時間には正確な人のようだから、そろそろ来てもいいころだ。

フロント横の、三基あるエレベーターのうち、真ん中の箱が開き、北欧系の金髪美女が現れた。黒の革パンツに胸元の開いた白シャツ。目はエメラルドグリーンというのだろうか。ボリューム満点の俺を見て微笑んだ、ような気がしたが、そのまま颯爽と通り過ぎていった。

俺はヒップを見送りながら、いくらなんでも彼女じゃないよな、と思った。

「笠くん？」

金髪美女のヒップから目を引きはがし、振り返ると、これまた東洋系の美女が立っていた。

背は俺と同じくらい。ヒョウ柄のキャミソールに、同じ柄のひざ丈スカート。足もとは黒のパンプス。スカートにはスリットが入っていて、太股の曲面がのぞいている。剝き出しの胸元や肩は、白く艶を放って眩しいくらいだ。両端が切れあがった唇は、濡れたように赤く、赤っぽく染められた髪は、完璧にメイクされた目許には、魅入られそうな光が宿っている。水大胆に後ろで纏めてあり、イヤリングの大きな真珠や、細長い首筋が露わになっている。泳かエアロビクスでもやっているのか、均整のとれた体つきで、贅肉がほとんどない。年齢は三十歳くらい？　もっと若いような、もっと年上のような、しかしとにかく、自分で言う

だけあって、紛れもなく大人の、いい女だった。引き合いに出すのも気の毒だが、この美女に比べれば、明日香はまだまだ子供だと、痛感させられた。

「違うの?」

美女が首を傾げる。

俺は立ちあがって、気をつけの姿勢をとった。

「はい、笙です」

「やっぱりね、そうだと思った」

ちょっと嗄れた声が、クールに響く。

「どうしてわかったんですか?」

「あなたがいちばん場違いに見えたから」

「…………」

「あらためて自己紹介するわ。沢村です」

「川尻笙です」

沢村社長が、くすりと笑う。

「けっこう可愛い顔してるのね」

「……はあ」

沢村社長がくるりと向きを変え、ホテルの正面出口に向かった。俺は急いで、沢村社長を追った。

「話は車で聞くわ」

ホテルの外に出ると同時に、地下駐車場から白いベンツが顔を出し、俺たちの前に停まった。すかさずホテルのボーイさんが、後部座席のドアを開ける。沢村社長が、ありがと、と言って乗りこんだ。俺はそのあとに、どうも、と言って乗った。ドアが閉まり、ベンツが動きだす。運転席には、若い男が座っていた。バックミラーに映っている目と、横顔を見るかぎりでは、相当の美形だった。

高級ホテル、白いベンツ、ヒョウ柄の美女、そして美男子の運転手。俺とは住む世界が違う。まるで違う。ほんとうに松子伯母は、こんな人たちと交流があったのだろうか。

「さ、笙くん。始めようか」

沢村社長が、両手をお腹の上に重ね、長い脚を組んだ。スカートのスリットが、はらりと開く。扇情的な香水の薫りが、車内にたちこめた。

「最初にもう一度聞いておくけど、松子が死んだってのは、ほんとうなんだね」

「はい」

「殺されたっていうのも?」

「そうです」

「誰にやられたのかも、わかってないんだね」

「警察は、龍さんを疑っているみたいです」

沢村社長が、細長い煙草を手にした。　俺をちらと見る。

「あ、どうぞ。　吸ってください」

沢村社長が、鼻息をついた。ライターを取り出し、面倒くさそうに火を点けた。　煙をふう

と吹く。

「まあ、疑われても仕方ないけどね」

「龍さんは、やってません」

「んなことはわかってるよ。　あの男、あたしのことは何か言ってた？」

「ちょっと変わってるけど、辣腕家で、業界の有名人だって言ってました」

「ふうん、それだけなの」

沢村社長が、興味なさげに、煙草を燻らせた。

「ねえ笙くん、あたし、何歳に見える？」

「……三十歳ですか？」

沢村社長の腕が伸びてきた。　頭をつかまれ、引き寄せられ、抱きしめられる。　俺は沢村社

長の谷間で顔面を塞がれ、息ができなくなった。

「ふぐぐ……んがっ」

と腕が緩んだと思ったら、こんどは、ぶちゅ、とキスされた。ようやく解放され、呆気に

とられる俺を見て、沢村社長が満面の笑みを浮かべる。

「残念でした。正解は四十九歳」

俺は、顎が外れそうなほど、口を開けた。

四十九歳ってことは、お袋と同い年……。

「さ、挨拶はこのくらいにして、本題に入ろうか」

沢村社長が、笑みを吹き消した。

「聞きたいこととは？　あたしが知っていることなら話してあげるよ。死人に気兼ねしても仕

方がないものね」

俺は、唇を手で拭った。心臓はまだ暴れている。バックミラーを見ると、運転席の美男子

は、眉ひとつ動かしてない。

俺は、大きく息を吸い、吐いた。

「あの……松子伯母さんと最後に会ったのは、いつなんですか？」

「島崎　佳織のお見舞いに行ったの、いつだっけ？」

運転席の美男子が答えた。柔らかな声だった。

「七月九日でした」

「七月九日」

「そのときの松子伯母さんの様子を、話してもらえませんか？」

「その日は、足立区の病院に、お見舞いに行ったのよ。事務所の子が入院していたんでね。その帰りだったね。病院の待合室の前を通りかかったら、会計係が名前を呼ぶ声が聞こえたのさ、川尻松子さーんって。あたしは思わず立ち止まって、そっちを見た。同姓同名かと思ったけど、思い切って声をかけた。そうしたら……それが、十八年ぶりに会う松子だった」

「太っていたって聞いたんですけど」

「そうね。前に比べたら、だいぶ太っていたね。髪もぼさぼさでさ、着ているものも、よれよれのTシャツに安っぽいスカートだもんね。昔の面影は、ほとんどなかった。名前を聞かなかったら、絶対わからなかっただろうね」

「松子伯母さんは、沢村さんのことを、すぐにわかったんでしょうか？」

「たぶんね。あたしは変わってないものね」

「……そうでしょうね。松子伯母さんは、どんな生活をしていたんですか？」

「そこまではわからない。住所も教えてくれなかったし、ただ、あたしに見られたことを、負い目に感じているみたいだった」

「沢村さんは、松子伯母さんに、どんな話をしたんですか？」

「おこがましいとは思ったんだけどね、うちで働く気はないかって聞いたんだよ。見るに見かねたってこともあるけど、専属の美容師が欲しいと思っていたのも、事実だったからね」

「美容師？　松子伯母さんが、美容師？」

「そう。彼女は腕のいい美容師だったのよ、知らなかったの？」

俺は首を横に振った。

「学校の先生だったって、さっき龍さんに聞いて、びっくりしたばかりなんですけど……」

「学校の先生？　それ、あたしは初耳だわ」

俺と沢村社長は、数秒間、見つめ合った。

沢村社長が、目を前に向ける。

「ま、いいわ。ええと、どこまで話したっけ」

「川尻松子さんに、我が社で美容師として働かないかと、勧誘したところまでです」

「ありがと、島崎。でね、もちろん、ブランクがあるだろうから、すぐ使いものになるかど

運転席から声がした。

うかはわからなかったけど、チャンスだけはあげようと思った。松子にもはっきり言った

よ。あなたにその気さえあれば、いくらでもチャンスはあげる。すべてあなた次第なんだっ

て」

「松子伯母さんは、なんと?」

「最初はね、ごちゃごちゃ言ってたけど、最後には、考えてみるって言ったよ。あたしも牧

師じゃないからね、生きる気力のない人間まで救うことはできない。だから名刺を渡して、

その気になったら連絡してって言って、別れたの」

「結局、連絡は来なかったんですね」

「来なかった。死んじまったら、待っても来るわけないよね。来たら怖いわ」

沢村社長が、寂しげに笑う。

「でも、待っていたんでしょ」

「……待っていたよ。ていうより、信じていたんだ。松子は頭のいい人だからね、このまま

じゃいけないって、必ず気づくと思った」

沢村社長が、目を瞬かせた。煙草を口にくわえ、頰をすぼめて吸う。煙草の先端が、きら

りと光る。沢村社長が、煙草を灰皿に押しつけた。

「十八年前は、どういう関係だったんですか?」

「あたしがたまたま行きつけていた美容院に、松子が美容師として採用されてきたんだ。そのときは逆にあたしが、それが松子だとすぐにわかったけど、松子はあたしだと気づかなかったみたいだった。まあ、無理はないけどね。……そういえば、あの男が松子と会ったのも、同じ美容院だったはずだよ」

「え、そうなんですか。その美容院というのは、東京に？」

「そう。銀座に、いまもあるよ」

「そのころは、まだ太っていなかった？」

「そうだね。ずっと引き締まっていた。ぜんぜん変わってなかったな。前よりも綺麗なくらいだった。ま、化粧をしていたせいかも知れないけど」

沢村社長の表情が、緩んだ。

「すごくいい目をしていたんだよ、そのときの彼女。全身全霊を傾けて、何かに立ち向かっているって感じでさ。あたしは、そういう人間が好きなんだよ。ファイターがね」

「でも松子伯母さん、どうして美容師になったんだろう」

「さあね」

沢村社長が、とぼけたように言った。

「でも、さっきも言ったけど、美容師としての腕は大したものだったんだよ。あたしも必ず

松子を指名したもの。まあ、旧知のよしみってこともあったけど、それだけじゃなかったね。

ほかの客のあいだでも、けっこう評判がよかったらしいし」

「あのう、そもそも沢村さんが松子伯母さんと知り合ったのは、どこなんですか?」

沢村社長の動きが、止まった。

「だから、美容院で……」

「でも、そのときはすでに、知り合いだったでしょ」

「あたし、そんなこと言ったっけ」

「言いました。前よりも綺麗になっていたとか、旧知のよしみとか……てことは、それ以前

にどこかで知り合いになっていたってことでしょ?」

沢村社長が、舌打ちをする。

「あのう、もうひとつ基本的なことを聞いていいですか?」

「なに?」

「サワムラ企画って、どういう会社なんですか?」

沢村社長が、ため息をついた。

「笠くんねえ、それ、すっごい失礼な質問よ。いちおうあたしも会社のトップなんだからね。

そういう人間に会うときには、その会社の事業内容をチェックしておくなんて、常識以前の

問題だよ。うちはホームページだって開いてるんだから、いくらでも調べようがあるでしょうが。時間がなかったなんて言わないでね。そういう台詞（せりふ）は、無能の証（あかし）だよ」

俺は恐れ入って、身体を小さくした。

「……すみません」

「まあ、いいわ。うちはね、モデルやタレントを抱える芸能事務所なの」

「芸能事務所……有名人がいっぱいいる？」

「ねえ、笠くん、サワムラ企画って名前、ほんとうに目にしたことないの？」

沢村社長が、意味深な笑みを浮かべる。

「笠くんも好きだと思うんだけど」

「？」

「アダルトビデオ、観たことない？」

「アダ……じゃあ、サワムラ企画に所属してるタレントさんって……」

「そう。AV嬢、ストリップダンサー、あとはテレビの二時間ドラマで、有名女優の吹替えで裸になったり、混浴シーンで意味もなく登場したり、まあ主に、その手の女の子を抱えてる事務所なの」

全身に汗が滲（にじ）んできた。

「……ということは。

「そうか。松子伯母さんは、所属タレントの一人だったんだ」

沢村社長が、吹き出した。

「違う、違う。ぜんぜん関係ないよ」

松子伯母が、かつての所属タレントというのであれば、沢村社長との繋がりは納得できる。

しかし沢村社長の顔は、嘘を言ってるようには見えない。こうなると、俺にはもうわからなかった。

「どうしても言わせるつもりかい?」

「え」

「しょうがないね、あんまり言いたくないんだけど、何でも話すって約束しちゃったもんね」

沢村社長が、俯いてから、ゆっくりと目をあげた。

「もうあれから二十七年になるか。あたしと松子が会ったのはね……」

口元に、不敵な笑みが浮かぶ。

「塀の中さ」

「へ?」

沢村社長が、目許を顰めた。

「にぶい子だね。刑務所だよ」

主文。被告人を懲役八年に処する。うち殺人罪に対し懲役七年、覚せい剤取締法違反に対し懲役一年とする。未決勾留日数百十三日を本刑に算入する。

3

被告人は、昭和二十二年八月二日、川尻恒造、多恵の長女として、福岡県大川市大字大野島に生まれた。二年後には弟の紀夫、さらに三年後には妹の久美が生まれた。父親は市役所の総務課に勤める地方公務員で、家庭は経済的には安定しており、何も問題がなかったが、妹が三歳のときに大病を患って入院し、以後も入退院を繰り返すようになった。被告人はそのころから、父親の関心が急速に自分から離れていくのを感じ、それを繋ぎ止めることに心を砕くようになり、いっそう勉学に励むようになったために、成績はクラスで常にトップとなり、学級委員に選ばれたこともあった。

高校に進学しても成績は上位を維持し続け、大学進学に臨んで国立大学入学を希望するようになり、理数系を得意とする被告人は、東京の大学の理学部に進学することを望んだが、父親がそれを望まず、逆に、被告人が地元の大学の文学部に進み、教職員の資格を得て、地元の学校の教師となることを望んでいることを知ったことから、自分の志

望を貫くことをあえてせず、父親の言葉に従ってＫ大学文学部を受験し、合格した。
大学の四年間は家を出て、大学近くのアパートに一人で暮らし、この間に親しい同性
の友人もでき、それなりに有意義な学生生活を送ったが、特定の異性をつくるまでには
至らなかった。在学中に教職員の資格を取得し、卒業後は父親の希望通り、地元の大川
第二中学校に国語教諭として赴任した。

（略）

翌朝の十時頃、小野寺保が帰宅した。被告人は一睡もしていなかったが、小野寺に対
し、トルコ嬢を辞めて、二人で小料理屋を開くことを提案した。小料理屋は、亡くなっ
た親友Ｓの夢でもあり、親友に代わって自分が夢を叶えてあげようと考えたものであっ
たが、小野寺はその提案に難色を示した。小野寺の態度に不審を抱いた被告人は、預け
てあった預金通帳を見せるよう迫ったところ、小野寺に渡していた稼ぎだけでなく、そ
れ以前に貯めてあったお金まで勝手に使いこまれていたことを知り、まるで小野寺が親
友の夢を踏みにじったかのように感じ、逆上した。口論するさいのやりとりから、小野
寺の浮気まで発覚し、絶対にこの生活から抜け出したいと思うようになった。しかし小
野寺は、そんな被告人の心情にはまったく理解を見せず、逆に、覚せい剤を打てば気が
変わる、と言って、強引に注射しようとした。小野寺の手を逃れるため被告人は、出刃

包丁を取って相対したが、小野寺はひるむどころか、やれるものならやってみろ、と挑発したため、被告人は激情に任せて刃を突き出したが、容易に手を押さえられ、おまえにはもう飽きた、山科の女子学生といっしょに暮らすことにする、おまえを譲って欲しいという話もあるから、おまえはそいつのところにでも行けばいい、と、まるで自分が人間ではなく、物であるかのような扱いをされていると知り、悔し涙を流したが、男の力には抗うことができなかった。しかし手首をねじられた拍子に包丁が落下したとき、偶然にも刃先が小野寺の足の甲に突き刺さり、小野寺は悲鳴をあげての力いっぱい振り下ろし、被告人はこの機に乗じて床に落ちた包丁を拾い、小野寺めがけて力いっぱい振り下ろし、右頸（けい）動脈裂傷により失血死するにいたらしめて殺害したものである。

（略）

弁護人は、被告人は激情に駆られて全人格的判断を経ることなく、短絡的に本件犯行に及んだもので、心神喪失の状態か、少なくとも心神耗弱（こうじゃく）の状態にあったものと主張する。

（略）

たしかに小野寺保の言動、行為にも責められるべき点が多く、屈強な男性から覚せい剤を強制的に注射されようとして、自己防衛のために出刃包丁を持ち出した被告人の行

為は、じゅうぶん理解の範疇（はんちゅう）にある。また、無念の死を遂げた親友の夢を、自分が成り代わって果たそうとする行為は、美しいとさえ言える。しかし、すでに重傷を負って身動きの取れなくなった無抵抗の男性に、刃（やいば）を振り下ろすという犯行の態様はまことに残忍であり、結果もまたきわめて重大で、正当防衛の範疇を完全に逸脱するものであり、被告人の責任が重いものであることに疑う余地はない。覚せい剤を常用するに至った経緯についても、小野寺から勧められたとき、断ろうと思えば断れたのに、疲労を和らげるという誘惑に負けてしまった被告人の弱さは、指摘されねばならない。また経済的に比較的恵まれた家庭に育ち、高学歴を得ながらこのような境遇に至った背景には、病弱な妹のために父親の愛情をじゅうぶんに受けられなかったという同情すべき事情はあるものの、自己中心的で、場当たり的で、狭い視野でしか対人関係を築けない、被告人の性格が根本要因としてあり、自業自得と言われても否定できない側面がある。被告人のこの性格は、事件後に警察に出頭しようともせず、自殺したかつての恋人のところに行こうと玉川上水まで行きながら自殺を果たせず、たまたま声をかけられた男性Ｓとあっさりと男女の関係を結んで夫婦同然の生活を始めるなど、第三者から見れば理解しがたい行動にも表れている。

（略）

覚せい剤については、尿から検出されなかったにも拘わらず使用を自白し、マンショ
ンの冷蔵庫に残っていた覚せい剤の所持をみずから認めるなど、反省の姿勢がうかがえ
るが、被害者への謝罪という点ではじゅうぶんとは言い難く、殺人という犯罪の重大さ
を認識し、心から反省しているとは到底思えない。

（略）

以上の被告人にとって有利不利と思われるいっさいの事情を考慮すれば、主文記載の
通り量刑処断するのが相当であると思慮する。よって主文の通り判決する。

昭和四十九年八月

「そこの部屋よ、あなたが先に入って」

女子刑務官の投げやりな声が、背後から聞こえた。薄ぼけた緑色の上着とズボン姿のこの
刑務官は、眼鏡（めがね）をかけた四十歳前後の太り肉（じし）で、化粧が異様に濃かった。

わたしは「取調室」と札の出ている部屋の前に立ち、金属製のドアを開けた。一歩踏み入

れて、立ち止まった。真っ暗だった。ぱちんと音がして、蛍光灯が点る。天井に備え付けてある扇風機が、回りだした。

狭い部屋だった。壁際に木の机と椅子が寄せられている。中央の床には、二本の白線が引いてある。その横に脱衣かごのようなものが二つ置いてあり、一つに灰色の何かが入っていた。

わたしは、部屋の真ん中に進んだ。刑務官も入ってきて、ドアを閉め、鍵をかけた。

「そこの二本の線を跨いで立って」

言われたとおりにした。

刑務官が、わたしの周囲を一回りする。

「怪我をしているところはない？」

「ありません」

「では、そちらの舎房着に着替えて」

灰色のものを指した。

「着ているものを脱いで。もう慣れたでしょ」

わたしはうなずいて、スポーツバッグを床に置いた。セーターとジーンズ、下着を脱いで、空いている脱衣かごに入れる。

「下着も全部、支給されるものを着けるのよ」

さっき脱いだパンティーを取ろうとすると、

「これは？」

「出所までこちらで預かります」

舎房着と呼ばれた代物は、灰色の上衣に同じ色のズボンだった。洗濯はしてあるものの、見事なほどよれよれだった。

刑務官の指示で、紙のように薄いゴム草履をはき、バッグを持って部屋を出る。すぐ隣の保安課に連れて行かれた。ドアを入ると、保安課の職員がいっせいに目を向けてきた。わたしは立ち止まった。扇風機の音が聞こえた。

「まっすぐ進みなさい」

刑務官が、後ろから囁く。

わたしは俯いて、歩き始めた。

正面に「課長」と札のついた机があり、そこに紺色の制服姿の女性が着席していた。わたしが近づくと、立ちあがった。大柄ではないが、力のある眼差しが、凛とした空気を放っている。化粧もごく自然な感じだった。四十代半ばだろうか。

わたしは、机の前に立った。

「連れて参りました」

刑務官が、わたしの隣で敬礼していた。

「ご苦労」

女性が敬礼で応える。

「川尻松子さんですね。私は保安課長の瀬川です。確認のために、本籍、氏名、罪名、刑期を言ってください」

「福岡県大川市大字大野島××番地、川尻松子、殺人と覚せい剤取締法違反、懲役八年です」

わたしは、すらすらと答えた。

瀬川課長が、手元の資料を見ながら、うなずく。

「川尻さん、ここではまず第一に、職員の指示に従ってください。資料を下に置き、目をあげた。勝手な行動は許されません。それと、懲役は強制労働なので、病気にならない限りは、働く義務があります。はじめの数日間は、観察工場というところで、あなたの仕事に対する適性を見ます。同時に分類課によって、IQテストや心理テスト、面接が行われます。観察工場にいる間は独居房という個室にいてもらいますが、仕事が決まったら雑居房に移ることになります。

とにかく、まじめに、ほかの人たちとトラブルを起こさないように、一所懸命がんばってく

ださい。いまのあなたは四級ですが、月に一回ある審査会で認められれば、進級することが

できます。進級すれば待遇も違うし、早く仮釈放をもらえます。わかりましたか?」

「はい」

瀬川課長が息を吐いた。わたしの顔をじっと見る。

「あなた、国立大学を出て、中学の先生になったそうね」

さっきまでの、事務的な口調が消えていた。

「時代は変わったのね」

口元に、諦めたような笑みが浮かぶ。

「部屋は第二寮の第三室。連れて行きなさい」

事務的な口調に戻って、言った。

保安課の職員が、バッグの中身を一つ一つ点検した。わたしは歯ブラシだけを受け取った。

残りの荷物は、衣服といっしょに預けることになるという。

さっきとは別の刑務官に連れられ、保安課を出た。この刑務官は若く、わたしよりも年下

に見えた。化粧も薄い。わたしの真横に並び、歩調を合わせるようにして歩いている。気の

せいか、表情が硬かった。

寮と呼ばれた建物は、見るからに堅牢なモルタル造りだった。中央に高い塔が聳えており、そこから放射状に二階建ての舎房が延びている。刑務官に言われて、わたしが入り口のドアを開け、足を踏み入れた。

中は、しんと静まり返っていた。天井が異様に高く、真夏だというのに寒々しい。刑務官がドアを閉めると、その音が建物中にこだました。

ここでまた、別の刑務官が待っていた。最初の刑務官と別人ではあったが、似たような太り肉の四十代で、やはり化粧が濃い。硬そうな髪には強烈なカールがかかっており、目元はアイシャドーとマスカラで化け物のようだった。

わたしはこの刑務官に引き渡され、六番という番号を与えられた。そして、一階の第三室に連れて行かれた。

部屋は、二畳ほどの広さだった。四方の壁はコンクリート。明かり取りの高い窓には、鉄柵が張られている。畳の上には布団が一組。隅の板敷きには、簡単な囲いをした木桶の便器と手洗い、洗面器、机が置かれていた。

「備え付けの『収容者遵守事項』をよく読んでおくように。それから、就寝の時間が来るまで横になってはいかんぞ。わかったな」

わたしは、はい、と答えた。

刑務官が、鉄製のドアを閉める。鍵穴から、がちゃん、と大きな音が響いた。

わたしは、畳に腰をおろした。明かり取りの窓を見あげる。

茜色の光が、射しこんでいる。

わたしは三日前に、二十七歳になっていた。小野寺が最初にわたしの客になったのが、去年のいまごろだったはずだ。赤木がすでに店を辞め、綾乃も仙台に帰ったあとだった。まさか一年後に、綾乃が死に、自分が小野寺を殺して刑務所に入っているとは、夢にも思わなかった。

いや、そうでもないか……。

九州を離れる直前に、大野島の家に帰ったとき、久美に抱きつかれて、恐ろしいと感じた。自分がこれから地獄に向かおうとしていることを、うすうす気づいていたのではなかったか。

だとすれば、裁判官に言われたとおり、すべては自業自得なのだ。

事件のことは、大野島にも伝わっただろうか。警察官が、家を調べたりしただろうか。紀夫はどう感じただろう。久美は？　誰一人、裁判の傍聴にも、面会にも来なかった。全国に指名手配されたそうだが、赤木の耳にも入っているだろうか。島津賢治はどうしているだろう。わたしと関わりになったばかりに、店を畳むことになってはいないだろうか。殺人犯と関係を持ったことを、悔やんでいるだろうか。わたしと関わりになった母は？　島津賢治はどうしているだろう。申し訳ないことをしてしまった。

それにしても小野寺に対しては、いまでも謝罪したいという気持ちが起こらない。あのとき小野寺から投げつけられた言葉を思い出すと、憎しみだけが蘇る。やはりわたしは、おかしいのだろうか。自己中心的？　場当たり的？　狭い視野でしか対人関係を築けない？　ほんとうにそうなのだろうか。欠陥人間なのだろうか。思いやりのない人間なのだろうか。人間失格？　そうかも知れない。もう、どうだっていいけど。

気配を感じて振り向くと、ドアにある視察窓から、さっきの刑務官の、化け物のような顔がのぞいていた。何を言うでもなく、じっとわたしの様子を、うかがっている。

けたたましいベルに飛び起きた。すぐに静寂が戻る。朝だった。わたしは『収容者遵守事項』にあったとおり、顔を洗い、布団を片づけ、簡単に部屋の掃除をして、ドアに向かって正座をした。

「せいめいっ！」

号令が響いた。

ほどなく視察窓に、刑務官が現れた。わたしを舎房に連れてきた、あの若い刑務官だ。綺麗な目をしているな、と思った。

「第三室、せいめい」

刑務官の言葉が何を意味するのかわからず、わたしは首を傾げた。

「番号と姓名を言ってください」

「早くしろ！」

若い刑務官の後ろから、声があがった。わたしを裸にして調べた、太り肉の刑務官らしか

った。若い刑務官が、おどおどした様子で、

「番号と名前です。早く」

「六番、川尻松子」

視察窓から、若い刑務官の顔が離れた。

「異状ありません」

太り肉の刑務官に報告する声が聞こえた。二人の足音が、隣に移っていく。

しばらくすると、配膳口から朝食が入れられた。味噌汁と、麦の入った御飯と、漬け物だ

った。拘置所の朝食と大して変わらない。わたしは黙々と平らげた。空きげ、という号令が

聞こえたので、容器を配膳口から出した。

「ごちそうさまでした」

視察窓に現れたのは、マスクに三角ずきんをした女性だった。遠慮ない目でわたしを見て

いる。化粧をしていなかった。この人も受刑者なのだな、と思った。

刑務所第二日となったこの日、わたしは、支給された衣類、下着類すべてに、糸で氏名を縫いつけた。その後は、畳に座り、窓を見あげて過ごした。午後八時を過ぎるまでは、横になることもできない。夕食の後ふたたび点検があり、一日が終わった。

三日目から、観察工場に出ることになった。朝七時半、ほかの受刑者といっしょに廊下に整列し、点呼を受けた後、保安課の職員に見張られながら、工場まで行進した。観察工場に出ている新入受刑者は、わたしを含めて十二人。工場では、紙細工の仕事を与えられた。要領をつかむまでは戸惑ったが、気がつくと作業に没頭していた。我ながら出来映えはよかった。

四日目の午後には、分類課によるIQテスト、心理テスト、面接調査があった。IQテストを受けるのは、小学校以来だった。

五日目には、教育課による新入教育の講義があった。講師は年配の男性刑務官だった。講義の内容は主に、所内での過ごし方についてのものだ。わたしは特に、進級に関する件に興味を持った。

「何か質問はありますか？」

最後に講師が部屋を見渡したとき、わたしは手をあげた。

「番号と姓名を」

わたしは、心臓の鼓動を感じながら、立ちあがった。

「六番、川尻松子です」

「質問は何ですか？」

「評価が高ければ、すぐにでも進級できるのですか？」

「川尻、おまえの刑期は？」

「八年です」

「それなら、少なくとも一年は、様子を見なくてはならない。三級に進むのに早くて一年、そこから二級に進むのにも半年はかかるだろう。一級となると、さらに二年は覚悟したほうがいい」

「二級になれば、美容師の職業訓練を受けられるのですね？」

講師が、嬉しそうに目を細めた。

「そうか。その点について、少し補足しておこう。たしかにここでも美容師訓練を行っているが、美容学校は笠松刑務所にしかない。だから希望者はまず、笠松で一年間、美容生として勉強して、卒業しなくてはならない。そのあとここに戻ってきて、美容室でインターンとして一年間実習を積み、国家試験を受けて合格すれば、めでたく美容師の資格を得ることができる。ただし」

講師が、言葉を切った。厳しい目で、部屋を見渡す。

「美容生となるには審査を受け、所長の許可をもらう必要がある。それにはまず初犯であること、まじめで規律違反を犯さないことが最低条件だ。この刑務所には四百人の受刑者がいるが、美容生はインターンを含めて十名程度しかいない。笠松の学校に行けるのも、年に二、三人。わかるな？　それだけ険しい道のりだということだ」

講師の顔が、緩んだ。

「あまり怖がらせてもなんだから、少し希望のもてる話をしようか。ここの表美容室には、表社会のお客さんが大勢詰めかけている。なぜか？　値段が安く、その上、美容師の技術が優れているからだ。ここで資格を取り、出所してから自分の店を持った者もいる。ここはあくまで刑務所であって、制限は多いが、本人のやる気次第では、いろいろなことが可能だ。

これでいいか？　川尻」

「はい。ありがとうございました」

深く頭をさげ、着席した。

わたしは興奮していた。刑務所で美容師の資格が得られる。そんなことは、想像もしなかった。

無意味だと知りながら、夢想せずにはいられなかった。島津賢治と二人で、理容店を切り

盛りしていく。

　美容師の資格を得たわたしは、女性客の開拓をしていく。いずれは店を大きくするか、別に美容室を開業する。二人で力を合わせ、幸せを築いて……。

　馬鹿なことを考えるな、おまえの刑期を考えろ、仮釈放をもらえるとしても五、六年、島津がそんなに待つはずがない、それどころか、おまえと暮らした日々を悔いているだろう、そんなはずはない?　それならどうして、面会に来てくれないのだ?　東京から遠い?　ほんとうに愛しているのなら、距離なんか関係あるものか。しょせんおまえは島津にとって、たった二カ月いっしょに暮らしただけの、通りすがりの女だったのだ。

　わたしは、そう叫び続ける理性を、封じこめた。

　夢でもいい。幻でもいい。どん底の掃きだめで見つけた、たった一片の生き甲斐、希望なのだ。しがみつこう。その先のことは考えない。ほかのことは考えない。

　九日目の午後、わたしは保安課に呼び出され、第一工場に配属となったことを知らされた。ここは初犯の受刑者ばかりを集めた工場で、紳士物スポーツシャツなど高級品をつくっているという。部屋も、雑居房に移ることになった。

　夕食後、わずかな私物を持って、独居房を出た。目の綺麗な若い刑務官に連れられ、第一寮第十四室に向かった。

　第十四室には、四人の先客がいた。

　刑務官がドアを開けると、みな正座していた。

「今夜からこの部屋でいっしょに生活することになった川尻松子さんです。仲良くしてくだ
さい」

「川尻です」

　わたしは頭をさげた。

　四人の受刑者は、小さく頭をさげ、探るような目で、わたしを見あげる。

　ドアが閉まって刑務官が去っても、誰も正座を解こうとしなかった。口を開く者もない。

　相変わらずドアに向かって、並んで座っている。

　わたしがわけがわからず立っていると、左端に座っていた受刑者が、自分の左側を指さし
た。

「ここに正座するんや、はよう」

　押し殺した声で言った。

　右端の受刑者が、舌打ちをする。

　わたしが言われた場所に正座すると、すぐに、

「点検っ！」

と号令が聞こえた。

ほどなくドアが開いた。

二人の女性刑務官が現れた。二人とも初めて見る顔だったが、やはり化粧が濃かった。後

ろに立っている刑務官が、名簿のようなものとボールペンを手に持っている。

「第十四室！」

前に立っている刑務官が声をかけると、右端の受刑者から、

「いちっ」

「にっ」

と、番号を言っていく。

あっという間にわたしの番になる。

「ん……ごっ」

手前の刑務官が、名簿を持った刑務官に向かい、

「以上五名、異状ありませんっ！」

ドアが閉まると同時に、受刑者が声を揃え、

「ありがとうございました！」

叫ぶが早いか、いっせいに正座を崩し、伸びをしたり腕を回したりした。

わたしも遠慮がちに、足を崩した。

これから九時の就寝までが、唯一の自由時間だった。

「あんた、男、殺してきたんやってなあ」

さっき右端で舌打ちをした受刑者が、声をかけてきた。足を前に投げ出し、両腕をつっか
い棒のようにして、上半身を支えている。四十歳くらいだろうか。浅黒い頬は丸くふくれて、
ブタのような顔をしていた。

「クスリで眠らせて、首絞めて殺して、出刃包丁でバラバラにして捨てたんやって?」

「え?」

わたしは思わず聞き返した。ほかの三人の顔を見ると、敬遠するような、怯えるような目
を、わたしに向けている。

「違うんかい?」

「男を殺しましたけど、クスリで眠らせたり、バラバラにして捨てたりしてません。覚せい
剤を打たれそうになったので、包丁で斬りつけたら、首に刺さってしまって……」

「ええっ! シャブ、嫌いなん?」

さっき左端で、わたしの座る場所を示した受刑者が、大きな声をあげた。三十歳くらいで
顔色が悪く、頬が病的なほど、痩けていた。

「そのときは、とてもそんな気になれなかったので」

「へえ、変わってるんやねえ」

「変わってるのはあんたやろ」

ブタ顔が言うと、頬こけが横目で睨んだ。わたしに目を戻し、

「じゃあ、禁断症状は?」

「拘置所にいるときに、少し」

不思議なことに、島津賢治といっしょに暮らしているときは、禁断症状を感じなかった。使用期間が短かったせいかもしれないが、自分が覚せい剤を常用していたことさえ、忘れていた。それが警察に逮捕されたとたん、猛烈に覚せい剤が欲しくなり、床を転げまわったのだった。

「もう取れたん?」

「はい」

「ええなあ、うちは未だに、どうしても打ちたくなることがあってなあ」

ブタ顔が頬こけに向かって、

「出所して、まずしたいことは?」

「とりあえず一発!」

頬こけが胸を張り、腕に注射する真似をする。

「あかんわ、こりゃ。馬鹿は死ななきゃ治らない」

「馬鹿で結構。うちはシャブと心中する覚悟、決めたんやもん」

頬こけが、にかっ、と笑う。前歯がなかった。

ブタ顔が、うっと唸って上半身を起こし、あぐらをかいた。

「自己紹介しとこか。うちは遠藤和子。結婚詐欺」

わたしは口をぽかんとあけた。

「な、な、信じられへんやろ？　この顔で結婚詐欺やて、これで引っかかる男の顔が見たい

わ、ほんま」

頬こけが、手を打って騒ぐ。

「うるせえな、ここにいるあいだに太っちまったんだよ。ほら、シャブ中、おまえの番」

「ええっと、もうわかってはるよね。牧野みどり、ふざけた名前やけど、本名でーす。もち

ろん、シャブ中でーす」

「正真正銘のアホや」

「一言多いの、あんたは」

頬こけの牧野みどりが、ブタ顔の遠藤和子に舌を出した。

「ほら、自分らも自己紹介しときや」

遠藤和子が、残りの二人に言った。

右側に座っている受刑者は、若かった。二十歳そこそこだろうか。刑務所では髪の長さは決められているはずなのに、どういうわけかこの受刑者だけ短くて、男のようだった。髪だけではなく、涼しげな目許やきりりと結ばれた唇は凛々しく、くだけた感じであぐらをかく様などは、どう見ても男、それも、相当なハンサムだった。

「東めぐみ、傷害」

低い声で言ってから、熱のこもった目で、微笑んでくる。　胸がどきりとした。

「川尻松子です。よろしく」

「東ぁ、色目使いやがって。また刃傷沙汰になっても知らんで」

遠藤和子が、うんざりした様子で言う。

最後に残った一人に、視線が集まった。四十歳くらいだろうか。壁際で、膝を抱えるように座っている。俯いているので、顔はわからない。

「自分も自己紹介しとき、そのくらい、できるやろ」

遠藤和子に促され、ゆっくりと顔をあげた。その顔は痩せてはいないものの青白く、精気がなかった。

「真行寺るり子、三歳の息子を、殺しました」

消え入りそうな声だったが、たしかにそう言った。

「ま、そういうことや、せいぜい仲良くやって、早く仮釈もらえるように頑張ろうや」

就寝前の一分間は、反省の時間だった。自分の犯した罪や、この日一日の行状を省みるための時間だそうだが、わたしは美容師になる決意を固めることに使った。

雑居房の広さは六畳ほど。わたしの寝る場所はトイレのすぐ隣で、間には衝立が一枚あるだけだった。わたしは、いちばん最後に用を済ませ、布団に横たわった。小便の臭いがした。

三十分ほどで減灯の時間となったが、真っ暗にはならない。やがて寝息が聞こえてくる。わたしはなかなか寝付けなかった。そういえば最近、夢を見ないな、と考えていたら、いつのまにか眠ったらしく、気がついたら朝になっていた。

起床してすぐ、洗顔、布団の片づけ、掃除を済ませ、ドアに向かって一列に正座する。例によって、

「点検！」

の号令が響き、きのうと同じ点呼が繰り返された。そのあと配食当番の東めぐみが運んできた朝食を、みなで手際よく配膳し、黙々と口に運ぶ。このときも例に漏れず、ドアに向かって一列に並んで食べるのだった。

七時半になると、

「出寮っ!」

の号令がかかった。受刑者たちは保安課の前の廊下に一列に並び、点呼と捜検、つまりボディチェックを受けたあと、第一から第三である工場に向かって行進した。新入教育のときの話では、各工場とも八十人前後が配属されているという。

工場に着くと、ラジオ体操をさせられた。そのあと各自のミシンにつき、与えられた仕事を始めた。わたしは初日ということで、はみ出た糸をハサミで切る仕事をすることになった。

単調で退屈な作業だったが、看守の目を意識して、真剣に取り組んだ。

進級するには、月一回の累進準備会で取りあげられ、審査をパスしなくてはならない。そのあとで累進審査会にかけられ、最終的に進級させるかどうかが決められるのだが、準備会で取りあげられるためには、現場の担当職員によい点数をつけてもらう必要があるのだ。

工場には、ミシンを踏む音が渦巻いている。私語はまったく聞こえない。工場担当の女性看守部長とその補助の看守一名が、眼光鋭く、受刑者たちの仕事ぶりを見張っている。わたしは、看守の視線を感じながら、仕事をこなしていった。

九時五十分から十五分間は、休憩だった。たちまちわたしの周りに、四、五人の受刑者が集まってきた。

「あんた、出刃包丁で男を八つ裂きにして、生ゴミといっしょに捨てたんやってな」

見ず知らずの受刑者から、言葉をかけられた。休憩時間でも、看守の目は光っている。わたしは内心うんざりしながらも、殊勝な顔をつくり、誤りを訂正した。

「なんや、それだけかいな。地味やなあ」

みな急に白けた顔になり、離れていった。

昼食は、工場の食堂で、全員いっしょにとった。時間は十一時五十分から十二時半までとなっていたが、食事が終わればあとは自由時間となるので、みんな食べるのが早かった。ただし全員が食べ終わるまで席を立てないので、いつまでものんびり食べていると、みんなに睨まれることになる。わたしは余計なトラブルを起こしたくなかったので、周囲の状況を見て、自分が食べ終わっていなくても箸を置いた。

午後も十五分の休憩を挟んで、午後四時半に作業終了となった。夕食も工場の食堂でとり、寮に戻り、保安課の前でふたたび点呼、捜検を受けていたとき、小さな事件があった。

「なんだ、これはっ!」

保安課の瀬川課長の声だった。

列の外に引きずり出されたのは、同室の東めぐみだった。口をへの字に曲げて、ふてくさ

れている。瀬川課長が、小さな紙切れを、東めぐみの目の前に突き出した。

「誰ですか、これをあなたに渡したのは?」

「知らねえな」

瀬川課長が、鬼のような目で、東めぐみを睨む。

「連れて行きなさい!」

瀬川課長が言うと、保安課の職員が東めぐみの腕をつかみ、どこかへ連れて行った。

「あの色男、また懲罰房かよ。トイチも楽じゃねえなあ」

わたしの背後で、ぼそりと声がした。

各々の舎房に戻ってから、あらためて点検があった。わたしのいる第十四室は、一人減って四名となった。

点検が済むと自由時間。この時間には、舎房で読書やおしゃべりをして過ごす者、お茶や生け花、日本舞踊などのクラブ活動をする者、内職に精を出す者と、様々だという。洗濯やヘアカットも、この時間に済まさなくてはならない。もちろん、洗濯場や美容室に行くときは、看守に監視されながら、一列に並んで行進するのだ。

わたしは、遠藤和子と牧野みどりのおしゃべりに、耳を傾けることにした。この二人は、クラブには入っていないようだった。話題はもちろん、懲罰房送りになったばかりの東めぐ

みだ。わたしはここで初めて、同性愛を意味する「チンタラ」という刑務所用語を知った。
話によると、東めぐみは人気ナンバーワンのトイチ（男役）で、ハイチ（女役）からのラブ
レターが後を絶たないという。たとえ手紙が看守に見つかっても、誰々からもらったと決し
て口を割らない。そんな男気（？）が余計に女心を惹きつけるらしい。だからいつまでたっ
ても進級できないそうだ。

「恋愛がそんなにいいかねえ。世の中、最後はカネだぜ」

と遠藤和子が言えば、牧野みどりが案の定、

「うそ。最後は絶対シャブよ」

と切り返す。わたしは、警察に連行されてから初めて、声をあげて笑った。真行寺るり子
は、そのあいだもずっと、黙って俯いていた。

やがて反省の時間が来て、就寝となり、明かりが落とされた。小便の臭いのする布団に横
たわりながら、こうやって一日一日が過ぎていくのだな、と思った。

4

「松子伯母さんは、刑務所に入ったことがあるんですか?」

沢村社長が、うなずいた。

「何をしたんです?」

「ヒモを殺したって」

「人殺し?……松子伯母さんが……」

俺は、腹の底に、苦い塊を感じた。

聞かなければよかった。

「ずいぶんとひどい男だったらしいよ。あたしに言わせれば、殺されて当然だと思うんだけ
ど、裁判官は男だからね、八年も喰らってた。ふつうは長くて四、五年だよ。八年は長すぎ
る。なんで弁護士が控訴させなかったのか、不思議なくらいだよ」

龍さんが殺人事件を起こしたことは知っていた。しかしまさか、松子伯母まで殺人を犯し
ていたとは、予想もしなかった。

俺は松子伯母のことを、社会の隅で孤独に生き、最後は何者かによって殺されてしまった、

哀れな女性だと思っていた。しかし松子伯母本人が、過去に人を殺めていたのだ。どんな事情があるにせよ、人殺しが許されるはずがない。みすぼらしいアパートで殺されたのも、何かの因果ではないのか。

松子伯母のことを調べていくと、もっと汚れた姿を見ることになるかも知れない。そう思うと、松子伯母のことを知りたいという気持ちが、萎えていった。

「刑務所では、真面目で、おとなしかったね。ただ、看守の目を意識してか、神経質なくらい規則を守っていた。炎天下での草むしりも、一心不乱って感じで取り組んでいた。ほかの連中はさ、看守の目をごまかして、適当に手を抜いてたもんだけど、松子だけは違ったね。まあ、そういう優等生を忌み嫌うやつがいるのも世間の常で、嫌がらせを受けたこともあったらしいけど、松子は堪えてたみたいだよ。あたしの知る限り、喧嘩や違反は一度もなかったからね。……どうした、ずいぶん静かじゃないか」

「まさか、松子伯母さんが人を殺していたなんて、思わなかったから……」

「ショックだったかい？」

「まあ……」

「たしかに人殺しは悪いことさ。でも笙くん、君は松子のことを知りたいんだろ？　理解してあげたいんだろ？　じゃあ、なぜ彼女がそんなことをしてしまったのか、きちんと調べて

あげたらどう？」

「でも、人殺しは人殺しでしょ。それに、なんだかもう、松子伯母さんのことは……」

「どうでもいいって言うのかい！」

俺は、口をつぐんだ。

「笙くん、君は松子を、清く正しく生き抜いた聖女だと思っていたのかい？」

「……」

「松子は生身の人間だったんだよ。セックスもすれば糞もする。人を愛することもあれば傷つけることもある。笙くんだって、嘘をついたり、ちょっとした法律違反をしたことはあるだろう」

「……」

「でも人殺しは……」

「そりゃないだろうよ。でも、はずみで誰かを殺してしまうことが、絶対にないと言えるかい？」

「……」

「松子は人を殺してしまった。だが、女が男を殺すからには、それなりの事情があるものなんだよ。それを調べもしないで、一方的に松子を悪者にするってのは、感心しないよね。とにかく、こうやってあたしまで引っぱり出したんだ。これで幕を引こうなんて、考えないでお

くれ。ここまで知った以上、松子のことをとことん調べて、彼女の生きざまを君なりに理解してあげなよ。そうでもしなけりゃさ……」

沢村社長が、大きく息を吸った。囁くように、

「松子が、あんまり可哀想だとは、思わないかい?」

ことり。

そのとき、松子伯母の骨壺から漏れ聞こえた幽かな音が、耳の奥に蘇った。

それはまるで、松子伯母の魂が、何かを俺に訴えているようだった。

「どうだい、笙くん?」

俺は、顔をあげた。

沢村社長が、憂うような目で、俺を見ている。

俺は、うなずいた。

「でも、調べるといっても……」

「事件のことを知りたいのなら、裁判所が下した判決文を読めばいい」

「読めるんですか?」

「読めるよね、島崎？」

「刑事裁判のものなら、検察庁に行って申請すれば、閲覧可能なはずです」

「そういうわけだよ。詳しいことは、大津の地方検察庁にでも聞いてみな」

「大津？　滋賀県の？」

「松子が事件を起こしたのが、滋賀県だったから」

「事件を起こしたのは、いつなんですか？」

「松子が刑務所に来たのが、あたしが入所して二年目だったから、昭和四十九年……かな」

「美容院で再会したのは？」

「たしか東京ディズニーランドができる前の年だったから……」

「昭和五十七年です」

「ありがと、島崎。昭和五十七年ね」

「その美容院は、いまもあるんですよね」

「ある。銀座にね。場所はちょっと変わったけど」

「その店にも、行ってみます」

沢村社長が、笑みを浮かべた。

「でも、すごい偶然だったんですね、東京には数え切れないくらい美容院があるのに」

「そんなことはないさ。東京に美容院は星の数ほどあったかも知れないけど、『あかね』って名前の店は、一つしかなかった。いまは『ルージュ』って変わっちゃったけどね」

ベンツが速度を落とした。いつのまにか、パレスホテルに戻っていた。どうやらベンツは、内堀通りをぐるぐる回っていただけらしい。

「笙くん、申し訳ないけど、時間だよ。久しぶりに君のような子と話ができて、楽しかった。また会おうね」

沢村社長はそう言うなり、両手で俺の顔を挟み、またしても濃厚なキスをしたのだった。

キスの余韻に頭がくらくらしていたが、西荻窪のアパートに帰り着くころには、正気に戻ることができた。明日香を東京駅で見送ったのは、ずいぶん前のような気がするが、じつは今朝の話なのだ。きょうは、いろいろなことがありすぎた。しかしまだ、やっておくことがある。

俺はまずインターネットで、大津地方検察庁の場所と、電話番号を調べた。午後五時をだいぶ過ぎていたが、とにかく電話してみることにした。

呼び出し音が四回鳴ってから、繋がった。

『大津地検です』

ぶっきらぼうな男の声だった。

「判決文の閲覧について聞きたいんですが」

『公判資料の閲覧ね。検察庁らしくない、軽快な音楽が流れてくる。

声が途切れ、検察庁らしくない、軽快な音楽が流れてくる。

『はい。総務部記録課です』

こんどはお姉さんの声だった。　若そうだが、沢村社長に会ったあとなので、年齢のことは考えないことにする。

「判決文閲覧の手続きについて知りたいんですが」

『すでに決着済みの件ですか？』

「はい。昭和四十九年の……」

『ああ、そんなに昔のものなんですか。当事者の方ですか？』

「いえ、当事者ってわけでは……」

『それじゃあ、ちょっとできないですね』

「え、どうしてですか？」

『刑事訴訟法という法律で、決着後三年を経たものは閲覧させられないことになっているんです。当事者か関係者なら別ですけど』

「俺、いちおう親戚なんです」

『親戚というと?』

「事件の被告、ていうんですか、それが、俺の伯母さんなんです」

『どういった事件ですか?』

「殺人事件です」

『その伯母さんという方は、いまはどうしてらっしゃるんですか?』

「亡くなりました」

『……ああ、そうなんですか』

「俺は、伯母さんのこと、ぜんぜん知らなかったんです。亡くなったのは最近なんですけど、伯母さんが殺人罪で刑務所に入っていたことがあると聞いて、どういう事情があったのか知りたくて」

『なるほど……わかりました。身内の方で、そういう事情でしたら、許可が出ると思います。

ただですね、資料がまだ保管されているかどうか……』

「廃棄されてる場合もあるんですか?」

『ええ、あんまり昔のものですと……。ちょっと調べてみますから、判決日か、刑が確定した日はわかりますか?』

「昭和四十九年ということしか、わからないんですけど」

「罪名は殺人でしたね」

「はい」

「被告人の名前は？」

「川尻松子です」

「川尻松子さん……と。コンピュータで検索しますので、少し時間をください。こちらからかけ直します』

俺は、名前とアパートの電話番号を告げて、受話器を置いた。

五分もしないうちに、呼び出し音が鳴った。

『さきほどの公判資料の件ですけど、まだ保管されているようですね。閲覧申請書を提出していただく必要がありますから、身分証明書と印鑑と収入印紙を百五十円分用意して、来てください』

「収入印紙？」

『ここの一階で売ってますから、こちらで買っていただいても結構です』

「身分証明書というのは？」

『運転免許証か保険証、パスポートでもいいですよ』

翌朝、俺は九時三分発「ひかり一一七号」に乗り、東京を後にした。京都駅で琵琶湖線に乗り換え、大津駅に着いたのが十二時半。駅舎内の軽食堂でカツカレー定食を食べてから、駅前に掲げてあった周辺地図で場所を確認し、大津地方検察庁に向かった。

大津地検は、駅から二百メートルくらいの、法務局地方検察庁に向かった。

大津地検は、駅から二百メートルくらいの、法務局合同庁舎の中にあった。合同庁舎は五階建ての建物で、地検のほかに大津地方法務局が入っている。このあたりはいわゆる官庁街らしく、裁判所や県庁、県警本部が集まっていた。

庁舎の入り口に、警備員が立っていた。記録課に行きたい旨を告げると、中の案内窓口で聞くよう言われた。案内窓口は、庁舎に入って左手すぐ。そこに座っていた男の人に教えてもらい、売店で百五十円分の収入印紙を買ってから、エレベーターで三階にのぼった。エレベーターを出て右手に、ドアの開け放たれた部屋がある。壁から突き出た表札には「検務官室」とあり、すぐ下のカッコの中に「記録課」という小さな文字が見えた。

部屋に入ると、ワイシャツにネクタイ姿の男性や、白いブラウス姿の女性が、コピーを取ったり、机で事務仕事をしたり、パソコンに向かったりしていた。どの机の上にも、資料が積みあげられている。

「なにか?」

浅黒い顔の若い男性が、俺の前に立った。声は柔らかだが、視線に隙が感じられない。

俺が、判決文のことできのう電話した者ですが、と告げると、机のほうから、あっと声が

あがった。見ると、体格のいい女性が立ちあがっていた。二十代後半くらいか。彼女が、記

録係だという。

その女性に、あらためて判決文の閲覧希望を告げると、閲覧申請書の用紙を渡された。

俺は、検務官たちの机の隣に並べてある、大きめのテーブルに座り、用紙に記入した。被

告人欄に「川尻松子」、閲覧の目的は「その他」に○をつける。当事者との関係は「甥」。そ

の下に自分の住所を書き、「川尻笙」と署名した。事件番号や刑の確定日は、コンピュータ

で検索した結果を教えてもらって、書きこむ。印鑑を押し、さっき買った収入印紙を貼り、

健康保険遠隔地証を提示して、担当の女性検務官に提出した。

これでいよいよ松子伯母の判決文と対面できる、と思っていたら、

「この事件の資料は倉庫にあるので、閲覧は明日になりますね」

「うそっ!」

まさか閲覧が、翌日になるとは思わなかった。それならそうと電話で言ってくれよ、と毒

づきながら、庁舎を出た。財布の中身を確認すると、帰りの切符分を残すとして、なんとか

一泊分はある。

俺はとりあえず、大津駅まで戻った。　駅前に交番があったので、そこのお巡りさんに安い
ビジネスホテルを教えてもらった。場所を聞くと、歩いて五分くらいだそうだ。お巡りさんは
親切にも、ホテルに電話までしてくれた。

チェックインするにはまだ早かったので、せっかくだから琵琶湖まで出てみることにした。
駅前ロータリーの噴水を横目に過ぎ、並木の緑が眩しい大通りを北に進むと、緩やかな下り
坂になる。十分ほどだらだらと下ると、道が平坦になり、踏切にさしかかる。ちょうど遮断
機がおりて、警報機が鳴っていた。緑色の電車が通り過ぎてから踏切を渡ると、大きな通り
に出た。ここを横断したとたん、磯の香りが鼻を掠めた。

俺はなんだか、遠足にでも来ているような気分になってきた。前方にマリンブルーの湖面
が見えてくると、思わず声をあげ、足を速めた。そしてついに湖畔に辿り着くと、そこは、
白い石畳の敷き詰められた広場になっていた。広場から湖に向かって、桟橋のような歩道が
突き出ている。

俺は迷わず、湖上の歩道に進んだ。　歩道は百メートルくらいあるだろうか。先端に立つと、
まるで自分が、琵琶湖の真ん中に浮いているようだった。湖を流れてくる清風が、全身を洗
い流す。足もとのアスファルトから、ゆったりとした波の振動が伝わってくる。すぐ左手に
は、白や黄色のヨットが、ずらりと停泊している。遥か遠くの湖面には、白い航跡が走って

いた。空は眩しいくらいの青。大きな入道雲も昇っている。

明日香の声が、聞きたくなった。携帯電話で、明日香の携帯を呼び出す。留守番サービス

に繋がった。俺は電話を切り、舌打ちをした。

翌朝は、九時きっかりに大津地方検察庁を再訪した。記録課に行き、担当の女性検務官に

来意を告げた。きのう申請書を記入するときに使った大きめのテーブルに座り、五分くらい

待っていると、担当検務官が分厚い書類の束を抱えて、戻ってきた。

「メモは結構ですけど、コピーは取れません。規則なので」

「ここで閲覧するんですか？」

「そうです。終わったら、声をかけてくださいね」

担当検務官が、自分の机に戻っていった。かなり厚い。ぱらぱらとめくると、調書から陳述書、判決文ま

俺は、資料と向き合った。

で、すべて揃っていた。

この古びた紙切れに、松子伯母の犯した殺人の全容が記されている。

俺は、判決文から、読むことにした。検務官室には、何人もの人が立ち働いていて、常に

ざわざわとしている。しかし俺は、判決文の冒頭の、「主文」という言葉を目にした瞬間か

　　ら、すべての雑音が聞こえなくなった。

　そこに記されているのは、事件の全容だけではなかった。至るまでの経過を、驚くほど事細かに、書き連ねてあった。松子伯母の幼少時代から事件に独り占めされたと思いこんでいた少女時代。望んだ生き方を貫かず、父親の愛情を、久美叔母さんに至るまでの経過を、驚くほど事細かに、書き連ねてあった。松子伯母の幼少時代から事件にた青春時代。修学旅行先で起こした盗難事件というのは、龍さんが言っていたものだろう。やはりこの事件がきっかけになって、失踪していたのだ。そのあとに、作家志望の青年Yと同棲を始めたが、Yが自殺。Yの親友、Oと不倫関係を結ぶが捨てられ、自暴自棄になって中洲のトルコ嬢（！）となる。トルコ風呂というのは、いまでいうソープランドのことだろう。俺は行ったことないけど……。松子伯母は、このトルコ風呂でSという女性と知り合い、親友になる。トルコ風呂で一時はナンバーワンとなる。やや人気が下降してきたところに、小野寺保という客に誘われ、滋賀県の雄琴に移る。雄琴での生活は多忙を極め、その疲労を取るために、覚せい剤を使うようになる。事件のあった前日、親友Sが、同居していた覚せい剤中毒の男に殺されたことを知る。松子伯母は、覚せい剤をやめる決意をし、小野寺保と口論となり、小野寺保が自分を食い物にして小料理屋を開こうとするが、それがきっかけで口論となり、小野寺保が強引に覚せい剤を打とうとしたので、松子伯母は出刃包丁いるだけだと気づく。小野寺保が強引に覚せい剤を打とうとしたので、松子伯母は出刃包丁

を持って抵抗する。小野寺保に腕をつかまれ、身動きできなくなるが、手から落ちた包丁が小野寺保の足の甲に突き刺さるという偶然も重なり、松子伯母は小野寺保を殺してしまう。

そのあと、自殺したかったのかつての同棲相手Yの後を追って死ぬために、玉川上水に向かうが、未遂に終わる。その際に心配して声をかけてくれた、理髪店を営む男性Sと同棲をはじめるが、二カ月後に、手配写真と名前を見た近所の人の通報により、警察に逮捕される。

判決文では、松子伯母の性格が、事件の根本原因にあったような書き方をされている。場当たり的で、自己中心的で、流されやすい性格が、道を誤らせたのだと。

しかし俺には、そうは思えなかった。この資料を読むかぎり、松子伯母は、それがトルコ嬢という仕事にしろ男性関係にしろ、不器用なほど真正面から、ぶつかっていっただけではないのか。

もしかしたら俺は、贔屓目に見すぎているのかも知れない。しかし、親父が言っていたような、どうしようもないだけの女性ではないと感じた。

小野寺保という男を殺した経緯についても、正当防衛に近いのではないか。沢村社長の言ったとおり、覚せい剤取締法違反を含めたとしても、懲役八年は長すぎる。

松子伯母は控訴もせず、刑に服し、出所後、美容師として見事に再出発した。美容師になったのは、逮捕直前まで同棲していた男が理容師だったことと、無関係ではないだろう。そ

して美容院で沢村社長と再会したのは……。

すべての資料を読み終えたのは、午後二時過ぎだった。

疲れ切った目をあげると、テーブルの向こうに、松子伯母が座っているような気がした。あの成人式のモノクロ写真の顔で、頬杖をつき、問いかけるような眼差しを、俺に向けている。

大津から琵琶湖線、新幹線、中央線を乗り継いで、西荻窪のアパートに帰り着いたときには、午後八時を過ぎていた。

部屋の蛍光灯を点してから、少し迷ったが、明日香の実家に電話した。呼び出し音が六回鳴って、繋がった。

『渡辺です』

明日香の声だ。

「俺だよ」

『は？』

「は、じゃないだろ、笙だよ。彼氏の声を忘れたのか？」

『ああ、明日香のお友達？』

顔から火が出た。

「……え、明日香……さんじゃ」

『ちょっと待ってくださいね』

受話器の向こうで、笑い声が聞こえた。

ばたばたと足音がしたと思ったら、

『笙？』

「明日香か。いまの人は？」

『姉貴。あたしと間違えたんだって？』

「だって、声がそっくりだったから」

『そそっかしいんだから』

「どうしてる？」

『忙しい。いろいろとね。笙は？』

「きょう、大津の地方検察庁に行ってきた」

『滋賀県の大津？　検察庁って、笙、何か悪いことしたの？』

俺は、順を追って説明した。

あの聖書を落としていった男に会えたこと。名前を龍洋一(よういち)といって、松子伯母の教え子だ

ったこと。龍さんが警察に連行されたこと。龍さんの紹介で、芸能事務所の沢村社長と会っ
たこと。松子伯母が殺人事件を起こして刑務所に入っていたこと。そして大津地検で、松子
伯母が事件を起こすまでの半生を知ったこと。

明日香は、聖書を落としていった男の正体にこそ驚きの声をあげたが、そのあとの件にな
ると相づちも打たず、じっと聞いているだけだった。

『松子さんが、人殺しをしていたなんて……』

「でもこれは、松子伯母さんだけのせいじゃないよ。俺は、殺された男のほうが悪いと思う。
松子伯母さんは、ちゃんと服役してから、美容師として再出発したんだ。これってすごいこ
とだと、俺は思う』

『……そうね。なんか、松子さんの人生って、あたしの想像をぜんぜん超えちゃってるな』

「あしたは、松子伯母さんが出所後に勤めた美容院に行ってみる。まだ銀座にあるそうだか
ら、ひょっとしたら、松子伯母さんを憶えている人がいるかも知れない」

『場所はわかってるの?』

「これから探す。明日香、いつまでそっちにいるんだ? まだ戻ってこないのか?」

『うん……』

「どうした? なんかあったのか?」

『ううん、なんでもない。もう少しこっちにいると思う』

「そうか。　明日香……」

「なに？」

「やっぱり明日香がいないと、つまんねえよ」

『……ありがとう。あたしも、いつも笙のことを考えてるよ』

俺は、吹き出しそうになった。　明日香らしくない台詞だ。

「ほんとかよ」

『ほんとうよ』

静かになった。

「じゃあ、また電話するわ」

『うん。またね』

受話器を置いた。

たったいま声を聞いたばかりなのに、よけいに寂しくなった。なんなんだろ、この感覚は。

俺は気を取り直して、駅前のコンビニで買ってきた弁当を食べながら、インターネットで銀座の美容院を検索した。いまどき、ちょっと気の利いた美容院なら、ホームページくらい持っているはずだ。

検索画面には、ずらりと美容院の店名が並んだ。ほとんどはアルファベットで、英語かフランス語をそのまま使っている。

美容室ルージュ。Rouge。

一つだけ、あった。

翌朝、俺は西荻窪から中央線に乗り、東京駅で山手線に乗り換え、有楽町駅で降りた。新宿や渋谷ならともかく、銀座にはあまり足を運んだことがなかったので、首都高速をくぐったところにある交番で、「ルージュ」の場所を尋ねることにした。銀座五丁目の何番地と言ったら、眼鏡をかけたお巡りさんが、地図を広げて指し示してくれた。

教えられたとおり、晴海通りを少し歩き、銀行を越えたところの路地を入った。時間が早いせいか、人通りは多くない。左手のビルを見あげながら歩いていると、銀座クレストビルという文字を見つけた。掲げられた電光看板を見ると、たしかに「美容室 Rouge」が三階に入っている。電光看板によると、この雑居ビルの地下一階には居酒屋が、二階には歯医者が入っているらしい。四階と五階にも怪しげな名前が掲げてあるが、何の店か見当もつかなかった。

俺は、狭い入り口をくぐり、エレベーターで三階にあがった。

降りてすぐ目の前に扉があ

った。複雑な模様の入ったガラスに、紅色の文字で「Rouge」と書かれている。準備中とい

う札が掛かっているが、照明が点いているから、人はいるのだろう。

扉を押してみた。開いた。来客を告げる涼しげな音が響く。

店内には、軽快なフレンチポップスが流れていた。入ってすぐ右手に、円形のボックス席

のようなものがある。フロントらしい。人はいなかった。フロント奥の空間には、壁一面の

鏡に向かって、四脚の椅子が並んでいた。インテリアは白を基調として、ところどころに赤

と青を織り交ぜた配色が施されている。店名はルージュでも、赤にこだわっているわけでは

なさそうだ。

椅子の向こうに、歪みガラスの衝立がある。そこに人影が映ったと思うと、衝立から飛び

出してきた。俺と同世代くらいの女の子だった。黄色いTシャツに白いパンツ姿。手には雑

巾。髪はぎょっとするようなピンク色で、耳たぶのあたりで横一文字に切り揃えてある。

「すみません。まだ準備中なんですが」

「俺、客じゃなくて、ちょっと聞きたいことがあって来たんだけど」

女の子が目の前に立って、首を傾げた。額に汗が滲んでいる。

「昔この店に勤めていた、川尻松子って人のことを知りたいんだけど」

「川尻松子さん？ 聞いたことないですけど。いつごろの話です？」

「二十年くらい前」

女の子が笑った。

「そりゃ知るわけないや。あたしまだ生まれてないもん」

「誰か、知ってそうな人、いないかな」

女の子が、両手を腰にあてる。

「そうねえ、二十年以上のキャリアの人って、大先生しかいないんじゃないかな」

「大先生というのは？」

「この店のオーナー。創業者」

「ここに来ることはあるの？」

「いまもいるよ」

「ほんと？　会えるかな」

「アポなしじゃ難しいと思うけど。いちおう、聞いてみようか。ちょっとこれお願い」

女の子が、雑巾を俺に押しつけて、「STAFF ONLY」と書かれたドアを入っていった。

雑巾はおろしたてらしく、真っ白だ。微かに薬品の匂いがする。ふと足もとを見ると、床に靴跡がついていた。せっかくだからと思い、雑巾で汚れを拭き取った。きれいになった、と思ったら、少し離れた場所にも汚れを見つけた。ついでにそちらも拭いていると、さっきの

女の子が戻ってきた。

「あ、だめえ！　それで床を拭いちゃ」

俺から雑巾を奪い取ると、

「これ、シャンプー台専用だったのに」

と泣きそうな顔になった。

「ごめん。知らなかったから」

「まあ、いいわ。あなたに預けたあたしが悪いんだから。大先生が、会ってもいいって。なんだか、あなたが来るのを、待ってたみたいな口ぶりだったよ。大先生の部屋は、そこのドアを入って、突き当たりの右の部屋」

俺は、礼を言って、スタッフ専用の扉をくぐった。突き当たり右の部屋には、「店長室」とプレートが掛かっていた。

ちょっと緊張する。

ノックをすると、

「開いてるよ」

と張りのある声が返ってきた。

俺は、失礼します、と言って、ドアを開けた。

　部屋は、六畳くらいの広さだった。正面の壁の窓の

右の壁際に、質素な事務机が置かれている。机に向かって

立ちあがった。

　背は低く、俺の肩くらいしかなかった。マッシュルームヘアが艶やかに光を反射していて、

黒飴みたいだった。縦ボーダーのざっくりしたシャツに、黄緑色のスパッツ。足もとはかか

との低いパンプス。手足は細い。髪と着ているものだけを見れば、十代の女の子のようだっ

たが、目尻には深い皺が刻まれ、頬は弛んで唇の両端を押し下げていた。真っ白に化粧して

いるが、六十歳は過ぎていそうだ。

「あなたが笠くん?」

「え、俺のこと、知ってるんですか?」

「沢村さんから電話があったんだよ。川尻笠って子が行くと思うから、松子の話をしてやっ

てくれってね。それで、世間知らずで失礼なことを言うかも知れないけど、許してやってく

れって」

「あの人が……」

「はじめまして。私は内田あかね。この店のオーナー。まあ、座りな。私は沢村さんと違っ

て、時間はたっぷりあるんだから」

5

わたしは入所一年半で、四級から二級まで進んだ。二級に昇格することが決まると、美容学校への入学希望を出し、所長の許可を得た。その年の九月末、同じく美容生となる二名の受刑者とともに、笠松刑務所に護送された。大阪駅から岐阜駅までは、新幹線を使った。そこで初めて、新幹線が博多まで開通していることを知った。

十月一日に開校式が行われ、全国の刑務所から集まった十一名とともに、正式に美容生となった。以後一年間にわたり、ヘアカット、パーマ、セット、シャンプー、リンシングといった頭部技術、日本髪、メイクアップ、マニキュア、マッサージなどの美粧技術、着物の着付け技術のほか、伝染病学、消毒法、皮膚科学をはじめとする衛生理論を叩きこまれた。

ヘアカットの実習では人形を使ったが、それ以外は美容生が二人一組になり、互いをモデルにして練習した。とくに難しかったのは、ロッドで毛束を毛先から巻くロッド巻き、二センチ四方の毛束を毛先からくるくる巻いて小さく納めるピンカール、櫛と指を使ってウェーブを作り出すフィンガーウェーブだ。いずれもローションをつけて練習するため、はじめのころは手がぬめるばかりで、まったく形にならなかった。ロッド巻きでは巻いた髪がぶらぶ

らと垂れさがってしまったり、ピンカールでは髪がぼそぼそとはみ出ていたり。それでも毎日練習するうちに、見栄えのいいものができるようになり、卒業するころには、ロッド巻きではクラスで一番になっていた。

笠松から戻ったあとは、刑務所の表美容室で、インターンとして働いた。インターンの仕事は主に、床掃き、中間リンス、片づけなどの雑用とシャンプー。そのあとブローもさせてもらうようになったが、最初はお客の髪が風船のように丸く膨らんでしまい、先輩にやり直してもらったこともある。ブローがうまくできるようになると、セットも手がけるようになり、最後にはカットを任されるまでになった。

わたしの服役している刑務所には、二つの塀がある。外塀の門には監視がなく、誰でも出入りできる。この門を入ると、古めかしい灰色の建物が見える。ここには、庶務課、分類課、教育課、所長室などの中枢機能が集まっている。わたしも入所初日には、庶務課に連れて行かれ、例によって本籍から氏名、罪名、刑期まで言わされた。この中枢部の向こうに、さらにもう一つ、塀が聳えている。

この内塀には、人ひとりやっとくぐれる程度の鉄扉がついており、厳重に施錠されている。この内塀の中には、寮や工場のほか、看守たちの司令塔である保安課や管理部長室、医務課がある。基本的に受刑者の生活は、この中で完結する。内塀の外まで活動範囲を広げられる、

　数少ない例外の一つが、美容生だった。

　表美容室は、刑務所の敷地内にあるのだが、内塀の外側にあった。「あかね」という店名の掲げられた美容室は、刑務所の職員のほか、一般の社会人も利用できる。「あかね」という店名内塀を出て「あかね」に通い、出所後に備えて実地訓練を積むのだ。ちなみに受刑者のヘアカットは三カ月に一回、パーマは五カ月に一回、認められているが、表の「あかね」とは別に、受刑者用の美容室が内塀の中にある。店名はとくにないのだが、受刑者は表社会への憧れもこめて、「中あかね」と呼んでいた。こちらの担当も、わたしたち美容生だった。

　わたしは「あかね」で一年間のインターンを終え、国家試験を受けて合格した。時を同じくして一級に昇格し、一級者の証である赤バッジを与えられ、舎房から居室に移った。

　居室は一級者用の一人部屋で、障子張りの部屋には机のほか、小さな置き床、タンスまで揃っている。ドアには錠がなく、看守の許可を求めなくとも自由に出入りができた。一人前にはほど遠い。さいわい「あかね」には、高い技術を持つ先輩たちが多かったし、火曜日と金曜日には、外来の美容学校の校長が実技指導に来てくれたので、そういう人たちから技術を盗み、学んだ。

　とくに美容学校の校長からは、技術面だけでなく、接客の大切さを教えられた。シャンプ

ーひとつとっても、お客の案内の仕方から、タオル、クロスのかけ方、シャワーの持ち方、湯加減、シャンプー剤の塗布の仕方、手の力の強弱を使い分けるポイントなど、注意する点は山ほどあった。

その校長が言ったことがある。

「店内のどこにいても、必ずお客様に見られていることを忘れるな、お客様の目は厳しいものだ、一秒でも気を抜いたら怖いくらいに伝わるぞ」

わたしはこの言葉を聞いたとき、「白夜」で綾乃に言われたことを思い出した。そして、究極の接客業でナンバーワンになったことのあるわたしが、美容院でやっていけないはずがない、と思った。

一級者ともなると、図書の貸し出しの手伝いや、講堂の椅子並べなど、所内の雑用もこなさなくてはならない。昼間は表の「あかね」で、夜は「中あかね」でハサミを振るうので、一日中とにかく忙しく、真冬でも寒さを感じないほどだった。

気がついてみれば、消化した刑期は、未決勾留期間を含めて五年五カ月に及んでいた。美容生は、インターンを含めて十三名いる。二列に並び、点呼を受け、内塀の鉄扉をくぐって「あかね」に到着するのが朝七時五十分。そのころにはすでに、十名ほどのお客が、ドアの外で待っている。もちろんみな、表社会の人間だ。近所の主婦も多いが、明らかに水商

売関係のお客も目立った。

「あかね」でも、背後には常に、看守の目が光っている。いかに客の厚意であろうと、飴玉一つでも貰ったが最後、美容室への出入りは即禁止され、級は格下げとなる。また客に注文を聞くのはいいが、私語は厳禁だった。

「川尻、おい、川尻、聞こえないのか?」

看守の声に、はっとして振り返った。

きょうの美容室担当は、二年前に栃木から転勤してきた江島刑務官だった。ころころと太っていて、受刑者からつけられたあだ名はダルマ。三十代半ばの独身だ。

「はい。申し訳ありません。なんでしょうか?」

「分類課長がお呼びだそうだ。すぐに行きなさい」

「えっ、うちの髪型、どないしてくれるねん?」

お客が首をひねった。

「申し訳ありません。ほかの者に交代させます」

「そんなあ、うちの髪型は、このお姉ちゃんやないとできへんのやで」

「すみません、規則なので。川尻、行きなさい」

「はい」

わたしは、お客に一礼してから、その場を離れた。更衣室で白衣から舎房着に着替え、別の看守に連れられて、灰色の建物に向かう。

わたしは二週間前にも、分類課長から呼び出しを受けていた。その席で、仮釈放のことを聞かされた。ただ、不安もあった。仮釈放されるには、引受人が必要なので、引受人が決まった後に、本面接を経て、正式に審理にかけられ、仮釈放を許可するか棄却するかが決定される。

わたしは、弟の紀夫を、引受人に指定していた。

「あかね」から分類課へ行くときには、石畳の歩道を五十メートルほど歩くことになる。途中、右手に外塀の門が見えるのだが、門のすぐ向こうには国道が通っていて、車の行き交う様子が、いやでも目に入った。門には監視がないため、ちょっと走れば簡単に脱走できそうな気もするが、もちろん上級者は、そんな馬鹿なことは考えない。下手に脱走を企てて降格させられるよりも、真面目に務めて早く仮釈放をもらったほうが、絶対に得だからだ。それでもこの石畳を歩くときは、風に乗って漂ってくる排気ガスにさえ塀の外の匂いを感じ、たまらない気持ちになるのだった。

わたしは、看守とともに分類課室に入り、分類課長である清水麻子の前に立った。この四

十過ぎの女性も独身だったが、ダルマと違って、恐ろしく美人だった。白い肌や彫りの深い

顔立ちは、一昔前のさる大映画女優を彷彿させるほどで、アップに纏めた髪もセンスを感じ

させる。

刑務所には二十代の刑務官も何人かいるが、刑務所歴五年五カ月のわたしが知る限

り、清水課長以上の美人はいない。

その清水課長が、険しい表情で、わたしを見あげた。

「川尻、用件はわかっていると思う」

声が沈んでいた。

わたしは身を固くした。

「はい」

「引受人の件だが、福岡の保護観察所が弟さんに確認したところ、残念だが、その意思はな

いとのことだった」

「……そうですか」

予想はしていた。しかし、実際に拒絶されると、思ったより堪えた。心の底では、紀夫が

引受人となって迎えに来てくれることを、期待していたのだろうか。

「ほかにあては、ないのか?」

清水課長の優しい声が、残酷に響く。

　わたしは俯いた。縋（すが）るような気持ちで、一人の男性の名前を、胸につぶやく。

　島津賢治。

　虫のいい話だろうか。忘れてくれと置き手紙をしておきながら、いまになって引受人になってくれだなんて。

　でも……。

　あなたは、わたしの過去なんかどうでもいいと言ってくれた。わたしといっしょに暮らしたいだけだと言ってくれた。あんなに素敵な言葉をもらったのは、生まれて初めてだった。あなたはプロポーズをして、わたしはそれを受け入れた。そうだ。たとえ籍は入れてなくとも、わたしはあなたの妻なのだ。いまのわたしには、美容師の国家資格がある。客の評判だっていい。きっと、あなたの力になってあげられる。

　わたしは、顔をあげた。

「島津賢治さん、東京の三鷹で、理容店を営んでいました」

「どういう関係の方だ？」

「内縁の夫です」

「籍は入れてないのだな」

「結婚の約束をしました」

「面会に来たことは？」

「いえ……」

清水課長が、渋い顔をした。

「でも、彼ならきっと、迎えに来てくれると思います」

「わかった。そこまで言うのなら、東京の保護観察所に連絡して、引受人となる意思がある
かどうか、確認してもらおう」

わたしの申し出を知った島津賢治は、どんな顔をするだろうか。どんなことを考えるのだ
ろうか。そして、どんな返事をするのだろうか。想像を巡らすたびに、息が苦しくなり、胸
を掻きむしりたくなった。

そろそろ保護観察官が、島津のもとを訪れているころだろうか。もしかしたら、いままさ
にその瞬間が来ているかも知れない。そう思うと仕事にも集中できず、シャンプーとリンス
を間違えるという、普段なら絶対にしないミスも犯した。このときは口頭注意だけで済んだ
が、下手をすれば、仮釈放の審理にも影響しかねなかった。

五年という歳月が、あまりにも重かった。たった二カ月いっしょに住んだ女、しかも殺人
で服役している女を、五年間も待ち続けるだろうか。そんな映画のような話があるだろうか。

冷静に考えるほど、絶望的に思えた。

しかし……。

島津賢治は、わたしに結婚を申しこんでくれた、ただ一人の男性なのだ。誠実で、勤勉で、思いやりのある男性なのだ。その男性の愛を信じられなくて、これから何を信じて生きていけばいいのか。でも、もし断られたら……。

結論が出るまでの毎日、わたしは生殺しにされているようなものだった。島津賢治を引受人に指名したことを後悔し、取り消してもらおうかと本気で思った瞬間もあった。

島津賢治の愛を、信じよう。

「連れて参りました」

二週間後。

「あかね」でお客の髪にロッドを巻いていたとき、清水課長の呼び出しを受けた。わたしは、看守に連れられ、分類課に向かった。用件は、引受人のこと以外に考えられない。「あかね」から灰色の建物に向かう石畳の歩道を踏みしめながら、心の中で繰り返した。

わたしは、清水課長の前に立った。

清水課長が、わたしを見あげる。

「引受人の件だが……」

「はい」

「島津賢治さんには、断られたそうだ。東京の保護観察官が、島津さんに確認したところ、引受人となる意思はない、との返答があった。残念だったな」

清水課長の発する言葉の一つ一つが、現実という鉛となり、わたしの胸を貫いていく。

「どうして……」

店を畳んだのか、それでわたしを置く余裕がないのか。

「お店は健在なのですか?」

「健在だそうだ。だが、五年前とはずいぶん状況が違っている。私に言えるのは、ここまでだよ」

何もかもが、凍っていく。身体が震える。肺が強ばり、息ができなくなる。

「そんな、そんなはずはありません、わたしはあの人の妻なのに、あの人は、わたしといっしょに暮らしたいと言って、籍も入れようって、愛してるって……わたしは信じてるんです

っ! 人違いです、きっと、ほかの人を島津と間違えて」

「川尻、落ち着きなさい。島津さんには断られたんだ。　間違いではない」

「じゃあ赤木さんを呼んでください」

「赤木?」

「わたしが働いていたトルコ風呂のマネージャーをやってました。わたしのことを好きだって言ってくれたんです。困ったときにはいつでも飛んできてやるって言ってくれたんです。赤木さんなら、きっと迎えに来てくれる」

「連絡先は?」

「それが、北海道の八雲というところに実家があるそうなんですが、住所や電話番号はなくしてしまって……」

「それじゃあ、どうしようもないじゃないかっ!」

清水課長が、拳で机を叩いた。

息を吐き、諭すように、

「なあ川尻よ、和歌山には、引受人のいない受刑者のための、更生保護施設もある。あるいは宗教関係でも、引受人になってくれる人たちがいる。そういう方に頼んでみてはどうかな?　もちろん、ご家族や友人に引受人になっていただいたほうが、主査委員の心証はよいのだが、当人にその意思がなかったり、ましてや連絡先がわからないとなれば、仕方がない

ではないか。川尻は一級者だし、日頃の勤務態度も申し分ないから、これから違反さえしなければ、仮釈は間違いないんだ。どうだ？」

わたしは、うなだれた。嗚咽を堪えきれない。

「川尻、返事をしなさい」

「……はい、お願いします」

それだけ答えるのが、やっとだった。

わたしは、清水課長に促され、職員の視線を浴びながら、分類課を後にした。看守に連れられ、灰色の建物から外に出て、「あかね」に向かう。

雲ひとつない秋晴れだった。

風に流される枯れ葉の群れが、石畳を滑っていく。

「川尻、ショックだったようだな」

隣を歩く看守が言った。五年前には目が綺麗だった彼女も、化粧が濃くなり、太り、言葉遣いが荒くなっていた。

「たしかに、誰も迎えに来てくれないというのは、寂しいものだ。だが、それだけおまえの犯した罪が、周りの人たちに迷惑をかけたということだぞ。もう一度よく反省したらいい。なにしろ、人を一人殺しているのだから。仮釈をもらえるだけでも、ありがたいと思わない

とな」

わたしは立ち止まった。左に目を向けた。外塀の門が見えた。監視もなく、誰でも行き来できる門。すぐ外の国道を、自動車やトラックが走っている。

「どうした？」

看守が、わたしの顔を覗きこんだ。

わたしは、両手で、看守を押しのけた。足を踏み出す。駆ける。

止まれ。叫び声。非常笛の甲高い音が鳴り響く。わたしは走った。引き寄せられるように、走り続けた。

何かが腰にのしかかった。顔から地面に突っこんだ。白い火花が散った。

「川尻、気でも狂ったか！」

腕をねじあげられた。地面に押しつけられた。必死に顔をあげる。門は目前だった。国道を走るダンプのタイヤが、視界を横切った。

「馬鹿が、これで仮釈も帳消しだぞ、美容室からミシン踏みに逆戻りだぞ、わかってるのか！」

引き起こされた。強い力。男性の刑務官。初めて見る。二人もいる。触るな。叫んで抵抗した。上衣のボタンが弾け飛んだ。両腕を男性刑務官に捕まれた。足をばたつかせた。

「おとなしくせんかっ!」

引きずられたまま、連行された。内塀の鉄扉をくぐった。懲罰房ではなく、沈静房に放りこまれた。

大きな音がして、分厚いドアが閉まる。施錠の音が響く。息の続く限り叫んだ。コンクリートにぶつかって、跳ね返ってきた。

四方をコンクリートで囲まれた狭い箱に、自分の息づかいだけが聞こえる。窓はなく、高い壁に明かり取りが付いているだけ。トイレもセメント製。周りは畑なので、いくら叫ぼうが暴れようが、誰にも聞こえない。わたしの声は、誰にも届かない。

わたしは、板間に転がった。

大の字になった。

ばかやろう。

コンクリートの天井に叫んだ。

涙がいつまでも流れた。

この事件のせいで、わたしは四級に降格となり、雑居房に戻された。作業場も、美容室から、第一工場に戻った。

舎房仲間だった東めぐみは、わたしが入所して十カ月後に、満期出所していた。牧野みど
りも一年とちょっとで仮釈放をもらったが、風の噂では、出所後まもなく亡くなったという。
遠藤和子は、わたしと同時に二級に昇格し、刑期を半年残して仮釈放された。「また来る
ぜ」と、冗談なのか本気なのか分からない台詞を残していったが、いまのところ戻ってきた
様子はない。真行寺るり子は、ちょうど仮釈放が決まったところで、社会生活に慣れるため
の専用の寮に移っていた。

わたしはふたたび、四級者用のよれよれの舎房着を着て、ミシンを踏む毎日を送った。雑
居房は八人部屋だったが、はじめは誰も、わたしと口を利こうとしなかった。仮釈放を目前
にしての脱走未遂事件はすでに広まっていて、わたしは気味悪がられていたのだ。

その後は淡々と、目の前のミシンだけを見て、日々を過ごした。仕事は真面目にこなした
し、トラブルも起こさなかったので、一年後にはふたたび三級に昇格し、その半年後には二
級となった。そして刑期を三カ月残したところで、仮釈放をもらった。仮釈放後の帰住先には、
和歌山の更生保護施設を指定した。ここには二十ほどの部屋があり、最低限の衣服と食事が
与えられるが、いつまでもいられるわけではなかった。

保護観察期間をこの施設で過ごした後、わたしは一人、東京に向かった。

昭和五十七年四月。

三十四歳の春だった。

東京駅で新幹線を降り、中央線で三鷹に出た。あのときと同じように、玉川上水沿いを歩いた。水路には相変わらず水がなかったが、沿道はアスファルトで舗装されている。新橋に辿り着いたころには、陽が傾きはじめていた。わたしの足は、島津賢治の理容店に向かった。

あのころの道路沿いには、畑や田圃しかなかった。しかし今や、住宅や店舗、ちょっとしたビルまで建っている。道幅も広くなって、オレンジ色のセンターラインが引かれていた。

当時の面影は、どこにもない。八年前のわたしの記憶は、役に立ちそうになかった。

見当違いのところを歩いているのかと思い始めたとき、トリコロールが目に入った。心臓の鼓動を感じながら、近づいた。「ヘアサロン島津」という文字が見えてくる。間違いない。島津賢治の店だ。改装したのだ。

しかし、わたしの記憶とは、何かが違う。あっと気がついた。店の位置がずれているのだ。その瞬間、記憶と目の前の光景が、重なった。かつて「理容しまづ」があった場所には、やけに明るい雰囲気の店が建っていた。駐車場が広く、二十四時間営業という謳い文句を掲げている。初めて見るタイプだ。お婆さんが一人で店番をしていたタバコ屋は、焼き肉屋に変わっている。平屋の民家があった場所には、二階建てのア

パートが建っていた。草の生い茂っていた空き地は、駐車場に変わっていた。

わたしは、島津の店の向かいに立った。通りを挟んで、店内の様子が、ガラス越しに見える。セット椅子は三台。客は、いちばん手前の台に座っている、年配の男性一人だけ。ヘアカットをしているのは、紛れもなく島津賢治。懐かしさに、胸が熱くなる。変わっていないな。いや、少し痩せただろうか。そのぶん、精悍せいかんさが加わったような気がする。ときおり口が動き、笑みがこぼれているが、目だけは真剣そのもので、客の髪と向き合っている。島津のハサミ捌きは、鮮やかだった。客も上機嫌の様子で、にこにこして鏡に向かっている。美容師となった今だからこそ、よくわかる。

一言だけでも、言葉を交わしたい。

わたし、美容師の資格を取ったのよ。

それだけでも伝えたい。このまま帰ったら、必ず後悔する。たとえ冷たく追い返されても、いい。会おう。会わなくてはならない。

通りを渡ろうと、足を踏み出した。

島津が、店の奥に顔を向けた。

わたしは、足を止めた。

店の奥から、島津と同じ白衣を着た女性が、現れた。小柄で、可愛らしい人。わたしと同

じくらいの年齢だろうか。笑顔で島津と言葉を交わしている。その女性の後ろから、小さな男の子が顔を出した。島津にそっくりだった。女性の腰につかまり、島津賢治を見あげている。客もいっしょになって、男の子に話しかけている。店内の笑い声が、聞こえてくるようだった。

わたしは、店に背を向けた。

三鷹駅への道を、歩きだした。

第四章　奇縁

1

　美容室「ルージュ」の店長室は、フランス国旗をモチーフにした店内と比べると、そっけないくらい質素だった。しかし俺は、明るく色彩豊かな店舗よりもむしろ、華やかな雰囲気が漂っているように感じた。内田オーナーの個性的なファッションのせいだろうか。しかし店で開店準備をしていた女の子も、個性的なファッションでは負けていないはずだ。あの女の子には無くて、内田オーナーにあるもの。もしかしたらそれが、オーラというものかも知れない。

　そんなことを考えながら俺は、勧められるまま、ソファに腰をおろした。

　内田オーナーが、みずからお茶をいれてくれた。

　礼を言ってから、一口啜る。旨かった。

「刑務所で美容師の資格が取れるんですか?」

「履歴書にちゃんと書いてあったよ。刑務所内で国家資格を取って、出所したばかりだって」

「それは本人から?」

「人を殺したってこともね」

内田オーナーが、うなずく。

「松子伯母が刑務所に入っていたことは、知っていましたか?」

「松子伯母が、昭和五十七年の四月だったよ」

「沢村さんから電話があったあとね、私も当時の日記を引っぱり出して、読み返してみたの

ね。そしたら、」

「松子伯母さんが、この店に来たのは、いつごろでしたか?」

顔が、悔しそうに歪んだ。

「これからじゃないか……」

「五十三歳だったそうです」

「まだ若かったんだろ?」

内田オーナーが、口を開く。

「松子、死んだんだってね」

内田オーナーが、笑みを浮かべた。

「あなたも沢村さんのことは聞いたんでしょ。あの方も昔、塀の中にいたことがある。沢村さんだけじゃないのね。以前から私の店のお客様には、明らかにその筋ってわかる人から、話をしているうちに、実は窃盗で捕まったことがあるって言われて、こちらがびっくりするような人まで。私も不思議に思っていたんだけど、いつだったかな、沢村さんが教えてくれたのね。和歌山の女子刑務所には、受刑者の職業訓練に使う美容室があって、その店名が『あかね』っていうんだって。笙くんも沢村さんから聞いていると思うけど、ここも以前は『あかね』って名前だったからね。それで刑務所に入っていた人が、懐かしくなって足を運ぶんだって。私も驚いて、逆に刑務所の美容室と同じ名前ではお嫌じゃないんですかって伺ったら、いや、刑務所の中で、美容室というのはいちばんリラックスできる天国だったんだって。沢村さんご自身も、店の名前『あかね』という名前には、ぜんぜん悪いイメージがないんだって。おっしゃっていたね」

「でも、そのあとで、名前を変えたんですよね」

「十三年前に、それまで入っていたビルが取り壊されることになったのね。それでこのビルに移ってきたんだけど、ちょうど昭和も終わったし、新しい時代に向かって気分を一新しよ

うと思って、ちょっと気取った名前だけど、フランス語のルージュにしたのね。ルージュは同じ赤でも、茜色より明るい赤なのよ。少しでも明るい時代になればと思ってね、そうつけたの。別に、塀の中にいた人に、来て欲しくなかったわけじゃないのよ」

内田オーナーが、いたずらっぽく笑った。

「松子伯母さんがこの店に来たのも、店の名前のせいだったんですか?」

「そう思うね。本人から聞いたわけじゃないけどね」

「出所して、すぐにここに来たんでしたよね。ということは……」

「どうしたの?」

「松子伯母さんは、警察に捕まったとき、理容師の男性と同棲していたんです。たぶん、刑務所の中で美容師の資格を取ったのは、出所してから、その男性といっしょにやり直すためじゃないかと思うんです。でも、出所してすぐにこちらに来たということは、その男性とは……」

「そういえば面接のときに、どうしても見返してやりたい人がいるんだって、言っていたね」

「見返してやりたい人……」

「松子が最初に来た日のことはね、よく憶えてるんだよ。いきなり店に入ってきてね、使ってくれって言ったのね。ふつうは募集広告を見て来るもんだろ。うちは当時、私のほかに技

術者が二人とインターンが一人いて、スタッフは間に合っていたからね、募集はしていなかったんだ。それを、どうしてもこの店で働きたいって言うのさ。そんな図々しい子は初めてだった。私も最初は断ろうとしたんだけど、目つきが凄いのなんのって。絶対に諦めないって感じの目でね。門前払いにしたら、こちらが殺されるんじゃないかと思うほどだった。だからまあ特別に、営業時間が終わるまで待ってもらって、モデルウィグを使ってテストすることにした。あ、モデルウィグというのは、人形のかつらのことね。でね、私もそこは人が悪いから、思い切り難しい課題を出したのね、あのころ店にいた技術者でも、できたかどうか怪しいくらいのをね。最初は、さすがにあの子も戸惑ったみたいで、もたついていたけど、五分もしないうちに、目の覚めるようなシザー捌きに変わってね。何かに憑かれたような顔になって、近づきがたい雰囲気っていうのは、ああいうことを言うんだって、納得したもんだよ。人一倍集中力があったんだろうね。終わったとたん、おもしろ半分に見ていたスタッフたちが、じゅうぶん及第点を与えられる仕上がりだった。抜群の出来とは言わないけど、二度びっくりさ。そのあとすぐ面接拍手したものね。シザーを持つのは三年ぶりと聞いて、二度びっくりさ。そのあとすぐ面接して、履歴書を見て、採用することにした。誰も文句は言わなかったよ」

「刑務所に入っていたことで、断ろうとは思わなかったんですか？」

それまで穏やかだった内田オーナーの表情が、一変した。険しい目で、俺を見据えた。

「なあ、笙くんよ」

「……はい」

「この内田あかねを、見損なってもらっちゃ困るよ」

老人とは思えない、凄みのある声だった。

「ご……ごめんなさいっ」

俺は、膝に手を突き、頭をさげた。

「ただね、松子の過去は、私しか知らなかったはずだよ。わざわざおおっぴらに宣伝することもないと思ったからね」

内田オーナーの顔から、険が消えた。

「あの……店での働きぶりは、どうでしたか?」

「手先は器用だし、もともと頭のいい子だったんだよ。ただ、いつも周りに壁をつくっているところがあってね。必死に突っ張っている感じだった。でも、トラブルを起こすわけでもないし、お客様の応対も笑顔でそつなくこなして、評判もよかったのね。仕事さえきっちりやってりゃ、こっちは文句ないんだからね。そんな状態が、一年くらい続いたかな」

内田オーナーが、深く息を吐く。

「おかしくなったのは、あの男が店に現れてからだったね」

2

　銀座の「あかね」は、雑居ビルの二階にあった。セット椅子が三台と、シャンプー台が一台だけの、こぢんまりとした店で、広さだけで言えば、刑務所敷地内の表「あかね」のほうが、広いくらいだ。ただしインテリアは、比べものにならないほど、洗練されている。

　店のオーナーは四十代の女性だが、パリで修行を積んできたというだけあって、入り口には堂々と、フランス国旗が掲げてあった。壁には、パリの名門アカデミー・フォーミュラのアヴァンセコース修了証と、日本国内で行われたカットコンテストの賞状が、飾られている。その下には大きなトロフィーが、金色の光を放っていた。

　試験と面接をパスしたわたしは、翌日からスタッフの一員として、働くことになった。オーナーである内田先生のほかに、スタッフは三人。このうち三十歳前後と二十代半ばの女性は美容師で、二十歳くらいの女の子はインターンだった。三十四歳のわたしは、スタッフの中では最年長になる。

　最年長でも新入りには違いなく、最初はシャンプーやマッサージを担当しながら、店のシステムや接客の方針を学んだ。一週間くらいすると、簡単なカットを任されるようになり、

道具の場所や使い方を一通り身につけたころには、ほかのスタッフと変わりなく、動けるようになっていた。

島津賢治と会うことは、あきらめていた。

島津賢治の幸福な生活を見せつけられたことは、何かの形で伝えたかった。しかし自分が立ち直り、美容師として再出発したことは、何かの形で伝えたかった。

わたしは不動産屋で部屋を探し、赤羽にアパートを借りることにした。保証人が必要だったので、交付されていた保護カードを持って保護観察所に行き、相談して保証人になってもらった。

わたしに残されていたのは、トルコ嬢時代に稼いだお金と、美容師の国家資格と、その技術だけだ。女一人で生きていく覚悟を決めた以上、自分の食い扶持は自分で稼ぐしかない。残る選択肢は、美容師だけ。どうせなら、都心で腕を試したかった。ふと思いついて、東京まで出た。駅前の公衆電話の電話帳をめくり、美容院の項目を探すうちに、「あかね」という店名に目が留まった。刑務所の美容室と同じ名前。最後の三年間は、表の「あかね」には足を踏み入れることさえできなかった。

年齢的にトルコ嬢はできないし、他の水商売もする気がしない。残る選択肢は、美容師だけ。

赤羽の職業安定所で、美容院の求人案内を見たが、惹かれるような店はなかった。どうせなら、都心で腕を試したかった。

わたしは、そのページを破り、電話ボックスを出た。

実際に「あかね」に入ると、最初に金色のトロフィーが目に入った。そこで初めて、カット

コンテストというものがあると知った。コンテストに出場して優勝すれば、島津の耳にも届くのではないか。そうすれば、少なくとも業界内では、名前が知られるようになるのではないか。

わたしは、オーナーの内田先生に直談判して、テストを受けさせてもらった。モデルウィグを使った実技テストでは、アウトサイドストロークカットを用いて、毛先に跳ねるような動きをつける髪型を、課題に出された。ストロークカットは、毛束を削り取るようなカット方法で、難度の高い技術だ。刑務所の講習で教わったことはあるが、実際に使ったことは数えるほどしかないし、得意な技でもない。それも三年前の話だ。しかし、やるしかないと腹を括って取り組んだ結果、辛うじて制限時間内に仕上げられた。自信はなかったが、テストは合格だった。

内田先生はカットコンテストの常連で、何度も最優秀賞を獲得している。スタッフも勉強熱心で、営業時間後も勉強会と称して、夜遅くまで内田先生の技術指導を受けていた。もちろんわたしも参加した。この時間がいちばん楽しくて、「白夜」のテクニック勉強会を思い出したものだ。

話を聞くと、コンテストはカットだけではなく、ワインディング、つまりロッド巻きの速さと正確さを競うコンテストもあるという。ロッド巻きは得意だったので、こちらを目指そうかとも考えたが、理容師である島津賢治はロッドを使うことがなく、きっとロッド巻きに

は興味がないと思い、あくまでカットコンテストを目指すことにした。

「あかね」に就職して二カ月目に、初めて指名を受けた。「白夜」で最初の指名を受けたのも、二カ月目だ。接客の心構えといい、営業時間外の勉強会といい、指名を受けるシステムといい、トルコ風呂と美容院の思わぬ共通点を発見し、愉快になった。

わたしを指名した女性は、二十代後半くらいで、シルクの白いスーツを着こなしていた。頬はぽっちゃりしているが、目鼻立ちは女優のように整っており、大きく揺れるウェーブの髪が、上品さを引き立たせている。彼女は「あかね」の常連客らしく、以前にも見かけたことがある。そのときは内田先生が担当だった。

わたしは、自分のキャスター付きワゴンを押して、彼女の脇に立った。ケープの着用はすでに、インターンの女の子が済ませていた。

「ご指名、ありがとうございます。川尻です。どのような髪型をお望みでございますか」

「夏らしく、短くして」

「ショートですね。どのような雰囲気がお好みですか?」

どこかで聞いたことのある声だった。しかし思い出せない。

「任せるわ。あなたが似合うと思う髪型にしてちょうだい」

女性が目を閉じた。

「……はい」

　試されている、と感じた。

　わたしは雑念を追い払い、あらゆる角度から女性の顔を観察した。丸顔の部類に入るだろうか。丸顔といっても、決して太っているのではなく、品のいい顔立ちだ。大きなウェーブは似合っているのだが、お高くとまった印象も与えている。ショートで同じような雰囲気が欲しいのなら、前髪をすべてバックブローにして額を出す。仕上げは手ぐしを使い、ムースを軽くつけてかきあげればいい。でもこの女性には、もっと優しさの漂う髪型が、似合うような気がする。たとえばショートレイヤーにして軽くパーマをかけ、フィンガーブローでラフな感じを出せれば……。

　わたしは心を決め、ワゴンからシザーとブラシを取った。

　シザーを使って大胆にウェーブを切り落とし、丁寧にレイヤーをつけていく。いつもなら軽い会話をしながらシザーを操るのだが、自分のセンスを試されていると思うと、神経が髪に集中してしまい、会話が途切れたままになった。はっとして鏡を見ると、女性は機嫌を損ねるでもなく、目を閉じたままで、口元には笑みさえ浮かべている。

　レイヤーが出来あがってから、パーマネント液をつけて毛束を巻き、ローラーボールを被せて浸透させる。パーマが終わったら、スタイリング剤をつけて、フィンガーブローで仕上げた。

162

完成の瞬間、深く息を吐いた。自分のセンスと技術をすべて注いだ作品。果たして銀座で通じるのか。

わたしは、ワゴンから合わせ鏡を取り、女性の後ろで開いた。

「いかがでしょうか?」

女性が、目を開けた。

硬い表情で、鏡を見つめている。

沈黙の数秒が過ぎた。

鏡の中の女性が、目をあげた。責めるような視線を、放ってくる。

「あなた、どこの美容学校を出たの?」

「……岐阜にある、学校です」

「笠松でしょ」

背中に汗が滲んだ。

「どうして、おわかりになるのですか?」

女性の表情がくだけ、笑みがこぼれた。

「そうか。ついに夢を叶えたんだ。よかったな」

わたしは、鏡に映った女性の顔を、見つめた。瞬きを繰り返す。

「松ちゃん、まだわからないのか。俺だよ」

女性が囁いた。熱のこもった目で、微笑む。

わたしは、はっと息を吸った。

「めぐみっ!」

大きな声をあげてしまった。店内の視線を感じ、周囲に頭をさげる。小さな声で、

「東めぐみさん?」

「いまは結婚して、沢村めぐみになっているけどね」

「びっくりした、見違えちゃったわ。ぜんぜん気がつかなかった」

「やっぱり?」

「めぐみはわたしのこと、いつ気づいたの?」

「この前来たときにね」

「声をかけてくれたらよかったのに」

「わるい。ちょっといたずらしたくてさ」

めぐみが舌を出した。

「松ちゃんは、ちっとも変わらないね」

「嘘ばっかり。もう三十四歳よ」

「嘘じゃない。前よりも綺麗になったよ」

「相変わらず女心をくすぐる人ね。結婚したって言ってたけど、お相手は男性？」

めぐみが苦笑した。

「決まってるだろ。トイチは中だけの話。外じゃ馬鹿らしくてやってられないよ」

「おめでとう。ほんとうに見違えちゃったわ。こんなに女っぽくなってるんだもの」

「そんなに言うなよ。照れる」

めぐみが、自分の髪に手を触れた。

「松ちゃん、これならじゅうぶん、銀座でやっていけるよ。あたしは、自分の顔がこんなに優しく見えるなんて、夢にも思わなかった」

その言葉を聞いて、全身の緊張が解けていった。

「よかった」

「松ちゃんがこの店を選んだのは、店名が？」

わたしはうなずいた。

「懐かしいというわけじゃないんだけど、ここ以外にないと思って」

「あたしはね、去年まで別の美容院に行っていたんだ。これも銀座にある店なんだけど、大手の化粧品メーカーが経営してるとかで、馬鹿でかくてさ、従業員だけで五十人はいたよ。

完全な分業になっていて、カットしてくれる人と、シャンプーしてくれる人と、顔剃ってく
れる人と、マッサージしてくれる人と、とにかくみんな違うんだよ。なんだか、流れ作業の
ベルトコンベアに乗せられてる気分になってね。もっと落ち着ける店がないかなって探して
たら、この店を見つけて」

「やっぱり、一度は入っちゃうよね」

「でさ、よくよく話を聞いたら、この店を作った内田さんって、あたしが行っていた馬鹿で
かい美容院を辞めて、一人でパリまで行っちゃった人なんだってね。親会社の方針が気に入
らなくて、啖呵切って飛び出したんだって。それ聞いて、ますますここが気に入ったよ。お
かげで、松ちゃんにも再会できたし」

「いまはどうしてるの?」

「ミカン山はこりごりだからね。かといって、澄ましてOLなんかやってられないし。手っ
とり早く金になって、犯罪にならないとなると、水商売しかないだろ」

「ホステスとか?」

「最初はね、そういうおとなしいのから始めたけど、酔っぱらい親父に絡まれると、ぶっ飛
ばしたくなるんだよ。それを我慢するのが大変でさ」

わたしは、わかるわかる、と笑った。

「つくづく客商売には向かないと思ったね」

わたしは声を落として、

「トルコ嬢は考えなかった？」

「考えなかったわけじゃないけど、松ちゃんの話を聞いていたからさ、あたしには務まりそうにないって思ったし、松ちゃんの前でこんなこと言うのもなんだけど、金のためにそこまでしたくはなかった……ごめん」

「謝ることないよ。わたしもそう思うから。でもね、あれはあれで、プロ意識を持って仕事をしている人もいたんだよ。わたしも、最初のころはそうだった。結局、自分を見失ってしまったけど」

めぐみが、神妙な顔でうなずく。

「あたしはね、身体を売ることは嫌だったけど、裸を見せることには抵抗がなかった。だから、ストリップ・ダンサーになったんだ」

わたしは、目を丸くした。

「もともと身体を動かすことは好きだったし、恥ずかしいからみんなには言わなかったけど、中学までバレエを習っててさ、ダンスもなんとかなると思った」

「……すごい。お金持ちだったの？」

「中学まで。父親が賄賂をもらったとかで警察に捕まって、そのあとは、ごろごろって感じの下り坂さ。で、行き着いた場所が塀の中。ダンサーとしちゃ評判よかったんだよ、あたし。ストリッパーはたくさんいたけど、ちゃんと踊れる子って意外に少なかったからね。それに気持ちいいんだ、男の目を一身に集めて踊るのって。そのうちに、ヌードグラビアの仕事も来るようになって、正式にモデル事務所と契約した。そのときの社長が、いまの旦那」

「お仕事はいまも？」

「まさか。とっくに引退したよ。いまは二十歳の可愛い女の子が、簡単に股をおっぴろげる時代だからね。オバサンは消え去るのみ」

「いまでは社長夫人ってわけね」

「そんな気楽なもんじゃないよ。これからまた事務所に顔出さなきゃならないんだ。こんどゆっくり会おうよ。休みはいつ？」

めぐみは、社交辞令を使わない人だった。「ゆっくり会おう」と言って帰っていった三日後に、銀座の喫茶店で会って、近況を存分にしゃべった。

めぐみの夫が経営しているモデル事務所は、所属する女の子が四人、スタッフは夫とめぐ

みと、電話番の若い男の子が一人だけという、小さなものだった。社長である夫みずから営
業に走り、めぐみは女の子たちのマネージメントをこなしているという。

めぐみが、コーヒーをスプーンでかき回しながら、ため息を吐いた。

「女の子を売りこむには、専用の宣伝写真が必要でね、それを撮影するだけでも、カメラマ
ン、メイク、スタジオ代、打ち合わせ費なんか入れて、一日で軽く十万円は超えちゃう。普
通のモデル事務所なら、そういうのは本人持ちなんだけど、うちみたいなアダルト系はそう
もいかなくてね。女の子たちにプロ意識がないっていうか、放っておいたらそんな面倒なこ
と、誰もしないんだ。困ったのは、綺麗な子ほど時間にルーズってこと。この業界はいいか
げんなようでも、そういうところは厳しいからね。とうぜん、トラブルを起こす子には仕事
が来なくなるんだけど、こんどは仕事がないことを事務所のせいにしたがる……ごめん、愚
痴になっちゃったね」

「大変そうね」

「マネージャーともなると、恋愛相談を受けることもあるんだけど、『彼の気持ちがわから
ないんですう』なんて泣きつかれてもね。たしかに塀の中じゃ男役だったけど、最近の若い
男の心なんか、あたしだってわかんないよ」

めぐみが、首を振りながら、笑った。顔から笑みを消し、物思いにふけるような目を、宙

に向ける。

「一人でいいんだ。一人の売れっ子を抱えれば、業界で大きな顔ができる。その一人が、なかなかいない」

「いっそのこと、めぐみが現役復帰したら？」

わたしは冗談のつもりだったが、

「考えなきゃいけないかも知れない」

めぐみが、真剣な顔でうなずいた。

「松ちゃん、初めてトルコ嬢の仕事をしたとき、どんな気持ちだった？」

「え……そうね、とにかく夢中で、何かを感じる余裕なんかなかった。気がついたら、お客さんの背中を見送っていたもの」

「嫌だとは思わなかった？」

「そのときは男に捨てられて、自棄になって自分で乗りこんで行ったから、嫌だとは思わなかったな。ただ、その前にも一度、面接には行ったことがあってね。そのときは同棲していた彼に行かされたんだけど、面接の場で服脱いでって言われたときは、さすがに嫌だった。泣いたよ」

めぐみが鼻息を吐く。

「自分の女をトルコ風呂で働かせようなんて、とんでもない男だな」

「いまから思えば、そうかも知れない。でも、わたしにとっては、大切な人だったんだよ。もう死んじゃったけどね」

「そう……」

「たしかにトルコ嬢って大変な仕事だったけど、ときどきトルコ嬢時代に戻りたくなることがある。雄琴じゃなくて、博多にいたころにね」

めぐみの目が、どうして、と問いかけてくる。

「あそこでは、自分を飾る必要がなかったから。いままでの人生で、あのころの自分が、いちばん素直に生きていたと思う」

めぐみが、唇をすぼめる。その瞳が一瞬、鋭い光を放ったような気がした。

その後しばらく、めぐみと会う機会はなかった。七月の終わりごろ、久しぶりに「あかね」に来店して、わたしを指名してくれた。

鏡の中のめぐみは、顔が一回り小さくなったように見えた。ぽっちゃりしていた頬が引き締まり、刑務所で初めて会ったころのような精悍さを、取り戻していた。

「めぐみ、痩せたんじゃない?」

「わかる？　食事制限とエアロビクスで、体重を落としてるんだ」

めぐみが、にこりと笑う。

「現役復帰することにしたよ」

わたしは声を落として、

「ストリップ・ダンサーとして？」

「いや、アダルトビデオ。単体で主演することが決まってね」

「アダルトって……」

「そう、ポルノ」

わたしは息を詰めて、めぐみの横顔を見つめた。

「ご主人は何も言わなかったの？」

「反対されたけど、できることは何でもやらなきゃ。事務所が潰れてから悔やんだって仕方がないだろ。彼だって、あたしが言いだしたら聞かない性格だってことは、わかっているはずだし」

めぐみが、鏡を睨みつけた。首を回して、わたしを見あげる。

「ねえ、松ちゃん。スケベそうな女が裸になるのはありふれてるだろ。絶対に裸になりそうにない女が脱いで、はじめて商品価値があがると思うんだ。あたしの歳じゃ清楚なお嬢様は

無理だけど、プライドの高い大人の女って感じを出したい。そういう髪型にできないかな」

「そうね……頬がすっきりして、顎の線がシャープになったから、ベリーショートはどうかしら。トップに柔らかくパーマをあしらえば、大人っぽくて、しかもキュートになると思う」

めぐみが、口を真一文字に結んだ。

「任せる」

空に灰色の雲がひしめいて、夏の終わりを予感させるような、肌寒い日。わたしは三十五歳の誕生日を、二週間前に済ませていた。誰からもお祝いの言葉をもらわなかった。

「あかね」は一週間の夏休みに入っていた。内田先生はパリに旅立ち、スタッフたちも帰省やら旅行やら、それぞれの休暇を楽しんでいるようだ。わたしには、何の予定もなかった。

この日も午前中は、テレビを眺めて過ごした。洗濯機を回そうかとも思ったが、空模様とテレビの天気予報を見て、あきらめた。冷蔵庫に冷や御飯が残っていたので、お昼にチャーハンをつくって食べた。お茶で口をすすいでいるとき、めぐみから電話がかかってきた。いまからそっちに行っていいか、という内容だった。わたしは、ほかに用事もなかったので、いつでもいいと答えた。

めぐみは、午後三時前に、やってきた。白のショートパンツに、胸元の開いた赤紫のカッ

トソー。その上からジージャンを羽織っている。めぐみにしては、ラフな格好だ。手には、駅前のケーキ屋の箱をさげていた。

「美味しそうだったから、買ってきたよ」

めぐみがやけに明るい声で言い、わたしにケーキ箱を押しつける。

大きなケーキ箱には、ストロベリーショートケーキ、チーズケーキ、チョコレートケーキ、シュークリームが二つずつ、入っていた。

「これ全部、二人で食べるの?」

「余ったらあたしが食べる」

めぐみが平然と言った。

わたしのアパートは、六畳の居間とキッチンにバス・トイレが付いて、家賃は四万三千円。

居間では、単身者用の小さなコタツを、テーブル代わりに使っている。

わたしはティーバッグで紅茶をいれ、小皿とフォークといっしょに、コタツテーブルに持っていった。

めぐみが、箱からストロベリーショートケーキを取り出し、自分の皿に置く。いただきまあす、と声をあげ、フォークで生クリームをすくってぱくついた。子供のような笑顔を輝かせる。

「うん、おいしい!」

わたしは、チョコレートケーキを選び、一口運んだ。コクに深みがあった。

「松ちゃん、刑務所を出て、最初に何を食べた?」

「何だったっけ、憶えてないな」

「ほんとかよ。あたしは憶えてるよ。生クリームが山盛りになったショートケーキ。塀の中にいるときから、絶対に十個食べてやると決めてたもん」

「食べたの? 十個も?」

「もちろん。そのあと吹き出物が出て困ったけどな」

わたしは笑った。

「刑務所にいたころからは、想像つかないわね。憶えてるわよ、たしか大福餅が配られたときに、めぐみはハイチの女の子にあげたのよね。月に一回しかもらえないのに、甘いものは嫌いだって。でもそれが看守にばれちゃって、懲罰房に入れられた。ほんとうに甘いものが嫌いだったの?」

「そんなわけないだろ。やせ我慢だよ」

「前から聞こうと思ってたんだけど、どうしてそこまでして、トイチを続けたの? 別に、そういう趣味があったわけじゃないんでしょ?」

「たしかにレズビアンじゃないけど、誰かに思いを寄せられるのって、気分がいいんだよ。

　めぐみがショートケーキを平らげ、チーズケーキに手を伸ばした。一口食べて、フォークを置く。口を動かしながら、バッグから一本のビデオテープを取り、わたしに差し出す。

　わたしは、チョコレートケーキの最後の一口を飲みこんでから、受け取った。

　パッケージに、めぐみの全身写真が載っていた。わたしがセットしたベリーショートの髪に、グレーのテーラード・ジャケットとタイトスカート。真っ赤なルージュの輝く口元には、自信に満ちた笑みが浮かんでいる。立ち姿は凜として、惚れ惚れとするほどだった。その横に仰々しく打たれたタイトルが、

『水沢葵・社長秘書は超淫乱！』

　その脇には、口にするのも憚られる宣伝文句が綴られている。

　パッケージをひっくり返すと、心臓が跳ねた。めぐみのあられもない姿が、いくつも載っていた。自分の裸体をまさぐって恍惚とするシーン、男優に激しく責められているシーン。

　わたしは、めぐみの顔を、見つめてしまった。

　めぐみは、我関せずといった顔で、チーズケーキを口に運んでいる。

「水沢葵っていうのは、あたしの芸名。これ一本で二百万もらったよ。このギャラは破格ら

しい。撮影は大変だったけどね」

「ほんとうにセックスしたの?」

「まさか。本番はしなかったよ。そこまでやっちゃったら、旦那がかわいそうだろ」

わたしはもう一度、パッケージに目をやった。

「観(み)てもいいよ」

わたしは、首を横に振った。ビデオテープを返した。

「うち、ビデオないから」

めぐみが、ふうん、と言って、ビデオテープを引っこめる。

「めぐみは、観たの?」

めぐみが、考えこむような顔をしてから、

「見始めたけど……からみが始まったところで、目を背けちゃったよ。そうしたら、旦那に叱られてね」

わたしは目を剝いた。

「ご主人もいっしょに観たの?」

「そんな声、出すなよ」

「だって、よく観られるね」

「旦那が言うにはさ、これからこの業界でやっていこうと思ったら、自分の恥ずかしいシーンもちゃんと観ておかなくちゃ駄目だって。　事務所の女の子たちが、自分のビデオをどういう気持ちで観ているか、理解しろって」

「厳しい人なんだ」

「仕事にはね。それ以外はへろへろだけど」

　めぐみが、慈しむような目をする。すぐに険しい顔になり、

「たしかにステージで裸になるのと、ビデオでアヘアヘ喘ぐのは、ぜんぜん違うんだよ。ステージではお客の反応が返ってくるからね、自分はダンサーだ、エンターテーナーだって思えた。でもビデオの撮影現場って妙に白けててさ、演技すればするほど気持ちが醒めてきて、自分が惨めになって……。ただし、一本出るだけで二百万になるとは思わなかった。同じお金をステージで稼ごうと思ったら、大変だよ」

　めぐみが、ふうと息を吐く。

「とにかく、いい勉強になった。これからはビデオの時代なんだって、実感できたし」

「まだビデオに出るの？」

「けっこう話が来ててね。できるだけやるつもりでいる。でも……一年が限界だろうな。旦那とも、一年って約束をしたし。そのあとは裏方に徹するよ。これからはきっと、アダルト

ビデオ女優がスターになる時代が来る。 そういう逸材を見つけて、 大儲けしてやるさ」

そして自分に言い聞かせるように、

「負けてたまるかよ」

めぐみが、窓に目を向ける。

「雨が降ってきたね」

その横顔が、わたしには眩しかった。 そして、めぐみとは親友になれない、 と直感した。

めぐみはその後、八本のアダルトビデオに出演した。「水沢葵」主演のビデオは、いずれも売り上げ好調らしい。撮影があるたびに、わたしがめぐみの髪をセットした。ベリーショートは、淫乱女優・水沢葵のトレードマークになっていた。めぐみが言ったとおり、水沢葵一人のおかげで、事務所経営も一息つけたそうだ。有望な新人も見つけたので、ビデオ出演は打ち止めにしたという。

わたしとめぐみの付き合いは、表面上は変わりなく続いた。めぐみは「あかね」に来店すると必ずわたしを指名し、ときには銀座の喫茶店やわたしのアパートを訪れた。初めて紹介されためぐみの夫は、序二段の相撲取りのような巨漢で、笑った顔が恵比寿様のようだった。夫を前にしためぐみは、

少女のように屈託なく笑った。そのあとにもう一度、自宅に招待されたが、わたしは適当な

理由をつけて行かなかった。

「あかね」での仕事は、無難にこなしていた。営業時間後の練習にも参加していた。しかし、

秋にあった関東地区のカットコンテストには、出場しなかった。各店の出場枠が決められて

いて、「あかね」からは二名しかエントリーできなかったのだ。「あかね」からは内田先生と、

二十代半ばのスタッフが出場した。内田先生は二位に入賞し、スタッフは十位にも入らなか

った。春にワインディングのコンテストがあるので、そちらにエントリーしてはどうかと勧

められたが、断った。

島津賢治のことは、思い出さなくなっていた。自分が何のために美容師を続けているのか、

わからなくなるときがあった。

クリスマス・イブは、一人で過ごした。アパートの部屋で布団を被り、耳を塞いだ。年末

年始も、一人で過ごした。餅も食べなかった。初詣(はつもうで)にも行かなかった。バレンタインデーに

は、チョコレートを買わなかった。暖かくなってきたと思ったら、桜の開花が宣言されてい

た。花見はしなかった。

真夜中、どうしてもお腹がすいて、冷蔵庫を開けたら、空っぽだった。文字どおり、何も

入っていなかった。わたしは、空腹のまま、布団に戻った。

3

「おかしくなったのは、あの男が店に現れてからだったね」

「龍という人ですね」

「名前は知らないけど、背の高い、ちょっと陰のあるいい男だったよ」

「美容院の客として、来たんですか?」

「いや、女の人の連れで来ていたね」

「恋人、ですか?」

「そういう雰囲気じゃなかったね……推測だけど、女の人は、どこかの組の姐さんか何かだと思うね。その男は、ただのボディガードか、運転手みたいな感じだったよ」

「組っていうのは……」

「暴力団。その男、暴力団の下っ端だったと思うよ」

「その人、龍洋一っていうんですけど、松子伯母さんの教え子だった人です」

「そういえば、履歴書にも書いてあったね。中学校の先生をやっていたって。じゃあ、そのときの?」

「はい」

内田オーナーが、ゆっくりと首を振った。

「……奇縁だねえ」

「松子伯母さんは、最初からそれが龍さんだと、わかったんでしょうか?」

「それは無理だったんじゃないの。中学生といい大人じゃあね。でも、その龍って男のほうは、わかったみたいだね。これも憶えているんだけど、その男が突っ立ったまま、口をあんぐり開けて、松子のほうを見てたものね。そしたら、いっしょに来ていた女の人から、ひどく叱られてね。人の言うことをろくに聞かないで、よそ見しているってね。その男、顔を真っ赤にして、ぺこぺこ頭さげてたよ」

「二人は同棲していたそうなんですけど、気づいていましたか?」

「いつからいっしょに住んでたのかは知らないけど、あの男が松子の送り迎えをするようになったから、付き合いだしたんだなとはわかったね。さすがに店の中までは入ってこなかったけど、ドアのすぐ外で立ってるんだものね。別に誰と付き合おうがいいんだけどさ、なんとなく、嫌な感じになってきたなあとは、思ってたのね」

4

昭和五十八年五月

その日わたしは、営業時間後の勉強会を休み、一人で家路についた。

店の入っているビルを一歩出ると、縁日の夜のような喧噪が、通りに満ち溢れていた。スーツ姿のサラリーマンは赤ら顔で笑い、流行のブランド服に身を包んだ若い女性たちは、我こそ銀座の主役という顔で闊歩している。

どうしてそんなに笑えるのか。どうしてそんなに自信ありげに振る舞えるのか。いったい、何がそんなに楽しいのか。

わたしは、自分とあまりに無縁な光景に、軽い目眩を覚えて、立ちすくんだ。

自分の居るべき場所は、たぶん、ここではない。わたしにとって安住の地は、どこか他にある。きっとある。あるはずだ……。

「川尻先生」

びくりとして、振り返った。

　背が高く、肩のがっちりした男が、立っていた。頭髪はパンチパーマ。ペイズリーのプレーンシャツに、白のチノパンツ。足もとは焦げ茶色のウィングチップ。

「やっぱりそうだ。川尻先生でしょ。大川第二中学の」

　男が近づいてくる。顔が見えた。見覚えがあった。きのう「あかね」に来ていた男だ。たしか若い女性の連れだったはずだ。女性から派手に叱られていたので、印象に残っている。

　わたしは、後ずさった。

「あなたは？」

「わかりませんか。俺です」

「……誰？」

「龍洋一です、三年二組の」

　顔を凝視した。

　そう言われれば、面影が残っているような気がする。

「龍くん？……ほんとうに、あの、龍洋一くんなの？」

「はい。そうです」

　わたしは、いま自分がどこにいて何をしているのか、見失いそうになった。

　龍洋一。

その名を聞くのは、口にするのは、何年ぶりだろう。

龍洋一と最後に交わした言葉は、憶えている。

『こんど来たら、殺す』

龍洋一は、わたしに憎悪の目を向け、そう吐き捨てたのだ。あの日の校長室では、言葉を交わすどころか、目を合わせようともしなかった。

「美容院で最初に見かけたとき、似ているとは思ったのですが、まさか先生のはずはないと……川尻と呼ばれている声を耳にして、ほんとうにびっくりしました」

龍洋一が、嬉しそうに歯を剝いた。

わたしの頰が強ばった。

「ここで、わたしを、待ってたの?」

「話がしたくて……あの、メシ、まだだったら、いっしょにどうですか?」

龍洋一の真意が、わからなかった。

わたしを憎んでいたんじゃないの?

どうしてそんな、嬉しそうな顔をするの?

「……ごめんなさい、わたし、急ぐから」

龍洋一の顔に、失望の影が射す。しかしすぐに笑顔を繕い、

「どちらまでですか？　よかったら、送らせてください」

龍洋一が、路上駐車してある車に、目をやった。古い型の国産高級車だった。

「ほんとに、わたしを、待ってたの？」

「すみません。でも、店の中で声をかけたら、迷惑をかけるかも知れないし……」

わたしは、頭が混乱するばかりで、継ぐ言葉を見つけられなかった。

沈黙が流れる。

龍洋一が、ばつが悪そうに俯いた。

「あの……いえ、俺やっぱり、これで失礼します。先生に会えて、嬉しかったです。ほんと

うに嬉しかったです。それじゃあ、お元気で」

龍洋一が、頭をさげ、背を向ける。

「待って」

龍洋一が立ち止まった。振り返る。

その一瞬、すべてが静止した。

わたしは、笑みをつくった。

「せっかくだから、送ってもらうわ」

龍洋一の顔に、喜びが広がる。

「ど、どうぞ!」

龍洋一が、助手席のドアを開けてくれた。わたしがシートに座るのを見届けてから、軽や

かな足取りで車の前を回り、運転席に乗りこんだ。

わたしは、アパートの住所を告げた。

「赤羽ですね。わかりました」

龍洋一の声が、弾んでいた。

わたしは、背もたれに身体をあずけた。龍洋一は、ときどきクラクションを鳴らしながら、

銀座の狭い通りをのろのろと進む。車窓を横切る人々は、みな楽しそうだった。

わたしは、龍洋一の横顔を、見つめた。

龍洋一が、ちらとわたしを見て、照れたような笑みを浮かべる。

「龍くん、いくつになった?」

「二十七です」

「もうそんなになるの。変わるはずだわ」

「先生は、変わってませんよ」

「大人になったのね、見え透いたお世辞を使うなんて」

「お世辞じゃありません」

龍洋一が声を張りあげた。

「お母さんと妹さんは?」

「母親は、男をつくって出て行きました。いい歳して、懲りない女ですよ。妹も行方知れず

で……行方知れずは、俺のほうかも知れませんけどね」

龍洋一が、ふっと笑った。

「きのういっしょにいた女の人は?」

「カシラの愛人です。俺は、運転手兼荷物持ちです」

「ヤクザになったの?」

「やっぱりって思ってるでしょ」

わたしは黙った。

車内に漂う、甘い香りに気づいた。目の前のキャビネットに、芳香剤が置いてあった。容

器の中に赤い液体が、たっぷり入っている。それが小刻みに、揺れている。

「……龍くん、人を殺したこと、ある?」

龍洋一が、躊躇（ためら）いがちに、首を振った。

「わたしはあるわ」

龍洋一が、こちらに顔を向けた。あわてて前に戻す。

「わたしは雄琴で、トルコ嬢をやってたのよ。そのときのヒモを包丁で刺し殺して、懲役八

年。ちゃんと務めあげて出てきたのが一年前」

車は狭い通りから、晴海通りに出た。少しだけ、スピードが上がった。

「これでもわたしは、変わっていないって言える？」

「……俺のせいですね」

龍洋一の声が、低くなった。

「なにが？」

「俺のせいで、先生は学校を辞めなきゃならなくなった。でも、まさかあんなことになるな

んて……」

間が空いた。

「修学旅行のときにお金を盗んだのは、龍くんなの？」

「……はい」

「そう。ほんとうに、そうだったのね」

「すみません」

「昔のことよ」

「でも……」

「もうひとつだけ、正直に答えて」

「はい」

「そんなに、わたしのことが、嫌いだったの？　憎んでたの？」

長い沈黙。

「正直に言ってくれて、いいのよ」

「違います」

「でも、最後に龍くんは、わたしを殺すって言ったわ。あんな怖い目で睨まれたの、初めて
だった」

「好きだったんですよ」

絞り出すような声だった。

「え？」

「俺、先生のことが、好きでした。好きで、好きで、たまらなかった」

まったく予想外の告白だった。

心臓の鼓動が、速くなる。

「……じゃあどうして、あのとき」

「俺だってわからない」

「知らなかった。まさか龍くんが、わたしのことをそんなふうに……」

龍洋一の目に、光が宿った。強面のヤクザには似つかわしくない、澄んだ光だった。

わたしは急に、いじわるをしたくなった。

「ねえ、龍くん」

「はい」

「わたしのどこが好きだったの？」

「……ぜんぶ」

「かわいいことを言うのね。あのころの龍くんからは、想像できない言葉よ」

「先生……」

「わたしの裸を想像して、自慰をしたことある？」

龍洋一が、言いよどむ。

「正直に言いなさい」

「……ある」

「よろしい。ご褒美に、寝てあげようか」

龍洋一が、息を呑んだ。

「もうオバサンだし、数え切れないくらいの男に弄られた身体だけど、それでもよければ寝

てあげるわよ。もちろん、タダで。龍くんも、それを期待してたんじゃないの？」

「そんな言い方、よしてください」

感情を必死に押し殺したような声だった。

沈黙が車内に満ちていく。

「怒った？」

龍洋一は答えない。

「ごめんね」

わたしは呟いた。シートに座り直した。ぼんやりと前を見る。

「夢を壊しちゃったね。思い出は、綺麗なままのほうがいいものね。きっと、あなたが好きだった川尻先生は、わたしとは別人なのよ」

それから龍洋一は、ひと言も口を利かなかった。

車でアパートに帰るのは初めてだったので、どこを走っているのか、見当もつかなかった。このままどこかのホテルに連れこまれるのだろうかと考えていたら、見覚えのある街並みが現れた。

「次の路地を右に入って」

龍洋一が、言われたとおりにハンドルを切った。

「そこの二階建てのアパートの前で降ろして」

車が停まってから、自分でドアを開けて、降りた。頭をかがめ、運転席に向かって、

「ありがとう、龍くん。先生もあなたに会えて、嬉しかったわ」

龍洋一が、前を向いたまま、小さく頭をさげる。口がへの字に曲がっていて、いまにも泣きだしそうだった。

わたしは、ドアを閉めた。

龍洋一の車は、クラクションも鳴らさず、走り去った。

わたしは、赤いテールランプを見送ってから、アパートの階段をのぼり、バッグから鍵を出して、部屋に入った。

居間の照明を点けると、物音ひとつしない空間が、浮かびあがった。蛍光灯が、ちらつい
た。

わたしは、バッグを隅に放り投げ、うずくまって膝を抱えた。

『わたしのどこが好きだったの?』

『ぜんぶ』

龍洋一の言葉を、反芻する。

『わたしの裸を想像して、自慰をしたことある?』

『……ある』

『よろしい。ご褒美に寝てあげようか』

膝に顔を埋めた。

なぜあんなことを言ってしまったのか。

どうしてわたしは、こんな性格なのだろう。

車のエンジン音が聞こえた。

わたしは顔をあげた。ドアに走った。部屋を出て、前の通りを見おろす。古い型の国産高

級車が、停まっていた。ライトは点灯したままで、エンジンもかかっている。息を呑んで、

その車を見つめた。やがてライトが消え、エンジン音も途絶えた。しかし、中にいるはずの

龍洋一が、降りてくる気配はない。

十分が経った。

何も起こらない。

龍洋一の車であることも、間違いない。どういうつもりなのか。

まさか朝まで待って、店に送るとでも言いだすのだろうか。いや、わたしがここに立ってい

ることには、気づいているはずだ。気づいていて、なぜ車から出てこないのだ。

二十分が過ぎた。

車内で、ちらと人影が動いた。こちらを窺い見たのだろうか。あわてた様子で、また身を小さくする。

わたしは、鼻を鳴らした。頰が緩んだ。

「世話の焼ける子ね」

階段をおり、龍洋一の車に近づいた。助手席のドアを開け、中を覗きこむ。

「龍くん?」

「先生、俺……」

龍洋一の頰は、涙で光っていた。

「わかったから、話は中でしましょ。ね?」

わたしは、龍洋一を部屋に招き入れ、これまでにあったことを、すべて話した。

修学旅行の下見のとき、田所校長にレイプされそうになったこと。その確執から、盗難事件の責任を問われ、失踪に至った経緯。徹也との同棲と、彼の自殺。徹也の友人、岡野との不倫関係と破局。トルコ嬢となって小野寺となじみになり、雄琴に移って覚せい剤に手を出したこと。自殺するために訪れた玉川上水で、理容師の島津と知り合い、いっしょに住んだこと。小野寺を殺してしまったこと。そして島津からプロポーズされた直後に、逮捕された

こと。

刑務所で美容師の資格を取り、出所後に島津の店を訪ねたが、島津はすでに結婚して、子供も生まれていたため、会わずに帰ってきたこと。銀座の「あかね」に就職して、一年が過ぎたこと。

龍洋一は、顔を伏せ、黙って聞いていた。

「わかったでしょ。わたしは、男から男へ、流されるように生きて、人殺しまで犯して、結局、何ひとつ手にできなかったのよ。残ったものは、美容師の資格だけ。二中にいたころとは、違うのよ」

龍洋一が、膝の上で、拳を握った。

「あの田所校長が、先生にそんなことをしていたなんて……俺はあいつを喜ばせただけだったのか。ちくしょう！」

「龍くん、そのことは、もういいのよ」

「よくないですよ！　知ってますか？　あいつ、あのあと県議会議員になったんですよ。教育の専門家というふれこみで。俺が少年刑務所にいたときにも、視察に来たことがあるんです！」

「お願いだから、そんなに大きな声を出さないで」

「すみません、でも……」

「ここに戻ってきたのは、もっと大切な用事があるからじゃないの?」

龍洋一の顔が、強ばった。座り直し、背すじを伸ばす。伏し目がちに、荒い呼吸を繰り返す。一分くらい、微動だにしなかった。頻繁に瞬きを始めたと思ったら、いきおいよく顔をあげた。

「俺、いまでも、先生が好きです」

「それで?」

わたしはわざと、冷たく返した。

龍洋一が、肩を落とし、目を伏せた。

「龍くん、ちゃんとわたしの目を見て、言いなさい」

龍洋一が、目をあげ、口元を引き締める。

「俺と……寝てください」

「寝るって、どういうこと?」

「その……先生を、抱かせてください」

「むかし憧れた女教師を、ものにしたいってわけね」

龍洋一が、何を言われたのか、わからないような顔をした。

「一度セックスできたら、それで満足なのね」

　龍洋一が、首を横に振った。激しく振った。

「違う、そんなつもりじゃない。俺は真剣なんです。　先生を愛してるんです！」

「愛してるなんて、軽々しく言うものじゃないわ」

「軽々しくなんて……」

「ただ一度きりのセックスなら、やらせてあげる。好きにしていいよ。でも、愛してるなんて言葉、二度と口にしないで」

　龍洋一の顔から、表情が消えた。

「口にしますよ」

　低い声で言った。

「俺は、先生のことを、愛してます」

「そんなこと、言っちゃだめ」

「本気です」

「龍くんは、自分が何を言っているのか、わかっていない。あなた、先生の命を俺にくれって言ってるのよ。女に求愛するって、そういうことなのよ」

「わかってるつもりです」

　わたしは、龍洋一と、見つめ合った。

「先生こそ、俺の気持ちを、誤解してる。　先生は俺にとって、一生に一度の恋なんです。そのためなら俺、自分の命だって……」

「馬鹿ね」

わたしは無理に、笑みを浮かべた。

「こんなオバサンなのよ」

「歳なんて関係ない」

「何百人という男に身体を売ってきた、汚れた娼婦なのよ。　人殺しまでしてかした女なのよ」

「人殺しだろうと娼婦だろうとかまわない」

「こんなわたしでも、愛してくれるの?」

「はい」

「ほんとうに?」

「もう、嘘は、つきません」

龍洋一の目は潤み、顔は紅潮していた。　まるで、中学生に戻ったかのように。

なんだろう、この胸の奥に灯った、温かな光は。　久しく感じていなかった光は。

なんだろう、この締め付けられるような、甘い高揚は。

なんだろう、この揺るぎない気持ちは。

「後悔、するわよ」

「しない」

「龍くん……」

胸から、言葉が、溢れてくる。

止められない。止めたくない。

「抱いても、いいよ。でも、二つだけ、お願いをきいて」

「言ってください」

「先生って呼ぶのはやめて。松子でいい」

龍洋一が、うなずく。

「それから……」

「はい」

「これからずっと、わたしといっしょに、いてくれる?」

「います、ずっといっしょにいます」

「信じるわよ、ほんとうに、信じていいのね」

「信じてください。俺、ずっと先生……松子、といっしょに、いる」

わたしの身体の中で、抗いきれない衝動が、爆発した。龍洋一の胸に、飛びこんだ。厚い胸板に頬を寄せ、背中に腕を回した。目を閉じる。逞しい心臓の鼓動が、心地よかった。

龍洋一の腕が、遠慮がちに、わたしを包む。

「もっときつく抱いてよ」

龍洋一の腕に、力が入った。

大きな温もりが、全身に浸み透っていく。心を覆っていた殻に、ひびが走る。ぽろぽろと崩れ始める。裸の感情が、殻を破って、流れ出る。

「わたしのこと、好き？」

「好きだ」

「愛してる？」

「愛してる」

「ずっと、そばにいてね」

「ずっと、そばにいる」

「約束よ」

「約束する」

「破ったら、わたし、死ぬからね」

「破らない。　俺は、松子を、愛してる」

「ねえ……」

「うん」

「もう一度、言って」

5

「松子はカットコンテストを目指していたのね。そのために、営業時間後も残って練習していたんだけど、その男と付き合いだすころから、練習を休みがちになってね。松子が入って最初のコンテストが秋にあったんだけど、それには遠慮してもらったのね。当時は出場枠があって、私の店からは二人しか出られなかったから、私と、もう一人はスタッフの若い子に出てもらったのね。その子には前から約束してあったし。松子はスタッフの中では最年長だったけど、やっぱり新入りだからね。次の機会に回ってもらったの。それが面白くなかったのかね。それを境に、ぎらぎらしていたものが、薄れていった感じでね。そこにあの男が現れて、だめ押しになったのね。初めて店に来たときとは、別人のようになっちゃって」

「どうして、そんなふうになったと思いますか?」

「結局、男だね。男ができるとね、いっそう仕事がおろそかになるタイプがいるけど、松子は後のほうだったみたいだね。なまじ手先が器用で、上達が早かったぶん、美容師が好きでなったわけじゃないようだしね。醒めるのも早かったんだろうね。悔しいというか、残念だったよ」

「そのあと、すぐに店を辞めたんですか？」

「二カ月くらい後だね。でも、辞めたわけじゃないよ」

「？………」

「本人からそういう話があったんじゃなくて、急に店に出てこなくなったんだよ。最初の日はね、たしか本人から電話があった。気分が悪くて休むってね。そこまではよかったんだけど、次の日も出てこなくてね、その日は何の連絡もなかったから、それならそれで電話くらいしろとは思ったけが出て、風邪で寝こんでしばらく休むってね。それならそれで電話くらいしろとは思ったけどね、まあ、風邪なら仕方がないか、くらいに私は考えてたんだ。ただ、その日はたまたま、沢村さんの指名が入ってたのね。事情を話したら、沢村さんは何か引っかかったようでね、夕方になってから、松子のアパートまで行ってみたんだって。そうしたら……」

「風邪じゃなかったんですか？」

内田オーナーが、うなずいた。

「沢村さんも、そこで何があったのかは話してくれなかったけど、とにかく松子にはがっかりさせられたって言ってたね。松子を見損なったって。もっと骨のある奴かと思っていたって。結局、松子はその日から、店に出てこなくなった。一週間たっても、何の連絡もなかった。私も、雇った責任があるし、けじめだけはつけたかったから、それまでのお給料を持っ

て、アパートに行ってみたのね。ひとこと言ってやりたかったしね。そしたらさ……」

内田オーナーが、顔を曇める。

「チャイムを鳴らしても反応がなかったのに、ドアの鍵が開いていたのね。でも人のいる気配はないのよ。なんだか胸騒ぎがして、思い切って中に入ってみたの。

もうびっくりさ。ガラスは割られてるわ、土足で歩き回った跡はあるわ、何から何までひっくり返されてて、ほんと、嵐が通り過ぎたような有様だった。あわてて警察に電話したよ」

「それで、松子伯母さんは?」

「影も形もなかった」

「……どういうことなんですか?」

「わからないよ。三日後に警察が店に来てね、松子について調べていったよ。私には、何がどうなってるんだか、見当もつかなかった。後になって沢村さんから、松子が警察に逮捕されて、刑務所に入れられたことを教えてもらったのね」

「また刑務所に……こんどは何を?」

「知らないよ。聞きたくもなかったしね。松子とは、それっきりさ。沢村さんも、ずいぶん悔しがっていたよ。無理にでも、あの男と引き離せばよかったってね。私が松子について知

つてるのは、これだけだよ」

内田オーナーが、ちらと窓に目をやった。

「じつはね、その男、最近になって、ここに来たのね」

「龍さんが？」

「うちの店を探してたらしいんだけど、昔のビルはもう取り壊されてたからね、苦労して、この場所をつきとめたんだって。松子を探してるから、沢村さんの連絡先を教えてくれってね。沢村さんなら、何か知ってるんじゃないかって思ったらしいのね。もちろん、お客様のプライバシーを教えるわけにはいかないから、断ろうと思ったんだけど、かわいそうなくらい一所懸命だったし、かつてのスタッフのことでもあるから、沢村さんに事情を話したのね。そうしたら、一度だけ会うってことになってね。沢村さんも、その男に聞きたいことがあったらしくて。私はもう、興味なかったから、その場には居合わせなかったけど」

内田オーナーが、息を吐いた。視線を宙に向ける。

「……そう、松子は死んじゃったの」

俺は「ルージュ」を出てから、銀座の通りをあてもなく歩いた。

松子伯母は、龍さんと付き合いだしてわずか二カ月で、ふたたび行方をくらませた。せっ

206

かく得た美容師の職を捨てて。部屋が荒らされていたことを考えると、何者かに拉致された

可能性もある。そして最終的には、警察に逮捕された。

松子伯母は二度までも、服役していたことになる。一度目は殺人。二度目は何だろうか。

アパートから姿を消した松子伯母の身に、何があったのか。

龍洋一。

すべては、龍さんが知っているはずだ。どうしても、もう一度会わなくてはならない。

俺は、携帯電話と、後藤刑事からもらった名刺を取り出し、名刺に書かれた電話番号にか

けた。女の人の声が返ってきた。後藤刑事をお願いします、と言うと、後藤は外に出ている

ので後からかけ直させる、とのことだった。俺は、自分の名前と携帯電話の番号を告げて、

電話を切った。

十分くらいで携帯電話が鳴った。

『よっ、少年。何か情報でも？』

「そうじゃないけど……龍さん、どうなったの？」

『ああ、あの男？　アリバイが成立したから、とっくに出しちゃったよ。教会で、牧師の手

伝いをしていたんだってさ』

「何ていう教会？」

『ちょっとタンマ』

　紙をめくる音が漏れてきた。

『ええとね、杉並のイエス・キリスト教会……そのまんまだな』

「杉並のどこ?」

『ううんと、これは環八の神明通交差点をだね、左に入って……かな』

　静かになった。

「もしもし?」

『わるい。電話番号教えるから、直接聞いてもらえる?　おれ、場所を説明するの、苦手なんだわ』

　俺は電話番号を教えてもらい、携帯電話に記憶させた。

『それから新しい情報が一つ。被害者、つまり君の伯母さんはね、あの部屋で暴行を受けたわけじゃないらしい。別の場所で殺されて部屋に運ばれたか、あるいは自力で戻って部屋で息絶えたか。もともとあの部屋には争った形跡がなかったから、そうじゃないかとは思ってたけどさ。きのう目撃者が出てね。暴行現場もだいたい特定できた』

「どこですか?」

『千住旭公園って知ってる?』

『けっこう大きな児童公園なんだけど、被害者のアパートからはちょっと離れてるんだよね。夜の散歩をしていたのかも知れないけど、どうして真夜中にそんな場所に行ったのか、ある

いは連れて行かれたのか、誘い出されたのか、そのあたりはわからないんだけど』

「犯人は？」

『まだ捕まえてはいないけど、目星はついている。近いうちに、逮捕できると思う。期待し

てくれていいよ。じゃあね』

切れた。

俺はすぐに、後藤刑事に教えてもらった番号に電話した。

たしかに龍さんは、教会で働いていた。龍さんと話がしたいと告げると、いまは牧師といっしょに外出しているが、午後二時くらいには戻ってくるはずだと返答された。教会の場所を確認したところ、京王井の頭線高井戸駅から環状八号線を北上し、神明通交差点を左折して西荻窪方面に向かい、荻窪小学校の手前の路地を入って、二百メートルほど進んだところにあるという。

よく考えたら、西荻窪の俺のアパートの近くにも、神明通りが走っている。荻窪小学校の前の通りも、明日香と二人で歩いたことがあるが、それほど遠いとは感じなかった。俺のア

パートから龍さんのいる教会まで、二キロも離れていないのではないか。

俺は、大急ぎでJR有楽町駅に戻り、山手線、中央線を乗り継いで、西荻窪のアパートに帰った。駅前のコンビニで買ったおにぎりとウーロン茶で腹を満たし、パソコンの脇に放ってあった茶封筒を拾って、部屋を出た。少し迷ってから、アパートの自転車置き場から、自転車を引っぱり出した。上京してすぐに買ったはいいが、ほとんど乗らずに放置しておいた代物だ。財布の中に入れていた鍵を差しこむと、がちゃんと音がして、スポークの間に突き出ていたロック棒が引っこむ。俺は、サドルの埃をはらって、またがった。

教会は、L字型の平屋だった。壁は白く、赤い三角屋根のてっぺんには、十字架が載っている。出入り口は二カ所あった。奥の出入り口の脇には「イエス・キリスト教会」の文字があって、白木の扉が開け放たれている。手前の出入り口の脇には「イエス・キリスト教会」の文字があって、白木の扉が開け放たれていた。教会の入り口は、こちらなのだろう。

俺は自転車から降りて、中を覗いた。長椅子が整然と並べられていた。正面の壁には、銀色の十字架。その前に、大理石製の演壇が置いてある。演壇では、銀色の燭台が、鈍い光を放っている。

演壇の脇の扉が開いた。

ころころと太った女の人が現れた。四十歳くらいだろうか。茶色い髪にはパーマがかけて

あるが、顔は浅黒く、化粧はしていない。キティちゃんのエプロンを着けていた。

俺を見て、驚きもせず、にっこりと微笑んだ。足早にいちばん後ろの長椅子まで来ると、

膝を折って屈みこむ。手にしていた雑巾で、長椅子を拭き始めた。両手で雑巾を押さえ、ゆ

っくりと座面を滑らせる。その顔つきは、真剣そのものだ。

「あのう……」

俺が声をかけると、女性が顔をあげて、

「はい」

と嬉しそうな声をあげた。

「龍さんに会いに来たんですけど」

「あ、龍さんですか。奥にいますよ。どうぞご自由に」

女性がふたたび、雑巾がけに戻った。

俺は、女性の出てきた扉を開け、入った。すぐのところに三和土があり、その先に、黒光

りする板張りの廊下が延びていた。右手にガラスの引き戸が並んでいて、突き当たりがトイ

レになっている。

俺は、足もとの段ボール箱からスリッパを取り、履き替えた。

「龍さーん、お客さんですよー」

背後から大声が響いた。

さっきの女性のほうが立っていた。

また長椅子のほうへ駆けていく。

目を廊下に戻すと、奥のガラス戸が開き、龍さんが現れた。グレーのズボンに、白いTシャツ姿。裸足(はだし)だった。大股(おおまた)で近づいてくる。笑顔が弾けた。

「笙さん!」

俺は、ちょこんと頭をさげた。

「よくここがわかりましたね」

「刑事さんに聞きました。警察の疑い、晴れたそうですね」

「ええ。ここの牧師様が、証言してくださったのです」

「沢村社長に会ってきましたよ」

「松子が死んだことを?」

「伝えました。ショックだったみたいです」

龍さんが、小さくうなずく。

「これ、渡そうと思って」

俺は、部屋から持ってきた茶封筒を、差し出した。

龍さんが、受け取る。

「これは?」

「松子伯母の部屋で見つけたんです。たぶん、龍さんが持っていたほうが、いいんじゃない

かと思って」

龍さんが、茶封筒の中身を、つまみ出した。

セピア色に変色した、振り袖姿の川尻松子。二十歳。

龍さんは、黙ったまま、写真に見入っていた。写真を封筒にしまい、鼻を啜った。

「ありがとう、笙さん」

「綺麗な人だったんですね」

「ええ」

「俺、大津の地方検察庁に行って来たんです。松子伯母さんの事件を調べるために」

龍さんの両眉が、すっと上がる。

「龍さんは、松子伯母さんが殺人事件を起こしたことを、知っていたんですか?」

「松子の口から、聞いたことがあります」

「龍さんは、刑務所を出てから、銀座の『ルージュ』という美容院に、行ったんですね

「ええ、そこの内田さんを通じて、沢村さんに会うことができたのです」

「俺、きょうは、龍さんにお願いがあって来ました」

「……なんでしょうか?」

「さっき『ルージュ』の内田さんに、話を聞いてきました。龍さんと松子伯母さんは、美容院で再会して、付き合いだした。でもしばらくすると、松子伯母さんが店に出てこなくなった。連絡がつかないのでアパートを訪ねたら、部屋の中がむちゃくちゃに荒らされていた。そう聞きました。お願い松子伯母さんも行方不明になったと思ったら、警察に捕まっていた。そう聞きました。お願いというのは……」

俺は、息を吸った。

「そのとき、龍さんと松子伯母さんに何があったのか、話してくれませんか?　松子伯母さんは、二度目には何の罪で捕まったのか。それと……」

躊躇ってから、付け加えた。

「龍さんが犯した殺人事件と、松子伯母さんが関係あるのかどうか、教えてもらえませんか?」

龍さんが俯いて、何かをぼそぼそと唱えた。

顔をあげる。

覚悟を決めた目で、俺を見た。

「外を歩きながら、話しませんか？」

俺は、うなずいた。

6

その日から龍洋一が、わたしの部屋で寝起きするようになった。　付き合っている女が何人
かいたらしいが、金を渡して別れてきたと言った。

いっしょに住み始めて三日目の夜、愛し合っている最中に、ピーピーピーと甲高い音が響
いた。龍洋一が弾かれたように離れ、ジャケットをひっつかんだ。　内ポケットに手を突っこ
み、小さな箱のようなものを取り出す。　音が鳴りやんだ。

「なんなの、それ?」

わたしは、絶頂を迎える寸前に抜かれて、苛立っていた。

龍洋一は答えず、小箱をポケットに戻し、裸のまま電話に駆け寄り、受話器をあげて、ダ
イヤルを回す。

「俺です」

低い声が、薄闇に染みた。

わたしは、背中一面に彫られた、天女と龍の刺青を、ぼんやりと見た。　龍洋一が、ときお
り小さな声で、はい、とか、ええ、とか答えている。

「いつものホテルの五二四……わかりました」

受話器を置くと、あわてた様子でトランクスを穿いた。シャツを被り、靴下を穿く。

「どうしたの？」

わたしは上半身を起こし、胸を毛布で隠した。

「出かける」

「いまから？　真夜中よ」

龍洋一が、ピンストライプのプレーンシャツに腕を通し、チノパンツを穿き、ベルトを締める。麻のジャケットを着て、わたしの目の前に腰を落とした。

「仕事なんだ。ごめん」

両手でわたしの頬を包み、キスをする。わたしは、目を瞑ってキスを受けながら、龍洋一の右手を、乳房に誘った。強くつかまれた。

「痛……」

声を漏らす。目を開けると、龍洋一が、優しく微笑んでいた。

「気をつけてね」

龍洋一が、うなずいた。立ちあがり、ドアに向かう。

わたしは、パジャマの上衣だけ肩に羽織り、龍洋一の後を追った。三和土のところで、も

う一度キスを交わした。

「行ってくる」

「気をつけて」

龍洋一が、ドアを開け、出て行く。

わたしは、ドアの施錠をしてから、布団に戻った。龍洋一の温もりの残る床で、三十五年の人生で初めて、自慰をした。満足すると、ぐったりとして、目を閉じた。

まさか、教え子の龍洋一と同棲することになるとは、あのころは想像もしなかった。金木淳子（じゅんこ）が知ったら、どんな顔をするだろう。人生はわからないと、つくづく思う。

目を開け、身体を起こした。部屋を見回す。龍洋一の荷物の入った旅行鞄（かばん）が、隅に置いてある。洗面台には、電動ひげ剃りと歯ブラシもある。現実なのだと、あらためて感じた。この部屋ではたしかに、わたしと龍洋一が暮らしている。

龍洋一が戻ってきたのは、二日後だった。わたしが美容院から帰ると、布団で鼾（いびき）をかいていた。わたしは、脱ぎ散らかされた衣服を拾い、ハンガーにかけた。その時、ジャケットの内ポケットから、封筒が落ちた。ポケットに戻そうとして、息を呑んだ。封筒から、一万円札がのぞいている。三十万円くらい。私は、何も見なかったことにして、封筒をポケットに戻した。

その後も龍洋一は、十日から二週間に一回の割で、呼び出しを受けた。ポケットベルが鳴るのは夜中で、出て行くと二日間は帰らない。呼び出しを受けていない日は、「あかね」まで送ってくれた。帰りも店の外で待っていてくれた。

初めて出迎えをしてもらった日には、外で食事をして、渋谷のホテルで一夜を明かし、そのまま出勤した。するとインターンの女の子に、

「川尻さん、部屋に帰ってないんですか?」

と囁かれた。

わたしが返事に戸惑っていると、

「だって、服が同じだから。最近、勉強会に顔を出さないなあと思ってたら、そういうことだったんですね。やりますねえ、このこの」

と肘でつつかれた。

以来、仕事帰りにホテルを使うことがあっても、必ずアパートに戻ることにした。

わたしは、龍洋一と暮らし始めたことで、東京という大都会に、やっと根をおろせたような気がしていた。東京に限らず、龍洋一といっしょならば、地の果てでも生きていける自信があった。ひょっとしたら自分は、いま幸せなのかも知れないとさえ思った。

しかし、同棲生活が二カ月を過ぎるころ、やはりそれが幻想であることを、思い知らされ

その日、美容院から帰宅すると、三和土に龍洋一の靴があった。

きょうは、龍洋一は部屋にいないはずだった。呼び出されたのが昨夜だから、いつもなら戻ってくるのは、明日の夜か明後日の朝になる。

わたしは、龍洋一の靴の隣に、自分のパンプスを並べ、部屋にあがった。

龍洋一が、布団に寝ていた。仕事が予定より早く終わったのだろうか。まいったな、と思った。帰りに食材を買ってこなかった。自分一人だから、簡単なもので済ませるつもりでいたのだ。龍洋一がいるとなると、そうもいかない。

わたしは、冷蔵庫を開けた。缶ビールが三本。牛乳の一リットルパックに食パンが三枚。マーガリン。卵が四個。未開封のハムを見つけた。まだ賞味期限前。よし、ハムエッグをつくるか。

あっと気づいた。

その前に、御飯を炊かなきゃ。

米びつの受け口に、炊飯器の釜（かま）をセットし、二合のボタンを押しこんだ。釜の中に、ざざっと米が落ちてくる、はずだったが、一合ほど落ちてきただけで、止まった。

た。

いけない、お米も切らしてしまった。

頭を抱えそうになったが、何か変だと気づいた。米びつには縦長の窓がついていて、残りの量が見えるようになっている。窓を見る限り、米はぎっしり入っている。出口が詰まったのだろうか。

米びつの上蓋を外した。米はたっぷり残っていた。米の中に手を突っこむ。指先が、米ではない何かに触れた。つまんで取り出す。米粒がぱらぱらと零れた。それは厚手のビニール袋で、何重にも包まれていた。透けて見える中身は、無色の結晶。どこかで見たことがある。

足もとから、冷気が這いあがってきた。

居間に顔を向けた。

龍洋一はまだ、鼾をかいている。

わたしは、ビニール袋を持って、居間に戻った。コタツテーブルの上に置き、正座し、龍洋一が目を覚ますのを待った。

龍洋一の鼾が止んだ。静かな寝息に変わる。わたしはその顔を、凝視し続けた。

龍洋一は、午後十時をまわったころ、ようやく目を開けた。わたしを見て、笑みを浮かべる。目を擦り、上半身を起こす。

「どうした?」

コタツテーブルの上に目をやる。あっと声をあげた。飛び起きた。袋を手にした。点検する。ほっと息を吐く。

「何なの、これ？」

龍洋一が、ちらとわたしを見た。

「俺のシノギだ」

「シャブでしょ。こんなにたくさん……密売？」

龍洋一が、俯く。

「洋くんも使ってるの？」

「……」

「正直に答えて」

「ときどきだ」

わたしは、息を吸いこんだ。

「わたしの友達が、シャブ中の男に殺されたこと、話したわよね」

龍洋一が、うなずく。

「洋くんがヤクザを続けたいのなら、続けてもいい。ほんとうはやめてほしいけど、洋くんがその世界で生きていきたいのなら、わたしは反対しない。でもシャブだけは、許せない」

龍洋一が、唇を噛む。

「シャブをやめてちょうだい。打つのも、売るのも」

「それは……」

「やめて、お願いだから」

「金はどうする？ この歳になって、いまさら他のシノギはできない」

「それならいっそのこと、ヤクザをやめればいいわ」

龍洋一が、目をあげて睨んだ。

「洋くんはしばらく、のんびりしたらいいよ。わたしにも蓄えがあるし、美容院で働いているから、生活はなんとかやっていける。ね、そうしましょ」

龍洋一は、答えない。

「お願い。シャブから手を引いて……シャブを扱った手で、わたしに触らないで」

ポケットベルが鳴った。

龍洋一が、ベルを止めて、電話に走った。受話器を取り、ダイヤルを回す。

「俺です……はい……いえ、ちゃんと手元にあります。問題ありません。そちらはもう大丈夫ですか……わかりました。いまから持っていきます」

シャブの包みが、コタツテーブルの上に残されていた。わたしは、それを両手でつかみ、

胸に抱いた。

龍洋一が、受話器を置く。わたしを見る。目に険が走った。右手を突き出した。

「出かける。それを渡せ」

わたしは、首を横に振った。

龍洋一が、右手を突き出したまま、近づいてくる。

わたしは、立ちあがって、後ずさった。

「渡せ」

「いや」

龍洋一の顔が、真っ赤に染まった。突き出されていた右手が、ゆっくりと振りあげられる。

「洋くん……」

身体が硬直した。風を感じた。暗くなる。火花が散る。身体が宙に浮いた。

龍洋一が、シャブの包みを、つかみあげた。泣きそうな顔で、わたしを見おろす。何も言わず、部屋を飛び出していった。足音が、小さくなっていく。聞こえなくなる。

わたしは、床の上で、仰向けになった。天井から吊るされた蛍光灯を、ぼんやりと見る。時計の秒針が、音を刻んでいた。

わたしは、起きあがった。左頬が、熱を帯び始める。化粧台の前に座り、三面鏡を開けた。

左頬が、赤紫色に腫れあがっている。唇の端が切れ、血が滲んでいた。

綾乃は、浅野輝彦がシャブに手を出していたことを、知っていたのだろうか。やめさせようとしたのだろうか。殴られることもあったのだろうか。それでも浅野は、シャブをやめなかったのだろうか。愛する男に胸を刺されたとき、どんな思いが過ぎっただろうか。わたしもいつか、龍洋一に殺されるのだろうか。それでもわたしは、彼とともに生きていく覚悟が、できているのだろうか。

イエス。

彼は約束してくれた。ずっといっしょにいると。わたしを愛してくれると。なにを迷う必要がある？　殺されてもいい。彼を信じて、ついていこう。それ以外の生き方は、わたしにはもう、残されていないのだ。

わたしは、掌で、唇の血を拭った。

翌朝、「あかね」に電話し、気分が悪いので休むと告げた。その日はずっと部屋にいて、龍洋一の帰りを待った。

龍洋一は、真夜中の零時過ぎに、帰ってきた。顔が赤く、息が酒臭い。部屋に入るなり、ポケットから札束をつかみ出して、床にばらまいた。

「松子、ほら、金だぞ。俺が稼いできたんだぞ。すげえだろうが」

高笑いを響かせる。

わたしは、龍洋一の前に立った。歯を食いしばり、見あげた。

龍洋一が、顔を突き出してくる。

「なんだ、文句あるのか」

「洋くん、お願い。シャブをやめて」

「まだそんなこと言ってんのか。この世界はな、やめます、はい、そうですかって、そう簡単にはいかねえんだよっ」

わたしは、震える手を伸ばし、ジャケットの襟を握りしめた。

「ねえ、洋くん、このままじゃ、ほんとうに、だめになっちゃうよ、ねえ……」

目を開けると、天井が見えた。歪んだ蛍光灯が、ぐるぐると回っていた。わたしは床に倒れていた。ああ、また殴られたんだ。そう気づくのに、時間がかかった。腹部が重苦しかった。龍洋一が、わたしのお腹に、馬乗りになっていた。拳を握っている。頭上高く、振りあげている。蛍光灯の光に溶けて、見えなくなった。次の瞬間、黒い拳が落ちてきた。

洋くんたら……そんなことしたら、死んじゃうよ。

気がつくと、わたしは布団に寝かされていた。頰に濡れタオルがあてられていた。

脇に目をやると、龍洋一が正座していた。心配そうな眼差しで、わたしの顔を覗きこんだ。

「洋くん」

龍洋一が、両手を膝の上に突っ張り、頭をさげた。

「松子、すまん」

「いま、何時?」

龍洋一が、首を回した。

「五時十五分」

「朝の?」

「夕方」

「……わたし、一日中、寝てたの?」

思考が、少しずつ、動きだす。

「あ、お店」

「電話があった。風邪で寝こんでるから、たぶん明日も無理だと言っておいた」

「そう……」

救急車のサイレンが、遠くから聞こえてきた。

「わたし、気を失ったの？」

龍洋一が、力無くうなずいた。

沈黙が、続いた。

顔面が、じりじりと痛みだす。

わたしは、目を閉じた。眠りに落ちた。

チャイムの音が聞こえた。目を開ける。

傍らに、龍洋一の姿は、なかった。

チャイムは夢の中で聞いたのだろうか。

「どちらさん？」

龍洋一の声が聞こえた。

わたしは、顔を向けた。

龍洋一が、ドアの覗き穴に、目をあてていた。

「沢村めぐみっていう者だけど、松ちゃんが病気だって聞いたから、お見舞いに来た。松ち
ゃん、いるんだろ？」

龍洋一が、振り返る。

わたしは、肘を突いて、上半身を起こした。頭がずきりと痛み、顔を顰める。龍洋一に向

かって、首を横に振った。

龍洋一がドアに向かい、

「松子は寝てるから、出直してもらえますか？」

「そうはいかねえよ。寝顔くらい見せろよ。こらぁ！」

ドアを激しく叩く音が響いた。

「このやろうっ」

龍洋一が声を荒らげて、ドアのチェーンを外した。

わたしは、布団から飛び起きた。頭が割れそうだった。我慢して、ドアに走る。

「洋くん、だめ！」

わたしは、ドアノブをつかんだ。

「松ちゃん、そこにいるんだろ？　心配して来たんだよ、顔くらい見せろよ」

龍洋一の顔が、紅潮している。ドアの向こうを、睨みつけている。

「洋くんは、中に入ってて。お願い」

龍洋一が、鼻の穴を膨らませた。息を吐き、居間に戻っていった。

わたしは、ロックを外して、ドアを開けた。

めぐみが、怖い顔をして、立っていた。裾と襟に濃紺のベルベット・タンクブラウスに、端正なグレーのヒップハングパンツ。メイクは完璧。トップを長めに残して、メッシュでアクセントをつけた絶妙なグラデーション・ショートヘアは、一目で内田先生の手によるものとわかる。

めぐみが、わたしの顔を見て、息を呑んだ。ため息を吐いた。唇の端を吊りあげる。

「最近の風邪は、顔にくるんだな」

わたしは、つくり笑いを浮かべた。

「そんなこったろうと思ったよ。時間になっても松ちゃんが店に出てこなくて、電話したら男の声で『風邪で寝こんでる』だと？　冗談じゃないよ」

「きょうお店に来たの？」

「予約入れてあっただろ？　忘れたのか？」

「……ごめん」

「その顔、さっきの男にやられたんだな」

「違う。わたしが道を歩いてたら、躓いて顔から突っこんじゃって……それじゃあ格好悪い

「いいんだよ、松ちゃんは刑務所にいたころから、嘘をつくのが下手なんだから」

「嘘じゃ……」

めぐみが左手をあげて、わたしを制した。

「邪魔するぜ」

右手に持っていたものを、わたしに押しつけた。駅前のケーキ屋の箱だった。めぐみが靴を脱いで、部屋にあがる。わたしの脇をすり抜け、居間に向かう。

「めぐみ、ちょっと待って……」

わたしは、ケーキ箱を手にしたまま、追いかけた。

居間で、龍洋一とめぐみが、睨み合っていた。めぐみは女性としては背が高いほうだが、龍洋一と並ぶと頭一つ低い。しかし、龍洋一に向けられた不敵な表情からは、怯えや恐れは感じられない。

「お、おまえにあんた呼ばわりされる義理はないぞ。なめた口利いたら、女でも容赦しねえぞ、こらぁ」

めぐみが、わたしを一瞥した。苦笑いを浮かべ、肩をすくめる。

「松ちゃんの顔をあんなにしたのは、あんただな」

龍洋一の顔に、戸惑いが過ぎった。

「なんだ、その態度は。俺を誰だと思ってる！」

　龍洋一が、めぐみの胸ぐらをつかんだ。めぐみの表情は変わらない。

「洋くん、その人を傷つけないで！」

　龍洋一が、わたしを見た。

　めぐみが、龍洋一を睨みつけたまま、胸ぐらの手を、引き剥がした。龍洋一にくるりと背を向け、わたしの前に立つ。右手の親指で、背後の龍洋一を指した。

「松ちゃん、こんな馬鹿と関わってちゃ駄目だ。すぐに別れな」

「めぐみ、もういいの。きょうは帰って」

　めぐみが、わたしの両肩をつかんで、前後に揺さぶった。

「目を覚ませよ。せっかく自分の生き方を見つけたんだろ。苦労して美容師になったんだろ。男なんか他にいくらでもいる。よりによってこいつを選ぶことはないよ。こんな男といっしょにいたら、地獄の底まで付き合わされるぞ」

　めぐみの澄んだ瞳に、わたしの顔が映った。

「……わたしは、洋くんといっしょなら、地獄でも、どこへでも、ついて行く。そう決めたの」

　めぐみが、頬を歪ませた。わたしの肩から、手を離した。龍洋一を、ちらと見る。深く息

を吐く。わたしを横目で睨んだ。

「勝手にしろっ！」

わたしの手からケーキ屋の箱を奪い取り、床に投げつけた。背を向けて、部屋を出て行く。

ドアの閉まる音が、空気を震わせた。

わたしは、ケーキ屋の箱を拾いあげた。蓋を開けると、何種類ものケーキが、ぐちゃぐちゃになっていた。箱ごと、ゴミ袋に捨てた。振り返ると龍洋一が、神妙な顔で俯いている。

わたしは、笑みを浮かべた。

「嫌われちゃったみたい」

龍洋一の顔は、青ざめて氷のようだった。

わたしは、努めて明るい声で、

「いまの人ね、刑務所で知り合った友達なの。中では、男みたいな格好をしていて、すごくもててたのよ。ね、おかしいでしょ」

「だめだな、俺」

「なにが？」

「あの女の言うとおりだ。俺、やっぱり、松子といっしょにいちゃ、いけなかったんだ。俺は……俺は、だめなんだよ」

一瞬、龍洋一の顔に、徹也の顔が重なる。

わたしは、龍洋一の腕に縋った。

「そんなこと考えないで。わたしは殴られるのなんか平気だよ。なんとも思わないよ。だから、ずっといっしょにいて。もう一人で勝手に、どこかへ行かないで」

龍洋一が、わたしを見つめた。

「俺、松子のこと、何回殴った？」

「数えてないよ、そんなの」

「俺を、殴ってくれ。松子の気の済むまで。頼むよ」

龍洋一が、跪いた。目を閉じた。

「頼む、松子」

わたしは、うなずいた。右手を振りあげ、龍洋一の左頰を、思い切り張る。左手を振りあげ、右頰を張った。

「もっとだ。もっとだ、松子！」

左右の頰を、交互に張り続けた。肉を打つ音だけが、部屋に満ちていく。

龍洋一の頰が、赤くなる。目から涙が、流れ落ちる。

わたしは、手を止めた。息が切れていた。掌が痺れていた。

龍洋一が、目を閉じたまま、子供のように泣きじゃくった。鼻水が垂れた。

わたしは、龍洋一の顔を、胸に抱いた。髪に頬を寄せた。

「洋くん、約束しただろ、わたしといっしょにいるって」

龍洋一が、わたしの胸の中で、うなずいた。

「じゃあ、シャブをやめてよ。ヤクザもやめてよ。友達がいなくなっても、お金がなくなっても、二人いっしょなら、生きていける」

龍洋一が、わたしの身体を離した。跪いたまま、わたしの目を、見あげる。

「わかったよ。シャブをやめる。ヤクザもやめる。松子といっしょに、やりなおす。ただ、時間がかかる。もう少し待ってくれ。約束は守る」

龍洋一が、財布から覚せい剤入りのパケを取り、わたしに差し出した。

「捨ててくれ。これが、手元にある全部だ」

わたしは、首を横に振った。

「これは、洋くんが、自分で捨てて」

龍洋一が、目の前のパケを、睨んだ。顔が苦しげに歪む。

「いますぐじゃなくてもいい。でも、必ず自分で捨てて。そうしないと、また他から、シャ

ブを手に入れてしまうよ」

龍洋一が、パケを財布に戻し、大粒の涙を零した。

「情けねえなあ、なんで捨てられないんだ。簡単なことなのに。俺は、自分では中毒じゃないと思っていた。シャブ中をさんざん見てるから、俺はまだあんなにひどくない、だから平気だって。でも、いつのまにか、これがないと……」

その声は、覚せい剤の魔力に今更ながら気づき、心の底から怯えているようだった。

「だいじょうぶ。必ず自分で捨てられるようになる。わたしは、洋くんを信じてる」

龍洋一が、目をぎゅっと瞑った。

次の日も、わたしは店を休んだ。とても表に出られる顔ではなかったし、龍洋一が、

「いっしょにいて欲しい、一人になったら、またシャブをやるかも知れない」

と声を震わせたのだ。

午前中は、部屋の掃除をするついでに、ちょっとした模様替えをした。龍洋一は初めて、風呂掃除とトイレ掃除をしてくれた。お昼には店屋物。龍洋一はカツ丼を、わたしは親子丼を食べた。龍洋一が、カツを一切れ分けてくれた。

午後になって、龍洋一の様子がおかしくなった。貧乏揺すりがひどくなった。煙草をくわ

えても、火を点けて一度吸っただけでももみ消し、すぐに次の煙草を手にする。あっという間に、吸い殻の山ができた。

龍洋一が、うなずいた。財布からパケをつまみ出し、目の前に掲げた。一分くらい、無言で見入っていた。

「シャブが欲しいの?」

「くそっ」

パケを財布に戻した。深呼吸をする。顔が苦しげに歪む。頭を掻きむしった。

わたしは、部屋のカーテンを閉めた。服を脱いで裸になり、龍洋一の前に立った。

龍洋一が、むしゃぶりついてきた。押し倒された。シャブのことを頭から振り払おうとするかのような、荒々しい愛撫だった。

シャブを断てるかどうかは、最後は本人の意思にかかっている。わたしにできるのは、これくらいしかなかった。

情事が済むと、少しは気が紛れたようだった。龍洋一が、買い出しに行くと言った。夕食をつくろうにも、何も食材がなかったのだ。外でシャブを打ってくるつもりだろうか、と思ったが、すぐにその考えを打ち消した。

龍洋一は、分厚いステーキ肉とワインを買ってきた。肉は彼が焼いてくれた。ちょっと焼

きすぎて硬くなったが、おいしかった。

「きょうだけだ」

ワインを飲み干して、龍洋一が言った。

「なにが、きょうだけなの？」

「シャブをやらない日」

「……明日から、また使うの？」

「違う。毎日、きょう一日だけは、シャブを我慢しようと自分に言い聞かせる。明日のことは考えない。きょう一日だけ我慢する。そうやって過ごしていれば、やめられそうな気がしてきた」

わたしは、胸が一杯になった。うん、と答えるのが、やっとだった。

「松子のおかげだ」

わたしは嬉しくて、声をあげて泣いてしまった。

その夜、わたしがお風呂からあがり、脱衣所で身体を拭いていると、居間から龍洋一の声が聞こえた。電話をかけている。その声は、何かを言い争っているようだった。約束が違う、という言葉が聞こえた。

わたしは、バスタオルを胸に巻いて、浴室を出た。龍洋一が、受話器を置いた格好で、立

ちすくんでいた。

「どうしたの？」

龍洋一が、はっとした様子で、わたしを見る。

「いや、なんでもない」

無理に笑みを浮かべた。

その二日後の夜中、龍洋一のポケットベルが鳴った。どこかへ電話して、いつものように出かける準備を始めた。

これが覚せい剤の取引に関わる合図だということは、わたしにもわかった。しかし、時間はかかるけれど必ずやめるという、龍洋一の言葉を信じていた。

服を着替えた龍洋一の顔に、不安げな影が射す。

「洋くん？　顔色がよくないけど……」

「前回から、まだ何日も経っていない」

「ポケベルの呼び出し？」

「いつもなら、十日以上あいだを空けてる。こんなことは初めてだ」

「どうするの？」

「行くしかない。上の指示だから」

龍洋一が、三和土で靴を履き、わたしと向かい合う。

「じゃあ、行ってくる」

「気をつけて」

「……うん」

龍洋一が、出て行った。

ドアのチェーンを掛けると、急に心細くなった。どうしようもなく不安になり、心臓が勝手に暴れだす。居間に駆け戻り、テレビのスイッチを入れる。いきなりバカ笑いが聞こえた。スイッチを切った。しんと静まり返った。

目を開けた。

暗かった。

電話が鳴っている。

枕元の目覚まし時計をつかんだ。

午前四時十二分。

まだ鳴っている。

頭の奥が、冷たくなった。

跳ね起きて、受話器に飛びついた。

「はい」

『松子、俺だ』

龍洋一。声が掠れている。

『金だけ持ってすぐにアパートを出ろ。円山町の「若葉」というホテルに来い。大川という名前で先に入っている。急げ、時間がないんだっ！』

「円山町の……」

『「若葉」だ。美容院の帰りに、最初に入ったあのホテルだ』

「わかる」

『とにかく、すぐにそこを離れろ、いいな！』

切れた。

わたしは受話器を見つめた。

龍洋一の言葉を、再現する。

悲鳴をあげて受話器を放り出し、ジーパンとブラウスに着替えた。化粧は口紅だけを引き、現金と通帳をバッグに入れ、アパートを飛び出す。朝の冷えた空気が、頬を撫でた。東の空

が、明るくなっている。バイクの音が聞こえた。反射的に身を隠す。新聞配達だった。バイクが通り過ぎるのを待って、駆けだす。誰も追いかけてこなかった。近くのコンビニエンス・ストアまで走り、公衆電話でタクシーを呼ぶ。タクシーが来るまで、店内で雑誌を立ち読みするふりをした。こんな時間でも、学生らしき数人が、店内にいる。

タクシーが駐車場に現れると、店を出て、タクシーに乗りこんだ。

「渋谷の円山町まで」

運転手に告げた。バックミラーの中の運転手が、充血した目をわたしに向け、

「円山町ね」

と、無愛想な声で答えた。

渋谷の道玄坂をのぼり切り、右へ入ったところで、タクシーを降りた。このホテル街も、中洲の南新地と同じく、夜と朝では見せる顔がまったく違う。記憶を頼りに、古ぼけた石段をおり、細い路地を進み、「ホテル若葉」を探した。この一帯は、ただでさえ起伏が激しく、道も複雑に折れ曲がっている。一瞬、方角の感覚を失い、迷路に入りこんだような気がして、足を止めた。周囲に視線を巡らせ、ようやく緑色のネオンを見つける。駆け寄ろうとしたとき、中からカップルが出てきた。わたしは、電柱の陰に隠れた。真っ赤なミニワンピースを着た若い女と、スーツ姿の中年の男。男は女の腰に手を回し、女は男の肩に顔を寄せている。

そのカップルをやり過ごしてから、ホテルに駆けこんだ。

部屋に入ったとき、わたしは息を呑んだきり、言葉を失った。龍洋一の顔面が、紫色に腫れあがっていた。左目の瞼が垂れて、目を塞いでいる。口のまわりに、血がこびりついている。よろよろとして、歩くのも辛そうだった。

「つけられなかったか?」

「だいじょうぶだと思う」

「そうか……」

龍洋一が、キングサイズのベッドに、身体を投げ出した。うっと唸った。天井を仰ぎ、目を閉じる。胸が上下するたびに、肺が鳴った。

わたしは、浴室に走った。タオルを濡らし、龍洋一の顔にあてた。

「どうしたの、こんな、ひどい……」

「もうだめだ。見つかったら、殺される。いまごろは、あのアパートも、むちゃくちゃになっている」

「何があったの?」

「組織の制裁だ。ほんとうなら、いまごろ殺されていた。隙を見て、逃げてきた」

「密売をやめるって言ったから?」

「……まあ、そんなところだ」

「ごめんなさい」

涙声になった。

「どうした?」

「わたしが、あんなことを言ったから……密売をやめることが、こんなに大変なことだなん

て、知らなかったものだから」

「違う、松子のせいじゃない」

「でも……」

「ほんとうに、ちが……」

龍洋一が、顔を歪ませて呻いた。

「洋くん!」

龍洋一が、小さくうなずいた。浅い呼吸を、繰り返す。

「ごめんな。俺と関わったばかりに、松子も巻きこんじまった」

「……わたしたち、これから、どうなるの?」

「しばらく、ここで、じっとする。動いたら、すぐに見つかる。頃合いを見計らって、東京

を離れよう。……北に行くか」

「北……」

「行くあてが、あるのか?」

「北海道は?」

「悪くない」

「北海道で、探したい人がいる」

「男か?」

「中洲でトルコ嬢をやってたときに、お世話になった人。マネージャーだったの」

「好きなのか」

「違う。ひとこと、お礼を言いたいだけ」

龍洋一が、目を閉じる。

「俺は、こんどこそ、地味で、まっとうな生き方をしたい。ヤクザは、もういいかげん、嫌になった」

龍洋一が、微かに笑った。すぐに、苦しげな表情になる。

「わたしは美容師を続けるわ」

「うん」

「洋くん一人くらい、面倒みられるよ」

静かになった。

龍洋一は、目を瞑ったまま。

「起きてる？」

「ああ」

「わたし、子供が欲しいな」

龍洋一が、目を開ける。白目が、血に染まっていた。

「俺の子供？」

「決まってるじゃない。歳が歳だから、無理かも知れないけど」

「俺と、松子の、子供か……」

「どう？」

「いいな。俺も、欲しい」

「ほんと？」

「ほんとうだ」

「男の子？　女の子？」

「どっちでもいい」

「じゃあ、両方いっぺんに産もうかな」

「双子か。にぎやかでいいな」

ポケットベルが鳴った。わたしと龍洋一の会話を、嘲笑うような音色だった。

龍洋一が、腕だけを動かして、ポケットベルを取り出した。目の前に持っていき、ちらりと見てから、横様に投げつける。壁にぶつかって、音が止んだ。

龍洋一が、顔を顰めて、起きあがった。ベッドサイドテーブルの電話に、手を伸ばす。受話器をあげて、ダイヤルを回す。無言で、耳にあてている。受話器を置いた。振り向く。そ

の顔に、諦観したような笑みが、浮かんだ。

「見つかった……二十四時間だけ待っとさ」

心臓を鷲づかみにされたような気がした。

「わたしたち、殺されるの?」

龍洋一は、答えない。目を伏せて、何かを考えている。

「……死ぬのね、わたしたち」

わたしは、無理に笑い声をあげた。

「わたしは平気だよ。洋くんといっしょなら、死んでもいい。でも、離ればなれにされて、乱暴されて殺されるのは、絶対にいや」

「俺が、一人で出て行けばいいんだ。奴らの狙いは、俺だけなんだから」

わたしは、龍洋一を睨みつけた。

「勝手なことを言わないでっ。洋くんが一人で死んでいって、わたしが喜ぶと思ってるの？ その程度の覚悟で、洋くんと寝たと思ってるの？」

龍洋一が、唇を嚙んだ。何分も、動かなかった。

互いの心臓の鼓動が、聞こえそうだった。

龍洋一が、思い出したように、目をあげた。よろめきながら、冷蔵庫に向かう。缶ビールを取り、戻ってきた。プルタブを引いて、わたしに差し出す。

「持っててくれ」

龍洋一が、財布から、覚せい剤のパケを取り出した。パケを破り、米粒くらいの結晶をつまみ出し、缶ビールに落とす。しゅ、と音がした。

わたしと龍洋一は、無言で、銀色の缶を見つめていた。

「もう、いいだろう。飲め」

龍洋一が、感情を失った目で、わたしを見た。

重い時間が、流れていく。

わたしは、缶に口をつけた。呷る。口の端から、滴った。シャブの溶けたビールが、喉を刺し、わたしの身体に入っていく。

龍洋一が、缶を奪い取った。呷った。喉が上下に動く。缶を床に落とす。息を吐く。ベッ

ドに腰掛けた。

わたしも、龍洋一の隣に、身体を寄せ合うようにして、座った。二人とも、口を開かない。

やがて、体内でシャブが、牙を剝いた。

世界が鮮明になった。

身体が宙に浮く。

陰鬱な気分が、吹き飛ぶ。

龍洋一が、さっきまでの憔悴が嘘のように、すっと立ちあがった。

「先にシャワーを浴びるよ」

そう言って、浴室に向かった。

わたしと龍洋一は、何時間も交わり続けた。命を絞り尽くすような、激しく執拗なセック

スだった。

力を使い果たすと、ベッドの上に、身体を横たえた。経験したこともないほどの倦怠感が、

全身を蝕んでいる。わたしは、自分の股間を指ですくい、混ざり合った二人の体液を、口に

含んだ。部屋には、底知れぬ安らぎが、漂っている。互いの息づかいと、喉の奥に広がる体

液の匂いだけが、現実だった。

「わたしたち、これで死ぬのね」

「死ぬのは、嫌か」

「……ちょっと怖いな。でも、洋くんといっしょなら、平気だよ。洋くんは？」

「俺も、死ぬのは怖い。できれば、死にたくない」

「仕方がないよね。わたしたち、こういう運命だったんだよ。そろそろ準備する」

わたしは、起きあがって、シャワーを浴びた。バスタオルを胸に巻いた格好で、化粧をした。といっても、口紅しか持ってきていない。丁寧に紅を引いてから、服を着た。

龍洋一も、すでに服を着ていた。ベッドに腰掛け、わたしを見ていた。

わたしは、笑みを浮かべた。

「どうやって死ぬの？　できれば、綺麗な死に方がいいな」

「すまん」

龍洋一が、受話器をあげて、ダイヤルを回した。

「警察ですか。円山町の『若葉』というホテルの、二〇一号室に来てください。……人を殺しました」

受話器を戻した。ちんと鳴った。

俺と龍さんは、礼拝堂を通り、教会を出た。車両一方通行の路地を、ゆっくりと歩き始めた。道沿いには、けっこう大きな家が並んでいる。どこからか、バイオリンの音色が漏れてきた。小さな子供が弾いているのだろうか。まだ騒音の域を出ていない。自転車に乗ったお婆さんが、俺と龍さんを、追い抜いていった。遠くで、車のクラクションが鳴った。

俺は、龍さんが口を開くのを、待った。

7

＊

十五歳から少年院、少年刑務所と渡り歩いた私は、二十歳を迎えるころには、地元の組織に入って、いっぱしの極道となっていました。もっとも、することといえば、借金の取り立てや、事務所の電話番や掃除といった雑用ですが。

最初のころは、これで一人前のヤクザになれると興奮していましたが、慣れてくると、どうということはありません。早い話が、使いっ走りをやらされているわけですから。すぐに

毎日が面白くなくなり、悶々とするようになりました。いいかげんに嫌気がさしたころ、ちょっとしたトラブルを起こして地元にいられなくなり、東京にやってきたのです。博多で知り合ったばかりの、十九歳の女性といっしょでした。

上京しても、まともに仕事する気は、はなからありません。やるなら、極道しかなかった。女性に働かせておいて、自分は一日中ぶらぶらと遊んでいました。

半年ほどしたとき、新宿を歩いていて、博多でいっしょだった古賀という男と再会しました。古賀は、東京のある組織の下で、シャブ、つまり覚せい剤の密売をしていたのです。私は古賀の口利きで、組織の一員となり、覚せい剤の売買に手を染めてからは、博多にいたころには想像もつかなかったような金額が、目の前を行き交うようになりました。さすが東京、博多とはスケールが違うと思ったものです。私はまるで、自分が大物になったような気がしました。

最初の懲役に行ったのは、二年後のことです。売買の現場を押さえられ、懲役一年十カ月の実刑判決を受けました。女性とは、逮捕と同時に別れました。

二十五歳で出所すると、すぐに組織に戻り、またシャブの密売に関わるようになりました。当時の組織は、名古屋の卸元から覚せい剤を買っていました。この卸元は在日韓国人で、韓国の密造組織から覚せい剤を密輸し、私が属していたような暴力団、つまり中間卸元に売

りさばいていたのです。中間卸元は、さらに覚せい剤を小分けして密売人たちに売り、莫大な利益を得ていました。組織ではいちおう、覚せい剤は御法度ということになっていましたが、もちろん表向きだけです。

私は、名古屋まで車を飛ばし、金と覚せい剤を交換して、東京に戻ってくるという仕事を与えられました。私は指定されたホテルの部屋に行き、そこで待っている男に金を渡します。男は金を持って別の部屋に行き、そこから覚せい剤を持って、戻ってくるのです。すでに確立したルートでしたので、仕事は簡単でした。私も、東京で一人前のシノギを得て、満足するはずでした。しかし、どうも面白くない。

たしかに大金を動かしてはいるが、所詮は組織の金です。一円たりともごまかしは許されない。よくよく考えてみれば、博多にいたときと同じ、組織の使いっ走りに過ぎないのです。かといって、組織を出て一人でシノギが得られるかというと、そこまでの自信はありませんでした。何百万というシノギを目の当たりにすると、十万や二十万のために危ない橋を渡るなど、馬鹿らしくてやってられませんでした。鬱屈する日々を送るうちに、とうとう私自身が、覚せい剤を使うようになったのです。

はじめて覚せい剤を注射したときのことは、よく憶えています。覚せい剤の常習者が、なぜこんなものに何万も払うのか、不思議だったのですが、自分で試してみて、納得できまし

た。気分がとてつもなく爽快になるのです。まるで自分が、全知全能の神になったようで、この世に怖れるものは何もない、という気持ちになれるのです。後になって、覚せい剤が太平洋戦争中、特攻隊員に使用されたと聞きました。死への恐怖さえ、なくしてしまうクスリだったのです。

笙さんにこんな話をしていいのかどうかわかりませんが、覚せい剤の威力はセックスのときに、もっとも強烈に表れました。何時間も勃起したままで、射精の瞬間の快感が延々と続くのです。そして最後に果てるときの、背中から脳天に突き抜けるような快感は、想像を絶するほどでした。これを経験してしまうと、普通のセックスなど、幼稚園のお遊戯。女性に使わせると、指一本触れただけで悶絶して……あ、すみません。話がそれましたね。

もちろん覚せい剤が、身体にいいわけはありません。最初は好奇心からでも、一度使って虜になってしまうと、自分一人の力では、絶対に抜け出せません。さっきもお話ししたとおり、あまりにも快感が強すぎるからです。切れると最悪です。

クスリが効いているときは爽快ですが、切れると最悪です。

当たり前です。

覚せい剤は、身体にエネルギーを与えるクスリではなく、使ってはいけないエネルギーまで、無理やり使わせているだけなのですから。

クスリが切れると、反動が来ます。身体はだるく、ちょっとしたことに腹を立てるように
なり、何をしても面白くない。地獄の底にいるような気分になり、そこから抜け出るために、
また覚せい剤を打つ。悪循環です。

そのうちに、覚せい剤を打っても、はじめのころのような快感が得られなくなってきます。

そうすると、打つ回数を増やしたり、量を増やしたり。さらに中毒が進むと、クスリが切れ
たときの苦痛が倍増します。

さっきお話ししした古賀という男は、後に覚せい剤中毒から心臓麻痺（まひ）を起こして死ぬのです
が、クスリが切れたときには、床を転げ回って苦しがっていました。彼は、幻覚にも悩まさ
れていました。幻覚といっても、本人にとっては現実としか思えないほど、生々しいものだ
そうです。たとえそれが、宇宙人に追いかけられているとか、壁から妖怪（ようかい）が飛び出てきたと
か、馬鹿げた幻覚だとしてもです。

……さいわいというか、私はそこまで行く前に、刑務所に入ることになったのですが。

話を戻しましょう。

自分でも覚せい剤を使い始めたというところまで、お話ししましたね。

そんな私に、タイミングを見計らったように、一人の男が近づいてきたのです。

厚生省の麻薬取締官、麻薬Ｇメンです。

彼は私に、スパイになれと言いました。普通なら、断るでしょうね。しかし私は、その申し出を受けたのです。もちろん、覚せい剤不法所持の現場を押さえられたせいもあります。

スパイにならなければ、また懲役に行くことになったでしょうから。

私は組織の一員ではありましたが、組織に忠誠を誓ったつもりはありませんでした。そもそも昔から、組織というものになじめない質なのです。表向きは、兄貴やカシラのために身体を張る、くらいのことは口にしていましたが、本心からではありません。ほんとうは、シノギを得るのに都合がいいから、組織に属していただけなのです。利用していただけです。

だから、スパイを引き受けたときも、裏切るという気持ちはありませんでした。麻薬Gメンのスパイになれば、懲役に行かずに済むし、今後も刑務所にぶちこまれることはないだろうと、計算したくらいです。

おそらくその取締官は、私のことを調べあげ、そこまで読んだうえで、接触してきたのだと思います。

その日から私は、麻薬Gメンの飼い犬になりました。取引があるごとに、指示された方法で、飼い主に報告しました。しかし不思議なことに、取引の現場を押さえられたことは、一度もなかったのです。私が飼い主に、どうして摘発しないのかと聞くと、こっちにはこっちの考えがある、と言われました。

後でわかったことですが、彼は、数百グラム程度の覚せい剤に興味はなく、広範囲な密売ルートそのものの壊滅を狙っていたのです。そのために、私はそこに登場する何十人何百人という人間の、一人に過ぎなかったのです。

もちろん私には、それがどんなストーリーになっているのか、見当もつきませんでした。表では組織のために覚せい剤を運び、裏では麻薬Gメンに情報を提供し、自分でも覚せい剤を打つ、という日々が続きました。松子と再会したのは、そんなころだったのです。その日は、カシラの愛人のお供をして、美容院についていったのです。そうです。「あかね」という名前の店でした。松子は、その美容院で、美容師をしていたのです。そのあたりの事情は、沢村さんや内田さんからお聞きになったとおりです。

以前にもお話ししたとおり、私は中学生のときから、彼女のことが好きでした。スマートで、綺麗で、頭がよくて、怒るとちょっぴり怖い。わたしはその後、何人もの女性と付き合いましたが、川尻松子先生は私にとって、永遠の女性であり続けたようです。

松子は、私がかつての教え子、龍洋一だとは、気づかなかったようです。私は迷いましたが、思い切って仕事の帰りに待ち伏せし、声をかけたのです。ほんとうはいっしょに食事をしようと思い、レストランの予約まで入れていたのですが、彼女に断られたので、自宅まで

　車で送ることにしました。

　私は車の中で、自分の気持ちを告白しました。

　松子は、自分がどんな人生を送ってきたのか、その一端を語りました。……そうです。トルコ嬢になったことや、殺人で服役していたことです。彼女は自分を、汚れた女だと言いました。そして、ただで寝てあげてもいい、と……。

　私は、松子を自宅まで送り届けて、無言で別れてしまいました。松子のアパートから走り去りながら、涙が出ました。永遠の女性だと思っていた川尻松子先生が、あんな台詞を口にするなんて……。

　さんざん非道なことをしているヤクザが何を言うかと思われるかも知れませんが、川尻松子先生だけは、清らかな存在であり続けて欲しかったのです。私自身が汚れているからこそ、余計にそう感じたのかも知れません。

　しかし私は、車を走らせているうちに、思いました。川尻松子先生が学校を去るきっかけをつくったのは、ほかならぬ私ではないか。トルコ嬢になったのも、殺人を犯して服役したのも、元はといえば、すべて私のせいではないのか。その私に、川尻先生を責める資格があるのか。

　もう一つ発見したのは、それでもなお私が、彼女を愛しく思っていることでした。彼女へ

の想いを自覚すると、いてもたってもいられませんでした。

私は、車をUターンさせ、松子のアパートに引き返しました。

松子は部屋にあげてくれました。そこで、松子が学校を去る経緯から、その後の人生を、すべて聞かせてくれたのです。

そのとき初めて、当時の二中の校長、田所文夫氏が、彼女をレイプしようとして未遂に終わった事件があったことを、知りました。学校を追われたのは、田所校長との確執の結果だったのです。必ずしも私のせいだけではなかったわけですが、それで罪の意識が消えたわけではありません。川尻松子先生に卑劣な行為をした田所校長を、よりによってこの自分が助けてしまったと思うと、悔しくてなりませんでした。もっとも当の松子は、過去のことと割り切っていたようでしたが。

私は、憧れの人と、結ばれました。その日から、私と松子は、同棲を始めたのです。

覚せい剤の密売をしていることとは、松子には黙っていました。

覚せい剤の取引が決まると、私のポケットベルが鳴ることになっていました。私は事務所に電話し、指示を受け、金を受け取って名古屋まで車を走らせ、覚せい剤と交換して帰ってきます。

覚せい剤は事務所ではなく、兄貴分のマンションに持ち帰りました。そこで小さなパケに

詰め替える作業があったので、一度呼び出しを受けると、二、三日は家を空けることになりました。

あるとき、名古屋で覚せい剤を手に入れて事務所に向かっていると、ポケットベルが一度だけ鳴りました。これは、いつものマンションには来ないで、覚せい剤を持ってどこかに隠れていろという合図でした。後でわかるのですが、このとき兄貴分のマンションは、警察に見張られていたのです。私は、三百グラムの覚せい剤とともに、松子と住んでいるアパートに戻りました。

私はお守り代わりに、小さなパケを財布に隠し持ってはいましたが、これだけの量の覚せい剤をアパートに持ちこむのは、初めてでした。松子と同棲を始めて以来、自分で打つときは、兄貴分のマンションにいるときか、一人で車に乗っているときに限っていたのです。注射器もタッパーに入れて、車に隠しておいたのです。松子の友人が覚せい剤中毒の男に殺されたことを聞かされていたので、松子といっしょにいるときは絶対に使いませんでした。もちろん、松子に使わせることも、考えませんでした。

とにかく、三百グラムもの覚せい剤を、松子が仕事から戻らないうちに、どこかに隠さなくてはなりませんでした。私は迷ったあげく、ビニール袋ごと、米びつの中に埋めておくことにしました。奥のほうに沈めておいたので、上から覗かれてもわからないだろうと安心し、

一眠りしました。

ところが、私が寝ている間に松子が帰ってきて、覚せい剤を見つけてしまったのです。私は仕方なく、覚せい剤の密売をしていると白状しました。真剣でした。松子は怒りました。覚せい剤だけは扱わないでくれと言いました。

しかし、そのときの私には、松子の心情を思いやることは、できませんでした。大量の覚せい剤を手元に置いているせいで、神経が過敏になっていたのかも知れません。もしこの場を警察に押さえられたら、懲役十年は喰らうだろうし、万が一覚せい剤をなくしてしまったら、組織に殺されてしまうかも知れない。

ちょうどポケットベルが鳴り、覚せい剤の袋を持っていく新しい場所を指示されました。電話を切って振り向くと、松子が覚せい剤の袋を抱えていました。私は、渡すように言いました。松子は、嫌だと言いました。とんでもないことを言う女だと思いました。ここで覚せい剤を届けなければ、私も松子も殺されてしまう。どうしてそんなことがわからないのか。私は頭に血がのぼり、松子を殴り倒してしまいました。あれほど恋い焦がれた人に、手をあげてしまったのです。そして私は、覚せい剤の袋を取りあげました。床に倒れた松子が、恨めしげな目で、私を見あげました。しかし、そのときはなにより、覚せい剤を届けることが大切だったのです。松子を殴ったことを、後悔しました。

　無事に覚せい剤を届け、いつもどおりパケに小分けする作業をしました。兄貴分と酒を飲み、アパートに帰ったのは、次の日の夜のことです。

　松子は起きて待っていました。

　私は、殴ったことを後悔はしていましたが、酒が入っていたせいか、ひとことも謝りませんでした。それどころか、松子がしつこく覚せい剤から手を引けと言うのが癇に障り、また殴りつけてしまったのです。こんどは一発だけではなく、馬乗りになって、何度も顔を殴ってしまった。松子が完全に気を失ってから、自分が何をしているのか気づき、あわてて介抱しました。

　眠り続ける松子を見て、自分に絶望しました。もうここにいてはいけない、と思いました。このままでは、ほんとうに松子を殺してしまうかも知れない。しかし、どうしてこれほど松子を痛めつけてしまったのか、自分でもわかりませんでした。好きで好きでたまらないのに……。

　いまから思えば、やはり覚せい剤の影響で、おかしくなっていたのかも知れません。

　松子は、丸一日近く、眠っていました。

　夜の八時ごろ、誰かが部屋のチャイムを鳴らしました。それが、沢村さんでした。私と沢村さんが顔を合わせたのは、それが最初です。松子もそのとき、目を覚ましました。

沢村さんは、松子の顔を見て、何があったのか悟ったようでした。

沢村さんは、私のようなヤクザ者を前にしても、怯む様子がありませんでした。そのころの私が凄むと、たいていの堅気の人は青くなって震えたものですが、沢村さんは顔色ひとつ変えないのです。

逆に私が怖くなりました。極道というのは、威張っているわりには、臆病（おくびょう）なのですよ。凄んで通じる相手にはとことん凄むけれど、まるで通じないとなると、どうしていいのかわからなくなってしまう。沢村さんを前にした私も、そんな感じでした。

沢村さんは、松子に向かって、私と別れなければ駄目だと言いました。

しかし松子は、沢村さんに帰るように言いました。そして、私といっしょなら、地獄へでもついていく、と言ってくれたのです。沢村さんは、怒って帰ってしまいました。

松子は、親身になって心配してくれている友人より、何度も暴力を振るった私を、選んだのです。

このとき私は、決めました。

もう覚せい剤は打たない。密売もやめる。松子と約束もしました。隠し持っていたパケを出して、松子に捨ててくれるよう言いました。しかし松子は、自分で捨てなければ駄目だ、と言いました。私は、悩みました。覚せい剤常習者の情けないところなのですが、ここに至

ってもなお、自分で覚せい剤を捨てることができなかったのです。この気持ちは、常習者で

ないとわからないかも知れません。私は、必ず自分で捨てると約束し、また財布に戻してし

まいました。

　覚せい剤の使用をやめるのは、あくまで自分だけの問題です。しかし、覚せい剤の密売を

やめるとなると、簡単ではありません。組織に話を通すことはもちろんですが、その前に、

私が情報を提供していた麻薬Gメンに、断りを入れなければならなかった。

　私は、こちらはなんとかなるだろうと思っていました。たしかに不法所持の現場を押さえ

られてはいるけれども、かなりの情報を流してきたし、ここでやめたいと言っても、ご苦労

だった、くらいの言葉はもらえると思っていたのです。

　とんでもない勘違いでした。

『俺です』

『どうした？　まだ先じゃなかったのか？』

『いえ、そうじゃなくて、話があるんです』

『なんだ？』

『俺、もうやめたいんです』

『……感づかれたか?』

「それは、大丈夫だと思います。そうではなくて、もう、この仕事から、足を洗いたいんです。Sも、シャブの密売も」

『なに……おい、なに言ってるんだ、貴様。おれが何年もかけて進めてきたシナリオを、台無しにするつもりか!』

「もう、勘弁してください」

『駄目だ。そんな勝手は許さん』

「でも……」

『いいか。もしやめたら、おまえがスパイだと、組織にばらすぞ』

「そんな……池谷さん、それじゃ約束が違うっ!」

組織に知られたら、間違いなく殺されます。私は初めて、自分がとんでもない泥沼にはまっていることに、気づきました。

このままでは、覚せい剤の密売から足を洗えない。こうなったら、松子とどこかへ逃げるしかない。逃げ切れるものだろうか。これからずっと、日陰の生活をしなければならないのか。しかし、時間だけが過ぎて行きました。いろいろ考えているうちに、

　二日後、ポケットベルが鳴りました。覚せい剤取引の合図です。電話すると、いつもどおり、金を持って名古屋に行くよう指示を受けました。前回の取引から間がなかったので、変だとは思ったのですが、指示に従わないわけにはいきません。

　このとき異状を察して、松子といっしょに逃げてしまえばよかったのです。

　覚せい剤を買う金を受け取りに事務所に入ると、いきなりカシラに殴り倒されました。この瞬間、自分が麻薬Gメンのスパイであったことがばれたのだと、悟りました。事務所にいた全員から、むちゃくちゃに蹴られました。最後には、痛いという感覚さえなくなり、意識も朦朧としていました。私は両腕を抱えられ、事務所から連れ出されました。夜明け前でした。車の後部座席に放りこまれました。どこかの山奥に運ばれ、埋められるのだと思いました。私は観念して、目を閉じていました。松子の顔が、浮かびました。もう会えないのだな、と思うと、涙が出ました。

　そのときです。

　周りが妙に静かだと気づき、目を開けました。車には私しか乗っていませんでした。身体を起こすと、差しこんだままのキーが見えました。窓の外を見ると、さっきまで私を足蹴にしていた兄貴分たちが、少し離れたところで、煙草を吸って話しこんでいました。

　考える暇はありませんでした。

私は、反対側のドアから外に出て、運転席に転がりこみ、エンジンをかけて、車を発進させました。人間というのは、気を失いかけていても、命懸けとなれば、身体が動くものですね。怒鳴り声が聞こえましたが、後ろを見る余裕はありませんでした。

どこをどう走ったか憶えていません。適当な場所に車を乗り捨て、公衆電話から松子に電話して、すぐに部屋を出るように言いました。私が逃げたとなれば、真っ先に松子に手が伸びて、殺される。とにかくアパートを出て、渋谷のホテルに来るように言いました。松子と私が、一度だけ使ったことのあるホテルです。電話をしたあとタクシーを拾い、渋谷に向かいました。

さきにホテルに入った私は、飼い主の麻薬取締官に電話をしました。組織に追われて逃げている。助けてくれと。

『いま、どこにいる?』

私はここで、躊躇いました。飼い主が、私を組織に売ったのではないか。そういう疑念が、頭をもたげてきたのです。いまにして思えば、覚せい剤を使っていたせいで、猜疑心（さいぎしん）が強くなっていたのかも知れません。私は、電話を切りました。

飼い主の麻薬取締官も信用できないとなると、万事休すです。組織の連中は、東京中を必

死に捜しています。捕まれば、私だけでなく、松子まで殺されてしまう。私がみずから名乗

り出れば、松子は助かるでしょう。しかし私には、それはできなかった。勇気がなかったの

です。死ぬのが怖かったのです。

やがて、松子がやってきました。

私は、組織から制裁を受けたと話しました。麻薬Gメンのスパイだったことは言いません

でした。

私は、様子を見て、東京から出ようと言いました。主要な駅や、幹線道路、空港は、組織

の連中が張りこんでいるはずです。東京から無事に脱出することは、奇跡に等しいでしょう。

しかし、わずかな可能性に賭けるしかない……。

そのわずかな可能性も、すぐに潰えました。ポケットベルが鳴り、電話をかけると、カシ

ラが出ました。そのホテルにいることを、知られてしまったのです。私は、組織の情報網を

甘く見ていたのです。もう取り囲んだから逃げられない。二十四時間だけ待つから、女とや

れるだけやって、おとなしく出てくるか、そこで女と自殺しろ。せめてもの情けだ。そう通

告されました。

ここで私が、何をしたと思いますか。

私は、捨てられずに財布に入れていたパケを取り出し、一粒の覚せい剤を缶ビールに溶かし、松子に飲ませました。私も、残りを飲み干しました。

死への恐怖を取り除くためではありません。

私と松子は、覚せい剤の力を借りて、最後の愛を交わしました。そして、シャワーを浴び、服を着て、警察に電話しました。人を殺したので、すぐに来て欲しいと。もちろん、それは嘘です。確実に、早く来て欲しかったから、そう言ったのです。そして確実に、警察署に引っ張っていってもらう必要があった。

思ったとおり、警察官が大勢やってきました。

私は、覚せい剤のパケを、警察官に渡しました。その場で覚せい剤であることが確認され、私は不法所持で逮捕されました。松子も任意同行を求められました。もちろん、断る理由などありません。

私と松子は、警察官に囲まれて、ホテルを出ました。組織の連中も、さすがに手は出せませんでした。極道である私が、よりによって警察に助けを求めるとは、考えていなかったようです。たしかに極道としては、物笑いの種になりこそすれ、決して誉められた行為ではありません。しかし、松子と私が生き延びるには、これしかなかったのです。

私は警察署で、尿検査を受け、覚せい剤使用の罪も加わりました。松子も同じころ、尿検

　査の結果が出て、覚せい剤取締法違反で逮捕されていたはずです。

　私と松子は、別々に裁判にかけられました。私は、懲役四年を喰らい、府中刑務所に入り

ました。松子も、懲役一年の実刑を受け、栃木刑務所に行きました。いくら組織でも、刑務

所の中までは追ってこられない。少なくとも松子に関する限り、命は保障されたのです。

　私はどうなるか、わかりませんでした。府中刑務所は、いわゆる暴力団関係の服役囚が多

く、私の組織に関わっている者も大勢いたのです。私が裏切り者だと知れれば、命を狙われ

ることになったでしょう。

　幸運だったのは、刑務所のほうで、私を守るような措置を取ってくれたことです。ふつう

私のような受刑者は、入所してしばらくすると雑居房に移るのですが、このときはずっと独

居房のままでした。

　じつは独居房というのは、雑居房よりも待遇は悪いのです。建物は古いし、部屋は狭い。

窓に目隠しがあるせいで外が見えず、風通しも最悪です。いまはどうか知りませんが、その

ころの窓はガラスではなく、ビニールが貼ってあっただけでした。ほんとうですよ。そのせ

いで部屋の中は、夏は蒸し風呂、冬は冷蔵庫のようでした。独居者でも、昼間は工場に出る

者が多いのですが、私は厳正独居といって、一日中部屋で紙袋の糊貼りをしなければなりま

せんでした。

刑務所暮らしで話し相手がいないというのは、本来ならかなり辛いことです。しかし私にとって、誰とも顔を合わせなくてよいのは、好都合でした。雑居房や工場にいたら、どこからどんな仕打ちをされたかわかりませんからね。

はっきりとは言われませんでしたが、おそらく飼い主の麻薬取締官が、手を回してくれたのでしょう。私を売ったのが飼い主だったのかどうか、いまでもわかりませんが、そのおかげで私は、生き延びることができました。それに私が刑務所に入って三年後に、飼い主のシナリオが完結して、組織そのものが一網打尽にされてしまったのです。私を殺したいと思っている連中は、いまでもいるでしょうが、組織として私を追うことはなくなったのです。

しかし、一度裏切り者の烙印を押された以上、極道の世界で生きていくことは出来なくなりました。土壇場で警察に縋ったことも、致命的でした。私を相手にしてくれるような組織は、日本のどこにもありませんでした。

8

昭和五十九年八月

一年の懲役を終え、栃木刑務所を出たわたしは、前回と同じように保護観察所に保証人を
お願いし、国分寺市西元町にアパートを借りた。
1Kで風呂はなし。狭くて不便だったが、お金を節約するためには仕方がなかった。
部屋に落ち着いて一週間後に、東京地方検察庁に出向いた。そこで龍洋一の判決文を閲覧
し、刑の満期日を確認した。

龍洋一は結局、婚姻届を出さなかったようだ。だから服役中は手紙のやり取りができなか
ったし、出所しても面会に行けない。

なにを意固地になっているのか。ほんとうに世話の焼ける子だ。

アパートから府中街道に出て、自転車で五分ほど南に下ると、府中刑務所の見あげるよう
なコンクリート塀が、左手に現れる。高さは五メートルくらい。これが街道沿いに、三百メ
ートル以上続いている。そこからさらに五分ほど走ると、JR武蔵野線の北府中駅に出る。

わたしが新しく就職した美容院は、北府中駅前の雑居ビルに入っていた。「カット＆パーマ　みたむら」という名前で、オーナーとインターンが一人いるだけの、典型的な個人経営の店だ。たまたま技術者を募集していたので応募したところ、面接試験だけで合格した。銀座の「あかね」のような実技試験はなかった。オーナーの三田村秀子は、履歴書の賞罰欄を見て躊躇ったようだったが、

「もう絶対に覚せい剤はやりません」

と強調したら、納得してくれた。着付けができることも、プラスに働いたようだった。

わたしの一日は、午前七時半に始まる。

パンと牛乳とバナナの朝食をとり、身なりを整えて、自転車で出勤する。府中刑務所の前にさしかかるのが、午前八時半。

いちど散策ついでに、朝の六時くらいに前を通りかかったことがあるが、そのときは路肩に黒塗りの高級外車が連なり、強面の男たちが何百人と集まっていた。このあたりは緑が多く、ふだんは閑静そのものだが、その朝に限って異様な雰囲気に包まれていた。パトカーも何台か出ていたので、警察官に何ごとか聞くと、暴力団の大物幹部が出所するという。ほどなく西門のあたりから、地鳴りのような響きが沸きあがった。集まっていた男たちが、西門に向かって腰を折った。口々に、お勤めごくろうさまでした、と言っていた。すかさず警察

官がマイクを手にして、

「速やかに退去しなさい」

と勧告すると、近くにいた何人かが、じろりと睨んできた。わたしは怖くなって、早々に引きあげた。以来、早朝に散策するのはやめにした。

わたしは毎朝、美容院に向かう途中、府中刑務所の西門の前で、いったん自転車を停める。自分と龍洋一を隔てるコンクリートの塀を見あげ、

「おはよう。きょうも一日、頑張ろうね」

と声をかけ、美容院に向かってペダルを踏んだ。

「みたむら」の営業時間は、午前十時から午後七時までだが、午後五時過ぎからが、いちばん忙しかった。府中刑務所の向かいに、大手電機メーカーの工場があるのだが、そこの女子従業員で、仕事帰りに利用するという人が、けっこういるのだ。

営業時間後の勉強会などというものはなかったので、掃除を終えて、午後八時には家路につけた。夕食は駅前の食堂の定食で済ませ、自転車で夜道を戻る。

府中刑務所の塀の前は、夜になると特に陰気だが、朝と同じように塀を見あげ、

「おやすみ」

と囁いた。

アパートに帰ると、洗面道具を持って銭湯に出かける。アパートから五百メートルくらいのところに、「明神湯」という銭湯がある。大きな湯船に浸かり、壁の富士山を眺めていると、一日の疲れが溶けていった。湯あがりには、体重計に乗って、太っていないことを確かめた。そのあと、大きな鏡に自分の裸体を映し、じっくりと見る。美容院に置いてあった女性週刊誌に、一日五分間、自分の身体を見つめてあげることで、体型の崩れを防ぎ、肌の若さを保てるという記事があったからだ。全身に乳液を塗りこみ、カレンダーの日付に×印をつけ、一日が終わる。

銭湯から帰ると、午後十時を回っている。

部屋に帰っても、待っていてくれる人はいない。

友達もいない。

しかし、寂しいとは思わなかった。

いまのわたしには、はっきりと思い描ける夢がある。

自転車で五分の場所に、龍洋一がいる。あと三年もしないうちに、出てくる。そうしたら、こんどこそ二人で、肩を寄せ合って、生きていける。

龍洋一が出所したら、風呂付きのもっと広いアパートに移ることになる。

できれば東京を離れたい。

北に行きたい。

その日のために、少しずつ貯金もしている。

わたしは、すべての生活の照準を、龍洋一が出てくる三年後に、合わせていた。

9

話は前後しますが、起訴されて刑が確定するまで、私は東京拘置所に収監されていました。

笙さんと最初に出会った、あの荒川の堤防に立つと、対岸にひときわ大きな建物が見えたでしょう。改築中らしく、屋上からクレーンが伸びていましたね。憶えていますか。

あれが東京拘置所です。松子も、あのどこかにいたはずです。

拘置されているとき、松子から手紙が届きました。拘置所では、手紙のやり取りは自由にできたのです。松子は手紙で、籍を入れて結婚しようと言ってくれました。刑が確定し、刑務所に移されると、面会や手紙のやり取りは、親族に限られます。結婚して夫婦になっておけば、たとえ別々の刑務所に入っても文通できるし、松子が先に出所したら面会に来られると言うのです。

嬉しかったですよ。涙が出るくらいに。私は松子の人生を、一度ならず二度までも狂わせた男です。その私と、結婚したいと言ってくれたのですから。

でも私は、返事の手紙の中で、こう書きました。もう私に関わってはいけない。私に松子を幸せにする資格はないし、その力もない。これ以上いっしょにいても、不幸を繰り返すだ

けだ。お願いだから、龍洋一という男のことは忘れて、新しい人生を生きて欲しい。

松子から、すぐに返信が届きました。婚姻届が入っていました。私が名前を記入し、印鑑を押せば、提出できるようになっていました。本気なのだと思いました。

私は悩みました。

松子といっしょにやり直せたら、どんなにいいか。想像するだけで、胸が熱くなりました。

しかしそれで、松子がほんとうに、幸せになれるのか……。

残念ながら、私の答は否でした。これから刑務所に移れば、命を落とすかも知れないし、運よく生きて娑婆（しゃば）に戻れても、堅気としてやっていける自信がなかったのです。それに、気絶するまで殴り続けるような男ですよ。どう考えても、いっしょにいないほうがいいに決まっている。

私は、婚姻届の空欄をそのままにして、手元に置いておきました。

松子から、催促の手紙が届くようになりました。私は、返事を書きませんでした。言いたいことは、最初の返信ですべて、書いてしまっていたからです。

やがて、松子が懲役一年の判決を受けて、栃木刑務所に移されたことを知りました。これで、松子から手紙が届くことは、なくなったのです。私が婚姻届の空欄を埋め、提出すれば、ふたたび文通が可能になる。まさに、私の決断ひとつに、かかってきたのです。

　私は、自分の判決が下る前日、婚姻届に記名し、印鑑を押しました。これを役所に提出すれば、私と松子は、晴れて夫婦になれる。私は、朱の乾いていない婚姻届を、いつまでも見つめ、目に焼き付けました。そして、真ん中から二つに破りました。くしゃくしゃに丸め、口に放りこんで、食べてしまいました。

　これが私なりの、決着のつけ方でした。

　もう松子のことは考えまい。これで松子も目が覚めただろう。出所すれば、別の優しい男性と巡り会って、人生をやり直すはずだ。そうあって欲しいと、心から願いました。

　……ええ、身勝手なものですよ。

　刑務所での生活は、じつを言うと、それほどきつくはありませんでした。さっきお話ししたように、少なくとも命の危険を感じることはなかったし、なにより覚せい剤を打てなくなり、規則正しい生活を強いられたので、体調がよくなったくらいです。

　もともと集団生活が苦手な私ですから、ひとりぼっちも苦ではありませんでした。刑期の二年目から三年目が、いちばん落ち着いていました。何も考えず、淡々と袋貼りをして過ごしていました。朝起きて、気がつくと就寝の時間になっている。そんな毎日でしたよ。

　ふつうは刑期の三分の二が過ぎると、仮釈放の審査準備が始まるものですが、私の場合は

ありませんでした。仮釈放されるには引受人が必要で、誰になってもらうか入所時調査のときに届け出ておきます。たいていは身内になってもらうものですが、親族がいないも同然の私は、更生保護会に引受人をお願いしていました。しかも私の場合は再犯で、独居房に入っていましたから、仮釈放はまず無理でした。でもそれで、落ちこんだりはしませんでしたよ。なぜなら私は、仮釈放を望んでいなかったからです。

最初の懲役のときは、出所が待ち遠しくてなりませんでした。これで俺も前科一犯のムショ帰りだ、ハクがついた、などと思ったものです。出所のときには、カシラから放免祝いもしてもらいました。しかし今回は、刑務所を出ても、行くところがない。

これからどういう生き方をすればいいのか。不安だらけでした。このときほど、娑婆が怖いと思ったことはありません。まともに働いた経験もない私が、社会で生きていけるのか。ずっと刑務所にいたいとさえ思いました。そういうときほど、時間の流れを速くできれば、

感じるものです。

ついに刑期を満了し、出所する朝が来ました。

雲ひとつない晴天でした。よく憶えています。

10

昭和六十二年八月

午前三時をまわったところで、眠ることをあきらめた。部屋の照明を点し、布団を畳んだ。インスタント・コーヒーをいれ、テレビをつけると、コンピュータでつくったようなアニメーションが流れていた。軽快な音楽の中で、鳥や動物たちが眠りについていく。

何だろうと見ていると、テレビ局が本日の放送終了を告げる番組だった。午前三時台はまだ深夜なのか。

テレビを消そうとリモコンを手にすると、ふたたびアニメーションと音楽が始まった。さっき眠りについた鳥や動物たちが、次々と目を覚まし、動き始める。本日の放送開始を告げるオープニングだった。

アニメーションが終わると、見たことのない男性アーティストが、ピアノを弾きながら歌う映像が始まった。力強くも切ない歌声が、やけに心に染みた。歌が終わると、天気予報になった。

きょうの関東地方は快晴。

わたしはコーヒーを飲み干し、腰をあげた。

冷蔵庫から、昨夜のうちに研いでおいた米を出し、炊飯器にセットして、スイッチを入れた。ナベに水を張ってガスコンロにかけ、鰹節で出汁をとる。賽の目に切った絹ごし豆腐を入れて一煮立ちさせ、味噌を溶かす。味を見てから干しワカメを散らし、蓋をして出来あがり。時を同じくして、炊飯器から蒸気が吹きあがり始めた。

ビールはたっぷり冷えている。何を食べたいと言うかわからないが、好物の牛肉は買ってある。松阪牛のステーキ肉だ。卵焼きは熱々を食べて欲しいから、帰ってきてから焼くことにする。二人で朝食をとりながら、これからの計画を話し合おう。

時計を確認する。

急がなくちゃ。

顔を洗い、歯を磨いた。パジャマを脱いで、新品の下着に替えてから、この日のために買っておいたベージュのワンピースを着た。

鏡の前で、丁寧にファンデーションを塗り、化粧をする。睡眠不足のせいか、ちょっとのりが悪い。仕方がない。

最後に口紅を引いた。髪は、八二に分けたリップラインのボブ。鏡に向かって微笑んでみ

る。悪くない。真面目くさった顔をして、

「お勤めごくろうさまでした」

吹き出した。自分の笑顔を見たのは、久しぶりだった。それにしても、我ながら四十歳に

は見えない。若さを保つ努力の賜だろうか。それともやはり、子供を産んでいないせいだろ

うか。

子供。四十歳。

もう無理かな。

鏡の中の自分から、笑顔が消えていた。

睨んでやった。

「そんな暗い顔してると、洋くんに嫌われるぞ」

時計を見た。

時間だ。

わたしは、部屋を出た。東の空はすでに、白々としている。自転車には乗らず、府中街道

の歩道を、南に向かった。

朝まだき、街道の交通量は少なく、歩いている人もいない。ときおり、徹夜で走り続けて

きたらしいトラックが、猛スピードで駆け抜けていった。

府中刑務所の塀が、近づいてくる。心臓が高鳴ってくる。ほかの暴力団関係者の出所と重なっていたら嫌だなと思っていたが、出迎えらしき人影はなかった。

西門の前に立った。観音開きの扉は鉄製で、高さが四メートルくらいある。わたしは、扉から少し離れたところで、龍洋一を待った。

空の色が、紫から青に変わっていく。

西門はその名のとおり西に向いているので、朝日が昇ると日陰になる。

腕時計を見た。

六時ちょうど。

まだ扉は開かない。

わたしは、龍洋一が出てきたときに、最初にかける言葉を考えていた。いろいろ思いを巡らせたが、どれもぴんとこない。

会うのは四年ぶり。

わたしは、体型も体重も、四年前と変わっていない。自転車通勤を続けたり、食事に気をつけたり、肌の手入れを怠らなかったり、それなりに頑張った成果だった。無惨に太って、龍洋一を幻滅させたくはなかったのだ。

龍洋一はどうだろうか。太っただろうか。痩せただろうか。相応に年を取っただろうか。

いまのわたしを見て、綺麗だと言ってくれるだろうか。

気がつくと、周りがすっかり明るくなっていた。

腕時計を見る。

すでに午前七時をまわろうとしている。

遅いな。まさか、すでに仮出所してしまったのか。いや、彼の場合、暴力団員だから、引受人で引っかかるはずだ。母親も妹も行方不明、ほかに親族はいないのだから。

満期日を間違えた？　そんなはずはない。ちゃんと検察庁まで行って調べたのだ。昨日が満期日だから、今朝出てくるはずなのだ。

それにしても、遅くはないか。

まさか、獄中で死んでしまったのか……。

がちゃん、と金属音がした。

たしかに扉から聞こえた。

微動だにしなかった鉄扉が、ゆっくりと奥に開く。わずかにできた隙間から、背の高い男が出てくる。

四年前と同じ服を着ていた。短く刈り上げられた頭以外は、変わっていない。いや、少し太っただろうか。

その後ろから、制服姿の看守が現れた。

坊主頭の龍洋一が、看守に向かって頭をさげる。

看守がうなずいて、扉を閉める。

大きな音が響いた。

龍洋一が、閉じられた鉄扉を、見あげる。息を吐いて、うなだれた。俯いたまま、扉に背を向ける。こちらに向かって、足を踏み出す。

顔をあげる。

足を止める。

目を剝いた。

11

午前七時。私は刑務所の外に、足を踏み出しました。

しかしそれは、娑婆に戻ってきたというよりも、放り出されたという感じでした。手元にあるお金は、逮捕時に所持していた五万三千円と、袋貼りの賞与金六千円、あわせて五万九千円だけ。これで、とうぶんの寝る場所と、食べ物を手に入れなければなりません。

扉の前で突っ立っていても埒があかないので、とにかく駅まで歩こうと足を踏み出したときです。

気配を感じて目をあげました。

足が止まりました。

そこに松子が立っていたのです。

優しい笑みで、わたしを出迎えてくれたのです。

そのときの松子の、神々しいまでの美しさは、この世のものとは思えないほどでした。

松子が近づいてくると、私の足が震え始めました。それは、いままで味わったことがないほどの、恐怖でした。

そうです。

　私は、恐ろしい、と感じたのです。

12

「洋くん」

わたしは、龍洋一に近づいた。

走った。

胸に飛びこんだ。

声をあげて泣いた。

両腕をつかまれた。胸から引き剝がされた。

龍洋一の顔は、蒼白だった。口元が震えていた。わたしの腕から、手を離した。

「どうして、ここにいるんだ?」

「どうしてって……待ってたのよ、決まってるでしょ」

「ムショは一年で出たはずだろ。その後、どうしてたんだ?」

「近くにアパートを借りてるの。駅前の美容院で働いている。毎朝、自転車でここを通って

たのよ。行きと帰りに、塀越しに声をかけてた。知らなかったでしょ」

龍洋一が、怯えるような目で、わたしを見る。

「さ、行こう。朝ごはん、できてるよ」

龍洋一が、目を逸らした。

「手紙、読まなかったのか?」

「手紙って?」

「もう俺に関わるなと、書いたはずだ」

「あんなの、本心じゃないでしょ。そのくらい、わたしがわからないと思ってるの?」

龍洋一の頰が、小刻みに震えはじめた。

「どうしたの? 寒いの?」

龍洋一は、答えない。

青ざめた顔で、横を向いている。

ちらと、わたしを見た。

「なに?」

「金。あるか?」

「いま?」

「そうだ」

「……少しなら」

龍洋一が、手を差し出す。

わたしは、財布ごと渡した。

龍洋一が、お札を抜き、財布を突き返す。

「どうするの？」

龍洋一が、わたしを見つめる。哀しそうな目をした。

お札をズボンのポケットにねじこんだ。

身を翻して、駆けだした。

「洋くん、どこ行くの？ アパートはそっちじゃないっ」

龍洋一が、振り向きもせず、走り続ける。

後ろ姿が、小さくなっていく。

龍洋一が、わたしから、去っていく。

去っていく。

去っていく。

去って……

「……どうして」

わたしは呆然と、見ているしかなかった。

身体から力が抜けた。

アスファルトにへたりこんだ。

「どうしてっ!」

鳥の囀りが、頭上から降ってきた。

13

　私は、愛されることに、慣れていなかった。松子の愛情に、身を委ねることが、怖くてできなかった。暗闇に慣れた私の目には、松子の愛情は眩しすぎて、痛かったのです。

　私は、松子からお金を奪って、逃げました。街道沿いを駆けながら、泣きました。どうしてこんな人生になってしまったのか。最初に、何かが狂ってしまった。できることなら、十五歳のときからやり直したい。心から思いました。

　私の足は、生まれ育った福岡に向かっていました。そこで日雇いの力仕事を得て、やるせなさをぶつけるように、働きました。それでも心は乱れて、凪ぐことはありませんでした。

　私はほんとうは、松子といっしょにやり直したかった。しかし、松子の愛情を恐れて、近づけない自分がいる。松子を幸せにする自信の持てない自分がいる。私の中で、心が二つに割れ、ぶつかり、傷つけ合っていたのです。ふたたび覚せい剤に手を出すのに、時間はかかりませんでした。同じ現場の肉体労働者の中には、覚せい剤を使っている者が何人もいて、

　私を紹介してくれたのです。

　私にとって、生きていること自体が、苦痛でした。かといって、死ぬほどの勇気はありま

せんでした。自殺しようと、高いマンションの屋上にのぼったこともあります。しかし、下を見ると足が震え、汗が滴り落ち、どうしても一歩を踏み出すことができなかった。極道だ何だと粋（いき）がったところで、この程度です。私は、苦しみを逃れるために、何度も覚せい剤を打ちました。

精神的に追いつめられ、クスリによる妄想の中で、私と松子の人生を狂わせた元凶が何か、見えてきました。いえ、見えた気がしただけです。そして、その元凶を排除しない限り、心の平安は得られない。松子も幸せにはなれない。ならばせめて俺の手で、その元凶を取り除いてやろう。それが、松子のためにできる、唯一のことだ。そう思いこんでしまったのです。

私は、昔のツテを頼り、一丁の拳銃を、手に入れました。

14

龍洋一のために用意した御飯と味噌汁は、そのままにしておいた。一人で食べる気は、しなかった。お昼ごろ、部屋のチャイムが鳴った。駆け寄ってドアを開けると、新聞の勧誘員だった。わたしは黙ってドアを閉めた。

二日目の朝、電話が鳴った。飛びついたが、三田村秀子だった。時間になっても来ないので、心配してくれたようだ。わたしは、しばらく店を休みたいと言った。

『川尻さん、あなたまさか、また覚せい剤に手を出してるんじゃないでしょうね?』

わたしは、何も答えずに、電話を切った。

どうして龍洋一が、わたしから去っていったのか、理解できなかった。もうわたしのことを、嫌いになったのか。そうは思えない。

中学の修学旅行のことを思い出す。行きの列車の中で、龍洋一はどのグループからも離れ、一人つまらなそうに外を見ていた。わたしがトランプに誘っても、その気のない素振りをした。しかし龍洋一はあのころから、わたしのことが好きだったと言ったではないか。十五歳の龍洋一は本心を隠して、健気に孤高を気取っていたのだ。あのとき、わたしがもっと強引

に誘っていたら、トランプの仲間に入ったかも知れない。だからわたしは、龍洋一が手紙で

別れようと書いてきたときも、それが本心だとは思わなかった。自分の心に嘘をついている

と思った。なぜなら彼は、わたしと約束したからだ。ずっといっしょにいると。わたしを愛

していると。

龍洋一は必ず帰ってくる。自分の心に素直になり、わたしの胸に戻ってくる。そしてわた

しは、彼を抱きしめる。

その気になれば、わたしの居所は調べられるはずだ。もし龍洋一が保護観察所に問い合わ

せれば、わたしに確認の連絡が入る。ここを動いたら、もう二度と会えないかも知れない。

だから、このアパートを引き払うことはできない。このアパートを動けないということは、

ここでの生活を続けなければならないということだ。

わたしは、「みたむら」に電話をかけた。さっきの非礼を詫び、明日から店に出たいと告

げた。三田村秀子は、今回だけは大目に見る、二度と無断欠勤はしないで欲しい、と言って

くれた。

きのうから炊きっぱなしの御飯と、温めなおした味噌汁を口にした。松阪牛には手をつけ

なかった。咀嚼していると、少しずつ力が蘇ってきた。

だいじょうぶだ、と思った。

一カ月後、テレビを見ながら、牛乳とコーンフレークの朝食をとっていたときだった。リモコンでチャンネルを替えていると、ニュース番組の画面に、見覚えのある名前が映った。

『昨夜十一時二十分頃、福岡県の県議、田所文夫氏が、柳川市の自宅前でタクシーから降りたところを、元暴力団関係者、龍洋一容疑者三十一歳に拳銃で銃撃され、病院に運ばれましたが、まもなく死亡しました。龍容疑者はその場で取り押さえられ、殺人および銃刀法違反の疑いで逮捕されました。警察では、動機について詳しく調べるとともに……』

第五章　うたかた

1

「その後のことは、知りません」

俺と龍さんは、黙って歩き続けた。

龍さんは、口を開こうとしなかった。

俺も、何を話していいのか、わからなかったが、言葉が腹の底から浮かび上がってきた。

「松子伯母さんが……かわいそうだよ」

龍さんが、無言でうなずく。

「ねえ龍さん、そのとき、松子伯母さんといっしょにやり直していたら、いまごろ、どうなっていたと思う？」

龍さんの足が、止まった。目を閉じて、俯く。深く息を吐いて、目をあげた。

「笙さん、それは勘弁してください」

「だってさ……」

「お願いします」

龍さんが頭をさげた。

「でも、後悔してるんでしょ？　逃げちゃったこと」

「……してます」

「懺悔するために、クリスチャンに？」

龍さんが、考えこむような顔をする。

「少し違うかも知れません」

龍さんが、歩きだした。

「笙さんが拾ってくれたあの聖書は、府中刑務所にいたときに、頂いたものだったのです。刑務所でも月に一回、教誨という宗教教育があるのですが、独居拘禁者は参加できず、代わりに希望者に聖書がもらえたのです。そのときは深く考えずに、なんとなく手元に置いていただけです。たまに気晴らしに読むくらいでしたし、読んでも心が動かされることはありませんでした。だから、府中刑務所を出所し、松子から逃げて福岡に帰り、田所さんを殺してしまうまで、私の手荷物の中に、ずっとあの聖書はあったのです。もし、精神的にど

ん底にあったとき、何かの偶然で聖書を開いていれば、少なくとも田所さんを殺すようなこ
とはなかったかも知れない。そう思うと、残念でなりません」

「もう一度聖書を開くきっかけは、何だったの？」

「田所さんには、二十一歳になる孫娘さんがいらっしゃいました。その方が拘置所まで、私
の面会に来たのです。とても可憐な女性でした。その女性が、私を真正面から見据えて、言
うのです。

『あなたが殺した祖父は、もしかしたら昔、あなたにひどいことをしたのかも知れない。で
もわたしにとっては、親代わりとなって育ててくれた、優しい、かけがえのない祖父だった。
人々のために献身的に働く、尊敬すべき、素晴らしい祖父だった』

私は、耳を塞ぎたかった。そんな話は、聞きたくもなかった。しかし、その女性はそのあ
とで、こう言ったのです」

『でも、わたしは、あなたを許します。あなたのために、祈ります』

龍さんが、首を小さく、横に振った。

「私は、何を言われたのか、わかりませんでした。正直に言うと、馬鹿にされたような気さ

えしました。大切な人間を殺されて、その犯人のところまでやってきて、罵倒するのならともかく、許すなんて……そんな人間、この世にいるはずがない。そう思いました。この女性は、それだけ言うと、帰っていきました。私にはただ、腹立たしさと、戸惑いだけが残りました。

この女性の言葉を思い出すのは、小倉刑務所に移って三年後のことです。就寝前の自由時間に、あの聖書に手を伸ばしたのです。三年間、一度も開こうとしなかったのに、その夜に限って、手に取りました。別に救われたいとか、そんなことは何も考えていませんでした。ほんとうに何気なく、適当にページを開いたのです。そしていきなり、その言葉が目に飛びこんできました。

『神は愛である』

意味はわかりませんでした。ただ、その部分から目が離れないのです。神は愛。その文字だけが、大きく見えました。そのうちに、錆びついて停止していた心が、軋みながら動き始めたのです。だんだんと回転が速くなっていくのが、自分でもわかりました。

私は、急かされるように、聖書を最初から読み始めました。少ない自由時間を利用し、何

日もかけて、一字一句なぞるように、最後まで読みました。わからないことがたくさんあり
ました。最初から読み返しました。少しわかるようになりましたが、まだまだわからないこ
とだらけでした。

私は、知りたくて知りたくて、たまらなくなりました。知りたいのにわからない、教えて
くれる人もいない。もどかしさや焦りが膨らんできました。

小倉刑務所でも教誨があって、月に一回、牧師様が来てくださいました。ここでは雑居房
に入っていたので、私にも参加資格があります。すぐに参加希望を出しましたが、募集は半
年に一回だったので、何ヵ月か待たなくてはなりませんでした。その間に、さらに聖書を読
みこみました。どうしてもわからないところに、印をつけていきました。

教誨が始まると、私は溜まっていた質問を、次々とぶつけていきました。牧師様は、一つ一つ丁
寧に、答えてくださいました。

私がいちばん聞きたかったのは、神は愛である、とはどういう意味なのか、ということで
した。牧師様は、しばらく考えてから、おっしゃいました。

『あなたはこれまで、誰かを心の底から憎んだことがありますか?』

『あります』

『いま、その方たちのために、心の底から祈れますか？　愛することができますか？』

『それは……』

『できますか？』

『いえ、できません』

『それでいいのですよ』

『！』

『人間の心は弱いものです。憎むべき敵のために祈るなんて、できるものじゃない。そうでしょう』

『……はい』

『でも、神様の力に縋れば、できるのです。許せない敵を愛する。麻薬や覚せい剤をやめる。ギャンブルをやめる。人間の力ではなかなか難しいことです。でもそれもみな、神様に縋れば可能になるのです』

『俺のような悪人にも、力を貸してくれるのですか？　おまえはそんな価値のない人間だって、断られるんじゃないんですか？』

『神様は、すべての人を愛してくださっています。神様にとって、価値のない人間なんていませんよ。すべての人が尊いのです』

『すべての人……』

『そうです。すべての人です』

『じゃあ神様は、俺のことも愛してくれているのですか？　こんな俺でも、尊いのですか？』

『はい。あなたは尊い。神様はあなたを愛してます』

『嘘だっ！』

私は、思わず立ちあがっていました。たちまち看守たちが、駆け寄ってきました。私を外に連れ出そうとしました。

『待ちなさい！』

牧師様が、厳しい声で、看守を止めました。看守たちが顔を見合わせ、手を離しました。

『どうして、嘘だと思うのですか？』

牧師様が、優しく語りかけてくださいました。私は、堰（せき）を切ったように訴えました。これまでの人生で、自分が周りの人間をどれほど傷つけてきたか。すべてぶちまけました。俺はこんなに悪いことをしてきたんだ。人殺しまでしたんだ。こんな俺が尊いはずがない。いくら神様でも、こんな人間を愛するはずがない。

私は、声がかすれるほど叫んでいました。

牧師様は、おっしゃいました。

『あなたは、いま、苦しんでいますね』

『はい……』

『あなたがほんものの悪人なら、そんなに苦しみません。

神様は、そんなあなたを、愛おしく思っておられるのです』

私は、雷に撃たれたような気がしました。

『許されない者を許す。それが神の愛なのです。それができるのは、神様だけです。たしか

にあなたは、社会では許されないことをしてきたかも知れない。しかし神様は、とうに許し

てくださっています。その証拠に、あなたは、自分のしてきたことを、心から悔いてるじゃ

ありませんか。

いまのあなたには、神様の愛が、溢れんばかりに注がれています。それをわかってくださ

い。あなたの心が神様の愛で満たされたら、こんどはその愛を、あなたの周りの人に、分け

与えてください。あなたにとって許されざる人間を、神様の愛の力で許してください。愛し

てください。この世にいる人がみな、自分が神様に愛されていることを知り、心を愛で満た

し、さらにそれを周りに注ぎ、許し、愛し合えば、この世はパラダイスになる。そうは思い

ません。

私は悟りました。

田所さんの孫娘さんの心には、神様が宿っていたのだと。だから、憎むべき私のことを許せた。そして松子にも、神様が宿っていた。

『どんなときでも、あなたは一人ではない。いつも神様が、あなたを見守ってくださっています。神様を、信じてください』

その言葉を聞いたとき、涙が流れて止まらなくなりました。気がつくと、いっしょに教誨に出ていた他の受刑者たちも、みな泣いていました」

龍さんが、深く息を吐いた。

左手に荻窪小学校が現れた。運動場で、子供たちが遊んでいる。歓声が乱れ飛んでいた。

俺と龍さんは、足を止めた。元気よく走り回る子供たちを、眺めていた。

「でも……」

龍さんが、言った。

「すべては遅すぎました」

学校のスピーカーから、チャイムが鳴り響いた。子供たちが遊びをやめ、校舎に向かって

走りだす。あっという間に、運動場から人影が消えた。砂埃だけが、残った。

2

昭和六十二年九月

わたしは「みたむら」を辞めた。オーナーの三田村秀子が、慰留するために一度だけアパートまで来てくれたが、わたしの様子を見て無駄だと悟ったのか、五分もしないうちに帰っていった。

龍洋一を失ったわたしの生活は、水に浸した角砂糖のように、崩れていった。目を覚ますのは午前十時ごろ。トイレを済ませてからまた布団に戻り、正午近くまで横になる。空腹に耐えられなくなると起きだして、ジャンクフードを缶ビールで流しこむ。はじめは三百五十ミリ缶を飲むと、半日は頭痛がして動けなかったが、二週間も続けると平気になった。

夕方になると、化粧もせず、スウェットの上下のまま、コンビニエンス・ストアまで歩き、弁当と缶ビール、ジャンクフードやカップラーメンの類を、気の済むまで買う。レジ袋をさげたまま、通り道にある児童公園のベンチに座り、弁当を食べる。こぢんまりとした児童公

園には、ベンチのほか、ブランコやすべり台、ジャングルジム、砂場が揃っていた。昼間は母子連れが多いが、夕方になるとたいてい、子供たちだけで遊んでいる。

銭湯には三日に一度くらい、気の向いたときに通った。アパートに帰ると、テレビを見ながらジャンクフードを口にする。気力のあるときはカップラーメンをつくる。テレビは、チャンネルを数秒おきに替えながら、深夜二時近くまで見る。眠れそうにないときは、ウイスキーをコップ一杯呷る。するとたちまち足腰に力が入らなくなり、否でも布団に横たわる。気がつくと、めでたく朝になっている。

十二月下旬、酔ってアパートの階段から足を踏み外し、転げ落ちて気を失った。救急車で運ばれたが、骨には異常がなく、軽い脳震盪だと言われた。ただ、肝臓が腫れているとのことで、酒をやめるように警告された。酒がないと眠れないと訴えると、アモバンとサイレースという薬を処方してくれた。アモバンは入眠を促す薬で、サイレースは睡眠を持続させる薬だそうだ。たしかにこれを飲むと、アルコールなしで眠れるようにはなった。ただしそれは、眠ったというよりも、深夜二時から朝の十時までタイムスリップしたような感じで、眠りにつくときの倦怠、疲労、絶望が、目覚めたときにそのまま残っていた。眠っているはずなのに、まるで二十四時間、一睡もせずに生活しているような気がした。

世間では、いつのまにか、年が明けていた。テレビの出演者がみな、正月用の衣装を着て
いた。おめでとうのオンパレードだった。

わたしは、テレビをつけたままにして、部屋を出た。冷たい空気が、肌を刺す。赤い太陽
が、西に沈もうとしている。薄闇の忍びよる路地を、ぶらぶらと歩き、いつも弁当を食べて
いる児童公園に入った。

四歳くらいの女の子が一人、砂場で遊んでいた。白いジャンパーに、赤いスカート、黒い
タイツ。頭のてっぺんに、ピンク色のリボンを結んでいる。親の姿はない。

わたしはブランコに座り、地面を蹴った。ブランコが、きいと鳴く。女の子が振り返った。
じっとこちらを見る。目がくりくりとして、頬のふっくらした、可愛らしい子。わたしは、
笑いかけた。女の子は表情を変えない。興味をなくしたように、また砂に向かう。

女の子は、おもちゃの赤いスコップを握り、憑かれたような顔で、黙々と砂を掘っている。
その横顔には、干渉を拒絶する雰囲気さえ、漂っていた。

太陽は完全に沈み、東の空から闇が降りてくる。空気がさらに、冷えこんできた。

わたしは、ブランコから立ちあがった。砂場に近づく。女の子の隣に、腰を落とした。

「ねえ、なにしてるの？」

「あなをほってる」

「穴を掘ってどうするの？」

「はいるの」

「……誰が？」

「みいちゃん」

「みいちゃんて？」

「わたし」

女の子は、手を休めずに、掘っている。

「こんな穴に入ったら、お洋服が汚れちゃうよ」

「いいの」

「おばさんも手伝おうか？」

女の子が、手を止めて、顔をあげた。

「ほんと？」

「うん。そのスコップ、貸してくれる？」

「いいよ」

　わたしは、赤いスコップを手にして、砂を掘った。穴が見る見る深くなっていく。女の子
は、穴の底をじっと見ている。

わたしは、自分の墓穴を掘っているような気がしてきた。この女の子は、わたしを地獄に誘う、死に神だろうか。……ああ、また馬鹿なことを考えている。

汗が滲んできた。

わたしは、手を休めた。

「ふう、ちょっと疲れちゃった」

女の子が、口を尖らせた。作業を中断したことが不満なのかと思ったら、

「おなかすいた」

その言い方が愛らしく、わたしは笑ってしまった。

「ママは?」

「しばらくそとで、あそんでなさいって。よびにくるまで、いえにかえっちゃだめだって」

「そう……寒くないの?」

「ちょっとさむい」

「そうだね。ねえ、おばさんのうちにくる? カップラーメンでもつくってあげようか」

女の子が、満面の笑みを弾けさせた。

「うん!」

わたしは、みいちゃんと手をつないで、公園を出た。みいちゃんが、道を歩きながら、歌

を口ずさみ始める。メロディがめちゃくちゃだったが、よく聞くと、テレビアニメの主題歌らしい。わたしも、できるだけ声を合わせて、歌った。みいちゃんが、つないだ手を、前後に振り始めた。

歌声も大きくなる。足がスキップを踏んでいる。

視線を感じたのか、急に足を止め、口をつぐんだ。不安げな眼差しで、わたしを見あげる。

わたしは、微笑みを返した。

みいちゃんが、ほっとしたような笑顔を、見せてくれた。

アパートに帰ると、薬缶に水を入れて、火にかけた。沸騰するあいだに、敷きっぱなしの布団を畳み、押入に押しこんだ。溜まっていた空き缶やゴミは袋に入れて、ドアの外に出す。隅に追いやってあったコタツを真ん中に戻し、電源を入れた。久しぶりに身体を動かして息が切れたが、これでなんとか、みいちゃんとわたしの座る場所ができた。

カップラーメンは、ちょうど二つ残っていた。神様に感謝した。

お湯を注いで、三分間待ってから、いただきます、と声を揃えた。

みいちゃんは、ほんとうに美味しそうに食べた。食べ終えると、きちんと手を合わせて、ごちそうさまでした、と言った。

わたしは、残ったスープを、流しに捨てた。居間に戻ると、みいちゃんが、コタツの天板に頬をぺたんとつけて、寝息を立てていた。わたしは、毛布を持ってきて、背中にかけてあ

げた。みいちゃんのそばに、腰をおろす。口を少しだけ開けた、無邪気な寝顔。見ていて、飽きなかった。丸みを帯びた頬を、指で触れた。押してみる。信じられないくらい、柔らかだった。

みいちゃんが、顔を顰めた。瞼を開けた。顔をあげた。きょろきょろと、周りを見回す。

壊れそうな目で、わたしを見る。いきなり泣きだした。

「みいちゃん、どうしたの？」

「ママっ、ママぁ！」

「みいちゃん、ねえ、何か食べる？　ポテトチップスがあるよ」

わたしの声は、みいちゃんの耳には届いていないようだった。みいちゃんは、天井を仰ぎ、ひたすら母親を呼び続けた。大粒の涙を流し、ママ、ママ、と繰り返すばかりだ。

部屋のチャイムが鳴った。

わたしは、泣き続けるみいちゃんとドアを、交互に見た。チャイムがまた鳴る。

「みいちゃん、ちょっと待っててね」

わたしは、ドアに走った。

「誰？」

覗き穴から見ると、警察官が立っていた。

「夜分にすみません。ちょっとお隣のことでお伺いしたいことがあるのですが」

「いま、取りこんでいるんですけど」

「お時間は取らせません。すぐに済みます」

わたしは、仕方なく、ロックを外した。

ドアがいきおいよく開いた。

「ちょっと、なにを……」

「美岬っ！」

「ママぁ！」

警察官の後ろから、目を泣き腫らした女性が、走り出てきた。土足で部屋にあがっていく。

みいちゃんが、その女性に飛びついた。女性が、みいちゃんを抱きしめた。

「美岬ぃ、ごめんねえ、ごめんねえ」

「お子さんに、間違いありませんね」

警察官が言った。

女性が、みいちゃんの髪に顔を埋めたまま、間違いありません、と叫んだ。

わたしは、ゆっくりと、警察官を見た。

「署までご同行願えますか？」

「どうして、わたしが？」

「幼児略取誘拐の容疑がかかっています」

「そんなつもりじゃ……」

「署のほうで伺います」

部屋の外に出ると、眼下にパトカーが見えた。赤い光を、周囲にばらまいている。野次馬らしき人影が、集まってきていた。わたしは、視線を浴びながら、パトカーに乗せられ、連行された。

取調室では、ありのままに話した。女の子が一人で寂しそうにしていたので、遊び相手になってあげたこと。寒くてお腹がすいたと言ったので、部屋にあげてラーメンを食べさせたこと。警察官が来たときになぜ泣いていたのか、虐待していたのではないか、と聞かれたが、わたしにもわからない、たぶん母親の姿がなくて心細くなったのではないか、虐待なんか絶対にしていない、と答えた。かつて二度服役していることも、自分から話した。どうせ調べればわかる。そのせいか、尿検査も受けさせられた。その夜は、留置場に泊まった。留置場は寒く、鼻水が出て仕方がなかった。

翌日の取り調べは、正午前に始まった。担当官から、尿検査の結果は陰性だった、部屋からも覚せい剤は見つからなかった、わたしの供述が女の子の証言と一致した、と言われた。

結局、厳重な注意を受けただけで、放免となった。

警察署から放り出されたあと、アパートまで一時間かけて歩いた。部屋は隅々まで捜索された　らしく、すべてのものが、少しずつ動いていた。

夕方になって、大家が訪ねてきた。六十歳くらいの老人だった。警察に連行された事情を聞きたいという。わたしは、警察で話したことを繰り返した。それでも大家は、わたしに出ていって欲しいと言った。一週間以内という期限まで、一方的に決められた。

「大野島まで」

タクシーの運転手に告げてから、座席にもたれた。コートの襟を立て、深く息を吐く。車窓の外を見あげると、JR佐賀駅の文字が見えた。一瞬、幻を見ているような気がして、サングラスを外した。しかし間違いなく、佐賀駅はそこにあった。どうしてこんなところにいるのだろう。何をしているのだろう。わたしは家に帰ろうとしているのか。

大野島？

タクシーは駅前通りを南下し、本庄町袋の交差点を左折した。国道二〇八号線を走り、光法の交差点から県道二八五号線に右折すると、いきなり道路沿いに、真新しいラブホテルが建っていた。新聞販売店や地元企業の社員寮の立ち並ぶ通りを抜けると、あとは見渡す限りの田畑だ。

　早津江に入ると、沿道にふたたび建物が増えてくる。郵便局や老舗のスーパーに混じり、東京のものと同じコンビニエンス・ストアができていた。

　車は、早津江橋西のT字路を左折し、早津江橋を一気に登った。早津江川のゆったりした流れが、眼下に広がる。

　前回大野島に帰ったのは、小野寺と雄琴に行く直前だったから、十五年ぶりの帰郷となる。

「筑後川に架かる橋は、もう出来たのかしら？」

「新田大橋ですね。もうずいぶんと前に、出来たとですよ。太か橋でね。長さが八百メートル以上あるとです」

「この道をまっすぐ行ったら、行けるの？」

「はい」

「じゃあ、その橋を渡ってちょうだい」

「大野島を過ぎるとですよ」

「かまわないわ。どんな橋が出来たのか、見てみたいから」

　車は、早津江橋をおりて、大野島に入った。沿道には見覚えのない建物が並んでいる。故郷（さと）に帰ってきたという感じがしなかった。

　大野島を横断する道路は、全長二キロもない。緩やかな左カーブを曲がったら、目の前に、

天空に向かうような、長い直線の上り坂が現れた。その頂点に、真っ赤な鉄のアーチが、神殿のように聳えている。その巨大さは、早津江橋とは比べものにならない。

「あれですよ」

車が、橋の直前の青信号を直進し、坂道を登り始めた。登るに連れて、筑後川の全貌が見えてくる。三百メートルはあるであろう幅いっぱいに、薄茶色の川面が膨れあがっていた。中央を走っているはずの導流堤は、水没して見えない。

「雨が降ったの?」

「正月早々、大雨が二日も続いたとです。昨日の午後になって、やっと止んでですね」

遥か右手には、有明海が迫っている。左手すぐ下を見ると、渡し船の桟橋が残っていた。

金木淳子はまだ、この土地にいるだろうか。

「渡し船は、どうなったの?」

「橋が開通して、しばらくしてから廃止になったとです。はじめのころは、橋を渡るのが怖かちう人が多くて、船を使っとりました。とくに年寄りがね」

車が、橋の頂上に登りつめる。濁った川面は眼下に遠ざかり、まるで飛行機で空を飛んでいるようだった。

車が、下り坂に入る。

「橋を渡ってからどげんしますか？　大野島にUターンしますか？」

「いいわ。そこの信号を右に曲がったところで降ろして」

タクシーを降りたわたしは、歩いて新田大橋を渡り、大野島に戻ることにした。西の空に向かって、一直線に延びる坂道は、三百メートルくらいあるだろうか。その先の、高く突き出た巨大なアーチが、空中に浮かんでいるように見える。

わたしは、軽い緊張を感じて、歩きだした。坂にさしかかると、足の裏にはっきりと、勾配を感じた。歩道の幅は、人ひとりがやっと通れる程度しかない。しかも車道との間にはフェンスもなく、ただ一段高くなっているだけだ。通行する車両が、すぐ脇を追い越していく。誤って手を伸ばそうものなら、弾き飛ばされそうだ。とくにダンプカーに追い越されると、風圧で引きこまれそうになる。なるほどこれでは、年寄りが怖がるはずだった。

この坂道を二百メートルほど登り、橋の本体に到達するころには、脚の筋肉が張り、心臓も激しく拍動していた。ここからは歩道の幅も広くなり、車道との間にもフェンスが設けてあった。さらに橋の頂上を目指して、歩いた。

そしてついに頂上に達すると、あまりの高さに、目が眩みそうになった。車で通ったときには感じられなかった、上空の気流や、音や、振動が、全身の皮膚から浸みてくる。空を飛んでいるというより、いままさに空中を落下しているような錯覚に陥った。思わず立ち止ま

り、欄干から下を覗く。冷たい雨水を呑みこんだ流れに、吸いこまれそうになる。

ここから落ちたら、即死は免れない。

いま誰かに背中を突かれたら、その数秒後に、わたしは死ぬ。

この欄干を乗り越えるだけで、その数秒後に、わたしは死ぬ。

ひょっとしたら、自分はこの瞬間、これまでの人生でもっとも、死に近づいているのではないか。

強い横風に煽られた。足がよろめき、身体がふわりと浮く。下半身に、快感にも似た電流が走り、腰が抜けそうになった。コートの襟を、ぎゅっとつかむ。荒い呼吸を繰り返す。背中に汗が流れた。心臓が暴れていた。

わたしは、笑いたくなった。身体は死を、望んでいないのだ。この期に及んでなお、生きようとしている。

わたしは、有明海に向かって、深呼吸をした。風のなかに、微かな故郷の匂いを、感じ取ったような気がした。

見慣れた赤い屋根ではなかった。箱のような形をした、モダンな二階建ての家に生まれ変わっていた。庭には芝生が植えられ、小さな花壇までしつらえてある。駐車スペースには、

真新しい四輪駆動車。門柱の表札には、たしかに『川尻』とあった。

陽が傾いてきた。腕時計を見ると、すでに午後五時をまわっている。東京ならばとうに暗くなっている時刻だが、ここではまだ空が明るかった。

門柱の前に佇んだ。自分が何をしたいのか、わからなかった。どうしてここに戻ってきたのだろう。何を求めているのだろう。

しかしこの家に、自分が縋りたいと思っている何かが、存在するはずだった。

玄関のドアが開いた。小さな男の子が出てきた。黒いズボンにフード付きのジャケット。一目で、紀夫の子供だとわかった。芝生に向かって駆けだし、しゃがみこんで玩具のようなものを拾いあげる。それを持って、すぐに家に入ろうとする。はっと立ち止まり、わたしを見た。

「こんにちは」

男の子が、恥ずかしそうに、頭をさげた。

「こんにちは」

わたしは、笑みを返しながら、門を入った。男の子の前で、腰を落とす。男の子の、澄み切った瞳に、わたしの顔が映った。

「あなたは、ここのお子さん？」

「うん」

「名前は何ていうの？」

「しょう」

「しょうっていうの。かっこいい名前だね。歳はいくつ？」

「ごさい」

　男の子が、右掌を広げて、押し出すような仕草をした。

「このお家で、お父さんとお母さんと住んでいるの？」

「それと、おばあちゃん」

「あのね、ショウくん、もう一人……」

「おい、お客さんか」

　声がして、玄関のドアが開いた。

　紀夫だった。

　グレーのズボンに茶色のセーター。正月気分で酒でも飲んでいたのか、目の周りが赤い。口に爪楊枝をくわえていた。磐井屋の屋上で会ったときと、あまり変わっていないような気がする。

　わたしは、立ちあがった。

紀夫が、目を剝いた。爪楊枝をつまんで、足もとに投げ捨てる。男の子に向かって、

「笙、中に入っとらんね」

男の子が、ばいばい、とわたしに手を振って、家に入っていった。

紀夫が、ドアが閉まるのを見届けてから、ズボンのポケットに手を突っこんだ。出した手には、車のキーが握られていた。

「ここじゃ話もできん。乗らんね」

紀夫が、四輪駆動車に乗りこんだ。わたしも、助手席に乗った。紀夫がキーを回すと、エンジンが吼えた。荒っぽい操作で車を出す。車内が、酒臭くなった。

「何しに戻ってきたと？」

紀夫が、前を向いたまま、言った。

「まだ許してくれないの？」

「人殺しまでしとって、許してくれち？　なんちゅう神経しとるね」

「さっきの子、あなたの息子ね」

「ああ……」

「わたしにとっては甥ね」

「あんたはおらんことになっとるけん。いらんこと、しゃべっとらんやろうな」

「何も言ってないわ」

「ならよか」

車が、早津江橋を渡り、県道二八五号線を北上した。

紀夫は、黙りこくって、表情のない目を、前に向けている。

「ねえ、紀夫」

返事はない。

「久美は、どうしてるの?」

紀夫が、ちらとわたしを見た。鼻息を吐く。

「あの家には、いないの?」

「久美は、死んだと」

「久美は、死んだ?」

「……死んだ?」

「そう。久美は、もう、死んだ」

わたしの手足を動かしていた糸が、ぷつんと切れた。わたしは、自分が最後に縋りたかったものを、はっきりと意識した。そしてそれはもう、この世にはいなかった。

「去年の秋ばい。風邪ばこじらせて、肺炎ば起こしよった。久美の最期の言葉、わかるか?」

わたしは、首を横に振る。

「姉ちゃん、おかえり。そげん言うて、笑いながら死んでいった」

車は、光法の交差点を、左に曲がった。

紀夫がスイッチを操作して、ヘッドライトを点灯した。意味のない風景が、目の前を流れ

ていく。エンジンの音が、大きく聞こえた。フロントガラスに、太宰府天満宮のお守りが、

揺れている。縫いつけられた金文字が、きらりと光った。

気がつくと、車が停車していた。

「降りんね」

見あげると、ＪＲ佐賀駅の文字が見えた。

わたしは、車を降りた。

「紀夫……」

「二度と来るな」

紀夫が、身体を伸ばして、助手席のドアを閉める。激しい音がした。

紀夫の四輪駆動車が、わたしを置いて、走り去った。

3

時計を見た。午前二時だった。シャツに触れると、じっとりと濡れている。首の後ろまで、汗にまみれていた。

俺は起きあがり、蛍光灯を点した。エアコンのスイッチを入れて、シャワーに直行する。

熱い湯を浴びてから、缶ビールを開けた。テレビをつけ、ベッドに腰掛けた。

寝汗をかいたのは、暑さのせいだけではない。夢を見たのだ。内容は忘れてしまったが、松子伯母の夢だったことは確かだ。

いまの俺は、たぶん他の誰よりも、松子伯母のことを知っている。ただ、龍さんに去られたあとの消息だけは、わからない。沢村さんの話から推測すると、荒んだ生活をしていたのだろう。しかし沢村さんとの再会をきっかけに、何かが変わろうとしていたのではないか。そうあって欲しい。

松子伯母の人生は、何だったのだろう。悲劇とか、不幸とか、そんな言葉では言い表せそうにない。そもそもの躓きは、教師生活二年目の、修学旅行先での盗難事件だ。いや、その前に、当時の校長に乱暴されかけた事件もあった。それらの事件さえなければ、平穏な人生

を歩んでいたかも知れない。失踪することもなかったかも知れない。いっしょに久美叔母さんの看病をして、そのうちにいい人を見つけて結婚して、子供もできて、たまに遊びに来たら、俺が子供の相手をしてやって……。

気がついた。

俺はまだ、松子伯母が最初に躓いた年齢にも、達していない。松子伯母の人生を他人ごとのように考えてきたが、この先、俺に同じことが起こらないという保証はない。沢村さんから言われたように、何かの拍子で人を殺してしまうことだって、ないとは言い切れない。殺人まで犯さなくとも、生きている以上、予想もしなかった出来事に、数多く遭遇することになるのだろう。

確実に言えることは、俺も松子伯母と同じように、時間が経てば老いていくし、いつかは必ず死ぬということだけ。時間は限られている。その限られた時間と、どう向き合っていくか。

たぶん、俺はまだ、わかっていないのだろうな、と思う。松子伯母のほんとうの哀しみも、人生のことも。

（松子伯母さん、ごめんな。いまの俺には、これが精一杯だ。もう少し大人になったら、もっと理解してあげられるかも知れないけど）

ほんとうは、生きているうちに、会いたかった。会って、話を聞きたかった。俺の話も、聞いて欲しかった。

（それにしても……）

いったいどこの誰が、何のために、松子伯母を殺したのか。死因は内臓破裂だと親父が言っていたが、なぜそこまで暴行を加えなければならなかったのか。

松子伯母は骨になり、松子伯母を殺した犯人は、いまもどこかで生きている。俺の心の中で、犯人への憎しみが、徐々に濃度を増してきていた。

気がついたら、カーテンが白っぽく輝いていた。テレビでは、騒々しいトーク番組が始まっている。

寝こんでしまったようだ。

俺は、目を擦りながら、起きあがった。

「おはよう」

「おは……えっ！」

ベッド脇に、明日香がいた。膝を抱えるようにして座り、俺を見ている。

「なに、おまえ、いつ入ってきたの？」

「一時間くらい前。チャイムを鳴らしても反応がなかったから、合い鍵使って入っちゃった。

だめだよ、ちゃんとチェーンを掛けておかないと」

「いままで、なにしてたの?」

「笙の寝顔を見てた」

明日香が、へへ、と笑う。

「かわいかったよ」

「帰省してたんだろ?」

「きのうの夜、戻ってきた」

「早かったな。もっとゆっくりしてくるのかと思った」

「そのほうがよかった?」

「んなことはないけどさ」

俺は、明日香の顔を、まじまじと見た。

「どうしたの?」

「いや、人生には、予想もつかないことがあるなと思って」

「なにそれ?」

「なんでもない。朝飯は?」

「もうお昼」

「じゃあ昼飯は？」

「まだ」

「外で食うか」

「いいよ」

とりあえず駅前まで歩き、そこで適当な店に入ることにした。

俺は道すがら、龍さんから聞いたことを、かいつまんで話した。

明日香は、黙って聞いていた。俺が話し終えると、ぽつりと言った。

「笙、変わったね」

「なにが？」

「だって最初は、松子さんのことなんか、ぜんぜん興味がないって言ってたのに、いまはま

るで、亡くなった友達のことを話しているみたい」

「自分でも、よくわからない。やっぱり、血の繋がりがあるせいじゃないか」

「でも、他人も同然だったんでしょ」

「それはそうだけど、龍さんの話を聞いてしまったから……。あ、それで思い出した。龍さ

んのいる教会、けっこう近いんだぜ。あとで行ってみる?」

「……いや、いい」

俺は思わず、明日香の横顔を見つめた。

龍さんと話がしたいと、神様にお願いしたのは明日香なのに……。

明日香は、口元を真一文字に結び、考えごとをするような目を、前に向けている。

「明日香、何かあったのか?」

「うん……」

なんだろう。俺と明日香のあいだに、透明な膜が挟まっているような感じがする。手を伸ばせば触れられるはずなのに、それができない。

「最近あらためて思ったんだけど、俺って明日香のこと、何も知らないよな」

「どうして?」

「明日香にお姉さんがいることも知らなかったし、ほかに兄弟がいるのか、何人家族なのか、聞いたこともなかっただろ。あと、小さいときはどんな子供で、食べものは何が好きだったとか」

「どうして聞かなかったの?」

「……きっと俺は、目の前にいる明日香が、明日香のすべてだと思いこんでいたんだろう

な」

「いまは、そうじゃないの?」

「うん……何て言ったらいいのかな、ここにいる明日香は、生まれてから今までの、いろいろな人との関わりや経験の積み重ねの上に、存在しているんだなって……俺の言ってること、わかる?」

明日香が、ふっと笑った。

「なんとなく」

「明日香と付き合い始めて、ああ、明日香にはこんな面もあったんだって、新たに発見することは多かったけど、明日香はまだ、俺がびっくりするような面を、いろいろ持っているんじゃないかって気がする」

明日香が、顔を空に向ける。明日香の胸が、膨らんだ。何かを吹っ切るように、長く息を吐く。

「あたしのお母さんね、あたしが小さいときに、出て行っちゃったの、男の人といっしょに」

「あたしね、テレビに出たことがあるんだよ。ほら、昔よくあったでしょ。奥さんに逃げら

れた男の人が、涙流して『ヨシコ、帰ってきてくれぇ』って叫ぶやつ。よく憶えていないん
だけど、親戚から強引に勧められたらしくって、お父さんと姉貴といっしょに出たんだっ
て」

「……小さいときって、何歳?」

「幼稚園に通っていたから、五、六歳だったと思う」

「で、お母さんは?」

「いまも行方不明」

俺は、はっと気づいた。

「明日香、松子伯母さんのことを気にしていたのは、もしかして……」

明日香が、沈んだ顔で、うなずく。

「そうなんだろうね、たぶん……自分でも知らないうちに、松子さんにお母さんを重ねて、
見ていたのかも知れない。生きていればちょうど、同じくらいの歳だもんね」

明日香が、瞬きをしながら、笑みを浮かべた。

「あたしね、お母さんのこと、嫌いなの。だってそうでしょ、自分が幸せになるために、お
父さんやあたしたちを置いて逃げてしまうなんて、許せることじゃないでしょ」

「うん」

「……でもね、あんまり不幸にも、なってて欲しくないなって、思う」

「どうして?」

「どうしてだろうね。不幸のどん底にいたら、憎むのがかわいそうになっちゃうからかな」

「幸せでいて欲しいんだ、お母さんにも」

「きっと、すごく悩んだと思うんだ、お母さん。悩み抜いた末に、家族を捨てて、男の人と暮らすことを選んだ。たぶん、一生に一度の、大きな決断だったんじゃないかな。それで幸せになってくれなきゃ、何のためにあたしたちが苦労したか、わからないじゃない……あたし、変かな?」

「変じゃないよ」

明日香が、明日香らしい笑顔を、久しぶりに見せてくれた。

「どう、びっくりした?」

「した」

明日香が、真剣な顔に戻る。

「ついでにもう一つ、びっくりさせてあげようか」

「……なんだよ?」

「あたしもね、大きな決断をすることにしたんだ」

俺は、足を止めた。

明日香が、唇を固く結んだ。ひとつ息を吸ってから、

「大学を、やめることにした」

「マジ？」

明日香が、俺と向き合った。

「なんで？」

「もう一度、受験勉強して、医学部に入り直す」

俺は、とっさに言葉が出なかった。

「い？」

「医学部」

「……医者になんの？」

「なる」

「明日香が？」

「うん」

「冗談、じゃないよな」

「真面目な話」

俺は、どう反応していいのか、わからなかった。そんな自分をごまかすように、笑った。

「でも、明日香と医者って、なんか結びつかないよな。そもそもなんで、医者になろうと思ったわけ？　やっぱり、お母さんのことが、関係してる？」

明日香が、首を横に振る。

「お母さんは関係ない。フレデリック・グラント・バンティングという人、知ってる？」

「フレデ……知らん。誰、それ？」

「カナダの医学者。一九二一年に、医学生だったC・H・ベストと力を合わせて、たった二カ月で、インスリンの抽出に成功した人」

「インスリンっていえば、糖尿病の……」

「そう。バンティングたちが抽出したインスリン標品が、糖尿病で死にかけていた十四歳の少年に投与されて、彼の命を救ったのが八カ月後。糖尿病はそれまで死の病とされていたから、これは画期的なことだったの。二年後には、その業績を評価されて、ノーベル医学生理学賞を受賞してる。でもその後、第二次世界大戦に出征して、飛行機事故で亡くなったの。まだ四十九歳だったって」

「そういえば生物の参考書で、そんな話を読んだことがあるような気がするけど。で、その人、明日香が医者になることと、どう関係があるんだ？」

「バンティングとベストという、たった二人の人間が発見したインスリンは、お年寄りから若い人まで、何億人もの糖尿病患者の命を救ってきて、これからも救い続けていくのよ。発見者が死んだ後も、ずっと。これって、凄いことだと思わない？」

「まあ、そう言われてみれば……」

「高校の生物の時間にね、先生がバンティングのことを話してくれたの。そのとき、あたしも一つでいいから、世の中の役に立つことを成し遂げたいって、強く思った。バンティングみたいに、自分の生きた証を、世界に残したいって。せっかく人間に生まれてきたんだから」

「だから、医者に？」

「そう。でも、現役で医学部に入るには、ちょっと力が足りなかった。お父さんや姉貴は、挑戦してみろって言ってくれたけど、どうしても自信が持てなくて、無難な道を選んでしまって……」

「無難ね」

ちなみに俺の大学合格は、担任教師から奇跡と評された。

「でも、妥協してしまったことは、心の底で、ずっと引っかかってた。いまの大学に入って、笙に会えたことは、ほんとうによかったと思ってるよ。でも、最近になってやっと、このま

まだと死ぬときに、絶対に後悔するってわかったの。どうしてあのとき、思い切って、自分の夢に突き進まなかったんだろう。どうして自分の可能性を、とことん試さなかったんだろうって」

明日香の目が、きらきらと輝いた。

「いまならまだ、それができるのよ」

明日香は、俺の手の届かないところに、行こうとしている。直感的に、そう思った。俺はこれから、別れを体験しようとしているのだ。おそらく人生で、もっとも大切な別れの一つを。

「わかった」

俺は言った。

「明日香の夢を、応援するよ」

明日香が、笑みを浮かべる。

「ありがとう」

「どこの医学部に?」

「まだ決めてないけど、関東には来ないと思う。できれば、名古屋大学に行きたい。難しいだろうけど」

俺は、次の問いを投げるのが、怖かった。でも、逃げることはできない。

「で、俺たち、どうなるんだ？」

明日香が、目を伏せる。しばらく黙ったあと、静かに言った。

「友達に、戻らない？」

足もとが崩れていくような気がした。

明日香は、自分の人生を獲得しようと、歩き始めたのだ。俺に止める権利はないし、止められるものでもない。

いいじゃないか。喜んでやろうよ。

「仕方が、ないよな。なんたって医学部だもんな。勉強しなくちゃ、いけないもんな」

明日香の頬が、震えた。潤んだ目をあげた。何かを言いそうになった。

俺はそれを遮るように言った。

「夢、絶対に、叶えろよな」

明日香が、俺を見つめる。

「うん……」

感情が胸に充満してきた。やばい、と思った。俺は先に歩きだした。

明日香がついてくる。

「退学願は?」

わざと軽い声で言った。

「休み明けに、出すつもり」

「じゃあ、あと一ヵ月はあるわけだ」

「笙、あたし、最低かな?」

俺は立ち止まった。振り返った。

「なんで?」

「笙よりも、自分の夢を優先させることになるから」

「……家族を捨てたお母さんといっしょだって、思ってるのか?」

「笙だって、ほんとうは怒ってるでしょ? 勝手な奴だって」

「明日香」

俺は、めいっぱい低い声をつくった。

「この川尻笙を、見損なってもらっちゃ困るぜ」

明日香が、じっと俺を見る。目から涙を零しながら、笑った。俺の胸に、顔を寄せてきた。

俺は明日香を、抱きしめた。キスをする。見つめ合う。言葉は必要なかった。

俺の携帯電話が鳴った。

催眠術が解けたように、互いの身体を離す。

俺は、ポケットから取り出して、耳にあてた。

誰だよ、まったく。

『あ、おれだけど』

後藤刑事。

『お待たせ。捕まえたぜ、君の伯母さんを殺した奴ら』

4

国分寺市西元町のアパートを追い出されたわたしは、家電や食器類などをすべて処分し、身の回りの品だけをバッグに詰めて、旅に出た。仙台、盛岡、青森と回り、津軽半島の龍飛崎まで行ったが、赤木がいるはずの北海道には、渡らなかった。

きっと赤木は、雪乃のイメージを、持ち続けてくれている。わたしが滅びても、赤木の心の中では、いつまでも若くて綺麗なわたしが、生き続ける。それが今のわたしにとって、たった一つの救いだ。もし赤木を探し出して会ったら、そのイメージを崩してしまうのではないか。それに赤木がすでに死んでしまっていたら、わたしの最後の希望まで、消えてしまう。

結局、東京に引き返すことにした。東北に住まなかった理由は、寒さが厳しいことと、言葉がわからないこと。やはり、誰の干渉も受けない東京が、性に合っていた。

常磐線で上野に向かっているとき、車窓を覗くと、眼下に大きな川が見えた。荒川だった。筑後川に似ている、と思った。まもなく電車が減速し、停まった。わたしは、バッグを持って、降りた。

駅前商店街を歩いていたら、不動産屋を見つけた。そこでアパートを探した。荒川の近く

に空き部屋があった。

築十年で風呂なしだが、家賃は安い。実際に見てみると、小ぎれいな部屋だった。即断して、その日のうちに入居した。保証人はいなかったが、敷金を払ってくれれば問題ないとのことだった。

このとき、わたしの預金通帳には、トルコ嬢時代に稼いだお金が、一千万円以上残っていた。刑務所での九年間は生活費が必要なかったし、社会に出ているときには美容院で働いていた。国分寺の三年間では、龍洋一との生活に備えて節約していたので、貯金が増えたくらいだ。

結局、わたしを裏切らなかったのは、お金だけなのか。メロドラマのような結論には、自嘲するしかなかった。

いいだろう。それならわたしにも考えがある。もう誰も信じない。誰も愛さない。誰にもわたしの人生に立ち入らせない。

わたしは、新聞の求人広告を見て、ときどきパートの仕事についた。スーパーのレジ。ビル清掃。何でもやった。バーのホステスにも応募したが、面接で断られた。履歴書の賞罰欄には、前科のことを書かなかった。どうせわかりっこない。就職してもたいてい、半年と保たずに辞めた。どの職場に入っても、なじめなかった。わたしは、お金さえ稼げれば、同僚に嫌われようと爪弾きにされようと平気だったが、周りはそうもいかないらしい。美容院に

　就職しようとは思わなかった。シザーを見るのも嫌だった。

　四十一歳の誕生日から二ヵ月ほど経ったころ、ひどい目眩に襲われた。吐き気がして、立っているのも辛くなった。熱を測ったところ、四十度近くある。布団に横たわると、起きあがれなくなった。水も飲めずに、一日中、天井を眺めていた。このまま死ぬかも知れない、と思った。二日間、何も口にできなかった。三日目の朝、少しだけ身体が軽くなったような気がした。這って冷蔵庫に行き、中にあったものを片っ端から食べた。その日の昼過ぎになって、やっと立ちあがることができた。なかなか死ねないな、と思った。そして、生理が久しく来ていないことに気づいた。妊娠はあり得なかった。この五年間、セックスはしていない。

　閉経。十五歳から続いてきた女の証が、終わっていたのだった。まさか終焉（しゅうえん）が、こんなに早く訪れるとは、思わなかった。わたしの肉体はもう、女ではないのか。では何なのだ？　ただ食って寝て生き長らえているだけの、醜い何かなのか。

　歩けるようになってから、コンビニエンス・ストアに出かけた。弁当やサンドイッチを山のように買った。それを部屋に持ち帰り、一日かけて食べた。大食いは快楽だと知った。寝る前には、毎日のようにアルコール、とくにウイスキーを口にした。気持ちが乱れるにつれて、時間の流れが加速していった。夜、ウイスキーをコップに注いで一息に呑み、布団

に横になったら、次の瞬間にはもう夜になっていて、ウイスキーをコップに注ごうとしてい
た。十一月に入ったと思ったら、いつのまにかクリスマスになっていて、気がついたら昭和
が終わり、桜が咲いていた。梅雨がうっとうしいと思ったら、また桜が咲いていた。季節が
まるごと、消えていくようだった。

新しいウイスキーの瓶を開けたとき、きょうは五十歳の誕生日だと気づいた。この十年近
く、自分が何をしてきたのか、まったく記憶がなかった。手から力が抜け、瓶を落として割
ってしまった。

以前に比べて、腹の回りに贅肉がついた。肌が荒れた。顔の皺が増えた。シミが増えた。
化粧をしなくなった。部屋が汚くなった。臭くなった。不潔になった。たしかに年月が過ぎ
ていた。信じられなかった。

このまま汚らしく老いて、一人さびしく死んでいくのだろうか。嘘だと思いたかった。こ
れは何かの間違いだ。悪い夢を見ているのだ。しかし、いくら待っても、目は覚めなかった。

翌日、新しいウイスキーを買おうと外に出た。行く手を、一匹の猫が横切った。足がすく
んだ。動けなくなった。なぜ猫ごときを怖がるのか、自分でも理解できなかった。猫だけで
はなかった。カラスが鳴くと、頭を抱えて蹲った。後ろで物音がすると、悲鳴をあげた。た

まらず部屋に引き返した。カーテンを閉め切り、部屋の真ん中で、膝を抱えた。知らず知らずに、心臓の鼓動を、数えていた。すると、ときどき脈が飛んだ。髪の毛が逆立った。心臓が止まろうとしている。本気でそう思った。一所懸命に念じて、心臓を動かし続けた。鼓動を意識していないと、心配で気が狂いそうだった。何も手につかなくなった。そして突然、怒りが爆発した。

洋くん、なぜわたしを置いて逃げた？

めぐみ、なぜわたしを見限った？

島津、なぜわたしを待っていてくれなかった？

小野寺、なぜわたしを裏切った？

綾乃姐さん、なぜ幸せになってくれなかった？

赤木、なぜはっきり求愛してくれなかった？

岡野、なぜわたしを弄んだ？

徹也、なぜわたしを連れて行ってくれなかった？

佐伯、なぜわたしを庇ってくれなかった？

田所、なぜわたしを乱暴しようとした？　なぜわたしを学校から追い出した？

平成十三年七月九日

病院の待合室に備え付けられたテレビは、正午のNHKニュースを流していた。画面に、

両親、なぜわたしを愛してくれなかった？
紀夫、なぜわたしを許してくれなかった？
久美、なぜ勝手に死んでしまった？
わたしがこんなになったのは、おまえたちのせいだ！

気がつくと、誰もいない壁に向かって、怒鳴っていた。
愕然とした。
わたし、壊れている……。
病院に駆けこんだ。精神科を受診した。症状を訴え、いくつかの抗不安剤を処方してもらった。薬を飲むと、頭がぼうっとした。ぼうっとしているあいだも、時間は容赦なく、駆け抜けていった。

懐かしい建物が映った。それは、福岡天神の老舗百貨店・磐井屋が、事実上倒産したというニュースだった。

「不景気だねえ。いったい、この国はどうなるんだ」

後ろの長椅子から、老人の声が聞こえる。

滅びてしまえ、と思った。

「川尻さあん、川尻松子さあん」

会計係の女が、声を張りあげた。

わたしは、椅子から立ちあがった。いつものようにお金を払い、薬の処方箋を受け取り、病院の出口に向かいかけたときだった。

「松ちゃん?」

ぎょっとして振り向いた。息を呑む。一目でそれが誰かわかった。

上品なグレーのボレロ・スーツ。スリムな体型は変わっていない。若い男を一人、従えている。

「めぐみ……」

「やっぱりそうだ、松ちゃんだ」

めぐみが、笑みを輝かせて、わたしの手を握った。大人っぽい香水が、鼻を掠める。

わたしは、自分の体臭が気になった。地の底に消えてしまいたかった。

「久しぶりだよねえ、どうしてたんだよ」

わたしは、手を引っこめた。目を伏せる。

「松ちゃんは今、何やってるの?」

「別に……」

「どうしたんだよ、あたしのこと、忘れたわけじゃないだろ?」

「ごめん。わたし、急ぐから」

愛想笑いを浮かべ、横を通り抜けようとすると、

「ちょっと待てよ!」

わたしは、目を閉じて、立ち止まった。

「どうしたの? それが十八年ぶりに会った親友に言う言葉?」

わたしは、振り向いた。めぐみを睨んだ。

「親友? わたしはあなたのことを、親友だと思ったことはないよ」

めぐみが鼻白んだ。唇を歪めて、けっと笑った。

「そうかい。ま、いいや。で、美容師、続けてるの?」

首を横に振った。

「一人暮らし?」

うなずく。

「どこで?」

「日ノ出町の……そんなこと、あなたには関係ないでしょ」

「働いてるんだろ?」

「……いまはとくに」

めぐみが、憐れむような目を、わたしに向ける。

そんな目で見るな。

「じゃあさ、うちで働かない?」

わたしは、目を剥いた。

「専属の美容師が欲しいんだ。松ちゃんなら、じゅうぶんやれる」

「無理よっ」

わたしは叫んだ。

「どうして?」

「美容師なんて、何年前の話? ハサミの持ち方も忘れてるよ」

「手が憶えてるはずだよ。その気になれば、できるよ」

「できない。できるわけない」

「どうして決めつける？　やってみないとわからないだろ？」

「もう放っておいて。わたしは、もういい。このままでいいの」

「何がいいんだよ。ぜんぜんよかないよ。いまの自分の顔、鏡で見たことある？　松ちゃん、いま、自分がほんとうに生きているって、実感できる？」

「わかったような口を利かないで。あなたにはご主人がそばにいる。わたしの気持ちがわかるわけがない」

めぐみの顔に、哀しげな笑みが浮かんだ。

「旦那はとっくに死んだよ。癌でね。あたしだって安穏と暮らしてきたわけじゃない。二人の子供と生きていくために、恥を晒しながら必死に働いてきたんだよ」

「わたしはあなたとは違うのよ！　あなたのように、何にでも立ち向かっていける、強い人間じゃないの。もう放っておいて、お願いだからっ！」

わたしは、めぐみに背を向けた。腕をつかまれ、振り向かされる。手に、何かを握らされた。

「わかったよ。そこまで言うのなら、もう松ちゃんには関わらない。干渉しない。でももし、もう一度、美容師として働く気があるのなら、遠慮せずに、ここに連絡して」

それは、めぐみの名刺だった。

沢村めぐみ。サワムラ企画・取締役社長。

わたしは名刺を握り、逃げるようにその場を離れた。

「待ってるよ、松ちゃんっ!」

めぐみの声が、背中から心臓を貫いた。

病院を出ると、熱気がまとわりついてきた。太陽は真上に昇っている。

わたしは、波立つ感情を無視して、ひたすら歩いた。細い路地を抜け、大通りを横断し、JR北千住駅の前から駅前商店街を突っ切っていく。いつもなら病院帰りに、駅前のコンビニエンス・ストアに寄り、雑誌を立ち読みしたり弁当を買ったりするのだが、きょうはその気にならない。

慣れない速さで歩き続けて、さすがに息が切れてくる。しかもこの暑さ。立ち止まると、汗が滴り落ちた。いつのまにか、千住旭公園に出ていた。学校の運動場のように広い児童公園には、そこかしこに樹が植えられている。公園のすぐ北側には、八階建ての白亜のマンションが聳えている。

わたしは、車両止めの間を通り、公園に入った。公園中央に植えられた樹を囲むように、

円形のベンチが設けてあった。ちょうど日陰になっている。わたしは、そこに腰をおろした。

手にはまだ、めぐみの名刺を握っていた。汗が染みていた。

「なにが、松ちゃん、だ。馬鹿にしやがって……」

両手で名刺をくしゃくしゃに丸め、地面に叩きつけた。立ちあがって足で踏んだ。

誰が、あんたの世話になるものか。

もう一度踏みにじってから、歩きだした。

アパートの近くまで戻ったところに、もう一つコンビニエンス・ストアがある。そこで缶ビールやジャンクフード、カップラーメン、菓子パンを大量に買った。

部屋に帰ると、着ているものをすべて脱ぎ、湿らせたタオルで身体を拭いた。洗濯しておいた下着をつけ、買ってきた缶ビールを開け、一気に飲み干す。大きなげっぷが出た。頭がくらくらした。

畳の上に、大の字に寝た。

目を覚ますと、部屋が暗かった。照明を点け、時計を見る。夜の八時十五分。クリームパンを囓ってから、洗面器とタオルを持って、銭湯に行った。広々とした湯船に、一時間以上浸かっていた。何も考えなかった。

部屋に帰って、すぐにウイスキーをコップに注いだ。口まで持っていったが、飲まずに置いた。琥珀色の液体が、抗議するように揺れる。その様を見つめながら、めぐみから投げら

れた言葉を、思い返す。すぐに首を振った。

「無理だよ、できるわけが……」

『どうして決めつける？　やってみないとわからないだろ？』

両掌を広げた。目の前に掲げた。

カチッ。

何かのスイッチが入ったような音が、頭の奥で聞こえた。

ロッドを巻く真似をしてみた。シザーを操る真似をしてみた。ピンパーマ。ストロークカット。レイヤーをつけ、最後はフィンガーブロー。手を使い、思いつく限りの技術を、再現していく。

夢中になった。指が喜んでいた。この十数年間、滞っていた血流が、ふたたび動き始める。意識が鮮明になってくる。封印され、埃を被っていた財産が、小躍りしながら飛び出てくる。できる。憶えている。

我に返ると、二時間が過ぎていた。その間に、想像上で完成させた髪型は、十をくだらなかった。わたしは、震えるほど、興奮していた。

「やろう」

　もう一度、やろう。だめでもともとじゃないか。やるだけやってみよう。

「めぐみに謝らなきゃ……」

　あっと気づいた。めぐみの名刺を捨ててしまった。あれがなければ、連絡先がわからない。

　わたしは、部屋を飛び出した。千住旭公園に走った。朝まで待ちきれなかった。こんなに心が弾む夜は、龍洋一の出所前夜以来だった。

　公園に近づくと、嬌声が聞こえた。公園の中で、若者たちが花火を楽しんでいた。五、六人いるだろうか。街灯は、公園の真ん中に一本だけ、点っている。

　めぐみの名刺を捨ててたのは、どのあたりだったろう。たしか、樹の下のベンチだったはずだ。わたしは、見当をつけて、公園の中を走った。見覚えのあるベンチ。あった。地面を這って探した。たしかこのあたりで、踏みつけたはず。しかし、それらしきものは落ちていない。どこだ。めぐみの名刺は、どこだ。

「こいつ、ホームレスかな」

「石鹸の匂いがするじゃん」

　声が聞こえた。

　顔をあげた。

花火をしていた若者たちが、目の前に立っていた。十代の女の子も混じっていた。

「やだ、あたしと同じやつだよ、この匂い」

わたしは、立ちあがった。

「ねえ、あんたたち、このあたりに名刺が落ちてなかった？　くしゃくしゃに丸めてあった

んだけど……」

鳩尾に何かが食いこんだ。息が詰まった。地面に突っ伏した。胃から熱いものが逆流して

きた。口の中に、酸っぱいクリームパンの味が、広がった。足で転がされた。仰向けにされ

た。

熱に浮かされたような哄笑が、夜空に響きわたった。

「きったねえ、こいつゲロってるよ」

「いい気味。生意気なんだよ、あたしと同じ石鹸使うなんて」

「みんなでお仕置きしてあげようか」

魔物のような目が、わたしを取り囲んでいた。何が起ころうとしているのか、わからなか

った……。

わたしは目を開けた。暗い空間にいた。壁に手をついて、立ちあがった。腰が抜けて、また座りこんだ。硬い何かで、尻を打った。衝撃が腹を抉った。呻き声をあげた。咳きこんで、痰を吐き出した。尻の下の硬いものを、手で触れた。呻き声をあげた。もう一度立ちあがり、目の前の壁を押した。簡単に開いた。よろめきながら、外に出た。生温かな空気が、肺に入ってきた。街灯が点っていた。その光が、黄緑色に見えた。人の気配はなかった。思い出した。ここは公園だ。めぐみの名刺を探さなきゃ。思ったとたん、腹の底から熱い液体が、噴きあがってきた。呻きながら、地面に吐き散らした。口の中が、ひりひりと染みた。手で、口元を拭った。

夜空を見あげた。何も見えなかった。目を戻した。呼吸を整えた。足を踏み出した。歩けた。一歩、一歩、進んだ。公園を出た。アスファルトを踏みしめながら、路地を進んだ。ほかのことは、考えなかった。ひたすら前に、歩き続けた。足がもつれて、転んだ。顔から突っこんだ。砂を噛みながら、立ちあがった。電柱に手をつき、唾を吐いた。

歩かなきゃ。

ふたたび足を、踏み出した。休みながら、休みながら、歩き続けた。前だけを見て、崩れそうになる身体を支えた。永遠に等しい時間の果てに、ひかり荘まで、帰り着いた。部屋の前に、立った。ポケットを、まさぐった。鍵が、見つからなかった。

公園で落としたのか……。

後ろを、振り返った。涙が溢れた。縋るような気持ちで、ドアノブを握った。回った。開いていた。鍵をかけ忘れていた。頰を歪めて、笑った。声は出なかった。

ドアを開け、部屋に入った。靴を脱いだ。あがった。蛍光灯を点けた。すべてが黄緑色に見えた。

吐き気がした。流しに飛びついた。口を開けた。呻き声のほかは、何も出てこなかった。

腹の中が、腐っているようだった。

手足が、重くなってきた。心臓だけが、もの凄い速さで、動いていた。鼻の奥に、きな臭い匂いが、広がってくる。心臓の鼓動が、さらに速くなってきた。

蛇口からコップに、水を汲んだ。口まで持っていった。飲まずに流しに捨てた。

目の前が、暗くなった。身体が震えだした。

また、見えるようになった。何も見えなくなった。

目の前が、暗くなった。

起きようとしても、身体が動かなかった。いつのまにか、居間の畳に倒れていた。うつぶせに、なっていた。起きようとしても、身体が動かなかった。瞼も、動かなかった。指も、動かなかった。

寒くなってくる。また目の前が、暗くなった。

白い光が閃(ひらめ)いた。

わたしは、赤い屋根を見あげた。わたしがこの世に生を受けた家。赤ん坊、幼児、小学生、中学生、高校生のわたしが、家族に囲まれて過ごした家。大学を出て、大人として一年間、過ごした家。何も変わっていなかった。電線に留まったカササギが、長い尾羽根を上下に振っている。

わたしは、引き戸を開けた。足を踏み入れた。黒ずんだ柱も、そのままだった。あのころと同じ匂い。同じ空気。

柱時計が鳴った。

わたしは靴を脱ぎ、家にあがった。居間を覗くと、父が背すじを伸ばして、新聞を広げていた。気難しそうな顔を傾げて、記事を読んでいる。わたしに気づくと、目だけあげて、小さくうなずいた。すぐ新聞に、目を戻す。

階段を、元気のいい足音が、駆けおりてきた。目の前に、飛び出してきた。立ち止まった。

久美。

息を切らしている。信じられないという顔で、わたしを見ている。相変わらずの美しい目。青白い丸顔。細い身体。

「姉ちゃんっ!」

久美が歓声をあげた。子供のような笑顔を、弾けさせる。飛びあがった。わたしの首に抱きついてきた。

「やったあ、姉ちゃんが帰ってきた、姉ちゃんが帰ってきたあ！」

久美が、わたしにしがみつき、全身で叫んだ。無邪気な笑い声を、家中に響かせる。

「姉ちゃん、おかえりいっ！」

わたしの身体に、温かなものが、満ちていく。わたしは、久美を抱きしめた。久美の髪に、鼻を埋めた。幼いころから慣れ親しんだ匂いを、胸一杯に吸いこんだ。そして、笑いながら、囁いた。

ただいま。

終章　祈り

　松子伯母を殺した犯人は、十七歳から二十一歳までの、男女五人だった。後藤刑事による
と、うち三人の男は都内の大学生で、十七歳と十八歳の女はフリーターだった。女は二人と
も、主犯格の二十一歳の男と出会い系サイトで知り合い、男の友人二人に紹介されたという。
その友人の一人が千住旭町にマンションを借りていて、事件当日、五人はその部屋で飲んで
いた。深夜になって花火をしようということになり、近くの千住旭公園まで出向いたところ、
松子伯母と遭遇し、殺してしまったらしい。松子伯母を殺した理由は、わかっていない。裁
判ではっきりさせられるだろうと、後藤刑事が言った。

　事件から四カ月以上経過した十一月上旬、大学生の男三人の初公判があった。俺は、地下
鉄霞ヶ関駅で龍さんと待ち合わせて、東京地方裁判所に向かった。昨日まで降り続いていた
秋雨は、早朝までにあがっており、霞ヶ関駅を出たころには、透き通るような青空が広がっ
ていた。

　松子伯母を殺した連中が、俺や明日香と同世代だったという事実は、ショックだった。こ

れから彼らと、実際に会うことになる。どんな奴なのか。できれば直接、聞いてみたい。ど

うして松子伯母を殺したのか。どんな気持ちがしたのか。自分たちのしたことを、どう思っ

ているのか。松子伯母に、言いたいことはあるのか。

そして、おまえ達はいったい、何者なのか。

「明日香さん、もう大学をやめて、帰ってしまったのですね」

龍さんが、ぽそりと言った。

「ひとことでも、聖書を届けてくれたお礼を言いたかったのですが」

「勉強が忙しいんだよ。なにしろこれから、医者を目指すんだから」

「すごいですね。夢を夢で終わらせず、挑戦していくなんて、尊敬しますよ」

正直言って俺は、明日香の決断力に、圧倒されていた。俺にも子供のころに抱いた夢はあ

るが、いまからそれに挑戦できるかと問われれば、『無理に決まってるだろ』と冗談にする

しかない。夢には捨て時がある。夢を捨てられたとき、はじめて大人になれる。そんな文章

を、読んだことがある。嘘だよな、と思う。

「私は、十五歳のときに何かが少しだけ狂ってしまい、それが時間とともに、取り返しのつ

かないくらい、大きくなってしまいました。もし、明日香さんのような知恵と勇気があれば、

どこかで修正できたかも知れないのに……」

「でも龍さんは、りっぱに修正したじゃない？　ちょっと遅かったけど」

「私の力じゃありませんよ。神様が助けてくださったのです」

俺は、あっと声を漏らした。

「どうしました？」

龍さんが、首を傾げる。

「いま気がついたけど、明日香も神様の力を借りて、決断したんだよ」

「俺が明日香といっしょに、龍さんの聖書を教会に届けたとき、牧師さんに勧められて、お祈りの真似事をしたんだ。その帰り、明日香が言った。神様は教会にいるのではなくて、自分の心の中にいる。悩んでいるときにお祈りをすることで、自分の心の声を聞くことができる。明日香はきっとそのとき、迷いを吹っ切って、医者を目指すことを決めたんだ。とつぜん帰省したのは、家族に自分の決断を理解してもらうためだったと思う」

「そうでしたか」

「だから、もし龍さんが聖書を落としていかなかったら、明日香もこんな決断はしなかったかも知れないね」

「……すみません」

俺は、大げさに手を振った。

「そういう意味じゃないよ。俺は明日香の夢を、応援してるんだから」

龍さんが、嬉しそうにうなずく。

「離れてしまうと、お付き合いも大変ですね」

「別れることにした」

龍さんが立ち止まった。怪訝な目で、俺を見る。

「なぜですか? 好きなんでしょ。お互いに」

「いま龍さんが言ったとおりだよ。距離がありすぎて、簡単に会えないから。たしかに俺たちはいい感じだったけど、明日香は受験勉強に没頭しなきゃいけないし、そういう現実を考えると、付き合い続けるのは難しいってことになって。それに俺たちは、まだ若いしさ」

「明日香さんと別れても、またすぐに別の人が見つかると、思っていますか?」

「……まあ、ね、女の子は明日香さんだけじゃないから」

「明日香さんは、この世に一人しかいませんよ。明日香さんに似ている人はいるかも知れないけれど、明日香さんはたった一人です」

「それはそうだけど……」

「私を反面教師にしてください。人生に出会いはたくさんありますが、ほんとうにいい出会いは数えるほどです。明日香さんとの出会いは、笙さんにとって、数少ない、よい出会いの

一つではないのですか。もっと大切にしなくて、いいのですか？　このまま明日香さんを失っても、後悔しませんか？」

俺は俯いて、黙りこんだ。

「すみません」

龍さんが、あわてたように言った。

「余計な口出しをしてしまいました。笙さんと明日香さんが決めたことですから、私がとやかく言うことではありませんでした」

龍さんが、小さく頭をさげて、歩きだす。

俺は、龍さんの少し後ろを、付いていった。

龍さんに言われなくとも、そのくらいはわかっている。でも明日香は、これから勉強が大変だし、俺が邪魔しちゃ悪い。

いや、そんなの嘘だ。俺は、明日香と恋人同士でいたい。でも、もし遠距離恋愛を続けたとしても、明日香が地元で新しい恋人に巡り会うかも知れないし、医学部に入ったら優秀な連中がごろごろいるだろうし、こっちだってどんな出会いがあるかわからない。そのとき、互いの存在が重荷になったり、憎しみ合ったりするようなことは嫌だ。いまなら、楽しい思い出として、関係を終えることができる。要するに、遠距離恋愛を成就させる自信がないの

だ。

いや、これも本音じゃないな。もっともらしい理屈をつけて、ごまかしているだけだ。自分で自分の気持ちがわからない。整理がつかない。ぐちゃぐちゃだ。

「ここですね」

龍さんの声で、我に返った。

その無機質なビルは、東京高等裁判所との合同庁舎になっていた。建物の入り口付近に、守衛が立っている。裁判所。人が人を裁く場所なのだ。

入り口は、職員用と一般来訪者用に分かれていた。俺と龍さんは、一般来訪者用の自動ドアを通った。守衛は、ちらとこちらを見ただけで、何も言わなかった。

入ったところで、警察官のような制服を着た職員が、何人も集まっていた。手荷物検査だという。俺は何も持っていなかったが、龍さんが小さな書類鞄を持っていたので、それを渡した。荷物は、すぐ脇のベルトコンベアに載せられ、エックス線透視装置に通された。俺と龍さんは、金属探知機のゲートをくぐった。何も鳴らなかった。

「どうぞ。結構です」

ゲート担当の職員が、丁寧な口調で言った。龍さんが、手荷物検査担当の職員から、書類鞄を受け取った。

手荷物検査を過ぎたところは、吹き抜けのロビーになっていて、天井が異様に高かった。

だだっ広い空間のあちこちで、スーツ姿やラフな格好の男女が、立ち話をしている。俺と同じように、ジーパン姿の若い男もいた。入って正面に、守衛ボックスがあった。

「あそこで調べるんですよ」

龍さんが、迷いもせずに、守衛ボックスに向かう。若い守衛が座っていたが、俺たちが前に立っても、何の反応もしない。龍さんが勝手に、ボックスの上に並べてある、公判開廷予定表を開いた。俺は、横から覗きこんだ。

この表には、裁判の行われる法廷、担当裁判官の氏名、時間、事件名、罪名、被告人名などが記されていた。開廷時間は後藤刑事から教えられていたので、被告人の名前を見て、該当する裁判を探した。後藤刑事から『わるい。法廷の場所は裁判所で探してよ』と言われていたからだ。

龍さんが、ページをめくる手を止めた。指さした先に、被告人の名前を見つけた。

橋本雅巳。ほか二名。

これが、松子伯母を殺した奴の名前。

見たことも、聞いたこともない。

罪名欄には、殺人。事件名欄には、リンチ殺人事件とある。リンチという言葉が、冷たく

浮きあがっていた。開廷時間は、午後三時。法廷は、四〇×号法廷。

俺と龍さんは、エレベーターで四階にあがった。扉が開くと目の前に、物音ひとつしない空間が広がった。天井の高い、幅広の廊下が、左右に百メートルは延びている。その冷たい空間には人影もなく、ひっそりと静まり返っていた。

天井からさがっている掲示板に、法廷番号の案内が記されている。矢印に従って進むと、ガラスの両開き扉があった。扉を押し開けて進んだところが、法廷の並ぶフロアだった。

各法廷の出入り口は、傍聴人用と、弁護人・検察官用に分かれている。傍聴人用の扉には、四角い覗き窓がくりぬいてあった。

俺は法廷番号を確かめ、覗き窓を開けて、中をうかがった。灯りは点っているが、誰もいなかった。

俺と龍さんは、扉を開けて、法廷に入った。誰もいないと思っていたが、眼鏡をかけた女性職員が一人、動き回っていた。開廷の準備をしているらしい。

傍聴席は三列、四十席くらいあった。傍聴席と法廷は、低い木の柵で隔てられている。俺と龍さんは、真ん中の列の、いちばん後ろに座った。

「誰もいないけど……」

「時間が早かったようですね。入って待ってましょう」

弁護人・検察官用のドアが開いた。豊かな白髪を後ろに撫でつけた、いかにも紳士という雰囲気の男性と、若い男性二人が、入ってきた。いずれもグレー系のスーツに身を包んでいる。向かって左側の席に着いた。

「被告側の弁護人です」

龍さんが、囁いた。

左手の傍聴人用の扉が開いた。年配の男女が入ってきた。男性は五十代半ば。値の張りそうなスーツを着て、胸を反り返らせている。俺たちに目を留めると、口をへの字に曲げた。女性はまだ五十歳には届いていないようだが、顔に精気がない。目線は宙をさまよっていて、ただ男性の後に付き従っているだけといった感じだった。二人が揃って、弁護人に頭をさげた。白髪紳士の弁護人が、手を軽くあげて応える。年配の男女は、左側の最前列の席に、腰をおろした。

開廷の時間が近づくにつれて、傍聴人が増えてくる。犯人の両親や、親族、友人と思しき人たちもいた。最初に入ってきた年配の男女は、弁護人となにやら話している。

「こんなことで、あの子の将来に傷がつくなんて……」

ハンカチを目にあてている中年女性に、白髪の弁護人が慈しむような顔で、言葉をかけている。

「これは事故なのよ」

どこからか、女性の声が漏れ聞こえた。やはり、犯人の親族らしい。

弁護人・検察官用のドアが開いた。濃いグレーのスーツを着た若い男が入ってきた。手に分厚い書類を抱えている。法廷を横切って、向かって右側の席に着いた。検察官だ。髪は短く、色も白い。頬が痩けていて、どことなく不健康そうだが、目だけは大きく、エネルギーを感じさせた。

検察官席の近くにあるドアが開き、黒いマントのような服を着た男性が、台車を押して入ってきた。台車には、書類が積みあげられている。男性はそれを、いちばん高い壇に並べていった。それが終わってから、一段低い壇についた。書記官らしい。

書記官の入ってきたドアが、ふたたび開いた。警察官のような制服を着た二人の廷吏が、男を挟むようにして、入ってきた。男は三人。

「こいつらが……」

「犯人です」

松子伯母を殺した奴ら。手首には手錠がかけられ、腰には黒っぽい縄が結ばれている。

最初の男は、ジーンズに白い長袖のトレーナー姿。短い髪の先だけが、金色に染まっている。

体つきは華奢なくらいで、顔色も悪い。縁なし眼鏡のせいか、秀才タイプにも見える。

二人目は、紺色のスーツを着ていた。髪はごく普通だが、背が高く、顔は日に焼けて浅黒く、体つきもがっちりとしていて、野球でもやっていそうだった。

三人目は、細身のジーンズに、スタジャンを羽織っていた。三人の中ではいちばん背が低く、痩せていた。は虫類のような顔を傾げ、口元を歪めながら、入ってきた。

三人とも、まったく見覚えがなかった。

こいつらの足が、松子伯母の内臓を蹴破（けやぶ）ったのだ。こいつらさえいなければ、松子伯母は今でも、生きていたはずなのだ。

俺の心臓が、暴れ始めた。心は冷静なのに、心臓だけが興奮していた。

三人は、廷吏に手錠と腰縄を外されてから、被告人席に座った。柵のすぐ向こうだ。

法廷正面の扉が開き、三人の裁判官が入ってきた。

「起立」

さっき動き回っていた女性職員が、声をあげた。

法廷にいた全員が、立ちあがる。

黒い法服を着た裁判官が、いちばん高い壇に着席すると、みなも腰をおろした。

「揃っていますね？」

真ん中に着席した裁判官の声が、法廷に響いた。弁護人と検察官が、神妙な面持ちでうな

ずく。

「はい、それでは開廷します。被告人、立ってください」

三人が、腰をあげた。背中を丸めて、俯いている。

「順番に、本籍、住所、職業、氏名を述べてください。まず、左端の方から」

「ええと……本籍は、神奈川県横浜市、港北区、日吉本町一丁目××番×号。住所は、東京都文京区、本郷三丁目××番×号、サンライズコーポ三〇二、大学生です。名前は、橋本雅巳」

最初に、秀才タイプが答えた。橋本雅巳の声は軽く、深刻な響きはなかった。それどころか、大学の講義で講師の質問に答えているような、媚と甘えがあった。少なくとも俺は、そう感じた。

裁判官が、名前を復唱し、漢字を確認してから、では次の方、と促す。

がっちりした男は須藤典之、は虫類のような男は森陽介、とそれぞれ名乗った。須藤典之は兵庫県、森陽介は富山県に本籍があった。

「検察官、起訴状を朗読してください」

若い検察官が、立ちあがる。

「左記被告事件につき公訴を提起する。公訴事実。被告人・橋本雅巳、須藤典之、森陽介の

　三名は、平成十三年七月九日午後十一時三十分頃、東京都足立区千住旭町三十番の千住旭公園において、二名の未成年女子とともに花火に興じていたところ、東京都足立区日ノ出町×番ひかり荘一〇四号、川尻松子、当時五十三歳に対し、自分たちが屯している公園に勝手に入ってきて、かつ、自分たちを無視していることを生意気と感じて殺害を決意し、集団で殴る蹴るなどの暴行を繰り返して、内臓破裂による失血性ショックを与え、意識を失った被害者を死んだものとみなし、千住旭公園の公衆便所内に放置した。被害者はその後、いったんは意識を取り戻し、自宅まで歩いて辿り着いたが、そこで力尽き、死亡したものである」

「罪名と罰条を」

「罪名、殺人。罰条、刑法第一九九条」

　検察官が、着席した。

　裁判官が、咳払いをする。

「これから審理に入りますが、その前に被告人に注意をしておきます。被告人には黙秘権があります。審理中、被告人は様々な質問を受けますが、答えたくないことは答えなくてかまいません。また話したいことがあるのなら、裁判所の許可を受けて、いつでも話すことができます。ただし、被告人がこの法廷で述べたことはすべて、有利不利に拘わらず、この事件の証拠になるので、よく考えて発言してください。よろしいですね」

三人が、揃わない声で、はい、と応えた。

「では尋ねます。　朗読された公訴事実に、間違いはありませんか？　何か異議があれば、述べてください。　まず、橋本さん」

「あのう……殺すつもりは、ありませんでした。死ぬなんて、思わなかったんです。ただ、遊びの延長のつもりで、みんなで盛りあがっていたから、ついでにちょっと、からかってやろうと思っただけで……。　軽い気持ちだったんです。ほんとうに、あんなことで死ぬなんて……でも、申し訳ないことをしたとは、思っています」

俺は、息を呑んだ。心臓が凍りついた。

なに言ってるんだ、こいつ。

「弁護人はいかがですか？」

弁護人が立ちあがった。あの白髪紳士。

「ただいま被告人が述べましたとおり、殺意については否定します。詳細につきましては、冒頭陳述の際に述べたいと思います」

須藤典之も、同じように、殺意を認めなかった。須藤典之の弁護人を務めているらしい若

い男性も、白髪紳士と同じことを口にした。森陽介も同じだった。判で押したように、殺す

つもりはなかった、軽い気持ちでからかっただけだ、でも、申し訳ないことをしたと反省し

ている、と繰り返した。

「では、被告人は着席してください」

橋本雅巳、須藤典之、森陽介が、軽く頭をさげる。橋本雅巳が、耳の後ろを、指で掻いた。

「ちょっと待てよ」

声が聞こえた。

俺の声だった。

「なにが、申し訳ない、だよ」

「笙さん」

龍さんが、俺の腕をつかむ。

「傍聴人、静粛に」

俺は立ちあがった。

龍さんが俺の身体を抑えた。

「笙さん、落ち着いて!」

「ふざけんじゃねえよっ!」

三人が振り向いた。目を丸くした。

「おまえら、自分が何をしたかわかってんのかよっ！ からかったくらいで人が死ぬかよ、松子伯母さんがどんな気持ちで……おまえらなぁっ！」

「傍聴人に退廷を命じます！」

廷吏が飛んできた。

俺は両腕をつかまれた。席から引き離された。

橋本雅巳、須藤典之、森陽介が、口を開けて、ぽかんとしている。その姿が、遠ざかっていく。小さくなっていく。

「なんとか言え、この野郎っ！」

目の前で、扉が閉じられた。

俺は、法廷の外に、取り残された。煮えたぎった怒りが、行き場を失っていた。俺の身体の中で、荒れ狂っていた。扉に向かって拳を振りあげた。

腕を止められた。

龍さんだった。

「龍さん」

「笙さん」

龍さんが、首を横に振った。

「もう行きましょう」

俺は、龍さんの腕を、振り払った。

「あんな奴を、許すって、言うんですか?」

すんですか?」

声が震えた。

龍さんが、哀しそうな目をした。

「許せない人間を許す。それが……」

「いやだ」

「……笙さん」

「俺は許さない。あいつらを絶対に許さないっ!」

龍さんが、黙ってうなずいた。

俺は、龍さんの横を抜けた。ガラスの扉を押し開けた。廊下を走った。階段を駆けおりた。裁判所から出た。闇雲にアスファルトを歩いた。怒りにまかせて、突き進んだ。どこをどう歩いているのか、わからなかった。しかし、止まらなかった。止まったら、身体が爆発しそうだった。

いつのまにか、陽が沈んでいた。高層ビルの黒い影が、残照に浮かんでいた。車のヘッド

ライトが、列を作っていた。

俺は雑踏のなかを、ひたすら進んだ。人の笑い声。話し声。車のクラクション。ブレーキ音。都会の騒音と喧噪が、すれ違っていく。

悔しかった。

俺は、ただひたすら、悔しかった。

涙が溢れて、前が見えなくなった。立ち止まった。両手で目を拭いた。

そのときだった。

体の中を、風が吹き抜けていった。

俺は、息を止めた。

ゆっくりと、空を見あげる。

いま、たしかに聞いた、と思った。

ことり、という優しい響きを。

あとがき

昭和四十年代の鉄道事情について、貴重な助言をしてくださった川口明彦さんに、この場を借りて心より感謝を申し上げます。

なお、この作品はフィクションであり、作中に登場する人名、地域、施設、省庁および設定等は、実在のものとは一切関係ありません。地方検察庁における公判資料の閲覧手続きについても、実際には作中の描写より時間のかかる場合が多いことを、お断りしておきます。

参考文献

『郷土大野島村史』　武下一郎　非売品
『うれしなつかし修学旅行』　速水栄　ネスコ
『博多チンチン電車物語』　平山公男　葦書房
『なりたい!!　理容師・美容師』　大栄出版編集部　大栄出版
『美容師』　山野靖子　実業之日本社
『トルコロジー』　広岡敬一　晩聲社
『戦後性風俗大系』　広岡敬一　朝日出版社
『東京夜の駆け込み寺』　酒井あゆみ　ザ・マサダ
『逮捕られたらどうなる』　安土茂　日本文芸社
『長い午後』　早瀬圭一　毎日新聞社
『実録塀の中の女たち』　花田千恵　恒友出版
『女子刑務所』　藤木美奈子　講談社

『塀の中のイラスト日記』　野中ひろし　日本評論社

『実録！　刑務所のなか』　別冊宝島編集部　宝島社

『現代ヤクザのウラ知識』　溝口敦　宝島社

『実録シャブ屋』　木佐貫亜城　ぴいぷる社

『特集アスペクト71　シャブQ&A』　アスペクト

『薬物依存』　近藤恒夫　大海社

『うつ病者の手記』　時枝武　人文書院

『愛されて、許されて』　鈴木啓之　雷韻出版

『図解裁判傍聴マニュアル』　鷲島鈴香　同文書院

『生化学辞典第二版』　東京化学同人

『東電OL殺人事件』　佐野眞一　新潮社

『TOKYO OMNIBUS　一人で来た東京』　小林紀雄　リトル・モア

『東京装置』　小林紀晴　幻冬舎

解　説

香山二三郎

　近頃話題のTVドラマといえば、月曜夜九時枠のCX系——いわゆる　"月九"　ではなく、NHK系の韓国ドラマと相場が決まっている。

　その韓国ドラマ人気に火をつけたのは、いわずと知れた　"冬ソナ"。"冬ソナ"　こと『冬のソナタ』は二〇〇二年の初春に韓国で放映された人気ドラマで、初恋を成就させたはずのカップルが男の事故死により破綻、一〇年後、死んだはずの彼とそっくりの男が現われたことから愛が再燃するという悲恋もの。恋人の死、三角関係、親子の秘密に闘病等、ロマンチックの王道をいく物語に、韓国ドラマならではの喜怒哀楽過剰演技や季節の特色を強調した美しいロケ、そして何より主役のヨン様ことペ・ヨンジュンとチェ・ジウ、ふたりの美しさで

話題を呼んだことは記憶に新しいところだ。

美男美女の激しい感情描写で迫るとなれば、自ずとドラマの味わいは濃い口になるわけだが、実は濃い口にかけては日本のドラマも負けてはいない。二〇〇四年初春、午後一時三〇分からのドラマ、いわゆる昼ドラの枠で放映された『牡丹と薔薇』は大河内奈々子と小沢真珠演じる美人姉妹が幼時の不幸な事件で別れ別れになり、やがて富豪の娘とそのお手伝いとして再会するというお話。これまたどろどろの愛憎劇演出で評判になった。

この『牡丹と薔薇』の脚本を担当した中島丈博はその二年前、菊地寛原作の『真珠夫人』でやはり大人気を博したが、してみると日本の通俗恋愛ドラマも元はといえば、韓国ものに優るとも劣らぬ濃い口であったことが察せられよう。むろんTVや映画がない時代から濃い口ドラマを馴染ませてきたのが小説であることは論をまたない。

本書はその古き良き濃い口ドラマの正統をいく本格派小説といえようが、〝冬ソナ〟的な恋愛ものというより、良家の子女が賤しい境遇に落ちていく悲劇の女性ロマンというべきか。良家の子女とか賤しい境遇などというと、半世紀以上前の話かと思われる向きも多かろうが、時代背景は一九七〇年代から今日に至るまで。ばりばりの現代ものというところが、実はミソなのである。

物語は、一九歳の主人公川尻筌が突然現われた父親から伯母の松子が殺されたことを知ら

されるところから幕を開ける。松子の存在すら知らなかった筺は恋人明日香に焚きつけられ、嫌々ながら松子のアパートに後片付けにいくが、その近所でかつて松子と同棲していた元殺人犯の男と遭遇する。明日香は男が落としていった聖書を頼りに居所を見つけようとするが、彼女は何故か、突然帰省宣言をして田舎に帰ってしまう。孤独感に駆られた筺は、松子の境遇を初めて深く慮り、元殺人犯の男を探し出そうと決意、やがてふたりは荒川の堤防で再会を果たす。

そう、川尻松子は嫌われ女どころか、国立大学出身の才媛で、地元福岡県大川市の中学校教師だったのだ。本書は、彼女のその後の軌跡を追う筺の追跡譚と松子の実際の足跡を、ふたりの視点から交互に描いていくスタイルを取っている。筺がつかんだ事実から謎が広がり、その広がった謎を松子の一人称の章が詳らかにしていくという塩梅。そうした演出はミステリー的ともいえようが、それもそのはず、著者はもともとミステリー作家の登竜門横溝正史賞（現・横溝正史ミステリ大賞）の出身。詳しくは後述するとして、ここでは、いちど読み出したら止まらなくなるリーダビリティを生み出しているのは、ふたりの交互の語りを巧みに活かした叙述スタイルに因ることを強調しておきたい。

男は筺に、自分は松子の教え子だったというが……。

さて、ここからは松子の転落内容に多少触れなければならない。**未読の人は、出来たらこの先は本書を読み終えた後お目通しいただきたい。**

才媛の美人教師が最初に直面したのはセクハラの罠。修学旅行の下見先で起きたその事件の犯人は校長で、それも旅行業者と結託のうえ、というのだから始末が悪い。近年教師による性犯罪が報道されるケースが増えているが、ホント威厳とかカンロクとかを楯にしがちな仕事にろくなものはない。もっとも松子は泣き寝入りしたわけではなく、陰で校長をねちねちといじめにかかるのだが、彼女に追い討ちをかけたのは本番の修学旅行で起きた旅館の現金盗難事件。そこで安易に身代わりを演じたことから冤罪を着せられ、校内はおろか、地域全体に汚名が広がってしまう。追い詰められた彼女はついにキレ、博多へ家出、そこから過酷な流転の人生が始まることになる。

その転落劇のポイントを挙げると──

（一）家族の支えがない。

（二）男を見る目がない。

（三）運やツキもない。

（四）人生の方針がない。

等のないない尽くし。松子はとりわけ父親の期待に報いようと勉学に励んできたが、その父の目は病弱な妹のほうに向きがち。彼女にはむしろ厳しく当たっていたのが仇となり、冤罪事件は松子と家族の溝をかえって深めてしまうのだ。その後彼女が風俗の世界で働き出す

となればなおさらで、頑固で偏狭な弟は彼女を救うどころか、縁切りに出る。

次に、家出した彼女が最初につかんだスカが自称太宰の生まれ変わりという絵に描いたような古典的文学青年くずれ。ファザコンのなせるわざか、はたまた教師愛の発露なのか、とにかくその手のクズ男に立て続けに引っかかったことが、風俗世界で働く引き金となる。その風俗世界でも、実のない男の口車に乗り、シャブにはまったあげく、殺人まで犯す始末。逃亡中に妻子を亡くした誠実な理容師と出会えたのはラッキーだったが、ほどなく警察につかまる運命にある辺りは運のなさ、ツキのなさの証しといっていい。

そうしたないない尽くしでいちばん問題なのは、しかし、松子が人生の方針を欠いていることだろう。前述したように、大学を出て教師になったのも父のためだし、男運がなかったり、ツキに見放されたりするのも、元はといえば、人生観の欠如が原因だったりして（そういえば、彼女には故郷の友人も存在しないのか、出て来ない）。見た目清楚なお嬢様は生真面目で世間知らずな反面、物事を短絡的にとらえがちな激情家でもある。型にはまった生きかたがひとたび狂い出すと、アンバランスなキャラクターは暴走しかねない。

いや、ソープ嬢にしろ、美容師にしろ、手先が器用で呑み込みの早い松子は、いったんその仕事に就けば有能なのだ。が、その仕事への執着、キャリアウーマンへの執着があるわけではないので、いったん男にのめり込むと簡単に情に流されてしまう。そこが、たとえば刑

務所で知り合ったAV界の女王!?　沢村めぐみとの違いといえよう。

もっとも、筆者はすべての責は松子にありといいたいわけでは決してない。

女の転落劇といえば、第二次大戦後の混乱期を背景に描いた林芙美子の傑作『浮雲』(新潮文庫他)等を思い浮かべる人もいるかもしれない。考えてみれば、『浮雲』のヒロインゆき子も敗戦後の生活に幻滅、生きる基盤を見失いつつも食べていくために娼婦にまで身を落とし、腐れ縁の男との関係を続ける。一九四七年生まれの松子はいわゆる全共闘世代に当たるが、彼女が学園闘争に参加したという記述はない。そんなノンポリ学生でも、高度成長期からバブル経済、その破綻後の頽廃期へと続く時代の波に翻弄されざるを得なかった。人生基盤を失った彼女もまた、ゆき子と同様、浮雲のように東へ東へと流れ、はかない死を迎える羽目になるのだ。

著者は、破廉恥だがエネルギッシュだったこの当時の時代もまた、松子に過酷な生きかたを強いたことを呈示していよう。

むろん、それは松子を追う川尻笙にも当てはまる。両親に甘え、ガールフレンドと能天気なセックスライフを楽しむだけの軽薄青年だった笙が、もし伯母の死を通過しなかったら、果して自立した社会人として目覚めることはあっただろうか。道徳も倫理も乱れ、犯罪が増加するいっぽうの現代社会。彼もひょんなことから身を持ち崩すことがないとは決していえ

まい。

そう、松子はアナタであり、ワタシでもある。

本書は韓国ドラマに優るとも劣らぬ濃い口の女性ロマンに仕上がっているが、そのいっぽうで、いつ自分の身に起きても不思議のない転落劇のシミュレーションとしても、存分に味わっていただきたいと思う。

著者のプロフィールについても最後に触れておこう。山田宗樹は一九六五年、愛知県犬山市生まれ。筑波大学大学院農学研究科（博士課程）を中退後、製薬会社の研究職に就く。一九九八年、長編『直線の死角』で第一八回横溝正史賞を受賞、デビューを果たす。その後も脳死問題、心臓移植を扱った『死者の鼓動』（一九九九／角川書店）、黒手病という伝染病をめぐるパニックの顛末を描いた医学サスペンス『黒い春』（二〇〇〇／同）と順調に長編を発表。本書は長編第四作に当たるが、ここでは今日的な素材を活かした社会派推理の作風から一転、オーソドックスな女性悲劇に転じてブレイクを果たした。

本書に続く長編第五作『天使の代理人』（二〇〇四／幻冬舎）は妊娠中絶という現代的テーマに沿った社会派系サスペンスに戻っているが、様々な立場にあるヒロインたちを登場させ、過去と現在を往還させつつ、複数のエピソードを並行して描いていくスタイルは本書の

延長上にある。シリアスなテーマ設定はあるいは本書以上に重いかもしれないが、スリリングな展開の先にある結末は感動的。出生率の低下にお嘆きの人ならずとも、お奨めの一冊だ。

———評論家

この作品は二〇〇三年二月小社より単行本として、二〇〇三年六月幻冬舎ノベルスとして刊行されたものを文庫化にあたり二分冊したものです。

幻冬舎文庫

●最新刊
病葉流れて（わくらば）
白川　道

将来に焦燥感を覚えていた梨田が運命的に出逢った麻雀。博打の時だけ生の実感を覚え、のめり込んでいく梨田。そして果てしなき放蕩の日々が始まる――。自叙伝的ギャンブル小説の傑作!

●好評既刊
天国への階段(上)(中)(下)
白川　道

復讐のため全てを耐えた男。ただ一度の選択を生涯悔いた女。二人の人生が26年ぶりに交差し運命の歯車が廻り始める。孤独と絶望を生きればこそ愛を信じた者たちの奇蹟を紡ぐ慟哭のミステリー!

●最新刊
火の粉
雫井脩介

元裁判官・梶間勲の隣家に、かつて無罪判決を下した男・武内が引っ越してきた。武内は溢れんばかりの善意で梶間家の人々の心を摑むが、やがて次々と事件が起こり……。驚愕の犯罪小説!

●好評既刊
ZERO(上)(中)(下)
麻生　幾

公安警察の驚愕の真実が日中にまたがる諜報戦争とともに暴かれていく――。逆転に次ぐ逆転、驚異の大どんでん返し。日本スパイ小説の最高峰、文庫化!

●好評既刊
童話物語(上)(下)
向山貴彦・著
宮山香里・絵
(上)大きなお話の始まり
(下)大きなお話の終わり

世界は滅びるべきなのか? 決定を下すために来た妖精は観察相手に極めて性格の悪い孤独な少女を選んでしまった……。圧倒的筆力と世界観で"冒険と成長"を描く感動のファンタジー。

嫌われ松子の一生（下）

山田宗樹

平成16年8月5日　初版発行
平成18年5月20日　20版発行

発行者───見城　徹

発行所───株式会社幻冬舎
〒151-0051東京都渋谷区千駄ヶ谷4-9-7
電話　03（5411）6222（営業）
　　　03（5411）6211（編集）
振替00120-8-767643

装丁者───高橋雅之

印刷・製本───図書印刷株式会社

万一、落丁乱丁のある場合は送料当社負担で
お取替致します。小社宛にお送り下さい。

定価はカバーに表示してあります。

Printed in Japan ©Muneki Yamada 2004

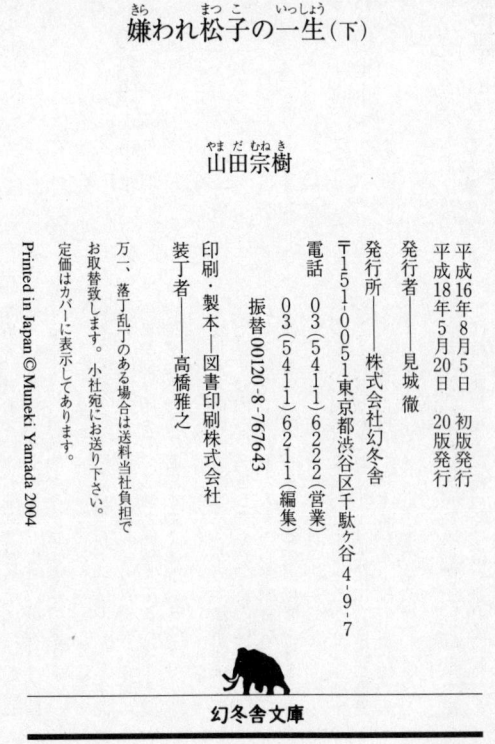

幻冬舎文庫

ISBN4-344-40562-5　C0193

KAT
MARTIN

Heart of
Fire

MIRA®

MIRA

ISBN-13: 978-0-7783-2452-2
ISBN-10: 0-7783-2452-4

HEART OF FIRE

Copyright © 2008 by Kat Martin.

To children everywhere.
May they all find love, joy and peace.

One

London, England
January, 1844

An icy drizzle hung over the churchyard. The gravestones stood dark and unreadable in the shadows of the high rock walls of St. Michael's Church.

Gowned in layers of heavy black crepe, her face hidden beneath the veil of a wide-brimmed black bonnet, Coralee Whitmore stood next to her father and mother, the Viscount and Viscountess of Selkirk, listening to the drone of the bishop's words but not really hearing them.

In the casket beside a mound of damp earth, her sister's body lay cold and pale, retrieved only days ago from the chilly waters of the Avon River, the victim of a suicide, the authorities claimed. Laurel, they said, had jumped into the river to hide her shame.

"You're shivering." A stiff wind ruffled the viscount's copper hair, the same fiery shade as Coralee's. He was a man of average height and build whose imposing presence made him seem much larger. "The bishop has finished. It is time we went home."

Corrie stared at the casket, then down at the long-stemmed white rose she carried in a black-gloved hand. Tears blurred her vision as she moved forward, her legs stiff and numb beneath her heavy black skirt, the veil on her hat fluttering in the cold February breeze. She laid the rose on top of the rosewood casket.

"I don't believe it," she whispered to the sister she would never see again. "Not for a single moment." Corrie swallowed against the painful, choking knot in her throat. "Farewell, sweet sister. I shall miss you ever so much." Turning, she walked toward her parents, the father both sisters shared and the mother who was Corrie's alone.

Laurel's mother had died in childbirth. The viscount had remarried, and Corrie had been born soon after. The girls were half sisters, raised together, always close, at least until the past few years. Then Corrie's job as society editor for *Heart to Heart,* a London ladies' gazette, had begun to absorb more and more of her time.

Laurel, who had always preferred the quiet life of the country, had moved in with her aunt Agnes at Selkirk Hall, the family estate in Wiltshire. The girls kept in touch through letters, but in the last year even those had grown sparse.

If only I could turn back time, Corrie thought, the lump in her throat swelling, becoming even more painful. *If only I could have been there when you needed me.*

But she had been too busy with her own life, too busy attending the balls and soirées she wrote about in her column. She'd been too self-absorbed to realize Laurel was in trouble.

And now her sister was dead.

* * *

"Are you all right, Coralee?"

Standing in the Blue Salon of the Whitmores' Grosvenor Square mansion, Corrie turned at the sound of her best friend's voice. Krista Hart Draugr walked toward her across the drawing room, where the pale blue damask curtains had been draped with black crepe, as had the brocade sofa and Hepplewhite chairs.

Corrie reached beneath her heavy black veil to brush a tear from her cheek. "I'll be all right. But I miss her already and I feel so…responsible."

Most of the mourners, few in number because of the circumstances of Laurel's death, were in the Cinnamon Room, a lavish salon done in gold and umber, with huge, sienna marble fireplaces at each end. An extravagant buffet had been set out for the guests, but Corrie had no heart for food.

"It wasn't your fault, Coralee. You had no idea your sister was in trouble." Krista was blond, fair and tall; taller, in fact, than most men, except for her husband, Leif, a blond giant of a man who towered over his wife and actually made her look small.

One of the handsomest men Corrie had ever seen, he stood across the drawing room in conversation with his brother, Thor, who was dark instead of fair, nearly equal in size and, in a fiercer way, even more handsome.

"I should have grown suspicious when her letters dwindled to nearly nothing," Corrie said. "I should have known something was wrong."

"She was twenty-three, Coralee. That is two years older than you, and she was very independent. And she wrote you from Norfolk, as I recall."

Last summer, Laurel had traveled to East Dereham in

Norfolk to live with her other aunt, Gladys. Along with
Allison, a cousin about Corrie's age, they were the only
relatives on her mother's side that Laurel had. Laurel had
never gotten along with Corrie's mother, but her aunts,
both spinsters, loved her like a daughter, and Laurel had
loved them.

"She wrote to me from Norfolk, yes, but only on rare
occasions. We had just resumed a serious correspondence
last month, after her return to Selkirk Hall."

According to the Wiltshire County constable, when
Laurel was in residence at Selkirk, she had gotten herself
with child. Agnes had kept Laurel's secret until her pregnancy began to show, then sent her north to live with
Gladys until the baby was born.

Corrie looked up at Krista, who stood a good six inches
taller than she, a buxom young woman with lovely blue
eyes, while Corrie was small-boned, with eyes a vivid
shade of green. Krista was a mother now, but she still ran
the gazette, a magazine for ladies that was well known for
its views on social reform.

"The police believe she committed suicide," Corrie said.
"They say she took the child she had carried in her womb
for nine long months and jumped into the river because she
couldn't bear the shame. I don't believe it. Not for a moment. My sister would never harm anyone, much less her
own baby."

Krista's gaze held a trace of pity. "I know you loved her,
Corrie, but even if you are right, there is nothing you can do."

Corrie ignored the feeling those words stirred. "Perhaps
not."

But she wasn't completely convinced.

She had been thinking about the circumstances of her
sister's death since news of the tragedy had arrived—her

sister drowned, remnants of an infant's blue knit sweater clutched in her hand.

Corrie had been devastated. She loved her older sister. She couldn't imagine a world without her in it.

Dreadful things were being said about Laurel but Corrie refused to believe them. Laurel's death could not possibly have been suicide.

In time, surely the truth would be unearthed.

Two

London
Three Months Later

The offices of *Heart to Heart* weekly ladies' magazine were located in a narrow brick building just off Piccadilly. Corrie had begun working at the gazette shortly after Margaret Chapman Hart had died and her daughter, Krista, had taken over the business, running the company along with her father, Professor Sir Paxton Hart. Last year, Krista had married Leif Draugr, now the owner of a successful shipping enterprise, and nine months later had borne him a son, but Krista still worked most days at *Heart to Heart,* her pride and passion.

As Corrie entered the office in search of her friend, she spotted Bessie Briggs, the typesetter, working to get the big Stanhope press, the soul of the gazette, ready for the next edition. Bessie looked up and smiled but kept on working, paying no attention to the dismal black mourning clothes Corrie had worn for the past three months and would wear for three months more.

Corrie tapped on the open door to Krista's ground floor office.

Her friend looked up and smiled. "Since you rarely knock, I assume this must be important. Come in, Coralee."

Her stiff black skirts rustled noisily as Corrie moved to close the door behind her. "I have something I need to discuss, and since you are my very best friend…"

Krista eyed her with speculation. "What is it?"

Corrie sat down and smoothed a nonexistent wrinkle from the front of her skirt. "I've tried to put Laurel's death behind me, but the fact is, I simply cannot. I have to find out the truth, Krista. I've never believed Laurel killed herself and her month-old child, and I am going to prove it."

Krista's features softened. "I know losing your sister has been hard on you. I know that in some way you feel responsible. But Laurel is gone and there is nothing you can do to bring her back."

"I realize that. But I failed her once when she needed me, and I will not do so again. My sister did not kill herself, which means someone else must have done it, and I intend to discover who it was."

One of Krista's blond eyebrows arched. "And how, exactly, do you plan to do that?"

"I shall start by doing some investigating right here in London. I am good at that, am I not? It is part of my job to unearth both facts and tidbits of gossip for my column."

"Yes, but that is hardly the same."

"I think it is exactly the same. I intend to go over every letter my sister wrote before she died and look for clues." Corrie glanced up, a fierce light coming into her eyes. "Then I shall leave for the country. I'm going to find out who fathered Laurel's child, and then I will know where to start looking for the answers to how and why she died."

Learning the name of the father was an important piece of the puzzle, the man her sister must have loved. Not even Aunt Agnes knew who he was. According to her, Laurel had adamantly refused to divulge his identity.

"You don't need to worry about the gazette," Corrie continued before Krista could speak. "I already have a temporary replacement in mind. Assuming you approve, I shall ask Lindsey Graham to fill in for me while I am away." Lindsey was a school chum, a former classmate at Briarhill Academy, where Krista and Corrie had met.

"Lindsay is currently penning textbook articles," Corrie said, "and extremely bored, I think. Her father is a baron and very well connected so she is able to move freely about in society. I believe she will handle my job very well."

"I imagine she could, but—"

"Actually, I considered hiring Lindsey while you and Leif were gone off to his dreadful island." Corrie smiled. "Running this place without you was a nearly impossible task. I have never been so happy in my life to see anyone return."

Leif and Krista's story was a well-guarded tale. That the big man and his brother had come from an uncharted island far north of Scotland where people still lived as Vikings was, at best, totally incredible and better left unsaid.

All that mattered was that Leif had found Krista and she had found him, and they loved each other desperately. Corrie wondered if the right man would ever come along for her.

Which returned her thoughts to her sister. In Laurel's early letters from Selkirk, she had mentioned meeting a man. She had described his many virtues and said how much she enjoyed his company. Corrie intended to review the letters, see if there might be a description, something that might help her find out his name. Who had stolen Laurel's heart, taken her virtue, then abandoned her?

Corrie wondered if the man who had fathered Laurel's child would have gone so far as to murder them.

"You can't be serious, Coralee. Tell me you do not intend to dredge up this painful affair all over again." Agnes Hatfield sat on the rose velvet settee in a small salon near the back of the Whitmores' town mansion, a room done in white and rose, an elegant, feminine salon that overlooked the garden. Three days ago, the black crepe strung round the room had been removed after three long months of mourning.

"I realize it will take some doing, Aunt Agnes, but I have given the matter considerable thought and I have no choice but to act."

Aunt Agnes, which Corrie had always called her though they were not actually blood-related, was a lady in her sixties, plump and silver-haired, and until the death of her beloved niece, always smiling. Seated next to her, Laurel's cousin, Allison Hatfield, a thin young woman with a razor-straight nose and pointed chin, very dark hair and hazel eyes, listened to Corrie with obvious trepidation. Allison's parents had died of cholera, leaving her in the care of her aging aunt.

At the viscount's invitation, both of the women had elected to remain in the city rather than return to Selkirk Hall and the awful memories the place still held for them.

"So you intend to begin some sort of investigation?" Aunt Agnes asked.

"Yes."

Allison made no comment. She was a shy, unobtrusive young woman rarely inclined to disagree with anything anyone said. Which was perhaps the reason she had agreed to leave East Dereham and accompany Laurel on her return to Selkirk Hall, pretending to be the baby's mother.

Or perhaps it was because Allison was tired of scraping by on her aging aunt Gladys's generosity, and Laurel had promised her a goodly sum and a better future in exchange for her help with the child.

"I do not believe for an instant the authorities' version of what occurred," Corrie said, "and after months of consideration, I have decided to act. I plan to take whatever steps are necessary to discover the truth of what happened to my sister. Aunt Agnes, you and Gladys helped Laurel. Now you must help me find out what happened to her and her baby."

Allison pulled a lace-trimmed handkerchief from her reticule and dabbed at her eyes. She had been as fond of Laurel and her month-old infant, Joshua Michael, as Agnes, who also dug out an embroidered square of cotton and blew her powdered nose.

The older woman took a fortifying breath. "I will help in any way I can…though perhaps my helping your sister is what, in the end, got her killed."

Corrie's eyes widened. "So you do not believe it was suicide, either! And if she did not take her own life, someone *must* have killed her. Laurel and the child were victims of foul play. It is the only explanation."

From her place on the rose velvet settee, Allison's soft voice whispered across the room. "There is a chance…I cannot say for certain…but it is possible that Laurel may have been meeting someone the night she disappeared. She wouldn't tell me where she was going, but she was excited. I didn't realize she had taken the baby until later, when I went into the nursery and saw his cradle was empty."

Corrie felt a rush of sadness that brought the sting of tears. She purposely leaned into the stiff bone stays of her corset, and the tiny jolt of discomfort set her back on course. "Please…we must try to stay focused."

Agnes blew her nose. "You are right, of course. We have all cried more than enough. And we can hardly find justice for my dear, lost angel by sitting here weeping."

Corrie's gaze fixed on dark-haired Allison. "Did you tell the authorities that Laurel might have been meeting someone the night she died?"

"It didn't seem important at the time. The constable said she had jumped into the river. The week before it happened, she had been a bit distraught, though she wouldn't tell me why. When the constable arrived with the terrible news, I thought perhaps… I accepted the constable's explanation for what had occurred."

Corrie made a mental note to find out what had upset her sister the week before her death. "You've had three months to consider, Allison. Do you still believe Laurel killed herself?"

She shook her head. "At the time, I was so distressed I could scarcely think straight. Laurel and baby Joshua were gone and nothing else mattered."

"Well, it matters to me," Corrie said. "And it would matter to Laurel. Are you certain, Aunt Agnes, my sister gave no clue as to the name of the man who fathered her child?"

"None whatsoever. I'm an old woman. I paid little attention to my niece's comings and goings."

"What about men who might have paid calls at the house?"

"Oh, there were a few who stopped by now and then. Squire Morton's son Thomas paid an occasional visit. The vicar's son…oh, dear, what is his name? It will come to me in a moment…. At any rate, the boy stopped by on occasion, as well."

"Anyone else?"

"Well, yes. Castle Tremaine is nearby." In fact, it was the estate closest to Selkirk Hall. "Lord Tremaine paid his respects whenever he was in residence, occasionally accompanied by his cousin. His brother, Charles, and his sister-in-law, Rebecca, paid an occasional call, and they always stop by at Christmastime each year."

Corrie frowned as bits of information came together in her head. "Lord Tremaine, you say?"

"Well, yes. He always calls at least once when he is in the country, but he never stays overly long."

Grayson Forsythe, Earl of Tremaine. The name stirred memories of the man who had come into the Tremaine title five years ago. Corrie had never seen the earl, who seemed to keep a good deal to himself, but she had heard he was tall and incredibly handsome. The man had a wicked, extremely sordid reputation when it came to women, and in her gossip column, "Heartbeat," Corrie had alluded more than once to rumors of his many affairs.

And if memory served, the earl was often in residence at Castle Tremaine, where his brother and sister-in-law made their home.

"I can see what you are thinking," Agnes said. "I will admit the earl is attractive, but he is also a dark, rather brooding sort of fellow. I cannot imagine your sister would be interested in a man like that." She glanced away. "Laurel was always so bright and fun-loving, such a warm-hearted, spirited young girl." Her eyes teared up and she used her handkerchief again.

Corrie felt a crushing weight in her chest. "Perhaps

you're right," she said, determined not to let her emotions rise to the surface. "But from the gossip I have heard, the man is quite ruthless when it comes to women. I imagine if he wanted to seduce an innocent young girl, it would be easy enough for him to do."

"Perhaps." Agnes fought to bring her own emotions under control. "But I just cannot…" She shook her head, her silver eyebrows drawing together. "His cousin, Jason, is quite dashing. He is also in residence much of the time. I suppose if I were to guess—" She broke off again. "I am sorry, Coralee, but I simply cannot imagine any of the young men who paid calls at the house murdering our dear, sweet Laurel and her innocent little baby. That is what you are thinking, is it not?"

"It's a possibility. Perhaps the man she fell in love with did not love her in return. Perhaps he did not wish to be forced to marry her."

"And perhaps she simply went for a walk that night and was waylaid by footpads. Perhaps they tried to rob her, but when they discovered she had no money, they tossed her and the child into the river."

It was a notion Corrie had already considered. "I suppose that could have happened. Anything seems possible at this point in time, except that Laurel would kill herself and her child."

"Coralee is right," Allison said softly, from where she perched like a bird on the edge of the sofa. "Laurel loved little Joshua with every ounce of her being. She would never have done anything to hurt him. And she was so clearly determined that no one would find out the identity of the father. It does make one wonder…."

Corrie nodded. "It does indeed."

Aunt Agnes eyed her warily. "I am loath to ask, but I

suppose I must. Tell us, Coralee, what exactly is it you propose to do?"

She stiffened her spine. At the moment she wasn't certain. But she was going to do *something*. Of that she was completely sure.

Excited at her discovery, Corrie climbed the steps of *Heart to Heart* and opened the heavy front door. As she walked into the long, narrow printing area, she spotted Krista coming out of the back room, heading for her office. Corrie followed her and hurriedly closed the door.

"Krista—you are not going to believe what I've found!"

Her friend whirled toward her, apparently not aware until then that Coralee had entered. "So you are still digging. I know you are determined to come up with something to validate your belief that Laurel was murdered, but are you sure your sister wouldn't rather you simply accepted her death and got on with your life?"

"They say she killed her own child. Do you believe my sister would want the world to believe she did something as heinous as that?"

"The police found no sign of robbery, Corrie. There were no incriminating marks on the body."

"She had been in the water for several days when she was found. The constable said it was impossible to tell exactly what had happened, and there *was* a bruise on the side of her head."

"Yes, and if I recall, the constable believed she must have hit her skull when she fell into the river. The police believe the baby drowned and simply washed out to sea."

"And I say the police are wrong. Laurel was killed by someone who didn't want the secret of the child's birth known, or had some other nefarious motive."

Krista sighed. "Well, there have certainly been murders committed for far less reason than preventing some sort of scandal."

"Yes, and when Agnes mentioned the Earl of Tremaine, I began to think. Some years back, I'd heard gossip about him. He was whispered about at a number of affairs, and I even made mention of his scandalous reputation once or twice in my column. I decided to go back through some of our older editions. Lady Charlotte Goodnight wrote the "Heartbeat" column in the days when your mother ran the paper. I took a look at those."

For the first time, Krista appeared curious. "What did you find?"

"The articles mentioned the gossip I had heard, said the man was a complete and utter rogue where women were concerned. They called him a 'sensualist,' a master of the art of love. Apparently, Grayson Forsythe was a major in the army before he inherited the title. He spent several years in India before his older brother fell ill and he came back to assume his duties as earl."

Krista smiled. "Sounds like an interesting man."

"Yes, well, I suppose you might say that. But as I was reading about him, I remembered something else."

"And that was…?"

"This morning I went down to the magistrate's office and searched for records filed under his name and there it was—the certificate of his marriage to Lady Jillian Beecher three years past."

"Now that you mention it, I remember hearing something about that. But Tremaine is a bachelor—one of the most eligible in London. What happened to his wife?"

"That is the point I am trying to make. I did some more digging, spoke to some of my sources, very quietly, of course. I discovered that the earl was married less than a year when Lady Tremaine died. The countess was the daughter of a wealthy baron, an heiress worth a good deal of money. She died leaving the earl with a sizable increase in his fortune—and he was free again, able to continue his sensual pursuits."

"I don't think I ever heard the story."

"I believe the family kept the matter fairly quiet." Corrie's eyes gleamed. "And since that is the case, what you also don't know is that Lady Tremaine *drowned,* Krista— right there in the Avon River!"

Three

A cool spring breeze floated through the open windows of the carriage as it rumbled toward the village of Castle-on-Avon, a small, picturesque market town surrounded by rolling green fields and thatch-roofed cottages. On a knoll near the edge of the village, Selkirk Hall loomed majestically over twelve hundred acres of rich grassy earth. A structure three stories high, it was built in the Georgian style, of golden Cotswold stone.

Coralee, Aunt Agnes and Allison were returning to the country in Agnes's carriage, not the viscount's fancy four-horse rig. Corrie couldn't risk her father's coachman telling him she had left the carriage before its arrival at Selkirk Hall. In fact, she meant to depart at the Hen and Raven, a nearby coaching inn, where she would hire a room for the night and continue to her destination as a different person in the morning.

It had been less than a week since Corrie had come up with her outrageous plan. Three days ago, she had presented it to Aunt Agnes and Allison.

"It will work—I know it will!"

Aunt Agnes had twisted her handkerchief in her plump hands. "I don't know, Coralee...it sounds extremely dangerous."

"To begin with, no one is going to know who I am," Corrie explained. "I shall pretend to be Letty Moss, the wife of Lord Tremaine's very distant cousin Cyrus. Letty is destitute in the wake of her husband's abandonment, and desperately in need of the earl's help." A story that could likely be true.

Corrie had run across the information during her research on the earl and his family. Through a friend who knew a friend who knew one of the earl's distant cousins—a man named Cyrus Moss—she had learned that Cyrus had left his much younger wife in residence in York and set off for America to make his fortune. After two years, Cyrus had not yet returned.

According to her source, Lord Tremaine had never met Letty Moss and knew little of his very distant cousin. The information gave Corrie the perfect means of getting into Castle Tremaine. Doing so, she believed, was the only way to discover if Lord Tremaine was the father of Laurel's child, and if so, whether he might be responsible for her and little Joshua's death.

"It will work, I tell you. It has to."

Aunt Agnes had fretted and argued, but in the end she had agreed to the plan. If Corrie could discover the truth of what had happened to her beloved niece, then she would go along with her scheme.

Corrie watched the landscape passing outside the carriage window—rolling hills beneath shadowy clouds, an occasional barking dog, a merchant's cart pulled by a tired-looking horse.

"I don't see how this can possibly succeed," Aunt Agnes grumbled from the opposite side of the carriage. "Surely someone from Selkirk Hall or someone in the village will recognize you."

"I haven't been to Selkirk since I was twelve years old. Mother and I both prefer London to the country. Whenever Laurel and I wished to visit, my sister always came to the city."

To distance herself even further from events at Selkirk, Corrie had decided to come out of mourning. She didn't want anyone connecting her to Laurel's death, and wearing those dreadful black garments just might put the notion in someone's head.

Corrie didn't think her sister would mind. She believed Laurel would rather the truth be discovered than that her younger sister mope about in dismal black, doing nothing to clear her name.

Agnes cast Corrie an inquiring look. "You are determined to discover the truth, but what if that truth turns out to be something you do not wish to learn?"

There was certainly a chance facts would surface that Corrie would rather not know. She would have to trust that Laurel was an innocent seduced into the affair, as Corrie believed she was.

"I'll deal with that circumstance should it arise."

"And the danger?" Agnes pressed. "If the earl is truly a murderer, what will stop him from also killing you?"

Corrie waved her aunt's worry away, though the thought had crossed her mind. "I told you, Tremaine will not know who I am. Besides, if he did murder his wife, he did it for money. And if he murdered Laurel and Joshua, he did it to keep his freedom, or perhaps to protect his family from scandal. As I am merely a destitute relative there for a visit, he would have no reason to murder me."

"And I will be there with her," Allison added softly, referring to the role she had agree to play: Corrie's maid.

"That's right. Allison will act as my liaison with you should any problem arise."

Fortunately, during the time Allison had been at Selkirk with Laurel, she had been pretending to be a widow with a newborn child. She had been dressed in mourning clothes and had never gone into the village, which meant she was safe from recognition at Castle Tremaine.

Agnes released a deep sigh. "I hope you two know what you are doing."

So did Corrie. At least she knew the Earl of Tremaine was in residence at Castle Tremaine, and had been for several weeks. Agnes had told her the man had been at the castle at the time of Laurel's death, and for several months before that. Lately he seemed to be spending even more time in the country.

Perhaps he had found a new victim on whom to ply his seductive skills.

Ignoring her companions, Corrie turned to look out the window and caught sight of the inn up ahead, the Hen and Raven. A tremor of nervous anticipation flitted through her. She was still gowned in black, her face hidden beneath a veil of black tulle, and would be until she left the inn on the morrow.

Then she would be dressed in the clothes of a gently reared young woman fallen on hard times, clothes Allison had collected from the local rag merchant: several slightly worn traveling suits, well-worn muslin day dresses, and a number of unimpressive but serviceable dinner gowns with barely frayed cuffs and soiled hems.

Though the gowns were not at all the sort she was used to wearing, in a way Corrie didn't mind.

Anything would be better than the dismal black that reminded her how she had failed her sister.

Four

⤜∽⊱♡⊰∽⤏

Ignoring the creak of leather as he shifted in his saddle, Grayson Forsythe, sixth Earl of Tremaine, surveyed his estate, the lands surrounding Castle Tremaine.

All the way to the low stone wall on his left, past the dense copse of trees in the distance, to the river running along the perimeter on the right, fields of gently rolling hills, verdant with the new grass of spring, beckoned as if whispering his name. Beneath him, his big black stallion, Raja, pranced and sidestepped, eager to continue the ride they had begun early that morning. Almost as eager as Gray.

For the past ten days, the only peace he could find came from riding the hills, escaping the confines of the house, escaping his family…and the memories. Every year, as the dreaded day drew near, the past began to haunt him like a specter.

May 19, the day his pretty young wife, Jillian, had died.

Gray nudged the stallion down off the hill, into a ground-eating gallop. Wind tugged at the thick black hair he wore unfashionably long and tied back in a queue, and fluttered his full-sleeved, white lawn shirt.

Out here, he could examine the memories and wash them clean, know they would eventually fade, as they did every year. Back at the castle, which stood next to the river where she had died, it was nearly impossible to do.

Gray rode for the next hour, reached the far edge of his property, turned the stallion and began to walk the horse at a cooling pace back toward the house.

In time, the memories would leave him. Day-to-day problems with his tenants and his fields, Tremaine account ledgers, and the businesses he had inherited along with the title, would engage him once more, and the past would return to its place in the corner of his mind. But May 19 was almost a week away.

Gray steeled himself and urged Raja toward the ancient castle on the hill next to the river.

Corrie stared through the window of the shabby carriage she had hired at the Hen and Raven. Up ahead, at the end of a long gravel drive, Castle Tremaine perched on the top of a hill like the fortress it had once been. Inside the thick stone walls she would find Grayson Forsythe, the man who might well have murdered her sister.

"Are you certain about this, Coralee?" Allison leaned toward her, her hands clasped nervously in her lap. "Aunt Agnes could be right, you know. We might be putting ourselves into dreadful danger."

"It's Letty or Mrs. Moss. You must remember, Allison, to call me that. And they have no reason to harm us. They are going to think I am a destitute relative. And if something happens that gives us the least reason to believe we might be in danger, we shall leave in very short order."

Allison smoothed her simple printed cotton skirt, even worse for wear than Corrie's pale blue gown trimmed with ecru lace. Though the lacy overskirt had been carefully mended, it was clearly past time for the garment to be replaced. Corrie adjusted the matching blue-and-ecru lace bonnet, ignoring a soiled spot that barely showed on the lower edge of the brim.

Like the rest of the clothes in her trunks, the well-worn dresses had been altered to fit. She looked just as one would expect—like a distant country cousin in need of a wealthy relative's aid.

With a lurch that nearly unseated them, the carriage rolled to a halt in front of the huge stone structure that was Castle Tremaine. Though the moat had been filled and planted with daffodils, the ancient building modified over the hundreds of years since its construction, the castle was impressive, with huge carved doors and two-story wings added onto each side of the high round keep that had once been the center of life there.

The Forsythe family had a respectable fortune—increased by the timely demise of Grayson Forsythe's wife.

The coachman helped Coralee and Allison from the rented carriage, tossed down their trunks, then climbed back up onto the driver's seat. "Ye want I should stay till yer settled, missus?"

Corrie shook her head. "We'll be fine. I am his lordship's cousin, you see, here for a visit." And she wanted the carriage to leave so there would be no way the earl could toss them out on their shabbily dressed derrieres.

She collected herself, gave the coachman a moment to set the carriage into motion, then heard the fading jangle of the harness as the conveyance disappeared down the long gravel drive. Ignoring the rubbery feeling in her knees, she climbed the steps to the majestic carved wooden door.

A few sharp raps and a butler, dressed immaculately in black tailcoat, black trousers and snowy white shirt, pulled open the heavy portal.

"May I help you?"

Corrie pasted on a smile. "I am here to see Lord Tremaine. You may tell him Mrs. Moss—Letty Moss, his cousin Cyrus's wife—is arrived to see him."

She wasn't sure the earl would even recognize the name, was hoping it rang only a distant bell.

"I'm afraid his lordship is not in at the moment, but his brother, Charles, is here. I shall inform him of your arrival. If you will please follow me."

The gray-haired butler, thin to the point of gaunt, led her and Allison into a drawing room that was furnished in quite a tasteful manner. It was done in a neoclassical style, with ornate white molded ceilings, a marble fireplace and graceful sofas and chairs upholstered in amber tones brightened with rich ruby accents.

Allison sat down in one of the chairs, her gloved hands clasped nervously in front of her. Corrie silently prayed the girl wouldn't completely dissolve into a fit of nerves before the first act of the drama had played out.

Seating herself on the brocade sofa, Corrie kept her smile carefully in place and waited, then rose at the swish of heavy skirts and the sound of feminine footfalls approaching down the hall. Allison rose, as well. Corrie could see she was fighting not to tremble.

A woman with golden-blond hair, parted and pulled into a cluster of glossy curls on each shoulder, swept into the drawing room. She had very blue eyes and a strikingly beautiful face. She surveyed the two women and, noticing Corrie's gown was simple and slightly frayed, but of better quality than Allison's, sharpened her gaze accordingly.

"Mrs. Moss, I presume?"

"Yes. Mrs. Cyrus Moss. My husband is Lord Tremaine's cousin."

"And this is your maid?"

"Yes…Miss Holbrook." Allison dropped into a curtsy, which the woman ignored. "I am here to speak to the earl on a matter of some importance."

"Lord Tremaine is not returned from his morning ride. As my husband is presently occupied, perhaps I could be of some assistance. I'm Rebecca Forsythe. If your husband is the earl's cousin, then he must be Charles's cousin, as well."

"Why, yes. It is a pleasure to meet you, Mrs. Forsythe." Corrie flicked a glance at Allison. "Perhaps my maid might wait in the kitchen so that we may speak in private."

"Of course." Rebecca called for the butler. "If you would, Mr. Flitcroft, show Miss Holbrook down to the kitchen for some refreshment. And bring tea and cakes for us."

Corrie kept her smile in place. She had been hoping to speak to the earl. Ultimately, it would be Lord Tremaine who would decide whether or not she would be allowed to stay. But she could hardly ignore this woman, who was her supposed cousin Charles's wife. Corrie would have to tell her story and hope to gain the woman's sympathy.

Allison cast her a worried look and followed the butler out of the drawing room. Corrie returned to her place on the sofa and Rebecca joined her there.

The blond woman smiled. She was incredibly beautiful, no more than five or six years older than Corrie, with a full bosom and very small waist. She was wearing a gown of aqua dimity with a full skirt heavily embroidered with roses.

"I'm afraid I've never met Cousin Cyrus," Rebecca said. "But I believe Charles had a distant acquaintance with his father. Where did you say you lived?"

"Cyrus and I make our home in York...though unfortunately, he has been away for more than two years. That is the reason I am here."

"I'm afraid I don't understand."

Corrie thought of Laurel, which helped her work up a tear. She pulled a handkerchief from her reticule and dabbed it beneath her eyes. "This is all so dreadfully embarrassing."

"Just take your time," Rebecca said encouragingly.

"I met Cyrus through friends of my parents, and in the beginning of our marriage, we were happy. Being older by nearly twenty years, he doted on me. Perhaps he loved me too much and that was the problem. You see, Cyrus had very little money, only what he inherited from his father, and that seemed to dwindle quite rapidly once we were wed. But Cyrus was determined to give me the things he believed I deserved."

Rebecca's blue gaze drifted over Corrie's worn garments. "And where is Cyrus now?"

"Well, you see, that is the crux of the matter. Cyrus wished to give me the best of everything—which is the reason, I suppose, that he left England and headed for America to make his fortune. Cyrus had plans, very big plans, and he had friends there he believed would help him."

"I do seem to recall Charles mentioning a distant cousin who left England for America in search of adventure."

Corrie nodded vigorously. "That was Cyrus. According to his letters, he arrived there safely. Then his letters stopped coming. I haven't heard from my husband in nearly two years."

"I am sorry to hear that, Mrs. Moss."

"Even worse than losing Cyrus, my funds have run out. Frankly, Mrs. Forsythe, I am quite destitute. I am here to humble myself and beg the earl to offer me shelter. If he refuses, I don't know what I am going to do." She dabbed the handkerchief again, ready to break into sobs if she thought it would help.

Rebecca began to frown. It was not a good sign. "You are not asking to take up residence *here,* are you?"

"Well, I—"

Just then voices drifted in from the stone-floored entry. One Corrie recognized as belonging to the butler, but the other was deeper, more resonant.

"I believe the earl has returned," Rebecca said, rising gracefully from her place on the sofa. A faint knock sounded as she floated across the drawing room, and an instant later, the butler slid open the door.

"His lordship is returned," the gray-haired man said. "I have informed him of his visitor."

Corrie still sat on the sofa.

It was a very good thing.

The man who walked through the door was not at all what she had expected. This man, with his black hair tied back in a queue, was dressed not in a tailcoat and trousers, but mud-spattered black riding breeches, black knee-high boots and a full-sleeved white shirt. With his fathomless dark eyes, he looked more like an eighteenth-century high-wayman than a wealthy English lord.

"Gray! I was hoping you would return. We have a guest, just arrived—your cousin Cyrus's wife, Letty Moss."

Those piercing eyes swung in her direction and seemed to hold her prisoner there on the sofa. "I didn't know I had a cousin Cyrus."

"I'm sure Charles has mentioned him. He is the son of your deceased third cousin, Spencer Moss. Spencer lived near York, as did Cyrus, if I recall. Mrs. Moss has come quite a distance to see you."

Tremaine didn't apologize for his rather disheveled appearance, simply turned and made a faint bow in her direction. "Mrs. Moss. Welcome to Castle Tremaine. Now, if you will excuse me, there are several pressing affairs I need to—"

"I should like a word with you, my lord." She rose from the sofa. "It is a matter of some importance and I have traveled quite far."

One of his black eyebrows arched up. It was clear he wasn't used to a woman speaking out as she had just done. For a moment he simply stared, as if taking her measure in some way.

The edge of his mouth faintly curved. "I suppose… since you have traveled, as you say, quite some distance, I can spare a moment." There was something in that hard-edged smile that made her stomach lift alarmingly.

Tremaine turned to his sister-in-law. "If you will excuse us, Becky…"

Rebecca's smile slipped. "Of course." She retreated toward the sliding doors, but didn't look happy about it. Corrie got the distinct impression the earl's sister-in-law wasn't pleased to think his impoverished distant cousin might move into the house, no matter how large it was.

The earl waited until the butler closed the drawing room doors. "You wished to speak to me. What can I do for you, Mrs. Moss?"

He didn't invite her to sit. It was clear he didn't expect the interview to take that long. Corrie steeled herself against a hint of irritation, followed by a rush of nerves. The earl was even more handsome than rumors about him had said. He was very tall and extremely broad shouldered, with a flat stomach and long, muscular legs clearly outlined by his snug black riding breeches. Looking into those penetrating dark eyes, she found it easy to imagine an innocent young woman like her sister succumbing to such sheer masculinity.

"It is difficult to know where to begin…." Corrie gathered her courage and prepared to get into her role.

"Just tell me why you're here, Mrs. Moss."

Fine. So much for the long, heartrending performance she had planned to give. "Well, my lord, to put it bluntly, your cousin Cyrus—my husband—left me high and dry and ran off to adventure in America. I have waited nearly two years for his return and still have received no word of him. I have no family, no one to help me. I have spent my last farthing getting to Castle Tremaine, my lord, and I am desperate for your help."

Those dark eyes traveled over her, taking in her simple garments, the tatters that had been carefully repaired, making a thorough assessment of her bosom, which was quite full for her size and apparent even in a gown that was buttoned to the throat.

"As I said, I have never heard of Cyrus Moss. I do not doubt that he is some distant relation, since my sister-in-law has said so, but how do I know you are actually his wife? For that matter, how do I know he even has a wife?"

She had come prepared for this. According to her sources, Grayson Forsythe was a highly intelligent man. He'd been a major in the army, a man who had traveled to far distant countries. He would not be the sort to be easily duped.

Corrie reached into her reticule and pulled out two folded pieces of paper. The forged marriage certificate hadn't been cheap—or easy to come by. But she *was* in the newspaper business and she had some very good connections.

She crossed to where he stood and handed the papers

to the earl, hating the fact she had to tilt her head back to look at him.

"The first document is a certificate of my marriage to Cyrus Moss three years ago, which was duly recorded in the church. The other is a letter from Cyrus, addressed to me as his wife and posted to me from the city of Philadelphia in America."

She had worked on that bit of tomfoolery herself, writing the letter with the heavy pen strokes of a man.

The earl perused the letter, reading where Cyrus professed his love and promised to return. Happily for Corrie, her sources assured her he hadn't yet set foot on English shores.

"Cyrus met your father on several occasions," she said as he finished and refolded the papers. Corrie hoped her information was correct. "I believe my husband held a high opinion of the man. Since the late earl is no longer with us, I am coming to you for help."

Tremaine frowned at the mention of his father, and she wondered if there had been some ill will between the two men. He seemed none too pleased as he handed back the documents, and Corrie held her breath.

Finally, he sighed. "If you will follow me into the study, I will write you a bank draft and you can be on your way." He turned and started walking.

Corrie fought a surge of panic. "Wait!"

Lord Tremaine turned. His attention fixed on her face and she felt again that odd floating in her stomach.

"I said I would give you money. What more do you want?"

Her eyes welled with tears. It wasn't that hard to do since her plan was about to fail. "I—I am in need of a place to stay, my lord—but only for a while. In a few weeks' time, I shall come into a small inheritance. My father set

up a trust, you see. When I am two-and-twenty, I shall be
eligible for a monthly stipend that will see to my comfort.
It isn't much, but it should be enough to keep me in
simple fashion until Cyrus returns."

The earl's slashing black eyebrows drew together.
"Your father and mother are dead, then? You have no one
else who might aid you?"

"As I said, I have no living relatives. It is one of the reasons I married Cyrus. With no one to look out for me, I
needed his protection. Unfortunately, his protection
didn't last all that long."

"How long were you and Cyrus together before he
left?"

"Just a little over a year."

The earl studied her for several long moments.

Corrie took a deep breath, her eyes tearing as she prepared
to release a wailing sob she hoped would add a bit of per-
suasion. The earl held up his hand to forestall the outburst.

"There is no need for that. You may stay…at least until
I can figure out what to do with you."

Her face lit up. She gave him a watery smile, brightened
by an inward surge of relief. "Thank you, my lord. I shall
be forever in your debt."

He merely nodded. "I'll speak to Rebecca, tell her we'll
be entertaining our *cousin* for a while."

"This is very kind of you, my lord. I'm sure Cyrus
would be even more grateful than I am."

Tremaine ignored the remark, turned and started for
the door. As soon as he stepped out of the drawing room,
Corrie sank down on the sofa, her legs no longer willing
to hold her up.

She had done it! She had managed through a bit of deception to weasel her way into Castle Tremaine! As soon

as she was settled, as soon as the Forsythe family had begun to let down its guard and trust her, she would begin her search.

Corrie's lips thinned. Gray Forsythe might be one of the handsomest men she had ever met, but that didn't mean he was innocent of murder. And if he had killed her sister and baby Joshua, the Earl of Tremaine was going to pay.

Gray stalked through the halls, his ill humor worse than it was before he left the house. He wasn't exactly sure how it had happened, but somehow, during her appearance in his drawing room in her mended garments, during the minutes she had looked up at him so pleadingly with her thick-lashed, jewel-green eyes, he had let down his guard and allowed a woman he had never met move into his house.

He didn't understand it. He had seen through her theatrics from the start, the false tears and wringing hands, the beseeching looks and trembly voice. But during her performance he had also caught a flash of something that intrigued him. He thought it might be desperation, for he was certain that was there, but this seemed more like determination. Whatever it was, it had interested him enough to let her stay.

Gray shook his head. For all he knew, Letty Moss was a charlatan, there to cajole him out of his money, rob him or worse.

He thought about the petite young woman with the fiery copper curls peaking out beneath the soiled brim of her bonnet, and almost smiled. He had been a soldier, a man who'd commanded troops in the British Army. If she gave him any trouble, he would simply toss her out on what held the promise of being a very attractive derriere.

The thought stirred him in a way he didn't expect. Since Jillian had died, he had slept with few women. It was his conscience, he knew, that kept him from indulging more in the pleasures of the flesh he so enjoyed, guilt that he was alive and Jillian was not. That he had not been there to protect her when she'd needed him.

He looked up to see Rebecca approaching down the hall.

"I hope you were a gentlemen about it," she said with a smile. "I realize she hoped you would let her stay here at the castle, but—"

"She's staying."

"What!"

"It won't be for long. She'll soon come into a monthly stipend that should be enough to provide for her until her husband returns."

"But…but we don't even know her. How can you simply let her move in?"

The smile he gave her was sardonic. "You are always chiding me about my manners. It would be the height of bad taste to toss a member of our family in need of assistance out into the street."

"Yes, but I thought you would give her money, not invite her to move in."

Though Rebecca was tall for a woman, Gray looked over her shoulder toward the massive, carved wooden staircase leading up to the floors above. "There are two separate wings and seventy bedrooms in this house. Put her somewhere she won't bother you."

"But—"

He started walking. "I won't be down for supper. See that our guest has something to eat." Rebecca generally ran the household, another reason he was surprised by his actions today. On the other hand, he *was* the earl, which his family seemed mostly to forget. Perhaps it was time he made the matter clear.

Gray continued down the hall, suddenly desperate to get back outside in the sunshine, away from the thick stone walls of the house. He wondered again why he had offered the woman his protection.

Undoubtedly, it was nothing more than boredom.

Still…

Five

"I cannot believe you actually did it." Allison perched on a tapestry stool in front of the dressing table in the bedroom they had been assigned. It sat at the farthest end of the east wing of the house, a room that had not been refurbished, as had most of the other bedrooms Corrie had passed along the corridor.

The massive carved four-poster bed was a remnant of some lost century, and the Persian carpet was faded. The tassels on the dark green velvet draperies were frayed in several places, the curtains themselves so heavy they blocked the sun.

Still, it would do and quite nicely, since its distant location would also make it easier for Corrie to move about the house without being seen. She surveyed her quarters. The sheets on the bed were clean and, at her request, an adjoining room had been prepared for Allison, who was a companion, Corrie had explained, as well as her lady's maid.

Corrie felt a shot of triumph that they had succeeded thus far.

"I don't think your dear cousin Rebecca is happy to have another relative in the house," Allison said, lifting one of Corrie's mended gowns out of the trunk and hanging it in the rosewood armoire in the corner.

"Apparently not." But it didn't really matter. Corrie was there and she meant to stay until either she had the answers to her questions or she was forced to leave.

"So what do we do now?"

She had given the matter a good deal of thought. "To begin with, since you are supposed to be a servant, I am hoping that the upper-staff will eventually accept you, and perhaps you will be able to get them to talk a bit about the scandal at Selkirk Hall. Laurel's death would be commonly known hereabouts, though Father did his best to keep the fact of the child a secret after the medical report was made. There is always gossip in a household this size. If Laurel was involved with the earl, perhaps one of them will know."

"That is a very good notion, Cor—I mean, Letty."

"And I shall seek out the people who live in the house. I have yet to meet Charles. I was invited to supper, but I declined. I didn't wish to seem too eager. And I wanted a bit of time to compose myself, perhaps take a stroll round the house. In the meantime, why don't you go down and have some supper? I'll see you before I retire."

Allison left the bedroom, and Corrie, dressed in a more comfortable gown of printed blue muslin and leaving her bonnet behind, followed the carpet along the hall to the stairs at the end of the east wing. By now, supper was under way and she could move about without causing a stir. Still, she didn't want to appear as if she might have some ulterior motive—which of course she did.

With her nerves still strung taut from her encounter

with the earl, she decided to go out to the garden. Descending a narrow staircase at the end of the hall, she pushed through a door into the cool night air. It was pleasant outside the house, and she was, she discovered as she moved along the terrace, in desperate need of a calming breath of air.

The first thing she noticed was how different it was in the country at night. The air was so clean and fresh, with not a particle of soot in the gentle breeze blowing over the landscape.

She hadn't been to the country in so many years it had never occurred to her to notice, not until tonight. Even house parties she attended had been, for the most part, held in homes at the edge of the city. Out here, the stars were so bright she could make out the constellations she had learned to name at Briarwood Academy. There was Orion, she saw, silently picking out each star, and the Big Dipper.

She wondered if Laurel had looked at the stars with Grayson Forsythe.

The thought darkened Corrie's mood. She stepped off the terrace and began to meander along one of the paths. The garden was lush, the leaves of the thick green plants flowing over the gravel walkways lit by burning torches. There were no gas lamps out here, as there were in her father's garden in the city, and somehow she liked the way the light flickered yellow and orange and cast dancing shadows against the leaves.

Corrie wandered the rambling paths, trying to collect her thoughts, plan her next move. She was rounding a corner of the path when she suddenly bumped headlong into a tall figure she hadn't seen standing in the darkness. Sucking in a breath, she scrambled to keep from falling.

A big hand shot out and caught her round the waist, pulled her upright before she took an embarrassing tumble.

"Easy."

Her stomach jerked at the sound of the deep male voice. Her gaze traveled upward, over a broad chest, up even farther to the dark, probing eyes of the earl.

"What are you doing out here?" he asked with a hint of accusation in his tone. "Why aren't you at supper?"

"Why aren't you?" she countered, wishing the man was anywhere except here. She caught herself. She wasn't a reporter doing a job; she was playing a role and she had better remember that. "I mean, I wasn't really hungry and I needed some air. It was a long ride in the carriage. I didn't think you would mind."

He studied her a moment, then turned his gaze toward the fountain bubbling a few feet farther down the path. "You enjoy being out-of-doors?"

Not really. She enjoyed dancing in lavish ballrooms, attending the opera, the theater, and dining in fine restaurants. At least she had until tonight.

"It's extremely pleasant out here. I never realized how clean the air would be."

One of his sleek black eyebrows went up. "I spoke to Charles. He said that from what he recalled, Cyrus Moss lived on a farm."

Oh, dear Lord. "Well, yes…yes, of course, but…but there were animals, you know…and they smelled quite unpleasant, all those cows and sheep." What in the world was the matter with her? She sounded like a complete and utter ninny. Then again, it was probably better that way. The less intelligent she seemed, the less threatening she would appear.

Tremaine's gaze narrowed a moment, then the corners

of his lips edged up—full sensuous lips that sent a funny little shiver into her stomach. "Somehow I have trouble imagining you tending a flock of sheep."

Never had a truer statement been made. She wished she'd had more information on Cyrus. It simply wasn't available, at least not quickly enough. "Well, I didn't do *that* sort of thing. Cyrus was very protective. He barely allowed me outside the house."

"I see. How long did you say you and Cyrus were together?"

What had she told him before? Sweet saints, she couldn't recall. "It was not quite a year."

For an instant his eyes seemed to sharpen, and she was terrified she had said the wrong thing.

"I suppose you miss him," the earl continued mildly, and she relaxed once more into her role.

"Why, yes, of course I…" She meant to continue the lie, then decided it was wiser to stay closer to the truth. She would hardly miss a man who had left her high and dry as Cyrus had done! "That isn't completely true. I know I should miss him, since he is my husband, but Cyrus was much older than I, and after the way he abandoned me, it is difficult to feel more than resentment toward him."

"I can understand your feelings." The earl's gaze assessed her, moved along her throat and over her bosom, down to the span of her waist, a slow, thorough perusal that made it suddenly hard to breathe.

"You…you do?" He was standing close enough that she could feel the heat of him, the power in his tall, masculine frame.

He was wearing a clean white shirt and a pair of black trousers fitted closely, as was the style, but no coat or waistcoat. His hair was clubbed back as it had been before.

Corrie realized he was a man who paid little heed to convention. Combined with the rumors she had heard, it made him terribly intriguing.

She didn't think he was wearing cologne, and yet she caught the faint, pleasant scent of sandalwood, and wondered at the source. The fragrance seemed to wrap around her, fill each of her senses, and she trembled.

"You're cold. Perhaps you should go back inside."

She swallowed. "Yes…yes, I believe that's a good idea." But she wasn't cold in the least. In fact, she felt overly warm. He made a faint bow, his black hair gleaming in the light of the torches, and she felt a strange pull low in her belly.

"Good night, Mrs. Moss."

She stepped backward as if to protect herself. "Good night, my lord." Then she turned and started down the path.

She was used to men's attentions. She was the daughter of a viscount, after all, and though she was a bit too outspoken, perhaps a bit willful, she knew that when she was ready for marriage, she would not lack for suitors. She enjoyed the company of men, had never been afraid of a man before, yet now, as she fled the garden, Corrie had to force herself not to run.

Gray watched the petite young woman with the fiery curls hurrying off down the garden path. In the light of the torches, she was lovely—skin as smooth as glass, luminous green eyes, and a lush mouth the color of roses. She was a beautiful woman, small but elegant, the sort to make a man think of silk sheets and even silkier thighs, though Gray suspected that perhaps she did not truly know that.

Still, she was not at all what she wanted him to believe, and that made him wary.

Gray made a rude sound in his throat. She had told him she'd lived with his cousin for more than a year, then said it was less. It was obvious she had never lived in the country, to say nothing of on a farm. Who was she? he wondered again.

For the past two years, since Jillian had died, Gray had felt restless in a way he never had before. The few women he had bedded had given him little satisfaction, just a few brief hours of sexual relief. He felt as if he had no purpose, no direction.

When he had first inherited the earldom, he'd had so much to do he'd had little time to think, had been exhausted at the end of each day. There was a great deal to learn about being an earl, and Gray had enjoyed the challenge. He had enjoyed his life, and his bachelorhood. He'd had any number of mistresses back then, and though he had tired of them easily, he always saw them well settled when the brief affair was over.

Then he'd been introduced to Jillian. She was young and beautiful, though a little too shy and a bit more reserved than perhaps he would have liked. But it was time he took a wife, time he did his duty and provided an heir, and Jillian and her family had seemed eager for the match.

Ten months later his wife was dead and he was once more alone.

Gray moved silently along the west wing hallway toward the master's suite. Since Jillian's death, he'd grown more and more restless, prowling the estate, searching for something but unable to discover what it was. With the arrival of the woman, for the first time in weeks he felt his interest piqued. Letty Moss posed a mystery and Gray meant to solve it.

He reached his suite, pulled open the heavy carved door and went into the rooms that had belonged to his father. The sitting room, with its gold velvet draperies and dark oak furniture, stirred unpleasant memories and somehow weighed Gray down. He walked on through, his mind returning to Letty Moss and what he might discover about her.

"Good evening, *sahib*." His manservant, Samir Ramaloo, walked out of the bathing chamber adjoining the bedroom. Wisps of steam from the marble tub, prepared for Gray's nightly bath, followed in his wake.

"Good evening, Samir." The small, dark-skinned man had been Gray's manservant in India during the three years he had served there in the army. Each officer kept a full retinue of servants, staff necessary for surviving the hot, arid, demanding climate.

With his impeccable service, Samir had made himself indispensable. He had also become Gray's teacher, introducing him to the customs and conventions of the exotic land, and giving him the insight to appreciate a country so different from his own. More than a servant, Samir was his friend—and the wisest man Gray had ever known.

"Your bath is ready, sire," he said now, glancing up with eyes so black they looked like bottomless pits.

Gray merely nodded and continued past him toward the marble bathing room.

"Your mind is far away," the Hindu said, knowing him well enough to sense that something was on his mind. "You think of the woman. I saw her this morning when she arrived and again tonight. She is very beautiful."

"Yes, she is." She was lovely, like a perfectly modeled porcelain doll. Likely with the same empty head. She had presented herself as a young wife married briefly, then abandoned by her husband. Gray knew women, and as skittish as this one was, he was sure she had barely known the touch of a man, and probably had never known fulfillment.

It made her story somewhat convincing, and yet he believed there was far more to her tale.

Interesting. That was Letty Moss.

Samir helped Gray disrobe, then stood aside as he stepped into the steaming water and settled his shoulders against the back of the marble tub.

"It is said the woman is your cousin."

Gray scoffed. "By marriage, and so far distant the relationship is meaningless."

"She has no husband?"

"She's married. The man left her penniless and went off to seek his fortune."

"Ah, then she is in need of a protector—and you are in need of a woman. You ignore the desires of the flesh, but they gnaw like a beast inside you. Perhaps you can give this woman what she needs and she will do the same for you."

"She has a head full of feathers," he said, trying to convince himself Samir's words held no appeal, "and she is not what she seems."

"Ah, a puzzle for you to solve. That is what makes her interesting."

"She is that. I'm not sure why she's here, but I intend to find out."

"That is good. Then you can allow yourself to pleasure the woman and enjoy her yourself. I will see what I can learn that might be of use."

Gray made no reply. He needed to keep a close eye on his so-called cousin, make sure she didn't cause any problems. Samir's watchful gaze might be helpful.

Whatever her story, Gray would soon find out the truth.

And perhaps, as Samir suggested, once he knew it, there

could be other, more intimate things about Letty Moss he might find out.

Corrie's heart pounded madly as she hurried along the hall toward her bedroom. She didn't like the feeling at all. She reached her room, pulled open the door, and found Allison waiting inside.

"I thought you might need help getting out of your gown," she said.

"Thank you, Ally." Though she could certainly use the help with her buttons and corset, Corrie wasn't all that happy to find the dark-haired girl there. Not while her own mind was still swirling, replaying those unsettling moments with the earl in the garden.

"Did you find out anything useful?" Allison asked as she crossed the room.

"What…? Oh, no, I just went for a walk outside." Coralee hadn't discovered a thing, except that Grayson Forsythe had a very worrisome effect on her.

She turned so that Allison could work the buttons at the back of her gown. "The earl was there. He didn't go to supper with Rebecca and his brother."

Allison's head snapped up. "You spoke to him out in the garden?"

"Why, yes."

"That is the second time you've met him. What is he like?"

Corrie bit her lip. How to describe the earl? "He is…the earl is a most unusual man. Besides being handsome in the extreme, there is something about him…. I cannot quite grasp what it is. He is very intense and has a decided air of mystery about him."

Allison helped her out of her dress and tossed it onto the bed. "Do you think he might commit murder?"

A shiver ran through her. "I am not sure. But he is a big man and clearly strong enough to accomplish such a feat if he wished. He is a man of the world, and certainly the sort to attract a woman. I'll need to investigate him further, and of course, we must find some proof that he and Laurel were involved."

Allison began to loosen the strings of her corset and Corrie drew in a welcome breath.

"You are just arrived," her companion said. "In time, you will find out the truth."

"I certainly hope so." Time was what she needed. She had to find answers about Laurel, answers about the earl.

Which meant spending more time in his company.

Corrie ignored the odd rush of heat that thought filtered into her stomach.

The morning was blustery, the breeze whipping the newly leafed branches on the trees outside the windows. Needing a moment to fortify her courage, Corrie stood outside the door to the breakfast room she had been directed to by one of the servants, a small, very thin, dark-skinned man.

Speaking with an accent unlike any she had ever heard, he'd told her his name was Samir. When she asked him where he came from, he'd said he was from the Oudh District of India, that his family was no longer living and he had come to England with Lord Tremaine.

A manservant from India. More and more the earl intrigued her. She could think of no one of her acquaintance who was anything like him.

Corrie walked into the breakfast room, a cheery place done in yellow and peach, with a table loaded with gold-rimmed porcelain and gleaming silver. Delicious smells rose from an elaborate sideboard covered with silver chafing dishes and steaming urns of coffee and tea.

"Good morning, Cousin." A handsome blond man spotted her and rose from his chair. Charles Forsythe was shorter than his brother, and as fair as his wife instead of dark like the earl. Tremaine followed suit and rose as well, but more slowly, with a casual sort of insolence that seemed to be part of his nature.

"I'm your cousin Charles," the blond man continued. "You've already met my brother, Gray, and my wife, Rebecca."

"Why, yes. It's good to meet you, Cousin Charles. Good morning, everyone." She didn't look at the earl. She didn't like the oddly disoriented feeling she experienced whenever she did.

"Do join us," Charles said. "You must be hungry. You missed supper last evening."

She managed a smile. "Yes, I discover I am ravenously hungry this morning."

She dared a glance at Tremaine, saw his eyes darken with something she couldn't read, and continued over to the chair Charles pulled out for her.

"You're beginning to settle in?" he asked. "Your maid has found the kitchen and acquainted herself with our servants?"

"Yes. It is very kind of you to allow me this visit."

Charles smiled. He had very white teeth and hazel eyes, and though he was not as imposing as his brother, he was a very attractive man. "I'm sure Becky will enjoy the chance for female companionship."

But when Corrie glanced at Rebecca, the tight smile she received made it clear that Cousin Becky wished Letty Moss had never arrived at Castle Tremaine.

Breakfast continued with pleasant conversation, Charles being as charming as his older brother was not. Tremaine said little, but she could feel his eyes on her, and the sensation sent nervous tremors through her core. There was something about him…. And yet the more she was around him, the less she could imagine her sister enjoying his company, let alone falling in love with him.

Laurel had always been sweet and terribly shy. A man like Gray Forsythe would have frightened her, not charmed her. But perhaps there was another side of the man that Corrie had not yet seen.

The earl had arrived earlier than the rest of his family and was nearly finished with his meal by the time a servant filled a plate for her and set it down on the table. Obviously, the man was an early riser. He finished the last of his eggs, cast her a final glance and excused himself from the group. The minute he disappeared from the breakfast room, the pressure in Corrie's chest began to ease.

She took a deep breath and released it slowly, fixed her attention on Charles and Rebecca, and joined in their light conversation.

"I'm afraid I have a prior engagement this afternoon," Rebecca said. "Perhaps tomorrow we'll have a chance to get to know each other a bit."

"That would be nice," Corrie said, not at all looking forward to the event. Still, getting to know Rebecca Forsythe might lead to information about Laurel and the earl.

As the meal continued, neither Charles nor Rebecca mentioned Letty's missing husband, Cyrus—a blessing, since Corrie knew almost nothing about him.

As soon as everyone finished, she excused herself and returned upstairs. Since Rebecca had dodged her company, Corrie intended to take advantage of the time she had to her-

self and walk to the village. It wasn't that far, and she was
ready to begin her investigation. She hadn't been to Castle-
on-Avon since she was a girl. No one would recognize her
and she was anxious to discover what she might find out.

Changing into a day dress of apricot muslin, and grabbing her shawl, straw bonnet and reticule, Corrie set off
for the village.

Six

A blustery wind blew the fringes of her shawl, but her full skirts and petticoats kept her legs warm. Corrie was enjoying her walk along the trail more than she had expected, noticing how green the fields were, how the wildflowers seemed to dance in the breeze. She was shading her eyes to get a better view of the copse of trees on the horizon when she saw him, a tall male figure mounted on a huge black horse.

Silhouetted against the sun, dressed in the sort of riding breeches and full-sleeved shirt he had worn yesterday, his hair tied back as before, the earl seemed out of time and place, as if he should have lived a hundred years ago.

The moment he spotted her walking along the path, he turned the stallion and began a leisurely gallop in her direction. The beautiful horse effortlessly climbed the rise to where she stood, and the earl drew the animal to a halt a few feet away.

"Mrs. Moss. I thought you would be spending the afternoon with Rebecca. Instead you are out for a stroll." He smiled, but it didn't look sincere. "You appear to be enjoying yourself."

"Why, yes I am." The words came out in an embarrassingly breathy voice and she stiffened her spine. "Your sister-in-law was busy and I was glad for a chance to get a little exercise. It's a bit windy, but the sun is warm, making it a perfect day for a walk in the countryside."

He frowned, his sleek black brows drawing together. "Where is your maid?" His voice held a hint of disapproval that sent her irritation up a notch.

"The village isn't that far, and need I remind you, my lord, I am a married woman."

His mouth barely curved. "You needn't remind me, Mrs. Moss. I have imagined you often in that manner." He said it as if he meant something else, but she couldn't quite figure out what that could be.

"I'm afraid I had better be going," she said. "I have some shopping to do and I don't wish to be late in my return."

"Perhaps I should accompany you—just to be certain you are not accosted."

"No! I mean, no thank you. I shall be fine on my own. Good afternoon, my lord."

Corrie continued walking, trying to ignore the butterflies swirling in her stomach. She couldn't figure out why the man affected her as he did, but she didn't like it. And she certainly didn't want him to go with her. She had questions to ask, and she could hardly do so with the earl tagging along.

As she continued along the trail, she dared a glance over her shoulder, saw that he was riding the opposite way, and breathed a sigh of relief. Turning her thoughts to the questions she meant to ask, she increased her pace toward the village.

The moment Letty Moss disappeared from view, Gray pulled Raja to a halt and spun the stallion in the opposite

direction. Staying as far back as he could, careful to keep
from being spotted, he followed the woman into the village. He saw her walk into one of the shops across from
the market square and while she was inside, rode to the stable.

"I won't be long," he told one of the stable boys, hand-
ing him the horse's reins and flipping him a coin. "Take
care of him till I get back."

Returning to High Street, the main street of town, he
spotted Letty coming out of the shop and stepping into the
one next door. As soon as she was inside, Gray made his
way to the window. Inside the shop, she examined bolts of
cloth, fingering the colorful swatches of silk with tender
care. Then she made her way toward the clerk. He watched
the two women talking, but couldn't hear what was being
said.

Letty left the shop and went into the butcher's store,
from which she soon exited munching on a piece of ham.
Next she stopped by the hatmaker's. Letty didn't seem to
be buying much, just having a look around, but then if her
tale was true, she had very little money.

She appeared to be having no illicit meetings, no rendezvous with a man, nor was she doing anything that might
give Gray pause.

He told himself to return to the house and leave the
woman alone, but something held him back. Instead, he
waited the nearly two hours Letty remained in the village,
then retrieved Raja and followed her home.

He watched her walking along the path through the tall
green grasses, her hips swaying as if to some silent song.
His groin tightened. He couldn't believe such an innocent,
unconscious movement could stir him that way. He nudged
the stallion forward, eager to catch up with her.

She must have heard hoofbeats behind her, for she whirled toward the sound and her foot caught on an unseen obstacle in the grass. She went down with an unladylike yelp, falling backward over a big granite boulder. Her skirts went into the air and her frothy white petticoats flew up to her chin.

Gray found himself grinning. He couldn't remember the last time he had done that. He sobered, pulled Raja to a halt on the path, and swung down from the saddle.

"Here—let me help you."

She slapped away the hand he offered, shoved down her skirts and propped herself up on her elbows, her knees still draped over the rock. "I don't need your help. You are the reason I am in this humiliating position in the first place."

"How is it I am at fault because you tripped?" He reached down and caught her wrist, hauling her somewhat awkwardly to her feet.

She didn't bother to answer, just cast him a look that said it was true. The ribbons on her bonnet had come undone and her hat tumbled into the grass. Her glorious copper hair came loose on one side and hung down in a riot of curls against her shoulder. Gray fought an urge to tangle his fingers in the heavy mass and haul her mouth up to his for a kiss.

It was insane. He barely knew the woman, and he definitely didn't trust her. Perhaps Samir was right about denying himself for too long. He made a mental note to pay a visit to Bethany Chambers, wife of the aged Earl of Devane, whose country home, Parkside, was just beyond the next village. Gray had heard the countess had returned for the summer. Though he hadn't seen her in several months, she was a woman of strong appetites, and he knew she would welcome him into her bed.

Letty began to brush off her dress, drawing his atten-

tion to the bosom straining against her bodice. He tried not
to wonder if her breasts were as full and tantalizing as they
appeared, or how they might feel in his hands. Letty made
no comment, just turned to begin her journey back along
the path, then winced as her ankle crumpled beneath her.
Gray caught her before she could fall.

She looked up at him with those jewel-green eyes. "I—
I think I twisted my ankle."

"Sit down on the rock and let me take a look."

Letty sat carefully and Gray knelt in front of her. He
picked up her foot, slid off her low-heeled leather boot and
began to gently examine her ankle.

"What…what are you doing?"

"I was in the army. I want to make sure nothing's broken." Her stockings had holes, he noticed, though they
had been carefully mended. At least part of her story appeared to be true. She was certainly in need of money.

"It is only twisted," she said, trying to pull the sprained
limb free of his grasp. "I'm sure it is fine."

Gray didn't let go. "Hold still, will you? You're only making this harder." It wasn't the only thing getting hard. As he
ran his hand over the fine bones in her feet, his groin tightened. Gray set his jaw against the unwanted arousal and continued to test each tiny bone, feeling for possible injury, trying
not to think what it might be like to slide his hand upward,
over the smooth silk stocking that covered a very shapely calf,
all the way to the slit in her drawers, then inside to touch—

He clamped his jaw against a shot of lust and the painful throbbing of his erection. Silently he cursed. He needed
a woman and badly, and though this one fired his blood,
he could not have her. Not yet.

He felt her trembling and realized he still cradled her
small foot in his hands.

Gray cleared his throat. "I don't think there are any broken bones."

"I told you, I am fine."

He slid her boot back on and tied the laces, carefully helped her up from the rock. She took a step and nearly fell. "Oh, dear."

"You need to keep your weight off that ankle. You'll have to ride home with me."

He didn't give her time to argue, just scooped her up in his arms and settled her in the saddle, one leg on each side of the horse, her full skirts bunching around her knees. Raja danced and sidestepped as Gray swung up behind her, but Letty didn't seem to be afraid. At least not of the horse.

"What a beautiful animal," she said, trying to keep her balance without touching him.

Gray almost smiled. It wasn't going to happen, and since he had no choice but to see her safely home, he might as well enjoy himself. He wrapped an arm around her waist and nudged the stallion forward. Letty tried to scoot away, and nearly unseated them both.

"I would advise you to sit still, Mrs. Moss, before we both wind up on the ground."

She glanced at him over her shoulder. "What are you doing out here? I thought you were returning to the castle."

"Lucky for you, I wasn't ready to go home just yet."

She turned, tilted her head to look up at him. "You weren't following me, were you?"

"Now, why would I do that?"

Letty made no reply, but her wariness did not lessen. They rode silently along the trail until the horse started up a rise and Letty began to slide backward in the saddle. She grabbed a handful of the stallion's thick mane to hold herself in place, but it did no good, her bottom coming to a snug rest between his thighs. Even through the fabric of her skirt and petticoats, he could feel the heat of her, the roundness of her flesh, and he went hard just thinking of the soft, womanly curves beneath her gown.

"I hope I'm not making you too uncomfortable," she said.

Uncomfortable? Good God, he ached with every heartbeat. "I'm afraid that is an understatement."

She started to move, squirming to put some distance between them, making him harden even more. Gray stifled a groan. "Hold still, dammit. Just stay where you are."

Letty's head came up. "You don't have to swear. If you will recall, this is your fault in the first place."

She had accused him of that, he remembered with a hint of amusement. "Sorry, I forgot."

They didn't talk again until the castle came into view. Gray rode directly up to the front, where a groom stood, waiting to take the reins. Gray swung from the saddle, then reached up to lift Letty down, finding her waist was so small his hands wrapped completely around it.

"Thank you," she said softly. He noticed she was breathing a little too fast, and figured he must be right about her. Her experience with men was obviously limited. Cyrus was a much older man. Perhaps his desire for a woman had declined with his years.

As Samir suggested, perhaps Letty's needs would surface, and if that happened, Gray would be delighted to oblige. At least he would be once he had assured himself she was no threat to him or his family.

He looked down at the top of her head, at the fiery curls resting against her small shoulders, and fisted his hands to keep from reaching out to touch them. She might not be a woman of great intellectual capacity, but she set fire to his blood, and should she wind up in his bed, he wouldn't waste time talking.

She looked up at him as he lifted her against his chest to carry her up the front steps, and another surge of lust hit him like a fist.

Holy God. Samir was right. It was past time he took a woman. He would send a note to Bethany Chambers. Gray just hoped he would receive her reply very soon.

In her quilted satin robe, Coralee sat in the middle of the massive four-poster bed, her legs tucked up beneath her. She had babied her ankle for the past few days, and the limb seemed to have fully recovered. Perhaps she owed some thanks to Gray Forsythe, but she didn't want to think of him now.

Instead, she fixed her attention to the bundles of pale pink letters, bound with pink satin ribbon and carrying traces of Laurel's favorite perfume, that rested on the faded counterpane. Corrie had brought the letters with her from London, all that remained of the sister she had loved.

An ache throbbed in her heart as she reached for a bundle, each letter filed by the date of its arrival. She located the two stacks she had received in the past eighteen months, and untied the first one. Last year, her sister had been living at Selkirk. In August, she had journeyed to East Dereham in Norfolk to spend time with Agnes's older sister, Gladys. There was only one letter written each month during the time she'd been there.

Corrie now knew she'd been pregnant, growing heavier each day with the child she carried. Her time must have been absorbed with thoughts of the babe, and yet she'd been afraid to tell even Corrie about the infant she would bring into the world.

Corrie's eyes misted as she reread one of the letters, this one dated March 20, when Laurel had been preparing to leave Selkirk Hall.

> *I feel restless and uncertain. I had such dreams for the future and now they seem sullied, darkened by pain and despair. And yet I have known love. I cannot tell you how that feels. Love makes the parting worth the sadness.*

Corrie remembered receiving the letter. She had penned a reply, asking her sister about the man she had fallen in love with, and why they couldn't marry if the two of them cared for each other. She had also asked the man's name.

Laurel's next letter had not come until a full month later, after her arrival in East Dereham. She had ignored Corrie's questions and instead talked about life on her aunt's farm.

Corrie had assumed her sister's infatuation had faded and that she hadn't been truly in love. Corrie's own life was so busy the subject never came up again. Instead, sparse as they were, Laurel's letters grew more and more cheerful. On September 18, she'd written:

> *Though it is autumn, it is sunny today, with warm bright rays filtering through the branches of the trees outside my window. Orange and yellow leaves are beginning to fall and I can hear birds singing, the hum of crickets in the dry fall grasses. Lately, the world seems somehow brighter, and I find myself awakening each day with a sort of wonder at all God has created.*

As Corrie looked back, she found it clear, from the difference in the first letters and those coming later, that something in Laurel's life had changed. Now Corrie knew that her sister was expecting a child, and it was obvious from her letters how much she looked forward to being a mother, how much she looked forward to the future.

A lump swelled in Corrie's throat to think how very short that future had turned out to be.

She finished rereading the letters but found no clue to the man Laurel had loved.

Was Gray Forsythe that man? When Corrie was around him, she found it hard to think. It was as if he had some sort of magic power, some mysterious quality she found nearly impossible to resist. Had Laurel felt it, too?

Corrie thought of the afternoon two days ago she had spent in the village. While pretending to shop, she had begun a subtle investigation into Laurel's death. She had casually mentioned the young woman from Selkirk who had drowned in the river several months back and, as always, people were eager to gossip.

"She done kilt herself," the butcher's wife said. "They say she lost her innocence to some man and couldn't stand the shame she brought down on her family." The rawboned woman shook her head. "Don't seem right for a young girl to meet such a tragic end."

At the hatmaker's shop, the story was the same—though it was clear her father's attempt to hide the secret of Laurel's illegitimate child had failed.

"It must have come as a terrible shock to his lordship...findin' out his daughter weren't pure as the driven snow the way she seemed." As the heavyset woman worked on the hat she was making, she leaned over the counter. "There were a babe, I hear," she whispered. "Drowned right along with her."

Corrie felt a wave of sadness followed by a jolt of anger that the villagers should think the worst of someone as sweet as Laurel. Reminding herself why she was there, she widened her eyes, pretending shock and disbelief. "What a dreadful thing to happen. Does anyone know the father?"

The beefy woman stuck a feather into the band of blue velvet around the brim of the hat. "Heard tell it were the vicar's son, but most don't believe it. They think it was one of them fancy lords up to the castle."

Corrie's stomach knotted. "Which one?"

The hatmaker shrugged. "No one knows for certain. That dark one'll take a woman's fancy. Ain't no doubt of that."

No doubt at all, Corrie thought.

"There's the married one, but his wife keeps a pretty close watch on him." The milliner smoothed the feather, checked its position in the hatband. "The other one, young Lord Jason, they say he's stolen the virtue of half the milkmaids in the county. Like I said, nobody knows for sure, probably never will."

But Corrie intended to find out. Thanking the woman for the bit of conversation, she had walked out of the village convinced her suspicions were not unfounded.

Local gossip named one of the men in the castle as the mostly likely father of Laurel's child. Corrie would do some checking on the vicar's son, and Thomas Morton, one of Squire Morton's four boys, since Agnes had made mention of him. But it was Gray Forsythe whose wife had drowned in the same river as Laurel, Gray Forsythe who remained at the top of her suspect list.

As she sat there now, in the middle of the bed, her sister's letters scattered around her, Corrie remembered the feel of the earl's hard body, the warmth and strength of his arms as she had ridden back to the castle with him. It wasn't difficult to believe he could have seduced her shy, innocent sister.

Corrie glanced at the clock on the mantel. She had begun to gather the first pieces of the puzzle. As soon as she got the chance, she would take a look around the house, see what else she might find out.

Seven

⸙

At Charles's insistence, Rebecca gave Corrie a brief tour of the house. It was clearly the last thing the woman wished to do. Still, she remained distantly polite, and Corrie did the same. Any chance to glean information was a welcome opportunity.

"The castle was built in 1233," Rebecca told her as they stood in the great room in what had been the original keep. A huge fireplace dominated one wall, and heavy carved beams supported the floors above. The medieval style had been preserved through the years, and now the space served as the formal dining room.

"Of course, the house has been refurbished and added onto dozens of times. Gray's mother took great care to see it modernized. I've made a number of changes myself." There was pride in Rebecca's voice when she talked about the castle, which was magnificent, a grand medieval palace with all the modern luxuries and most elegant furnishings.

"How long has the Forsythe family lived here?" Corrie asked.

"It's been family-owned for more than two hundred years."

"So the earl lived here as a boy?"

"Yes."

"What was his family like? I mean, Gray and Charles were brothers. Were they brought up in happy circumstances?"

For a moment, Rebecca seemed uncertain how much she should say. "There were three brothers but no sisters. James was the eldest, the apple of his father's eye. Charles was the baby and he was indulged a good deal."

"And Gray?"

Rebecca shook her head, moving the golden curls on her shoulders. She was gowned in pink-and-white silk. With her creamy complexion and cornflower-blue eyes, she was a confection of loveliness, the perfect English rose. And yet Corrie sensed a core of steel inside her.

"Gray was different," she said. "He was dark where the rest of the family was fair. He was outspoken and often headstrong. He and his father...didn't get along."

"Is that why he joined the army?"

She shrugged her shoulders. "He was a second son. It is commonly done."

"I heard he was in India."

Rebecca nodded. They moved out of the great hall down one of the numerous corridors. "He was stationed there for three years before James fell ill. I think Gray resented having to return. He was always a bit of a wanderer. Once he became the earl, he was forced to settle down and accept his responsibilities."

Corrie followed her down the hall, past several beautifully furnished drawing rooms. "Was that the reason he married?"

"I suppose it was. It was his duty to produce an heir, and

Gray wasn't the sort to shirk his duty. Jillian was beautiful and she had money and social position."

Corrie's interest stirred. "Was she in love with him?"

"I think she was mostly in love with the idea of being a countess. Jillian was still a child in many ways."

Corrie had come here for answers. She pressed for more. "Just before Cyrus left the country, he received a letter from one of his friends." Hardly true, but a way to broach the subject she needed to discuss. "The note mentioned the countess's death."

"Yes. There was a boating accident. Her death was extremely hard on Gray."

"He must have loved her very much."

Rebecca turned toward her. "I don't know if Gray is capable of love. Certainly, he cared for her a very great deal. He blamed himself for not being there when it happened, not being able to save her."

So the earl wasn't there when his wife died. More information to file away. There would be time to examine it later.

They moved along the hallway into the long gallery, where portraits of the men in the earl's family hung, floor to ceiling, on the walls. Most of them were blond or had light brown hair and looked nothing at all like Gray, whose hair was midnight-black, his features dark and more defined, more masculine.

"Gray's mother must have been dark complexioned."

Rebecca arched a delicate eyebrow. "Clarissa Forsythe was as fair as Charles. She claimed Gray got his coloring from the women on her mother's side of the family."

Claimed. It was an interesting choice of words. Corrie studied the wall, finding not one portrait that remotely resembled Gray. Perhaps there was some doubt as to the earl's parentage. Perhaps that was the reason he and his father had not got along.

Corrie made a mental notation to include with the rest of the information she had collected.

Rebecca glanced at the clock. "I hope you've enjoyed seeing some of the house. Perhaps another time I can show you a bit more. For now you'll have to excuse me. There are several pressing matters I must attend to."

"Of course." Corrie hid her feeling of relief. Though Rebecca had been unerringly polite, it was clear the woman disliked her. Perhaps she suspected Letty Moss wasn't what she appeared, and if so, Corrie could hardly fault her. Or perhaps Rebecca simply didn't want another woman living under her roof.

Whatever the reason, they were not destined to become close friends, and considering the reason Corrie was there, perhaps it was better that way.

Left on her own, she wandered the maze of halls, memorizing which rooms were where, slowly making her way along one corridor into the next, hoping she would be able to find her way back. As she passed the library, she paused, then, drawn by the floor-to-ceiling rows of books, stepped inside.

The grand room was impressive, each oak bookcase tightly jammed with leather-bound volumes of various sizes and shapes. It sat in one of the oldest parts of the castle, with walls of stone and wide-planked oak floors that had been worn in places over the years. And yet the wood was polished to a glossy sheen, the brass lamps on the tables gleaming. Each of the long rows of shelves had been carefully dusted, as if the books they held were of importance to the master of the house.

Corrie appreciated the value of books. Her home in

London was filled with them; even her bedroom had a bookcase stuffed with volumes she treasured. She was a writer. It only made sense she was also a voracious reader.

She prowled the library, enjoying the comforting feel of the room and its familiar volumes, the slightly musty smell of old paper and ink. Laurel had also liked books. Corrie wondered if perhaps it was an interest her sister had shared with Lord Tremaine. If so, the library might hold some clue that would provide a connection between the pair. For reasons she refused to examine, a bitter taste rose in her mouth at the thought.

And the same persistent feeling that Laurel would never be attracted to a fearsome man like the earl.

She was simply too gentle, too kind, while the earl was contrary, forceful and intense.

Corrie wondered at his childhood. Gray's mother had died when he was ten, she knew, leaving him with a father who—what? Believed he was another man's son? Had Gray been mistreated? Had he joined the army to escape an unloving parent?

And what of his wife?

Rebecca had said Gray was incapable of love, and yet Jillian had seemed to have no qualms in marrying him. Was he in some way responsible for her death? Was that the reason for his guilt?

Corrie wandered the endless rows of bookshelves, picking up a volume here and there, recognizing a goodly number she had read. One section held classical Roman texts including Virgil's *Aeneid* and a volume of poetry by Lucretius, *On the Nature of Things,* printed in the original Latin. Both were books Corrie had enjoyed. She had always loved school, loved learning. Her father had ignored social custom and provided her with the best tutors money could buy.

She perused the next section, pulled a volume out of the stack and flipped it open: Homer's *Odyssey*. She had read the book years ago, an epic adventure that had spawned her desire to write. Just as before, the words on the page began to draw her in and she found herself rereading a favorite passage. She was so immersed in the tale, she didn't hear the earl's heavy footfalls, muffled by the thick Persian carpet.

"Find something interesting?" Reaching out, he plucked the book from her hand. Turning it over, he read the gold letters printed on the leather cover. "The *Odyssey?*" He started to frown. "You read Greek?"

Good heavens. "I—I…was just looking at the letters. They look so different than they do printed in English."

He turned away from her, shoved the book back into its place on the shelf. "You're in the library, so I presume you like to read. What sort of books do you prefer?"

She was Letty Moss, she reminded herself, a poor relation from the country. "I, umm, actually I don't read all that much. Mostly I enjoy the ladies' magazines…you know, *Godey's Lady's Book* and the like." She flashed a beaming smile. "They show the very latest fashions."

Gray's mouth thinned. He nodded as if he were not the least surprised. Somehow that look rankled more than anything he could have said.

"I'm sure Rebecca has something you might enjoy," he told her. "Why don't you ask her tonight at supper?"

"Yes…I'll do that. Thank you for the suggestion."

He stood there, waiting for her to leave, tall and dark and imposing.

"I—I do enjoy reading poetry on occasion," she said, searching for an excuse to remain in the library. "Perhaps I might find something to keep myself occupied until tonight. You don't mind if I look a bit longer, do you? It's a very pleasant room."

He studied her face. "I don't mind. I spend a good deal of time in here myself."

She summoned a sugary smile and waited for him to leave. As soon as he disappeared out the door, she set to work. No more time for dallying. She needed to see what was in the drawers of the big oak library desk, examine the writing table in the corner. As soon as she got the chance, she intended to visit Lord Tremaine's study, but that would be dangerous and certainly no daytime venture.

Corrie hurried over to the desk and began to pull open the drawers. There were all sorts of musty papers, an ink pen with a broken nib, and some old books with pages missing. She wondered why the earl had not thrown the books away then thought how hard it was for her to get rid of a beloved text. Perhaps, as she had once thought, there was a side to the earl she hadn't yet discovered.

Then again, perhaps it was Charles who had kept the books. He seemed far more sentimental.

She made her way to the writing desk. The inkwell was dry and this pen also required a new tip. Nothing had been written at the desk for some time and there was nothing to signify a connection to Laurel.

Corrie moved back to the bookshelves. Laurel loved poetry. Had she and her lover met in the castle, perhaps sat together in the library? Or had their affair remained in the dark shadows of the woods, or somewhere else lovers might tryst?

There was a top shelf full of books, a bit out of the way, that looked intriguing. It was just out of reach, so she shoved the rolling ladder over and climbed up until she could see the volumes clearly, but she didn't recognize any of them.

The Kama Sutra was the title of one of the works. She recognized a book by the French author Voltaire, the scandalous, erotic novel *Candide* she'd heard whispered about, one no decent person would read. Beside it, her eye caught on a book entitled *The Erotic Art and Frescoes of Pompeii*.

A flutter of interest ran through her. She loved to read about foreign places. Someday she hoped to travel and write stories about the people and places she visited. The book was about an ancient town in Italy, but the title implied it was far more than a travelogue. Corrie couldn't resist reaching for the volume, opening it up for a single quick glance.

The book fell open in her hand and she saw that the pages were filled with drawings. Her eyes grew wide at the first one that came into view. A wall painting from the Stabian baths, said the copy beneath the etching—a naked woman with bulbous breasts, resting on her hands and knees. A naked man knelt behind her, and the woman's head was thrown back in what appeared to be a grimace of pain.

Corrie couldn't imagine exactly what he might be doing, but her heart began to beat oddly and a drop of perspiration slid between her breasts. Hastily, she turned the page to the drawing of a mural. In it, Mercury strode naked across the picture, a huge appendage thrusting forward between his legs. Corrie just stared.

"I see you found something, after all." The earl stood at the foot of the ladder. Corrie shrieked at the sight of the tall figure looking up at her, lost her balance and tumbled backward off the ladder. She landed squarely in the arms of the earl, the erotic book flying into the air, then falling back to earth with a soft thud, landing open in her lap.

The earl looked down at Mercury, and Corrie's face turned beet-red.

"Interesting choice," he said, and she could hear the amusement in his voice.

"Put me down!" She struggled to get free, trying to regain at least some portion of her dignity. She could feel the strength in the arms around her, the hard muscles in Tremaine's powerful chest, and her stomach contracted.

The earl set her firmly on her feet, catching the book before it tumbled to the floor. He held it open, his eyes moving over the drawing.

"I approve your selection, Mrs. Moss. I think you'll find this far more interesting than poetry, as much as I enjoy a good poem. I admit, however, I didn't think you would be quite this adventurous."

Corrie closed her eyes, her skin burning all the way to the tips of her breasts. "I—I just happened to see it. I couldn't imagine what I might find inside." She stiffened her spine. "You should be embarrassed, my lord, to keep books of this nature in your library, where any unsuspecting person might stumble upon them."

One of his black eyebrows went up. "This particular unsuspecting person had to climb to the top of a ladder to reach them. That is hardly stumbling, Mrs. Moss." The corner of his mouth curved. "Though should you wish to examine the rest of the pictures, I would not tell anyone."

"How dare you!" As insulting as the suggestion was, in truth, she would dearly love to look through the book. What had the naked man and woman been doing? she wondered. And what else might she learn?

"My apologies," said Tremaine with a trace of mockery. "I merely thought you might find it educational…since you are a married woman and already familiar with the intimacies shared between a man and woman."

Her face turned even redder. She remembered the book

she and Krista had found in the basement of the dormitory at Briarhill Academy. It described the basics of making love, but little more. At the time, they had both been appalled by the thought of a man and a woman joined in that way.

But Krista had said that lovemaking was glorious, and considering Corrie's reaction to Gray Forsythe, the way she grew flushed and dizzy whenever he came near, she wondered if it might not be so. Whatever the truth, it was frightening, these strange feelings he stirred.

And dangerous.

"I think it is past time we ended this conversation," she said. "It is, at best, highly inappropriate to speak of such matters. If you will excuse me, my lord…"

Tremaine made a formal bow. "Of course. Have a good afternoon, Mrs. Moss." The amusement had returned to his voice but there was something more.

Corrie couldn't miss the hot look in his eyes, and for a moment, she couldn't glance away. Her heart was beating like rain on a roof, and her mouth felt dry.

She tried to imagine her sister with Gray, but the image would not come. Laurel would have required a gentle lover, someone who understood her shyness, her tender sensibilities. Corrie couldn't imagine Gray Forsythe in any sort of understanding role. As a lover, he would be demanding, not tender. She wasn't sure how she knew, she just did.

Turning away, careful to keep her gaze fixed straight ahead, she walked out of the library. Though she could no longer see the earl, she could feel his gaze on her, burning with the force of a flame. The gossips called him a sensualist, a master in the art of love. It was clear from the books she had seen that he was a student of the erotic.

The man must know a dozen ways to touch a woman, a hundred ways to heighten the wild sensations that swirled through her body whenever he came near. Had her sister succumbed to the aura of masculinity that surrounded him?

Each time Corrie was with him, the notion seemed more absurd.

And yet his wife was dead and so was Laurel.

The thought sent a cold dash of reality through the fire that seemed to burn through Corrie's veins.

Eight

Krista sat next to Leif in the drawing room of the town house they had purchased in Berkeley Square. Upstairs, their five-month-old son, Brandon Thomas Draugr, Viscount Balfour, heir to the Earl of Hampton, lay napping in the nursery with his nanny.

"I hope we are doing the right thing."

"You have not stopped worrying about Coralee since she left. You will feel better if you do something."

"I should have *already* done something," Krista said. "I should have stopped her from going in the first place."

Leif scoffed. In the light streaming into the drawing room, his golden hair glinted and his eyes looked as blue as the sea. "Your friend is much like you, my love. Once her mind is made up, there is little chance of changing it."

Krista sighed. Leif was right. Coralee was as stubborn as Krista. Perhaps that was one of the reasons they had become such good friends.

"Apparently Allison has been able to keep in touch with Agnes Hatfield, Laurel's aunt," Krista said. "We know, for the moment at least, Coralee is safe, but she is taking a terrible risk."

Leif didn't disagree. "Perhaps your Mr. Petersen can help as he did before." Leif had insisted on hiring the investigator. Now Krista was glad.

A noise in the doorway drew her attention. "Your guest, Mr. Petersen, is arrived," the butler announced, a gray-haired man with impeccable credentials who had come to work for them shortly after she and Leif were wed.

"Send him in, Simmons." Krista rose along with Leif to greet the investigator they hadn't seen in nearly a year.

Dolph Petersen had helped Krista and her father discover the identity of a man trying to destroy the gazette. The villain had been ruthless and determined, willing to go to any lengths, including murder. With Dolph's help, they had been able to stop him. Krista hoped the investigator would be able to help them again.

Petersen appeared just then in the doorway, tall and lean, his face hard-edged yet handsome. Leif's hand settled possessively on Krista's waist, and Dolph broke into one of his rare smiles.

"It looks like the newlyweds are still in love. It's good to see you both. Congratulations on the little one. I heard it was a boy."

"Thank you." Leif's massive chest expanded with a hint of pride. He was a wonderful father, an attentive husband and a passionate lover. Krista knew how lucky she was.

Which made her think of Corrie and the trouble she faced, and why Leif had asked the investigator to come to the house.

"Why don't we sit down?" she suggested, guiding the small group farther into the drawing room. "Would you like some refreshment, Mr. Petersen? Some tea, or perhaps something stronger?"

"It's just Dolph. I think we know each other well enough by now. And I'm fine."

Krista and Leif took seats on the sofa and the investigator settled his lean frame in a chair. "So what can I do for you this time?"

Krista cast a glance at Leif, who nodded for her to begin. "You remember Miss Whitmore?" she asked. "My friend Coralee?"

"Of course."

"Well, she has become involved in a very dangerous intrigue and we are hoping you might be able to help."

Petersen leaned forward in his chair. "Go on."

Trusting the man's discretion, for the next half hour Krista and Leif explained about Laurel Whitmore's death and that of her illegitimate child. They told him the authorities had concluded it was suicide, but Corrie adamantly refused to believe her sister would do anything that would harm her baby.

"She thinks her sister was murdered," Leif said. "She is convinced the Earl of Tremaine is the man who killed her."

"Grayson Forsythe?" Petersen asked in surprise.

Leif straightened on the sofa, emphasizing his incredible height. "You know this man?"

"Yes. Aside from a rakish reputation with women, Gray Forsythe is as honorable as they come. He served in the military in India and was decorated several times before he came home. Why would Miss Whitmore believe the earl would murder her sister?"

"To begin with, the earl's estate, Castle Tremaine, sits next to Selkirk Hall. And both Laurel and the earl's wife were drowning victims. Both died in the Avon River."

Krista went on to explain that Jillian Forsythe's death had left Gray with a goodly sum of money and the chance to resume his numerous affairs. She told him Corrie knew his reputation with women and thought that he must have seduced her sister, gotten her with child, then killed her to prevent a scandal.

"Interesting. Not much is known about the circumstances of Tremaine's wife's death. The family kept the matter fairly quiet."

"Well, Coralee has managed to scheme her way into Castle Tremaine pretending to be some long lost cousin, and that is the reason Leif and I are so worried about her."

"If the earl is guilty of murder," Leif added, "Coralee could be in very grave danger."

Petersen grunted. "The lady has guts, I'll say that for her. I'll do some digging, see what I can find out. I'll also try to find out if Tremaine had a relationship with Laurel Whitmore."

"If he didn't," Leif said, "find out who did."

Petersen nodded. "I'll do my best." He stood up, and so did Krista and Leif. "I'll let you know as soon as I find anything."

Krista gave him a relieved smile. "Thank you, Mr.…Dolph."

He smiled. "As I said, I'll be in touch."

Krista and Leif bade the investigator farewell and returned to the drawing room.

"I'm so glad you thought of hiring him," she said.

"Petersen is a good man. He'll do his best to find out about the earl."

Krista knew he would. She just hoped whatever he discovered wouldn't be more bad news for Coralee.

Corrie sat in her bedroom after supper. The meal had been an uncomfortable affair. Since her arrival, she had noticed a certain tension between Charles and his wife that seemed amplified when they were together for any length of time. Gray rarely appeared for the evening meal. An hour ago, she had seen him ride out of the stables, heading off toward the village.

Thinking of his reputation with women and remembering the erotic books she had found in his library, she figured he had probably gone off in search of female companionship, a notion she found oddly annoying.

A light knock sounded on the door to Allison's small, adjoining bedroom. Relieved that her friend had returned to her room, Corrie hurried over to open it.

"I've been worried about you," she said. "Where on earth have you been?"

"I was talking to Hilde Pritchard, one of the kitchen maids. The woman is a dreadful gossip—for which I am eternally grateful."

Allison sank down on the bench at the foot of the big four-poster bed, and Corrie sat beside her. "So what did you find out?"

Allison tucked a lock of dark hair up into her mobcap. She was still dressed in the simple black skirt and white blouse that had been provided for her as Corrie's maid.

"Hilde is quite friendly. She has worked here a very long time, so she knows a lot about the family. She says there was a great deal of animosity between the earl and his father. Apparently after his mother died, Gray's father treated him very badly. He was punished for the slightest infraction. Once he was caned so badly the housekeeper felt compelled to summon a physician."

Dear Lord. "Why did his father treat him so cruelly?"

"According to Hilde, the late earl didn't believe Gray was truly his son—though until the day she died, Lady Tremaine swore she had always been faithful."

Sympathy for the young boy Gray had been rose up inside Corrie. A child with a father who beat him, living in a home without love....

She forced herself to think of Laurel, of her pregnancy and abandonment, her senseless death. Ruthlessly, Corrie tamped any sympathy down.

"Did you ask Hilde about the earl's wife?"

Allison nodded. "It seems Rebecca had planned an outing that day. A number of guests were invited. There was to be a picnic and a boat ride down the river. At the last minute, Gray declined to go with the rest of the group. Half an hour into the journey, the craft sprang a leak and very rapidly sank. Charles was able to help Rebecca reach safety, but Jillian's garments must have caught on something beneath the surface, and she sank out of sight so fast no one was able to save her."

Corrie felt a rush of sadness for the loss of such a young life. It was followed by an unexpected pang of relief.

"So it truly was an accident."

"Apparently so."

Still, Tremaine *could* have murdered Laurel. Coralee revised the thought. She was coming to suspect the earl less and less, if for no other reason than she couldn't imagine the man in the role of Laurel's beloved.

"Perhaps the earl wasn't the one," Allison said finally, parroting Corrie's thoughts.

"Perhaps not. But there were two other men in residence at the castle much of last year. According to Aunt Agnes, both Charles and Jason Forsythe, the earl's cousin, were living here when Laurel died. If it wasn't the earl, it could have been either one of them."

"I heard Lord Jason is due to arrive on the morrow."

Corrie had heard that, too. "So it would seem. I'll have a

chance to meet him, see what he is like. In the meantime, the earl has gone out for the evening. If we're lucky, he'll be gone all night—which means I'll be able to search his room."

"His room? But you just said—"

"When it comes to women, Tremaine is a rogue without conscience. I have to make certain he wasn't the man who fathered Laurel's child."

Allison eyes widened. "What if he comes back while you are in there?"

"I'll stay alert, but I don't think he will. He doesn't appear to be the sort to go long without female companionship, even should he have to pay for it." Which, as handsome as he was, she doubted very much. Corrie ignored a second stab of annoyance.

"Perhaps I should come with you," Allison suggested, but the uncertainty in her hazel eyes said she didn't really want to.

"I'll have less chance being discovered if I go by myself."

It was true, and relief shone in Allison's face. "His valet was in the kitchen when I left. He's an interesting little man. I'll try to keep him talking until you are finished."

"Good idea."

"I'll wait up for you. I won't be able to sleep until I know you are safe."

Corrie just nodded, glad to have a friend there in the castle.

With a last glance out the window to be certain no lone rider approached, she lifted the skirt of the drab gray dress she had chosen to make her less noticeable and headed out the door.

Gray rode Raja into the stable and swung down from the saddle next to a sleepy groom.

"I would 'ave waited up, milord," Dickey Michaels said in his thick Cockney accent. "I thought ye was gonna be gone fer the night."

"I thought so, too, Dickey." He handed the reins to the sandy-haired youth. "See Raja is watered, grained and rubbed down before you put him away."

"Yes, sir. I'll take real good care o' 'im." The boy led the stallion away and Gray started back to the house.

He'd been on his way to Parkside to see Bethany Chambers when he changed his mind. He needed sexual relief and badly, but somewhere along the route, he'd recalled the lady's spoiled disposition and constant demand for attention. On a hill halfway to her house, he'd pulled Raja to a halt. Need or not, the lady was just too much trouble.

On top of that, he realized, he no longer had the least desire for the lovely Lady Devane.

Dammit to hell and gone. Another female had caught his fancy and it seemed no other would do.

Gray didn't really understand it. He was a man of lusty appetites. Why this one had snagged his interest so strongly he could not say. There was something about her he couldn't quite figure out, and perhaps the mystery drew him. Whatever it was, he wanted her and he was fairly certain she wanted him.

They were both mature adults. At thirty, he wasn't too old for Letty—or whoever she turned out to be. It really no longer mattered. She posed no threat that he could discover. Whoever she was, if he had run across her in London, he would have made her his mistress. She needed money. He would set her up in a cottage somewhere near. He would treat her well, see her financially cared for and, in return, she would service his needs.

Gray almost smiled.

On the morrow, he would send a note of apology to Bethany for failing to arrive for their intended assignation. In the meantime he would begin his campaign to bring Mrs. Moss to his bed.

With that thought in mind, Gray headed toward the stairs leading up to his suite in the west wing of the castle. It was dark in the house. Only the gas wall sconces Rebecca had installed were burning, leaving just enough light to find his way. He climbed the stairs, strode down the corridor and pulled open the heavy door.

The curtains were drawn and an oil lamp burned on the bedside table, the wick turned down low. For an instant, he figured Samir must have anticipated his return in that uncanny way he seemed to have and lit the lamp for him. Gray frowned. Even Samir couldn't have read his thoughts tonight. They were too uncertain.

Stepping quietly into the sitting room, he surveyed the interior. The hair prickled at the back of his neck. The sixth sense he'd developed in the army was kicking in, telling him someone else was in the room.

At first, the space appeared to be empty. Then his gaze lit on the heavy gold velvet draperies and an unnatural bulge there. A pair of feet peeped out from underneath—small, feminine feet, he saw, encased in soft kid slippers.

The shoes were too fine to belong to a servant, yet a bit scuffed with wear. With a flash of certainty, Gray knew those small feet belonged to Letty Moss.

What was she doing here? Trying to steal his money or something else of value? Her worn garments betrayed her desperate need. He stared at the curtain, a wicked thought coming into his mind.

Dressed in his riding clothes, Gray sat down on the stool in front of the dresser and began to tug off his boots.

One after the other, they hit the floor with a heavy thud. His coat came off, then his shirt, leaving him bare-chested. Rising from the stool, he started toward the window, unbuttoning the fly of his riding breeches along the way.

A faint gasp sounded through the curtain as the flap came undone and his breeches slid a little lower on his hips.

"You may come out, Mrs. Moss—unless you wish to remain there while I finish disrobing."

Slight movement rippled the curtain. With a sigh of resignation, Letty stepped out from behind the gold velvet, her chin lifting as she turned to face him. Though she stood ramrod straight, her eyes widened at the sight of his bare torso, the curly black hair on his chest. She spotted the unbuttoned fly of his breeches and her cheeks turned scarlet.

"Might I ask what you are doing in my room?" he asked calmly, though having her there was making him feel anything but calm. Letty moistened her lips, and heat pooled low in his groin.

"I, um, got lost. I was out in the garden, you see. I came up the back stairs and I—I must have turned the wrong way when I reached the second floor landing."

"Ah…that must be it. Your room is in about the same location at the opposite end of the house."

"Yes, it is." Her relief turned to suspicion. "How do you know the location of my room?"

He gave her a wolfish smile. "I like to personally assure myself my guests are comfortable. You *are* comfortable, are you not, Mrs. Moss?"

Her eyes narrowed. "Not at the moment."

He closed the distance between them, stopped directly in front of her. Gray caught her shoulders and felt her tremble, but she didn't back away. "I want to know what you're doing in my room, and this time I want the truth." He gently shook her. "Were you looking for money? I know you have very little. I suppose I could understand that."

Her chin firmed. "I am not a thief."

"What then?"

"I just…" She released a shaky breath. "I wanted to know something about you. You've allowed me into your home. I thought I might learn something of what you are like if I took a look round your suite."

His fingers dug into her shoulders. "Why would you care?"

Letty stared up at him with the greenest eyes he'd ever seen. "There are…a number of reasons. Some of them even I don't understand." The words rang with a sincerity that seemed to surprise them both.

Gray looked into her beautiful face, the softly winged russet eyebrows, the small indentation in her chin. He watched the rise and fall of her breasts, and a wave of lust hit him like a blow.

He wanted Letty Moss. With her lovely copper hair and small but voluptuous body, she drew him like a moth to the flame. Gray slid an arm around her waist and hauled her against him. Her eyes widened in shock the instant before his mouth crushed down over hers. For a moment, Letty stiffened, her small hands pressing against his chest as she tried to push him away, but Gray refused to let her go.

The heat of her surrounded him, the taste of her inflamed him. He drew her closer, enfolded her in his arms and kissed her until her mouth began to soften under his. Letty began to kiss him back, and a groan escaped from deep in his throat. Slanting his mouth over hers, he continued the gentle assault, inhaling her soft rose scent and hardening to the point of pain.

Coaxing her lips apart, he slid his tongue inside to taste her more fully, and Letty melted against him, her full breasts pillowing into his chest. Gray's whole body tightened and he fought the urge to open the front of her simple gown and take the creamy weight into his mouth.

Her hands ran over his bare chest, slid around his neck, and she went up on her toes to increase the contact. She was all warm, willing woman, exactly what he needed.

Gray lifted her into his arms and strode toward the door to his bedroom—and Letty began to scream.

"Quiet! What the hell are you doing? Do you want to bring the entire household down on us?"

"You put me down this instant!"

For a long moment, he just held her, his body aching with need, his shaft hard as stone. Just seconds ago, Letty had been warm and pliant. Now he could feel her stiff restraint and knew that whatever fires had burned between them had begun to flame out.

Reluctantly, he set her on her feet. "You seemed willing enough a minute ago."

She glanced away. In the dim light of the lamp, he could see the hot wash of color in her cheeks. "I—I don't know what happened. I just…I didn't realize it would feel so…" Letty shook her head and Gray frowned.

For all her passionate responses, he had always sensed her innocence. Was his bloody cousin Cyrus such a miserable lover he had never bothered with foreplay, never managed to arouse his wife in any way?

"I must go," she said. "I apologize for coming here. It was stupid and meddlesome. I hope you will forgive me."

"Listen to me, Letty. If you're frightened, you don't have to be. I won't do anything to hurt you."

"I have to go," she repeated, backing toward the door. "My maid will be waiting to help me undress." Her cheeks colored again at the mention of disrobing, and Gray felt a renewed flare of lust.

Letty spun toward the door and he didn't try to stop her. It was clear his seduction was going to take more time than he had planned.

Still, he had no doubt of the outcome.

Letty Moss was going to be his. If money was what she had come for, he would see that she had it. Whatever she needed, he would give it to her.

That and something far more enjoyable.

Gray felt the rare pull of a smile. Soon Letty Moss would be spending her nights in his bed.

Oh, dear God! Trembling at the memory of what had just occurred, Corrie stood outside the door to her bedroom, trying to catch her breath. Her heart was hammering, her composure shattered. Allison would be waiting inside. She would want to know what had happened. Dear Lord, what would Ally say if she knew?

Corrie leaned her head against the wall and forced herself to take long, calming breaths. She had done as she planned and gone into the earl's private chambers, but she had found nothing of interest. At least nothing that connected Tremaine with Laurel. Careful not to disturb anything or leave something out of place, she had searched every dresser drawer, gone through two tall rosewood armoires, the earl's portable writing desk, even his clothes. She had found nothing.

Nothing except the earl himself.

Sweet saints in heaven!

How could she have allowed him to kiss her? How could she have kissed him back the way she did?

A fresh wave of heat curled through her at the remembered feel of his mouth moving hotly over hers, the hard muscles of his naked chest pressing against her breasts. She remembered the way her nipples had tightened and begun to throb, aching with a need she had never felt before. She'd wanted to touch him all over, to feel those hard muscles against her bare skin, to taste him, to—

She broke off at the horrifying thought. Sweet God, the rogue deserved every bit of his scandalous reputation. He was a devil with the skill of a sorcerer.

Unconsciously, she reached up to touch her kiss-swollen lips, which tingled and felt oddly tender. She could still taste him there. If she closed her eyes, she could recall his male scent, tinged with the fragrance of sandalwood.

He was a skillful seducer, and yet, after a sample of his scorching passion, Corrie had never held a stronger conviction that Gray Forsythe was *not* Laurel's lover, not the man her sister had fallen so deeply in love with, a man she had protected until the end of her life.

Corrie knew Laurel too well, and was beginning to know the powerful earl. The two were completely ill suited. There was no way her sister could have withstood the intensity of a man like Gray.

Still, Corrie couldn't completely exonerate him until she found the man who was Laurel's beloved.

The man who might have murdered her.

Taking a slow, deep breath, smoothing wisps of hair back into the chignon at the nape of her neck, Corrie opened the door and stepped into her bedroom.

Nine

After a long, mostly sleepless night, Corrie awakened to a rainy May morning. Anxious to escape the house and avoid the Earl of Tremaine, she skipped breakfast, dressed simply and set off for the village, despite the darkened sky.

The town, some of the stone buildings of which were as old as the castle, was quiet this early. Corrie strolled through the shops that were just opening their doors, bought a crumpet and tea in a tiny salon and a length of pretty blue silk ribbon to tie back her hair. She spoke to a number of the local women, hoping to pick up a bit of gossip, then headed for the church.

Vicar Langston had been assigned to the parish three years ago, Corrie had learned. His son, Patrick, was currently a deacon in nearby Berkshire County, but he had been living in the village at the time Laurel was murdered.

Corrie was standing in the aisle a few feet in front of the altar when the vicar approached, a fine-boned man with silver hair and kindly blue eyes.

"May I help you, young lady?"

"Well, I…actually, I came to say a prayer for a friend of mine. She died a few months ago. Her name was Laurel Whitmore."

The vicar shook his head. "Terrible tragedy that. My son and I often stopped by to visit Laurel and her aunt. She was such a sweet girl, a friend of my son's fiancée, Arial Collingwood."

"Your son is engaged to be married?"

"Why, yes. For more than a year. The wedding is set for next month. Miss Whitmore helped Arial make plans for the nuptials."

Corrie's chest tightened. If Laurel was a friend of the girl Patrick Langston was going to marry, she never would have gotten involved with him in any way. She simply would not have betrayed her friend.

"I've heard rumors about what happened," Corrie said carefully. "I know there was a child. I still find it difficult to believe Laurel would kill herself—and nearly impossible to imagine she would have done anything that might harm her baby."

"Yes, it came as a shock to everyone. I blame myself, somewhat. I should have sensed her distress. She was a member of my congregation, after all. Of course, I didn't know about the child…not until later. In fact, the truth didn't surface until after both of them were gone. The family tried to keep the information private, but it's difficult to keep a secret like that in a town this small."

"I imagine it would be." She cast a glance at the altar, where a row of flickering beeswax candles cast shadows against the stone walls. "You would think the father of the child would come forward. I don't suppose anyone knows who he is."

"I'm afraid not. Perhaps he never knew about the

babe…at least not until it was too late. By then it didn't really matter."

Good heavens, she had never thought of that. Was it possible Laurel had never told the man she loved that she carried his child? And if so, why not?

"I am truly sorry about your friend," the vicar said. "I liked Miss Whitmore very much."

"Thank you. So did I."

Corrie left the church, her heart aching. Laurel was dead, and speaking about her with the vicar made the pain resurface again. At least Corrie could mark another suspect off her list. She didn't believe Patrick Langston was the man who had fathered her sister's child, not when his fiancée had been Laurel's friend.

Corrie was thinking about her sister as she walked along the path through the fields, her mind miles away, when she heard a soft whimper. She paused, her gaze searching for the source of the noise. A second whimper reached her and she left the path and headed in the direction the sound had come from. Not far away, a big gray mongrel lay on his side in the tall grass, blood oozing from a gash across his ribs.

"Easy, boy." Corrie knelt beside the dog, ran her hand over his matted fur. He was a tall animal, but thin, his gray hair long and stringy, his tail curved up over his back. He was malnourished and homely, but his eyes were dark and compelling, and when he looked at her, she saw such pain and resignation it twisted her heart.

"It's all right, boy. You're going to be all right. I'm going to take care of you." *I'm not going to let you die.* She didn't know whose dog he was, probably just a stray, but she couldn't stand to see an animal suffer.

Reaching beneath her skirt, she tore off a long strip of

her petticoat, then another and another. Very carefully, she bound them around the dog's ribs, gently tying each strip of cloth. The injury needed to be washed and cleaned, but first she had to get the animal back to the house.

"Just stay here," she said, smoothing her hand over his fuzzy gray brow. "I'll be back as soon as I can." Picking up her skirts, she ran for the path, then raced all the way back to the house. She was breathing hard by the time she reached the stable and rushed inside in search of a groom. She found the earl instead.

"What's happened?" he asked, coming out of Raja's stall, where he had been working. "Are you all right?"

She choked out the words, trying to catch her breath. "I need a wagon of some sort. I found a dog who's been injured. He needs help and I—"

"Wait a minute—you ran until you are barely able to stay on your feet for a *dog?* What about your ankle? You could have sprained it again."

"My ankle is fine, but the dog is injured. I need to get him home so that I can take care of him."

The earl studied her face, reading her fear for the animal. His features softened. "Come," he said gently. "I'll help you bring him back."

Relief washed through her. The earl would help her. For reasons she could not fathom, it didn't really surprise her.

Hitching one of the horses to a gig, he helped her onto the seat and they set off down the muddy road. Taking the path would be shorter, but it was narrow, not wide enough for the cart. They would have to carry the dog to where the vehicle waited on the road.

As soon as they reached the spot, about halfway to the village, they left the cart and crossed the field to the path. It took a while to locate the place where Corrie had left the dog. He was still there, still lying on his side, her makeshift bandage soaked through in several places with bright red blood.

"It's all right, sweetheart," she said, sinking down in the grass beside him. She petted his neck and talked to him softly, then glanced up at the earl, who was looking at her strangely, wondering, she supposed, why she bothered with such a homely mutt.

Tremaine turned his attention to her makeshift bandage, went down on one knee and began to gently check for broken bones, as he had done that day with her.

"I wonder what happened to him," she said.

"I don't know. We'll know more when we get him home and take a look at the wound." He rechecked the bandage. "You used your petticoat?" he said with amazement, noticing the blood on her skirt.

"I realize I don't have all that many clothes, but I really had no choice."

His lips edged up. "No choice, indeed." But he looked as if none of the women of his acquaintance would have sacrificed their garments for a dog.

Tremaine bent over and carefully lifted the animal into his arms. The dog whimpered but didn't try to fight him.

"It's all right, old fella," he said. "We'll get you back so the lady can take care of you." The earl looked down at her. "Don't get your hopes up. He's lost quite a bit of blood. He might not make it."

She squared her shoulders. "I'm not letting him die." Lately, there had been too much death around her. Laurel. Little Joshua Michael. She wasn't letting this poor animal die, as well.

The earl started walking and Corrie hurried to keep up with his long strides. He placed the dog on the blanket they had spread in the back of the gig, helped her up onto the seat, then climbed up beside her.

He hadn't mentioned the scene in his room last night, had, in fact, treated her as if nothing at all had occurred. Instead of feeling grateful, she was annoyed the encounter had left him so little affected.

Still, he was helping her with the dog. For now that was all that mattered.

They reached the barn, and two of the grooms raced up to the cart. One carried the dog into a stall and placed him carefully on a bed of straw. Corrie sank down beside him.

"Easy, boy." She petted the mangy gray hair on his head as the earl unwrapped the bandages around his ribs. One of the grooms brought a bucket of water and a stack of rags, and Corrie used the cloths to cleanse the wound, rinsing away the blood and dirt.

Her gown was ruined. She had brought only a few with her, and Letty Moss could certainly not afford to buy more. But when the dog rested his paw on her hand with what she thought was a look of gratitude, she decided he was worth the loss of the gown.

"The cut's pretty deep," Tremaine said, after assessing the long gash, "but it's not as bad as I thought. We'll bind the wound, and if he rests and recovers his strength, he might be all right."

Corrie looked up eagerly. "Do you think so?"

"I'd say there's a very good chance."

She smiled in relief. "Thank you for helping him."

The earl's gaze found hers. "I was helping you, Letty, not the dog." But the gentleness he had shown made her believe that if he had been the one who found the animal, he wouldn't have simply left him there to die.

"He needs a name," she said. "What do you think we should call him?"

"You shouldn't name him until you're certain he's going to live. It'll just make it harder if he doesn't."

"In that case I shall most certainly name him." She ran her hand over his unkempt fur. "I think I'll call him Homer."

"Homer? From the *Odyssey* and the *Iliad?*"

Oh, dear, that was exactly the reason. The dog seemed to be a wanderer. After she'd found the book in the library, the name had just popped out. Corrie thought quickly. "Homer was the name of my dog back in York. Is he also a character in a book?"

Gray shook his head. "He's an ancient Greek writer. And I suppose it's as good a name as any."

"It is a wonderful name." She stroked the dog's matted fur. "Isn't it, Homer?"

The animal licked her hand as if in agreement. When she looked up at the earl, there was a tenderness in his expression she had never seen before.

"You've a soft heart, Letty Moss." He rose from his place in the straw beside her. "Let me know if you need any more help." And then he was gone.

Corrie should have felt relieved.

Instead, she found herself wishing he had stayed.

Lord Jason arrived the next day, and good grief the man was handsome. Corrie had heard the servants tittering about him, but seeing him in person made their comments as bland as mush.

In a different, less fearsome way, Jason Forsythe, youngest son of the Marquess of Drindle, was even more handsome than Gray. Though not as tall nor as solidly built, with his light brown hair and stunning blue eyes he was every woman's fantasy. His warm smiles came often, carving an amazing pair of dimples into his cheeks, and his laughter had a merry ring.

He was five-and-twenty, Allison told her, just two years older than Laurel, a discovery made through a growing friendship with the servants. As charming as he was, it was easy to imagine the two of them together.

It was easy to imagine Laurel falling in love with Lord Jason—and nearly impossible to believe the man was a murderer.

"I didn't realize what charming company I would find here at the castle," he said on their first meeting. "If I had, I might have come home sooner." He made an extravagant bow over Corrie's hand, pressing a kiss against the back. "I'm afraid I've never had the pleasure of meeting your husband, Mrs. Moss, but I must say he has exceptional taste in women."

Corrie lowered her eyes, enjoying but not the least taken in by the man's flattery, which, unlike the earl, he seemed to hand out in great measure.

"I only hope Cyrus is safe," she said, keeping to her role. "It is difficult not to worry after not having heard from him for so long."

"I imagine you must be terribly lonely," Jason said, extending an arm to escort her in to supper. "Perhaps I can help in that regard while I am here."

Corrie smiled up at him, liking him as much as everyone seemed to. "I'm certain you will."

They walked into the dining room the family used for less formal evenings, a lovely space holding a long rosewood table with twelve matching high-back chairs upholstered in forest green. Only the main rooms and hallways had been converted to gas lighting and none of the bedrooms, but here a gas-burning crystal chandelier hung above the table, illuminating the interior with a soft yellow glow.

Jason seated her, then took a chair across from her. Rebecca and Charles took their usual places, Rebecca wearing a cream-and-gold taffeta gown that set off the golden highlights in her hair. Corrie tried not to think of the gown she herself was wearing, a turquoise silk that had never been the height of fashion. Though the gown rode low on her shoulders, as was the current mode, mended roses cupped her breasts and the hem was slightly frayed.

For once, the earl had decided to join them. Taking his place at the head of the table, he cast Corrie a penetrating glance. With a burst of clarity, she realized Tremaine wasn't happy she was paying so much attention to his extremely handsome cousin. Why that pleased her so inordinately, she refused to consider.

But as the servants began arriving with the first course of the meal, a delicate cream of leek soup, Corrie gave Jason an even brighter smile.

"Rebecca says you are just returned from the Continent. How long were you there?"

"Only the past two months. I was in Italy mostly, but I also spent time in France."

Gray took a drink of his wine. "Mrs. Moss is particularly interested in Italian history." His dark eyes burned into her. "Did you happen to visit Pompeii while you were there?"

Corrie choked on the sip of wine she had taken.

"Are you all right?" Jason reached over and took the glass from her unsteady hand, set it back down on the table.

"I—I am fine. It must have gone down the wrong way."

"You were saying…?" Gray pressed, and Corrie wanted to hit him.

"I'm afraid I didn't get as far as Pompeii. Mostly I was in Rome."

Corrie cast a furious glance at Gray, then returned her attention to Lord Jason. "I should love to see Rome. The history of the Colosseum is fascinating. I read once that in its glory the arena seated more than fifty thousand people, and the opening games lasted a hundred days. I thought it was amazing they could actually fill the arena with water and stage naval battles. The ruins must be an incredible sight."

Gray was frowning. "I thought you only read ladies' magazines." His suspicious tone jarred her back to reality. She was Letty Moss, for heaven sake! Letty didn't read Roman history in the original Latin!

Corrie pasted on a smile. "Well, that is mostly true. What I meant to say is I have a friend who knows a lot about history. She particularly enjoyed reading about Rome. We discussed it on occasion."

"The Colosseum *was* fascinating," Jason said, picking up the thread of conversation—thank God. "There were all sorts of cells and tunnels under the floor where the Romans kept the animals and gladiators. You could almost imagine Julius Caesar sitting up in the gallery."

"I would love to see it someday."

While they dined on stuffed capon and drank expensive French wine, Jason described the sights of Rome, and Corrie was enthralled. She would so much love to travel. Reading about a foreign country wasn't the same as seeing it in person.

She asked about other of his visits, and he told her a bit about France.

Jason smiled at her across the table. *"Vous êtes une trés belle femme,"* he teased, his blue eyes twinkling. *You're a very beautiful woman.*

"Et vous, monsieur, êtes un flattereur," she couldn't resist retorting. *And you, sir, are a flatterer.*

Gray eyed her with suspicion.

"I only know the basics," she explained with a sweetly regretful smile. "How to count to fifty, how to find the ladies' retiring room or respond to a compliment. I should love to be able to speak French—it is so romantic, is it not? But alas, I've never had a knack for language."

Liar. She was fluent in both French and Italian, and lately, even spoke a bit of Old Norse that Krista's husband, Leif, had taught her. She had always had an ear for language. She yearned to travel to France and talk to the people who lived there.

"Gray is really the traveler, not me," Jason said. "He lived abroad for several years before he joined the army. You know he was stationed in India?"

She looked over at Gray, realized he was watching her. "Yes…Rebecca mentioned he was there."

"Perhaps he'll tell you about it sometime."

And she would dearly love to hear what he had to say. But the earl made no effort to continue the subject, just leaned back in his chair and looked down the table at her in that arrogant way of his.

Dressed entirely in black except for a showy white shirt and dove-gray waistcoat, his black hair glinting in the light of the gas chandelier, he was the most compelling man she had ever met. He wore his hair queued back, accenting the hard line of his jaw and his high carved cheekbones, and it occurred to her that Lord Jason might be more handsome in the conventional sense, but Gray was by far the more masculine.

She felt a tug of awareness and realized his gaze had moved down to the line of cleavage between her breasts, exposed above the bodice of her turquoise gown. Beneath that sensual stare, her nipples hardened into tight little buds, and as she reached for her wineglass to steady herself, the top of her corset rubbed against them. With Gray's attention fixed there, the sensation was wildly disturbing.

A corner of his mouth crept up and his eyes seemed to darken. It was as if he knew, as if he'd reached out and touched her, cupped her breasts in his big dark hands. The man was a devil. Corrie told herself it was hardly her fault that some wicked part of her responded to him.

For the rest of the meal, she kept her attention firmly fixed on his cousin. As far as she was concerned, the devil earl could go straight to hell.

Ten

The house was completely silent, the family all abed. Reading to stay awake, Corrie waited impatiently for the clock to strike two. When she finally heard the soft chime, she set aside her book and made her way toward the door.

She hadn't told Allison what she intended to do. Her friend would only worry, and she didn't want that.

Dressed in a white cotton nightgown, her blue quilted wrapper buttoned up for warmth, she lit a beeswax taper, opened the door and peered out into the hall. There was rarely anyone in this part of the house, and certainly not at this time of night. Holding the candlestick in front of her, Corrie made her way to the stairs at the end of the corridor and descended to the bottom floor.

She had carefully memorized which hallway led to the study, a room she had discovered in her wanderings, and she headed straight for it. She had never been inside, and as she stepped into the interior, she wondered if Gray had taken a hand in the heavy dark furnishings that gave the interior a forbidding air. Somehow she didn't think so.

It wasn't until she spotted a door in the study wall, pushed it open and walked into a smaller chamber, that she felt his presence. It was as if she had stepped into another world, the foreign world of India. The furniture was lighter, much of it made of cane, and the faint smell of sandalwood hung in the air. She recognized the pleasant, slightly musky fragrance she had come to associate with Gray, but until now hadn't connected to India.

A thick Indian rug, intricately patterned in burgundy and navy, covered the floor, while brass urns of odd shapes and sizes sat on the tables. She held up the candle, fascinated by the array of items Gray must have collected during his travels. In a glass-fronted bookcase, pieces of carved ivory in lacy patterns rested on the shelves, and above the case, a pair of crossed military sabers hung on the wall.

She could feel Gray Forsythe in the room as if he stood behind her, and for an instant she turned, holding up the candlestick to be sure she was still alone. Relieved to discover she was, she turned back and began her search.

As she moved through the room, she found several items of interest, though nothing that connected Gray to Laurel.

In a small brass box, she found two carefully folded letters. In the first, his mother told him she loved him and that when he grew older, when he heard unpleasant rumors of his birth, he was to open the second letter. She told him to believe every word and never to doubt it, to trust his heart to know what she told him was true.

The date on the letter said Lady Tremaine had written it just before she died. Gray would have been ten.

Corrie sank down on the edge of chair, feeling like the voyeur she was, and completely unable to resist reading the words in the second missive. In it, the countess told Gray in no uncertain terms that he was a true son of the Earl of Tremaine.

I was never unfaithful to your father. No matter what he believes, I have always loved him. It is his jealousy that drives him to behave as he does. I hope someday you can find it in your heart to forgive him for being such a fool.

Corrie read the page, her chest oddly tight. As a child, Gray had suffered for his father's unfounded jealousy. He had lost his mother and his wife. Corrie felt a pang of pity for the loneliness he must have suffered in his life. She wondered if perhaps Laurel had been drawn to that loneliness. But even as kindhearted as her sister was, Corrie could not see her with Gray.

Carefully replacing the letters in the box and setting it back on the shelf, Corrie moved into the main portion of the study and began to search there, starting with the big mahogany desk that dominated the room.

Finding nothing, she searched the bookshelves along the wall, and was ready to give up and return upstairs when her eye caught on a volume pushed back from the rest, shoved between two other books in a way that made her wonder if someone had not wanted it to be seen. Reaching up, she pulled down a volume of William Shakespeare, *Sonnets and Romantic Poetry.*

Her heart began pounding. Corrie knew the book, one of Laurel's favorite works of literature. And the faded leather cover was worn in a manner that seemed somehow familiar. Her hand trembled as she opened it and her gaze fastened on the feminine scroll on the first page.

My dearest beloved,
We have shared so many beautiful moments. An afternoon of reading this together is a memory I shall always treasure. I give it to you in the hope you will remember me in the years to come. With my deepest love, Laurel.

Corrie's heart wrenched. Memories of her sister rushed in and her eyes burned with tears. Laurel sitting in the window seat reading the book, telling Corrie that someday she hoped to find the kind of love Shakespeare had written about in the pages. Though the inscription did not give the name of the man Laurel had fallen in love with, the man she had gifted with a book she treasured, there could be no more doubt that it was one who lived at Castle Tremaine.

Was it Gray? Corrie tried to imagine Gray and Laurel reading the romantic poems printed in the book. There was simply no way she could convince herself.

She glanced round the study, toward the door leading into the room next door. The things that seemed most important to Gray he kept in his private office. If the book had been a gift, wouldn't he have kept it there?

Then again, perhaps the gift meant little to the Earl of Tremaine. She thought of the other two men in the house. Charles spent a good deal of time in the study. He was the sort of man her sister would find attractive, but he was married. She would never give herself to a married man.

Which left handsome and charming Lord Jason. This afternoon, as Corrie had walked past, Jason had been sitting behind the desk.

Which of them did you love, sweet sister?

And was this man you loved responsible for your death and that of your child?

But no answer came.

Hating to part with the precious memento, Corrie went up on her toes and replaced it on the bookshelf. At least her wild scheme to get into the castle had not been completely insane. It was clear she was on the right track. In time she would discover which man had fathered Laurel's child. Once she knew, she would find out the truth of what had happened to her sister the night she died.

Drawing her blue quilted wrapper a little closer around her, Corrie left the study and hurried along the passage toward the east wing back stairs. She had almost reached her destination when a familiar male voice sent a prickle of alarm down her spine.

"Well, Mrs. Moss…I see you are out on another of your nightly forays. And just where, exactly, are you headed at this hour?"

She turned to find the earl behind her, his tall figure unmistakable in the shadowy darkness of the hallway.

"I—I was just returning upstairs." She managed to smile. "I couldn't sleep. I came down to see if I might find a glass of milk in the kitchen."

"So you were in the kitchen," Gray said with obvious disbelief.

"Why, yes. You don't mind, do you? I suppose, after you found me lurking about in your room, you probably believe I came down her to steal the family silver or something."

His eyes ran over her, sending a little curl of heat into her stomach. "Or something…"

There wasn't the least trace of amusement in his voice and she wondered if he was still angry over the attention she had paid his cousin at supper two nights past.

"It's extremely late. I suppose I should be going."

"On the contrary," he said, an edge creeping into his voice. "Since you are unable to sleep, and I am, as well, we may as well enjoy a little conversation…or something."

Her pulse began to thrum. There was a hard twist to his lips, and yet his eyes said exactly what that *something* was. She started to argue, but the earl took a firm grip on her arm and began to guide her down a corridor in the opposite direction. Propelling her into one of the drawing rooms, he firmly closed the door.

"I—I don't think this is a good idea."

"Why not? You said you couldn't sleep. I know a sure cure for insomnia."

Her nerves quivered as he walked past her, over to the hearth, where the remnants of a fire still flickered behind the grate. She thought that he must have been in the room while she was in the study, and said a silent thank-you that he had been far enough away not to hear her.

Or had he?

Crouched in front of the fire, he added a bit of coal to the low-burning flames. Part of her wanted to run while she still had the chance; another part watched in silent fascination the play of sinew flexing in his thighs, the tightening of the muscles across his broad back beneath the fabric of his white lawn shirt.

He used the bellows to heighten the blaze, then rose and walked over to where she stood next to the sofa. He stared down at her, and the firelight glinting in his eyes made them look forbidding. "You seem nervous. Am I keeping you from something? Perhaps a late night rendezvous with my cousin?"

Surprise widened her eyes. "Your cousin? I told you I went to the kitchen for a glass of milk. I haven't seen your cousin for the past two days."

"No? And yet he seems to have won your favor."

She watched the earl's face for a clue as to where this conversation might be leading, and noticed the hard set of his jaw. He *was* still angry. Surely he couldn't be jealous!

"Jason is a very charming man," she said carefully. "It's only natural I would enjoy his company."

"Of course." The hard edge remained in Tremaine's voice. He reached out and caught a wisp of hair that had come lose from her braid and curled next to her cheek. The heat of his hand sent a ripple of warmth through her. "I wonder…has he offered to make you his mistress?"

Her whole body stiffened and she drew away from his touch. "What are you talking about? Your cousin has never behaved as anything but a gentleman."

The earl shrugged. On the surface, the gesture seemed nonchalant, and yet she couldn't miss the tension in those very wide shoulders.

"You need money," he stated casually. "Jason has plenty. You're obviously attracted to him. I should think—"

She tried to control her temper but the words just popped out. "I am not sure *thinking* is something you do all that often, my lord."

Tremaine's dark eyes narrowed dangerously.

"If you did, you would know I am not attracted to your cousin in the least."

"Is that so?"

"Quite so." She lifted her chin, chiding herself for momentarily forgetting her role. "Aside from that, I'm a married woman and not the sort to trifle with another man."

His expression changed and his tension seemed to ease. There was something different in his eyes now, something hot that he had kept hidden before. "And yet that night in my room, you returned my kisses, did you not? And with a surprising amount of passion."

Faint color rose in her cheeks. "Well, I—I was caught unawares, my lord."

"Gray," he corrected softly. "Go on, Letty…you were caught unawares and so when I kissed you, you kissed me back like a tigress coming into her first season. And you wanted more, sweeting." His gaze came to rest on her lips. "I think you still do."

She opened her mouth to argue, but his lips came down over hers, silencing her words. It was a soul-stealing, ravishing kiss, part anger, part need. He was all virile male, all strength and domination, and his sandalwood scent wrapped around her. She told herself to think of Laurel and the book she had found, and what it might mean, but when she tried to imagine Gray with her sister, the image would not come.

Instead, she saw herself in his arms as she was now, and desire for him roared like a drug through her veins. She had never experienced passion, never understood it, but she knew it now. Another woman seemed to have entered her body, a wicked, shameless creature who burned with the same fierce desire she sensed in Gray.

"I want you," he whispered, pressing hot kisses against the side of her neck. "I want you, Letty Moss, and I intend to have you."

Corrie moved her head from side to side in denial. Gray captured her face between his palms, bent his head and kissed her, a wet, hard, hungry caress that left her body weak and her mind in a numbing fog. His tongue tangled with hers as he plundered her mouth, and her hands pressed uselessly against his chest.

"Gray…" she whispered, searching for the strength to stop him. "Please…we can't…we can't…"

"Oh, yes, Letty, we can." With those words his lips began a slow journey along the line of her jaw, leaving a damp trail of heat. She didn't realize he had managed to unbutton her quilted wrapper until he slid it off her shoulders. His mouth claimed hers as he tugged at the ribbon on her nightgown, allowing the top to slip precariously low. Hot kisses trailed down her neck and across her bare shoulder, burning her skin like a brand.

She moaned as he eased the soft cotton lower, exposing her breast, settling his mouth there, suckling the tip until it puckered into a tight little bud.

"Lovely," he whispered, licking the peak, swirling his tongue around it. "I've imagined you this way."

Corrie trembled at the fierce need swirling through her, the desire that threatened to overwhelm her. Gray loosened the ribbon at the end of her braid and drew his fingers through her hair, spreading the heavy mass around her shoulders.

"Like fire," he said, burying his face in the rippling strands. "Like silken flames."

He kissed the side of her neck and her body tightened with longing. She swayed toward him, pressed herself more fully against him, and even the hot, hard length thrusting determinedly against her could not sheath the claws of her desire.

His dark head returned to her breast, taking the fullness into his mouth, and pleasure shook her with such force she thought she would surely swoon. Her other breast throbbed for his attention, and as if he knew, his long fingers tightened over her nipple, pinching harder than she expected, sending a rush of pleasure out through her limbs.

Gray sat down on the sofa and drew her onto his lap. Corrie moaned and shifted restlessly, an ache beginning to throb between her legs. One of his hands moved along her calf, raising her nightgown, sliding along the inside of her thigh, leaving a trail of fire in the wake of his touch.

Her mind signaled a sluggish warning. *You can't do this! You've got to stop him before it's too late!*

"No!" Corrie shot up from the sofa. "I—I can't…. Dear Lord, what am I doing?" On legs like rubber, she jerked her nightgown up to cover her breasts, and tied the pink ribbon with trembling hands.

Gray moved toward her. "It's all right, sweeting, I'm not going to hurt you. I'm only going to make love to you."

"You'll do no such thing!" She backed away from him, her cheeks burning at the shameful liberties she had allowed him to take. And how much she had enjoyed it. "How do you do it? What evil tricks do you use?"

Amusement touched those sensuous lips. "There is nothing evil about making love. I'll teach you, Letty. Come. You don't have to be afraid."

But she was already backing toward the door. Swinging it open, she rushed out into the hall. She heard Gray swearing as he strode into the passage behind her.

"You'll need your candle." He held the taper out to her. "Without it you might fall."

But Corrie just kept running, her hair streaming behind her, her body still throbbing in places that had never throbbed before.

Dear God, she had to be more careful, had to stay away from the earl and not succumb to the fierce attraction she felt for him. She thought of Laurel, pregnant and alone. Heaven above, she didn't want to wind up the victim of a man's desire.

And yet when she thought of Gray and the wild yearning he sparked inside her, she couldn't help but wonder if the danger might not be worth it.

Corrie trembled, her body still pulsing, knowing if she wasn't careful, the devil earl was going to be her downfall.

Gray walked down the hall toward the study, his mind exhausted, while his body still hummed with remnants of unspent need. He had told Letty the truth. He had been downstairs wandering in the garden, then reading for a while because he could not sleep. It happened far too often. Sexual congress gave him temporary relief, but he hadn't been with a woman in weeks.

Gray sighed. He had burned his bridges with Bethany. He would get no relief there. And in truth, there was only one woman he wanted. The mysterious creature who lived beneath his very roof.

In the darkness, he made his way toward a lamp, lit the wick and sat down behind the desk. Drawing a piece of foolscap from the drawer, he used pen and ink to scratch out a message.

He was writing a friend in London, a man named Randolph Petersen he had known since before he went into the army. At the time, Dolph had worked for the War Office, doing work he could never discuss. Several years ago, the man had become a private investigator, a good one from what Gray had heard. Dolph was the sort who had always been good at his job—no matter what it entailed.

In the letter, Gray said he wanted to hire him to investigate a woman named Letty Moss, the supposed wife of his cousin Cyrus Moss. He gave Dolph the few sketchy details he had, told him Letty had apparently lived near York with Cyrus until he left England to make his fortune in America, that she appeared to be destitute and in need of help.

Find out what you can and get back to me as soon as possible, he finished. Then signed it, *Your friend, Gray Forsythe, Earl of Tremaine.*

He sealed the letter with a drop of wax, pressed it closed with the Tremaine seal—the emblem of a lion beneath a pair of crossed sabers—and carried it with him up to his suite. In the morning, he would have Samir hire a private dispatch to carry the note to London.

Tremaine thought about the letter as he entered his sitting room, wondering what Dolph might find out, and half tempted to rip the message to shreds. He wanted Letty Moss. He didn't want Petersen to discover something so distasteful he would have to send her away.

Standing there in the faint glow of the lamp on the dresser, he tapped the letter, then set it on top, knowing he had no choice but to send it.

"You are disturbed," Samir said, stepping silently out of the shadows. "The woman did not give you release this night."

"No."

"She desires you. It is there when she casts her eyes upon you. What does she wish in exchange for the use of her body?"

Gray almost smiled. Samir thought every problem came with a solution. There was only the matter of discovering what it was. "I think she's afraid. She has only been with her husband, and he was a very poor lover."

"This I can see, as well. But you are skilled in the art of passion. You will teach her what she needs to learn."

"I suppose…in time…" But time always seemed to slip out of his grasp when he was with Letty Moss.

He handed Samir the letter. "See it posted tomorrow, will you? Perhaps we'll learn the truth about Mrs. Moss."

Samir bowed from the waist. "As you wish, *sahib.*" He slipped off into the darkness, leaving Gray alone.

Letty was only a woman, he thought, not much different from a dozen others he'd had. And yet there was something about her…something that made him think she might be more than what she seemed.

He scoffed. It was only her luscious little body that drew him, that and the fiery passion inside her he had glimpsed and ached to release. Whatever Dolph learned about Letty, Gray meant to have her. Once he had sampled her charms, she would be just another woman, one that in time he would tire of and be able to forget.

Gray thought of the life he had led, the countries he had traveled, the women he had known. Until his return to England, he had never felt this restlessness, this emptiness that continued to gnaw at him.

Or perhaps he had. Perhaps all those years he'd spent traveling, the years he had lived in India, he had felt it deep down inside. But it wasn't until after Jillian had died that he'd longer been able to ignore it.

What was it he searched for? What was it he wanted that remained so elusive, that always seemed to hover just out of his grasp? He didn't know, and perhaps it was better that he didn't.

Gray sighed. Closing his mind to his unwanted musings, he shed his clothes, blew out the lamp and climbed into his empty bed.

Eleven

When Allison rushed into her bedroom early the following morning, Corrie was still groggy from another night of restless sleep.

"Come on! Get up! There is a woman here to see you, a dressmaker from London! The entire household is abuzz."

Corrie opened her eyes and blinked at the sunlight streaming in through the window.

"Hurry!" Allison dragged back the covers and tugged on her hand.

"For heaven's sake, what are you doing?" Groggily, she swung her legs to the side of the feather mattress. After her encounter with the earl last night, she was exhausted. Even after she had gone to bed, it was impossible to fall asleep.

"I told you—a dressmaker is here from London, some fancy French designer. The earl must have sent for her. You need to get dressed. She is waiting—and so is the earl."

"What?"

Allison began rushing around the bedroom, collecting

and laying out undergarments, choosing a soft peach muslin morning dress along with matching kid slippers.

"Apparently, the earl told Rebecca that since you are a member of the family, it is his duty to see you properly clothed. I think they argued about it. The earl just ignored her."

Corrie thought of the determined man she had run into in the hall last night. "I am not surprised. He is entirely too used to getting his way."

"Perhaps you can tell him that when you go downstairs."

"I am *not* going downstairs." After their passionate encounter, the last person on earth she wished to see was Lord Tremaine.

"If you don't come down, the housekeeper said to tell you that the earl and the dressmaker will come up to your room."

"Good grief!"

"Exactly. We had better hurry."

And so, as rapidly as possible, Corrie slipped into her undergarments, stockings and slippers, then put on the peach muslin gown. Allison brushed her sleep-tangled hair and hurriedly pulled it back on the sides, fixing it in place with a pair of tortoiseshell combs.

"I cannot believe this," Corrie grumbled. "I have a houseful of clothes in London. I scarcely need more."

"No, but the earl doesn't know that. He thinks you are Letty, remember?"

Corrie groaned.

"You had better be on your way."

Resigning herself, she took a deep breath and headed for the door. At the bottom of the stairs stood the housekeeper, Mrs. Kittrick, a large-boned, buxom woman with iron-gray hair.

"They are waiting for you in the Sky Room." A drawing room in an older part of the castle whose ceiling had been painted during the Renaissance, with cherubs floating on fluffy white clouds in an azure sky. "If you will please follow me."

She fell in behind the robust woman, who rarely made an appearance above stairs. She was always busy working, and she seemed to be extremely efficient. Corrie doubted that Rebecca would settle for anything less from the staff.

Steeling herself to face the earl, Corrie walked past the housekeeper into the drawing room. Tremaine waited next to a tall, reedy woman with a slightly wrinkled face and dark hair streaked with silver.

"I am here—at your insistence," Corrie said. "But I do not need you to buy me any clothes." She forced herself to look at him, refused to think of last night, and prayed she would not blush.

"Actually, you do," he said. "If you will recall, you ruined one of your shabby dresses the day you saved that mangy dog. I doubt you brought many with you, and even if you did, they are barely fit to wear." His hard look softened. "Let me do this for you, Letty. I can well afford it. I should like to give you the dresses as a gift."

She felt like the worst sort of fraud. She was one of the best dressed young women in London. In fact, she prided herself on her wardrobe. How could she let the earl spend his money on a woman who had plenty of her own, and who had come to prove him guilty of murder?

She tried to think what Letty would do, or at least the Letty she portrayed. Reaching over, she caught hold of his hand. "Please, my lord. I have been forced to humble myself by coming here and asking for your help. I would take it as a personal favor if you would not add to my humiliation by forcing me to accept more of your generosity. I would not have you purchase the very clothes on my back."

Gray looked stunned, as if no woman he knew would refuse such a gift. "You need the dresses, Letty."

"I'll have my own income soon. Once I do, I'll be able to buy what I need."

He was frowning. "Are you certain? Most women would gladly accept such an offer."

"I am not most women, my lord."

"No," he said in that soft, deep voice that made her insides curl. "You most assuredly are not." He turned to the dressmaker. "I will, of course, pay for your time in coming all the way out here, plus a generous bonus."

The dressmaker nodded, satisfied, it would seem. "Thank you, my lord."

Corrie watched as the woman picked up her sewing basket, waited while her assistant reloaded a trunkful of sample fabrics, and the pair left the drawing room.

"Thank you, my lord," she said.

Gray just nodded. He was looking at her in a way he hadn't before, with a hint of admiration.

For the first time, Corrie realized how badly she wanted to prove Gray Forsythe innocent of her sister's murder.

It rained the following morning, but by the time Corrie was dressed and ready to set off for the village, a bright sun shone over the rolling green fields.

Grateful for the gift of such a day, which helped dispel her lingering bad mood, she stopped by the stable to check on Homer and found him anxiously prowling the stall where he was being cared for.

"'E needs some exercise, missus." The groom, a young man named Dickey Michaels, stood at the door of the stall.

"'Omer ain't used ta being cooped up." The lanky youth scratched the dog's ears, and it was clear the animal had made a new friend.

She smiled. "I'm on my way to the village. Do you think Homer is well enough to come along?"

Dickey opened the stall door and the dog rushed out, yapping merrily and dancing around her legs.

"Seems to be feelin' just fine. I think a walk would do 'im good."

"What if he runs away?"

Dickey just shrugged. "I suppose if 'e wants 'is freedom, ye ought to give it to 'im."

"Yes, I suppose that's true."

But Homer seemed perfectly content to roam along beside her, racing after an occasional butterfly, sniffing wildflowers in the field, digging up holes in the soft, damp earth.

Corrie ruffled his long gray fur, clean now, thanks to Dickey. "Maybe we'll get some answers this time," she said to the dog as they headed away from the house, though, of course, Homer didn't reply.

After finding Laurel's book, Corrie knew the hatmaker had been right. One of the lords at Castle Tremaine was the man Laurel had fallen in love with. The question remained, which one?

Perhaps someone in the village knew, but if so, who? And how would she get them to tell her? It occurred to her that the lovers had probably not trysted at the castle. Perhaps someone at the inn had seen them together.

She headed in that direction, making her way along the row of shops, passing several freight wagons in the street. Homer barked at a huge brown mastiff in the back of one—tied tightly, thank the Lord. Walking toward the far end of the village, Corrie spotted the Green Dragon Tavern up ahead.

"You stay here," she told Homer, wondering if he really would. Then she climbed the wooden steps, opened the door and stepped into the interior.

Off to the left of the stone-floored entry was a taproom, a low-ceilinged, smoky chamber with rough-hewn beams and worn oak floors. She walked over to one of the tavern maids hoping that for a price the woman might be willing talk.

Corrie pulled a silver coin from her reticule and held it up in front of the woman's plain, dish-shaped face. She was younger, blond and fair, with a great deal of bosom exposed above the gathered neckline of her white cotton blouse. For an instant, Corrie's mind flashed back to the other night, to the feel of the earl's hand cupping her breasts, the heat of his mouth on her skin.

Fighting not to blush, she forced the shameful memory away and turned her attention to the serving girl. "Would you like to earn this coin?"

The girl eyed her with suspicion. "Course I would."

"What's your name?"

"Greta. Greta Tweed."

"Do you know the lords who live at Castle Tremaine, Greta?"

She nodded. "The earl and his brother and young Lord Jason live there most of the time." She reached for the coin, but Corrie drew it back.

"One of them was seeing a young woman named Laurel Whitmore. She lived at Selkirk Hall. Would you have any idea which of them it was?" She held out the coin and the girl eyed it with longing.

"Were that young Lord Jason, I'll wager." She grinned. "The man's got the stamina o' a bull. He could turn the head o' just about any woman." It was clear she was speaking from experience, and Corrie felt her face heating up again.

"But you're guessing," she pressed. "You have no way of knowing for sure."

Greta shrugged her round, freckled shoulders. "All three of 'em's 'andsome as sin. Coulda been the earl 'isself. He don't pay for his fun like the younger one. Mostly, he beds down with them what calls themselves ladies. I s'ppose the daughter of a viscount would do, but he don't seem the sort to trifle with an innocent girl that way. I'd say he'd be more inclined to a woman with experience."

Greta leaned closer. "Talk is, he's built like a stallion. They say he studied all manner of lovemakin' over there in India. Knows exactly how to pleasure a woman." She grinned. "Wouldn't mind trying a bit o' that meself."

Face flaming, wishing she could turn and run for the door, Corrie handed the girl the coin. "Is there anyone who might know for certain which man it was?"

"I mostly know what's happenin' in these parts. One of them lords was sleepin' with the girl, he kept it quiet."

"Thank you for your help, Greta." Turning away, Corrie made her way to the door, ignoring the curious stares of the men in the smoky taproom as she pushed her way out into the sunshine.

She shouldn't have come. It was hardly proper for an unescorted female to enter a tavern, but it was the sort of place money could often buy information, and she'd had to take the chance.

Was it Gray? she asked herself for the hundredth time. Had he used his devil's powers to steal Laurel's innocence? After their late-night encounter, Corrie believed he certainly had the skill.

A yap at the bottom of the steps drew her attention. Homer sat on his haunches, awaiting her return, his long pink tongue hanging out. His ears perked up when he saw her, and she smiled, glad he had decided to stay. It was good to have friends, even a furry one, in a house where so much intrigue swirled around her.

She thought of the earl and felt a pang of guilt for what she'd let happen.

Perhaps that was the thing about desire. It chose you, not the other way around.

Leaving the tavern behind, Corrie made her way along the main street of the village. There seemed to be some sort of argument going on at Pendergast's Grocery. She was surprised to see the earl talking to a boy of ten or so. The grocer was also there, a fat man with curly gray side-whiskers.

Curious, she walked in that direction, staying close to the buildings, where she wouldn't draw attention.

"You know stealing is a crime?" Gray said to the boy, a skinny, dirty ragamuffin whose brown hair alternately poked out or stuck to his head.

"Yessir, milord."

"Are you hungry? Is that the reason you stole the bread?"

"Doesn't make a fiddler's damn," the shopkeeper interrupted. "The boy's got to be punished. A good hard birching's the only way to learn the difference between right and wrong."

The lad's face went pale, making his dark eyes look huge in his thin face. Gray flicked a warning glance at the grocer, a muscle tight in his jaw. Corrie thought he must be remembering the beatings he had suffered when he was a boy.

"I asked why you stole the bread."

One look at the earl's hard features and Corrie felt a wave of pity for the boy.

The lad looked up at him, his expression a mix between fear and defiance. "Me da died of the lung disease. Me and Ma come here from London to stay with Ma's sister, but when we got ta the house, Aunt Janie was gone. We didn't have no food. Ma was weak as a kitten. I—I didn't want 'er to die like me da."

The fat man harrumphed. "I'm going for the constable. I won't put up with thievery, no matter the lad's excuse."

"Hold on, Pendergast. There's no need to run off half-cocked." The command in Tremaine's voice made his request more of an order. The boy trembled as he looked into the earl's hard face.

"What's your name, son?"

"Georgie Hobbs, milord."

"Where's your mother now?"

"In the cottage where Aunt Janie lived. 'Bout a mile out o' town."

"You know stealing is wrong."

The boy looked down, dragged the toe of his worn leather shoe. "Yessir."

"If you do it again, I'm going to let Mr. Pendergast call the constable, and they'll lock you away. You understand?"

Georgie Hobbs nodded. "Y-yessir."

Pendergast opened his mouth to argue and the earl held up a hand. "I'm going to pay for that loaf of bread you stole, as well as some cheese and some meat. You're going to take them back to your mother. When the two of you have eaten your fill, you're to come to the castle and work off the debt you owe for the food. If you don't appear, I'll come after you. I'll personally give you that whipping Mr. Pendergast thinks you deserve. Is that clear?"

"Yessir."

"Do I have your word?"

"Aye, milord. On me honor, I swear it!"

"Get him what he needs," Tremaine said to the store owner, "and put it on my account."

"Yes, my lord." The shopkeeper looked smugly pleased at making a sale he wouldn't have made before.

Leaving the boy to complete the task, the earl turned away and started walking in Corrie's direction. Good grief, she should have left sooner. Now here he was, and she had no escape.

His head came up when he saw her. "Well, Mrs. Moss... I hadn't thought to see you again for a while. Aside from your forced encounter with the dressmaker, I imagined you would stay in your bedroom for at least several days, holed up like a frightened rabbit."

Irritation trickled through her. She wasn't a coward and never had been. "Then you would be sorely mistaken, my lord."

One of his eyebrows went up and it occurred to her that while Coralee Whitmore wasn't a coward, Letty Moss wouldn't be nearly so brave. "I mean...I—I realize what happened wasn't entirely your fault."

"No?"

"Well, I *am* a married woman, after all. I should have known better than to allow matters to get so out of hand."

Tremaine made no reply, but it was clear he didn't regret what had happened at all.

Homer raced up just then, yapping and begging for attention. Grateful for the distraction, Corrie reached down and petted his head.

"I'm afraid I had better get going," she said. "I was just heading back to the castle." She glanced toward Pendergast's Grocery, and a grudging compliment escaped. "That was quite well done of you, my lord. It doesn't seem fitting to punish a child for trying to feed his mother."

"No. Though stealing isn't right, either. Don't think for a moment I won't keep my promise should the lad not stand by his word."

She never doubted it. Tremaine had been a major in the army. Discipline and honor would have been part of his life. *Honor.* When had she begun to think of the devil earl as a man with any sort of honor?

"I was heading back home myself," he said. "I'll see you get there safely."

Corrie clamped down on an urge to refuse his escort, to tell him she didn't need nor want him anywhere near her. It was unsettling enough just living in the same house with him. Still, she was his guest. She had no choice but to agree.

The earl retrieved his horse, then walked beside her along the path, Homer trailing in their wake. Neither of them said much along the way, and she found the companionable silence unexpectedly pleasant.

"You seem to enjoy the village," he finally said. "You spend a good deal of time there."

She shrugged, not pleased he had noticed. "I like to get out-of-doors. And the villagers are friendly."

They left the stallion and the dog with Dickey, who waited in front of the house. Tremaine took her arm to help her climb the steep stone steps to the door, which opened before they reached it. When she walked into the entry, Gray's servant, the dark-skinned man from India, waited for their approach.

"What is it, Samir?" Tremaine asked.

"A letter for the *memsahib.* It came while she was away in the village."

Corrie looked at the little man and frowned. "How did

you know I went to the...? Never mind." She reached for the letter addressed to Letty Moss. "If you will excuse me, my lord?"

He made a faint bow. "Of course."

Turning, she headed upstairs to her bedroom. The only people who knew where to find her, knew she was using that name, were Aunt Agnes, Allison, Krista and Leif. She wrote to her parents, of course. She didn't want them to get suspicious, but any letters from them came to Selkirk Hall and Allison brought them to her.

Corrie looked down at the letter in her hand. It came from Krista, she saw as she closed the bedroom door and broke the wax seal. The message was brief.

> *Leif hired Dolph Petersen to investigate Grayson Forsythe. Mr. Petersen says the earl's wife's death was a boating accident. There was no evidence of foul play. He says the earl was with Bethany Chambers, Countess of Devane, the night Laurel died. He didn't leave her house until morning. Dolph says Tremaine was barely acquainted with Laurel. Please come home. Your friends, Krista and Leif.*

Her mind spun. *Not Gray, not Gray, not Gray.*

The words revolved in her head and with them came a rush of relief so powerful it made her head swim. She sank down on the bench at the foot of the bed just as Allison knocked on the door and walked into the room.

"What is it? What's happened?" Mobcap slightly askew over her shiny dark hair, she hurried to where Corrie sat on the bench. "Are you all right? You're looking a little flushed."

Corrie held out the letter. "It wasn't Gray...I mean, Lord Tremaine. He was with his mistress that night." And though the knowledge rankled, it was an incredible weight off her shoulders to know the man who attracted her so fiercely had never been Laurel's lover.

Which meant it was unlikely he was responsible for what had happened to Laurel and her baby that night.

Allison read the letter and handed it back. "You thought it was the earl, but it wasn't, so now can we go home?"

Corrie sighed. "It wasn't Gray, but the book I found in the study proves Laurel was in love with one of the men in the house. All we have to do is find out which one."

"That's all we have to do?" Allison said sarcastically.

"Well, it has to be one of them."

"So why don't you just ask them? Maybe the man who is guilty will tell you."

Good heavens, she couldn't possibly do that. Could she? But the notion intrigued her. She couldn't ask Jason or Charles, but what about Gray? She trusted Dolph Petersen to find out the truth, which meant Gray had never been involved with Laurel. But perhaps the earl knew which of the other two men had been.

A tremor of unease ran through Corrie. If she wanted to find out what the earl knew, she would have to talk to him, spend time with him, gain at least a bit of his trust. Dear God, she could barely think when he was around. She didn't trust herself when she was with him, didn't trust the wild, wanton feelings he so easily aroused.

Still, if she approached the matter carefully, if she kept her wits and her body under control, perhaps he might tell her what she wished to know.

"You have that look in your eye," Allison said, beginning to know her too well.

"I think, dear Ally, you may have a very good notion."

"What? I was jesting, Coralee. You can't simply *ask* them!"

"No, but if I handle the matter with care, perhaps I can get the information out of the earl."

Allison pointed toward the letter in Corrie's hand. "Maybe this Mr. Petersen can figure out which of the men it was."

Corrie nodded. "Good idea. I should have thought of that myself. I knew there was a reason I brought you along."

Moving toward the bed, she knelt and dragged out her trunk, opened the lid and stashed the letter in the bottom. "I shall write to Krista tonight, tell her about the book I found, and have her ask Mr. Petersen to continue his investigation into the other two Forsythe men. In the meantime, I'm going to see what I can find out from the earl."

Allison groaned.

Fighting a smile, Corrie headed for the door. "I'll be back in a while."

"Are you sure you know what you're—"

Corrie closed the door with a quiet click, then paused in the hallway to gather her courage. She didn't want to spend more time with Gray, but she needed information, and to get it, she had no choice.

Twelve

Corrie found the earl out in the stable, grooming his big black horse. He didn't seem to notice her arrival, so she simply stood there watching him, trying to dredge up the courage to approach where he worked, brushing the stallion, then setting the blanket in place and his flat leather saddle on top.

Though he was a tall, broad-shouldered man, there was a certain gracefulness in his actions, an ease about his movements and no wasted effort. A lock of black hair had come loose from the black velvet ribbon at his nape. It teased one of his high cheekbones, and her stomach contracted.

She had the strangest urge to pull the ribbon free and run her hands through his glossy hair, discover if it was as silky as it looked. She wanted him to drag her into his arms and kiss her the way he had the other night.

Good grief! It was happening again, and she wasn't even near him!

"Keep looking at me that way and I'll do exactly what it is you're thinking about."

She must have jumped several inches and a guilty flush

spread into her cheeks. "I—I was only thinking that it is quite…quite a nice day for riding."

He paused as he tightened the cinch. "Do you ride, Letty?"

"Yes, but not all that well." She'd had lessons, of course. Krista loved to ride and was a very accomplished horsewoman, but Corrie had ridden mostly in the park, as it was fashionable to do.

"You're here in the country," he said. "I think today would be a good day for you to begin developing your skill."

"Today? But I couldn't possibly—"

"You lived on a farm. Surely you own a riding habit."

"Well, I…yes, of course." Allison had insisted she bring one along. Since Letty was supposed to have lived on a farm, it was probably a good thing she had.

"I'll wait here while you go in and change."

Corrie hesitated at the thought of an afternoon riding with Tremaine, being alone with him, feeling those strange unwanted urges she couldn't seem to control.

On the other hand, she needed to win his trust. She couldn't do that unless she spent time with him.

It was a terrifying thought.

She drew in a breath and pasted on a smile. "As you wish, my lord." Homer yapped at her side as she hurried back to the house.

With Allison helping, she was able to return to the stables twenty minutes later dressed in a slightly frayed, dark green velvet riding habit. A pretty little sorrel mare stood docilely next to the earl's big black. Her ears perked up at Corrie's approach.

"She's lovely."

"Tulip's very gentle." Tremaine slid a hand along the mare's sleek neck, and Corrie felt as if he was touching her. "She won't give you any trouble."

"I'm sure she'll be fine." She was thinking the only one who might give her trouble was the Earl of Tremaine.

She walked over and patted the sorrel's neck, careful to keep her distance from Gray, and glanced toward the black stallion. "What about Raja? Will he be all right with Tulip?"

"She isn't in season," he said baldly, sending a wash of color into Corrie's cheeks. "He'll behave himself."

She only prayed Gray would also behave. "Where are we going?"

"I need to make a call on one of my tenants. His wife is with child and I want to make sure they have whatever they might need."

He was worried about his tenants. It surprised her. She thought of him as the devil earl, and devils didn't care about other people.

"Ready?" he asked, and she nodded. Walking up behind her, he set his hands at her waist and lifted her up on the sidesaddle. Corrie remembered to release the breath she was holding. Even through her corset, the heat of his hands lingered well after he had walked away.

Gray swung up on the black, nudged the horse toward a path leading from the stable, and Tulip fell in beside him. Corrie hadn't ridden in months, but the lessons she'd had over the years began to come back, and she settled more easily in the sidesaddle. The leather reins felt good between her gloved fingers, and a warm sun beat down on the back of her neck.

"You've a very nice seat, Mrs. Moss," Tremaine said with a smile as they rode along. But there was a glint in his eyes that hinted the seat he was speaking of had nothing to do with riding.

Or perhaps it did.

She colored faintly and hoped Gray wouldn't notice. "Thank you," she answered with polite formality.

The horses moved easily across the rolling green fields, and once the earl was satisfied with her ability, such as it was, he increased the pace. Tulip cantered along as if she hadn't a care in the world, and Tremaine kept his stallion to the same easy stride.

They had ridden for nearly an hour when he pulled up at the top of a rise. "That's Peter and Sarah Cardigan's house, just over there at the edge of that copse of trees." He pointed in that direction and Corrie spotted a little thatch-roofed cottage with a plume of smoke rising from the chimney.

Gray urged the stallion on and Tulip again fell into step beside him. They drew up in front of the small, white-washed house, and Gray came round to help Corrie down. She steeled herself as his hands found her waist and he lifted her off the horse. Instead of setting her on the ground, he eased her down the length of his body, letting her feel his hard frame inch by inch.

Her breathing hitched. Her heart began to pound. "Put me down, Gray."

A corner of his mouth edged up as if he had won some small victory, and she realized that in calling him by his first name, he had. "As you wish."

He set her on her feet and turned away, tied the horses' reins to a post in front of the cottage, guided her over and knocked on the door.

A soft groan greeted them.

"Mrs. Cardigan?" Gray called out.

"Please…" whispered a woman's voice, so softly it went almost unheard. "Please…help me…."

Gray thrust open the door and strode inside the house, and Corrie hurried in behind him. They raced through a small living area made comfortable with handmade furniture upholstered in chintz and covered by crocheted doilies, past an area that served as a kitchen, into a cozy bedroom off to one side. A woman lay amid the bedcovers, the huge girth of her belly sticking up beneath the sheet, her dark hair tumbling wildly across the pillow beneath her head.

Tremaine reached her side and took hold of her shaking hand. "Mrs. Cardigan, where is your husband? Where is Peter?"

She swallowed, moistened her dry lips. "He went—went for the midwife. I told him…there wasn't time, but…but he didn't know what else to do." She groaned in pain and started panting to catch her breath. "Please…help me."

The earl turned to Corrie. "We'll need hot water and towels of some kind. The stove is already burning. The well is just outside."

"What…what are you going to do?"

"Help Mrs. Cardigan have her baby." He turned away, stripped off his riding coat and tossed it over a chair, then reached down to lift the sheet.

Corrie's eyes widened. "But…but you can't possibly mean to…"

The earl swung back to her, his gaze hard. "Do what I told you. The woman needs our help. Get out there and bring me what I need!" The command in his voice settled her, as he had meant for it to do.

Corrie swallowed, took a deep breath and nodded. "Yes, yes, of course. Water and towels. I'll get them as quickly as I can."

The earl seemed relieved. Corrie ran out of the bedroom, into the tiny kitchen. A fire was burning in the old iron stove, but it wasn't hot enough. Tossing off her jaunty little hat and removing her jacket, she added a few pieces of wood, grabbed the water bucket off its hook and raced outside. She had never done household chores, but it didn't take long to figure out how to haul up the bucket from the bottom of the well and transfer water to the pail she had brought with her.

A sharp shriek split the air and Corrie jerked so hard she almost spilled the water. Frightened for both mother and child, she carried the heavy pail into the kitchen and dumped its contents into a pan sitting on the stove.

Towels.

She glanced around. Thank God, there was a stack of clean white linen resting on the end of the counter, preparations Mrs. Cardigan had apparently made for the coming birth of her child.

Corrie's chest tightened. She had never been anywhere near a woman giving birth, but she had heard stories of the terrible pain and suffering. The woman cried out again, her wrenching cries coming far more often, and Corrie thought of Laurel and the pain she must have suffered to bring her child into the world. Surely, she would have done anything to protect a gift that had come at so high a price.

Grabbing the stack of linens off the counter, Corrie rushed into the bedroom. "Here are the towels. The water's almost—" She broke off in horror as she realized the woman's nightgown was shoved up to her waist, leaving her naked, and her legs were spread wide apart. There was blood on the sheets and on Gray's white linen shirt.

"Oh, my God!"

He didn't spare her a glance, but his voice was soft when he spoke to her. "It's all right, Letty. Sarah is doing just fine."

"But…but there's so much blood."

"That's just part of having a baby." He looked up, a

slight frown marring his forehead. "Surely on a farm, you saw animals being birthed."

"Well, I…" She took a deep breath. "As I said, Cyrus was very protective. He didn't believe it was a proper thing for a lady to see."

Gray's gaze held hers for an instant, then he returned his attention to the woman on the bed.

"You're going to be all right," he said to her. "Letty and I are going to help you."

Corrie swallowed and set the towels down on the nightstand. Sarah Cardigan screamed in pain, and Corrie started shaking. Dear God, she had no idea how to help a woman birth a child!

She forced herself to calm down. Hurrying out of the bedroom, she ran back for the water, which was boiling away on the stove. She ladled some into a smaller pan and carried it back into the bedroom, then went for cold water and a cloth to sponge the poor woman's face.

By the time she returned to the bedroom, Mrs. Cardigan's skin was the color of paper and she was soaked in perspiration. Corrie sponged her forehead, then wiped down her throat and shoulders.

"Thank you…" Sarah said through dry lips. Corrie laid the damp cloth over them, giving her a bit of moisture. The earl glanced her way, saw what she was doing, and something softened in his face.

A piercing cry rent the air and she realized that the head of the baby had begun to shove its way out of the woman's body. Unconsciously, Corrie reached for Sarah's hand, whose icy fingers tightened into a grip of steel.

"It's all right," Corrie soothed. "The earl knows what to do."

He flashed her a glance, then returned his attention to

the woman. Well, he did seem to know, she thought as he urged Sarah to push at just the right time, whispering words of encouragement in a voice so deeply male it resonated through Corrie's entire body.

"The baby's coming," he said. "Get me a knife and make sure it's clean."

"A knife?"

He glanced up. "And a piece of string."

Having no idea what the items might be used for, Corrie raced back to the kitchen and found a knife and string set out where she had found the linens. She picked up the butcher knife, tested its sharpness, washed it in some of the boiling water, and grabbed the length of string. Hurrying back to the bedroom, she set the knife down beside the linens, turned and saw Tremaine leaning over the woman.

When he stepped back, he was holding a newborn infant, his long fingers wrapped around the baby's ankles. A quick slap to the bottom and the baby let out an earsplitting scream. Corrie watched in fascination as he used the knife and string to sever the long cord that connected the child to its mother, then wrapped the infant in one of the linen towels and set the bundle in Corrie's arms.

"I—I don't know how to hold a baby," she said nervously.

Tremaine made a sound in his throat. "Every woman knows how to hold a baby. I think it's something to do with your makeup as a female." He turned to the woman on the bed. "You've a daughter, Sarah. A beautiful little girl."

Tears rolled down the woman's cheeks. "God bless you both for what you've done." She was a big woman, but pretty, her limbs firm and strong, the sort of female made for birthing babies.

While Tremaine worked to clean up the infant, Corrie

changed the linens on the bed and helped the mother into a fresh nightgown. When she finished, she looked up to see Gray looking down at the infant he cradled in his arms. There was so much emotion in his face her breath caught.

Dear Lord, surely it wasn't yearning.

Wrapping the baby in a yellow woolen blanket he found folded and waiting on the dresser, he carried her over to the bed and settled her in the crook of her mother's arm.

Corrie watched Sarah and the baby, feeling an odd melting in her chest. She moved quietly toward them.

"She's so tiny." She reached out, yearning to touch the child, her heart swelling with emotion. "She's beautiful, Sarah."

"Thank you. Thank you for everything."

A lump rose in Corrie's throat, making it impossible to speak. She blinked to hold back tears. She had helped bring a new life into the world. It was amazing, exhilarating, the most incredible experience of her life. She turned toward Gray and saw the same exhilaration reflected in his eyes.

Neither of them spoke, unwilling to end the moment. Then the door burst open and Peter Cardigan rushed into the room.

"Midwife's gone off to birth another babe. God Almighty, Sarah, what are we gonna—" His eyes locked on the earl and he blinked, as if he couldn't believe what he was seeing.

"You've a daughter, Peter. And with a little rest, your wife is going to be fine."

Peter Cardigan just stood there, a look of disbelief on his ruddy, dirt-smudged face. Without a word, he rushed to his wife's side and knelt next to the bed. "Sarah…God above, I never should have left you."

His wife managed a tired but reassuring smile. "It's all

right, luv. Your daughter is here—thanks to the earl and his lady. Everything is fine."

Peter Cardigan seemed to regain his wits. He turned to Tremaine and began a round of thanks that seemed to have no end. Eventually, Corrie and the earl were able to retrieve their belongings and slip away, leaving the proud parents with the daughter they named Mary Kate.

"You knew what you were doing in there," Corrie said to the earl as they walked toward the well to wash up. "You've delivered a baby before."

He nodded, tossed his riding coat over one shoulder. "In India. There was a woman…a camp follower. I found her in the bushes along the road. There wasn't time to fetch the surgeon. There was no one to help her but me."

Corrie studied him with renewed respect. "Another man might have left them."

He shrugged. "Perhaps. I'm not a man who could."

She mulled that over, adding it to the list of things she was beginning to know about him. "What happened to the child and its mother? Were they all right?"

"They were the last time I saw them, just before I left India to return to England."

He was talking, opening up to her. She needed him to continue. "You seemed comfortable with the infant. Did you want a family when you were married?"

Tremaine stopped dead in his tracks. Corrie held her breath, waiting to see if he would answer. "I wanted children then. Not anymore."

"Why not?"

"I'm not cut out to be a father. I should have realized that before I married. I wouldn't know how to raise a child."

She looked up at him. "Because you never really had a father of your own."

His jaw tightened.

"I've heard the stories. I know the late earl treated you very badly."

Gray scoffed as if she had just made a grand understatement. "Douglas Forsythe was a real bastard."

She should have been shocked at his language. Instead when she thought of the beatings he had suffered, the loveless home he had grown up in, she silently agreed.

"Whatever sort of man your father was, I saw you in there with Sarah and her baby, and I think you would make a wonderful father."

"Well, it isn't going to happen. I've no intention of marrying again, so you needn't concern yourself."

"But—"

"That's enough, Letty." Gray started walking, his jaw clenched as it hadn't been before. And yet he had opened himself up to her a little. In time, perhaps she could get him to talk about his brother and his cousin.

As she walked along beside him, she thought of what he had said, that he would never remarry, that he no longer wanted a family.

It shouldn't have bothered her, but it did.

Gray studied the woman beside him. Once she'd gotten over the shock of the baby's impending birth, she had given herself over to the task without reservation.

Not one of the upper-class women he knew would be willing to dirty her hands to help a simple peasant woman, but Letty seemed not to mind. In fact, she had been fascinated by the miracle of the infant's birth.

Letty had surprised him today. But then, she continued to surprise him, which, he supposed, was one of the reasons he was so attracted to her. That and her innocent responses. And of course, there was the not-so-small matter of her extremely passionate nature and luscious body. If only he could make her see how good it could be between them.

Thinking of the frustration he continued to suffer, Gray silently cursed.

Letty had said she wasn't attracted to his cousin, and after Gray had overcome his unwanted and completely unexpected jealousy, he believed her. Letty belonged to him in some way, and though she protested mightily, it was only a matter of time before she would acknowledge the pull between them and let him make love to her.

His mind returned to the questions she had asked him about his marriage. It was a forbidden topic. He didn't discuss his late wife or the grief he had suffered when she died. People who knew him knew better than to bring up the painful subject, or risk calling down his wrath on their heads.

But Letty hadn't realized the subject was taboo, and Gray had surprised himself by answering her questions. He didn't know why, but with Letty, it didn't seem as difficult as it was with someone else.

Gray pondered the notion as he walked to the well, his mood turning dark once more. After his mother had died, he had built a protective wall around his emotions. He'd done so in order to survive the terrible years with his father.

Even after his marriage, that had not changed. Jillian was his wife and Gray had cared for her greatly, was devastated by his failure to protect her as he should have.

Still, he had never allowed her to get too close, had

never let down his guard where his wife was concerned. He didn't intend for that to change.

He wasn't about to let anyone, not even sweet little Letty, find a way inside the wall that had protected him all these years.

Thirteen

───────⟡⟡⟡───────

Corrie studied Gray's grim features as they approached the well. "You're different than I thought you were. I can't seem to figure you out."

His head came up. The hardness left his face. "I haven't managed to figure you out yet, either."

Thank goodness for that, she thought. She could only imagine Tremaine's dark rage if he knew who she was and why she had schemed her way into his home.

"You did well in there," he said. "Most of the women I know would have fainted dead away at the sight of all that blood."

Corrie tried not to be pleased. "As you said, Sarah needed our help."

Tremaine paused beside the well, tossed his jacket aside and pulled up a bucket of water. She didn't realize his intention until he grabbed the hem of his bloodstained shirt and pulled it off over his head. Smooth dark skin covered a wide chest rippling with muscle. A crisp mat of coarse black hair arrowed down over a flat stomach ridged with muscle and disappeared into the waistband of his snug black riding breeches.

A ripple of desire washed through her, settled deep in her core. A large, very masculine bulge at the front of his breeches caught her attention, and Corrie remembered the tavern maid's words, *"Talk is he's built like a stallion."*

"You're looking at me that way again, Letty. I hope you like what you see."

Hot color washed into her cheeks. "I was *not* looking at you, and you, my lord, are extremely conceited. Besides, looking is hardly my fault when you strip off your clothes at every opportunity."

He actually grinned. Her breath caught at the changes it made in his face. He looked younger and even more handsome, and as his grin slowly faded, she wondered what it might be like if he laughed. Would those same faint lines crinkle beside his eyes? Would his laughter sound deep and husky, the way his voice often did?

"Sorry," he said with amusement. "I forgot your delicate sensibilities. Unfortunately, I didn't think to bring along a clean shirt." He dumped water onto the stained white linen to rinse out the blood, washed his face and chest, then put the wet shirt back on.

"Does this satisfy your modesty?" he asked, though of course the wet shirt clung to every ridge and sinew, and was so transparent she could see his flat copper nipples.

Heat curled low in her belly and she had to glance away. She washed her face and hands as best she could, then dried them on the handkerchief he handed her.

Afraid to look at him, she studied the horizon, where gently rolling hills met the bright blue sky. "It's time to head back to the castle."

She could feel his eyes on her. "I suppose you're right."

Taking her hand, he led her back to the horses, lifted her
up on Tulip, then swung onto the black. After her unsuc-
cessful effort to replace her hat, he plucked it from her
hand, stuffed it into his saddlebags, and they set off for
home. As far as Coralee was concerned, it had been a very
long afternoon.

Gray nudged Raja into an easy gallop, and Tulip took
up the pace. The blissful afternoon he had envisioned had
come to a fruitless end. He had imagined, after a brief stop
to check on his tenants, sharing lunch and a flask of wine
with Letty, making love to her until his wild craving for
her had at last been satisfied.

Gray sighed as they rode along. If a man's plans could
be destroyed in a heartbeat, certainly finding a pregnant
woman in the throes of labor had done so better than anything he could have imagined.

And yet, as he spotted the secluded copse of trees up
ahead where he had planned to accomplish his seduction,
it occurred to him that perhaps his plans could be sal-
vaged.

Just thinking about making love to Letty made him
hard. Gray turned the stallion, and Letty followed him
into the grove. Pulling Raja to a halt, he swung down
from the saddle.

"Why are we stopping?"

Gray just kept striding toward her. "You haven't ridden
much. You looked as if you could use a rest."

"I am fine. I don't need a rest."

"There's some meat and cheese in my saddlebags. You
haven't eaten since we left."

"I told you I am fine."

Ignoring her protests, he wrapped his hands around her

waist, lifted her down from the sidesaddle and straight into his arms.

"Letty…" Bending his head, he settled his mouth very softly over hers. Her lips were as sweet as heaven, and the scent of her filled his senses. His tongue traced the corners of her mouth, coaxing her to open for him, and the taste of her made him even harder.

He could feel her resistance, her uncertainty in the slight pressure of her hands against his chest. Gray ignored her subtle protest, kissing her until she made a soft little sighing sound in her throat, rose up on her toes and kissed him back.

Inwardly he groaned. The heat of her, the feel of her feminine curves pressed against him, sent a jolt of fire through his blood. He pulled her into the vee of his legs, letting her feel how hard he was, how much he wanted her, ached to be inside her.

"Gray…" she whispered as he kissed her neck, nipped the lobe of an ear.

"I need you, Letty." He kissed her again, more deeply this time, and her body seemed to melt into his.

Need poured through him, the powerful urge to make her his. "Let me take care of you," he whispered. "I'll find you a nice place to live…." He cupped her breasts, gently kneaded them. "A house not too far from the castle…"

Another searing kiss had her swaying against him.

"I'll see you have whatever you require," he said softly, "whatever you want."

His words finally seemed to reach her. But instead of looking up at him as if he were her savior, Letty jerked away as if he had slapped her.

"You aren't suggesting…you're not thinking I should—should become your *mistress?*"

Gray caught both her hands, hating the look of betrayal

on her face. "Your husband is gone. You have no idea when, or if, he'll ever return. You need a man to protect you. Would it really be so bad if I were that man?"

Her cheeks flamed. "I—I am not interested in any sort of arrangement. In a few weeks time, I shall…shall come into my inheritance and be gone from here for good." She glanced away and he could see that he had hurt her. It was the last thing he'd meant to do.

"I was a fool to allow you to take liberties," she finished. "I am sorry if I gave you a false impression."

He caught the glint of tears in her eyes the instant before she turned and walked away.

"Letty!"

She ignored him, caught her horse's reins and led the mare over to a stump to regain her seat.

Dammit to hell and gone. Gray caught up with her and turned her to face him, desperate to make her understand. "You want me, Letty. You can't deny it. Let me make love to you. I can show you pleasure unlike anything you've dreamed."

She took a step back, as if to shield herself from him. "I'm sorry, my lord, I can't."

Gray lifted her chin with his fingers. "Are you certain?" Bending his head, he kissed her very softly on the lips. "We'll be good together, Letty. I promise you."

She stared at him for several long moments and his hopes soared.

Then she shook her head. "I told you…I can't."

Clamping down hard on his disappointment, Gray said nothing more. He fought an urge to call her back, try once more to make her agree.

Instead, he lifted her onto her sidesaddle, his mood even darker than before. His shaft pulsed with unspent

need, and every time he looked at Letty, the sharp edge of
lust cut into him. He would get no satisfaction today, he
knew. Yet Letty's flat refusal to become his mistress made
it imperative he succeed in seducing her soon.

He would woo her and take her, he vowed, give her the
pleasure he had promised.

Once she was his, she would not refuse him again.

Gray clenched his teeth. Letty Moss had gotten under
his skin and he would not be rid of her until he had pos-
sessed her. Once he had tasted her shy passion, once he had
satisfied his craving for her, he would be free of whatever
mysterious hold she had over him.

He flicked her a glance, caught the gleam of her fiery
hair, and his loins swelled painfully. He wanted Letty Moss
and he intended to have her.

Today was only a skirmish in what he intended to be a
very short campaign.

Homer was yapping at the end of his tether, fiercely
wagging his tail, when Corrie and the earl rode into the
courtyard. Gray swung from his horse, walked over and
lifted Corrie down. She turned away from him as soon as
her feet touched the ground.

She hadn't been prepared for the earl's indecent propo-
sal, or her wild yearning to agree. It was ridiculous. She
wasn't Letty Moss, gently reared, impoverished, abandoned wife. She was Coralee Whitmore, the daughter of
a viscount, and she wouldn't cast her virtue aside for a
scoundrel like the Earl of Tremaine no matter how appealing he was.

She hadn't forgotten the womanizing rogue she had
written about in her column, nor his recent affair with
Lady Devane. The man was a scandalous knave who

wanted nothing more from her than the use of her body. It was insane to feel this ridiculous longing for him.

Hurrying toward the dog, she untied the rope round his neck and ruffled his long gray fur. "Did you miss me, boy?" She scratched his head, careful not to look at Gray. Homer yapped one last time, then raced off in search of a rabbit or whatever he might find in the field.

"'E'll be back," Dickey said. "'E's happy 'ere. 'E's found 'imself a 'ome. Don't think 'e ever really 'ad one before."

"Perhaps not." A memory of her conversation with Gray returned and Corrie wondered if perhaps the reason he didn't want a family was because he had never really had one. He had lost his mother as a boy, been raised by a father who didn't love him, then married and lost his wife.

Perhaps he feared that if he remarried, he might lose something precious again. The thought softened her anger toward him, and she turned at the sound of his deep voice.

"Thank you for your help this afternoon. I didn't invite you along to help birth a babe, but I'm glad·you were there."

Reluctant pleasure filled her. "I did little. You handled everything that mattered."

"It would have been a lot ·harder without you." He caught her hand. "I had planned a quiet outing. It didn't turn out that way, but perhaps I could make it up to you on the morrow."

She quickly shook her head. "You know how I feel, Gray."

"Even if I promise not to touch you?"

She was torn. If she hoped to discover the name of the man who had been Laurel's lover, she needed to spend time with the earl. And yet his indecent proposition still stung. She wasn't ready to beard the lion again quite so soon, and she couldn't resist a little sting of her own.

Corrie gave him a too-bright smile. "I appreciate the thought, my lord, but your cousin Jason has offered to show me round the conservatory. He seems to have quite an interest in flowers."

A muscle tightened in Tremaine's hard jaw. "The only flower Jason has an interest in is the one beneath your skirts."

Her false smile faded, replaced by a flash of anger that colored her cheeks. "Is that so? Then it would seem the two of you have at least one thing in common." The man was incorrigible! He said whatever he pleased with no concern for decorum.

Still, it was his very unconventionality that made him so appealing.

Turning away from him, she started toward the house.

"We aren't finished, Letty."

She glanced back, once more, pasting the false smile on her face. "Oh, but we are, my lord."

Behind her, she heard the earl's soft curse.

Fourteen

Corrie sat across from Charles, next to Jason in the break-fast room. As he entered, Gray cast her a dark, forbidding glance and took his place at the head of the table.

Rebecca floated airily into the room and the men rose politely. Charles seated his wife next to him.

"Thank you, darling."

Charles filled a plate of sausage and eggs from the sideboard, then set the plate in front of his wife. She cast a brief glance at Gray, her mouth curving into one of her feline smiles.

"I'll expect everyone for luncheon," she said. "The Countess of Devane will be arriving sometime late this morning."

Corrie's stomach knotted. Lady Devane was the woman Gray had been with the night of Laurel's murder. The countess was Gray's mistress! Corrie's gaze shot to his face and she saw that he was frowning.

"The countess is a friend of Becky's," Charles ex-plained. "Her country estate, Parkside, is less than an hour's ride away."

Coralee knew who she was, though they had never been introduced. Lady Devane was quite well known in society.

Gray's jaw looked tight. "I'm afraid I have plans for the afternoon." He flicked a glance at Corrie. "Mrs. Cardigan had a baby yesterday. I thought I would take her and her husband a basket of food, see how their newborn is faring."

Though his concern pleased her, Corrie said nothing. The earl's mistress was coming to luncheon. Dear God, she would have to smile and converse and try not to wonder at the things the two of them had done together.

"Surely your visit can wait until tomorrow," Rebecca said. "I've planned a very nice meal to be served on the terrace. You don't wish to insult the countess, do you?"

"Come on, have pity, Gray," Jason teased. "You know the only reason she's coming is to see you."

"Jason, behave yourself," Rebecca chided. "The countess is a married woman."

Jason grinned, digging dimples into his cheeks. "A married woman with a husband as old as Methuselah."

Rebecca tried for a look of reproach, but Corrie thought that secretly she seemed pleased Jason had made the relationship clear. Corrie wasn't a fool. Even if Krista's letter had not revealed the information, she would have known from the conversation that the countess was Gray's mistress.

The earl leveled his hard gaze on Rebecca. "I suppose I can stay until after luncheon…as I'm sure you and the countess planned."

Rebecca merely smiled.

Corrie felt sick to her stomach. She swallowed a bite of eggs, but it seemed to stick in her throat. The meal passed in a blur, little of which she recalled, and as soon as she could politely excuse herself, she left the breakfast room.

She headed straight for the garden, desperate for a breath of fresh, untainted air. It was a cloudy, late spring morning, but the crocuses had bloomed, the trees were leafing out above the walkways. She was standing next to the fountain, taking deep, calming breaths, when she heard familiar footfalls approaching behind her.

She kept her back to Gray. "Please go away."

"At least let me explain."

It was insane to feel jealous. She knew the sort of man he was, knew he was a complete and utter rogue who hadn't the least desire for anything from her but the use of her body. Yet thinking of Gray with another woman made her insides swirl with nausea.

"She's your mistress, Gray." She turned and looked up at him. "What is there to explain?"

"She isn't my mistress—not anymore." He released a slow breath. "After Jillian died, I couldn't bring myself to… I wasn't interested in physical gratification." He glanced away, as if picturing that dark time. "Bethany and Rebecca were friends. The countess came to the house quite often and eventually she made her interest clear. I wanted to forget the past. Bethany provided a way for me to do that. But our relationship was based on physical need, nothing more. We were never so much as friends."

Corrie was surprised by the turbulence she saw in his dark eyes, as if he cared what she thought, as if he was worried that he had hurt her.

"Most of the time, Bethany lives in London," he added. "Since her return to Parkside more than a month ago, I haven't seen her. I don't intend to."

Corrie lifted her chin. "Your relationship with the countess is none of my business."

"Perhaps not. I just…wanted you to know that Bethany means nothing to me. She never has."

Corrie looked into his handsome face and saw that he was truly concerned. But why should he care?

"Thank you for telling me."

He nodded. "Bethany has worse claws than Rebecca. I won't leave you alone with her."

So he had noticed his sister-in-law's behavior, the treatment that bordered on rudeness. "I suppose I should be grateful, but I don't think I am."

His mouth curved faintly. "I was hoping you would be. I could show you ways to repay me that—"

She pressed a hand over his lips, felt the warmth of his breath against her fingertips.

He straightened away from her, made her a formal bow. "I shall see you at luncheon, Mrs. Moss."

She watched him walk away, thinking how he must have suffered after his wife died, that he must have loved her at least in his own way. Corrie thought how lonely he often seemed, and wished she didn't feel such a fierce urge to comfort him. The man was a notorious rogue. He needed her body, not her heart.

And yet lately when he looked at her, she saw a need in him she hadn't recognized before. It called to her, made her want to hold him, erase the pain he had suffered through the years. It made her want to give him the one thing he had never had.

Love.

The realization burst over her, sank into her, made her gasp for breath. Dear God, she couldn't love Gray! Would not allow herself to love him. The man would ruin her without a backward glance. He would never love her in return—she wasn't sure he even knew how. If she fell in love with the Earl of Tremaine, he would break her heart into a thousand little pieces.

Corrie took a deep, strengthening breath. She wasn't in love with Gray, and from now on she wouldn't take any chances. She wouldn't allow him to get too close, to use those yearning looks and persuasive glances.

She would be careful to guard her heart.

Gray watched Letty in the drawing room. Bethany had just arrived, driving up in her husband's coach and four, wearing an elaborate gown of pale blue silk and ivory lace, the bodice cut a little too low for an afternoon luncheon. With her mahogany curls, finely arched brows and expanse of creamy bosom displayed by the gown, she looked every inch the countess.

Standing next to her, Letty wore a dress of yellow gauze and lace he had seen before, slightly outdated, the cuffs a bit frayed. She was shorter, more petite than the countess, a little unsure how to behave under the circumstances, and to his way of thinking, far more desirable than Bethany ever would be.

Letty looked fresh and lovely and innocent, and he wanted her more than he ever had before.

"So you are married to Gray's cousin." The countess raised her chin so she could look down her fine, straight nose at Letty.

"That is correct. My husband is traveling at present. I thought it a good time for a visit."

Bethany smiled with cunning. "Yes, well, Gray has a reputation for picking up strays."

He inwardly cursed. The claws were out, but Letty pretended not to notice.

"Unfortunately, I shan't be able to visit much longer."

She smiled as if it were she who was doing him the favor by paying him a call. "I shall be off to London soon."

Gray almost smiled in turn. She was holding her own, he was only a little surprised to see. She might not have much of an education, might not be as well read or as versed in the social graces as some of the women he had known, but she was no fool.

Bethany's blue eyes ran over the shabby yellow gown. "Perhaps once you are in London, you will have a chance to shop. It must be difficult to maintain a fashionable wardrobe when one lives so far from the city."

Faint color rose in Letty's cheeks, but she merely smiled. "Yes, it is."

She didn't trade barbs, and that very fact seemed to elevate her above them in some way.

"So what do you think, Gray?" It was Rebecca, hoping to draw him into the conversation.

Unfortunately, his attention had been so fixed on Letty, he had missed what the countess had said. He moved into the group, nearer Letty's side, caught a whiff of her soft rose perfume.

"I'm sorry, my mind must have wandered. What was it you were saying, Lady Devane?"

"I said I've been thinking of having a costume ball. Arthur is still in the city and it gets rather lonely out here by oneself."

"You have at leave fifty servants, Countess. You are scarcely alone."

Bethany's smile slipped a little. "Yes, well, I still think a ball is a marvelous idea."

"As do I," Rebecca agreed. "I shall come as Marie Antoinette."

"And I as Diana the huntress." Bethany cast him a seductive smile that made clear whom she was hunting, and Gray inwardly cursed. How he had ever found the woman the least appealing he didn't understand.

Just then a footman announcing luncheon appeared at the door of the drawing room, and Gray said a silent prayer of thanks.

"Shall we go in?" he suggested, managing to smile, offering his arm to the countess, the lady of highest rank in the room.

She gave him a man-eating smile in return and rested her gloved hand on the sleeve of his coat. "Yes, let's. I discover I am starving."

And it was more than clear to Gray which appetite she wished to sate. When he glanced at Letty, there was an unusual spark in her brilliant green eyes. He hoped it was jealousy, and thought that perhaps having the countess to lunch wasn't such a bad idea, after all.

Gray almost smiled.

He glanced up just as Samir appeared silently at the door of the drawing room. Gray excused himself and walked over to where the small man stood waiting.

"What is it?"

"I am sorry to disturb you, *sahib,* but a message for you has just arrived."

Gray took the wax-sealed letter from Samir's leathery hand. "Thank you, my friend."

He broke the seal and read the note.

> *In the matter of your investigation of Mrs. Letty Moss, I am sorry to disappoint, my lord, but I am not at liberty to accept the position, as it would be*

a conflict of interest. Respectfully, your friend, Dolph Petersen.

There was a post script.

I wouldn't concern myself overly about Mrs. Moss.

Gray read the note, then read it again. Dolph was in some way connected with Letty? Or had he been hired by another person to investigate the lady? And why the subtle message that she was no threat?

Tremaine was more curious than ever, and at the same time vastly relieved. He trusted Dolph Petersen. If Dolph said not to be concerned about Letty, then he wouldn't be. He would simply continue with his planned seduction.

Sliding the note into the pocket of his tailcoat, he returned to the others. He just hoped that while he was gone, Rebecca and Bethany hadn't sunk their sharp claws too deeply into sweet little Letty Moss.

She had to get away. As she sat across from Gray and the countess, luncheon had seemed interminable. Every time the woman cast him one of her come-hither glances, every time she wet her ruby lips and smiled at him as if he were a succulent piece of meat, Corrie had wanted to rip out the catty female's gleaming dark hair.

The woman was a she-devil, the perfect match for the roguish devil earl.

As soon as the meal was over, Corrie excused herself and slipped away, went upstairs and changed into her riding habit. Yesterday she had discovered the joy of riding as she never had in the city. She felt confident with Tulip, able to relax and enjoy herself. Yesterday, she had ridden with Gray. Today she intended to rid herself of his haunting image.

Out at the stable, she asked Dickey Michaels to saddle Tulip, then waited while he went to see it done. He brought the horse round, saddled and ready, then frowned when he looked up at the sky.

"I don't know, missus. Looks like a storm's comin' in. Might be best if ye waited till mornin'."

"I'm going now, Dickey."

He nodded. "Whatever ye say. Won't take a minute to saddle meself an 'orse. I'll be ready in a jiff."

"Wait, Dickey—I appreciate your offer, truly I do, but I don't need you to come along. I'll be fine by myself."

The youth's sandy eyebrows drew together. "'Is lordship will skin me I let ye go alone."

"I'm afraid I'm not giving you a choice. You may tell him that if he gives you any trouble. I'll be back in a couple of hours."

Homer yapped just then and wagged his tail, wanting to go along. "Not this time, boy." She turned to the groom. "Hold on to him, Dickey, until I'm out of sight."

She needed to be alone. Even Homer was more company than she wanted at the moment.

Urging Tulip into a trot, she rode out of the stable yard, heading off in the direction she had taken yesterday with Gray, figuring she would be able to find her way back to the castle. The wind had kicked up and the sky looked a little dark, but the storm still seemed some distance away.

She wouldn't stay out long, she told herself. Just long enough to clear her head and bring her turbulent emotions under control. Not for the first time since she had arrived at the castle, she wished she could go home.

Corrie sighed as she rode along the trail. In London she

would be free of Gray and the uncertain feelings he stirred, free to return to the life she had lived before. London and her work at *Heart to Heart* had never seemed more appealing, but she just wasn't ready to give up yet. She had pledged to Laurel to find out the truth. Corrie had made some progress but it wasn't enough. She had to continue—and she would.

All she needed was some time away from the castle, away from Rebecca's pinched expression and the countess's smirks, away from Gray and the unwanted feelings he stirred.

And so when the wind picked up, she merely shrugged. When Tulip shied at a rabbit and she nearly lost her seat, she didn't care. Instead, she urged the mare into a gallop, feeling free for the first time in days.

She wasn't ready to return, not yet.

Not until she'd had time to gird herself to face the devil earl.

Fifteen

Gray searched for Letty in the castle. He looked for her in the garden. By the time he thought of Homer and considered she might have gone out to the stable to see the scruffy mutt, nearly an hour had passed.

"Have you seen Mrs. Moss?" he asked Dickey Michaels, who was busily sweeping the earthen floor in one of the stalls.

"That I 'ave, milord. The missus rode out on Tulip a while ago."

"By herself?"

He nodded. "Tried to get 'er to let me go with her, but she wouldn't 'ave it. Wouldn't even let 'Omer go along."

Gray bit back a curse. It wasn't Dickey's fault, it was his. He should have known she'd be upset after the dismal luncheon with his ex-mistress that she had been forced to endure. He just hadn't expected her to go off on her own like this.

"Which way did she ride out?"

"Same way the two of ye went yesterday. I told 'er a

storm looked t' be comin' in. Said she'd be back in a couple of hours."

Gray glanced at the flat dark clouds swelling on the horizon. "Saddle Raja. I'll bring her back." And wring her pretty little neck for putting herself in danger.

Damn stubborn female.

He thought of his offer to make her his mistress. Letty had been insulted, though it was a very sensible solution to her troubles. *Too damn proud for her own good. Too damn naive.*

He looked up at the sky as Dickey brought the stallion over and handed him the reins. "If she comes back, tell her I went looking for her. Tell her I intend to have a talk with her when I return."

One of Dickey's sandy eyebrows went up. "Aye, milord."

Why was it everyone was afraid of him, except Letty Moss?

Gray set his jaw and headed off in the direction of the Cardigan cottage, hoping he would catch up with her as she made her way back home.

Instead, an hour passed and then another.

The wind began to howl. Grass and leaves blew into the air, and the first drops of rain began to fall. He stopped at the Cardigans' long enough to discover that the baby was doing well and Letty hadn't been there, then returned to his search.

If she had stayed on the main path, she would have missed the turn to the cottage. The trail would have taken her toward the old hunting lodge, a structure that had been built just a few years after the castle.

He started in that direction, wondering if he might have missed her and she was already safely back home. But Gray's sixth sense was kicking in, telling him that hadn't happened. It was easy to get lost out here, especially in a storm. The landscape looked different, the tree branches distorted by the wind, the trails hidden by billowing grasses.

It was starting to rain in earnest, the wind shrieking through the trees, dragging the tie from his hair. It whipped the heavy black strands into his face with stinging force, mimicking the ferocity of the storm, and his worry kicked up another notch.

Letty was only a passable rider. What if she had taken a spill? What if Tulip had stepped in a hole and gone down? What if Letty was injured and lying out in the storm somewhere?

His pulse accelerated. Worry made his insides tighten into a knot. He shouted her name again and again, but the wind blew the sound away.

He wished he had thought to bring Homer. The dog loved Letty and might have been able to find her.

A dark shape moved among the trees ahead. It was Tulip, Gray saw, and his chest squeezed. The mare was riderless, her saddle gone, her reins trailing on the ground as she steadily made her way back toward the castle. Tulip knew the way home—but sweet God, what had happened to Letty?

He rode toward the sorrel, caught her reins. She didn't appear to be injured, didn't look to have taken a fall, but why had the saddle come off?

"Where is she?" Gray asked, patting the horse's wet coat. "Where's our girl?"

The sorrel nickered as if she wanted to tell him. Leading Tulip, Gray started in the direction she had come from, looking for any sign of Letty up ahead. A low stone wall loomed in the distance, just off the main path. When the mare's ears perked up and she nickered again, Gray kicked Raja into a gallop and rode for the wall.

His heart constricted when he spotted Letty, pale as death, lying on the opposite side. Quickly dismounting, he raced toward her, fear crawling down the back of his neck.

Let her be all right. Please, let her be all right.

Thoughts of the day Jillian had died came back to him, and the bitter taste of bile rose in his mouth. Kneeling in the wet grass, he reached for Letty's pale hand. It felt as cold as death.

"Letty…Letty, can you hear me?" For an instant, he thought she was dead, and a wave of nausea hit him. He checked her pulse with a shaking hand. It was there, strong and steady, and the knot in his stomach began to uncurl. She was breathing evenly, and the painful constriction in his chest began to ease.

He checked for broken bones, found none, and just as he finished, her eyelids started to flutter.

"Letty! Letty, it's Gray!"

"Gray…?"

He reached down and captured her hand. "I'm right here, sweeting. Are you injured? Tell me where it hurts."

She swallowed, tried to raise her head.

"Easy… Just tell me where you're hurt." Lightning flashed in the distance, warning him of the storm's approach, and the roll of thunder followed.

"The wind was…blowing," she said. "We were galloping along and I felt…so free. The wall was there and I thought we could make it. If the cinch hadn't broken—"

"Dammit, Letty, tell me where you're hurt!"

Her luminous green eyes came to rest on his face. "My head hurts a little. I must have hit it when I fell. Aside from that, I think I'm all right."

A wave of relief rolled through him, so strong a tremor followed. He released a slow breath. "Good. That's good."

Another flash of lightning was followed by a reverberating crack of thunder. The storm was closing in, coming dangerously close. They had to get to shelter.

He glanced toward the horizon, saw the silhouette of the old hunting lodge in another bright flash of lightning.

"We've got to get out of this storm. I'm going to lift you up. Stop me if I hurt you." Reaching down, he hoisted her gently into his arms. "All right?"

She nodded, rested her head against his chest. He settled her on the saddle, then swung up behind her.

"Just lean against me. I know a place we'll be safe."

She didn't protest when he turned Raja toward the hunting lodge and set off in that direction, Tulip trotting behind them. It didn't take long to reach the rustic structure. Gray swung down, eased Letty into his arms and strode for the building that had been his place of refuge when he was a boy, and still often was.

The heavy wooden door was never locked. He lifted the latch, eased the door open with his boot, carried Letty inside, then shoved the heavy wood closed against the rain.

"How are you feeling?"

"Better. I don't think I broke anything."

He'd been sick with worry. His fear congealed into anger at her carelessness, and a muscle twitched in his jaw. "It's a wonder you didn't break your pretty little neck riding off that way. I swear I ought to thrash you for scaring me the way you did."

She colored slightly, but made no reply.

Gray settled her carefully on the brown leather sofa in front of the hearth. "I'll see to the horses and bring in some wood for a fire."

Letty still said nothing, and he couldn't tell if she was grateful he had found her or wished that he hadn't.

Sheltering the animals in the lean-to beside the lodge, he fed them some of the oats he kept there, then returned to the house carrying an armload of wood. It didn't take long to build a roaring blaze, and the heat of it began to drive the chill from the room.

The lodge wasn't all that big, only a single chamber, low-ceilinged with a roof fashioned of heavy timbers. A kitchen with an iron stove and an old oak table sat off to one side. The main room was furnished with a leather sofa and overstuffed chairs in front of the big stone fireplace, and a four-poster bed in the corner.

He built a fire in the iron stove for additional warmth, set water on to boil for a pot of tea, then returned to where Letty rested, soaked and bedraggled, on the sofa.

"We need to get out of these wet clothes."

She was shivering even as she shook her head. "I can't. I don't have anything else to put on."

He strode to the linen cupboard and dragged out a pair of woolen blankets. "These will have to do." He tossed her one and it landed next to her on the sofa.

Moving toward the fire, he began to strip off his coat, waistcoat and shirt. Letty just sat there, careful not to look at him.

"I am fine just as I am," she said. "Eventually my clothes will dry."

"And by that time, you'll have the devil's own ague."

Her chin shot up. "And if I do take them off, I'll have the devil *himself* to deal with."

His lips quirked. He didn't have to ask who that was.

Still, her health was more important than her modesty. "Sorry, sweetheart, this is one argument you're not going to win. I'll help you take off those wet clothes or I'll take them off for you. Which is it going to be?"

"You wouldn't dare!"

He began to pull off his boots. "You know I would. I don't think you have the slightest doubt."

Her eyes snapped with anger. Why was it there were times Letty seemed almost like two different women, one sweet and docile, the other full of fire?

She muttered something. Surely it wasn't a curse.

"You really are a devil," she said. She looked away while he finished undressing, picked up one of the blankets, wrapped it around his waist and tucked it in so it wouldn't fall off.

"Your turn," he said.

Letty got up slowly and Gray helped her carefully to her feet. "How are you feeling? Are you dizzy?"

"I was fine until you demanded I take off my clothes."

He bit back a smile. He had smiled only rarely since Jillian had died, but Letty managed to make it happen more and more.

"Just stand still and I'll do the work." He reached for the buttons on the bodice of her dark green riding habit, but she slapped his hands away.

"I can do it myself."

He stepped back, letting her salvage her pride, and waited as she unfastened the buttons with trembling fingers. He helped her out of the bodice, leaving her in her chemise, and draped the top over a hook next to the fire. She unfastened the tabs on the skirt and swayed precariously as she tried to step out of it.

"Easy." Gray caught her arm to steady her, and she didn't object, though it was clear from the stiffness of her spine that she would rather he kept his hands to himself.

Her petticoats went next. Soaked completely through, they sagged into a pile of soggy white cotton at her feet.

He helped her step out of them, leaving her in her wet, clinging, nearly transparent undergarments.

He was trying his damnedest to behave himself—after all, the lady had suffered a fall—but his male instincts were springing to life, along with his male anatomy. Her chemise barely hid the sweet curve of her bottom, and Gray's loins began to fill.

Clearing his throat, he pulled the damp strings on her corset, loosened them, then took a step away. He thought he could trust himself. She'd been injured, if only slightly. But as he studied the feminine curve of her spine, the tantalizing swell of her hips, he began to doubt his strength of will. God, he ached for her. His erection pulsed with every heartbeat.

A bolt of lightning lit the room and the wind rattled the shutters.

"Would you please hand me the blanket?"

"What?"

"I need the blanket. Would you hand it to me, please?"

"Sorry." He unfurled the second blanket and held it up in front of him. "You need to take off the rest. I promise I won't look."

"I don't trust you."

"I don't trust myself, but I'll do my best."

He thought he heard her laugh.

"I want your word as a gentleman," she said.

"All right, you have my word as a gentleman."

He raised the blanket. Letty kept her back to him and he could hear the rustle of fabric. He lowered the cover enough to see over the top, and watched with growing lust as she stepped out of her corset and tossed it aside, then stood in front of the fire half-naked. She moved a little and he caught a glimpse of her naked breasts, which were even lovelier than he recalled, plump and rose-tipped, the color of day-old cream. A memory of the taste of them sent a fresh surge of blood to his groin.

Her drawers followed—not mended, he saw, but made of finest lawn trimmed with expensive lace. If she prized them so highly, he would buy her a dozen pairs, though once she belonged to him, he would forbid her to wear anything at all beneath her skirts. Her pink satin garters came off, and she bent over to roll down her stockings.

The sight of her sweet behind poised so temptingly in the air made his mouth water and his erection jerk. He prided himself on his control, but it seemed to elude him where Letty was concerned. Then she turned, and he couldn't take his eyes off the glossy auburn curls glinting between her pale thighs.

Letty's shriek of outrage hurt his ears.

"You gave me your word!"

He held the blanket up in front of his eyes, reluctantly blocking his view. "I gave you my word as a gentleman— which I never have been. You should have asked me to give you my word as a soldier. I would have been honor-bound by that."

"You are a…" she sputtered, "you are a—"

He walked toward her, wrapped her snuggly in the blanket and also in his arms. "You are the most desirable woman I've ever met. So beautiful and sweet. God, I've never wanted anyone the way I want you."

And then he kissed her. Bound up in the blanket, she struggled to get free, but he just kept kissing her. Soft, teasing kisses, sweetly passionate, became hot, deep, hungry ones that made his erection go rock hard. The moment she stopped struggling, the moment her lips began to soften under his, Gray gentled the kiss, and Letty kissed him back.

He eased his hold and her arms went around his neck. He felt her fingers sliding into his wet hair.

"Letty…" He hadn't lied to her. He wasn't a gentleman and he never would be. He took what he wanted, and he wanted Letty Moss. In return, he would take care of her in the manner she deserved. It was the perfect arrangement for both of them.

Gray lowered the edge of the blanket and began to kiss his way toward Letty's ripe breasts, determined to accomplish the goal he had set for himself. His seduction would end her protests and she would be his.

Why that seemed so important he refused to consider. He only knew he meant to give her the pleasure he had promised, make her ache for him as he ached for her.

Gray set himself to the task.

The blanket slipped to her waist and Corrie melted into the warm arms around her. Firm lips melded with hers, and a warm, solid body took away the last of her chill. Her headache was gone, her mind filled instead with numbing pleasure.

She knew it was wrong, knew she would have to stop him, but nothing had ever felt so good, so right as this moment with Gray. He nuzzled the side of her neck. She tilted her head back to give him better access, and his thick black hair, free of its ribbon, teased her skin. She thought of the way he had looked when she had been lying there in the rain. With his legs braced apart and his unbound hair swirling round his shoulders, he was the highwayman she had always imagined him to be.

Gray deepened the kiss and the muscles across his chest pressed into her breasts. They tingled and her nipples went hard. A soft ache pulsed between her legs. Liquid heat sank low in her belly and desire swirled through her, as tempting as the snake in the garden.

She was nearly twenty-two years old. In all the parties she had attended, and all the men who had paid her court, she had never met a man like Gray. None of their kisses had stirred her; not one of them could move her as he did.

She thought of the man he was, remembered the dog and how he'd helped her care for him, the boy he had rescued in the village. She thought of the baby he had delivered, the care he had shown mother and child. She remembered the pain he had lived through, the losses he had suffered.

The blanket slipped a few more inches and she felt the heat of his mouth on her breast, the strong pull of his teeth, and a rush of pleasure tore through her. The wanton creature she had been before rose up inside her, daring her to take what she wanted. To experience what no other man could give her.

It was true, she realized. If she denied herself now, she might never know the sort of pleasure Gray offered. She didn't intend to marry for years—there were too many things she wanted to do. Even after she wed, she might not feel the passion for her husband that Gray made her feel.

His hands slid into her wet hair, pulling out the pins. Then he was running his fingers through the heavy strands, spreading them around her shoulders.

"I love your hair," he whispered against her ear. "I love every sweet curve of your beautiful body."

His words seduced her along with his hands. He skimmed them over her naked flesh, teased and caressed her, made her skin tingle at his slightest touch. His mouth claimed hers in another ravishing kiss, his tongue delving in, coaxing hers to respond.

She arched backward, bringing her body into full contact with his, and realized both blankets had fallen to the floor. The two of them were completely naked. She could feel Gray's arousal, the hard male length that so intrigued her, and eased back a little to see what it looked like.

Her eyes widened at the heavy appendage thrusting toward her, reminding her of the image of Mercury she had seen in his erotic book. "Oh, my heavens!"

His mouth curved. "It's all right. We'll just take our time."

It was now or never. If she didn't stop him this instant it would be too late. She looked up at him, saw the hot desire burning in his eyes, and there was something more, a yearning so powerful it seemed to reach inside her. She felt mesmerized by it, captured and unable to resist.

"I need you, Letty," he whispered, drawing her into his arms and kissing her again. "I need you so damn much."

The longing was there in his voice, the loneliness. Her mind whirled, fought to discover what this feeling was that gripped her, held her in its thrall.

And then there it was, so crystal clear she couldn't believe she had been able to deny it before.

Dear God, she was in love with him!

Not a little in love, as she had feared, but desperately, wildly in love.

It was too late to protect her heart, too late to save herself, and because she could not, the only choice she had was for her to save *him*.

She looked up at him and tears stung her eyes. "I need you, too, Gray."

Something moved across his features, dark and turbulent. Gray stared down at her with an intensity she had never seen before. His kiss was hard and deep, no longer seductive. It was the savage kiss of a man claiming his mate, and Corrie responded with eager abandon.

Wet, sensual kisses left her dizzy. Hot, passionate caresses sent liquid heat into her core. He touched her, teased her sensitive skin. His fingers sifted through the curls at the juncture of her legs and breached her as no man ever had.

Wild desire burned through her. This was what she needed, what she had been waiting for all of her life.

"Make love to me, Gray."

She heard his deep groan, tinged with male satisfaction.

Then he was lifting her into his arms, carrying her over to the bed in the corner. Gray followed her down on the soft feather mattress, kissing her even more deeply than before. Corrie burned for him, ached for more of the searing pleasure his hard body promised.

And yet she was no longer the naive young woman that she had been in London.

"I'm afraid, Gray. What if there is a child?"

He brushed her tumbled damp hair back from her temple. "There are ways to prevent it. A French letter, other ways. I won't let it happen. Even if it did, I would take care of you."

God help her, she believed him. Perhaps she truly was a fool.

Whatever happened, it no longer mattered. She loved him and she wanted him. Corrie kissed him with all of the newly found love she felt for him, and let him work his magic.

Gray tried to remember the skills he had learned in India, the dozens of tricks that could give a woman pleasure, but his mind was clouded by his need for Letty. He had waited too long, wanted her too badly. He kissed her deeply, stroked her until she was wet and ready, writhing beneath him and begging him to take her. Parting her legs with his knee, he came up over her, found the entrance to her passage and began to ease himself toward his goal.

She was tight. Amazingly so, but then it had been two years since she had been with her husband. Gray kissed her slowly, thoroughly, and she kissed him back, thrusting her small tongue into his mouth and driving him insane. He prided himself on his control, on his skill at lovemaking, but all he could think of was Letty and how badly he needed to be inside her. He could feel the tightness of her feminine sheath and desire overwhelmed him.

"Gray," she whispered, sliding her fingers into his damp hair, dragging his mouth down to hers for another burning kiss.

Gray's tight control slipped, then disappeared completely. With a single hard thrust, he drove himself home, impaling himself full length in her sweet little body. When Letty cried out, it took a moment for his lust-filled brain to realize he had hurt her, that the thin barrier he had felt and ignored was her maidenhead.

That Mrs. Letty Moss was a virgin.

"What the hell?" Fury shot through him. He lifted himself away enough to gaze into her tear-damp eyes. "You're no married woman! Who the hell are you, Letty? Or is that even your name?"

She swallowed, reached up to touch his face with a trembling hand. For a moment she seemed uncertain, as if there was something she wanted to say. Then she shuddered and shook her head. "We…we never made love. Cyrus was old. I should have told you."

Gray reached down and wiped away the tears on her cheeks. It made sense. He had recognized her innocence from the start. And suddenly he was glad his cousin was such an old fool.

"If I had known, I would have taken better care." He bent and very softly kissed her. "I'm sorry I hurt you."

She gave him a gentle smile. "It's all right. It doesn't hurt now. I just feel…full of you."

Relief mingled with an odd feeling of protectiveness. "You're the most amazing woman, Letty Moss." And she was his, a virgin wife. The perfect mistress.

Gray kissed her gently, taking his time, working to arouse her again. Perspiration popped out on his forehead and the muscles across his shoulders ached with his effort at control. He wanted to please her, to give her satisfaction.

"Please, Gray," she whispered, arching beneath him, urging him to give her what she needed, and the instant she said the words he started to move.

A single deep thrust and Letty came up off the bed in a shattering climax. He could scarcely believe it. He felt a rush of triumph that he had been the man to bring her to fulfillment, but he didn't stop, just drove into her until she peaked again, her nails digging into his shoulders, stealing the last shred of his control.

Deep, powerful strokes fired his blood; the heavy thrust and drag of his shaft sent him over the edge. His body shook with the onset of his climax and the effort it took to pull himself out of her welcoming heat before he spilled his seed.

He had promised to protect her and he meant to keep his word. He kept French letters in the top drawer of his dresser. Next time he would be sure to bring them along.

Gray smiled as settled himself next to Letty in the bed and drew her snugly against his side. He couldn't remember the last time he had felt so completely relaxed, so utterly replete.

The restlessness was gone, at least for the moment. Contentment filled him in a way he couldn't explain.

He pressed a kiss to her temple. "Everything is going to work out, sweetheart. I promise you."

Gray closed his eyes, enjoying the soft feel of the woman in his arms. It was getting dark and the storm still raged outside the lodge. Letty drifted into an exhausted sleep and though he wanted to rouse her, make love to her again, he thought of her innocence and let her be.

He must have drifted off himself. When he awakened, he was amazed to discover he had slept straight through until dawn.

It was the first peaceful night's sleep he'd had since Jillian had died.

Sixteen

"Where is she, Charles? Where the bloody hell is my daughter!" Justin Whitmore, Viscount Selkirk, stood in the foyer of Castle Tremaine in his damp greatcoat and high beaver hat.

As Charles walked toward him, he noticed Justin's distress, and his smile of welcome slipped away. "What the devil are you talking about? Surely you aren't speaking of Laurel. Her death came as a terrible blow to us all, but—"

"I am talking about Coralee! She is here in your home, posing as some long lost cousin of the earl's. I demand to see her, Charles. Now!"

Charles Forsythe looked stunned. For the first time, Justin realized how utterly and completely his daughter had pulled off her charade.

It didn't matter. She was an unmarried young woman. She had no business traipsing around the countryside in some wild attempt to redeem her sister's lost honor.

Charles cleared his throat. "I presume you are speaking of the young lady who calls herself Letty Moss."

"Yes, though we only just discovered her ruse. Her mother and I had been growing more and more worried about her. Her letters were spare, at best, and told us nothing of her well-being. Coralee was never one for the country, and yet she has stayed here some weeks. We decided to see how she fared, and instead discovered she is not in residence at Selkirk Hall and never has been."

"I see. Well, I had no idea, of course." His blond eyebrows drew together over his hazel eyes. "What motive, exactly, did your daughter have for such an elaborate hoax?"

"I am not quite certain of that myself."

Charles motioned for the butler to take the viscount's coat and hat, which in his haste to see Coralee, he still had on.

"Perhaps the matter would be better discussed in private" Charles suggested.

"Yes, I'm certain it would be."

"If you will please follow me." He walked into the drawing room and Justin followed. As the men settled themselves, the butler closed the door.

"I must say, your daughter is quite an accomplished actress," Charles said. "Coralee was only a child when last we saw her. You can hardly fault us for not realizing who she was."

"The fault was not yours, Charles. In fact, you have my most sincere apologies for the trouble she has caused. And you may believe when I speak to her I shall have a good deal to say in that regard. Now if you would ask her to come in here…"

Charles's gaze became shuttered. "I'm afraid, at the moment, there is a bit of a problem with that."

Justin's senses went on alert. "What do you mean?"

"Your daughter went out riding just before the storm hit. Gray was worried, so he went after her. I'm sure he must have found her, since he didn't come back home. They must have taken shelter someplace to wait out the storm."

"What if he didn't find her? What if she is out there injured—or worse?" Thank God he had insisted Constance wait for him at Selkirk Hall. If she knew her daughter had been out all night, she would be worried sick.

"My brother was a major in the army. If he hadn't found her, he would have come back for help. The storm raged for hours and only broke this morning. The best thing to do is give them time to get home. If they don't return in the next several hours, we'll form a search party and go after them."

It chafed Justin to wait. His daughter might be lying out there, injured or even worse. But waiting was a better alternative than riding off haphazardly with no idea where to look.

"You really believe your brother found her?"

"I'm sure of it. Gray was in the army, I repeat. He's an extremely capable man."

Justin thought of the handsome earl he had met in London on several occasions. And Grayson Forsythe's wicked reputation. An unpleasant thought occurred. "If they spent the night together, you realize what it will mean."

Charles's blond head came up. "Good God—he'll have to marry her."

Justin gritted his teeth. He'd had one daughter ruined, a scandal he and his family would suffer for years to come. He wouldn't tolerate another. If the rogue had spent the night with her, he would marry Coralee.

Justin thought of his daughter's independence, of her unruly, stubborn nature.

Dammit to hell, in this she would not defy him.

She would marry the earl—whether she wished it or not!

Corrie rode on Raja in front of Gray, while Tulip trailed along behind them. After their wild lovemaking, both of them had slept through the night. Gray had awakened early and gone out to check on the horses. With the cinch broken, the sidesaddle was useless. He planned to send Dickey Michaels back to pick it up.

Seated in front of Gray as they rode back to the house, Corrie wondered what he thought about last night. It occurred to her that a man with his reputation might cast her aside, now that she had gifted him with her virtue. If he did, he wasn't the man she had come to believe he was, and she would be better off without him.

The thought made her insides tighten. She was in love with Gray. She didn't want to lose him. But then, what would he do when he discovered that she wasn't the woman he believed, that she had come to the house to prove him guilty of her sister's murder?

All the way back to the castle, the worrisome thought swirled in her head. Neither of them spoke as they climbed the hill from the stable and went into the house through the door at the rear of the castle.

Samir was waiting when they stepped into the hall.

"There is trouble, *sahib*. I am sorry I failed you."

"What are you talking about, Samir?"

"The woman...I should have tried harder to learn the truth."

"Do not talk in riddles, my friend. Tell me—"

"Gray! Thank God you are returned." Charles strode toward them. "And safely, I see."

Corrie could feel a flush creeping into her cheeks and

hoped Gray's brother would not see it. She was safe, but no longer the innocent young woman she had been before she had ridden out yesterday afternoon.

"Letty's cinch broke and she took a spill. She's lucky she wasn't severely injured."

Charles cast her a glance she couldn't read. "Yes, well, I am glad she is all right. However, there is a matter that requires your attention, and also…Letty's. If you will both come with me…"

"I'm not fit company for anyone," Corrie said, wanting nothing so much as to escape upstairs to her room. "I need to change out of these clothes and into something more presentable. If you will excuse me, Charles…." She started past the two men, but Charles caught her arm.

"I'm afraid this can't wait."

Gray cast her an uneasy glance and Corrie felt a prickly shiver of alarm. Wordlessly, they followed Charles down the hall to the Emerald Room, an extravagant salon done in bright colors and gilded furniture. It was a room Rebecca preferred and Corrie rarely entered.

She stepped into the drawing room, saw her father and very nearly swooned. Gray must have noticed. His hand shot to her waist to steady her.

"Are you all right? Perhaps you were injured, after all, and only now showing the symptoms."

"Truly, I—I am fine."

"Good morning, Coralee." Her father walked toward her, his features set as grimly as she had ever seen them.

"Good morning…Father."

Gray's eyes swung from her to the viscount. "Lord Selkirk?" He looked back at Corrie. "What the devil is going on?"

Corrie swallowed, feeling faint once more.

"That is a very good question, my lord," her father said. "Would you care to explain, Coralee?"

Gray's penetrating dark eyes fixed on her face. "Coralee? That is your name?"

"I was going to tell you, Gray, I swear. I wanted to tell you last night. I just…couldn't. Not yet."

"Coralee is my daughter," the viscount began. "She would have been a child when last you met. She is quite grown up now, as you can see. As a matter of fact, from her bedraggled appearance, there is every chance you have discovered that for yourself."

Corrie gasped. "Father, please—"

"You are not Letty Moss," Gray said darkly. "You are Coralee Whitmore, the viscount's daughter."

"Yes…" The word came out on the faintest breath of air. Her heart was pounding, each beat a dull throb inside her chest. Dear God, what was Gray thinking? And how could she possibly explain?

"Why did you come here?" he asked. "Why were you pretending to be someone else?"

"I was…" She nervously wet her lips. "I was trying to find out who murdered my sister."

Charles cut in just then. "That is absurd. Laurel killed herself. She drowned right there in the river."

Corrie turned in his direction. "I don't believe my sister would do such a thing. I think she was murdered."

Charles's face went pale.

Gray's dark gaze pierced her. "Tell me you didn't come here because you think her death had something to do with one of us."

She swallowed. "I thought…thought it was you." She closed her eyes to block out the rage that darkened his face.

"I found out about your wife, that she drowned just like Laurel. I came here to prove you had killed her."

"Bloody hell."

"I discovered it wasn't you. I found out you were with the countess that night, so I knew you weren't guilty."

Gray's jaw looked like granite. "Your sister had a child out of wedlock. It was common knowledge in the village. She killed herself when her lover refused to marry her. I'm sorry for your loss, *Miss Whitmore,* but that doesn't make up for what you've done."

Turning, the earl started to walk away, but the sharp edge in her father's voice brought him to a halt.

"Nor does it change the circumstances of what must now occur."

Gray turned, his eyes hard and glittering.

"Coralee is an unmarried young woman from one of London's finest families, a family that has suffered far too much scandal already. It will soon be well known that the two of you spent last night together. You are bound by your honor, my lord, to marry my daughter."

Corrie gasped. It took all of her courage not to cringe at the fierce look on Gray's face.

"You expect me to marry her? After the lies she has told? After the way she deceived us all?"

Corrie felt the sharp sting of tears. For the first time she realized how harsh the penalty was going to be for her deceit. "I'm sorry, Gray, truly I am. I meant to tell you the truth, but I just… I made a vow to Laurel to find out what happened. I could not break my promise."

He looked down at her and something moved across his features. She thought it was disappointment. "You're nothing like her, are you? You aren't sweet and kind, gentle and loving. You're deceitful and conniving, a vicious little tart willing to stop at nothing to get what she wants."

Corrie blanched.

"That's enough," said the viscount. "You will not speak to my daughter that way."

The earl ignored him. "I remember you now. You're the little harpy who wrote about me in your newspaper column. Let me see…what was it you called me? 'A conscienceless seducer of women.' Yes, I believe that was it." He raked her with cold, dark eyes, a silent reminder of the intimacies they had shared last night. "I suppose in your case, you were right."

He started walking again, stopped at the hard note in her father's voice. "Then you admit you took advantage of my daughter."

He turned. "I seduced Letty Moss, the lovely, destitute young wife of my very distant cousin. I don't know this woman at all."

A strangled sound caught in Corrie's throat as she watched Gray walk away. She wanted to call him back, tell him she and Letty were different parts of the same person, but she knew he wouldn't believe her.

It was over between them.

Corrie felt as if a knife had been thrust into her heart.

Gray stalked out of the house and headed for the stable. God, what a fool he was. He should have known the sweet, innocent young woman he had made love to last night didn't actually exist. She was simply too good to be true. Naive, gentle Letty was a figment of his imagination.

"Stop where you are, Tremaine."

At the sound of the viscount's voice, he halted on the stone walkway and turned to face him. He had always respected the man. It wasn't his fault his daughter was a cunning little baggage with the conscience of a whore.

"I realize my daughter duped you. I hope you will try to understand how devastated Coralee was by the news of her sister's death. Until recently, the two of them were extremely close. Coralee refused to believe Laurel's drowning was suicide. According to her aunt, she was convinced you were the man who had seduced her sister and then killed her, and she came here to prove it."

Gray ignored the grudging respect he felt that she would risk herself that way.

"Apparently, she proved just the opposite," the viscount continued. "If she hadn't believed you were innocent, there is nothing on this earth that could have moved her to give herself to you, as apparently she has."

Gray remained silent. A feeling of loss swept through him that Letty didn't exist, that the night he'd spent with her in his arms was nothing more than a fantasy.

"There's been far too much scandal in my family to let this matter go unresolved," the viscount continued. "I'll expect you to do the right thing by my daughter, Tremaine. If you refuse, I shall have to call you out."

Christ. A duel with Selkirk was the last thing he wanted. The man and his wife had already suffered more than their share of scandal and grief. Even now the man stood in front of him clothed in the black garments of mourning.

From the corner of his eye, Gray spotted a familiar small figure hurrying down the pathway toward them. She looked like Letty, but he knew she was nothing at all like the sweet creature who had made him burn for her last night.

She raced up and caught hold of his arm, and he ignored a thread of sympathy when he noticed the tears in her eyes.

"Please don't hurt him," she said. "You don't have to

marry me. I told him I wouldn't marry you even if you asked. Just please…please don't hurt him."

He looked down at her and something moved inside him. She was Letty, but she was not. Anger burned like a hot poker in his stomach. An urge to make her pay for the lies she had told combined with a fierce desire to bury his hard length inside her.

"So you won't marry me even if I ask?"

She swallowed. "I am employed in London. Aside from that, there are things I wish to do, places I wish to see. I am not ready for marriage yet."

One of his eyebrows arched up. "Is that so?" He turned to her father. "See to the license. We'll be married as soon as arrangements can be made."

"What!"

He started striding toward the house, a surge of triumph expanding in his chest. He would pay her back for her deceit, and in the process he would satisfy this wild craving for her that one night of lovemaking had not begun to satisfy.

"I won't marry you!" she said, lifting her skirts and running along behind him.

He stopped and turned. "You'll marry me. I'm not giving you a choice."

Her mouth fell open as he strode away. He thought he heard a swear word slip from between her lips.

A grim smile arose. She was a cunning little baggage, but the passion he had aroused in her last night was real. Whatever sort of wife she made, he meant to enjoy her until he'd had his fill.

Then he would send her on her way, back to London.

"I won't marry him!"

"You will, by God. You refuse and I swear I will take a

switch to you, as I should have done when you were a child."

Corrie couldn't believe it. Her father had always indulged her. Now he was telling her she had to marry a man who despised her?

"I can't marry the earl," she argued. "I have a job. I am employed at *Heart to Heart*. Doesn't that matter to anyone?"

"You never should have taken that job. You are above that sort of labor. Besides, you would have to marry sooner or later. After last night, you have no choice but to do it now."

"But he hates me! Once I'm his wife, he'll probably beat me!"

"Good for him. If I had done that myself, I would have a quiet, respectful daughter instead of a willful harridan who is determined to ruin not only herself but her family, as well."

That shut Corrie up. She had seen what the gossips had done to her mother and grandmother and the rest of her family after Laurel had died. There was simply no way she could allow that to happen again to the people she loved. If Gray meant to punish her for her deception, so be it. She certainly couldn't deny she deserved it.

She took a deep breath and slowly released it. "All right, I'll marry him."

Her father's dark look slowly faded. "You wouldn't have given yourself to the earl if you hadn't cared about him, Coralee. You aren't that kind of woman."

She didn't argue. She was in love with Gray. Or at least she had been. She didn't know the hard-faced stranger he had become.

"In time it will all work out," the viscount said.

Corrie managed a halfhearted smile. "I'm sure you're right, Father."

But she was fairly certain it wouldn't.

Lately, nothing ever seemed to work out the way she had planned.

Seventeen

It took only three days for a special license to be obtained and hasty wedding arrangements made. She would marry Grayson Forsythe this morning in the gardens at Selkirk Hall, then return to the castle as Gray's wife, the Countess of Tremaine.

The thought chilled Corrie to the marrow.

"I don't think I can go through with this," she said to Allison, pacing frantically in front of the window. Only half-dressed, in frilly white undergarments and a blue satin wrapper, she turned and paced back the other way. "After what I did, I don't think I shall ever be able to face him and his family again."

She and Allison had arrived at Selkirk Hall shortly after the awful confrontation at Castle Tremaine. It was impossible to believe the days had rushed past, and Allison was there to help her dress for her wedding.

"You don't have any choice," her friend said, speaking out as she rarely did. "You owe it to your family. Laurel's death hurt them very badly. Your father may not show it, but he is still grieving. You don't want your parents to suffer another scandal."

"Oh, God." Corrie sank down on the tapestry stool in front of her rosewood dresser. The bedroom, done in white and mauve, was far more elegant than the shabby room Rebecca had assigned her at Castle Tremaine. Corrie's stomach churned at the realization that when she returned she would be sleeping in the countess's suite, which connected to Gray's bedroom.

"Perhaps after you are wed you will be able to make the earl understand why you behaved the way you did. In time, surely he'll forgive you."

She shook her head. "I don't think Gray is a very forgiving man. Perhaps if I were truly Letty Moss, in time he might forgive me. I think he cared for her in some way. Unfortunately, I'm Coralee. I'm outspoken and stubborn and determined. I am not the sort of woman Gray would wish to marry."

"Stop that right now. You are as much Letty as you are Coralee. You are kind and considerate. You are loyal and giving. In time your husband will see that, and he will realize you are everything he thought and more."

Corrie looked up at her, blinking to hold back tears. "Do you really think so?"

Allison wrapped her in a hug. "Yes, I do. You were willing to put yourself in danger because you loved your sister. And you love the earl. In time he will realize it and accept you for the woman you truly are."

Corrie's gaze lifted to Allison's face. "How did…how did you know I loved him?"

"We have come to be friends, Coralee. I do not believe you would have given yourself to the earl if you did not love him."

An Important Message from the Editors

Dear Reader,

Because you've chosen to read one of our fine novels, we'd like to say "thank you!" And, as a **special** way to thank you, we're offering you a choice of <u>two more</u> of the books you love so well **plus** two exciting Mystery Gifts to send you— absolutely <u>FREE</u>!

Please enjoy them with our compliments...

Pam Powers

Lift here

Peel off seal and place inside...

The Editor's "Thank You" Free Gifts Include:

- ● *2 Romance OR 2 Suspense books!*
- ● *2 exciting mystery gifts!*

Yes! I have placed my
Editor's "Thank You" seal in the
space provided at right. Please
send me 2 free books, which
I have selected, and 2 fabulous
mystery gifts. I understand I am
under no obligation to purchase
any books, as explained on the
back of this card.

**PLACE
FREE GIFT
SEAL
HERE**

| ROMANCE |
| 193 MDL ELTD 393 MDL ELWD |

| SUSPENSE |
| 192 MDL ELRY 392 MDL ELUZ |

FIRST NAME   LAST NAME

ADDRESS

APT.#   CITY

STATE/PROV.   ZIP/POSTAL CODE

Thank You!

▼ DETACH AND MAIL CARD TODAY! ▼

© 2003 HARLEQUIN ENTERPRISES LTD.

(EC2-RS-07)

The Reader Service — Here's How It Works:

Accepting your 2 free books and 2 free gifts places you under no obligation to buy anything. You may keep the books and gifts and return the shipping statement marked "cancel." If you do not cancel, about a month later we'll send you 3 additional books and bill you just $5.49 each in the U.S. or $5.99 each in Canada, plus 25¢ shipping & handling per book and applicable taxes if any.* That's the complete price and — compared to cover prices starting from $6.99 each in the U.S. and $8.50 each in Canada — it's quite a bargain! You may cancel at any time, but if you choose to continue, every month we'll send you 3 more books, which you may either purchase at the discount price or return to us and cancel your subscription.

*Terms and prices subject to change without notice. Sales tax applicable in N.Y. Canadian residents will be charged applicable provincial taxes and GST. All orders subject to approval. Books received may vary. Credit or debit balances in a customer's account(s) may be offset by any other outstanding balance owed by or to the customer. Please allow 4 to 6 weeks for delivery.

If offer card is missing write to: The Reader Service, 3010 Walden Ave., P.O. Box 1867, Buffalo, NY 14240-1867

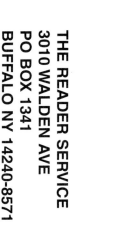

BUSINESS REPLY MAIL

FIRST-CLASS MAIL   PERMIT NO. 717-003   BUFFALO, NY

POSTAGE WILL BE PAID BY ADDRESSEE

THE READER SERVICE
3010 WALDEN AVE
PO BOX 1341
BUFFALO NY 14240-8571

NO POSTAGE
NECESSARY
IF MAILED
IN THE
UNITED STATES

She dashed the tears from her cheeks. "Gray believes I've betrayed him, and in a way I did. I pretended to be someone I am not."

"You only pretended a little."

She sighed. "Perhaps. But he has been hurt before and he guards his heart above all things. I don't know if I shall ever get a second chance to reach him."

"If you love him, you have to try."

Corrie swallowed past the lump in her throat, realizing her friend was right.

"You need to get into your gown," Allison said, reminding her how soon her life would change.

"I need a moment, Ally, if you don't mind."

Allison nodded. "Of course." She left to dress for the ceremony with a promise to return to help Corrie get into her wedding gown.

She had been gone only a moment when a soft knock sounded at the door. Corrie walked over to open it and cried out at the sight of her best friend in the world, tall, blond Krista Hart Draugr, standing in the doorway.

"Krista!" Corrie rushed into her arms and the women embraced. "I am so glad to see you! I knew you would arrive if you could, but I was afraid something might have come up and you wouldn't be able to make it."

"You shouldn't have worried. I left London as soon as I received your letter. The roads were still muddy after that dreadful storm and it took us longer than we thought to get here. Leif, Thor and my father are downstairs. All of us have been so worried. Are you sure about this? Are you certain this is what you want?"

Corrie sighed. "I have never been less certain of anything in my life."

"Then perhaps you should refuse the earl's offer."

A near-hysterical laugh escaped. "It was more of a command than an offer. It is clear you do not know him. I shudder to think what he would do if I actually had the courage to refuse him."

"As I said, Leif and Thor are downstairs. If the earl were to cause any trouble—"

"It isn't really the earl. The truth is, this entire affair is my fault. Even if I were selfish enough to see my family embroiled in yet another scandal, I would not wish for that to happen to Lord Tremaine. Marrying me, whether he wishes it or not, will quiet the wagging tongues. He is not the awful man I believed him to be. He did not murder his wife or my sister, and his reputation doesn't deserve to be blackened any more than it has been already."

Krista took hold of her hand. "It sounds as if you care for him—at least a little."

Corrie looked up and tears welled in her eyes. "I love him, Krista. He is brooding and difficult and entirely too demanding, and I am hopelessly in love with him. Unfortunately, Gray doesn't love me. In fact, he hates me for deceiving him."

"I see." She seemed to mull that over. "The earl is angry—I suppose he has every right to be. But surely in time he will understand why you behaved as you did."

"Perhaps." Corrie looked at herself in the mirror, noticed the unusual pallor of her face. She took a shaky breath and turned back to her friend. "Aside from marrying a man who despises me, there is the not so small matter of my employment."

"Lindsey is doing a fine job in your absence. She wanted to accompany us to the wedding, but someone had to stay and oversee this week's edition. I am sure she will be willing to continue until you can figure out what you're going to do."

Corrie glanced up. "Do you think I might be able to come back? I like working at the gazette. I like working with you, Krista. I wasn't ready for marriage."

Krista took hold of her hand. "You weren't ready to fall in love, either. Sometimes these things just happen."

As they had to Krista, Corrie recalled. In the beginning, her relationship with Leif had been a disaster. Now they were incredibly happy. Corrie thought of Gray and ached at the loss she suddenly felt.

She walked away, over to the window. From the garden below, voices of the guests, just beginning to arrive, drifted up to her second-floor balcony. "I never found out what happened to my sister."

Krista joined her at the window. "I got your letter. I know you think one of the men at the castle was her lover. That doesn't mean he killed her."

"I know. I've told myself that again and again."

"Today is your wedding day. It's not a time to dwell on the past. Your sister would want you to be happy."

Corrie's heart squeezed. Laurel would have wanted her to marry a man who loved her. It wasn't going to happen.

"Gray will want some sort of justice. He lives by his own set of rules, but in his way, he is a very honorable man."

"As you are a brave and honorable woman. In time he will see that."

But Corrie didn't really believe it. Whatever Gray had felt for her was gone. It had vanished the morning Letty Moss disappeared.

Dressed in a three-tiered gown of dove-gray organdy trimmed with rows of mauve ribbon, her copper hair pulled into clusters of curls on her shoulders, Corrie stood just inside the French doors leading out to the garden. She planned to return to mourning for at least another month, as was the custom, and had chosen the gown with that in mind.

"He still isn't here." Her mother, a pretty brown-haired woman in her late forties, relieved of her mourning clothes for the wedding, stood at the window wringing her hands. "Dear God, perhaps he isn't going to come."

Corrie's chest tightened. It was possible. Perhaps leaving her at the altar was the earl's punishment for her weeks of deceiving him. For her parents' sake, she prayed he wouldn't make her humiliation so public.

"He is only a few minutes late," she said, trying to keep her mother from bursting into tears. "Perhaps there was a problem on the road." But in truth, she imagined he was making a point. If he arrived at all, it was clear he wasn't an eager bridegroom.

"He is here!" Krista turned away from the window and hurried toward them. "He is just walking into the garden."

"Thank God." Her mother was shaking. Corrie walked over and gave her a reassuring hug, though she wasn't sure which of them needed it more.

"Everything's going to be all right, Mother."

The older woman managed a trembly smile. "Yes, yes of course it will be. You are marrying an earl, after all. In time, people will forget how hastily you were wed."

Corrie felt a fresh rush of guilt. If only she had listened to Krista and stayed in London, none of this would have happened.

"It is time to go, Coralee." Her friend's soft reminder sent a wave of alarm rushing through her.

She took a calming breath and prepared to face the ordeal ahead. Krista knelt and straightened the train of her organdy gown, then opened the door. Though the guests were few, the church had been decorated with huge urns filled with white chrysanthemums and yards of mauve ribbon. A white runner pointed the way to the altar.

Leif and Thor both waited by the door, two very large men, one dark, one fair, both with the bluest eyes Corrie had ever seen.

Leif leaned over and kissed her cheek. "You look beautiful. Your earl is a lucky man."

She managed a wobbly smile. "Thank you."

"If he does not treat you well," Thor said darkly, "you only need come to me."

Tears burned her eyes. She was lucky to have such dear friends. "Thank you. I shall remember your offer, Thor." Which she very well knew he meant.

Thor Draugr had come from the same undiscovered island as his brother. He'd been as backward and unschooled as Leif had first been. But Professor Hart was working the same miracle with Thor that he had worked with Leif. It was amazing the progress the big Norseman had made.

"You had better go." Krista gave her a last brief hug then returned to her husband. Seeing the way they glanced at each other made Corrie's heart ache with longing. If only Gray would look at her with that much love in his eyes.... But she didn't believe he ever would.

Her father stood waiting. "You make a beautiful bride, Coralee." He bent and kissed her cheek, his copper hair glinting, the same exact color as her own. "No matter how you feel about my actions, you know it doesn't mean I don't love you."

"I know, Father. I love you, too."

He lifted her white-gloved hand and kissed the back. "Whatever happens, I'm proud of your strength, Coralee. And your loyalty. The earl is getting a very fine wife."

She simply nodded. Her throat had closed up and she couldn't squeeze out the words she might have said. Then her gaze moved toward the front of the church and she saw the man who would soon be her husband, the tall, dark Earl of Tremaine. His jaw was set, his eyes as hard and dark as onyx.

She tried to recall the caring man who had searched for her in the pouring rain, the man who had made tender love to her, but there was no trace of him.

"Ready?" her father asked.

She nodded. It was all she could manage.

Corrie fought not to tremble as he walked her down the aisle. She spotted a few familiar faces: Allison next to Aunt Agnes, who worriedly wrung her hands; Rebecca and Charles next to Jason, who seemed almost amused.

Corrie had a grandmother she adored, but she was too frail to make the journey from London. Her mother waited at the end of the aisle for her husband to deposit the bride and join her. On the opposite side, Sir Paxton Hart, Krista's father, stood next to Krista, Leif and Thor.

Corrie's gaze swung back to the altar, where the earl stood waiting. Her father cast him a glance that held a trace of warning, then gave her into his care. Her hands felt like ice inside her gloves as she looked into the iron-hard lines of his face.

"I'm so sorry," she said softly. "I never meant for any of this to happen."

One of his black eyebrows lifted. "I suppose, in a way, I am sorry, as well. If I hadn't lusted after your lovely little body, you would still be a maiden and I would not be forced to marry you."

She recoiled at the reminder. He had always been blunt, but today she would prefer he save his well-deserved barbs until they were alone.

"Are we ready to begin?" Vicar Langston stood at the altar in front of them. He gave her a kindly, reassuring smile. "Sometimes the Lord works in strange ways. I hope you will both place your trust in him."

She felt the sting of tears, but steeled herself against them. She would not cry. Not in front of Gray. He thought little enough of her already.

"If you will please join hands."

Gray took her gloved fingers and she could feel the undisguised anger humming through him.

"Dearly beloved," the vicar began. "We are gathered together this day to join this man, Grayson Morgan Forsythe, sixth Earl of Tremaine, and this woman, Coralee Meredith Whitmore, in the bonds of holy matrimony according to God and the laws of England…."

The minister continued, speaking the words that would wed her to Gray, but Coralee barely heard them. Inside, she was trembling, her heart aching for the uncertain future ahead of her. Gray believed that he had lost Letty.

When the ceremony ended and he dragged her into his arms for a hard, punishing kiss, Corrie knew for certain that she had lost Gray.

The wedding was over at last. The wedding party, small as it was, adjourned to the dining room, where a lavish buffet had been set out: a round of beef, roasted lamb with mint sauce, poached salmon and a medley of vegetables, cheeses and fruits. A separate table held desserts: gingerbread pudding, egg creams, custards, cakes and pies. Her mother had spared no expense and the guests seemed to enjoy the sumptuous array of foods.

Playing the role of solicitous bridegroom, Gray filled a plate for Corrie and brought it over to the linen draped table where they were seated, but she had no appetite. Not when each of the glances her husband cast her way seemed darker than the last.

His gaze skimmed over her dove-gray gown. He didn't miss the implication. "You look quite lovely today, but if you are thinking to return to mourning for your sister, you may think again. I'll not have my wife moping around the house, bringing the dirge of death to my family. You have grieved more than enough. Your sister is gone and the matter is over and done."

"But—"

"It is finished, Coralee."

She didn't argue. She hated wearing the depressing clothes that continued to keep Laurel's death at the forefront of her mind. In truth, for the first time since her marriage, she found something to be thankful about.

Gray leaned back in his chair. "At least your quarters will be better than the ones you occupied before."

"Yes…I had thought of that myself."

His mouth thinned. "Of course, Letty didn't seem to mind."

Corrie's temper inched up. She set her wineglass down on the table a little harder than she meant to, and several drops spilled over the edge. "I know you think the worst of me. But I am not the spoiled, selfish creature you seem to believe."

"Are you not?"

"No." She glanced around to be sure no one could hear. "I will not apologize because my family has wealth and position. I did not choose to be born the daughter of a viscount any more than you chose to be an earl."

He was watching her with interest now, and she saw it as a chance to explain at least some of what had occurred.

"I know you are angry about a number of things, one of which is what I wrote about you in my column. In it, I mentioned what the gossips were calling you at the time. It was my *job* to report what I heard."

He leaned back in his chair. "And you did it so well. After all, you aren't the simple country wife you pretended to be." He frowned as a light seemed to suddenly dawn. "You named him Homer for the *Odyssey,* didn't you?"

"Yes."

His dark gaze sharpened. "Then you admit you read Latin."

Her chin inched up. "I also read Greek. It isn't a crime, you know."

"And you probably speak French!"

Jason must have heard the venom in Gray's voice. He walked up just then and rattled off his congratulations in the language. Corrie graciously accepted them, replying in perfect French, casting Gray a look nearly as black as the ones she'd been receiving from him.

Gray's hard gaze shifted to his cousin. "Be careful what you say to my *wife*," he warned. "Remember, I also speak the language."

Jason grinned, digging creases into his cheeks. "And here I thought you were only jealous of our ragamuffin little cousin. Interesting."

The earl's jaw hardened as the younger man walked away. "It appears my cousin still fancies you. Apparently whatever name you use doesn't matter to him."

"Don't be ridiculous. He was merely being polite."

"You're my wife now, Coralee. You had better remember that."

"I told you, I have no interest in Jason." She leaned

closer. "If you recall, it was you, not him, I welcomed into my bed. Or have you already forgotten?"

His dark eyes seemed to glitter. "I have not forgotten. Nor will you, once we get home."

Corrie sucked in a breath. Perhaps rousing the devil's ire on his wedding night was not a good idea. Sweet God, when would she learn to hold her tongue?

The party ended far too early to suit Coralee, but from the hot looks he gave her, not nearly soon enough for Gray.

"Get your wrap," he said. "We're leaving."

"But—"

"Now!"

She jumped at the command in his voice. She wasn't Letty, she wanted to remind him. She didn't have to dance to his tune. But he had a right to be angry, and it was clear that tonight he intended to make her pay for the trouble she had caused.

A tremor of uneasiness went through her. She didn't know this man she had married, far different from the one who had made love to her in the storm. What plans did he have for her? What would he expect her to do?

Her uncertainly grew. She barely noticed when he wrapped her in her cloak and began to usher her toward the door, leaving only time enough for a brief farewell to her family and friends.

As she passed Thor, he caught her hand. "Remember what I said." The glance he cast Gray left no doubt as to what he meant, and Corrie felt a little tug of gratitude that he was her friend.

"I won't forget."

Gray began propelling her once more toward the door. In the carriage, he lounged against the seat across from her, his eyes burning with heat and anger, the face of the devil in a towering rage. It took all of her courage to meet that hard gaze and not look away.

"I'm your wife," she finally said. "I won't shirk my duties on our wedding night, but neither will I let you hurt me."

His sleek black eyebrows flew upward in surprise. "That is what you think? That I mean to hurt you?"

She trembled. "It is clear how much you hate me. I know you intend to punish me for the things I've done."

For the first time, his hard look softened. "I would not hurt you, Coralee, no matter how angry I was." He relaxed against the seat. "In fact, my plans for you tonight have nothing at all to do with pain…though I've learned there are times it can be used in interesting ways. Tonight, pleasure is the only thing I have in mind for you."

But the hardness had returned to his features, making his words difficult to believe.

Eighteen

The sun had set. Darkness settled in around the castle as a brutal wind howled outside. Corrie sat stiffly on the stool in front of the dressing table in the countess's bedroom, which adjoined that belonging to the earl.

She had her own suite of rooms, and as Tremaine had predicted, they were far more elegant than the shabby quarters she had occupied before. Furnished with graceful French rosewood furniture, and draperies and a counterpane made of pale green silk, the room was lovely, and yet she couldn't help feeling like an interloper in the bedroom that must have belonged to the earl's late wife.

With Allison no longer playing the role of her maid, Gray had promised to have one of the chambermaids assigned the task. The girl had not yet arrived, and Corrie fidgeted, nervously awaiting her. A fire burned in the hearth, warming the room, and yet she felt chilled inside.

Soon Gray would come.

She wasn't sure what he would expect of her, only knew that making love with him would be nothing at all the way it had been before. There would be no gentleness, no tenderness, no concern for her feelings.

The thought twisted her heart.

She was dreading the night ahead, wishing her maid would arrive, when the door swung open and Gray walked in without knocking. He glanced round the room and started frowning, as if for the first time realizing where he was.

"You can't stay in here. Not until the room has been changed. This bedroom belonged to Jillian, and there is nothing of you that reminds me of her."

He looked as if he had delivered the gravest of insults, and Corrie's heart squeezed harder, even as her chin went up. "The housekeeper brought me here."

He frowned again as he moved closer.

"It wasn't her fault," she quickly explained. "She was only doing what she thought you would want."

One eyebrow lifted. "Did you think I would beat her for a simple mistake? Is that now the opinion you hold of me?"

Corrie swallowed. "You were different before. I don't know who you are anymore."

"As I don't know the woman I married." He ran a finger along her cheek. "Tonight perhaps we can change at least part of that."

He flicked a glance toward the door leading into his bedroom. "You may do whatever you wish in here. You will stay in my room until the necessary alterations are made."

Her stomach knotted. "I—I need at least a bit of privacy…and the maid you promised. Surely that is not too much to ask."

A hard smile lifted his lips. "Tonight I will serve as your maid. After that, I'll find someone to assist you." He held out his hand. "Come. It's time you made ready for bed."

She couldn't move. Her feet seemed rooted to the floor. She looked up at him and tried not to tremble.

"What is it?"

She had lied enough. "I'm frightened, Gray. I trusted you before. Now I..." She glanced away, struggling not to cry. She had never been a coward and yet tonight felt like the biggest coward on earth.

"Dammit to hell." Striding toward her, he bent and scooped her into his arms. Though her train had been removed, the tiered layers of her organdy skirt fell in frothy folds around them. Carrying her over the threshold into his bedroom, he set her on her feet in front of the dresser and began to pull the pins from her hair.

She stood stiffly as he sifted his hands through the curls, spreading them around her shoulders. He said nothing as he worked the buttons at the back of her gown, then helped her step out of her skirt and petticoats. She was left in her corset, drawers and stockings, while Gray remained dressed in the black trousers and white shirt he had worn to the wedding. His coat and waistcoat were gone, his black hair slightly mussed from the wind, and she thought of the highwayman who had stolen her heart.

If only he were here.

Gray bent and kissed the side of her neck, and Corrie started to tremble. It was insane. She was no longer a maiden. Gray had said he wouldn't hurt her, and yet...

She had loved the rogue who had taken her innocence that night in the storm. This was not the same man. She closed her eyes, but couldn't stop the tears from leaking from beneath her lashes. Gray saw them and his head came up.

"For God's sake, Cora, you're no longer a virgin. I told you I wouldn't hurt you. What the devil is wrong?"

She swallowed, found a handful of courage. "You aren't

him—that is what is wrong. You wanted Letty. Well, I want the man you were before." A bubble of hysterical laughter escaped. "It is poetic justice, is it not?"

Those dark eyes drilled her. He whispered a curse she couldn't quite hear, turned away from her and stalked over to the sideboard along the wall. A few moments later, he returned with a small glass of wine. "Drink this."

"What is it?"

"In India, they call it the *divine elixir.*"

"What is in it?"

"It's a powder made from crushed priyala seeds and kumhara—that's prickly pear—and something they call murahari. I mixed it with wine to help you relax."

When she looked up at him, he reached out and cupped her face. It was the first tenderness he had shown since the morning he had discovered her true identity.

"There's nothing in it that will harm you. You have my word."

She eyed him with suspicion. "As a soldier or a gentleman?"

His lips twitched, just the faintest crack in the armor he had built around him.

"As a soldier," he said softly, and she upended the glass and drank every drop of the slightly bitter wine.

By damn, he'd meant to punish her, pay her back in some way for the lies she had told and the damage she had done. But when she looked at him with those lovely, tear-filled green eyes, when her soft lips trembled, all he could think of was how much he wanted her.

He didn't understand it. She wasn't the sweet country wife he had fantasized about, the simple young woman whose innocent passion he craved.

Instead she was a shrewd, calculating creature who had schemed and lied her way into his affections. He looked down at her, all soft curves and lovely, feminine features, hair like silk and the color of flame.

She had the beauty of a goddess, the sensuous pull of a siren. She was Maya, the Hindu goddess of illusion. She was nothing at all what he had believed, and yet he ached for her as he never had another woman.

But Maya was also a demon, the creator of the magical arts.

This woman must be a demon. How else had she managed to enchant him to the point where punishing her, hurting her in any way, would be far more painful for him than for her?

He reached toward her, ran a finger along her cheek, felt the creamy smoothness of her skin. His blood heated. He wanted to taste her, to touch her all over, to bury himself inside her.

She handed the glass back to him with a hand that no longer trembled, and he could see the power of the aphrodisiac already beginning to work.

Her eyes no longer looked frightened, but languid, soft and welcoming. The stiffness was gone from her body, and as he set the glass down on the dresser, she swayed toward him, her gaze drifting up to his mouth. When she moistened her lips with her small pink tongue, his stomach contracted and his shaft went iron hard.

The potion had done its work. She was his now, a more than willing partner to do with as he pleased. He turned her toward the mirror and watched her face as he prepared to strip away her remaining garments.

The nape of her neck beckoned, slender and pale, dusted with fine burnished hair. He pressed his mouth there, felt the soft tickle of silken strands against his cheek, and hardened even more. Reaching down, he propped one of her feet on the stool, knelt and removed each of her stockings, kissing his way along her calf. He licked the arch of her small foot and heard her moan.

Her drawers and corset remained. Remembering his fantasy the day she had sprained her ankle, he slid his palm up her shapely leg, her thigh, until he reached the slit in her drawers. He slipped his hand inside and gently began to stroke her, finding her wet and slick, as he knew he would.

The drug would do his work for him. He tried not to think how much he preferred her natural responses to those conjured by one of the potions Samir had made from ingredients brought back from India.

She began to move against his hand and he stopped, unwilling to give her release so soon. Instead, he came to his feet, slid his hands into the heavy weight of her hair, tipped her head back and kissed her. At his touch, she pressed herself full length against him, went up on her toes and kissed him back. When her tongue dipped into his mouth, a shudder of lust tore through him.

He wanted to drag her down on the floor, to open his trousers and take her, pound into her until he could no longer hold on to his seed.

Instead, he removed the rest of her garments, kissing each section of bare skin exposed, inhaling her soft floral scent mingled with the musky odor of her desire. Lifting her into his arms, he carried her over to the bed, leaving her only long enough to remove his own clothes, then returning to join her on the mattress.

The moment he reached for her, she went into his arms and kissed him wildly, and Gray nearly lost control. He knew the power of the drug, had given her only the mild-

est dose. It occurred to him that it wasn't merely the potion, it was the woman he had given it to. Her name might
be Coralee and not Letty, but this was the same passionate creature who had responded so avidly to him before.

Something loosened inside him. He didn't really know
her, wasn't sure he could make any sort of life with her.
He wasn't a man who gave his trust lightly and what little
he had given to Letty, Coralee had destroyed.

Still, when he entered her lush, welcoming body, when
he moved inside her and she lifted her hips to take more
of him, he felt a stirring deep inside he hadn't expected to
feel.

He kissed her hungrily, as if he couldn't get enough, and
she kissed him with equal abandon. Heavy strokes took
him higher, his hips pumping, driving him closer to the
edge. He didn't give in to his powerful need until she
reached her peak and cried out his name, didn't give in
until she peaked again. Then desire overtook him and pleasure surged through him, so fierce his teeth clenched and
his muscles knotted.

It was a long time before he spiraled down. Gray lay beside this wife he did not know, felt his erection stir to life
once more, and told himself he could not possibly want her
again so soon.

The fear was gone. Instead Corrie felt a burning fire she
couldn't seem to put out. She had expected Gray's anger,
his need for revenge, not this wild passion he couldn't
seem to control. Her own passion burned. She couldn't
seem to douse the flames.

She told herself it was the drug, but in her heart, she knew
it wasn't. The potion was merely an excuse for her to do
what she wanted. Since that first night, she had dreamed of

kissing him, touching him all over, of feeling the movement of muscle over bone, learning the texture of his skin.

As he lay beside her, she came up over him, her breasts brushing against the curly black hair on his chest, his flat copper nipples, her own pebbling into diamond-hard crests. She kissed him deeply, kissed his brow, his eyes, the line of his jaw.

"Coralee…" he whispered, saying her name as she had yearned to hear him do, making her heart leap with hope.

Lacing her fingers in his thick black hair, she bent over him, ravished his mouth in a burning, hungry kiss, and Gray kissed her back, driving his tongue inside, setting her body on fire.

She loved the taste of him, the heat and masculinity, the strength in the arms that surrounded her. She felt his hands at her waist, lifting her on top of him, her hair swinging forward, forming a curtain that seemed to block out the rest of the world.

"Gray…" she murmured. She had loved him once… when he was a different man and she a different woman.

He kissed her deeply and lifted her again, and she felt the hard length of him probing for entrance. Understanding dawned and she took control, began to lower herself onto his shaft, to feel the exquisite fullness inside her.

Heat spiraled through her, a fierce burning desire to reach the pinnacle he had taken her to before. She moved, lifted herself up, then sank down again, felt a rush of triumph and an incredible surge of pleasure when he groaned. Gray's muscles tightened as he fought for control, and for the first time she recognized the power she held over him.

Corrie shifted, beginning to learn the rhythm, moving steadily toward the goal both of them longed to reach. The wind howled, her breathing heightened and pleasure sharpened inside her. Gray hissed in a breath as she took more of him, began to move faster, plunge harder, deeper.

"Mother of God," he growled, gripping her hips to hold her in place, thrusting into her again and again until he drove both of them over the edge.

Fulfillment came swift and hard, a shattering release that again forced his name from her lips. Gray reached the pinnacle an instant later and both of them careened off the cliff.

She slumped onto his powerful chest and was surprised to feel his lips press against her forehead. He eased her off him, then curled her against his side.

Gray said nothing and neither did she, both of them afraid of destroying the fragile moment.

Slumber beckoned. Her last thought was that whatever happened between them, she was no longer afraid.

Corrie awakened as the first faint light of dawn purpled the lands outside the window. Her mind felt a little muzzy, her muscles a little sore. A hard male body pressed against her. *Gray.*

She turned her head to look at him, recognized the thick black lashes fanned out against his lean cheeks, the hard line of his jaw, the faint shadow of his beard.

The covers were bunched around his hips, leaving him naked to the waist, and her attention moved there. He had the most magnificent body, all hard muscle and sinew, his abdomen flat, except for the slight rise of his hip bones. He had made love to her last night, and though it wasn't the same as before, he had given her the pleasure he had promised.

The potion had done its job and she had relaxed. No, more than relaxed. She had responded like the tigress he

had once called her. She blushed to think she had practi-
cally attacked him.

Her insides tightened with the thought. Perhaps that would
be his punishment. When he awakened he would ridicule her
behavior, remind her of the wanton creature she had become.

Corrie sighed. Whatever he had put in the wine had
helped dissolve her fears, but she couldn't blame her wild
responses completely on that.

She flicked a glance at the man she had married. As
much as she had enjoyed the pleasure he had given her, she
liked their lovemaking better when the passion between
them had sparked to life by simple desire.

That hadn't happened last night, but perhaps they might
have reached some unspoken agreement. He was a man
and she a woman. They desired each other. It would have
to be enough.

"Sleep well?" he asked from the opposite side of the bed
and the edge was back in his voice.

Corrie steeled herself. "Very well, thank you."

"Are you still frightened?"

"No."

That same eyebrow arched. To test her, he reached over
and cupped a breast, began to rub her nipple. It tightened
instantly and an ache began to throb between her legs. His
hand moved there as if he knew, and a soft moan escaped.

"Well, at least we have this." There was no taunt in his
voice, no hint of reproof, and she relaxed as he came up over
her, kissing her deeply, arousing her with an ease that should
have surprised her but did not. She gave in to the fires he
stirred, letting him catch her up, beginning to pick up the
rhythm of his movements, thinking perhaps he was right.

At least we have this.

But in her heart, she knew it was not enough.

Nineteen

Sunlight probed for entrance through the curtains at the windows of Gray's bedroom. Corrie stirred and reached for him, but his side of the big four-poster was cold, Gray already gone. She lay back against the pillow, staring up at the heavy gold velvet canopy above her. Though part of her was glad she didn't have to face him, another part wished he had been there to make love to her when she awakened.

A light knock sounded, drawing her attention, and a young woman in a black skirt, white blouse and mobcap entered the bedroom.

"His lordship sent me," she said. "I'm Anna. I'm to be your new maid." Tall and amazingly thin, with fine brown hair and pale skin, Anna smiled pleasantly. "If that be all right with you, milady." She was perhaps a little over thirty, her features plain but not unattractive.

"Very well, Anna. My clothes are in the countess's suite. Why don't we go in and you can help me pick out something to wear?"

"Yes, milady."

Half an hour later, Corrie was dressed and sitting in the breakfast room across the table from Rebecca, the two of them engaged in their first private conversation since the wedding.

"So you are now here for good. Or at least until Gray tires of you."

Corrie stiffened. From the moment she had filled her plate from the array of foods at the sideboard, Rebecca had been as unpleasant as Corrie had feared.

"What are you talking about? We are married. I am now Gray's wife." Which he had made abundantly clear with his fierce lovemaking last night.

"Surely you realize his interest in you is only temporary. He meant to make you his mistress, not marry you."

It was true. He had married her because her actions had left him no choice. "Even if that is so, he is still my husband."

Rebecca sipped the robust dark tea in her porcelain cup. She was dressed as extravagantly as always, in a gown of pale blue silk that set off the blue of her eyes. A cluster of gleaming blond curls rested on each of her shoulders.

"Gray is a man of powerful sexual appetites," Rebecca said. "For a time after Jillian died, he felt guilty. He buried his desires, but Bethany put an end to his celibacy. Then you came along. Surely, you realize you won't be the last."

Corrie managed to swallow the bite of eggs she had taken, though she was no longer hungry. "As I said, we're married. I'll expect him to uphold his wedding vows." And as she repeated the words, she realized she meant them. If Gray could not be faithful, she would leave him. The thought stirred an ache in her heart.

Rebecca just laughed. "If fidelity is what you expect, then you, my dear, are a fool. What man holds to his marriage vows? Sooner or later, another woman will catch Gray's fancy and he will ship you off to one of his other estates. Perhaps if you are fortunate, you can take up residence in his town house in London. At least you would be able to continue writing that ridiculous column of yours."

Corrie gritted her teeth. Now that she was married to Gray, the last shreds of Rebecca's civility had faded. The woman was clearly furious that she was no longer mistress of Castle Tremaine.

"Writing for the paper is my job. But I suppose you would see any kind of work as beneath you." Which reminded her that if she expected any sort of privacy, she would have to see to the refurbishment of the countess's bedroom.

She rose from her chair, her plate barely touched. "I'm afraid I have to go. I have a number of things to do this morning. If you will excuse me…"

A tight smile stretched across Rebecca's face. It didn't matter. They had never been friends and that wasn't going to change.

As Corrie made her way along the hall to retrieve her cloak, she thought of the project ahead. This morning, as she dressed for the day, she had noticed how dismal Gray's rooms were—the massive wooden furniture, the heavy draperies that hid the sun, the dark brown carpet on the floor.

After being in his sunny office—the India Room, she called it—where he kept his most personal belongings, she was certain the bedroom did not suit him. She would ask him first, of course, but if he gave her permission, she would change the dismal suite along with hers.

She found him in his private study, working on a set of ledgers lying open on his desk. She had never seen him in the room, and now that she did, she realized the extent to which his travels were a part of him. He looked perfectly natural seated at the light rattan desk, comfortable amid the jewel-toned colors, the brass urns, the pots of sandalwood incense. In fact, he seemed more at home in the room than anywhere else in the castle.

Girding herself for whatever mood he might be in, she knocked on the open door, pasted on a smile and walked in.

He glanced up from the ledgers, saw her and frowned. Not an auspicious beginning.

"Good morning, my lord."

His eyes ran over her apricot gown. "I thought only Letty dressed in simple muslin."

Corrie tried not to feel the barb. "I have work to do. That is why I am here. Silk and satin would hardly be appropriate."

"What is it you need?"

"You suggested I make some changes in the rooms that are mine upstairs. I was wondering…if you would agree, I should also like to make some alterations in your rooms, as well. Of course, if you prefer them the way they are—"

"Do whatever you please." He returned to his work, bending his dark head to the task as if she were already gone.

Letty might not have minded being so summarily dismissed, but Coralee Whitmore wasn't used to such rude treatment. Rounding the desk, she marched to where he sat.

His head came up as he realized she was still there. "Was there something else you wanted?"

Not when she had first come into the room. Now, seeing the tight lines of his face, the twist of his lips that made it clear he wanted her gone, there were any number of things she wanted.

"Perhaps there is." She pondered only a moment. "I am your wife, am I not? We have been wed but a day. I believe as a bride, I deserve a good-morning kiss."

She caught the shocked expression on his face as she leaned down and pressed a warm kiss on his lips. Gray sat there stunned as she turned and walked away.

"Have a good day, my lord," she called to him over her shoulder.

As she sailed out of the room, she smiled, unable to contain a small feeling of triumph.

The refurbishing project was under way. As soon as she left Gray's office, Corrie set off for the village to hire workmen and order new furnishings for both of their bedroom suites.

Earlier, she had considered having the carriage brought round—she was, after all, the Countess of Tremaine. But the day was simply too pleasant, the sun the perfect temperature on her shoulders.

She was passing the stable on her way to the path leading into town when Homer came bounding toward her.

"Homer!" She knelt in front of the scruffy gray dog and threw her arms round his neck. "I missed you, boy." She petted his shaggy coat. "Want to go for a walk with me?"

He barked as if he understood, and she laughed as they set off for the village. At least she could count on one friend at the castle.

The path was even more overgrown than it had been last month, the long grasses brushing against her full skirts. Her first task as Lady Tremaine was begun, but there was a far more important matter on her mind, one she had tried to set aside but realized she simply could not.

I have not forgotten you, sweet sister.

For the past few days, she had managed to ignore thoughts of Laurel. With the forced marriage and dealing with Gray, Corrie had had little time to think of anything else.

Now that she was actually a resident of the castle, it occurred to her that she had accidentally fallen into the perfect situation. Though it was nearly impossible to believe Charles or Jason capable of murder, finding Laurel's book had convinced her one of the men had been Laurel's lover.

Rebecca had remarked on men's infidelity. Perhaps she knew firsthand.

And Jason…Jason was boyish and charming, exactly the sort of man her sister might have fallen in love with.

As a member of the household, Corrie could go wherever she pleased. A little more snooping might tell her which of the men she should pursue. Once she knew for certain who it was, she would press him for answers, find some clue as to what had really happened to Laurel and her baby.

Corrie hurried her pace. As soon as she returned from the village, she was going to continue her quest for the truth.

Gray stood at the window in his bedroom. After his encounter with Coralee in his office, he had found himself climbing the stairs, thinking that if kisses were what his little wife wanted, he would give them to her—and far more than that.

But the room was empty, and he tried to tell himself he wasn't disappointed. Looking down from the window, he spotted his bride in the courtyard of the stables, behind the house. He was annoyed to see her kneeling, wrapping her arms around her big gray mutt of a dog.

What the hell was she doing? She wasn't Letty Moss. She was the hardhearted female who had slandered him in her column, a woman who made a living by digging up people's secrets and flaunting them in front of the world. She had lied to him, pretended to be sweet and naive when clearly she was not.

And yet…

Gray watched her with the dog and wondered. Was it possible Cora and Letty weren't as different as he believed?

The thought was disturbing. It was one thing to indulge a favorite mistress, to care for her in some distant fashion. It was another thing entirely to become enthralled with one's wife. During the year he was married, he had managed to keep Jillian at arm's length, had never really desired any sort of closeness. But there was something different about Coralee, something that drew him and filled him with a strange sort of yearning.

Gray steeled himself against the urge to join her on her walk to the village. He was a solitary person. He had been since he was a boy, and he intended to keep on that way. He wasn't about to let the deceitful little redhead charm her way into his heart.

He turned away from the window as a soft knock sounded on the door. He walked into the sitting room just as Samir turned the knob and walked in.

"I am sorry to disturb, *sahib,* but visitors have arrived downstairs. Your friends, Mr. Petersen and Colonel Rayburn. They wait for you in the study."

"Colonel, is it now?" Timothy Rayburn had been a major when Gray was in India, one of his closest friends.

The little man grinned, exposing two gaping holes in his teeth. "Yes, *sahib.*" Samir had always liked Rayburn.

Gray found himself smiling, as well, a rare occurrence these days. "Tell them I'll be right there." He was glad for the unexpected arrival of his friends, though a little surprised they were traveling together. Timothy Rayburn was military through and through, a major—now colonel—in the 99th Infantry stationed in India, where Gray had first met him. Dolph was retired from whatever unofficial position he'd held in the War Office.

Then again, perhaps it wasn't so surprising.

Gray headed downstairs and found the men lounging in deep leather chairs in front of an empty hearth, sipping from snifters of brandy Samir had provided them.

"Timothy. Dolph. It's good to see you." The men rose and shook hands with him. "Congratulations on your promotion, Colonel. You certainly deserve it."

Rayburn grinned. "Yes, well, it took long enough." He was a barrel-chested man with a freckled face, thick red hair and a quiet disposition. He was also the sort of soldier a man could trust with his life—as Gray had done on more than one occasion.

"What brought you two all the way from London?" he asked.

"Business in Bristol," the colonel answered. "A new trade agreement that involves the East India Company and the army's need for gunpowder."

Gray nodded. Saltpeter, a necessary ingredient, had been shipped from India since the early 1600s.

"Trade and a chance for a little advice from a friend," Dolph added.

Gray leveled a hard look at the tall, dark-haired man with the rugged face and weathered complexion. "Advice, is it? It seems I got a bit from you. As I recall, I received a message telling me not to be concerned about Letty Moss."

Dolph just smiled. "The lady is hardly a threat. You

wished to hire me to investigate her, but at the time, I had already been hired on her behalf to investigate *you*. I've been away from London for a bit, but from your manner, I presume you've discovered Mrs. Moss's true identity."

Gray walked over to the sideboard, lifted the stopper off a crystal decanter and poured himself a drink. "Perhaps you should have told me. Had I known, the lady might not now be my wife."

Dolph choked on the sip of brandy he had just taken. "You married her?"

He shrugged his shoulders. "Letty Moss was a delectable little morsel. I planned to make her my mistress. The viscount had a different notion—since the girl was his daughter."

Dolph bit back a grin. "Congratulations."

"Hear, hear!" Timothy Rayburn said, raising his brandy glass in salute.

Dolph's expression turned serious, laugh lines fading from the corners of his eyes. "She's a fine young woman, Gray. She'll make you a very good wife."

Gray made no reply. He didn't want a wife. He'd had one already, and losing her had brought him endless pain.

He carried his drink over to the sofa and sat down across from his friends. "So…what sort of advice are you looking for?"

The colonel replied. "You know India, Gray, better than any Englishman I know. Rumor is, trouble may be brewing there. We'd like your opinion on the subject."

"You say *we*." He turned, fixed Dolph with a stare. "I thought you were retired."

"I am. Occasionally I do a little work for the East India Company…matters here that might pertain to their interests over there."

"I see." Gray leaned back in his chair as the colonel picked up the conversation and began to fill him in on the situation in India as it was today, five years after Gray's departure.

He listened intently. From the moment he'd set foot on Indian soil, the instant he had inhaled his first breath of hot, pungent air scented with frangipani, sat and watched the dark-skinned children with their wide white smiles, the women with their kohl-rimmed eyes, he had felt a special bond with the country.

Samir had been assigned to him a few weeks after his arrival, and the frail little man had sensed his passion for the land. The Hindu had introduced him to Talika, a beautiful, exotic Indian woman whose husband had died, and a week later, she became his mistress.

Talika was well schooled in her duties, the skills she had learned from the *Kama Sutra,* the Hindu guide to living and the art of love. She had guided him, instructed him and taught him how to achieve the ultimate pleasure from a coupling. He'd been younger then, hot-blooded and eager, and he had learned well.

Through his Hindu mistress, he had also learned about India, experienced the sights and sounds, the colors and diversity of a place unlike any other in the world.

"We have concerns, Gray," the colonel was saying. "There are rumors, whispers of mutiny. The Bombay and Madras commands are a bit worrisome, but it is the Bengal forces that make us the most uneasy."

Gray lounged back in his chair. "In my opinion—which apparently is the reason you gentlemen stopped by—I think the army has every reason to be concerned. Until that fiasco in Kabul two years ago, the British Army was considered unconquerable, almost godlike in its power. The annihilation of Elphinstone's garrison and the retreat from Kabul put an end to that thinking."

The colonel's russet eyebrows slammed together. "For God's sake, man, you know what that place is like. The terrain is abominable, the weather unbearable. Along with the fighting, the troops died of heat, disease and lack of supplies."

"Not to mention," Gray added dryly, "the senior officers were poorly chosen and incapable of conducting a proper campaign."

Rayburn did not deny it. "Even so, I should think the stiff retribution the army dished out would have redeemed us in the opinion of the Indian population."

"I wish it were that easy. They're a people with long memories. I fear the damage will not be so easily repaired." Gray took a sip of his brandy. "Whatever happens, I don't think it's going to occur right away. Waves of dissension move slowly. It could take years before the army sees the result of its ill-advised war with Afghanistan."

The colonel sipped from his own glass. "I appreciate your speaking your mind as you have. I was not overstating when I said you know India better than any man of my acquaintance."

Certainly better than most of the men in England. In the three years he had lived there, Gray had made it a point to learn as much as he could, to understand the people and their customs. Since he had left, he'd stayed abreast of what was happening as much as possible.

He smiled. "I am no longer in the army. My opinions won't get me clamped in irons."

Rayburn chuckled. "You make a point."

"I hope you're planning to stay the night. Rebecca spent a fortune on the cook she hired. The food is incredible. And

Derek is due in sometime this afternoon. I imagine it's been a while since you've seen him."

Derek Stiles was Gray's half brother, a man whose existence he had discovered only after his father had died.

"We'd love to stay," the colonel said. "It's a bit of a ride on to Bristol."

"I haven't seen Derek in years," Dolph added. "Besides, I had a second reason for coming. I'd like a word with your wife."

Gray looked at his friend, at his carved features and swarthy complexion. He was a hard man, as his face betrayed, and yet there was something about him women found attractive. Gray decided their meeting would not be private.

"She went into the village. I'll see if she has returned." Gray left the men, wondering what Dolph had to say to Coralee. He wished he weren't so glad to have an excuse to seek her out.

His thoughts settled on the woman he had married. His Indian mistress had taught him patience, a skill essential to the art of making love. But when it came to Coralee, Gray's practiced skills seemed to elude him. Each time he made love to her, he was consumed with desire unlike any he had known since he was a youth.

Tonight, he was determined that would change. He intended to regain his legendary control, use his skills instead of letting his emotions guide him. He wondered if, without the influence of the drug he had given her, his wife would be as eager a pupil as she had been last night.

Twenty

Finished with her errands, Corrie headed back to the house, stopping briefly to leave Homer at the stables, where he was most content. She was surprised to see young Georgie Hobbs, the boy who had stolen the bread, busy cleaning one of the stalls.

"Hello, Georgie."

The lad's dark head came up. He looked around warily, as if searching for the earl.

"He isn't here. You don't have to worry."

The boy released a breath. "I've been comin' every day. I'm not sure 'e knows."

"I imagine he does. He seems to know most of what goes on around here."

He lifted another forkful of dirty straw and dumped it into the wheelbarrow. "You think…if I was to keep workin' real hard and pay off me debt, he might give me a job here at the castle?"

She bit her lip. It wasn't her place to interfere in Gray's decisions. Then again, she was his wife, and to her husband's chagrin, not nearly as timid as he wished. "I think he might. Why don't you ask him?"

His face went a little pale. "He pro'bly don't need no help, anyways."

"Actually, I could use another stable boy." Gray strode toward them, tall and masculine and incredibly attractive.

A memory arose of his hard body pressing her down in the mattress last night, the driving strength in those lean, muscular hips, and her stomach contracted.

"How is your mother?" Gray asked the boy.

"She's feelin' much better, milord. Did ye mean it about the job?"

"You've already worked enough to repay your debt. I'll give you a little money out of your first week's wages, enough to last you and your mother until you get paid again."

A watery sheen appeared in the young boy's eyes. "Thank you, milord. Ever so much."

"You keep working the way you have been, Georgie, and in time you'll earn a permanent position here at the castle."

The boy looked at Corrie and smiled so widely she caught sight of a missing tooth. She smiled back at him, an odd fullness in her chest. Georgie returned to work, and when she glanced at Gray, she saw him gazing at her in a way he hadn't since his discovery that she wasn't Letty Moss.

"Stray dogs and stray boys. I admit I am surprised, Countess."

He was surprised that she would be kind to a ragamuffin boy? That she wasn't the coldhearted shrew he believed her to be? "Is that supposed to be a compliment?"

He reached out and touched her cheek. "I suppose in a way, it is." He took hold of her hand. "Come. We have guests. One of them is a friend of yours."

"A friend?"

"As it turns out, he is also a friend of mine. Randolph Petersen." The edge returned in his voice. "The man you hired to prove me guilty of murder."

Corrie walked with Gray into the drawing room where Dolph Petersen waited. She wasn't actually the person who'd hired him—Leif and Krista were responsible for that—but she had written Krista and asked that the investigator continue his work even after he'd discovered Gray was innocent.

Her heart kicked up. Perhaps Mr. Petersen had brought news.

She spotted him as she walked through the doorway, her full skirts swishing around her ankles. He was nearly as tall as Gray, as rugged and attractive as she remembered.

"Mr. Petersen. It's good to see you." She took his hand in both of hers, and he bent and kissed her cheek.

"Your husband told me the news of your marriage. I wish you both the very best."

She flushed to think what else Gray might have told him. "Thank you."

"I had hoped to speak to you in private." He cast Gray a glance, must have read the implacability in his face. "Since you are now a married woman, I find myself in a bit of a dilemma."

"Perhaps not. Perhaps it is time my husband understood why I remained here even after I knew he was not involved in what happened to my sister."

One of Gray's black eyebrows arched. "And here I thought you stayed because you were so enamored of me."

She ignored the sarcasm. "I stayed because I wanted to find out the truth. To do that, I needed to discover whether it was Charles or Jason who was my sister's lover."

Gray's jaw hardened. "What the hell are you talking about?"

"I am talking about the man who got my sister with child, then abandoned her. If you gentlemen will please follow me, I will show you the proof I have found."

Corrie left the drawing room and the men fell in behind her. She could feel Gray's anger radiating in waves, and wondered what damage she had done to their already fragile relationship by accusing a member of his family of such heinous behavior.

Making her way into the study, she drew up a step stool to retrieve the book she had found. She frowned as she felt the empty space where it had been. Scanning the shelf, she read the gold printing on the spine of volume after volume, then moved the stool and looked again, though she knew in her heart the book had been removed.

"It was here. Only a short time ago, I found it. I returned it so no one would know what I had discovered."

Gray's features looked tight. "What are you searching for? You're making no sense, Coralee."

"I found a book that belonged to Laurel, a volume of sonnets she prized. She had given it as a gift to the man she loved. It was inscribed to him inside the front cover."

"If it was inscribed, then you know the man's name."

"She didn't pen his name. She called him her beloved. She mentioned they had read the book together. She said that she loved him."

Gray said nothing. She was sure he didn't believe her, and turned away so he wouldn't see the tears that sprang into her eyes.

She wiped them away with the tip of her finger, took a deep breath and turned back to him. "Since you can't be the man who took her innocence, then it has to be Jason or Charles."

"It could have been any number of men," Gray argued. "Dozens of people visit the castle. Perhaps your sister fell in love with one of the guests."

"If you knew Laurel, you would understand that she would never give her affections lightly. She had to have known the man, come to respect and love him. That takes time."

Dolph Petersen's voice was gentle. "That is what I wished to tell you." He looked up at Gray. "I know you don't want to hear this, but as your wife says, perhaps it is time you did."

Dolph returned his attention to Corrie. "There was another man at the castle quite often, during those months before your sister became with child. In fact, he spends a good deal of time here. Derek Stiles, Gray's half brother. Apparently, he will be arriving sometime this afternoon."

A long silence fell. Only the ticking of the clock on the mantel broke the silence. Why hadn't someone told her? Why had she never heard the name?

But she had, she began to recall. Several years back, she'd heard gossip about Derek Stiles, the bastard son of the late Earl of Tremaine. Derek had the same reputation Gray had with women. It had simply never occurred to Corrie that a son born out of wedlock would be welcome at the castle.

"Both of you are insane." Her husband cast her a piercing glance, then started for the door.

"I think your wife is right," Dolph said, stopping him before he reached it. "I believe the countess found the book, as she claims, and if she did, then one of the men in your family fathered Laurel Whitmore's child. Now that Laurel is dead, whether it matters remains to be seen."

A muscle ticked in Gray's cheek. "What are you implying, Dolph?"

"Nothing. But Coralee believes her sister was murdered. If that proves to be true, she deserves to see justice done. If Laurel had an affair with one of the men in your family, perhaps he knows something that would lead to the truth of what happened to her sister and her infant that night."

Gray pinned Corrie with a glare. "What happened is that Laurel Whitmore committed suicide. It can't be undone. If one of my brothers or my cousin was involved with her in a physical way, rest assured he has suffered for his indiscretion. But none of them are murderers." He turned to Dolph. "What's been said in this room stays among the three of us."

"That goes without saying."

Gray turned back to Corrie, his features even harder than before. "You're my wife, Coralee. I want this madness ended here and now. You and your obsession with your sister's death have caused more than enough trouble already."

He stalked out of the room, and Corrie fought to hold back tears. Her heart was aching, her throat too tight to swallow. *More than enough trouble.* That was how he thought of their marriage—as trouble. A problem she had thrust upon him.

She felt Dolph's hand on her shoulder. "I'm sorry, my lady. Perhaps I should have handled this in a different manner."

She shook her head. "It wasn't your fault. I was going to tell him, anyway. I thought he might be willing to help me."

"Give him a little time. Gray's a hard man, but fair. And justice is important to him."

She thought of all the good he had done in the time that she had known him. Gray was fair and he was just. Perhaps in time, he would understand why discovering the truth was so important.

As she made her way out of the study, she tried without success to convince herself.

As expected, Derek Stiles arrived at the castle that afternoon. He was about Gray's age, probably no more than thirty, another handsome man who might have been Laurel's lover. Derek shared the same blond hair as Charles, only a richer shade of gold. He had the same straight nose as Gray and the same brown eyes, though Derek's were more tawny.

On their first meeting, he was as charming as his half cousin Jason, as solicitous as Charles, both of whom were there to greet him.

"So you managed to tear yourself away from the ladies long enough to come out and meet your new sister-in-law," Jason teased during the introductions made in the Sky Room.

Derek drew Corrie's gloved hand to his lips. "I'm sorry I missed the wedding. Somehow my invitation got lost."

Corrie colored faintly. "There wasn't much time."

Gray just grunted. "It was a small affair, and besides you hate weddings."

"Only the thought of my own," Derek said with a roguish grin. Corrie thought of Laurel and wondered how far the man would go to avoid being forced into marriage. She tried not to think that Gray had done the honorable thing only because her father had made it nearly impossible for him to refuse.

Rebecca floated forward just then, her blue eyes finding Derek. "Stop it, you scoundrel. As Coralee said, there was scarcely time to make arrangements, but you will be invited to the reception I am hosting in the newlyweds' honor."

Gray opened his mouth, but Rebecca cut him off before he could protest. "Come now, Gray. You know it's an old tradition to invite the village for a celebration of the nuptials when the lord of the castle is wed."

And Rebecca would want to squelch any gossip that might arise from Gray's actions—or Corrie's stupidity in not stopping his seduction when she had the chance.

"You don't really mind, do you, Gray?" his sister-in-law pressed. "It truly is a custom and it will help still the wagging tongues."

"Do whatever pleases you," he said darkly.

"Thank you." She smiled. "We shall make it an afternoon affair two weeks hence. Oh, and I almost forgot—an invitation arrived just this morning to Lady Devane's costume ball. It is going to be held the last Saturday of the month. I have already sent our acceptance."

Gray scowled. "You might have asked."

"You're married now. You have an obligation to present your wife to society—such as it is out here." Her smile looked brittle. "You wouldn't want anyone thinking you have already grown tired of your bride."

Gray's gaze found Coralee's and she saw the heat, the hunger. He had certainly not tired of her yet.

His mouth edged up. "No, we wouldn't want that. Tell the countess we'll be there." He looked at Derek. "How long are you planning to stay?"

"Until you tire of my company. I thought at least until the end of next week."

Something shifted in Rebecca's features before her smile slipped back into place. "You know you are welcome for as long as you wish."

Charles smiled. "We have other guests in the house, as well. Dolph Petersen is here and Colonel Timothy Rayburn. I believe you're acquainted with them both. They'll be joining us for supper. Perhaps we can convince them to stay a bit longer and we'll get up a bird-hunting party. What do you say?"

"A splendid notion," Derek agreed. "We'll make a point of it."

Corrie left the men to their discussion of the week's activities. As she headed for the library in search of something to read, she tried to form a picture of Derek Stiles with her sister.

Aside from his comments about marriage, it wasn't that difficult to do.

In a gown of emerald silk that bared her shoulders and exposed a bit of her cleavage, Corrie sat across from Gray in the dining room. Beneath gas chandeliers, the guests dined at a linen-draped table set with gilt-rimmed plates, ornate silverware bearing the Tremaine family crest, and shimmering crystal goblets. A pair of footmen served the sumptuous meal prepared by Rebecca's French chef.

"You were right," the colonel said as he dipped his spoon into an exquisite cream of oyster soup. "The food is delicious. Of course, a military man is grateful for anything more than bread and boiled meat."

Jason grinned and Charles chuckled softly. Even Gray managed to smile.

Petersen and Rayburn were interesting men, Corrie saw as the evening progressed, well-educated and not afraid to discuss topics beyond fashionable London parties and the weather. As she had hoped it might, eventually the conversation turned to India.

"Gray lived among the natives," the colonel said, "something few Englishmen are willing to do. I think he fell a little in love with the place. He was determined to learn as much about the country as he could."

"It's unlike anyplace else in the world," Gray said between bites of roast lamb and parsley potatoes, bringing up a topic Corrie had longed to hear him discuss. "It's wildly primitive, some of its customs incredibly barbaric. At the same time there's a wisdom among the people I've never witnessed anywhere else in the world."

Corrie began asking him questions, and Gray surprised her by answering. A lively discussion ensued about the future of India and what should be done to insure British interests.

"They won't wear the yoke forever," Gray said. "One day they'll demand their independence and England will be forced to give it to them."

"Nonsense," Rayburn declared. "They're a colony and always will be. They're like children, dependent on the British to take care of them."

By the time the debate was over, Corrie had seen a side of her husband she hadn't yet discovered. He was far more open in his beliefs than she would have believed, and powerfully persuasive in presenting his views. He should take his seat in the House of Lords, she thought, but doubted that she could convince him to do so.

The evening was more enjoyable than she had expected—except for the dark, penetrating glances she received from Gray. Clearly, he was still brooding over her earlier accusations. But the other men made up for his occasional silence, keeping the women entertained.

In deference to the ladies, the men declined brandy and cigars, and Derek suggested a game of cards.

"I'm afraid we'll have to pass," the colonel said, having already declined an invitation to stay and join the bird-hunting party. "Our business in Bristol can't wait, which means we'll need to get an early start."

"We appreciate your hospitality, Gray," Dolph added. "Good evening, ladies and gentlemen."

The two men headed upstairs, but the rest of the household agreed to the card play. As they moved into the game room, Gray stayed surprisingly close to Corrie's side, even partnering her at whist.

With him seated to her left, she couldn't help noticing how handsome he looked in his perfectly tailored black evening clothes, the way his white cravat set off his dark hair and swarthy complexion. She could feel his masculine power, feel the force of his gaze as if he touched her, and her hand shook as she picked up her cards.

"All right, let's get started, shall we?" Charles began to arrange his hand, eager to get under way.

Turning her thoughts from Gray, Corrie forced herself to concentrate on the game.

She was good, she knew, and it showed when she won her first hand. Silently, she thanked Leif Draugr, a master player, for helping her improve her skills. As the evening progressed and Corrie chalked up another winning hand, Derek teasingly made mention of her prowess.

"Are you certain you aren't a sharper, my lady? You play cards like a man."

Gray glanced her way. "Another of your hidden talents, sweeting? I wonder what other interesting abilities you've kept hidden from me."

She ignored the subtle jibe. Letty had pretended to be a very poor card player. Corrie was better than most men. It was another reminder of her deception.

She pasted on a smile. "My friend's husband, Leif Draugr, helped me improve my game. He is very good at cards. The three of us played in the evenings quite often."

"I know Draugr," Derek said, his blond hair gleaming

in the lamplight, the color of pirate gold. "Made a fortune at the gaming tables. No one knows much about him."

"His wife, Krista, is my best friend. We work together at *Heart to Heart*. It's a ladies' magazine. Perhaps you've heard of it."

Derek looked amused. "I've read it."

"You have?" She was only a little surprised. A number of men read the gazette, or at least portions of it.

"I have a lady friend who's a dedicated fan. Whoever writes the editorials does a damn fine job."

Corrie's smile this time was sincere. "That would be Krista mostly. I wrote a number of them last fall when she was away. I did a series of interviews with reform leaders, including one with Feargus O'Conner, mostly as a means of lending support to the various bills before parliament."

Gray's dark eyes fixed on her face. "Becky subscribes to the gazette. News is hard to come by out here, so I read it often. You wrote that series?"

She steeled herself, certain he would have something viperous to say. "Yes… As I said, I managed the gazette for a time while Krista was away."

"They were very well written," he said softly, drawing her gaze to his. "You made some extremely valid points."

She stared at him, her heart squeezing painfully. "The gazette isn't just about fashion and gossip. We also do some very important work. In time I hope I'll be able to contribute again in some way."

Derek shot Gray a roguish grin. "Didn't know you married a reformer, eh, Brother?"

Gray stiffened, his grim look returning. "There is a lot I don't know about my wife. I do, however, know what a delightful bed partner she is, so if you will excuse us, it is time the two of us retired."

"Gray!" Her face flushed with embarrassment as he slid back his chair.

"Your wife is a lady," Charles said. "I shouldn't need to remind you."

Gray made a slightly mocking bow, not the least repentant. "My apologies, madam." Tugging on her arm, he urged her to her feet, her cheeks still flaming.

It was clear Gray was making a point. She had noticed his possessiveness all evening, but had no idea what it meant.

Leaving the others in the game room, they headed up the stairs. Even before they reached the master's suite, she sensed a subtle change in him, the control he seemed to draw around him like a protective cloak.

Uneasiness settled over her as he opened the door and waited for her to walk in.

Twenty-One

The bedcovers on the large four-poster were neatly folded back, the lamp on the dresser turned low in preparation for the lord and his lady wife. A soft yellow glow permeated the room and the faint scent of sandalwood hung in the air.

Corrie's heart beat softly. She knew what lay ahead and her senses sharpened in awareness.

"I need to ring for Anna," she said, hoping to give herself a little time. She started toward the gold-tasseled bell-pull, but Gray caught her arm.

"You don't need your maid." He shrugged out of his black evening jacket and his waistcoat and tossed them over a chair. "Turn around," he commanded, the husky note in his voice sending a curl of heat through her middle.

She did as he asked, allowing him to undress her. Anticipation mixed with trepidation as he pulled the pins from her hair. He took his time, kissing her shoulders, her neck, biting an earlobe as he unfastened the buttons at the back of her emerald silk gown. His warm breath fanned her skin and heat pooled low in her belly.

Gray peeled away each layer, kissing the areas he exposed, and yet there was an odd detachment to each of his movements, a control he seemed determined to keep.

He knew exactly where to press his mouth to make her tremble, exactly how to caress and mold her breasts, how hard to bite down on her nipple to make her breath catch. The heat was building, her body responding. Pleasure rolled through her, so powerful she bit her lip to stifle a moan.

She looked at Gray, saw the hard ridge of his sex outlined at the front of his black evening trousers, knew he was aroused and wanting her as much as she wanted him.

And yet there was something missing, some element that had been there when he had made love to her that night in the storm, and now seemed almost imagined. Her wedding night had been fierce and abandoned, but there had been little emotion in her husband's practiced lovemaking. Apparently tonight would be the same.

Unless she did something about it.

The moment he removed the last of her garments, Corrie turned and slid her arms around his neck. Pressing herself against him, she pulled his mouth down to hers for a deep, burning kiss. For an instant, he resisted, clasping her arms as if he meant to push her away. Corrie just kept kissing him, running her fingers into his silky black hair, dislodging the velvet ribbon, pressing her breasts into his chest.

Gray softly groaned.

And then he was kissing her back like a madman, parting her lips with his tongue, driving deeply inside, cupping her bottom and pulling her against his arousal. The stiff ridge thickened even more, began to pulse insistently against her. Corrie worked the buttons on the fly of his trousers, reached down and caught his hard length in her palm. It felt big and hot and male, heavy against her fingers. When she tightened her hold, Gray jerked backward, surprise and passion darkening his face.

"I'm sorry," she said, "did I...did I hurt you?"

"No, I..." He shook his head. "God, I want you." And then he was kissing her again, deep savage kisses that left her breathless and pliant, hot wet kisses that left no doubt as to his intent. For an instant, she recognized the man he had been that night in the storm. The fiery, passionate man who took what he wanted, but gave of himself in return.

Lifting her up, he carried her over to the bed and settled her in the middle of the deep feather mattress. For a time, he simply stood there, staring down at her. He drew a shuddering breath, fisting his hands as if he fought for control, then moved away from her to strip off his clothes.

He disappeared for a moment, then reappeared, striding naked toward the bed. Hard muscle rippled in his shoulders and the broad width of his chest. Ridges tightened across his stomach, and long sinews flexed in his thighs as he approached.

There was something in his hand, she saw. Several lengths of red silk floated from his palm, almost touching the floor. He came to the bedside, caught both her arms and looped the silk around her wrists. She didn't resist when he drew them over her head and tied them to an ornate post in the headboard.

"What...what are you doing?"

"Just let yourself relax. You'll enjoy it, I promise."

The distance had returned. Dear God, would she never be able to reach him? She stifled a sob, thinking of the man she had fallen in love with, the man she might never know again.

Gray leaned over and kissed her, a soft, deep, sensuous kiss with none of the wild abandon of moments before. For the first time, she realized how tightly he held himself in check, how carefully leashed each of his movements was.

Gray kept kissing her, arousing her body, taking complete control. In a flash of insight, she realized that in tying her up, he was able to keep himself apart from her. That he was protecting himself from his response to her.

That in his arms, he was in danger of losing control.

And knowing she could affect him so deeply made her heart leap with hope.

He climbed onto the bed and his mouth covered hers. Long, deep, erotic kisses followed, and Corrie gave herself up to his practiced skills. It wasn't what she wanted, wasn't what she needed from him, but she wouldn't deny herself the pleasure those hot looks promised.

She arched upward at the feel of his mouth on her breasts, the sharp tug of his straight white teeth. His hands worked their magic, teasing and caressing, skimming over her body, sliding hotly between her legs. She shifted restlessly on the bed, tugging at her silken bonds, crying out at his gentle penetration, the heated stroke of his fingers. Desire swelled, twisted like a hot coil in her belly.

She wanted him, wanted to feel him inside her.

"I need you, Gray…please…"

"Not yet."

She trembled as his mouth moved lower; his tongue slid into the indentation of her navel. He settled himself between her legs, kissed the inside of her thighs, and she squirmed.

"I need…" She moistened her lips. "I want to feel you inside me."

"Soon," he said, and set his mouth to an entirely new task.

Corrie writhed and arched against the sweet invasion of his tongue, her body tightening, the sensations sharpening until she couldn't stand an instant more. She cried out as a powerful climax shook her, stalled her breathing. Pleasure washed through her, so fierce she bit back a scream.

She was beginning to spiral down when he entered her, the bonds still holding her wrists, making it impossible for her to escape. Impossible for her to touch him. Dear God, she wanted to. She had never wanted anything so badly.

Perhaps that was the reason her body tightened instantly, began to climb to the pinnacle she had reached before. She could feel his hardness inside her, feel the breadth and length of him, the power of his maleness. Gray plunged into her again and again, and waves of sensation crashed through her.

Corrie bit her lip to keep from crying his name, and then she was soaring, arching upward, Gray pounding deeper and harder until he reached his own release.

She drifted, floating in a sea of contentment. She didn't notice when he untied the silk scarf, only roused a little when he curved his hard body around her.

She must have slept for a while. It was the middle of the night when she awakened to the feel of his mouth on her breast, his hands stroking gently between her legs. Passion flared and she welcomed him into her body.

Afterward, she slept again.

In the morning, Gray was gone.

It was early, though the servants were already up and about their daily tasks. In the kitchen, Gray accepted a linen bag filled with cold meats, bread and cheese that Cook threw together for him. Then he headed for the stable. What he needed was a brisk morning ride, a long run with Raja over the glistening dewy fields. He needed to escape his uncertain feelings for the woman in his bed.

Dammit to bloody hell.

He couldn't believe what had happened, couldn't believe how close he had come to losing control. He didn't understand it. As lovely as his wife was, he had been with more beautiful women, been with far more skillful lovers. What was it about her?

He strode along the stone path to the stable, his mind on Coralee and how best to deal with the woman who was now his wife, when he spotted Dickey Michaels racing toward him.

"Milord! Thank 'eavens ye've come. I was only waitin' till a decent hour to fetch ye."

Gray frowned. "What is it, Dickey? What's happened?"

"I need to show ye. This way, milord." The lanky youth raced ahead of him into the barn. "It's your lady, milord. The day after she took that spill, I went to fetch 'er side-saddle, like ye told me. Didn't think nothing o' it at the time. This mornin', I took it down to put a new cinch on and this is what I found."

Dickey held up the broken cinch for Gray's inspection. "It's been cut, do ye see? Weren't just a break, like I thought. It were meant to come apart the way it did."

Gray examined the cinch, saw it wasn't torn raggedly as a break would have been, but sliced almost all the way through. A chill slid down his spine. "Who else uses this saddle, Dickey? Maybe my wife wasn't meant to be the target."

"No one uses it, milord. Your sister-in-law used it before she got 'erself a fancy new padded one some months back. Ain't no one used it till I saddled Tulip for your ladyship the day the two o' ye went ridin'. Since it didn't break that day, someone musta cut it right after."

Someone who figured Coralee would be using it again. "Aside from you and the other grooms, who has access to the tack room?"

"Door ain't kept locked. Coulda been just about any-one, maybe someone passin' by from the village."

And Coralee had been in the village asking questions. For the first time Gray considered that perhaps his wife was right, and someone had indeed murdered her sister. He didn't believe for an instant it was anyone in his family. Even if one of his brothers or his cousin might have seduced the girl, none of them would murder a woman and her innocent child.

More likely, the killer—if there was one—was a foot-pad or criminal of some sort. Maybe someone from the village had committed the murder and was sending a warning that Coralee should stop asking questions.

"Thank you, Dickey. From now on, keep the tack room door locked, will you? And keep an eye out for anyone you see who shouldn't be around here."

"Aye, milord. Ye can count on Dickey."

Gray just nodded, his mind shifting from escaping the house to worry about his wife. The woman had been noth-ing but trouble since the day she arrived. Nothing but trou-ble since the day he'd been forced to marry her.

And his stomach knotted with fear that something might happen to her.

During the day, Corrie worked on her plans to remodel the upstairs suites, which gave her the chance to spend time with a number of the servants. Determined to continue her search for information, she subtly questioned the house-keeper, the butler, the upstairs and downstairs chamber-maids, even the kitchen maids. If one of the male members of the family had been involved with Laurel, the servants did not know.

Surprisingly, gleaning the information was more difficult than Corrie had expected. Every time she looked up, Gray was somewhere near. He was there in the master suite when the draper, with the help of a pair of footmen, hung new silk curtains at the windows. He appeared outside the door of the kitchen when she went in on the pretense of getting a glass of milk.

She was heading for the village to check on the arrival of the furniture she had purchased when her husband pulled up beside her in his two-wheeled phaeton and insisted she let him drive her.

He had never been more solicitous. She would even go so far as to say he was cordial. Still, at night he was the same remote lover he had been since their wedding. As intense as the pleasure was, there was always something missing.

The odd thing was, she believed Gray felt it, too.

Nearly a week had passed when the first shipment of furniture arrived at the castle. Movers cleared the heavy oak pieces out of Gray's suite, replacing them with lighter teak and bamboo ones she had purchased with the help of a dealer in London.

There was a rosewood dresser inlaid with intricate designs in brass, a mahogany chest delicately carved and inlaid with ivory, a teak writing desk with ebony drawers.

Screens with lacy filigree were scheduled to arrive later in the week to decorate the walls, along with brass lamps and several antique urns.

At Corrie's instruction, one of the workmen rolled up the ugly brown rug on the floors, and new carpets of a paisley pattern in rich blues, deep greens and burgundy went down in its stead.

The amber walls and draperies, tied back to let in sunlight, went well with the burgundy silk counterpane and the decorative pillows in colorful patterns of blue and deep green she'd had made to accent the massive four-poster bed, the only original piece of furniture she had kept.

She was helping one of the men move the heavy oak dresser and replace it with a teakwood writing desk, when she tripped over an ottoman that hadn't yet been placed, and fell back against the paneled wall on one side of the room.

When she stepped away, the panel popped open, and to her amazement, revealed a passage behind the wall. Looking around to be sure no one had seen it, she quickly set the ottoman in front of the panel. When the workmen had finished placing the furniture and gone to fetch another load, she hurriedly examined the latch so that once the panel was closed, she would know how to open it again.

Where in heaven's name did the passage lead?

Corrie vowed that as soon as she got the chance, she would find out.

Gray decided not to tell Coralee about the cinch. He wasn't certain the broken strap meant she was truly in danger, and he didn't want to worry her for nothing.

And he didn't want her jumping to conclusions—even if they were the same ones he had jumped to. He didn't want the entire matter of her sister's death stirred up all over again.

Instead, he wrote to Dolph Petersen in Bristol, telling him about the cinch and the possible threat to Coralee, asking him to return to Castle-on-Avon and continue his investigation into the possibility of Laurel Whitmore's murder.

In the meantime, Gray began asking a few questions himself, snooping around a bit in the village, seeing what he could find out. He spoke to Vicar Langston and discovered that Laurel Whitmore had come to see him after her return from East Dereham. She'd been troubled, the vicar said, though at the time, he didn't believe she was in any way suicidal.

At the Green Dragon Tavern, a barmaid named Greta told him—for a price—that gossip had it one of the men at the castle had been having an affair with Viscount Selkirk's daughter.

"Thought it was you, 'andsome," she said, grinning up at him. "Ye'd surely be the one I'd pick."

Gray paid her for her help, a little extra for the compliment, and headed back to the house. He had tried to convince himself neither his brothers nor his cousin had been involved with Laurel Whitmore. But Cora believed it was so. Dolph was fairly convinced, and local gossip agreed.

It bothered Gray to think that one of the men in his family might have seduced an innocent young woman and abandoned her.

Still, seducing a woman was far different from murder.

If it hadn't been for the broken cinch, Gray would have remained convinced the girl had killed herself. But he couldn't ignore what Dickey Michaels had found, and now he wondered…

Had a footpad come upon the young woman that night, as she wandered with her child beside the river? Perhaps he had tried to rob her, and the attempt had gone sour. If Laurel was anything like Coralee, she would have fought her attacker. In the tussle, Laurel and her child could have fallen into the water.

Or the man could have pushed her.

Coralee had been asking questions. Perhaps the man responsible was afraid he would be discovered. He would hang for the crime, no doubt.

How far would a desperate fellow go to escape the gallows? With two deaths behind him, another would hardly be a concern.

Gray thought of Coralee and his stomach twisted into a knot of fear.

The announcement, completely unexpected, came at luncheon the following day and sent the entire household into a tailspin. Corrie, Gray and the rest of the family sat round a table placed on the terrace to enjoy the sunny June afternoon. There were guests in attendance: Squire Morton and his wife, Mary, as well as two of their sons, Thomas and James.

Corrie studied Thomas carefully, since Aunt Agnes had made mention of his visits to Selkirk Hall. He was the second son, perhaps thirty-five, a large man with thick brown hair and skin slightly weathered by the work he did out-of-doors. Even with the faint scar on his chin, he was handsome. He was polite and well-mannered, the sort of man Laurel might have found attractive.

But the book Corrie had found in the study made it clear that Laurel had been in love with one of the men at the castle.

As the group sipped white wine and enjoyed dilled salmon and a fresh cucumber salad, Rebecca leaned toward Charles and whispered something in his ear. He rapped his wineglass to draw the company's attention.

"We've news to share," he said at her urging. "Why don't you tell them, my dear?"

Gowned elegantly in cream-and-rose silk, Rebecca surveyed the table of family and friends and smiled. "We're going to have a baby. For years, Charles and I have been hoping…praying it would happen. Now, after all of this time, God has finally blessed us." Tears brimmed in her brilliant blue eyes and she wiped them away with the tip of a finger.

"Why, that is marvelous news!" said beefy Squire Morton.

Gray rose from his place at the head of the table, dark and forbidding, looking nothing at all like the rest of his fair-haired family. "This is quite an occasion. Congratulations to you both. I know how much you've wanted a child."

There was something in his expression Corrie couldn't quite read, something deep and troubled. He had wanted children once. Perhaps he still did, but had vowed never to have them.

"I…my wife and I," Gray corrected, "couldn't be happier for both of you."

"A toast," Jason said, lifting his wineglass, "to the future Mama and Papa Forsythe."

"Here, here!" Derek chimed in. "To a healthy babe and many more to come."

The toasts were accepted graciously, Rebecca smiling all the while, Charles a bit more reserved, but smiling along with his wife. Corrie added her own good wishes, happy for Rebecca, though they were not friends, and delighted for Charles, who was certain to make an excellent father.

After luncheon, the group dispersed, heading off in different directions to entertain themselves.

"What are your plans for the afternoon?" Gray asked Corrie, solicitous as he had been all week.

"I need to take a few more measurements in the rooms upstairs." It was only a tiny lie. She meant to explore the secret passage, which meant she truly would be upstairs in the suite. "Why do you ask?"

"No plans to run off to the village?" There was a trace of worry in his expression. It had been there all week.

"No, but—"

"Fine, then I'm going for a ride. Stay out of trouble, will you?" For an instant, she thought he might kiss her. Instead, he turned and strode toward the back of the house.

Corrie watched his tall dark figure disappear, a feeling of yearning in her heart. She had tried to tell herself she was no longer in love with Gray, that the man she had married was an altogether different one, but it wasn't the truth. Day after day, the need she saw in her husband's face, the longing he tried to hide, stole a little more of her heart.

She thought of the lonely man he was and the lonely life he led. She thought of all he had lost, and believed it was his fear of losing even more that made him unable to love.

With a sigh, she crossed the terrace and entered the house. The mystery of the passage lured her, the possibility of where it might lead and what she might find once she got there.

Corrie picked up her pace as she climbed the wide staircase.

Twenty-Two

Thankfully, both Samir and Anna were busy somewhere else, so the master's suite was empty. Corrie breathed a sigh of relief. Hurrying over to the dresser, she lit a candle, placed it in a silver candlestick and quietly moved toward the wood-paneled wall.

The newly arrived furniture was draped with white sheeting, hidden from Gray until the project was complete. She wanted to surprise him, hoped so much that he would be pleased with what she had done. But there was no way to know until he saw it.

In the meantime, the passage beckoned. Corrie pressed on the spot she had carefully marked, and a portion of panel silently swung open. She expected cobwebs and spiders, but when she thrust the candle inside the opening, the narrow passage seemed merely dusty and inky dark.

Taking another quick look around, and a breath for courage, she stepped into the space, but didn't close the panel. She planned to be back in the room long before Gray returned from his afternoon ride. Aside from that, the last thing she wanted was to be trapped in the narrow, confining passage with no way to escape.

As she began to move down the pitch-dark corridor, the candle threw faint yellow light in front of her and cast shadows along the walls. She couldn't tell how far the passage went, but along the route, the candle revealed what appeared to be several openings…if she could figure out how to unlock them.

Ignoring the chill that invaded the passage and slowly crept up her spine, she continued along until she came to a set of stairs. The candle flickered and she paused, her heart racing at the thought of the flame going out, leaving her in total darkness.

The full skirts of her apple-green day dress swished against the walls as she descended to the floor below. She wasn't sure where she was, only that the faint sound of voices began to reach her.

Corrie moved toward the sound, stopping when she could hear what was being said. But the thick walls muffled the voices so much she couldn't tell who was speaking, only that they seemed to be a male and a female.

"It's mine, isn't it?" the man was saying.

"Of course it is, darling. Charles was never man enough to father a child."

Corrie sucked in a breath. *Rebecca.* It had to be.

"I knew I wasn't the one to blame," she said, "and you have proved it. I shall be forever in your debt for such a gift."

Corrie heard the muffled sound of footfalls—the man pacing back and forth across a carpet. "He doesn't suspect, does he?"

"Of course not, darling. He wants a child too badly to examine the matter overmuch. The last thing Charles would wish to know is that the child isn't his."

Corrie felt a pang of sympathy for Charles Forsythe, to be duped in such a manner. She also felt a trickle of relief. Laurel's baby wasn't Charles's. Though he and Rebecca had tried to have children, Charles hadn't been able to father a babe. Which meant he couldn't have been Laurel's beloved.

Corrie liked Charles Forsythe. She was thankful to know he hadn't seduced an innocent young girl and then abandoned her.

"He'll raise it well," the man was saying. "Charles was meant to be a father, as I never was."

Who are you? Corrie silently asked, still unable to actually recognize the speaker's voice. *Jason or Derek?*

The ugly thought arose—perhaps it was Gray.

She bit her lip. It couldn't be. She refused to believe it. Gray had never shown the slightest interest in Rebecca. And Corrie didn't believe for an instant he was the sort of man who would cuckold his brother.

"I miss being with you. I want us to be together again." The man's voice barely reached through the wall.

The idea arose: *What about Thomas Morton?* He was an attractive man, a friend of Rebecca's. Perhaps more than a friend. And he had just been there at the house.

"We've discussed this," she said. "It's over. You know it had to end."

"I don't want it to end. I don't see why we can't go on the way we were."

Corrie strained to hear Rebecca's reply, but the pair was moving away from the wall. All Corrie could hear now were whispers, and soon after, only silence. She thought she heard a door open and close, but she couldn't be sure.

For a moment, she stood there in the passage, the candle flickering, threatening to go out. With a calming breath, she turned back the way she had come. When she reached the tiny staircase leading upward, she picked up her skirt and petticoats and hurriedly climbed, anxious to leave the dismal corridor and consider what she had learned.

Things at Castle Tremaine weren't as they seemed and never had been.

She wondered what Gray would say if he knew.

Then again, perhaps he already did.

As he had done every afternoon this week, Gray rode Raja as fast as he could across the fields. Still, he couldn't escape thoughts of Coralee. Worry that something might happen to her made him physically ill.

Except for the few hours he took for himself when Cora was inside the castle and he knew she was safe, he stayed close by. Even now, worry nagged him. He drew Raja to a halt atop a hill, turned the horse and started back toward the house.

As he crossed the fields, his thoughts shifted from Coralee to the announcement his sister-in-law had made that afternoon. Before this time next year, Charles would be a father. If the infant was a boy, the Tremaine title and fortune would be secure. And Charles would make a very good father.

For the first time, Gray was forced to ponder the notion that Coralee might also be with child.

It was a frightening thought.

Terrifying.

Gray had never had a loving, supportive father of his own. He had no idea how to be one. Bloody hell, he wouldn't know where to begin. He thought of Jillian and the short time they had been married. As a newly titled earl, he'd believed it was his duty to provide an heir. He had been certain that in time it would happen, but beyond that, hadn't given the matter much thought.

Then Jillian had died and the guilt had set in. Her death had been his fault. If he had gone boating with her that day, he could have saved her. He didn't doubt it for a moment.

A wave of nausea rolled through him. He had failed Jillian, and if he had a child, he might fail again. For an instant, he thought he might be sick.

He couldn't take the chance of failing a daughter or son, of failing Coralee. It wouldn't be fair to any of them.

From now on, he decided, he would take measures to prevent Cora's womb from quickening. He certainly knew how to do it, though there was always a chance it might not work. He didn't think she had yet conceived. There was still time to prevent it from happening.

By the time he reached the house, Gray had mostly convinced himself. Leaving the stallion with Dickey, he headed toward the castle. His worry built as he went in search of her, hoping she was still involved in her refurbishing project and out of any possible danger.

"Have you seen the countess?" he asked Samir.

The little Hindu smiled. "She awaits you upstairs, *sahib.*" Samir had said little about the woman Gray had married. He was a patient man and not quick to judge another human being, but Gray was sure he'd just caught a hint of approval in the weathered lines of the man's dark face. If he had, Gray wondered what his wife had done to win such a wise man's favor.

Calling Coralee's name as he opened the door and stepped into his sitting room, Gray knew in an instant why Samir seemed so pleased.

His own chest tightened. For an instant, he thought he

had stepped out of England and into a world from his past.
Nothing of the old suite remained. The massive oak furniture and heavy gold draperies, always so oppressive, had
disappeared and with them, dark memories of his father
seemed to lift away.

With sunlight streaming through the windows, he saw
furnishings of teak and bamboo, a rosewood dresser decorated with shiny brass ornaments, a carved mahogany chest
inlaid with ivory, an ebony-fronted bureau. Screens of lacy
filigree lined one wall. There were beautiful brass lamps
and the kind of antique brass urns he hadn't seen since he
had left India.

He walked into the bedroom, his heart beating oddly,
and saw that both rooms had been done in royal blue, deep
green and rich burgundy, the walls and draperies of a soft
honey color.

Only the bed remained, and with its burgundy silk counterpane and decorative pillows in colorful blue-and-green
paisley patterns, even that looked different. It was as if his
wife had looked into his soul, as if she understood the
world that had made him most happy.

"Do you like it?"

He followed the sound of her voice and turned to see
her standing a few feet away. She looked so lovely that a
lump rose in his throat.

"You read my heart," he said.

Tears welled in her eyes. She walked to where he
stood and leaned toward him, gently slipped her arms
around his neck.

"I hoped you would like it. I wanted you to feel as if
you were home."

He held her. Just held her. Her small body curved into
his and it filled him with warmth. He knew he should let

her go. Knew it was dangerous to allow these feelings he held for her to grow into something more. He took a deep breath and stepped away, but he couldn't let go of her hand.

"It's beautiful. I couldn't be more pleased. Thank you for such a wonderful gift."

She simply nodded. With her hand still holding his, she led him toward the door between their bedrooms and pushed it open. The suites were nearly identical. The tones in hers were a little softer, but there was no mistaking the Indian influence.

"You don't mind, do you? You make it sound like a very special place."

"I don't mind."

"I should like to see it someday."

He shook his head. "It's an amazing country, but not a place for an Englishwoman."

She merely shrugged. "I've always wanted to travel. I had hoped to write a book one day about the places I had seen." She let go of his hand and glanced away. "That was before, of course."

"Before you married me."

She returned her gaze to his. "Yes."

"I guess we both gave up something."

"Some of our freedom, I suppose."

That was what he had thought, but now he wondered…. Perhaps he had gained something even more valuable in return.

He cleared his throat. "I love the rooms," he repeated, simply to have something to say.

"I'm glad."

Her smile was so sweet his heart squeezed. Bloody hell, he couldn't let this continue. He had to do something before he slid completely off the precipice that seemed only inches away.

"Your rooms are nice, but I like having you in my bed, nearby in case I want you. When we retire, you will continue to sleep with me."

She bristled, as he knew she would, and the tender moment was lost.

"I have my own bed. Just because I'm your wife doesn't mean you can command me as you once did your troops."

Grateful to be on more familiar terrain, he stood his ground. "Nevertheless, you'll sleep in my bed. If you refuse, I will simply carry you in and tie you to the bedposts as I did the other night."

She made a low, growling sound in her throat, and he almost smiled. She was so full of fire.

Nothing at all like Letty.

Yet in the ways that counted, exactly like Letty.

The thought disturbed him, considering the feelings he had harbored for the little country waif. Instead of dragging his wife into his arms, carrying her over to the bed and making love to her as he dearly wished to do, Gray turned and walked away, leaving her alone in the suite.

It occurred to him, as it had before, that perhaps he should tell her about the broken cinch. If he didn't hear from Dolph in the next day or two, he would. Gray was coming to appreciate Coralee's intelligence. It might be interesting to hear what she had to say.

In the meantime, he would keep her safe.

He cast a last glance at the door to her bedroom and forced his feet to keep moving away.

Supper was over. The men suggested a game of cards, but Rebecca pleaded a headache and declined. Corrie seized the opportunity and also declined, then headed upstairs to renew her investigation of the passage. She had secured a prying tool from one of the workmen who had helped with the refurbishing, and hoped to use it to open the panels along the secret corridor.

Anna helped her change out of her dinner gown into her nightgown. Corrie stood fidgeting as the maid pulled the pins from her hair and ran the bristle brush through it.

"Thank you, Anna, that will be all for tonight."

"Don't you want me to braid it?"

"I'll take care of it this evening." She didn't have much time. She would plait it the moment she got back.

"Good night, milady." The thin woman slipped quietly away, and the moment she was gone, Corrie lit her candle and headed for the passage. Pressing on the spot she had marked, she stepped back as the panel swung open, then quickly ducked into the shadowy space.

The last time she had entered it had been daylight. The corridor was no darker now, yet it seemed so. Each of her creaking footsteps tightened her nerves a notch. The eerie whisper of air that blew through the passageway sent a shudder down her spine.

She moved along the corridor, holding the candle out in front of her, searching the walls to find any cracks that indicated there might be an opening. The air shifting past her felt colder, the darkness more dense. She shivered and wished she had put on a robe. Some ways down the passage, she found the first opening and tried to think which bedroom it might lead to.

She pressed on the wall, ran her hand up and down each side and over the top, but found no way to get it to open. She tried the prying tool, pulling back firmly, but not hard enough to crack the wood, yet the door remained solidly closed.

She was debating whether to use more force when the candlelight reflected on a shiny piece of metal she hadn't noticed before. She lifted the inch-long latch and the panel popped open neat as you please.

She could see the glow of lamplight and flattened herself against the wall of the passage, fearful someone might be in the room. A lamp burned on the dresser, the wick turned low, but when she leaned forward to peek into the room, she saw that it was empty.

Unsure how much time she would have, she ducked through the opening, which was not quite as tall as she, and made a quick survey of the bedroom.

A leather traveling satchel sat on the floor, and she recognized some of Derek's garments in the armoire. A hat and gloves, black evening clothes and shiny black shoes… There were several well-made frock coats and trousers, but nothing that might be a clue to a connection with Laurel. Corrie moved to the satchel, opened and searched inside for something—anything—that might prove telling.

Nothing.

A riding crop lay on the dresser, and a pair of leather riding boots stood nearby. It was clear Derek traveled lightly and also clear she wasn't going to find any pertinent information here.

She wasn't sure how much time had passed or how long the men would continue their card playing, but she felt fairly safe in trying one more door. Returning to the secret corridor, she ducked inside and closed the panel, then continued through the inky blackness. The second door seemed miles away, and yet she knew it must access one of the other bedrooms along the upstairs hall.

Being even more careful this time, she pressed her car against the wall, straining to hear anyone moving about.

Relatively certain the room was empty, she found the metal latch, then held her breath as the panel popped open.

No lamp burned this time. She crossed the room, set her candle on the dresser and began to search the place in its soft yellow glow. She was busy looking through the armoire when the bedroom door swung open without the least amount of warning, and Jason Forsythe walked into the room.

"I'll see you in the morning," he said to someone in the hall, then turned and stopped dead at the sight of her in her nightgown standing in front of his armoire.

"Well, *chérie,* I admit you are a treat I hadn't expected to find. However, we both might have been better served if you had come when your husband was not standing in the doorway." Amusement curved his lips. "As it is, we shall both be lucky to escape with our lives."

Corrie gasped as Gray stormed into the bedroom, his dark eyes blazing with damnation. "What the bloody hell are you doing in my cousin's room?"

Jason held up a hand. "Easy, Gray. Perhaps she merely lost her way."

He pinned her with a glare. "Surely you can do better than that, sweeting."

Corrie swallowed. Gray was already furious, but the truth was better than what he was thinking now. "I was…" She turned, pointed toward the open panel leading to the secret passage. "I found a hidden corridor behind the wall in your sitting room. I wanted to see where it led."

He looked over at the black, forbidding hole that was the opening of the passage, and frowned. "You expect me to believe you traveled through that dismal tunnel merely to see where it went?"

"Well, I—I was…"

"The truth, Coralee."

"All right! I was looking for clues. I thought you would all be busy playing cards, and while you were downstairs I would see what I could find out."

"Your sister, again! Dammit to bloody hell!"

"Would one of you mind telling me what is going on?" Jason walked over to examine the opening, enjoying the situation now that he was sure Gray wasn't going to kill him.

Of course, Corrie thought, her husband might still do his wife bodily harm.

Gray focused his attention on Jason. "Coralee came here to prove I had murdered her sister—which you already know. Apparently, she discovered my innocence or she wouldn't have allowed me to bed her."

Corrie blushed.

"Unfortunately, she is now convinced one of the other men in the house was Laurel Whitmore's lover. She is trying to discover which one of you it is."

Jason's light brown eyebrows went up. "Interesting. I had trouble imagining you leg-shackled, Gray, but I think I'm beginning to understand. You certainly don't have to worry about your marriage being dull."

Gray's features tightened. "Since we're discussing seduction, I might as well ask—were you and Laurel Whitmore involved in an affair?"

Jason shook his head. "I knew her. I liked her. I wouldn't have minded taking her to bed, but I am not ready for marriage and knew well enough that is what it would mean."

Gray shoved back a lock of black hair, loose from its ribbon. He turned a dark glare on Corrie. "Satisfied?"

"I suppose I shall have to be."

He walked over to the passage, leaned down to peer inside, then shut the panel. As he walked back across the room, he grabbed Corrie's wrist and started tugging her toward the door.

"I'd appreciate it if you would keep my wife's little adventure to yourself."

Jason chuckled. "Of course."

Gray dragged Corrie out into the hall and along the carpet toward the master's suite, her nightgown billowing out around her ankles as she ran to keep up. He hauled her into the sitting room and slammed the door.

"You little fool, I swear I ought to give you the thrashing of your life." His gaze sliced down to her bottom, protected only by the thin white nightgown. "But I'd probably enjoy it too much." Angry strides carried him over to the panel she had left open as a means of escape.

"Did you know it was there?" she asked.

"No." He tried to see inside the passage, but it was as black as pitch inside. "Where does it lead?"

"I've only gone partway. It travels along the bedrooms on this side of the hallway, opens into some of them, and also goes downstairs. I went down and looked around a bit, but you can see how dark it is. I wasn't sure where I was, so I came back up."

His jaw clenched. "You could have been hurt, Coralee. If you had been injured while you were in there, we might never have found you." He paced back to where she stood. "Dammit, promise me you won't do anything that foolish again."

"I left the door open. I wasn't really in danger."

"You might have been." He sighed, dragged the tie from his hair and ran his fingers through it. The thick black mass fell around his shoulders, making him look like the highwayman he sometimes seemed. "The day you rode out in that storm, your cinch didn't break—it was cut."

"Cut? I don't know what you mean."

"Someone wanted you to take that fall. You'd been asking a lot of questions. Perhaps it was a warning, I don't know. Until we do, we have to be careful nothing like that happens again."

Corrie glanced toward the window, thinking of the day she had taken the fall in the rain. "You're saying someone tried to kill me?"

"Or at least hoped to see you hurt."

She mulled the information over and lifted her chin. "If that is so, it proves I am right. My sister was murdered, and whoever cut my cinch wants to stop me from finding out who killed her."

Gray released a slow breath and, to her amazement, agreed. "It's possible." He glanced toward the passage, pointed to the ominous dark opening. "And if you're right, with a stunt like that you're playing right into his hands."

He was angry again. And he was worried. She could see it in his eyes.

The anger won out. "It's time for bed." After shutting the panel, he grabbed her hand and hauled her across the carpet into his bedroom. "I want you from behind. Get up on the mattress."

She had no idea what he was talking about and simply stood there staring.

"The bed," he demanded, as if he had the right. Which, as her husband, he did.

She flicked a glance in that direction, but still didn't move. He might have the right, but she didn't like his tone of voice and wasn't about to be bullied. "I am not yours to command, and besides, I don't know what you want me to do."

He seemed only a little surprised by her defiance. Perhaps he was beginning to know her, after all. He was a difficult man, moody and often brooding, but she didn't believe he meant to hurt her.

His hard look slipped away. "I'll teach you," he said softly. "I'll make it good for us both. Trust me."

She did, she realized. Certainly, she trusted him in this. She started to pull the string at the neck of her nightgown, but Gray caught her hand.

"Leave it," he said gruffly.

Intrigued now, she did as he asked, climbing up on the high four-poster, watching as Gray stripped off his clothes. He turned away for a moment, then joined her naked on the bed. Catching her face in his hands, he kissed her, a long, wet, demanding kiss that sent heat into her stomach and desire sliding through her limbs.

Gray came up behind her, molding his powerful body against her back and hips. Through the nightgown, she could feel the heat of his groin against her bottom, and silently cursed the fabric that formed a barrier between them. One of his big hands slid into her hair where it fell in soft curls around her shoulders. He combed the heavy strands with his fingers, exposing the column of her neck.

She felt his mouth against her nape as he reached around to caress her breasts, to tease and mold them through the soft white cotton, and her nipples stiffened against his palms.

She yearned to be rid of the nightgown. "I need to feel you, Gray."

"Soon."

"But I need—"

He leaned over and caught her chin, settled his mouth over hers, silencing her protests.

"I'm going to give you exactly what you need," he promised in his deep husky voice.

But instead of removing the nightgown, he lifted it over her hips, bunching the fabric around her waist. His hands smoothed over her bottom, then moved between her legs, where he began to caress her.

Her insides tightened. The man knew every trick, knew that the longer the cumbersome nightgown stayed on, the greater was her need to take it off, and the hotter she became.

She moaned as he parted her burning flesh and began to stroke her. "You're mine," he said. "No more trips into another man's bedroom."

She tried to concentrate on his words, but the pleasure was building. She bit down on her bottom lip to keep from begging him to take her. "I wasn't…"

He nipped her bare bottom and a warm shiver went through her. "You are the most vexing female." The stroking increased. "Damn, but I want you."

Guiding himself into her damp heat, he filled her slowly, until he impaled her completely, then gripped her hips and began to move.

Hot sensation poured through her. Sweet God, it was heaven. Corrie arched her back to take him deeper still, and Gray hissed in a breath. His pace increased, the heavy thrust and drag infusing her with heat. She knew his desire was as strong as her own. Still, she could feel his determined control.

Her own control faded, caught up in the heat and need, the desire that scorched through her like a flame. The muscles in his buttocks flexed as he drove into her. Hard arms reached around her. He gripped the nightgown in his fists and tore the fabric away.

A whimper escaped. She was naked at last and she wanted

to sob with relief. Instead, she gave herself over to the hot feel of skin against skin, the deep stroke of flesh into flesh.

She cried out Gray's name as a powerful climax shook her, but he didn't stop. Not until another wave of pleasure rolled through her, melting the last of her need. Then his muscles tightened and he reached his own release.

Seconds passed. Slowly they spiraled down. Gray settled himself beside her, and as she curled against him, she saw him removing something from his still-firm erection.

"What is that?"

"French letter," he said absently.

Corrie stiffened. "You…you told me they were used to prevent childbirth."

He looked up at her. "That's right."

"But we're married now. Children are a normal part of marriage."

He glanced away. "I'm not ready to be a father, Coralee. I'm not sure I ever will be."

She swallowed. She couldn't believe she had heard him correctly. Tears welled in her eyes. "You're my husband, Gray. Would you deny me the joy of having your child?"

His gaze swung back to hers, turbulent and for the first time uncertain.

Corrie pressed on. "What about your duty as an earl?"

"Charles's son can carry on the title."

"But I love children, Gray. And I think you would make an excellent father. Please don't take this away from me—from us."

His gaze found hers. "I didn't think it would be this important to you."

He didn't think it would be important? A lump swelled in her throat. She loved him. He was her husband. Of course it was important. "I want your child, Gray—more than anything in the world."

He reached out and touched her face, and she was surprised to feel a tremor in his hand. Leaning over, he very softly kissed her. "All right, if that's what you want. I'll give you a baby. Or at least make a damn good try."

And then he came up over her, filling her again and stirring her blood. Corrie gave herself into his care, feeling love for him expanding in her heart.

She wasn't sure she could ever make him love her in return, but tonight they had touched on the future, spoken of children and family.

It just might be a start.

Twenty-Three

—⁊⊙⊙⊱—

It was a sunny afternoon in June, the day of the celebration being held in honor of the marriage of the Earl and Countess of Tremaine. Rebecca had worked tirelessly for nearly two weeks, and as Corrie looked out on the wide green lawns surrounding the castle, where the party would be held, everything appeared to be in perfect order.

The gathering was scheduled to start at four o'clock and continue into the evening. Colorful paper lanterns hung from the trees. The candles would be lit as soon as it was dark. Great kegs of ale had been brought in for the villagers, along with lemonade and jugs of wine. Long rows of tables had been set up under the trees, laden with outrageous quantities of food: roast pig, a haunch of beef, succulent pigeons browned on a spit. There were breads and cheeses, platters of vegetables and puddings, and an astonishing array of desserts.

It was a day when commoners would mingle with the aristocracy, a celebration not to be missed.

Though Corrie's parents had decided not to make the tedious journey, Aunt Agnes and Allison would be there.

Since Corrie's marriage, their visits had been few. They didn't want to take her away from her husband.

Corrie scoffed. All Gray really cared about was having her close by whenever he wanted access to her body, which he did with amazing frequency. Of course, she couldn't deny she enjoyed his skillful attentions. She just wished he would share a bit of himself beyond making love.

The party progressed and the ale flowed. More platters of food were brought out and consumed by the festive crowd on the lawn. Krista, Leif and Thor had been invited, but with Corrie gone and Lindsey still new to her job as editor, Krista was needed at the gazette. Reluctantly, she and Leif had declined the invitation, but promised a visit next month, which Corrie preferred, since they would be able to spend more time together.

The afternoon moved toward evening, perfectly choreographed by Rebecca, who was dressed like royalty in a confection of cream-and-amber silk. Corrie had chosen a gown of pale green moiré, the skirt swept together in long pleats up the front, and trimmed with green silk cord around the bodice and hem. Her full petticoats brushed against her ankles as she moved through the crowd of guests on her husband's arm.

In a navy-blue frock coat, satin-collared waistcoat, light gray trousers and white silk cravat, Gray looked elegant and handsome. His wavy black hair, tied neatly at the nape, shone like jet in the afternoon sun. Corrie didn't miss the provocative glances he received from several women.

If he noticed, Gray didn't let it show. He was playing the dutiful husband, and if she pretended, she could almost imagine him that way. In truth, it was only a performance. He had yet to accept her as more than a bedmate. She had to keep that firmly in mind.

Corrie studied the sea of guests milling about on the manicured lawns. All the important neighbors for miles around were there: the town magistrate, the vicar and his family, Squire Morton, his wife and sons, two of whom were married and had children of their own.

The Forsythe family was well represented, with Charles and Rebecca, Gray's half brother, Derek, and his cousin, Jason all in attendance. Corrie flicked a glance at the handsome man with the deep dimples and light brown hair. Jason had denied any involvement with Laurel, and he had been extremely convincing.

Which left Derek Stiles the likely suspect.

Corrie sighed, no longer certain that any of them were involved. Without the book she had found as proof, she had begun to doubt her own judgment. Perhaps she was wrong about it all.

Then again, there was the sabotaged cinch and the fall she had suffered.

It was several hours after the party had started and introductions had all been made that Gray allowed her to escape into the company of her friends.

"I am so glad to see you!" Corrie hugged Aunt Agnes, then Allison. "We live so close to each other and yet it seems there is never time enough to visit."

"You are newly married," said bulky Aunt Agnes, out of mourning along with Allison for the occasion of Corrie's wedding celebration. After Gray's edict, Corrie had never returned to wearing the dismal black garments. She couldn't say she was sorry.

"You are busy with your husband," Aunt Agnes continued, "as is to be expected. You need time to get to know each other."

Corrie just smiled. "Even so, I shall come by and see

you next week. I should love an excuse to get away for a bit."

Allison reached over and squeezed her hand. "How are you doing? Are you and the earl…beginning to settle your differences?"

Corrie's gaze shifted to where Gray stood in conversation with Jason. "I suppose. He is no longer angry, at least. Though I don't think he has altogether forgiven me."

"Give him time," Allison said.

Corrie nodded. What other choice did she have?

Her friend looked exceptionally pretty today, a bit too thin, but attractive with her very dark hair and high, carved cheekbones, elegant in a way Corrie had never really noticed before.

Derek did. As the afternoon progressed, he homed in on Allison, and Corrie saw the two of them sharing a plate on a blanket down by the river.

Her stomach twisted. What if Derek had been Laurel's lover? What if he had seduced and abandoned an innocent young woman, had perhaps been involved in her death and that of her infant son?

Was Allison in danger?

"You are frowning." Gray's deep voice reached her. She turned to see him walking up beside her. "What's wrong?"

"Nothing. I just…" She looked up at him. She wasn't sweet little Letty. She didn't have to pretend anymore. "I am worried about Allison. Derek seems to have taken an interest in her and there is a chance he was the man who fathered my sister's child. I don't want Allison getting hurt."

Corrie thought Gray would be angry. Instead, his dark gaze moved off toward the couple on the blanket. ·

"Derek has always enjoyed the company of a beautiful

woman. Without her mobcap, your friend Allison has quite an arresting face. I'll speak to him, make certain he understands that the girl is family and therefore off-limits." He cast Corrie a glance. "I'll talk to Derek. I suggest you speak to your cousin."

She nodded, knowing he was right, though it might not do a bit of good. Derek was blond, handsome and charming. What woman wouldn't be attracted to him? Then again, perhaps Corrie was jumping to conclusions. "I shall. Thank you."

He reached out and touched her face, then turned and walked away.

She saw him again when he arrived to escort her to supper. Filling their plates with all sorts of delicious treats, Gray seated her at a table that had been set up for the bride and groom.

The meal was delicious. When she had finished as much as she could possibly hold, she leaned back and sighed with contentment. The wine was as good as the food, and she drank a good bit, which made her notice the hot looks Gray began to cast her way. She yearned to slip off with him, to have him take her upstairs and make love to her.

Feeling a little bit wicked, she'd leaned over to suggest exactly that when a wave of dizziness hit her. Reeling a little, she sat back in her chair.

Gray's eyebrows drew together. "What is it? Are you feeling unwell?"

"No, I...I'm sure I am fine. I just..." Another round of dizziness hit her and she braced herself against the table. "I think I must have drunk too much wine."

He nodded. "I'll make our excuses and we'll go upstairs." His burning glance told her exactly what he had in mind once they got there. Corrie smiled as he made his way to Rebecca and Charles to express his thanks for the party and take his leave.

By the time he returned, Corrie was no longer smiling. "I am feeling unwell, my lord. I am extremely sorry."

"It's all right. I've noticed you aren't much of a drinker." Helping her to her feet, he guided her back to the house. Thankfully, the company, many of them feeling the effects of the food and drink themselves, paid little heed to their leave-taking.

Unfortunately, by the time Corrie reached her suite, she was well and truly ill. Hurrying into her bedroom, she lost the contents of her stomach into a chamber pot. The world swirled around her and she fought not to be sick again. Catching sight of Gray walking toward her, she felt embarrassment war with misery.

"Here, drink this." He handed her a glass of water. She drank it, then used the towel he handed her to wipe the perspiration from her face.

"I—I didn't realize I had drunk all that much." She sat down in a chair, suddenly exhausted. "I'll be all right in a minute. I just…just need to rest for a while." Her eyes slid closed. She was asleep in an instant, leaning against the back of the chair.

Gray shook her shoulder, but she barely stirred.

"Coralee? Coralee, are you all right?"

She tried to nod, but her head lolled sideways. All she could think of was sleeping. She couldn't remember ever being so tired.

"Dammit, Coralee, wake up!"

Gray shook her again and her eyes slowly opened. She stared up at him blearily. "I'm sorry… I'm just so… sleepy." Her lids drifted closed once more and she heard Gray curse.

Corrie moaned as he hauled her to her feet.

Gray examined her pupils, must have seen something that he did not like. "I don't think you drank too much." He tipped her chin up and looked into her heavy-lidded eyes. "I think someone drugged you." He shook her again and her eyes fluttered open. "Did you hear what I said? You've been drugged."

"Drugged…?"

"Given a dose of opium. The drug acts this way when a person has too much. Someone must have doused your wine or your food with laudanum or something similar. If you go to sleep, odds are you won't wake up."

She roused herself a bit at that, forcing her head up, her heartbeat sluggish inside her chest. "Someone is trying to kill me?"

His jaw hardened to steel. "It isn't going to happen." He settled her in the chair for a moment, strode over to the bellpull and gave it a single hard yank.

"On your feet," he said, hoisting her up again, forcing her eyes to open. "Sooner or later, the stuff will wear off. Until then, you have to stay awake."

"I—I don't think I can."

His hand was gentle on her cheek. "I'm going to help you, love. Just lean on me." And so she did, her body as limp as soggy bread, her feet barely willing to move round the floor.

She didn't remember exactly when Samir arrived in the bedroom, only dimly heard Gray speaking to him in a deep, worried voice.

"She's been given an overdose of opium," Gray said. "Can you do something to help her?"

Before her eyes closed again, she caught the little man's nod.

"I will do what I can. I will need time to mix the herbs."

"Do it as quickly as possible." As the dark-skinned Hindu shuffled away, Gray's grip on her tightened. "Let's go," he commanded, urging her to move again, holding her up as if she were an oversize rag doll.

She was so unbearably tired. She felt limp, her body out of control. "Can't I just…can't I rest…just for a moment? I'll get back up…I…promise."

She started to sink down, but Gray hauled her erect. "Keep walking. I'm not letting you die, dammit."

And so she did. Walking and walking, her body leaden, her eyelids barely open. She wasn't sure how long they went on that way, Gray moving her around the floor, his hard body and firm arm all that kept her from sliding into a puddle at his feet.

"Come, love. Drink this." He held a glass to her lips and tipped it up, forcing her to swallow the bitter liquid Samir had brought. "Finish it." She did as he commanded, knowing he wouldn't allow her to refuse.

They walked some more, on and on, an endless march as the hours slipped past, the hands on the clock moving even more slowly than her legs. Eventually, little by little, she was able to hold her head up, able to lift her feet a little more easily. The hours continued toward morning, but still Gray did not give up. She knew he must be as exhausted as she, but he was relentless.

It was after four in the morning when she finally looked at the clock and the numbers were no longer blurry. "I need to sit down, Gray. I promise I won't fall asleep."

"Are you sure?"

She nodded, her eyes for the first time completely open.

Gray leaned over and kissed her forehead. "Sit for a while. I'll be right beside you."

He settled her on the settee in front of the hearth and

sat down next to her, keeping an arm around her, watching for any sign she might slip into an unconscious slumber.

Corrie reached over and caught his wrist. "You saved my life tonight. If you hadn't been here—"

"I *was* here and that's what matters." He lifted her hand to his lips and placed a soft kiss in her palm. Then his jaw tightened and he glanced away. "I'm going to find out who did this. And when I do, the bastard is going to pay."

The sun was finally up when Gray put Coralee to bed. He left her maid sitting in a chair beside her, with instructions to awaken her every hour. If there was a problem, Anna was to find him immediately.

Even then, Gray worried. As he sat behind the desk in his private office and recalled what had happened, perspiration broke out on his forehead. What if he hadn't gone upstairs with her? What if he had been distracted and hadn't noticed her drug-induced state until it was too late?

Coralee might now be dead.

Gray's chest constricted at the thought of losing her. He told himself it was just that she was his wife and it was his responsibility to protect her. He reminded himself that he had failed Jillian and didn't want to fail again.

He was lying to himself and he knew it. Somehow, in the weeks Coralee had spent in his household, she had begun to reach him in a way no one ever had. She had told him she wanted to have his baby. *His.* As if no other man would do.

He didn't believe in love. He told himself he didn't love Coralee. And yet he would kill to protect her. He had known it the moment he had seen her in the bedroom, barely able to stay on her feet, vulnerable as he had rarely seen her.

As he headed downstairs, Gray thought of the way she had trusted him to take care of her, the way that trust had made him feel. Coralee was in danger—of that there was no doubt. But when he looked at her and felt the soft pulsing of his heart, he realized so was he.

"What on earth were you thinking? For God's sake, that was an idiotic, unbelievably stupid thing to do." Rebecca paced one way and then another, paused and looked out at the fountain at the rear of the garden.

"She needs to be stopped. Sooner or later, she's going to stumble onto someone who saw or heard something. She's going to put the bits and pieces together and figure out what happened to her sister that night."

Rebecca turned to face him. "You said we should do something that would warn her away, and I agreed, but I didn't agree to this."

The man sipped his brandy. "If it had worked, she would no longer be a threat."

"But it didn't work—and I am coming to believe you have lost sight of our goal."

They stood on the terrace. Just a polite conversation with a friend. They were safe, since Charles had gone into the village.

"It isn't Gray's wife we need to dispose of," Rebecca continued. "It is Tremaine himself. Once that distasteful bit of business is finished, Charles will be earl and I will be his countess. With the Tremaine fortune at my disposal, I shall be able to pay you the very sizable sum I promised."

The man swirled the brandy in his glass and took a drink. "Believe me, I haven't forgotten."

"What do you intend to do?"

He drained the snifter and set it down on a wrought-iron table near the balustrade. "I intend to do exactly as I agreed."

Rebecca eyed him with speculation. "You know, these attempts that were made on Gray's wife might actually work in our favor. If he were to die in an accident that appeared to be meant for her…"

For the first time, her companion smiled. "You are not only beautiful, but smart."

"Or better yet, both of them might perish."

He nodded. "Yes, that would be safer. I'll speak to Biggs, figure out how best to proceed. I believe you have hit on exactly the right solution."

Rebecca hoped so. For years she had run the earl's household, assumed the duties of countess with none of the respect or financial rewards. Now her place was being usurped by an interloper who had snared Tremaine through a web of deception, and sooner or later Rebecca would lose everything.

She was tired of being dependent on her brother-in-law's charity. Fortunately, the man at her side enjoyed living well and he was in need of money.

And he was tired of waiting, too.

Corrie slept the entire next day and all through the night. She didn't go down for meals. Instead, Anna brought a tray up to her room.

Corrie wasn't in the mood to face Gray and his dark, worried glances, or listen to Rebecca discussing London gossip. She wasn't interested in Jason's flirtatious banter or what Derek might have to say about his afternoon with Allison. Only Charles's kindness would be missed. He had always been the one who seemed to ease the discord between her and Rebecca, to try to lighten the tension between her and Gray.

So far, none of them had been told the circumstances of her illness. She had decided to leave it to Gray whether or not to tell them. She knew he was doing his best to discover the culprit, and prayed he would succeed. Odds were the man had already committed a double murder, and so far he had gotten away with it. Corrie was his biggest threat.

A chill went through her.

Once she was dead, he would be safe.

As the afternoon progressed, she wrote a letter to her parents, leaving out mention of the attempts on her life, wrote a similar letter to Krista, then retrieved her journal from the trunk beneath her bed.

She never quite knew where to start, but it didn't matter. It was the writing itself that was important. She loved the play of words, loved to fashion them into interesting sentences. She loved writing her column for *Heart to Heart,* but her real ambition was to pen a novel.

She would, she vowed. Now that she was married, she would never get to travel as she had planned, but there were other things she could write about.

One day, she thought with an inward sigh.

Dipping the quill pen into the inkwell, she began to scratch out the dark events swirling around her: the secret panel and the conversation she'd overheard about Rebecca's baby, the broken cinch and the overdose of opium.

Corrie shuddered as she tried to think who might be guilty of the attempts on her life.

And what the man might do next to see her dead.

Twenty-Four

Corrie received a summons from her husband to appear in the study at three o'clock that afternoon. When she walked through the door, she saw Gray standing behind the desk, while his half brother, tall, blond Derek Stiles, stood on the opposite side next to Charles, who stood next to Jason. Along with the fair-haired men was Dolph Petersen.

"Coralee," Gray said, rounding the desk to join her. His gaze turned worried as he noticed she was still a little pale. "Are you feeling any better?"

"Much better, thank you." She didn't say more. She was hoping he would tell her the nature of the meeting, but instead, he simply seated her and returned to his place behind the desk. The others took seats in the same row of chairs lined up across from him.

"I appreciate all of you coming. As you may know, my wife has been ill for the past few days. What you don't know is that someone tried to kill her."

"What?" That from Charles, who rose halfway out of his chair.

"Those are very strong charges," Jason said. "Are you certain, Gray?"

"Very certain. She was given an opium overdose sometime during our wedding celebration. When I was stationed in India, I saw the effects of the drug on several occasions. A man in my regiment died from a similar misuse of it."

"Perhaps it was some sort of accident," Charles suggested. "Somehow the drug got into her food by mistake."

"I might believe that…except this was the second attempt on her life."

Charles sat back in his chair, clearly shaken.

"Do you know who did it?" Derek asked, his jaw hard. He was the most hot-tempered of the Forsythe men.

"Not yet. I asked you here because I am hoping you might be able to help."

"Of course," Charles said. "Whatever you need us to do."

"Why would anyone want to kill Coralee?" Jason inquired, his tone still a little uncertain.

"From the time of her arrival at Castle Tremaine, my wife has been convinced that her sister was murdered. She has been trying to find the man who did it."

"I thought that matter was resolved," Charles said with some surprise. Like everyone in the household, he had assumed she had given up her quest after her true identity was revealed and she had been wed to Gray. "There was never any suggestion of foul play in Miss Whitmore's death," he added. "The authorities believe it was suicide."

"That is what I believed, as well," Gray said, "before the second attempt on Coralee's life. Now I think my wife is very likely correct. Dolph Petersen agrees."

Petersen turned in his chair, fixing his attention on the others. "I think this latest attempt speaks for itself. As long as the countess is alive, the villain is in danger of exposure. The penalty would surely be death."

Charles just sat there.

Jason and Derek seemed to ponder the notion.

The silence lengthened until Gray spoke again. "The reason I asked you here is because I need to know the truth. I would have sought each of you out in private, but I believe the matter is too important. I also believe Coralee has the right to hear what you have to say."

Gray's dark gaze swept the room. "Jason has already addressed the matter. That leaves you, Charles, and you, Derek. Both of you were in residence during the months before Laurel Whitmore left for East Dereham, carrying an illegitimate child. What I want to know is if either of you was the father of that child."

Coralee sat forward in her chair. Since Charles couldn't father a child, it had to be Derek. She wondered if he would be man enough to admit the truth.

But it was Charles who spoke up, a gruff note in his voice. "It didn't happen the way you are thinking." He swallowed so hard his Adam's apple bobbed up and down. "I loved Laurel and she loved me. I never meant to see her hurt in any way."

It wasn't possible. Rebecca had said Charles couldn't father a child. Yet with one look at his pale, haggard expression, Corrie knew it was the truth.

Anger forced her out of her chair. "You're a married man, Charles! How could you seduce an innocent young woman? How could you do it?"

"I never meant for it to happen." His voice was hoarse with emotion. "We came upon each other one morning while we were out riding. Laurel's horse had picked up a stone. I walked with her as she led the animal back to her house. We started chatting. She was so easy to talk to and we had so much in common." Tears welled in his eyes. "I rode to the same spot the following day, hoping I would see her again, and there she was. We talked and talked. It seemed as if there was so much to say. We started meeting whenever we could. I don't think either of us ever thought it would go further than friendship."

He shook his head and the tears in his eyes rolled down his cheeks. "And then one day it did."

He looked at Corrie, and there was so much pain in his face, her heart squeezed with pity.

"Your sister was the loveliest, kindest person I have ever known. I would have died in her place if I could have."

Corrie forced the pity away. "You abandoned her, Charles. You left her alone when she needed you most."

He stiffened. "I didn't know about the child. She never told me. She knew I was married. She didn't want my family to suffer for what we had done. She said she needed time to sort things out. I thought perhaps she was right." He swallowed. "I should have stopped her from leaving. If I had, she might still be alive." He started crying then, great sobs that shook his shoulders and were completely unlike him.

Corrie's heart went out to him. She had lost Laurel and grieved for her, as Charles must have done. She stood up and went to him, put her arms around his neck and simply held him. For a moment, Charles clung to her. "I'm sorry," he whispered, "so very very sorry."

Taking a deep breath, he straightened away from her, spoke to Gray and the rest of the men in the room. "I never meant to bring about such tragedy. Laurel and I…we never meant for anyone to get hurt."

Gray took control, allowing his brother to regain his composure, and Corrie sat back down.

"So you didn't know about the baby," he said.

Charles shook his head. "I only saw Laurel once after she came back from East Dereham."

"What happened?"

"It was just the way it was before. I still loved her and she still loved me. I told her I wanted to leave Rebecca and marry her."

Corrie's heart twisted. She should have known it was Charles her sister had loved. She should have realized Charles would have loved her in return.

"What did Laurel say?" Gray asked.

"She said I had to be sure it was what I wanted, be certain that it was the right thing to do. I told her making her my wife was exactly what I wanted. That I knew it was the right thing to do."

"Who besides Laurel knew what you intended?" Corrie asked.

"No one. It was only discussed between the two of us."

"So you never mentioned the possibility of divorce to your wife?"

Derek rose out of his chair. "Surely you aren't implying…"

"She didn't know," Charles said. "I was hoping to hear from Laurel, to meet with her again to finalize our plans. Instead, word came from the constable that she…" He swallowed and a fresh glaze of tears appeared in his eyes. "That she had drowned and there was a child." Charles squeezed his eyes closed and Corrie could feel his pain as if it were her own.

"No one is perfect," Gray said gently. "Your marriage to Rebecca was arranged when you were both children. You and Laurel fell in love. Sometimes things just happen."

Jason spoke up just then. "It's clear Charles had nothing to do with Laurel Whitmore's death. He was in love with her. He would certainly do her no harm. It seems to me that if, as your wife is convinced, Laurel was murdered, she must have been the victim of a footpad or a thief from the village."

"Jason is right," Derek agreed. "During your wedding celebration, the entire village was present. The person who drugged Coralee could have been any one of a hundred different people."

"Do you know what Laurel was doing at the river that night?" Corrie asked Charles.

He shook his head. "She wasn't that far from Selkirk Hall. Perhaps she just wanted to think things through, clear her head. Perhaps she had decided to tell me about the baby, I don't know. The entire chain of events could be purely happenstance, a footpad coming upon her, a struggle and then…" He swallowed hard and glanced away.

"Whatever happened," Gray said, a fierce gleam coming into his eyes, "my wife is not going to become another victim. I'm going to find out who the killer is and stop him from doing it again."

At Gray's insistence, Corrie spent the week close to the house. Her visit to Selkirk Hall was postponed. Even on a long walk in the garden, Gray accompanied her. In the meantime, Dolph Petersen was staying at the Green Dragon Tavern, trying to dig up information in the village.

Corrie wondered if Greta would offer the hard-faced man comfort, and if so, whether he would accept her invitation. She wondered what new information he might be able to charm out of the woman if he did.

Rebecca had been told of the attempts on Corrie's life, but she was not completely convinced.

"It could just be some sort of coincidence, you know. Your cinch broke. Later you ate something that didn't agree with you and had some sort of reaction."

Corrie didn't argue. Rebecca's opinion didn't really matter. She'd been informed out of necessity, but she had not been made aware of Charles's involvement with Laurel.

Corrie had pondered whether or not to tell Gray about Rebecca's affair and the child she carried, but Corrie had no idea who Rebecca's lover might be, and it seemed to have no bearing on the matter at hand. Even if she told him, she wasn't completely sure Gray would believe her. With so much turmoil in the household, she finally decided keeping silent, at least for the present, would be best.

She was considering her decision when Charles approached her on the terrace after supper.

"I asked Gray if I might have a moment with you in private," he said, stepping out of the shadows into the light of the torches.

"What is it, Charles?"

"I wanted to speak to you about your sister. I wanted you to know how much I loved her, and how truly sorry I am for everything that's happened."

Corrie looked up at him. She could still see the lines of grief in his face. It must have taken immense control to hide it for so long. "I'm glad it was you," she said. "I am glad you were the man my sister fell in love with."

"Do you mean that?"

"You're a good man, Charles, no matter the circumstances of your relationship with Laurel."

His eyes misted. "She meant everything to me. Everything."

Corrie nodded. "Yes, I can see that."

"When you came here, I thought you were merely distraught, grief stricken, as I was, over her loss. Now…to discover Laurel truly might have been murdered…it is nearly unbearable."

"We'll find him. All of us working together…we'll find him."

Charles stared down at his feet, as if there was something of importance he wished to say, and was trying to find the courage to do so. "I never asked before. I suppose I couldn't bear to know. Was the child a boy or a girl?"

She felt a tug at her heart. "You had a son, Charles. Laurel named him Joshua Michael."

Charles's blue eyes filled with pain. "That was my best friend's name. He died of an influenza while we were at boarding school. Laurel knew how close we were, how often I thought of him." There was overwhelming sadness in Charles's face. "You're very brave. If I had been a more courageous man—"

"You didn't kill her, Charles. It wasn't your fault."

He didn't say more, just nodded as if trying to convince himself, then turned and walked away. He left her on the terrace staring after him, feeling his pain and grief.

Gray joined her a few moments later. "My brother is a good man."

"Yes, he is."

"Then you no longer believe he had any part in your sister's death?"

"No. I just wish the information he gave us could have been more useful."

A muscle tightened in Gray's cheek. "So do I."

It was several days later when Dolph Petersen returned to the house. Unfortunately, Corrie wasn't invited to join him and Gray in their closed-door meeting in Gray's private office.

Still, she couldn't resist a bit of eavesdropping. As soon as the men were inside, she hurried over to the door and pressed her ear against it. She was surprised to hear them discussing the Countess of Devane and her upcoming costume ball.

"I think the two of you should go," Dolph was saying.

"Are you insane? You saw what happened at the last affair Coralee attended."

"This time we'll have men both inside and outside the house. Your wife will be completely protected."

"No. It's out of the question."

"If you don't find this man, Gray, sooner or later he is going to succeed. You need to catch him before he does, and unless you have a better idea, we are going to have to draw him out."

"With my wife as bait. The answer is no."

Corrie opened the door and walked into the office. "I am sorry to intrude, my lord, but Mr. Petersen is right. I can't live like a prisoner forever. Presently, I can't go riding, can't visit my family. I can't even walk out to the garden. I won't go on this way. I simply will not."

"Since you were eavesdropping, you heard what I said. It's just too dangerous."

"So is not finding him."

Gray blew out a breath. For several long moments, he said nothing. Then he turned a hard look on Dolph. "Fine, we'll do it your way. But if anything goes wrong—"

"Nothing is going to go wrong. We won't let it. If our theory is correct, the culprit is someone from the village. That means he will not be among the guests, but someone hired by the countess's staff to help with preparations for the ball."

"Which means it could be a footman or a groom or a housemaid. Bloody hell, it could be the cook!"

"As I said, we'll be careful. And you will be with your wife the entire duration of the ball."

Gray cast a firm look Corrie's way. "You may be certain of that."

Still, it was obvious he was worried. She knew he felt guilty for the death of his first wife. He was determined it wouldn't happen again. Certainly it wasn't because he held any special feelings for Corrie herself. Since Charles had confessed his deep love for Laurel, Gray had been more remote than ever. Even his desire seemed to have waned.

On the occasions they did make love, his passion was carefully controlled. He used his skills to pleasure her and himself, but his emotions remained locked away.

Only the concern she saw in his eyes gave her the faintest degree of hope.

Twenty-Five

The plans were set, arrangements made. Dolph brought men in from London, a small army of protectors. Though the footmen and serving staff would be wearing Lady Devane's pale blue livery, Petersen's men, dressed in simple peasant garments, were meant to go unnoticed among the stable hands and grooms outside, the below-stairs servants working behind the scenes in the house.

So many extra people had been hired for the occasion the men should be able to mingle without being noticed. It gave Corrie some comfort, but still she was worried.

So was Gray, she knew, though she hadn't seen him since earlier in the day. He was checking things over, making last minute changes, doing everything in his power to insure she would be safe. Charles, Jason and Derek all knew the plan and had agreed to watch for anything that might look suspicious.

By seven o'clock that evening, their whole party was costumed and ready to depart in the carriages that would take them to Parkside. All but Corrie, who was a little late getting dressed.

"Are you certain, my lady?" Anna was looking at her worriedly. "You said you planned to dress as Julia Augusta, the empress of Rome."

She had meant to. She had worn the slim white robes and gold sandals at a ball in London, and had found the costume in one of her trunks. "I changed my mind."

"But surely the wife of an earl—"

"I am going as a country maid. What is wrong with that?"

Anna bit her lip. "Why…nothing, my lady."

But gowned in worn apricot muslin and a simple straw bonnet, she didn't really look like anyone but Letty Moss—which was exactly her intent. She had no idea where the notion had come from, but once it stole into her head, she couldn't make it go away.

She had no idea what Gray would be wearing, no idea what his reaction would be when he saw her. Perhaps that was the reason she was so determined to go through with it.

She left Anna in the bedroom and headed down the hall to the stairs, her simple muslin skirts and ruffled petticoats whispering against her legs. When she reached the top of the steps, she paused.

Standing at the bottom of the staircase was the handsomest man she had ever seen, and her heart began to throb. He was tall and broad-shouldered, dressed in tight black riding breeches tucked into knee-high black boots, and a full-sleeved, white lawn shirt. His hair was in a queue. A mask of black silk hid the top half of his face, covering all but his intense dark eyes.

He was costumed as a highwayman, the man she had imagined him to be the day she had first seen him.

The man she had fallen in love with.

Her knees felt weak when he looked up to find her

standing at the top of the stairs. She wondered if he would be angry at the clothes she had chosen, but instead, the edge of his mouth faintly curved. He waited in silence as she made her way toward him, then took her hand as she stepped down from the bottom stair.

"I believe we have met somewhere before," he said, making her a sweeping bow.

"Mrs. Moss," she said. "Letty Moss, my lord."

Through the holes in his mask, his dark eyes glinted, seemed to drink her in. Did she really look so different? Or was it just the memory of the woman she had been that softened his gaze when he looked at her?

"I believe our party is waiting," he said. "Shall we, Mrs. Moss?" Extending his arm, he led her out to the row of carriages lined up in front of the house. The others were already there, and at their appearance, began to climb aboard the coaches. Petersen's men rode front and back, and armed men posed as footmen at the rear of each carriage.

Inside the coaches, the entire party was costumed, Rebecca garbed as Marie Antoinette in a blue satin gown encrusted with brilliants and decorated with ropes of gold. Her skirt was wide, draped over a wire-mesh farthingale, the fashion of that day, and she wore a tall silver wig also laced with gold.

Charles was garbed as the French king, Louis. Jason wore a red hunting jacket and cap and looked as if he intended to ride to the hounds, and Derek was a pirate with a gold earring in his ear, a patch over one eye and a sword belted at his waist.

All of them were dressed for the ball and ready for the evening ahead, and yet there was an unmistakable tension among the men. They were acting as Corrie's guardians.

She didn't believe they would shirk their duties tonight.

It took the better part of an hour for the party to reach the next village and find its way to Parkside, Lady Devane's magnificent Georgian estate. As their carriages pulled up in front, Corrie noticed the glow of lamplight in every room of the house. A half-dozen liveried footmen rushed to assist the guests up the red velvet carpet into the foyer of the mansion.

"I want you to stay close to me," Gray said. "No wandering off on your own."

She nodded absently, caught up in the pomp and extravagance of the event. She was carrying a feathered mask on the end of a stick. She held it over her face and peered through it at her surroundings.

Gray caught her chin, forcing her to look at him. "Promise me."

"I promise."

"If you see anything, notice anything, I want you to let me know."

"I'm not a fool, Gray."

His mouth edged up. "No. You've never been a fool." He took her hand and rested it on his arm, and they made their way toward the receiving line.

Gowned as the goddess Diana, Lady Devane stood in the foyer. Her gaze sharpened on Gray. "Darling—it's good to see you. I'm so happy you and—" She broke off in surprise at the sight of Corrie's simple clothes. "I'm so happy you and your *wife* could attend."

Gray just smiled. "I'm sure we're going to enjoy the evening." He urged Corrie inside, leaving the countess staring after them, stanching whatever vitriolic words she might have said.

The decorations were lavish, the mansion made to look like an ancient Greek city, with white-painted columns scattered about and ivy draping the walls. It was clear the countess had spared no expense. A ten-piece orchestra, the musicians garbed in white togas, began to play, and Gray led Corrie toward the sound as the strains of a waltz drifted to them.

"Would you like to dance?"

She looked up at him in surprise. She had never danced with her husband. It seemed odd, and yet, knowing Gray, she was surprised he would ask.

She smiled at him with delight. "I would love to dance with you, my lord."

His eyes ran over her face, came to rest on her lips, and a soft warmth spread through her. He settled a hand at her waist, led her onto the dance floor, and she followed him in the steps of the waltz.

He danced with the same grace she had noticed when he rode his horse, and though he was a great deal taller, they moved easily together, their rhythm well matched. Beneath her hand, she could feel the hard muscles in his shoulder and when she caught the faint scent of sandalwood, desire flared. Gray must have sensed it, for when she looked up at him, heat was there in his eyes.

She caught that same look off and on through the evening. Though he kept a close watch over her, the night was filled with subtle touches and hot, burning glances. A little after midnight, the rest of their party joined them as they went in to the long gallery to enjoy the lavish supper set out for the guests.

"Seen anything?" Gray asked Jason.

"Not a thing."

"Derek?"

He shook his head, moving the shiny gold hoop in his ear. "I almost wish I had."

Gray's jaw flexed. "I'd like to put my hands around the bastard's neck and squeeze the life out of him."

Corrie shivered and Gray's expression softened. "Sorry, love. I didn't mean to sound so bloodthirsty."

But she was sure he meant every word.

They dined on pheasant and lobster, served buffet style, which meant the food would be safe for her to eat. They enjoyed champagne from a communal fountain, though none of them drank very much.

As the evening progressed, Corrie began to relax. She didn't think the man they searched for was here. Perhaps he couldn't find a way in, or simply wasn't ready to try again so soon. Some of Gray's tension eased as he came to the same conclusion, and each of his glances seemed to burn hotter than the last. In his highwayman's costume, he was the most handsome man in the room, and Corrie felt the pull of attraction, the surge of love for him that she had felt that night in the storm.

They were standing near the staircase, taking a momentary break from the dancing, when she leaned toward him. "I want you to make love to me."

Surprise appeared on his face. "You don't mean here? Now?"

She cast him a wicked glance. "There are so many people. Surely we can disappear somewhere for a little while without being missed."

His eyes turned the color of jet and a fire seemed to burn inside them. He hadn't looked at her quite that way since the night of the storm.

Grasping her hand, darting a glance both ways, he led her up the sweeping stairs. A few guests were paired off together in the hallway, some she recognized, enjoying trysts of their own. Gray led her past them to the end of the corridor, to another hallway that was completely empty. He opened a door, checked to be sure the room was unoccupied, then hauled her inside and turned the lock.

Corrie reached up and pulled the ties of his black silk mask. "Kiss me."

Gray's gaze turned fierce. He took the feathered mask from her hand and dragged her mouth up to his for a deep, burning kiss.

"I want you," he said, kissing her until she was nearly too weak to stand.

She tugged at the black velvet ribbon tying back his hair, freeing the long black strands. "I want you, too. I want you the way you were that night in the storm."

He reached out and cupped her cheek. "How was I that night?"

Corrie's eyes filled with unexpected tears. "You were fierce and you were tender. You were the man of my dreams."

Gray's chest tightened. For long moments, he just stood there, staring down at the woman he desired above all others. "Sweet God, Coralee."

His hands shook as he reached for her, pulled her into his arms. She looked so beautiful tonight, so artless and sincere. And he wanted her so damn badly. Cradling her face in his hands, he kissed her, softly at first, then more deeply. A force burned inside him and the kisses turned wilder, hotter, became a fierce plundering that seemed to have no end.

For weeks he had held himself back, forced himself to keep his distance even when they were in bed. He knew their lovemaking had been different than before; he had purposely made it so by keeping himself under tight control. But he hadn't understood that his wife felt that difference, too. That she had been as dissatisfied as he.

Now her softly spoken words and the yearning in her eyes reached him as nothing else could have. Inside his chest, his heart squeezed and his breathing turned harsh. He felt shaken, completely off balance, as if he could no longer ignore his fate.

As if he no longer wanted to.

Grasping her shoulders, he ravished her mouth, drove his tongue inside to claim the sweetness within, kissed her the way he hadn't allowed himself to do since before their return that morning after the storm. He gazed down at her, thought how much he wanted her, how much he had come to need her.

Taking her lips in another burning kiss, he drank in the taste of her, inhaled her soft rose scent until his body ached and demanded release.

Backing her against the wall, he lifted her skirts, found the slit in her drawers and began to stroke her. She was wet and ready, her need as fierce as his own.

"We haven't much time," he said against her mouth, nibbling the corners before he kissed her again.

"We don't need much time," she said breathlessly, reaching out to unbutton the front of his breeches. Gray helped her free his erection, lifted her against the wall and wrapped her legs around his waist. He plunged himself deep inside her, felt her hands in his hair and heard her soft moan of pleasure.

Again and again, he drove into her, completely out of control. He no longer cared. This was what he wanted, what he needed from the woman in his arms, this unleashed passion that was so different from the practiced lovemaking they had shared since their wedding. A hot, wild consummation he hadn't known since that night in the storm.

"I need you," he said, driving into her again. "I've never wanted a woman so badly."

"Gray…" She kissed him as if she couldn't get enough, slid her small tongue into his mouth.

A deep groan rose from inside him. He tried to hold on, told himself it was too soon, but when he felt her passage tighten around him, felt the first sweet ripples of contraction, he couldn't hold back any longer. A powerful climax hit him, shook his body and tightened his muscles until he clenched his teeth to hold back a primal scream.

"Letty…" he groaned, driving into her one last time, holding her tightly against him. "My sweetest love…"

Gray felt her stiffen. She drew away from him, dragged in a shaky breath and struggled to get free.

It was then he realized she was trembling, fighting not to cry. Easing her legs from around his waist, he set her back on her feet.

"What is it, sweeting? Did I hurt you?"

She looked up at him and tears rolled down her cheeks. "You hurt me, Gray. You broke my heart." And then she turned, twisted the key in the lock and ran out of the room, slamming the door behind her.

For an instant, Gray just stood there, completely stunned. What in God's name had he done?

You called her Letty, you fool.

The name had just slipped out; he had no idea why. Surely it wasn't so important.

Whatever had occurred, his wife was under his protection and he had to find her.

Hurriedly rebuttoning his breeches, he ran out of the room and down the hall. Coralee was nowhere to be seen. At the bottom of the stairs, he spotted Charles next to Jason and ran toward them.

"Have you seen Coralee? She was with me and now I can't find her."

"We'll help you look for her," Jason said. "I'll go upstairs. You two search down here."

"We've got to find her!" Gray exclaimed. "There's no telling what might happen if we don't."

His brother must have read the panic in his face. Charles caught his arm to steady him. "We'll find her. We'll get Derek to help us."

But they had only begun to search when Coralee walked up to Gray as if she had returned from an afternoon stroll. She looked shaken and pale, and his heart squeezed inside him. Worry turned to anger.

"For God's sake, Coralee, where the hell have you been? You scared me to death."

She drew a shaky breath, her face even paler. Her expression tore at his heart. "I'm afraid I'm not feeling very well, my lord. I would like to go home."

Concern shot through him. "Are you ill? Has something happened?"

"It's nothing like that. I just…I want to go home."

"All right. Yes, that's a good idea." He took her with him to retrieve her cloak, made his farewells to his brothers, Rebecca and Jason, and the two of them left the house. The guards fell into their places around the carriage as the couple climbed inside.

All the way back to Castle Tremaine, Gray watched Coralee, but she made no mention of what had happened in the room upstairs.

Perhaps he had injured her in his furious, unrestrained lovemaking.

"Tell me what I did," he said as the carriage rumbled through the darkness. "If it was the way we made love—"

She shook her head. "You were wonderful. You were exactly the man I remembered." But when she gazed up at him, fresh tears gathered in her eyes.

"Tell me."

"You were just as I remembered. But I am not Letty and I never will be." And she said no more, not even when they retired upstairs to his suite, not until she told him she wanted to sleep in her own bed that night.

Gray let her. Inside his chest, an ache had formed around his heart. She had dressed as Letty and he had called her that. He didn't understand why the name had hurt her so badly. And he had no idea how to repair the damage he had done.

Whatever it took, he would fix it, he told himself. He would apologize and make things right.

But in the morning, when he asked her maid if she was feeling better, he discovered Coralee was gone.

Twenty-Six

London teemed with activity as the sleek black carriage rolled through the crowded streets. Corrie had forgotten how noisy the city was, how sooty the air. She had traveled all day, hoping to reach London before nightfall, but darkness had settled in an hour ago.

She sighed as she leaned back against the velvet seat. When she had left the castle early that morning, all she could think of was getting away from Gray and the hurt she had suffered. On the long journey, she'd had time to ponder what she should do once she got back to the city.

Gray had a town house in London. As the Countess of Tremaine, she would certainly have the right to use it, but Gray might come after her. He was, after all, a very protective man. Whatever his feelings for her, she was his wife and he would feel responsible.

Corrie wasn't ready to face him.

By leaving the country, she would likely be in far less danger. But there was always a chance she might be followed, and the only place she would truly feel safe was with Krista and Leif. Corrie hated to ask them for help, but she needed her best friend's advice, and she knew with Leif and Thor close by, she wouldn't have to be afraid.

It was after supper when the coach pulled up in front of the Draugr's two-story brick town house. Corrie climbed the steep front steps and knocked.

The butler opened the door. "May I help you, madam?"

She managed to smile. "You may remember me… Coralee Whitmore? I am now the Countess of Tremaine."

"Why, of course, my lady. Please do come in." He was a middle-aged man whose hair was turning gray. Simmons was his name, she recalled.

"If you will please follow me into the drawing room, I will tell Mr. and Mrs. Draugr that you are arrived."

"Thank you." She followed the butler into a salon done in red and gold, with fringed lamps on small ornate tables, shelves filled with an astonishing amount of bric-a-brac, and bins that held a number of London weekly magazines.

It was decorated in the latest Victorian fashion, probably furnished by someone other than Krista, who was always too busy to worry about such things.

As Corrie stood in her best friend's home, she realized that she was nervous. For an instant, she wished she hadn't come.

Then Krista came striding into the room on those long legs of hers and pulled her into a warm, comforting hug. Corrie clung to her, grateful for their enduring friendship, and fought not to cry. Krista must have felt her tremble, for she eased a little away.

"Coralee, what on earth has happened?"

Across the room, Leif stood in the doorway. Corrie caught a quick glimpse of Thor's tall dark figure just before Leif closed the drawing room doors, giving them the privacy he must have sensed they needed.

"Is it the earl?" Krista asked, leading her over to the sofa, where both of them took a seat. "He hasn't hurt you, has he? If he has—"

"He hasn't hurt me. Not in the way you mean."

Krista reached out and caught her hand. "Tell me, dearest. What has happened that has made you leave your husband?"

For the next half hour, Coralee told her friend about Gray and how deeply she had fallen in love with him. How, after they were married, she had tried to convince herself he was no longer the man she had believed him to be and that she no longer felt as she had before. How she had finally admitted the truth.

"I love him so much," she said, accepting the handkerchief Krista handed her to wipe the tears from her cheeks. "He's a hard man, but he can be gentle. Gray is intelligent and loyal. He is lonely and in so much need of love. He touches me and I…" She glanced away, blushing at the thought of what Gray could do with a single kiss or the touch of his talented hands.

She took a shaky breath. "The problem is he is not in love with me. He is in love with a woman who doesn't exist. He is in love with Letty Moss."

"Oh, Coralee…"

"It is true, Krista." Corrie next told her friend about how it had been before they were married. Krista listened patiently, though it was clear she wasn't completely convinced.

Not even when Corrie told her about the night they had gone to the costume ball. "For the first time since our wedding, he let down his guard and made love to me as if he truly cared. Then he called me…Letty, his *sweetest love*."

Krista squeezed her hand. "That is not so hard to understand. You said you were dressed as Letty. Perhaps, for a moment, he was confused."

"I'm sure he was. I'm also sure he was wishing Letty Moss was truly there instead of me."

They talked for several hours, Leif kind enough to leave them alone. Then a brisk knock sounded and Krista's huge blond husband slid open the drawing room doors.

"Ladies, I am sorry to interrupt. But Coralee, your husband is here, and if I do not let him in to see you, he and Thor will soon be brawling in the entry."

Corrie came up off the sofa. She had thought Gray would follow her. He would feel obliged to protect her. But she didn't think he would arrive in the middle of the night!

The door slid open farther and Gray strode into the drawing room. He was dressed in his riding breeches and high black boots, both of which were mud-spattered and wrinkled. His black hair was tied back, but strands fell loose around his shoulders as if the wind had torn them free. It was clear he had ridden hard to make up for the head start she'd had before he discovered her gone.

She ignored a little thrill that he had come so quickly, told herself he was merely doing what he felt was his duty.

Gray stood in front of her, his dark eyes blazing. "What the bloody hell are you doing in London?"

So much for his concern.

"I needed some time to think. This is the only place I could imagine where I would be able to do it."

"What about the danger, Coralee? Did you give any thought to what might happen to you when you took off on your own?" Before she could answer, Gray turned to Leif and Thor, who stood behind them, long legs splayed as if they were prepared to do battle. "Has she told you her life is in danger? Did my hotheaded little wife happen to mention that twice she has nearly been killed?"

Leif frowned, his golden eyebrows drawing together. "You should have told us, Coralee."

Thor pinned her with a disapproving glare. "If this is so, you should not have gone off by yourself. But you need have no fear. We will make sure you are safe."

Leif's blue eyes fixed on Gray. "Why does someone wish to kill Coralee?"

"Because of her damnable determination to find the man who murdered her sister."

Krista's head came up in shock. "I thought you were through with all of that, Coralee!"

"Tell them, Gray. Tell them I was right—that Laurel was murdered."

"I imagine it's true, though we've yet to find proof. The fact that someone wants Coralee dead gives credence to the theory. Dolph Petersen has continued his investigation and he believes it is so." Gray returned his angry gaze to her. "And the last thing you need to do is run off by yourself without the least protection!"

He stalked toward her. Corrie backed up until her shoulders brushed the red flocked wallpaper.

"Enough of this foolishness. You're coming home with me. I am not about to leave you here."

"I'm not going with you, Gray. Krista says I am welcome to stay, and that is what I'm going to do."

"I'm not giving you a choice!" Reaching out, he caught her arm and started hauling her across the room toward the door.

Thor stepped in his way. "Your wife does not wish to leave."

"I told you, her life is in danger. I'm her husband. It's my duty to keep her safe."

"Coralee will be safe here, with my brother and me."

Corrie felt a swell of affection for the handsome, dark-haired Norseman. In the months after Krista's wedding, Corrie and Thor had become friends of a sort, though much of the time he had been at Heartland with Professor Hart, studying the English language and customs.

Corrie had come to like him very much, and he seemed to like her. On top of that, she was Krista's friend and therefore part of his extended family. Like Leif, Thor was very protective of his family and friends.

"I'm not leaving without her," Gray said, ready to go head-to-head with Thor, who was at least four inches taller and a good deal heavier than he.

Corrie stepped between them. "I need some time, Gray."

"You're my wife, Coralee."

"I'm your wife, but you don't love me. I need some time to come to terms with that."

His mouth opened, but no words came out. She could read the turbulence in his expression, the responsibility he felt to keep her safe. But he wasn't a liar, which left him with nothing to say.

"These men are warriors," Corrie continued, tamping down her disappointment. "Surely you can see I'll be safe as long as I am with them."

"You belong with me."

"I'm not ready to leave."

He turned away, paced across the drawing room and back. "I don't like this—not one bit."

"I'm staying, Gray."

He turned, fixed a hard look on Thor. "If I leave her in your care, do you swear to keep her safe?"

"I give you my word as a warrior."

Gray would accept that. "And do you also give me your

word that you will treat her with the respect she deserves as my wife, and make no advances toward her?"

The edge of Thor's mouth curved. "She is beautiful, but she is yours."

Gray turned to Coralee. "I'll be here tomorrow. There are things that need to be said."

She wondered what he could possibly have to say and tried not to be hopeful. "All right."

Gray started for the door, stopped and strode back. He hauled her into his arms and very thoroughly kissed her. It was a fierce, possessive kiss, and by the time he let her go, her knees were weak.

"I'll be back," he said gruffly, and then he was gone.

Corrie just stood there, blushing furiously at his outrageous behavior.

Krista walked up beside her. "I'm sorry, Coralee, but I don't believe a man who kisses a woman that way doesn't love her."

A lump rose in her throat. "Gray doesn't know how to love."

Krista looked up at her handsome blond giant of a husband, a man who had come to London unable even to speak the language. He'd known nothing of English customs and had no idea how he was going to earn a living. Today, he was married to the granddaughter of an earl, was the father of an eight-month-old son and the owner of a successful shipping firm.

Krista just smiled. "It's amazing what a man can learn."

Gray lay awake well past midnight, trying unsuccessfully to read himself to sleep.

He was surprised when a light knock sounded and the door swung open. Samir moved so quietly across the bedroom, he seemed to appear by magic. "I traveled quickly. I thought you might have need of me."

The man was amazingly intuitive. "Thank you for coming, Samir. I had only planned to stay one night and return with my wife on the morrow. It doesn't appear that is going to happen."

"She refuses to come back with you?"

He nodded. "She's a woman. She is behaving exactly like one."

"And yet you do not force her, as you could."

Gray sighed into the quiet. "She says she needs time. Considering all she's been through, I didn't think it was too much to ask."

"She loves you."

He glanced away. He didn't even know what love was. His mother had loved him, but that had been so long ago, he didn't really remember. And yet when Samir said the words, Gray's heart swelled with hope that it was true.

"You must show her you have feelings for her, as well."

Gray shook his head. "I wouldn't begin to know how."

"You could tell her the way you feel."

"I won't lie to her. It wouldn't be fair."

"That is so, but also do not lie to yourself."

Gray said nothing. Whatever he felt for Coralee was unlike anything he had felt for a woman before. Was it love? He scoffed. He wasn't the kind of man who loved.

"If you cannot find the words to tell her, you must show her. Your woman has never been…what do you English call seducing a woman with gifts and small pleasures?"

He smiled. "Courting."

"This you must do."

"I'm worried about keeping her alive, Samir. I hardly have time to pay her court."

The little Hindu shrugged his thin shoulders. "That is for you to decide."

But by morning, Gray had come to the conclusion that Samir, as usual, was right. First he wrote to Charles, Jason and Derek to tell them he would be staying in London for at least a week. He knew they would be worried, would be on their way to join him if they didn't get word. Instead, he asked them to stay in the country and continue working with Dolph to find the man who had threatened Coralee's life.

His next piece of business was a stop at the florist shop. There he ordered half a dozen bouquets of yellow roses and had them sent to the Draugr's town house, then bought a bouquet of red roses to take with him.

The soft scent reminded him of Coralee, and he held them to his nose as he finished his shopping and made his way toward the residence where she was staying. He wasn't sure what he would say, how he was going to get his wife back, but he knew he wanted her home. She belonged in his house, in his bed.

And Gray was a man who went after what he wanted.

Corrie made her way downstairs to join Krista in the breakfast room and found the entry filled with yellow roses. More sat in vases in the drawing room, and when she went in to breakfast, a vase of red roses graced the middle of the table.

Leif's deep voice reached her from his place at the head of the table. "It is clear your husband cares for you more than you believe."

Her heart stumbled. Was it possible?

"Gray sent…sent all of these?" She indicated the other bouquets spread throughout the house.

"I looked at one of the cards," Krista said, smiling. "I was dying of curiosity."

"But he isn't the type of man who would send a woman flowers."

"Apparently, he is," her friend said smugly. "And as I recall, roses are your favorite."

"He couldn't possibly know that."

Thor scoffed. "You smell like roses. Any man would know." With his thick black hair neatly trimmed, if a little long over his collar; with his square jaw and incredible blue eyes, he was one of the handsomest men Corrie had ever seen.

But it was Gray who drew her, Gray she loved.

As they breakfasted on eggs and sausage, Corrie told them about the attempts that had been made on her life, and their efforts to catch the man who might still want her dead.

"We tried to draw him out at the Countess of Devane's costume ball. It didn't work, but the party was quite spectacular." She took a sip of her tea. "I, um, thought I might write an article about it for the next edition of the gazette."

Krista uttered a small yelp of glee. She came out of her chair, hurried over and hugged her. "Oh, Coralee, that would be wonderful. Lindsey is doing a marvelous job, but she's working extremely hard. The article would give her a bit of a break."

Thor made a sound in his throat. "The woman needs more than a break. She needs a man who will take her in hand."

Krista rolled her eyes. "They fight like children. I don't know why they can't get along."

"She doesn't know her place," he grumbled.

"And you are still living in the sixteenth century, Thor Draugr."

He didn't bother to argue. He had arrived with his brother from an island far to the north of Scotland, a place not found on any seaman's map. They had lived there in the same manner their Viking ancestors had been doing for more than three hundred years.

It was only by chance that Corrie and Krista had come upon Leif, who had survived a shipwreck and been washed up on English shores, and the pair had helped him escape the men who had taken him prisoner. Krista's father, Sir Paxton Hart, had helped him make a new life here in London, and during that time she and Leif had fallen in love.

Thor had eventually joined his brother in England, and Sir Paxton was schooling him and helping him become a gentleman—no easy job for Thor. For the moment, he was working at *Heart to Heart,* but he was also working with his brother in the shipping trade.

The butler appeared in the doorway, his attention focused on Corrie. "I am sorry to bother you, Lady Tremaine, but your husband—"

"Needs a word with you," said Gray as he walked into the breakfast room. "I'm sorry to intrude," he said to the others, not looking sorry at all, "but I need to speak to my wife." Seeing that her plate was nearly empty, he urged her up out of her chair. "If you will all excuse us…"

It was more a command than a request. He was, after all, the Earl of Tremaine and used to getting his way.

"Of course," Krista said diplomatically, while Thor looked daggers at Gray.

Corrie didn't protest. She wanted to hear what he had to say. "Excuse us," she repeated, and let him lead her toward the door of the breakfast room.

"He reminds me of someone I know," Krista whispered to Leif as the two walked out into the hallway.

Her husband just grunted.

As Corrie entered the drawing room, Gray tossed a look back over his shoulder. "The Draugr brothers are quite unusual. I imagine they have an interesting story. Perhaps in time you will tell me."

"Perhaps." But at the moment, there were other things she wished to discuss. She led him over to the sofa and both of them sat down. "Thank you for the flowers. I was surprised you would send them."

He glanced away. "I've watched you in the garden. I thought you would like them."

"Roses are my favorite."

His mouth edged up. "I guessed."

So he *had* noticed her perfume. "So what did you want to talk to me about?"

Gray met her gaze squarely. "Letty Moss."

Corrie tried not to wince. Gray had always been direct. "What...what about her?"

"Why did my saying her name upset you so much?"

She glanced down, plucked at a fold in her skirt. "Because it's always been Letty you wanted. Always her and not me. I had hoped that would change, but obviously it hasn't."

Gray caught her hand. His fingers felt warm around hers and his gaze was intense on her face. "Letty Moss was a woman I wanted to bed. I would never have married her."

"You wouldn't?"

"No."

"Because of her social status? I didn't think you were the sort of man who would be concerned."

"It wasn't *who* she was. It was who she wasn't. The Letty you portrayed would have satisfied me in bed, but nothing more. I need a woman who's intelligent and interesting, one who is loyal and steadfast, a woman I can count on. I need a woman who isn't afraid to stand up to me. I know I am not an easy man."

She smiled. "No, you are stubborn and difficult. You're possessive and far too domineering."

He grinned. "But I am extremely skillful in bed."

Corrie blushed. "Yes, you are, you rogue, though I like you better when you let down your guard and allow your feelings to show."

"I like you better that way, too."

"You could tell?"

He brought her hand to his lips and pressed a kiss into her palm. She could feel the heat all the way to her toes.

"Come home with me, Coralee. We'll start over, get to know each other as we should have done before."

Hope soared inside her. And yet she didn't quite trust him. "Give me a little more time."

"Dammit, Coralee."

"Please, Gray."

"I want you in my bed. Just sitting here, I find it's all I can do to keep my hands off you." As if it were true, one of his hands unconsciously fisted.

"I want to go with you, Gray—you'll never know how much. But I'm just not ready yet."

He studied her face. "You're that determined?"

"I need this, Gray."

He nodded. "All right, I'll give you the time you need on one condition."

"What is that?"

He smiled, making him look so handsome her breath caught. "You agree to go for a carriage ride with me this afternoon."

Pleasure moved through her, along with a hint of worry. "Do you think it's safe?"

"I won't come alone. I'll have at least two men with me."

She nodded. "Then I would love to go for a carriage ride with you."

Gray leaned over and kissed her. What started as a gentle brush of lips turned into a deep, openmouthed, soul-bending kiss that left both of them breathless and wanting.

"I'll see you at four," he said gruffly, rising to take his leave.

As she watched him walk out the door, Corrie thought how much her husband had surprised her. He was giving her the time she wanted. She hadn't believed her wishes were important to him.

I want you back in my bed, he had said. But she needed to be certain she was the woman he truly wanted, and not a phantom who had never existed.

As she recalled the events of the past two days, it occurred to her that Gray might not love her, but it appeared he cared more than she had believed.

Corrie clung to that hope as she headed upstairs to begin her article on the costume ball at Lady Devane's.

Twenty-Seven

As he did each afternoon, Gray took Corrie for a carriage ride round the city. He was attentive as she had rarely seen him, taking her shopping, buying her gifts and sweets. He refused to buy her perfume except for the rose fragrance she usually wore, and somehow she found that charming. It felt wonderful to be with him, to enjoy the attention he lavished upon her.

It worried her only a little that she was falling even more in love with him. He was her husband. If she wanted her marriage to work, loving him was a risk she would have to take.

Gray came in the afternoons, but in the mornings before he arrived, while Leif went to work at his company, Valhalla Shipping, Thor would accompany her and Krista to *Heart to Heart*. Corrie finished the article on the countess's costume ball, refraining with only a bit of difficulty from hinting at the names of the people involved in the trysts she had stumbled upon upstairs. Then she wrote a piece on the joys of living in the country—something she never would have imagined until she journeyed to Castle Tremaine.

Though she enjoyed working again, it occurred to her

that she had changed in the months she'd been gone. She was no longer as fascinated with society and the social whirl as she had once been, and because of Gray, she now knew the damage unfounded gossip could cause.

As always, it was fun working with Krista, and interesting to watch Thor and Lindsey Graham, the school chum who had taken over Corrie's job. Lindsey and Thor studiously avoided each other, as if neither could stand to be in the same room.

Lindsey, slender, with honey-brown hair and tawny eyes, was energetic and dynamic, a woman who clearly had goals and ambitions. Thor believed a woman's place was in the home—skinning furs, Corrie imagined, weaving or winnowing wheat.

And yet there was a certain sizzle in the air between them whenever they were accidentally forced together.

Interesting, she thought as she walked out of the office with Gray, who had come to pick her up for their afternoon in the city. Though the summer weather was lovely, warm but not too hot, and the flowers in the park bloomed in brilliant shades of pink and gold, he refused to put the top down on the low-slung Victorian that carried them about the town.

"It would make you too easy a target," he said. "I'm not willing to take any chances." And so there were two armed guards posing as footmen at the rear of the carriage, and she knew that Gray was also armed.

They settled themselves comfortably inside and let the relaxing whir of the wheels set the mood.

"I've enjoyed the time we've spent together this week," Corrie said, trying not to notice the way he watched her, the heat in his eyes he made no effort to hide. "Since our wedding, it's been the first chance we've really had to get to know each other." She glanced over to where he lounged in the carriage seat. "But we have yet to speak of your late wife, Gray. Will you tell me about her?"

For several long moments he said nothing. Then he sighed and let his head fall back against the squabs, reluctant, she could tell, but somehow resigned.

"Jillian was young and she was beautiful. I had just come into the title. I felt I needed a wife and Jillian seemed suitable."

"Suitable? That is the reason you married her?"

He shrugged. "It seemed reason enough at the time."

"What happened the day she was killed?"

He glanced away, toward the shops lining the street. A young boy darted after a ball, then returned to where his playmate waited.

"Rebecca had planned a boating party," Gray said. "A number of people had been invited. At the last minute, I decided not to go. I was feeling restless. I couldn't stand the idea of spending the day being polite and pretending to be interested when I wasn't in the least. I went riding instead. When I returned to the castle near dark, Charles was waiting. He told me the boat had sprung a leak shortly after leaving the dock and gone down very quickly. Everyone made it out safely except Jillian."

"Oh, Gray, I'm so sorry."

He stared out the window, but seemed not to notice the carriages they passed or the people hurrying along the street. "Charles said she went under and never came up. Her skirts must have caught on a sunken log or something, I don't know. The men searched for hours. We didn't find her body until the next day."

Gray looked up and she could see the pain in his face. "If I had been there, I could have saved her. I was her husband. I was supposed to protect her."

Corrie leaned toward him, reached out and cupped his cheek. "You are no more to blame for Jillian's death than I am responsible for what happened to Laurel. For months, I blamed myself for not being there when she needed me. I thought that if she had confided in me about the baby, I could have helped her in some way. But the truth is, life is full of misfortune. We can only do the best we know how. That is all God expects of us."

Gray gazed down at her. There was something in his eyes, a vulnerability he rarely let show. He glanced away, and when he looked at her again, his expression had changed and so did the subject.

"It is time you came home."

She didn't like the determination she saw in his fierce dark eyes. "But I've so enjoyed your courting—that is what you've been doing, is it not?"

A flush rose in his cheeks. "I am trying to make you happy. These are the things a woman likes, are they not?" He cast her a smoldering glance. "Of course, there are far better ways I might please you." His gaze lowered to her breasts. "All you have to do is come home."

Corrie gasped as he hauled her into his arms and very thoroughly kissed her, a searing promise of what would happen if she gave in to his demands. She was tempted. Very tempted—and light-headed by the time he let her go.

Still, she wasn't quite ready to return. "I can't, Gray. Not yet."

"I warn you, Coralee. I'm not a man known for his patience. And you are testing mine sorely."

She knew she was. She felt as if she faced a lion on a very short leash. "Just a few more days."

He made a growling sound in his throat that somehow seemed fitting.

"I know the words you want to hear…what every woman wants to hear. But I know nothing of love, Coralee. I only know I care for you deeply. I need you, Corrie. Please come home."

I care for you deeply. The words wrapped around her heart. Coming from a man like Gray, so unsure of his emotions and completely uncertain how to deal with them, they were words she cherished. He had given her more than she had ever believed he would.

She swallowed past the tightness in her throat. "All right. I'll come home with you, Gray."

His eyes closed in relief. "Thank God." He drew her into his arms and kissed her. She could feel his hunger, his powerful need, even as he slowly released her. He reached over and brushed a loose tendril of hair from her cheek.

"As much as I'd like to go back to the castle, I think we should stay in the city a little while longer. My family and Dolph are searching for the man who tried to kill you, but until they find him, I think you're safer here."

She had thought the same thing. "Probably."

"Since we're staying, we might as well enjoy ourselves. I made arrangements to take you to the theater tonight…if you would like to go."

"The theater?"

He must have read the surprise in her face, for he smiled. "I don't spend all of my time in the country, you know. I never expected you to do that, either."

She had always loved the city. She found herself smiling in return. "I adore the theater. I would love to go."

He seemed pleased. "We'll have men with us, so you won't have to worry." He settled back in his seat. "Tonight the theater. Afterward you return to my bed."

A tremor of heat slipped through her. She had missed his lovemaking, missed sleeping next to him at night.

Tonight she was going home.

She wondered when she had come to think of any place with Gray as being home.

The theater was crowded with ladies and gentlemen elegantly gowned for the evening. Corrie hadn't been to the Theater Royal since the interior had been redone with gold-flocked wallpaper, gilded ceilings and crystal chandeliers.

The earl's private box sat on the second floor, the interior draped with heavy gold velvet and furnished with matching velvet chairs. As soon as they were safely inside, the two guards who had escorted them upstairs returned to the carriage to await the end of the performance.

Corrie let Gray seat her, then he took the chair beside her. Wanting to please him, she had chosen a gown of aqua silk that left her shoulders bare and displayed a good bit of her bosom. The full skirt had a deep vee in the front that made her waist look exceedingly small, and she was wearing a lovely string of pearls Gray had bought her at Harrington's, an expensive shop in Bond Street.

She had taken extra care with her hair, curling the coppery strands into clusters against her shoulders. She seemed to have chosen well. Gray's eyes slid over her breasts again and again, making her nipples harden against the stays of her corset. She trembled at the hunger he so boldly displayed, and felt an answering hunger rising inside her.

Her need built with every second she sat next to him in the box. Dressed almost completely in black, with his onyx hair and intense brown eyes accented by the snowy cravat at his throat, he was so handsome she could barely keep her mind on the play. Tonight he carried a silver-headed cane, giving him an even more dashing appearance, which clearly impressed the ladies as he walked by.

The play, a comedic farce called *The Lark,* first performed in Vienna, was wildly entertaining and actually had Gray laughing. Corrie felt a swell of love as she looked up at him, and he leaned over and kissed her.

He ran the pad of his thumb across her bottom lip. "Thank you for what you said today."

That he shouldn't blame himself for what had happened to Jillian. Perhaps it was the reason he was able to laugh tonight. Perhaps he had taken the first step in forgiving himself, the first step toward healing.

The play was a delight, but by the time it was over, Gray was no longer laughing. Instead, he was looking at her as if he would ravish her right there in the box, and making her want him to do just that.

"I enjoyed the play," he said, "but as soon as we get home, there is something I intend to enjoy far more."

You, his dark eyes said, and a delicious warmth slipped through her. She was smiling when they pushed through the heavy velvet curtains into the crowded hallway. Then a man walked up beside her and pressed something into her ribs. She glanced down and gasped at the sight of a pistol.

He prodded her again. "When ye get to the end of the hall, ye'll see a door. It'll take ye out to the rear o' the buildin'."

Her heart set up a clatter. Was this the man who had tried to kill her? Dear God, how had he known where to find her?

"I'm not…not going anywhere with—" A fierce jab cut off her words.

"Ye'd best do as I say." He had bony hands and dirty hair and he smelled of stale liquor.

She trembled as she looked up at Gray.

"Do exactly what he says, Coralee." A second man, bigger than the first, stood next to Gray and she glimpsed a second weapon. Gray squeezed her hand where it trembled on his arm, warning her to stay calm. His eyes said not to fear, that he was biding his time, looking for the moment to strike.

They moved undetected through the crowd, though the men were dressed more shabbily than the rest of the theater patrons exiting their expensive boxes. It was late and everyone was tired, eager to get home, just as Corrie had been only a few minutes ago.

Gray pushed open the door at the end of the hall and she caught sight of a stairway outside, leading down to the alley behind the theater. They made their way to the bottom, and the instant Corrie's feet touched the ground, Gray shoved her hard out of the way.

"Run!" he shouted. A pistol shot rang out and Corrie screamed as Gray and the big man hit the ground rolling, one of them groaning in pain.

Please God, not Gray, she prayed, and saw him spring to his feet at the same instant the second man aimed his weapon.

"Gray!" Corrie cried, and launched herself at the man, knocking him off his feet, the gun flying out of his hand. He spun her around and slapped her hard across the face, sending her into the rough brick wall. Then Gray was on him, slamming a fist into his face, knocking him backward onto the ground. Gray retrieved his silver-headed cane from where it had fallen, turned the handle, and a blade popped out the end. He pressed the knife against the man's neck, the blade glinting in the light of a gas lamp next to the stage door at the rear of the building.

Corrie stood shaking, her hand over her mouth, watching the drama unfold as if it were part of the play.

"Are you all right, love?" Worry lined Gray's face.

She nodded, all she could manage as she wiped a trickle of blood from the corner of her mouth with a shaking hand.

He returned his attention to the man on the ground. "Who are you?" When the fellow didn't answer, Gray pressed the knife blade into the soft folds under his chin. "I want your names."

"'E's Biggs. Me name's Wilkins."

Biggs wasn't moving. A widening swath of crimson spread across his chest and pooled in the dirt of the alleyway. "Looks like your friend Biggs is dead. You don't answer my questions, you'll be joining him."

The man wet his lips, but was careful not to move his head.

"Did you and Biggs kill Laurel Whitmore?"

"Not us, mate. Biggs works for the man what did."

"Who is he?"

"Don't know nothin' about 'im. Biggs paid me to help 'im get rid o' ye. That's all I know."

"You had orders to kill both of us?" When the man didn't answer, Gray pushed the knife blade into his flesh, and Wilkins hissed as blood trickled from the wound onto the dirty collar of his shirt.

"Said to get rid o' the pair o' ye. That's what 'e said."

"How did you know where to find us?"

"Biggs knew where ye lived. We been watching ye all week."

Gray swore softly, his hand tightening around the handle of the silver-headed cane. For an instant, Corrie feared he would thrust the blade into the man's skinny neck.

"Don't do it, mate," Wilkins pleaded.

Corrie leaned against the wall, her cheek throbbing, her heart still hammering away.

"I'll make ye a trade," the henchman said, sweat beading on his forehead. "I've got information for ye…valuable information. I'll tell ye, if ye promise to let me go."

The knife blade didn't falter. "Information worth your useless life?"

Wilkins barely nodded.

"Tell me. If it's worth it, I'll let you go."

He swallowed. "The child…the one what was with the girl that night at the river. 'E's still alive. Least 'e is, far as I know."

Corrie surged away from the wall. "You're lying! You're just saying that to save your own skin!"

"'Tis the truth, lass, I swear it! Biggs said the man what killed the girl didn't 'ave it in 'im to murder an innocent babe. Paid Biggs to take the child to one of them baby farms 'ere in the city."

Gray cast Corrie a glance. "You never considered it?"

Her insides were shaking, quaking like a leaf in the wind. "I—I wondered if it might be possible. I was afraid to get my hopes up, afraid to think what might be happening to him if he lived. Oh, Gray, you don't think it might be true?"

Gray moved the knife an inch or so away, and the man exhaled in relief. "If the boy is alive, where is he?"

"Don't know. 'Twas Biggs who left 'im."

Just then the second-story door they had come out burst open, and one of the guards—Franklin, a man with a stocky build and side-whiskers—came rushing down the wooden stairs. "My lord—thank God we found you! Deavers and me, we got worried when you and her ladyship didn't come out with the others and took off looking for you."

Deavers, a beefy man with a hard face and bad complexion, came racing down the alley behind them, pistol drawn. "Lord Tremaine—thank God!"

"Ye gonna let me go?" Wilkins asked, looking hopeful.

Gray's jaw hardened. "Sorry, my friend. You tried to kill us. I don't keep promises I make to murderers."

"We'll take him, my lord," said Deavers. "The police will be glad to get their hands on him."

Deavers kept his pistol pointed at Wilkins while Franklin went for the police and Gray went to Corrie. As he drew her into his arms, he caught sight of the bruise beginning to form on her cheek.

"The bastard hit you. I should have killed him for that if nothing else."

She shuddered at the fierce look on his face. "I'm all right." She gripped his arm. "Oh, Gray, do you really think Laurel's baby might still be alive?"

"If he is, we'll find him, I promise you."

"His body was never recovered."

"No. I thought it was possible that someone might have taken the child, but I didn't want you to worry about that, too."

She went back into his arms. Now that it was over, she was shaking, fighting not to cry.

Gray pressed his cheek against her hair. "I knew I could count on you," he whispered.

"You did? Why?"

He smiled down at her, so softly her heart squeezed. "Because you're Coralee and not Letty." Very gently, he kissed her.

"The police have been summoned." The guard named Franklin returned down the alley. "The carriage is coming round to pick you up."

Gray turned to Corrie. "With this man, Wilkins, we

have proof that your sister was murdered. We can use help from the police to find the man who did it, and also to help find Charles's baby."

She looked up at him. "I've always thought of Joshua Michael as belonging to Laurel. But the baby is Charles's, too. We have to find him, Gray."

He squeezed her hand. "If he's alive, we'll find him. But it's been five months, love. Those places are death traps. They put bastard children there to get rid of them. Most of them die. You have to face that possibility."

She swallowed against the lump that rose in her throat. "Laurel was strong and so is Charles. Perhaps the baby got his parents' strength."

"For now, that's what we'll believe." As the carriage rolled up in the alley, Gray turned to the men guarding Wilkins. "We're going home. Tell the police they can speak to us there in the morning."

Deavers nodded. "We'll take care of it, my lord. Soon as we finish here, we'll come to the house to keep watch."

"They've been watching the house. Someone knew where to find us. Keep a sharp eye out."

"Aye, milord."

Corrie felt Gray's hand at her waist as he led her over to the carriage. She was going home with her husband. Not exactly as she had planned, but it was the place she wanted to be.

The butler opened the door and Gray led his wife into the entryway of his Mayfair town house. He could feel her trembling. Gray's jaw knotted as he thought of the bastards who had attacked them. Any other woman would have crumbled beneath the onslaught of violence and death. Not his brave little Coralee.

Gray looked down at her and worry tightened his chest. He had to find the source of the attacks and he had to do it soon.

The butler took his hat and coat, along with the silver-headed cane he had carried for exactly the purpose it had served, and Gray drew in a calming breath.

"Coralee, this is Stewart," he said. "Stewart, this is your countess."

The white-haired butler bowed extravagantly. "My lady."

"We had some problems tonight." He stared down at the blood on his black broadcloth coat, then over at the bruise on Coralee's pretty cheek. "We'll need hot water sent up."

"I believe Samir has bathwater for you upstairs."

He merely nodded. The little man was always one step ahead of him. Gray urged Coralee toward the stairs, felt her stumble, and swept her up in his arms.

"It's all right, love, I've got you." And he was not about to let her go again. In the days they had spent apart, he had come to realize the precious gift he had been given. He didn't deserve her, he knew, had never treated her as he should have, but she belonged to him and he meant to keep her.

He hurried up the stairs, her arms around his neck, her small frame nestled against him, and thought again how glad he was to have her returned. After the attack tonight, his desire for her was stronger than ever, the need to claim her, prove to himself she was his. He had dreamed of making love to her tonight, but now he only wanted to take care of her, make sure that she was all right.

Closing the door with his foot, he set her gently in front of the dresser and began to strip off her clothes. Her aqua silk gown was dirty and torn in several places, her shoulder scraped raw by the rough bricks the bastard had shoved her against. Gray bent his head and pressed a soft kiss on her tender flesh, fighting a surge of anger, wishing he had been able to spare her.

"There's a small room adjoining the bedroom," he said. "It's where I bathe and dress. Samir has a bath there waiting."

Gray tipped her chin up, forcing her to look at him. "I was so proud of you tonight. You were brave and you were smart. I've never known a woman like you."

She gazed up at him and tears filled her brilliant green eyes. "Gray…"

He drew her into his arms and just held her, prayed she would know how much she had come to mean to him. Then he stepped away.

Tossing off his jacket and waistcoat, he rolled up the sleeves of his shirt. "All right, let's get you cleaned up and into bed." Desire burned through him. He wanted her. He always seemed to want her. But he was determined to keep the beast inside him locked away.

Removing the rest of her clothes, leaving her in only her chemise, he pulled the pins from her fiery hair, letting it cascade round her shoulders, then carried her into the dressing room. As promised, Samir had the copper bathing tub filled with steaming water. Gray drew the chemise over Coralee's head, lifted her up and lowered her into the bath.

Even with the bruise on her cheek, she was beautiful. His loins clenched. *She is injured,* he told himself, knowing if he wasn't extremely careful, he might very well lose control.

Instead, he knelt beside the tub and gently bathed her, soaped a cloth and drew it over her tantalizing breasts. For an instant, the beast broke free and he moved the cloth between her legs, felt the brush of the russet curls at the juncture of her thighs. His shaft filled and desire heated his blood. Cursing, he pulled the cloth away.

"I'm sorry. You're hurt and the last thing you need is—"

"You're exactly what I need, Gray." Coralee rose from the tub, water cascading over the sweet curves of her body. She went into his arms, a wet, naked nymph, and his arousal strengthened to the point of pain.

"I just…I want you so badly. I missed you so damned much." And then he kissed her, a gentle kiss that heated and changed, seared through his determination and burned like a flame.

Coralee whimpered. Her fingers slid into his hair, freeing it of its tie, and the heavy strands tumbled forward around her face. She kissed him with all the passion he had dreamed of, kissed him as if she couldn't get enough, and desire thundered through his veins.

Carrying her into the bedroom, he set her on the edge of the bed and eased her back on the mattress, then stepped between her thighs. He wanted her now. He didn't bother removing his trousers, just unbuttoned the fly and freed himself, positioned his erection and drove himself home.

She was wet and slick and welcoming. He groaned at the tight, hot feel of her, clenched his jaw to hold on to his control.

It wasn't easy. He wasn't the same man he had been before, one who could ignore his emotions and enjoy the pleasure from a distance. He didn't want to be that man again.

"Sweet God, Gray…" she whispered as he thrust into her again and again. She cried his name as she found release. Reaching for him, she wrapped her arms around his neck and dragged his lips to hers for a burning kiss. At the feel of her small tongue inside his mouth, the last of his control shattered and he followed her over the edge.

For long moments, he remained joined with her. It felt so good to be inside her, to know that she was his.

Then he began to remember the rough treatment she had suffered earlier that night, and eased himself from her seductive warmth.

"Damn, I shouldn't have done that. After what you've been through, I should have been more patient, taken more care with you."

She draped her arms around his neck. "You were perfect."

Gray bent down and kissed her. "So were you." Perfect for him as he had never really realized before. Helping her snuggle beneath the covers, he pulled them up to her chin. She was asleep by the time he finished.

Gray didn't join her.

Instead, he drew his pistol from a drawer of the dresser, sat down in the chair beside the bed and settled the gun in his lap.

Twenty-Eight

G ray spoke to the police the next morning, giving them as much information as he could about the attack and how it related to the death of Laurel Whitmore some months back. Corrie added her version of events.

Afterward, Gray insisted on accompanying her to the offices of *Heart to Heart*. They needed information on baby farming, and Krista, who was active in social reform, could point them in the right direction.

They didn't travel there alone. Both Franklin and Deavers, the bodyguards Gray had hired, went with them. Corrie knew Gray would take every precaution until the man behind the attacks was apprehended.

They stepped through the door of the gazette and she caught the familiar scents of ink and oil and newsprint. The big Stanhope press took up a good deal of the main floor of the building, and immediately captured Gray's interest.

"I'd like to see it work sometime."

"We go to press on Thursdays."

He spared it a moment's more attention, then continued with Corrie through the open door into Krista's office.

"Well, good morning." Blond and pretty, Krista rose from the chair behind her desk. She wasn't as tall as Gray, but far taller than Corrie. "I'm a little surprised to see you two today." She must have thought they would be enjoying a leisurely morning in bed, which they should have been. "How was your evening at the theater?"

"I'm afraid it didn't go quite the way we planned," Gray said.

For the next half hour, he and Corrie filled Krista in on what had happened last night, nearly being killed at the theater, and the news that Laurel's child might still be alive.

"One of the men who attacked us knew about Laurel's murder," Corrie said. "He didn't know the man who had committed the crime, but he said that little Joshua Michael had been taken to a baby farm."

"Oh, dear God."

"Exactly so," Gray said darkly.

"Those places are a travesty." Krista got up from her desk and walked over to the window looking out onto street. "I've been asked to join a movement to try to make them illegal. Now I know I shall do exactly that."

"What can you tell us about them?" Corrie asked, her stomach churning at the thought of her sister's child suffering in any way.

"Baby farming started as a result of the Poor Law reform about ten years ago. It was done as an attempt to restore female morality by absolving the fathers of illegitimate children of any responsibility. It fell to the mother to feed and care for the child completely on her own. I suppose they thought that a woman facing that sort of consequence wouldn't be so easily seduced."

"I had no idea," Corrie said.

"Most people don't. Since many of the mothers work and earn barely enough to support themselves, the only solution is to get rid of the child."

Gray's jaw clenched.

"How could a mother do that?" Corrie asked softly. "How could she give up her baby?"

"That's just it," Krista said. "Baby farms are operated mostly by women. The ads in the papers say that for a small sum of money—which can often be extricated from the father—a child will be taken into a loving home. But the only way a baby farmer can make a profit is for the child to die before the money she receives runs out."

Corrie's heart squeezed so hard it hurt. "Dear God in heaven."

"Most of the babies are starved, or drugged with laudanum. Sometimes they're fed watered-down milk tainted with lime. The infants slowly die of hunger or some illness brought on by mistreatment. I'm sorry, Coralee, but most of them don't live more than a couple of months."

Corrie said nothing. Her throat was too tight to speak.

Krista sighed. "I know this isn't easy to hear."

She stiffened her spine. "I need to know, Krista."

Her friend returned to her seat behind the desk. "Sometimes one of the parents pays a monthly fee toward the infant's care. Those children have a better chance of surviving, since the fees, small as they are, continue as long as the child is alive. Still, they're kept at the barest level of subsistence and most are dead before they reach their first year."

Corrie thought of little Joshua Michael and despair settled over her. "I can't imagine a murderer paying to keep a child alive." She looked at Gray, tears welling in her eyes.

"There is still hope, Coralee."

"If he's alive, we have to find him before it's too late."

Gray reached out and caught her hand. "We'll search, love, until we find out what happened to him." He slid his chair a little closer to the desk, a little closer to Corrie. "Where do we start looking?" he asked Krista.

"As I said, the women run ads in newspapers. We refuse to carry them in *Heart to Heart,* but there are at least a dozen each day in the *Daily Telegraph* and the *Domestic Times.*"

"We'll buy copies of the papers," Gray said. "We'll track down every person involved in the trade and offer enough of a reward to encourage them to help us find the child. We know the baby was taken on January 30, the night your sister was killed. You said he was a month old at the time."

"That's right," Corrie said.

"So we're looking for a six-month-old baby."

"How will you know you've found the right child?" Krista asked.

"Allison said he was an adorable baby," Corrie said. "He was born with dark hair and eyes, but a newborn's hair and eyes can change. By now he could have blond hair and blue eyes."

"More like his mother and father," Gray said.

"Or he could be darker complexioned, like you," Corrie added, staring him straight in the face. She had read his mother's letter and believed the countess had been faithful, that Gray had indeed inherited his looks from his mother's side of the family, which meant Charles's son might also inherit dark features.

Gray stared back at her, understanding her message— that he had nothing to be ashamed of and never had.

He cleared his throat. "So we know his age but not what he looks like. In order to claim the reward, we'll require some sort of proof from whoever is caring for him. Perhaps they kept a record of who brought him or paid for his care, that sort of thing."

"There's a chance he'll have a mark on his left shoulder," Corrie said. "Allison never mentioned seeing it, but my father has it. I don't, but my sister did."

Gray reached over and caught her hand. "We'll start today. Thanks to Krista, at least we know where to begin."

"I want you to stay here, where you will be safe." They were standing in the study of Gray's town house. For the past three days, they had been going over ads in the newspapers, locating the women who had placed them, which turned out to be no easy task.

Baby farmers had to be careful. Though some handled a single child at a time, Corrie had learned that over a period of years some were responsible for the deaths of as many as fifty or sixty infants. It was all kept very quiet, since there was really no system in place to handle the unwanted offspring of unwed mothers.

"I am going," Corrie said. "This child is my nephew. If…if he *is* alive, when we find him he is going to need a woman's care. Aside from that, I feel safer being with you than I do here without you, no matter whom you hire to protect me."

Gray shoved a hand through his hair, knocking loose the velvet ribbon. He swore softly, picked up the ribbon and tied back the heavy strands again.

"You are upset because you think I am right—that I would be safer if I were with you."

He stalked over to the window. One of the guards stood watch in the garden, another kept the street covered out in front. Gray turned back to her. "All right, dammit.

You're right. I'd rather have you with me than here with someone else."

She smiled up at him. "You are a very smart man."

"And you are a handful of trouble, lady. But then, you always were."

Before he had come to London in search of her, she would have been hurt by the words. Now she saw that he said them with a hint of affection. She wondered if in time that affection might grow into something more.

"Are you certain we shouldn't tell Charles? If he knew, he would surely wish to help."

"We've been over this, Coralee. Charles has suffered enough. If chances of finding the boy were better…"

She felt a tightness in her throat. "I know."

Gray walked over to where she stood. "Are you certain you can handle this? God only knows what we'll find in some of these places."

She swallowed, afraid to imagine the horrors they might see. "I have to do it, Gray."

He simply nodded. "All right, then let's get started. We've a long day ahead of us."

With Deavers and Franklin riding at the back of the carriage, they began their search, which took them through the dregs of the city, from Southwark to the Turnbull and Cow Cross districts, to a woman in Holburn and one in St. Giles.

Most of the time, they had to knock on several doors in the area to locate the person they were looking for. Once they found the right house, they rarely went inside. The age of the child alone had the women shaking their heads.

"Sorry, but I can't help ye," a widow named Cummins

told them from the porch of her home in Bedford Street. "We've nary a child o' that age."

Which meant no babies in her care had survived to the age of six months old.

"Is it possible you took a boy child in around the first of February?" Gray asked, as he did at each stop they made. "He would have come from the area round Castle-on-Avon, brought to you by a man named Biggs? If you did and you have proof, it's worth a hundred pounds."

Her gray hair dirty and unkempt, the woman looked up with widened eyes. "A hundred pounds? Even if the babe is dead?"

Corrie's stomach knotted for the tenth time that day.

"Yes," Gray said. "If you can prove it was the child we're looking for."

The widow's gaze turned shrewd. "Weren't me what took 'im in, but I'll ask 'round a bit, see what I can find out."

Gray gave her one of his calling cards. "Should you come up with any information, you can find us here. If you do, you'll be well rewarded."

The conversation went much the same at each house they visited. They went inside only a few, and in those, the babies were kept in rooms upstairs. Corrie didn't have to see the poor sickly infants, but she could hear their pitiful, hungry wails, imagine their terrible suffering.

She was crying by the time they left the last house. "I can't stand this, Gray. All these poor, innocent children. We have to do something to help them."

Gray looked nearly as upset as she. "We'll talk to Krista about how we might do the most good."

Corrie nodded, turned away so that he wouldn't see the tears streaming down her cheeks.

They started back to the carriage. With a weary sigh, he helped her climb inside, then stepped in behind her. "We've done enough for today. Let's go home."

Corrie looked back at the run-down house they'd just left. "There's one more name on our list. It's on the way back. Baby Joshua might be there."

Gray cupped her cheek in his hand. "Are you sure, love? I can see what this is doing to you."

"Please, Gray."

He set his jaw and nodded. She knew this was affecting him nearly as much as it was her.

The house in Golden Lane was old and shabby, the paint peeling off, the shutters hanging loose at the windows. As they walked up on the porch, the boards creaked and Gray took a careful step back, afraid his foot would go through.

He had to deliver several sharp raps before someone came to the door. It opened with a groan and a woman in a mobcap, her front teeth missing, appeared in the doorway.

"Are you Mrs. Burney?" Gray asked

"Who wants to know?"

"We're looking for a child, about six months old."

A baby started crying then, a pitiful keening sound, and Corrie's chest squeezed painfully.

"Only one here and he ain't that old."

It was the same story again. Infants in these places simply didn't live that long. Corrie fought to hold back tears.

"There's a reward for the one we're searching for." Gray gave the woman the details of the baby they were trying to find, and handed her his card.

As he finished, the child cried out again, his soft little sobs so heartbreaking, Corrie simply shoved the door wide open and walked past the woman into the house.

"Here now! Wait a minute!"

Corrie just kept walking. In the parlor, she spotted the rough wooden boards that served as the baby's cradle, went over and looked down at the small scrap of flesh lying naked in the bottom without even the comfort of a blanket. Though the infant was probably two months old, his shrunken body made him look even younger.

"What ya think yer doin'?" The woman, Mrs. Burney, marched toward her.

Corrie ignored her, reached down and lifted the child against her breast. She wrapped her arms around him, trying to share some of her warmth. "Is this your baby?"

"I'm carin' for 'im."

Corrie held him tighter. "No, you are not. You are killing him, and I am not going to let you."

"Coralee...sweetheart..." Gray walked up beside her.

"I'm taking him, Gray. I'm not letting this poor little baby suffer a moment more."

"He isn't yours, love." His voice was so soft, his expression so tender it made the ache in her heart expand until she could barely breathe.

"He isn't *hers,* either." She looked up at him and tears rolled down her cheeks. "I can't leave him, Gray. He probably hasn't eaten in days. He's starving to death and I can't leave another child behind to die. Please don't ask it of me." She clutched the small, thin body against her, felt his faint breathing, the soft brush of fine hair against her cheek. She wouldn't let him die, she vowed. Somehow she would save him.

Gray straightened, turned his fierce gaze on the woman. "How much do you want for the child?"

"He ain't for sale."

"How much!"

"Give me twenty pounds, he's yers."

Gray drew a pouch of coins from the inside pocket of his coat, pulled it open and counted out twenty gold coins. "What's his name?"

"Jonathan. That's all, just Jonathan."

Gray took off his coat and Corrie wrapped the baby in the soft folds that still held Gray's warmth.

"You've got my card," he said. "You get the information we need, you'll be paid for that, too."

Corrie felt his hand at her waist, urging her toward the door, and she headed there gratefully. They climbed into the carriage and it lurched into motion, making the sad little creature in her arms begin to cry again.

"He needs milk," Corrie said.

"I made arrangements for a wet nurse, a woman named Mrs. Lawsen, in case we found Charles's son. I'll send one of the servants to fetch her as soon as we get home. And I'll send for the physician."

Corrie looked up at Gray and her heart squeezed. She wondered if he could see the love she felt for him shining in her eyes. "Thank you, Gray. I'll never forget what you did today."

He reached out and touched her cheek. "He's terribly ill, love. You mustn't get your hopes too high."

She nodded, swallowed past the tight knot in her throat. The child was so small and frail, and he had been so mistreated. As the babe lay in her arms, too weak to even cry out, she said a prayer that the precious little boy might be saved.

"And please, Lord, help us find little Joshua Michael," she whispered. "Don't let us be too late."

The baby was dead by morning. So terribly weak and malnourished, he passed away quietly in his sleep. At least he had been warm and dry, his stomach full, and when he slipped away, he was not in pain.

Corrie cried for the lost babe and all the others who suffered in the terrible places she had seen. In memory of the child, Gray promised to set up a fund to help unwed mothers care for their infant children.

Still, it didn't make the tiny baby's passing any easier.

And it didn't make Corrie's worry for her sister's son go away.

"You won't give up, will you?" Returning from the brief service that had been held in the churchyard at St. Andrews, she looked up at Gray. Her eyes were puffy and swollen, her cheeks wet with tears. She dabbed at them with the handkerchief he had handed her. "You won't stop until we know for sure what happened to him?"

"We won't stop, love. Not until we've done everything we can to find him."

And so they decided to run an ad in *Heart to Heart*. They gave the infant's age, the date he'd been brought to London, the name of the man who had brought him, and offered a reward for information—and a hundred pounds for the return of the child.

"It's worth a try," Krista said, studying the ad to make sure it read correctly.

"For a hundred pounds," Leif said, "if the boy still lives, someone will come forward."

But another week passed, and though a number of women appeared on their doorstep, none had credible information and none arrived with the child.

It seemed hopeless, and despair settled over Corrie with the weight of a shroud. Only Gray's tender affections kept the grief and worry at bay. He seemed to understand her pain, even share it.

Other visitors came and went. Colonel Timothy Rayburn stopped by, in London for a few days before his return trip to India. Gray filled him in on what had been happening since he had visited Castle Tremaine, the attempts on Corrie's life and the attack at the theater.

"I knew Dolph had been working on a case that involved the countess's sister," the colonel said as they sat in the drawing room after supper. "Damned sorry to hear he hasn't been able to catch the bast—er, villain who killed her."

Gray leaned forward in his chair. "We've got to catch him, Timothy. Neither of us is safe until we do."

"Wish I were going to be here awhile longer. Might be able to help."

"We could certainly use your assistance, but you're needed far more in India."

The colonel cast Gray a speculative glance. "Still have a yen to go back? You always did seem more at home there than you did here."

Gray swirled the brandy in his glass but didn't take a drink. "There was a time I wanted to return. I joined the army to get away from my father, then wound up enthralled with the country. I hated having to come back to England." He looked over at Corrie. "Now I'm glad to be here."

Corrie's heart swelled at the soft look in his eyes.

Rayburn chuckled. "Don't blame you. Not one little bit."

Corrie watched the exchange, not quite sure what the colonel meant. Exhausted, still grief stricken over the loss of the infant, she said farewell to the officer and went upstairs to the bedroom she shared with Gray.

Tomorrow, news will come, she told herself. But each day ended the same, with no word from Dolph or Gray's family, and no news of Laurel's baby boy.

Twenty-Nine

Gray stood at the window of the study in his town house. The garden behind the house was in full bloom this time of year, the flowers along the pathways brilliantly colored. Gray barely noticed. His mind was on his wife and the danger she still faced, perhaps both of them faced, and now, to top things off, was the matter of a lost little boy.

He hadn't told Coralee, but he had hired another investigator, a man named Robert Andrews, who had an excellent reputation and a staff of half a dozen men. Gray had hired the firm to search for information on the missing child. So far they had found nothing.

He turned away from the window. Every time he thought of Coralee, his chest ached. He was so afraid for her, and he couldn't bear to see the pain in her face that losing the infant had caused. Perhaps he shouldn't have let her bring the baby home. Its death had only caused her more grief. And yet he couldn't have denied her, couldn't have forced her to leave the suffering infant, no matter the outcome.

As he did more and more, Gray thought how much he

had come to care for the woman he had married. Was it love? He had tried to convince himself he wasn't the sort of man who could fall in love, but the flare of emotion he felt whenever she walked into a room, the powerful urge to protect her from any sort of pain or danger, made him wonder….

Was it love he felt for Coralee?

And if it was, what did she feel for him?

She had been forced to marry him. What if he loved her and she didn't love him in return?

A painful tightness constricted his chest. He had loved his father, but received only hatred in return.

He wasn't even sure he was capable of love, and yet when he looked at Coralee and saw her lovely green eyes well with tears, he felt he would do anything—anything!—to erase her pain and make her smile again.

Gray thought of the way he had found her asleep last night, curled up in the middle of their bed, tracks of tears dried on her cheeks. He hadn't made love to her in days, not since the night of the attack at the theater. Though he ached to touch her, to lose himself inside her, he wasn't sure how she would receive his advances, and he refused to press her for something she wasn't ready to give.

He was lost in his musing, uncertain what step to take next, when a rap came at the door.

Gray crossed the room and opened it. "Samir…what is it?"

"Come quickly, *sahib*. There is a woman downstairs. She has news of the child you seek."

His heart quickened to a faster pace. Was it possible? Or was it just another charlatan, out for what money she might procure, as most of the others had been?

Gray hurried along the hall and down the staircase.

When he reached the front parlor he was surprised to find the widow he had spoken to in Bedford Street, her gray hair as dirty and unkempt as before.

"Mrs. Cummins, if I recall. What news have you brought me?"

"The child ye seek…'e's alive. I can show ye where to find 'im."

His pulse kicked up again. "What proof do you have that the baby is the one we're looking for?"

She handed him a folded piece of paper, one edge ragged, as if it had been torn out of a book. Inside was written the date the child, a boy, had arrived in London—February 2—and his first name, Joshua. The name of the man who'd brought him was written on the next line down: Sylvester Biggs.

"You were told these things. How is this proof?"

She handed him a second piece of paper. "This here's a bank draft what come just yesterday. It's fer fifteen shillings." It wasn't much, just enough to salve a conscience.

"Name o' the man what's payin' is writ right there. Ye can see where he signed." She pointed a grimy finger at the name scrawled in blue ink, and Gray's whole body tightened.

Thomas Morton.

A wave of fury swept over him, so strong that for an instant his vision blurred. "Where is the child right now?"

She cast him a cunning glance. "What's in it fer me?"

"Fifty pounds."

Her eyes gleamed and she nodded. "I'll take ye there meself."

Gray turned to Samir, who watched from the hallway. "We'll need the carriage. Have it readied and brought round front."

"It awaits you there now, *sahib*. You will find blankets for the child."

The man never failed to amaze him. "Thank you." He turned to the widow. "Shall we go?"

Coralee's voice, floating down from the top of the stairs, reached him before he took two steps. "That is the woman we spoke to in Bedford Street." She hurried down to the entry. "Where is she taking you?"

He clamped down on an urge to lie. If the babe was as sickly as the last… If it was all some sort of hoax…

"Tell me, Gray."

"Mrs. Cummins believes she has found Joshua Michael. She has proof of a sort." He handed Corrie the page torn from a book. "If she is right, this may be the name of your sister's murderer."

Her hand trembled as she reached for the second piece of paper, read it and looked up at him. "Thomas Morton? Squire Morton's son? Dear God, why would he wish to kill Laurel?"

"That is what we're going to discover. First we need to find her baby."

Corrie whirled toward the door, but Gray caught her arm. "This may be even worse than before. Are you certain you're ready to go through that again?"

Her chin firmed. "I don't have any choice."

And so Coralee led the way out to the carriage, and Gray helped her and the widow climb aboard. He went back inside to get his pistol, stuffed it into a pocket of his coat, then ordered both Deavers and Franklin to join them.

If Morton was the man who'd sent the child, there was a good chance he was the man who had murdered Laurel. And there was also a chance he had seen the ads in the newspapers or somehow gotten wind of their efforts to find the babe. If so, this could be a way of luring them into a trap.

Gray wished he could leave his wife behind, just in case, but he knew she would fight him. And in truth, she deserved to be there.

Seated across from her, he reached inside his coat to check the pistol in his pocket.

She could smell the stench of rotting vegetation and human waste blocks before they got to the house. It was the sort of place where typhus bred and people suffered from endless poverty and despair, where children went without food in their bellies.

She closed her eyes, trying not to think what the babies here endured, what Laurel's child might be enduring even now. Instead, she concentrated on finding the baby alive, and how, once she did, she would nurse him back to health.

It wouldn't be like the last time. God wouldn't let them find him, only to have him die once they got him home. This time, they wouldn't be too late.

The widow began to stir on the seat beside her, her odor nearly as foul as the streets.

"Pull up 'ere." It was a wood-framed, two-story house in a neighborhood populated with pickpockets and women of the night. The carriage rolled to a stop, and Corrie took a calming breath, bracing herself for what they might find, knowing she could never be truly prepared.

"We stay inside the coach until Franklin and Deavers make sure this isn't a trap," Gray said, as Corrie leaned toward the door, anxious to get to the baby, praying it was truly Laurel's son.

"Ain't no trap," the widow grumbled, but Gray ignored her.

The hired guards circled the house. They went up to the door and knocked, then pushed their way inside. They reappeared a few minutes later, made their way over and opened the carriage door.

"Looks safe enough, my lord," Deavers said. "Still…place like this, we'd best be careful."

Gray nodded, turned to Coralee. "You're certain you don't want to stay in the carriage?" She opened her mouth. "Never mind. Let's go." He took her hand and helped her down, then helped the widow.

"She's expectin' ye," Mrs. Cummins said. "Wants the reward. Won't give ye no trouble."

Corrie hoped not. She just wanted to take the baby and go home.

Gray held open the front door, which tilted at an angle and scraped against the wooden floor as they walked inside the house. It was as dirty as the rest of the neighborhood, with unwashed plates on the tables, a filthy iron skillet on what passed for a stove, a dead rat in the corner on top of a pile of rags.

A baby wailed, a low keening sound that reminded Corrie of little Jonathan. Her heart snagged as the infant snuffled and began to cry, and her mouth flooded with bile.

"Where is he?" she asked. Gray must have heard the tremor in her voice, for his hand reached out to steady her.

"She'll be bringin' 'im."

Just then a woman appeared, slovenly and overweight, an apron tied round her considerable girth and a baby, wrapped in a dirty woolen blanket, held in her pudgy arms.

"This is him—Joshua." She held the infant against her enormous bosom.

"We need to get a look at him," Gray said.

The woman peeled away the blanket to reveal a child with blond hair and dark brown eyes. He was smaller than Corrie had imagined, thin to the point of gaunt. It was clear he had never had proper nourishment, never had the least loving care. His cheeks were sunken and his skin slightly sallow. His eyes had a hollow look, and his head lolled weakly against the woman's hand.

Corrie's heart twisted hard inside her. Reaching out, she pulled the edge of the blanket a little farther down and there it was, Laurel's tiny birthmark on his shoulder. Corrie's eyes filled with tears and her resolve turned fierce.

"Give him to me," she demanded.

"Not till I gets me money."

"You'll get your blood money," she said, looking up at Gray with pain-filled eyes. He handed the woman a pouch of gold coins and a bank draft for the balance of the reward, and she passed the baby to Coralee.

"It's all right, sweetheart." She pressed a kiss to the infant's cheek, her hands shaking as she settled him gently against her shoulder. "You're going home. No one's ever going to hurt you again."

As quickly as possible, Gray finished the transaction and they left the house. Inside the carriage, Corrie tossed the dirty blanket out the window, and Gray helped her wrap the infant in a soft clean woolen one Samir had left on the seat.

The baby seemed to snuggle against the softness, and Corrie's heart ached at the sight. How little comfort he had known, how hard he must have fought to survive. "He has my father's mark," she said softly as the conveyance rolled along the dirty street toward Mayfair. "It has to be Joshua Michael."

Gray's eyes found hers. "Even if he weren't, I wouldn't have left him there. Not after I saw the way you looked at him."

She glanced away, thinking how deeply she loved this

man she had married. She only wished she had the courage to tell him.

Instead she nuzzled the baby's soft cheek. "You're going to be all right, sweetheart. You're going to get well and grow strong for your papa." She turned, saw Gray looking at the child with a tenderness she had never seen in his face before.

"He has to be all right, Gray. I can't watch another child die."

He pulled the blanket carefully up around the baby's head. "Joshua's not going to die. He's survived this long with almost no care. Now he has you and his family to love him. We're going to make sure he grows strong and healthy."

Her heart trembled inside her. She loved this man so much. And already she loved the little boy in her arms. She brushed another kiss on top of the baby's head and settled herself against the velvet seat, whispering the same sort of soft, loving words her sister must have said.

I've found him, she silently told Laurel. *I've found your son, dearest. Soon you'll be able to rest in peace.*

Gray prowled the room impatiently. He wanted to leave London for the country. He had business with Thomas Morton—very personal business. So personal, in fact, he hadn't yet written to Dolph or any of the men in his family. He wanted to be there to confront Morton himself, wanted to hear what had happened the night Laurel Whitmore was murdered. He wanted to watch as the bastard was hauled away in chains.

At the very least, Morton was guilty of abducting an innocent baby and keeping him from his family. Gray was certain he was also the man behind the attacks on Coralee's life.

For those crimes alone, Gray wanted to see him hang.

But he couldn't leave the city yet. He had Coralee to consider, as well as his brother's son. He wouldn't leave without them. He wouldn't take a chance that Morton might have some other scheme in motion to rid himself of the threat they posed.

He knew Coralee was as eager to leave as he. She wanted justice for her sister and she wanted to unite Charles with his son. Yesterday and all of last night, she and Mrs. Lawsen had sat up with the baby. The wet nurse had fed him as much as he could possibly consume, and Coralee had held him, crooned to him and comforted him.

His wife was sleeping now, but he knew she wouldn't rest long. She was determined to give the child what he needed most and had never had. *Love.*

Gray felt an odd pressure in his chest. She would make a wonderful mother. He was grateful she wanted his child, and wondered if even now she might not be carrying his babe. Standing in the nursery, he looked down at the little boy asleep in the cradle Samir had found in the attic, and ached at the thought of what it might be like to have a son or daughter of his own.

He looked up as Coralee walked into the room, and a swell of emotion rose inside him. Even tired and worried, she looked beautiful.

"He's sleeping," Gray said softly. "I told Mrs. Lawsen not to wake you. I said I'd watch him until you got up."

She came toward him, smiled as she reached his side. He wanted to cup her face in his hands, to kiss away the worry he read in her eyes, to hold her and tell her how glad he was that she was a part of his world.

"Thank you for staying with him," she said.

He gazed down at the sleeping infant, his tiny fist pressed against his mouth, and felt something move inside him.

"We need to take him home, Gray."

His head came up. He wanted that above all things, but not at the risk of the child. "Do you think it's safe for him to travel?"

"It's warm and dry outside. As long as Mrs. Lawsen comes with us, there's no reason Joshua can't make the journey. He'll sleep most of the way and he's not as weak as…as poor baby Jonathan." She glanced away and he knew she was thinking of the pitiful little boy who had died that night in her arms. She looked back at Gray. "I think Joshua will recover even faster in the fresh country air."

He nodded, grateful they would soon be on their way, and more anxious to be home than he had ever been before. "All right, we'll leave first thing in the morning. That'll give him another day to recover."

And time for Gray to send a note to Dolph, telling him about Thomas Morton's apparent involvement in the murder and Gray's plans to confront him after they arrived at Castle-on-Avon.

His jaw knotted. By the day after tomorrow, Morton would be in prison and Coralee no longer in danger.

Soon after, the villain would be swinging from the end of a rope.

"What are you talking about—you want out? Are you insane?" Rebecca paced back and forth along the gravel path at the rear of the garden. It was late in the afternoon and they were far from the house, in a place safe for her and Thomas to meet. "We're both in this together. All we have to do is get rid of Tremaine—"

"Biggs is dead. His crony, Wilkins, is in prison. By now Tremaine has undoubtedly hired a small army of guards. We won't be able to get to him again."

She paced along the path, turned and paced back. "Perhaps you're right. We would be better to wait a bit, let things cool down. Charles says that man, Petersen, hasn't come up with anything in his investigation. Waiting a little longer won't matter. We'll bide our time, plan for just the right moment...."

"I don't know, Rebecca. It might be better if I just disappear."

She spun toward him. "God forbid you should do something so stupid! You leave and it will only arouse suspicion. We need to keep things perfectly normal, continue just as we have been."

She sidled over to him, allowing her hips to sway, though Thomas was not so easily played as some. Still, she knew she affected him and always had. Reaching out, she touched his cheek. "Think of the rewards, darling. You're not in line to inherit. That little house your father gave you is all you will ever own. We do this, and you'll earn the fortune I promised. And I shall have the title and money I deserve."

Thomas said nothing. His instincts were telling him to run, while his greed urged him to stay.

"Thomas?"

"I'll stay," he decided. *At least for a little while longer.* As the lady said, there was a fortune at stake.

The journey was long, but not unpleasant. The weather was mild, the sun shining and the roads dry. Corrie and Mrs. Lawsen rode in the first carriage, while Gray mostly rode outside on his stallion. A second carriage followed, carrying Samir, a nursemaid named Emma Beasley, whom Coralee had hired to help with the baby once they got home, and Mrs. Lawsen's children, a two-year-old and an infant of barely three months.

Mrs. Lawsen, a buxom, healthy woman in her thirties, had plenty of milk for both of the babies, and a sweet way of handling them that Corrie vowed to remember when she had a child of her own. The woman's husband, a clerk in the city, was staying behind with their other two offspring.

"You've quite a family," Corrie said with a smile, enjoying the older woman's company.

"I've been lucky. All of them were born healthy. My husband and I wanted a large family and God granted our wish."

Corrie made no reply. Gray had said he would give her a baby. As she cradled her sister's son against her breast, she realized she wanted that above all things. She wanted Gray's child. And she wanted him to love her.

In the days since he'd come to London, he had seemed different, as if he truly cared.

Perhaps in time…

Gray rode up to the window just then. "It'll be dark soon. It won't be much longer until we get there." He nodded toward the infant. "How's he doing?"

"He's sleeping a lot. He hardly ever cries. He's such a sweet baby."

Gray smiled, almost a grin. "Don't count on a son of mine being that cooperative." Pulling the horse away from the window, he nudged the animal into a gallop and rode off ahead of the carriage.

Corrie stared after him, not quite able to believe what she had just heard.

"Your husband loves you very much."

Corrie turned in the older woman's direction. "Why do you say that?"

"I can see it in his eyes whenever he looks at you. Surely he's told you."

She shook her head. "I'm not sure how Gray feels about me."

"Have you told him how you feel about him?"

"I love him, but…"

"But?"

"But I am afraid to tell him."

"Why on earth is that?"

Why *was* she so afraid? "Gray doesn't believe in love. He would probably think I was a fool."

"Or perhaps he would like to know you love him, just as much as you'd like to know he loves you."

Was it possible? Rebecca had said Gray didn't know how to love, and yet as Corrie looked back on their time together, he had shown her his care of her in a hundred different ways.

Loving Gray was easy. Telling him was hard. But perhaps, as Mrs. Lawsen said, he needed her love as badly as she needed his.

Snuggling the baby a little closer against her, she leaned back against the seat, resolved to tell him how she felt. Somehow she would find the courage. Perhaps tonight, she thought. After Charles and his son had been reunited. When she and Gray were upstairs in bed…

A warm yearning sifted through her. Gray hadn't made love to her since the night they had gone to the theater. Tonight she would let him know how much she wanted him. And then she would tell him that she was in love with him.

Uncertainty sliced through her. Dear God, what would he say when she did?

Thirty

Gray rode ahead of the carriages. Darkness had fallen and lanterns along the gravel drive lit the way. He urged Raja to the front of the house, swung down and handed the reins to the groom.

"Welcome home, milord."

"Thank you, Dickey." It was indeed good to be back, no matter the circumstances. He wondered when the place he had so gladly left behind had truly become home to him.

He clenched his jaw. He was back, but tonight he wouldn't be staying long. As soon as he had settled Charles with his son and seen to Coralee's safety, he was leaving. He had a grim date with Thomas Morton, and he wasn't about to wait until morning.

The front door opened and a pair of footmen raced down the steps. The butler wore a look of surprise at the unexpected appearance of his master standing at the bottom.

He should have sent word, Gray knew, prepared Charles for the arrival of his son. Perhaps he had delayed in an effort to postpone the confrontation his brother would undoubtedly face with Rebecca over the existence of the child.

Gray wasn't sure what his sister-in-law would do when she found out the boy he was bringing into the house was her husband's illegitimate son.

It didn't matter. Gray knew what Charles would want. He would demand the boy be raised in the care of his father, no matter what Rebecca said.

Gray waited as a footman helped Coralee down from the carriage. Her ugly mutt, Homer, raced up barking, and she leaned down to ruffle his scruffy fur, obviously glad to see him.

"Come, my lady," Gray said with the faintest of smiles as he escorted her up the front steps, the baby in her arms. The rest of the party trailed along behind them.

"Mrs. Lawsen, you and Nurse Beasley take Joshua upstairs to the nursery," he instructed, once the group had arrived in the entry. "Mrs. Kittrick, the housekeeper, will show you where it is."

"Gray…?"

He heard the uncertainty in Coralee's voice, read the question in her pretty green eyes.

"We need to handle this carefully, love, give Charles a little time to get over the shock, and set things in order."

She nodded. She knew Rebecca and understood what Gray was saying. She handed the baby to Mrs. Lawsen, who followed the housekeeper up the stairs, trailed by the baby's nursemaid.

"The family is currently in to supper," the butler told him. "Mrs. Forsythe is giving a small dinner party tonight."

"I see." Gray released a breath. "Tell my brother that I am here and need a word with him. Tell him it's important."

"Yes, my lord."

"We'll be waiting in the Sky Room."

"Yes, my lord." The gray-haired man moved swiftly down the hall and disappeared. The dining room was in another section of the house. It took a few moments for his brother to arrive.

"Thank God you are both home and safe," Charles said as he walked into the drawing room, where Gray stood waiting with Coralee. "We've all been extremely worried."

"It's quite a long story, Charles. I'm sorry to interrupt your supper, but this is urgent. I think you had better sit down."

Worry crept into his brother's features as he seated himself in a chair, and Gray and Coralee sat down on the sofa. For the next fifteen minutes, Gray told him some of what had happened during the time they had spent in London, planning to ease into the subject of the baby a little at a time.

"You should have written, told us you were in danger," Charles said. "We would have come immediately. Surely the three of us could have done something."

"You were doing something important here. I figured sooner or later you would find out something that would lead us to Laurel's killer. Instead, we found the answer in London."

Charles sat forward in his chair. "You know who killed Laurel?"

Coralee reached over and caught Gray's hand, warning him to go gently. Charles had loved her sister. Her murder could not be an easy subject. And the shock of learning he was a father would be more difficult still.

"We don't know for certain," Corrie said, "but we know Thomas Morton was there the night Laurel was killed."

"Thomas? Good God, Thomas was there that night with Laurel? But she barely knew him. I—I don't understand."

"We know he was there," Gray continued. "We don't know his motive, but we believe he may be the man who killed her. Tonight, I plan to pay him a visit. I intend to find out what happened that night."

Charles stood up from his chair, his face as hard as Gray had ever seen it. "You won't have to go far. Thomas is here. He's among the guests at Rebecca's dinner party."

Gray cast a glance at Coralee, thought of the broken saddle cinch, the night she had been drugged, the attack at the theater. Rage rose like a beast inside him.

"Good of him to save me the trip." In a haze of fury, he leaped to his feet and strode out of the drawing room, down the hall to the dining room.

The rage inside would not let him slow. He burst through the door to find Rebecca in her usual seat, Jason next to the Countess of Devane, Derek next to Allison Hatfield, apparently his guest for the evening. Thomas Morton sat calmly on the opposite side of Charles's empty chair.

"Gray!" Rebecca smiled. "I didn't know you were coming home tonight."

"Good evening, everyone." He tried to control the fury pumping through him, the anger in his voice. "Especially you, Thomas. I had planned to pay you a visit this evening. I am pleased you spared me the journey."

Morton set his fork down beside his plate, wariness settling over him. "You wished to see me tonight? It must have been a matter of some importance."

"You might say that. It involves Laurel Whitmore and the child you sent to London."

The man's face went pale. "What are you talking about?"

"I'm talking about murder, Thomas."

Both Derek and Jason went on alert, tensing in their seats at the table.

"That is insane," Thomas said.

"Is it? You hired a man named Biggs to deliver the child to a baby farm. I suppose you did it to salve your conscience. I'm sure you figured by now the child would be dead."

Rebecca shot to her feet, shoving her chair back so hard it tipped over onto the carpet. Her cheeks were red, her eyes wild. She stared at Thomas Morton as if he were something stuck on the bottom of her shoe. "You idiot!" Her hands balled into shaking fists. "You were supposed to get rid of it! You said you'd take care of it. You said you'd handle everything! Now look what you've done!"

"Sit down, Rebecca," Morton warned.

"You did it for her, then?" Gray asked, less surprised that Rebecca was involved than he should have been. He fixed a hard look on his sister-in-law, trying to fit the pieces together. "What happened, Becky? You found out about Charles's affair and wanted the girl and her baby dead?"

"Shut up," Morton demanded, his gaze piercing Rebecca. He turned to the others sitting in stunned silence at the table. "She's distraught. I can't imagine what she's talking about. I don't know anything about any of this."

Gray fought to control his temper. "We have proof, Morton. We know you were there. Did you kill her? Or was it Rebecca who pushed her into the river?"

Jason shoved back his chair. Gaslight glinted on his light brown hair, and in the soft rays, his face was pasty white. "*You* killed her? You would go that far to protect your interests, Becky? You would do murder?"

Rebecca whirled on him, her face contorted in fury. "I didn't kill her—he did!" She thrust a finger at Morton, so angry she shook. "If he had finished the job he was paid to do, she and her brat would both be dead and no one would be the wiser."

Shock quivered in Charles's deep voice. "You knew about my relationship with Laurel?"

From the corner of his eye, Gray saw his brother near the door, his skin the color of ash.

"Of course I did. For God's sake, Charles, you were so transparent, so utterly smitten. Any idiot could tell you were in love. I thought it was over when she left, but then six months later, she returned. I followed you that night. I heard you telling her you were going to get a divorce. I couldn't allow that to happen."

"So instead of a divorce, you hired Thomas Morton to murder her." Charles seemed to be on the ragged edge of control.

Rebecca's lips thinned to an ugly line. "We had a partnership of sorts. I intercepted a note she sent you. She wanted you to meet her at the river. I didn't know she'd birthed your bastard, but apparently she planned to show it to you that night."

Rebecca cast a disgusted glare at Thomas. "If you'd gotten rid of it as you were supposed to, no one would have ever found out."

"I'm not taking the blame for you, lady." Morton rose to his substantial height, a large man made to appear even taller by the anger that stiffened his spine. Across from him the Countess of Devane sat utterly frozen. Allison trembled. Jason and Derek sat on the edge of their chairs, ready in case Morton tried to run.

"Why did you try to kill Coralee?" Gray asked, pressing hard for the rest of the story. He felt her small hand on his arm and realized she had walked up beside him. Dammit to hell, he had meant for her to stay out of the way.

"She wouldn't let the matter rest," Morton said. "She was always digging, stirring things up. Sooner or later, she would have stumbled onto something—which is exactly what happened in London."

Gray's whole body tensed as Morton drew a pistol from inside his coat pocket. Bloody hell, he hadn't expected the man to be armed at a dinner party.

But then, Morton wasn't a man, he was a murderer.

Thomas held the pistol steady. It was obvious he wouldn't hesitate to use it. "Now that we've cleared the air, I'll be leaving."

Rebecca's blond eyebrows shot up. "What are you talking about? You can't just leave!"

"If you think I'm going to the gallows for you, my dear, you are sorely mistaken. I'm a businessman. As of now, our business is finished."

Instead of aiming at Charles or Gray, Morton pointed the pistol at Coralee. "I can't get you all with a single shot, but Lady Tremaine will be dead the minute one of you takes a step in my direction."

Allison made a strangled sound, drawing Morton's attention. Derek tensed, but the gun never wavered.

Fear flooded into Gray's stomach and he fought for control.

"Please," Charles implored, "don't anyone move."

"Very sensible, Charles," Thomas said. "But then, you always were a sensible man." He turned to the others. "Stay where you are and no one will have to die. I'll merely leave and you will never see me again."

He backed toward a door that led to a hallway outside the kitchen, the gun pointing dead center at Coralee's chest.

Gray's heart thundered. One wrong move and his wife would be dead.

Morton stepped back carefully. He had just reached the door when the panel swung open behind him, knocking him off balance. His arm jerked upward and Gray seized the moment, charging forward and knocking Morton to the floor, catching a glimpse of Samir as he did so.

The pistol roared and Coralee screamed. Rebecca crumpled onto the carpet, landing in a heap of pink silk and blond curls.

"Becky!"

Gray heard Jason's voice the instant before his own fist collided with Morton's chin and the beast broke loose inside him. He jerked Morton up by the lapels and hit him again, driving his fist into his face. Morton fought back, landing a blow to Gray's jaw. He was a big man and he threw a hard punch, but Gray's fury made him unbeatable. He drove a fierce blow into Morton's body, rained blow after blow into the big man's face.

He might have kept on hitting him if Charles hadn't smashed a Chinese vase over Thomas's head, knocking him unconscious.

Knuckles bleeding, Gray stood up and took a couple of staggering steps backward.

"Gray!" Coralee leaped toward him, nearly knocking him over. He held on to her hard. Nothing had ever felt so good as having her arms around him.

"It's all right, love…it's over."

She looked up at him, her eyes full of tears. "Rebecca's dead, Gray. Morton's shot went wild. The lead ball broke her neck."

He glanced over to see Jason kneeling beside the beautiful blond woman gowned in pink silk. Charles moved toward them, along with Gray and Coralee.

"She's…she's gone, Charles." Jason looked pale and shaken.

"The child she carried…" Charles stared down at her.

Jason swallowed and glanced away. "It wasn't yours, Charles. I'm sorry…it was mine." He took Rebecca's hand and cradled it gently in his. "I never meant to betray you— I swear it. I just… I fell in love with her."

Charles met his cousin's tortured gaze. "Rebecca was always discreet in her affairs, but I knew from the start it wasn't mine. I wanted a child so badly I didn't care."

Jason's eyes filled with tears. "She said you couldn't give her the son she needed. She begged me to help her. I knew she hoped someday to be countess. I never knew she would kill to make it happen." He shook his head. "I'm sorry, Charles, so sorry. Perhaps someday you'll be able to forgive me."

Jason rose and moved woodenly out of the dining room, and everyone seemed to break free of the trance that held them immobile.

"Dreadful business," said Lady Devane with a sad shake of her head. "Then again, I'll have gossip enough to keep London entertained for years."

Gray's head snapped toward her. "You say a word about what happened here, Bethany, and all of London will know every detail of your prurient tastes in bed."

The countess opened her mouth, then snapped it closed. "Fine," she said. "If that's the way you want it."

Derek looked shaken, yet solidly in control. He ran a hand through his thick golden hair, said something reassuring to Allison, then the two of them moved toward Gray.

"All of this was going on in the house and I didn't know," Derek said. "I feel as if somehow I failed you. I'm sorry, Gray."

"Everything that's happened was caused by a woman's greed. You are hardly to blame for that."

Allison came over and hugged Coralee. "I was so frightened for you, Corrie. To be truthful, I was never completely convinced you were right about Laurel being murdered. I won't ever doubt you again."

Gray could see how badly his wife wanted to tell her friend about the baby, but it was Charles who deserved the news first.

Derek tipped his head toward the unconscious man on the floor. "I'll send someone to fetch a constable. While I'm at it, I'd better get something to tie him up."

"I imagine this will do." Dolph Petersen strode through the doorway, a length of gold drapery cord dangling from his hand. A grim smile played on his lips. "It would appear I am a bit late for our appointment, my lord."

"If Morton hadn't been a supper guest, you would have been right on time."

"Yes…well, after I got your letter, a few bits and pieces I had been working on finally fell together." He handed the cord to Derek, who set to the task of tying up the unconscious man on the floor.

"Such as…?"

"All of this happened because your sister-in-law wanted to become the Countess of Tremaine."

"That's what Jason said. I suppose that's why the attack at the theater was made against both of us. With me out of the way, Charles would inherit the title and Rebecca would be countess."

"That's right, and if Rebecca's plan had been successful, you would have been dead long ago. You see, Gray, lovely Rebecca arranged the boating accident that wound up killing your wife. But you were the target, not her."

A chill ran down his spine. Coralee's hand slipped into his, warming his suddenly cold insides. "That makes no sense. I wasn't even there."

"No, but you only decided not to go at the very last moment. By then, plans were already in motion and there was no way to stop them. Apparently Morton's accomplice—the man named Biggs you shot that night at the theater—was working among the crew, paid to knock you unconscious before you went into the water. Jillian was a casualty no one expected."

Gray said nothing. For years he had blamed himself for his late wife's death. All the while, Rebecca had been responsible. If she weren't already dead, he might have killed her himself.

"It's finished, Gray." Coralee squeezed his hand. "It's over and now we can get on with our lives." She turned and he followed her gaze to find Charles kneeling beside Rebecca on the floor.

"She was never happy," Charles said. "She wanted to marry a man with a title. She probably could have if our fathers hadn't been such close friends. When James died and you became earl, she must have seen an opportunity to make her dream come true." He rose to his feet. "I can pity her, but I cannot mourn her, not after all she has done. Perhaps her death was God's will, for justice has surely been served here tonight."

Thirty-One

The constable had yet to arrive. Once he did, there would be statements to make, a man to be hauled off to prison. In all the confusion, no one had asked about the child Gray had mentioned, the child who now lay sleeping upstairs.

Corrie thought that Charles was simply too over-whelmed to realize the importance of his brother's words, that his son was alive and returned to him.

"We need to tell him," Corrie said to Gray as they stood near the balustrade at the edge of the terrace. The night was black and quiet, helping to soothe her ragged nerves. "We'll have to explain to the constable how we knew Thomas Morton was the killer. We'll have to explain about the baby."

Gray just nodded. In the flickering light of the torches, he looked heartbreakingly weary. She yearned to take him upstairs and put him to bed, to snuggle beside him and wrap him in her arms.

Tonight his family had nearly been destroyed. She ached for what he must be feeling.

"I had hoped for better circumstances," he said. "Charles has already been through so much."

Her throat tightened. *Poor dear Charles.* As he'd walked out of the dining room, he'd looked so lost, so utterly alone.

Gray took her hand and they set out in search of him, but as they crossed the terrace, Charles came walking toward them.

"We were just coming to find you," Gray said.

"I thought Jason might be out here."

"We haven't seen him."

"I need to talk to him, set things right between us. I am hardly blameless in this affair. I refuse to punish Jason for the same sin I committed."

Corrie managed to smile. "I'm glad you feel that way. I know the two of you will work things out. In the meantime, there is someone you need to meet."

He frowned. "Tonight?"

"We had hoped it would be a happier occasion," Gray said, "but yes, Charles, tonight."

They made their way back inside the house and started up the stairs, Charles behind them.

"Where are we going?" he asked.

"The nursery," Gray said, and Charles froze midway up the staircase.

"The nursery? I don't…I don't understand."

Corrie reached down and caught his hand. "It's all right, Charles. We're taking you to meet your son."

His fingers trembled in hers. "My son…?" His blond eyebrows drew together as he worked to put the pieces together. "Earlier…you said something about Laurel's baby. But everything got so mixed up, and then there was the shooting, and Rebecca, and I—I…" He faltered, then turned and started up the stairs at a breakneck pace, leaving them hurrying to catch up with him.

When they reached the door to the nursery, he stopped. "Is he…? For God's sake, tell me he's all right. He hasn't been terribly mistreated or…or anything like that."

"He's going to be fine," Gray said firmly. "He just needs love and attention. He'll have plenty of that here."

Charles just stood there, too full of emotion to speak.

Gray swung the door of the nursery open and led his brother into a room lit by the soft glow of a lamp. The nursemaid, Miss Beasley, eased silently out of the room as they moved forward to surround the cradle. Inside, nestled in the warm folds of a blanket, lay Charles's blond-haired baby boy.

"My God…" he said thickly as Corrie reached down to gently lift the child out of the cradle and place him in his father's arms. "My son…" Charles held him with such tender care that a painful lump swelled in Corrie's throat.

"I can scarcely believe it." He stroked the baby's soft cheek, tears glistening in his eyes. He kissed the top of the boy's blond head. "You're home at last, my son." He looked up as if he could see into the heavens. "Be at peace now, beloved. Your son is in his rightful place and you may be certain that he will be loved."

As if in agreement, the baby reached out and wrapped his small hand around his father's finger. Charles brought the tiny fingers to his lips. "I'll tell you everything about her," he promised. He looked over at Coralee. "Your sister and I, we'll tell you how beautiful she was and how kind, and how much she loved you."

Corrie wiped at the tears spilling onto her cheeks. She went into her husband's arms and for a moment he just held her. Then the two of them slipped quietly away, leaving father and son alone.

"Your sister can rest easy now," Gray said as they stood

together in the hallway. "You kept your vow to her, just as you promised."

"Without you, I couldn't have done it." Corrie looked up at him, her heart expanding inside her chest. "I love you, Gray. I love you so very much."

His arms came hard around her and he held her as if he would never let her go. "Coralee…" Cradling her face between his hands, he very gently kissed her. "You came into my life and filled the empty place in my heart. I never thought I could fall in love, but sweet God, Coralee, I love you, too."

Epilogue

One month later

The wind whipped the sails of the ship that carried them across the white-capped sea to France. It was past dawn, the sun a glowing orb riding low on the horizon. They had just finished making love. Corrie lay next to her tall, handsome husband in the wide berth in the owner's cabin aboard *Sea Dragon,* Leif's personal flagship, feeling as if her world had finally righted itself.

"We'll be docking sometime late this morning," Gray said. A strong arm draped around her shoulders, tucking her in beside him. "Are you excited to get there?"

She turned and smiled. "I've been excited since the moment you told me we were going. Oh, Gray, I've always wanted to see Paris." It wasn't India, but it was a start. Along with France, he had also promised to take her to Italy. She couldn't wait to see Rome.

Gray leaned over and kissed her forehead. "Remember you promised to write about your trip when we get home."

"Actually, I mean to start while we are away. Krista has asked me to do a series of articles about my travels."

"Then I suppose I shall have to make sure you have plenty of material for your stories."

And Corrie was certain he would see that she did. He was looking forward to the trip as much as she. A journey was exactly what they needed. So much had happened in both of their lives. So many changes had taken place since her sister had died.

Thomas Morton had been sentenced to hang, just as he deserved.

Charles was now a father, doting over his son worse than any nursemaid.

Both Jason and Derek had left the castle and returned to London. According to Allison, Derek had promised her he would come back, but Corrie wasn't certain of his intentions. She hoped her friend wouldn't be hurt too badly if things didn't work out with Gray's roguish half brother.

The most exciting news was that Gray had decided to take his place in the House of Lords.

"There are laws on the books that need changing," he'd said. "I can't ignore my duties any longer."

She knew he was speaking of the terrible business of baby farming, but there were other injustices that also needed to be dealt with, and Corrie believed Gray was exactly the man for the job. Duty had always been so much a part of him. She was only surprised he had waited this long.

She snuggled closer against him, enjoying the solid warmth of his body, the play of muscle whenever he moved. "There is one thing I keep wondering…."

One dark eyebrow arched. "What is that?"

"Rebecca said Charles couldn't father a child, and yet it is clear that he did."

"Charles was in love with your sister. Perhaps that made the difference."

"Yes, I suppose it must have." She traced a finger through the crisp mat of hair on Gray's chest and felt his heartbeat quicken.

"You are playing with fire, my love." The gruff note in his voice made her smile.

"And if love was truly the cause, it's a very good thing we left England when we did, because I love you desperately—which might just mean that very soon I'll be—"

He cut off her words with a kiss. "It might just mean that very soon you'll be heavy with my babe. I love you, lady trouble. And I think that perhaps we should give this baby-making another try."

She laughed as he came up over her and began to make a very thorough attempt at becoming a father.

Corrie had the strangest feeling that this time his efforts would succeed.

And inwardly she smiled.

Author's Note

Hope you enjoyed HEART OF FIRE, the second in the Heart Trilogy that started with HEART OF HONOR. The third in the series is HEART OF COURAGE, Thor and Lindsey's story. Theirs is a tale of two headstrong people who fight the attraction between them—until they realize love conquers all, even rebellious spirits such as theirs.

Hope you'll watch for HEART OF COURAGE and that you enjoy it.

All best wishes,
Kat

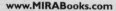

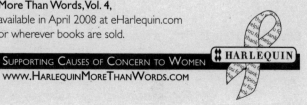

Kat Martin

32470 THE SUMMIT	___ $7.99 U.S.	___ $9.50 CAN.
32383 HEART OF HONOR	___ $7.99 U.S.	___ $9.50 CAN.
32326 SCENT OF ROSES	___ $7.99 U.S.	___ $9.50 CAN.
32207 THE HANDMAIDEN'S NECKLACE	___ $7.99 U.S.	___ $9.50 CAN.
32199 THE DEVIL'S NECKLACE	___ $7.50 U.S.	___ $8.99 CAN.
32125 THE BRIDE'S NECKLACE	___ $7.50 U.S.	___ $8.99 CAN.

(limited quantities available)

TOTAL AMOUNT	$ _____
POSTAGE & HANDLING	$ _____
($1.00 FOR 1 BOOK, 50¢ for each additional)	
APPLICABLE TAXES*	$ _____
TOTAL PAYABLE	$ _____

(check or money order—please do not send cash)

To order, complete this form and send it, along with a check or money order for the total above, payable to MIRA Books, to: **In the U.S.:** 3010 Walden Avenue, P.O. Box 9077, Buffalo, NY 14269-9077; **In Canada:** P.O. Box 636, Fort Erie, Ontario, L2A 5X3.

Name: _____
Address: _____ City: _____
State/Prov.: _____ Zip/Postal Code: _____
Account Number (if applicable): _____

075 CSAS

*New York residents remit applicable sales taxes.
*Canadian residents remit applicable GST and provincial taxes.

MIRA®

www.MIRABooks.com

MKM0108BL